PENGUIN CLASSICS

THE CRITICAL MUSE

Henry James was born in 1843 in Washington Place, New York, of Scottish and Irish ancestry. His father was a prominent theologian and philosopher and his elder brother, William, was also famous as a philosopher. He attended schools in New York and later in London, Paris and Geneva, entering the Law School at Harvard in 1862. In 1865 he began to contribute reviews and short stories to American journals. In 1875, after two prior visits to Europe, he settled for a year in Paris, where he met Flaubert, Turgenev and other literary figures. However, the next year he moved to London, where he became such an inveterate diner-out that in the winter of 1878–9 he confessed to accepting 140 invitations. In 1898 he left London and went to live at Lamb House, Rye, Sussex. Henry James became naturalized in 1915, was awarded the O M and died in 1916.

In addition to many short stories, plays, books of criticism, autobiography and travel, he wrote some twenty novels, the first published being *Roderick Hudson* (1875). They include *The Europeans*, *Washington Square*, *The Portrait of a Lady*, *The Bostonians*, *The Princess Casamassima*, *The Tragic Muse*, *The Spoils of Poynton*, *The Awkward Age*, *The Ambassadors* and *The Golden Bowl*.

Roger Gard was educated at Abbotsholme School, Derbyshire, in the Royal Artillery and at Corpus Christi College, Cambridge. He now lectures in English at Queen Mary College, University of London. Among his previous publications are books on Henry James, Jane Austen and the teaching of fiction in schools.

HENRY JAMES

THE CRITICAL MUSE

SELECTED LITERARY CRITICISM

EDITED WITH AN INTRODUCTION BY
ROGER GARD

PENGUIN BOOKS

PENGUIN BOOKS

Published by the Penguin Group
27 Wrights Lane, London W 8 5 TZ, England
Viking Penguin Inc., 40 West 23rd Street, New York, New York 10010, USA
Penguin Books Australia Ltd, Ringwood, Victoria, Australia
Penguin Books Canada Ltd, 2801 John Street, Markham, Ontario, Canada L 3 R 1 B 4
Penguin Books (NZ) Ltd, 182–190 Wairau Road, Auckland 10, New Zealand

Penguin Books Ltd, Registered Offices: Harmondsworth, Middlesex, England

Published in Penguin Books 1987

Filmset in Sabon (Linotron 202) by
Rowland Phototypesetting Ltd,
Bury St Edmunds, Suffolk
Reproduced, printed and bound in Great Britain by
Hazell Watson & Viney Limited
Member of BPCC plc
Aylesbury Bucks

EDITOR'S DEDICATION

To my fellow teachers at Queen Mary College who have survived a grudging and inimical administration with such good humour.

ACKNOWLEDGEMENTS

Every effort, with the aid of Macmillan London Limited, has been made to contact the Executors of the James Estate for permission to reprint excerpts from the letters.

ABBREVIATION

HJL refers to *Henry James, Letters*, selected and ed. Leon Edel, 4 vols., London and Cambridge, Mass., 1974–84.

CONTENTS

CONTENTS

ix

INTRODUCTION

❧

I

Henry James's literary criticism is so vivacious, informative and elegant that few readers will find it other than a pleasure to read. Some will predict for themselves imaginary difficulties, because of his great and misleading reputation for obscurity, but a glance at this volume will quickly show that they feared in vain. James is so interesting that he is interesting even when one has not read all or even any of what he is writing about – a curious test for a critic, but one which few pass. Like Dr Johnson he brings to his work a superabundance of mind which makes his comments on others a substantial part of his own proper *oeuvre* – as opposed to only a medium for information and judgement. His fine, impressionistic account of the Eighteenth Century (No. 13, below), for example, has a value independent of our knowledge or opinion of Mme de Sabran's *Correspondance*, and it is by no means a special case.

One of the reasons for James's accessibility is that he was an *occasional* critic. He finds a prominent place in any university course on English Literary Criticism and Theory but this position should not lead us to forget that from his early twenties he was a skilled practitioner of the higher journalism of his time, writing for editors and a modest fee. He responded to what was current rather than sought a field for research and evaluation. He wrote a short book on Hawthorne (No. 21), translated *Port Tarascon* by his friend Daudet, and even delivered – with immense private delighted flutterings and murmurings – celebrity lectures on Balzac (No. 53) and Browning (No. 73); but he was, besides being a great artist, a nineteenth-century man of letters, not a professor. An avid admirer, Professor R. P. Blackmur, wrote in his *Literary History of the United States* that James's criticism 'was almost entirely contemporary, of narrow range and narrower sympathies . . . worth reading chiefly as an illumination of his own mind and writing'. This is misleading to the point of absurdity and no doubt relects Blackmur's special interest in, and relative overestimate of, the Prefaces to the New York Edition of James's work (see the General Note to Nos. 56–71). Although he did not have an ordinary formal education, James has some of the widest sympathies known to intelligent literary man and his implied range is very wide – from Homer onwards; and he is often probably the *most* illuminating single writer on many of his subjects, Balzac or Flaubert or Zola for instance. Furthermore his actual range of interests is surprisingly broad; he being almost as at home with travel adventure or art history or political speculation as with literature proper. Blackmur may well have not had many of the relevant essays readily to hand. Nevertheless, the perversity of his remark should not obscure a substantial truth buried within it. Since the mushroom-like emergence of English Studies in mass academic education in this century we tend to think – often wrongly, but no matter – of the literary critic as a person able and willing to expound facts and judgements on the great mass of English (or Anglo-Saxon) literature. A professional teacher qualified to take most things on as well as a specialist and a scholar. This pleasant belief is not always unfounded; but it has the drawback of altering our more or less conscious *expectations* of the past, so that readers are dismayed to find that the great critics have little or nothing 'on' what they want to read them about. Matthew Arnold is practically no help at all on novels, Coleridge hardly there on dramatists after Shakespeare, Dr Johnson strange to our minds on early-seventeenth-century poetry – and Sir Philip Sidney had naturally heard of very little in English. So when it comes to James we may be dashed to find that he is decidedly slight and weak about poetry. His finest work on a poet is his essay on Browning's *The Ring and the Book* (No. 73), but this is fine precisely because of his interest in its subject as a 'grateful theme' for the 'fine strong economy of *prose* treatment'. As early as 1868 he was 'tempted to fancy' George Eliot's *The Spanish Gypsy* as prose; and his praise in the same year of William Morris's 'Chaucerian' *The Earthly Paradise* at the incidental expense of Keats and Swinburne sets the less than vital tone of his dealings with poetry from then on:

... frankly a work of entertainment. It deals in no degree with actual realities, with worldly troubles and burdens and problems ... Forget them for a few moments, and it will remind you of fairer, sweeter, and lighter

2

things, – things forgotten or grudgingly remembered, things that come to you in dreams and waking reveries, and odd idle moments stolen from the present ... in what better company could we forget the present? and remember not only the past, but the perpetual, the constant, the eternal, – the constant loves and fears and sorrows of mankind? It is very pleasant to wander ...

This is certainly a dignified form of escape; and James was obviously too intelligent to consider all forms of poetry in so wistful a light – in the following year he attacked Whitman's *Drum-Taps* (No. 5) for being insufficiently intense as poetry to take on the great subject of the Civil War. Nevertheless he never, in print, showed himself an especially percipient reader of verse. This may be odd in the creator of such marvellously achieved reverberant prose rhythms; but it is my point here that it would be crass to expect great critics to be universal critics.

Or would it? James himself had great ambitions to be a cultural force when he was a young man. In 1867 he wrote to T. S. Perry that:

... I suppose you will study Latin and Greek by the aid of German and *vice-versa*. But the English literature and spirit is a thing which we tacitly assume that we know much more of than we actually do. Don't you think so? Our vast literature and literary history is to most of us an unexplored field – especially when you compare it to what the French is to the French. – Deep in the timorous recesses of my being is a vague desire to do for our dear old English letters and writers *something* of what Ste Beuve and the best French critics have done for theirs.

This could be part of the proposals for the university English departments which began to emerge over half a century later. And it was not a casual idea. In 1880 he praised Sainte-Beuve himself precisely in terms of the width of his aspiration:

The part he desired to play was that of the vividly intelligent, brightly enlightened mind, acting in the interest of literature, knowledge, taste, and spending itself on everything human and historic. He was frankly and explicitly a critic; he attributed the highest importance to the critical function, and he understood in so large a way that it gives us a lift to agree with him. The critic, in his conception, was not the narrow lawgiver or the rigid censor that he is often assumed to be; he was the student, the inquirer, the interpreter, the taker of notes, the active, restless commentator, whose constant aim was to arrive at justness of characterisation. (review of

Correspondance de C. A. Sainte-Beuve (1822–69), North American Review. January 1880)

Any reader of James's criticism in any bulk will appreciate that in very many ways he lived up to this model. The case is similar with his other great admiration, Matthew Arnold, into whose 'critical arms' he remembers being thrown, as a young man, 'with force', in the autobiographical *A Small Boy and Others*. Arnold is of course primarily a critic of poetry. But what James seems to have especially loved is the depth and breadth of his sympathies. He quite explicitly took over a number of Arnold's key words and conceptions – crucially, 'interesting': Loti's insufficiently human ('quadruped') love affairs are 'not, as Mr Arnold says of American civilisation, *interesting*' he wrote in 1888 – and one of his own leading and inspiriting tendencies is towards the emulation of Arnold's 'ideal critic' (No. 4). Those who nowadays wish to attribute a Theory of the Novel to James would do well to take seriously his description of Edmond Schérer as such a critic:

There are plenty of theories, but no theory. We find . . . none but a moral unity . . . The age surely presents no finer spectacle than a mind liberal after this fashion; not from a brutal impatience of order, but from experience, from reflection . . . a mind inquisitive of truth and of knowledge, accessible on all sides, unprejudiced . . . (review of *Nouvelles Études sur la Littérature Contemporaine, par Edmond Schérer, Nation*, 12 October 1865)

So much, again, for Blackmur's 'narrow range and narrower sympathies'. But the question now arises: what became of a critical genius who so frequently and forcefully endorsed such ideals for himself? The answer is twofold and embraces the most important aspects of James as a critic.

II

First: James is rightly famous as an innovator in the criticism of the novel. He was uniquely equipped by his education in New England and New York, England, France, Italy and Switzerland—entailing as it did a rare intimacy with French – and by his subsequent ambiguous nationality as well as by his genius, to become a great champion of the new achievement of the age. No wonder he found Taine's theory of '*L'homme, le milieu, le moment*' etc. (No. 9) very obvious, for he embodied it. Although it has been pointed out (by Richard Stang in his *The Theory of the Novel in England 1850–1870* for example) that not all of our ideas about prose fiction sprang Minerva-like from James's head it is nevertheless true that he is the seminal force behind any discussion in English of this form. Hence our tiresome tendency to overvalue the Prefaces; but hence also the likeliest explanation of James's comparatively lukewarm dealings with poetry. He was far too busy, we might say, being an apologist for the new and striking and modern in literature to be more than duly respectful of what was, and in some ways still is, the more conventionally reputable form. This shows as it were statistically; at a rough count James published 149 pieces on novels against 22 mostly marginal ones on poetry; but it shows most, of course, in the brilliance and originality of what he had to say about fiction. By the time of his best early essay, 'The Art of Fiction' of 1884 (No. 26), he had clearly decided that it was time to set out some of the prime conditions for intelligent discussion of the novel, and that he was the man to do it. So with graciousness and charm he sets his contemporaries, and indeed us, right about the nature of fiction as a serious art. Of the common opinion of artistic preoccupations in novels he gaily observes:

They are too frivolous to be edifying, and too serious to be diverting; and they are moreover priggish and paradoxical and superfluous. That, I think, represents the manner in which the latent thought of many people who read novels as an exercise in skipping would explain itself if it were to become articulate.

On the contrary, novels are 'at once as free and serious a branch of literature as any other' and this he supports by a series of arguments which are as strong as they are subtle. The main thrust of the essay is that no requirement whatever – for a happy ending, for moral edification, for the placation of Mrs Grundy, for adventures, for a story, for certain restrictive forms – should be allowed to hamper the poetry of the novelist. 'Catching the very note and trick, the strange irregular rhythm of life' is his business and this is to be achieved by imagination, by being 'one of the people on whom nothing is lost'. This last formulation is extremely famous. Indeed it is part of an essay which more and more appears as *the* manifesto of what we assume to be 'modern' literature and thus almost consists of famous and immensely influential *dicta*: 'What is character but the determination of incident? What is incident but the illustration of character?' 'A novel is a living thing, all one and continuous, like any other organism.' 'Why [must a novel consist] of adventures more than of green spectacles?' 'The deepest quality of a work of art will always be the quality of the mind of the producer.' – such deft and serious strokes have become part of the medium through which the twentieth century views its literature. The charming ease of tone does not disguise the fact that James, because of the natural depth of his intellection, raises in some form – the form appropriate to the novel – many of the basic perennial questions of literary criticism from Aristotle onwards. The question of imitation and representation – in what sense is fiction true; the ways in which illusion is sustained; how fiction can properly be called good; the form (or shape or structure) of works of art; the epistemological relations of an artist both to his creations and to reality; the dubious nature of general laws or prescription in art; the qualifications requisite in an audience – and so on. The manner is that of the best kind of essayist – informal and non-abstract, even flattering: but the purport is entirely serious. When, for example, James accuses Trollope of a 'crime' in undermining his work by drawing attention to its arbitrary or artificial nature he means exactly what he says. And 'The Art of Fiction' is only one of a series of general essays, backed up by a multitude of pieces on individual writers, which culminate in the New York Prefaces on James himself. Much of the relevant material, it is pleasant to be able to say, can be found below.

Not that James was at all infallible as a critic of the novel. He fought a long and intimate war with the French, the most notable events of which are his lifelong revaluation of Balzac; the yielding of his early classification of Flaubert as 'minor' along with Charles de Bernard (No. 16) to the satisfying treaty about the relation of subject-matter and treatment represented by his 1902 essay (No. 49); and his successful defence against Zola and Naturalism (No. 50). But elsewhere he could be less alert. It would have been entirely appropriate for him as a francophile and pioneer to have led the rediscovery of Stendhal. But, like Sainte-Beuve who was unforgettably ridiculed by Proust for it, he did not see the point. And although he expressed admiration for *La Chartreuse de Parme* in 1874 he found 'the heroine . . . a kind of monster' and *Le Rouge et le Noir* almost 'absolutely unreadable', with an air of 'unredeemed corruption'. These are the kind of late-nineteenth-century fixed attitudes – the indiscriminate rejection of the 'unpleasant' – from which he himself later suffered and against which he was later energetically to fight. But he scarcely returned to Stendhal. In a different way, those who take the great Jane Austen seriously will be irritated by his habitual air of bland, benign patronage when she comes up; for James as critic she is always the 'little', 'unconscious' feminine genius, in implied contrast to the weighty, serious and technically aware male masters (including George Eliot) who succeeded her. This again endorses a literary cliché about 'everybody's dear Jane' of which he was scornfully aware, and which is particularly galling in James as a novelist who so obviously, in *The Europeans* and *Washington Square* for example, found a great deal to learn from her (but see No. 22).

The best-known instance of James's failure to concur with what is now established taste are his dealings, or lack of them, with Tolstoy. The allusion to 'large loose baggy monsters' in the preface to *The Tragic Muse* (No. 60) has been quoted to death. Another well known passage from a letter to Hugh Walpole is more interesting:

Form alone *takes*, and holds and preserves, substance – saves it from the welter of helpless verbiage that we swim in as a sea of tasteless tepid pudding . . . Tolstoy and D. [Dostoyevsky] are fluid-pudding, though not tasteless, because the amount of their minds and souls in solution in the broth gives it savour and flavour, thanks to the strong, rank quality of their genius and their experience . . . we see how great a vice is their lack of composition, their defiance of economy and architecture, directly they are emulated and imitated, *then*, as subjects of emulation, models, they quite give themselves away. There is nothing so deplorable as a work of art with a *leak* in its interest; and there is no such leak of interest as through commonness of form. (May 1912)

In an essay on *Anna Karenina* which sets out to confute such views, F. R. Leavis, with characteristic accuracy, observes that 'the sense of the possibilities of the novel that informed [James's] criticism was determined by his own creative preoccupations, and his conception was personal and his own in a limiting way . . .' (*'Anna Karenina' and Other Essays*, 1967) and he compares Matthew Arnold's equally unpopular refusal to see Tolstoy's novel as other than a 'piece of life'. This has justice; but I think it important to be less scathing than Leavis. James was writing *in private* to an eager young disciple, 'Beloved little Hugh'. More importantly, the determination 'by his own creative preoccupation' may have narrowed James's focus as he grew older – a *leitmotiv* in his later letters is his confession in the face of all sorts of demands from H. G. Wells, Edith Wharton, Howard Sturgess, Willa Cather, etc., that 'My only way of reading . . . is to imagine myself *writing* the thing before me' (Letter to Lucy Clifford, May 1912); but it was exactly this preoccupation which gave strength and seriousness and insight to his campaign on behalf of the beloved form. Who but James, after all, insisted that 'The house of fiction has . . . not one window, but a million' (preface to *The Portrait of a Lady*, No. 58)? – a conviction which appears time after time in his criticism. It is a commonplace that much distinguished criticism is the offshoot of creation. And if we can willingly assent to the preoccupations of Pope, Johnson, Coleridge, T. S. Eliot, and D. H. Lawrence (who also quarrelled with Tolstoy), why are those of James less allowable or even beneficial? Possibly because he is so open on the question of what he would take on. 'I haven't at the moment *time* to read all or any of this stuff, it's impossible to me,' he complained to Gosse in 1901 when asked to write on Tolstoy. Even so, it is not as though he were unaware of these Russians (Alice James used to copy out passages from *War and Peace* in French into her commonplace book in the late 1880s; and her doing so at once reminds us that her brother must have early been accustomed to admirers of Tolstoy, and that the problem is unlikely to have been that of bad translations of Russian into French; see also No. 40). And it really is time to emphasize the obvious fact that both in private and in public what James laments is the tendency to waste, because of the alleged lack of organization, what he acknowledges as a tremendous vitality and splendour, 'mind' and 'soul', in these writers, especially Tolstoy. James's favourite author was probably Turgenev. He loved and championed him from early on; and it is pardonable to allow him a preference, for as he says in 'The Art of Fiction':

Nothing, of course, will ever take the place of the good old fashion of 'liking' a work of art or not liking it: the most improved criticism will not abolish that primitive, that ultimate test.

Quite so.

Finally on the question of James's limitations as a critic of the novel, the reader of so much liveliness and sharp judgement will perhaps find himself irrationally disappointed that we do not have him 'on' the moderns such as Proust or Joyce or even Thomas Mann. We do have a parenthetical remark, again rather infamous, on D. H. Lawrence in 'The New Novel' (No. 76) to the effect that *Sons and Lovers* hangs 'in the dusty rear' of Hugh Walpole, Gilbert Cannan and Compton Mackenzie. But this is the work of a man in his penultimate year, preoccupied as we know with his own methods and moreover guilty of a critical negligence unusual for him. '"Have you ever read any of Lawrence's novels – really read them?"' Edith Wharton records a mutual friend as insisting. 'James's most mischievous smile crept down from his eyes to his lips. "I – I have trifled with the exordia," he murmured.' This is a pity as well as a laugh, although Lawrence does not seem to have resented it: 'Subtle conventional design was his aim,' he remarked with a notable lack of acrimony the following year. Except in the case of Turgenev (and himself) James, unlike for example Baudelaire, was never a great spotter and backer of undervalued genius. But it would still be good to know what he would have made of writers he is so often said to have been the precursor of. All we have is some evidence that his mind began to narrow before he really paid attention to Conrad, and a tradition that he was immensely struck by Proust – but this latter is hearsay, and probably a case of wishful thinking.

A more fruitful line is to consider a large instance of James confronting what was for him the modern in a manner and with a force available to him alone. His long essays on Maupassant and Zola deal with the challenge of Naturalism and are represented below (Nos. 29 and 50). But D'Annunzio is so little read nowadays that I have economized on space by omitting James's long essay on him, published in 1904. (It can be found in Morris Shapira's *Henry James, Selected Literary Criticism*, 1963, as well as, of course, in Edel and Wilson's *Henry James, Literary Criticism, Vol. II*.) Instead, it can be cited here as an example of how tactfully yet powerfully James reacted to another, related, school which he distrusted. He starts with a full surrender to what is offered: 'I propose . . . that it shall not be prematurely a question with us of what we miss; no intelligible statement of which, for that matter . . . is ever possible till there has been some adequate statement of what we find.' He then goes on by description, evocation and lengthy quotation to render the torrid and sensuous atmosphere of D'Annunzio's fictions, with their surrender to beauty and passion at all costs. 'Beauty at any price' had been a bore, a 'queer high flavoured fruit from overseas'; but now although interested only in 'the erotic and the plastic', it finds such energetic embodiment in D'Annunzio that Casanova's autobiography appears 'cheap loose journalism' by comparison. James is marvellously sympathetic and receptive as an audience. He gives everything possible in the way of appreciation and even indulgence to this Latin aesthetic assault. He sets D'Annunzio substantially before us. But then he begins to turn mildly, hardly perceptibly, from an applauding reader into a sensitive judge; and this judge is very serious and ultimately implacable. The beauty and richness of D'Annunzio's doomed lovers, it appears, depends on their passion having 'neither duration, nor propagation, nor common kindness, nor common consistency with other relations, common congruity with the rest of life.' It is 'vulgar'. And as James puts it with a delicate, cruel firmness, the 'association rising before us more nearly than any other is that of the manners observable in the most mimetic department of any great menagerie'. The effect of this is of course to condemn much more substantially and effectively and finally than any initially hostile approach could do. It is damning with lavish praise. But it is not a trick. It is a real exercise of the sympathetic imagination carefully and definitely discriminating. Readers of this selection will soon learn to recognize this structure as a basic habit of James's mind. In the earlier criticism it often produces sudden and dazzling plus/minus switches of approval; later it becomes almost a method or a trademark – as with Flaubert (No. 49 and elsewhere), Balzac (No. 50 and else- where), George Sand, Victor Hugo, Wells and Bennett (No. 76), and many others. Edith Wharton records a pertinent if painful memory of James in person:

. . . it would be a mistake to imagine that he had deliberately started out to destroy my wretched tale. He had begun, I am sure, with the sincere intention of praising it; but no sooner had he opened his lips than he was overmastered by the need to speak the truth, and the whole truth, about anything connected with the art which was sacred to him . . . on all subjects but that of letters his sincerity was tempered by an almost exaggerated tenderness; but when *le métier* was in question no gentler emotion prevailed. (*A Backward Glance*, 1934)

James as a critic of the novel is at the same time benign and formidable, just as he is as a novelist.

III

The second leading aspect of his criticism which demands discussion here concerns James's stance in what may crudely be called the 'life versus art' debate, or the debate between various kinds of 'formalist' and the rest of the world. Much of what James thought has already been implied; and as will appear, it amazes me that there is still any serious question as to his, admittedly very subtle and influential, attitudes. But it is as well to be quite explicit.

There is, unfortunately, a nagging opposition between two schools, or at least between two leading emphases. One tends to say perhaps rather excitedly that 'James's later work, especially his Prefaces, precurses and leads into Modernism, with its sophisticated stresses on textual analysis, rhetoric(s), the science of signs, new genre classifications, Structuralism and the-sky's-the-limit.' The other replies, 'Forget all this pseudo-scientific jargon; James was an Arnoldian, Sainte-Beuvian, 'life'-based, value-judgement kind of critic; and he is thus part of our magnificent Anglo-Saxon pragmatic tradition, a rich earth to come down to.' Both of these positions *can* be respectable, even useful, as a means of organizing our thought about James. But neither does anything like justice to the subtlety and power of his mind. Neither adequately recognizes the logical basis of his actual 'position', which is stated or implied at various times throughout his career, from 'The Art of Fiction' and earlier to his latest recorded utterance. This is that art is important, literally vitally important, and worthy of the deepest love and respect for and infatuation with and delight in all its methods and intricacies and registers and strategies and tricks, precisely because, and when, it renders experience most strongly and finely. There is no real conflict. Lifeless 'art' is bad art. Artless or crude art fails to do justice to life. James believed that Tolstoy lost significance through inattention to artistic discipline; but he also believed that *Madame Bovary*, with all its renowned discipline, is limited by having too dull and circum-scribed a subject. Both of these judgements are vulnerable; but they are certainly consistent. James himself is nothing if not a conscious and polished writer: but like Turgenev as described by him, 'He believes in the intrinsic value of "subject" in art; he holds that there are trivial subjects and serious ones, that the latter are much the best, that their superiority resides in their giving us absolutely a greater amount of information about the human mind.' This was written in 1874. In July 1915, only a few months before his death, he wrote to H. G. Wells a letter which contains the famous gnomic sentences 'It is art that *makes* life, makes interest, makes importance, for our consideration and application of these things, and I know of no substitute whatever for the force and beauty of its process.' Wells professed not to understand this; and it is frequently cited by those of the 'formalist' persuasion to further some notional superiority of 'art' over 'life'. But (as noted by Edel and Ray in 1959, among others) its context is the other side of the coin: 'I *have* no view of life and literature ... other than that our form of the latter in especial is admirable exactly by its range and variety, its plasticity and liberal-ity, its fairly living on the sincere and shifting experience of the individual practitioner.' There is no reason why James should have altered his basic position in forty years of devotion to literature. His practice was as consistent as his logic.

The failure to understand, let alone arrive at, this both simple and complex position is a characteristic elementary vulgarity of the 'aesthetes' of all generations, including our own; and, equally, of the moral, religious or political seekers of various more or less naïve affirmations from art. For instance it is possible to at once partly agree with, and feel a profound if weary irritation at, the following quite up-to-date, generally sensible account of the situation by Vivien Jones:

James's reputation benefited most from the taste for formal self-consciousness engendered during the 1940s and 1950s by the application of New Critical principles to the novel but ... *The Portrait of a Lady* is a part of Leavis's great tradition, and in 1963 Leavis appropriated James for his aggressively untheoretical criticism of moral evaluation by rejecting the Prefaces, as capable only of offering 'a new academicism', in favour of a defective version of James's essays on French novelists 'in which, defining his essential value-judgements . . . he invokes "life".' Leavis's damaging and early influential split between early and late James is extended from the novels to the criticism – where it is of course equally false. (*James the Critic*, 1984)

Although it may appear obscure to the general reader, unaware of academic ups and downs, this quick survey contains some sense. But in detail it is gross and tendentious in an embarrassing way. Leavis – whose 'great tradition' includes very much more of James's fiction than *Portrait* by the way – is depicted as some kind of bullying literary entrepreneur. In fact, one is inclined to say, he came from a different civilization from that of Jones. His brilliant short lecture, which was reprinted as an introduction to Morris Shapira's *Henry James, Selected Literary Criticism* (and in the posthumous *The Critic as Anti-Philosopher*, 1982) is actually the most packed and finely understanding essay on James's criticism available – making most of the points noted above better and implying more. Although it is challenging and severe in places, the only really accurate thing Jones tells us about it is its date. Leavis thought the Prefaces overrated, but he emphatically recommends that to *Roderick Hudson*; and the essays on Maupassant, Flaubert and Balzac which he spends most of his time praising were published in 1888, 1902 and 1902. He moves on from them to endorse James's treatment of Arnold Bennett in 'The New Novel' of 1914.

But an equal irritation should be felt about the other side, as it were. Morris Shapira's collection, for which Leavis was persuaded to allow his lecture to be used as preface, was designed and destined to be influential. One can see that the selection was done with sophisticated care. But its representative quality is quite ruined by reprinting disproportionately much of James's dismissals of various types of aestheticism. To the indispensable essay on the Goncourts (No. 31) and that of 1902 on Flaubert he adds the very long one on D'Annunzio, just discussed. Then he omits any mention, let alone reprint, of the Prefaces in the face of Leavis's recommendation of that to *Roderick Hudson*. It amounts to a very stiff piece of anti-aestheticism, though it is not at all crude. It is easy to see why Vivien Jones was so angry.

I have sketched in the lines of this academic debate because of its representative quality. The responses here opposed are *both* likely to be felt, at different but quickly succeeding times, by any alert reader. We should be aware of them, and become therefore primarily aware that James provokes them because of the generous width of his intelligence. The middle way which he steers is not that of timid mediocrity but of reconciling critical genius. His chosen role was that of the defender of the importance of both life to art, and of art to life – a central role which must not be misinterpreted. It is no contradiction to add in passing that, of modern critics of distinction, Leavis is the one who has always struck me as closest in nature to James. If we forget for a moment the disconcerting aura of quarrelsomeness which hangs around the former's name and pass quickly through the obvious differences of milieu, field and emphasis we find that they share extraordinarily a passionate belief in the dignity and almost the sanctity of art; a cultivated awareness of the complex and nuanced social, political, national and spiritual sources from which it springs; an inwardness with its most refined workings and its broadest effects; a love, therefore, of the concrete and actual, the facts of the case; a sophisticated impatience with poseurs; a hovering concern with what 'moral' means in relation to their vital subject; and a lifelong determination to say what they mean and nothing else. And because of the last they both evolved a prose style which is complex, not for love of the elaborate, but because of the complexity of what has to be expressed – 'like marching on seven different fronts at once' as Leavis once said, or 'involved because the impressions of a man of genius are so many, and the resources of speech so limited' as Mrs Humphrey Ward said of James. They were both, incidentally, evidently men of great wit and charm and real benevolence. Beside all this it is of marginal importance, or of importance only in other ways, that Leavis responded to neglect and misunderstanding and the praise of a cult with an embattled stance and James with a defensive excess of grace.

IV

Leavis makes the point that 'the way in which' James criticizes 'is hardly . . . a separable thing' from what is said. I should like to close my suggestions by expanding on this very briefly. It is of course true of all very good writers that their manner strictly creates the meaning; that a paraphrase would signify, however slightly, something different. With James the dominant mode is of a wit and urbanity which lifts his criticism from the merely instructive to the delightful. All good critics should, I think, try to entertain. Nobody needs a dull book to explain an interesting one. Johnson entertains by his humorously gloomy authority; Hazlitt by his dash; Matthew Arnold by his ironic teasing and special personal vocabulary. I have remarked before that it is possible to read James for entertainment and intrinsic interest without knowing the author under discussion. He has a polite vivacity even when making an austere judgement. How does this come about? Much of the wit is a matter of quick, imaginative, metaphorical turns of phrase. We get used to such felicities as this on Hawthorne's 'psychology': 'His tread is a light and modest one, but he keeps the key in his pocket' (No. 21). But what is especially distinctive is that these metaphors tend to become first extended metaphors, and then full similes. Well-known examples of the latter are, for instance, the 'house of fiction' and its windows in the preface to *The Portrait of a Lady* (No. 58) and the exposition of a complex theory of romance by means of early aviation – the 'Balloon of experience' and its tethering rope – in that to *The American* (No. 57). But he is always liable to take off in this direction. When writing to W. D. Howells in 1890, for instance, he anticipates the first of these ideas (a cousin to the mirrors invoked by Hamlet and Stendhal maybe) and elaborates it at greater length than I have space to quote:

The novelist is a particular *window*, absolutely – and of worth in so far as he is one; and it's because you open so well and hang so close over the street that *I* could hang out of it all day long. Your very value is that you choose your own street – heaven forbid that *I* should have to choose it for you. If I should say that I mortally dislike the people who pass in it . . . etc. (*HJL*, Vol. 3, 282)

This is simply not reducible to: 'I like your realistic mind and approach but dislike your subject matter.' The figure is *essential* – besides hinting at a general idea. Some readers do go away with the impression that James's elaboration is only decoration of a stupendous kind, or even indulgence in whimsy. On the contrary, the ideas would not exist even in the flattest form without the metaphors. Consider these valedictory words on Pater:

Well, faint, pale, embarrassed exquisite Pater! He reminds me, in the disturbed midnight of our actual literature, of one of those lucent matchboxes which you place, on going to bed, near the candle, to show you, in the darkness, where you can strike a light: he shines in the uneasy gloom — vaguely, and has a phosphorescence, not a flame. But I quite agree with you that he is not of the little day — but of the longer time. (Letter to Edmund Gosse, December 1894. *HJL*, Vol. 3, 492)

This contains its subject perfectly. I cannot imagine how a paraphrase would run. The only occasions on which the metaphorical habit may obscure James's precision is when his favourite analogies with painting or sculpture (or sometimes architecture) become so strong and literal that the qualities of these arts begin to modify and distort instead of illuminating and defining literature – to re-invade it with their associations of stillness and finish for example.

Besides the creation of exact and otherwise unavailable meaning, metaphorical writing tends to involve the reader more energetically than plain statement would do. It is thus a parallel and abetter to another notable characteristic of James's critical prose, the way in which we begin to take a lively interest in the movements and adventures of the writer's sensibility. The essays become a species of little story about how this colourful and charming 'speaker' fared in relation to this or that subject. The playfulness, hanging clauses, exaggerations, stalking around, and seeming over-delicacy create small dramas of the 'which way will he jump next?' variety. Especially when, as I have remarked, he jumps sometimes with disconcerting speed from praise to censure and sometimes moves with gradual deliberation from warm appreciation to austere judgement. This drama is most evident in the longer essays (of 10,000 words or over) which are James's best form – the quarterly-review type of survey in which the subject's life, work, and characteristics are described and evaluated, as in the various essays on Balzac, Flaubert, Emerson, D'Annunzio, George Sand, Daudet and so on. But it is also present in the shorter reviews and even in all its essentials in the classic anecdote told by Sir Edward Marsh about James's reaction to some unfortunate entertainment offered at Edmund Gosse's house:

. . . the literary lights of London, packed like figs in a box, observed with languor the performance of some third-rate marionettes. After a while Mr

James, who was standing beside me squeezed against a wall, turned to me with a malicious gleam in his eye. 'An interesting example, my dear Marsh, of Economy of Means – and – and – and –' (with an outburst) 'Economy of *Effect*.'

The advantage of so recognizable a manner is clear: probing by metaphor and the personal dramatic style both contribute to the sensitive telling of truths about the impressions made by literature as near precisely as we can ever get. But a slight practical disadvantage follows. The tone is infectious and when, as often happens, it is copied, it tends to become a kind of facetious trifling, affected and coy, which may in turn distort our vision of the original. James was deadly serious about art, and his reader is constantly jolted back to that. His critical prose, like that of his novels, is a unique instrument and should be considered so: it is not a good model nor is it the idiosyncratic and lovable (or forgivable) medium of a mind fine in spite of its medium.

Lastly on this subject it should be noted that James quite often uses some important words in a sense different from ours. Usually this is evident from the context, given attentive reading. But sometimes a little extra awareness is in place. The 'interesting' which he seems to have taken over from Matthew Arnold, for example, tends to have a high, dignifying 'moral' force rather than a merely descriptive one. 'Irresponsible' is used in a way colloquial then but not now – it is a praise word meaning free of irrelevant or cramping restrictions, *not* lacking seriousness. A good novel can be irresponsible. A few meanings are relatively archaic – when James refers to 'humorous' Norman peasants in Flaubert he means that they are full of characteristic traits and quirks, not that they are affable and witty. And every reader of the later fiction will know that pseudo-superlatives such as 'wonderful' and 'magnificent' are likely to be deceptive: they range from meaning what they seem to mean to meaning the exact opposite. On the whole, it is useful to bear in mind what sometimes becomes overt in the earlier criticism; that James was, after all, a Victorian American Gentleman and, in spite of the reach and urbanity which often makes him seem our contemporary, always wrote as one.

V

James's reviews often contain regretful words like 'I had marked a great many passages for quotation. Page after page . . .' Naturally in view of the qualities of his work its editor finds himself frequently echoing the sentiment. Although this is the most comprehensive selection published, roughly a fifth of what is available, it still leaves out a great deal which I feel, without fanaticism, should be generally known. In particular I regret the omission of a large body of writing which while not strictly literary criticism is informative and evocative about literary people, their lives and characters. Thus James is always good on George Sand, although he ended up being interested in her as a personage much more than in her novels (see Nos. 19 and 75). He wrote in the course of forty-five years what could amount to a short book on her; and here he is in 1897 conjuring up with controlled nostalgia his feelings about the special atmosphere of mid-century French artistic circles:

It is antedeluvian history, a queer vanished world – another Venice from the actually, the deplorably familiarised, a Paris of greater bonhomie, an inconceivable impossible Nohant. This relegates it to an order agreeable somehow to the imagination of the fond quinquigenerian, the reader with a fund of reminiscence. The vanished world, the Venice unrestored, the Paris unextended, is a bribe to his judgement; he has even a glance of complacency for the lady's liberal *foyer*. Liszt, one lovely year at Nohant, 'jouait du piano au rez-de-chausée, et les rossignols, ivres de musique et de soleil, s'égosillaient avec rage sur les lilas environants.' The beautiful manner confounds itself with the conditions in which it was exercised, the large liberty and variety overflow into admirable prose, and the whole thing makes a charming faded medium in which Chopin gives a hand to Consuelo and the small Fadette has her elbows on the table of Flaubert. (review of *She & He: Recent Documents*, Yellow Books, 1897)

Well, yes, and Balzac talks until five in the morning three nights in a row – as he actually did. This is James showing what S. Gorley Putt so memorably calls his 'occasional poetic glee'. Elsewhere he is less lyrical but equally interesting – as in the reconstruction of the life and times of his old friend the Shakespearian actress, hostess, beauty and wit, Fanny Kemble: or in his brief and touching essay on the French Romantic painter Henri Regnault, shot dead defending Paris in 1871 at the age of twenty-seven; or in his living accounts of the theatre in

Boston or Paris or London – and so on through affectionate renderings of Musset, J. R. Lowell, Frances Parkman, George du Maurier, W. D. Howells, Daudet and many other subjects. James does not make the notorious mistake of the Bellettrist critic of judging artists' work through or because of their lives; but his keen recall and creation of real figures in an environment does of course remind us that a great deal of his thought about the conditions and nature of artistic creation is contained in his novels and tales: and clearly *they* cannot be reprinted here.

This selection has been made mainly by consulting the following sources (listed here approximately in order of importance):

Henry James: Literary Criticism, 2 vols., ed. Leon Edel and Mark Wilson in the Library of America, 2 vols., 1984; *The Letters of Henry James*, selected and ed., Percy Lubbock, 2 vols., 1920; *Henry James, Letters*, 4 vols., selected and ed., Leon Edel, 1974–1984; *The Notebooks of Henry James*, ed. F. O. Matthiessen and Kenneth B. Murdock, 1947 and *The Complete Notebooks of Henry James*, ed. Leon Edel and Lyall H. Powers, 1987; *Henry James, Autobiography* (*A Small Boy and Others*, 1913, *Notes of a Son and Brother*, 1914, *The Middle Years*, 1915), ed. F. W. Dupee, 1956; *William Wetmore Story and his Friends*, Henry James, 1903; *The American Scene*, Henry James, 1907; *English Hours*, Henry James, 1905; *The Scenic Art*, ed. Allan Wade, 1949; *The James Family*, F. O. Matthiessen, 1948, and *A Little Tour of France*, Henry James, 1884. The order is chronological and the reader is invited to contemplate James's mind changing, sometimes back and forward, on subjects of importance. The selections from the Prefaces are printed in one sequence (nos. 56–71).

Each item is preceded by a Headnote giving details of publication etc., and any other relevant information and comment. Thus the tedium of footnotes has been avoided. Following the Library of America edition of the *Literary Criticism* the last version of the texts is used in cases where James revised them; but contrary to the practice of these valuable volumes, the spelling has been regularized into the English as opposed to the American form – a decision made for reasons of consistency rather than of patriotism.

ROGER GARD

I

✂

On Sir Walter Scott, from a review of Essays in Fiction *by Nassau W. Senior, 1864.* North American Review, *October 1864. Note the early distrust of overt moralism in the novel. Also that the twenty-one-year-old James, as well as considering Fielding 'one of the masses', does not seem to have read James Austen.*

HE WAS the inventor of a new style. We all know the immense advantage a craftsman derives from this fact. He was the first to sport a fashion which was eventually taken up. For many years he enjoyed the good fortune of a patentee. It is difficult for the present generation to appreciate the blessings of this fashion. But when we review the modes prevailing for twenty years before, we see almost as great a difference as a sudden transition from the Spenserian ruff to the Byronic collar. We may best express Scott's character by saying that, with one or two exceptions, he was the first English prose story-teller. He was the first fictitious writer who addressed the public from its own level, without any preoccupation of place. Richardson is classified simply by the matter of length. He is neither a romancer nor a story-teller: he is simply Richardson. The works of Fielding and Smollett are less monumental, yet we cannot help feeling that they too are writing for an age in which a single novel is meant to go a great way. And then these three writers are emphatically preachers and moralists. In the heart of their productions lurks a didactic *raison d'être*. Even Smollett – who at first sight appears to recount his heroes' adventures very much as Leporello in the opera rehearses the exploits of Don Juan – aims to instruct and to edify. To posterity one of the chief attractions of *Tom Jones* is the fact that its author was one of the masses, that he wrote from the midst of the working, suffering mortal throng. But we feel guilty in reading the book in any such disposition of mind. We feel guilty, indeed, in admitting the question of art or science into our considerations. The story is like a vast episode in a sermon preached by a grandly humorous divine; and however we may be entertained by the way, we must not forget that our ultimate duty is to be instructed. With the minister's week-day life we have no concern: for the present he is awful, impersonal Morality; and we shall incur his severest displeasure if we view him as Henry Fielding, Esq., as a rakish man of letters, or even as a figure in English literature. *Waverley* was the first novel which was self-forgetful. It proposed simply to amuse the reader, as an old English ballad amused him. It undertook to prove nothing but facts. It was the novel irresponsible.

We do not mean to say that Scott's great success was owing solely to this, the freshness of his method. This was, indeed, of great account, but it was as nothing compared with his own intellectual wealth. Before him no prose-writer had exhibited so vast and rich an imagination: it had not, indeed, been supposed that in prose the imaginative faculty was capable of such extended use. Since Shakespeare, no writer had created so immense a gallery of portraits, nor, on the whole, had any portraits been so lifelike. Men and women, for almost the first time out of poetry, were presented in their habits as they lived. The Waverley characters were all instinct with something of the poetic fire. To our present taste many of them may seem little better than lay-figures. But there are many kinds of lay-figures. A person who goes from the workshop of a carver of figure-heads for ships to an exhibition of wax-work, will find in the latter the very reflection of nature. And even when occasionally the waxen visages are somewhat inexpressive, he can console himself with the sight of unmistakable velvet and brocade and tartan. Scott went to his prose task with essentially the same spirit which he had brought to the composition of his poems. Between these two departments of his work the difference is very small. Portions of 'Marmion' are very good prose; portions of *Old Mortality* are tolerable poetry. Scott was never a very deep, intense, poetic poet: his verse alone was unflagging. So when he attacked his prose characters with his habitual poetic inspiration, the harmony of style was hardly violated. It is a great peculiarity, and perhaps it is one of the charms of his historical tales, that history is dealt with in all poetic reverence. He is tender of the past: he knows that she is frail. He certainly knows it. Sir Walter could not have read so widely or so curiously as he did, without discovering a vast deal that was gross and ignoble in bygone times. But he excludes these elements as if he feared they would clash with his numbers. He has the same indifference to historic truth as an epic poet, without, in the novels, having the same excuse. We write historical tales differently now. We acknowledge the beauty and propriety of a certain poetic reticence. But we confine it to poetry. The task of the historical story-teller is, not to invest, but to divest the past. Tennyson's 'Idylls of the King' are far more one-sided, if we may so express it, than anything of Scott's. But imagine what disclosures we should have if Mr Charles Reade were to take it into his head to write a novel about King Arthur and his times.

2

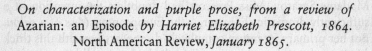

On characterization and purple prose, from a review of Azarian: an Episode *by Harriet Elizabeth Prescott, 1864.* North American Review, *January 1865.*

THERE IS surely no principle of fictitious composition so true as this, – that an author's paramount charge is the cure of souls, to the subjection, and if need be to the exclusion, of the picturesque. Let him look to his characters: his *figures* will take care of themselves. Let the author who has grasped the heart of his purpose trust his reader's sympathy: from that vantage-ground he may infallibly command it. In what we may call subordinate points, that is, in Miss Prescott's prominent and obtrusive points, it is an immense succour. It supplements his intention. Given an animate being, you may readily clothe it in your mind's eye with a body, a local habitation, and a name. Given, we say, an animate being: that is the point. The reader who is set face to face with a gorgeous doll will assuredly fail to inspire it with sympathetic life. To do so, he must have become excited and interested. What is there in a doll to excite and interest?

In reading books of the Azarian school, – for, alas! there is a school, – we have often devoutly wished that some legal penalty were attached to the use of description. We have sighed for a novel with a *dramatis personae* of disembodied spirits. Azarian gives his name to two hundred and fifty pages; and, at the end of those pages, the chief fact with which he is associated in our minds is that he wore his hair in 'waves of flaccid gold'. Of Madame Saratov we read that she was the widow of a Russian exile, domesticated in Boston for the purpose of giving lessons in French, music, and Russ, and of educating her boys. In spite of the narrowness of means attributable to a lady who follows the profession of teaching, she lives in a splendour not unworthy of the Muscovite Kremlin. She has a maid to haunt her steps; her chosen raiment is silks and velvets; she sleeps in counterpanes of satin; her thimble, when she sews, is incrusted at the base with pearls; she holds a *salon*, and treats her guests to draughts of 'richly-rosy' cordial. One of her dresses is a gown of green Genoa velvet, with peacock's feathers of gorgeous green and gold. What do you think of that for an exiled teacher of languages, boasting herself Russian? Perhaps, after all, it is not so improbable. In the person of Madame Saratov, Miss Prescott had doubtless the intention of a sufficiently dramatic character, – the European mistress of a *salon*. But her primary intention completely disappears beneath this thick *impasto* of words and images. Such is the fate of all her creations: either they are still-born, or they survive but for a few pages; she smothers them with caresses.

When a very little girl becomes the happy possessor of a wax-doll, she testifies her affection for it by a fond manipulation of its rosy visage. If the nose, for instance, is unusually shapely and pretty, the fact is made patent by a constant friction of the finger-tips; so that poor dolly is rapidly smutted out of recognition. In a certain sense we would compare Miss Prescott to such a little girl. She fingers her puppets to death. 'Good heavens, Madam!' we are forever on the point of exclaiming, 'let the poor things speak for themselves. What? are you afraid they can't stand alone?' Even the most clearly defined character would succumb beneath this repeated posing, attitudinizing, and changing of costume. Take any breathing *person* from the ranks of fiction, – Hetty in *Adam Bede*, or Becky Sharp the Great (we select women advisedly, for it is known that they can endure twenty times more than men in this respect), – place her for a few pages in Miss Prescott's charge, and what will be the result? Adieu, dear familiar friend; you melt like wax in a candle. Imagine Thackeray forever pulling Rebecca's curls and settling the folds of her dress.

This bad habit of Miss Prescott's is more than an offence against art. Nature herself resents it. It is an injustice to men and women to assume that the fleshly element carries such weight. In the history of a loving and breaking heart, is that the only thing worth noticing? Are the external signs and accidents of passion the only points to be detailed? What we want is Passion's self, – her language, her ringing voice, her gait, the presentment of her deeds. What do we care about the beauty of man or woman in comparison with their humanity? In a novel we crave the spectacle of that of which we may feel that we *know* it. The only lasting fictions are those which have spoken to the reader's heart, and not to his eye; those which have introduced him to an atmosphere in which it was credible that human beings might exist, and to human beings with whom he might feel tempted to claim kinship.

When once a work of fiction may be classed as a novel, its foremost claim to merit, and indeed the measure of its merit, is its *truth*, – its truth to something, however questionable that thing may be in point of morals or of taste. *Azarian* is true to nothing. No one ever looked like Azarian, talked like him, nor, on the whole, acted like him; for although his specific deeds, as related in the volume before us, are few and far between we find it difficult to believe that any one ever pursued a line of conduct so utterly meaningless as that which we are invited, or rather allowed, to attribute to him.

We have called Miss Prescott's manner the descriptive manner; but in so doing we took care to distinguish it from the famous realistic system which has asserted itself so largely in the fictitious writing of the last few years. It is not a counsel we would indiscriminately bestow, – on the contrary, we would gladly see the vulgar realism which governs the average imagination leavened by a little old-fashioned idealism, – but Miss Prescott, if she hopes to accomplish anything worth accomplishing, must renounce new-fashioned idealism for a while, and diligently study the canons of the so-called realist school. We gladly admit that she has the talent to profit by such a discipline. But to be real in writing is to describe; such is the popular notion. Were this notion correct, Miss Prescott would be a very good realist, – none better. But for this fallacious axiom we propose to substitute another, which, if it does not embrace the whole truth, comes several degrees nearer to it: to be real in writing is to express; whether by description or otherwise is of secondary importance. The short tales of M. Prosper Mérimée are eminently real; but he seldom or never describes: he conveys. It is not to be denied that the great names in the realist line are associated with a pronounced fondness for description. It is for this reason that we remind Miss Prescott of them. Let her take Balzac's *Eugénie Grandet*, for instance. It will probably be affirmed that this story, the interest of which is to the full as *human* as that of her own, is equally elaborate in the painting of external objects. But such an assertion will involve a mistake: Balzac does not *paint*, does not copy, objects; his chosen instrument being a pen, he is content to *write* them. He is literally real: he presents objects as they are. The scene and persons of his drama are minutely described. Grandet's house, his sitting-room, his habits, his appearance, his dress, are all reproduced with the fidelity of a photograph. The same with Madame Grandet and Eugénie. We are exactly informed as to the young girl's stature, features, and dress. The same with Charles Grandet, when he comes upon the scene. His coat, his trousers, his watch-chain, his cravat, the curl of his hair, are all dwelt upon. We almost see the musty little sitting-room in which so much of the action goes forward. We are familiar with the grey *boiserie*, the faded curtains, the rickety card-tables, the framed samplers on the walls, Madame Grandet's foot-warmer, and the table set for the meagre dinner. And yet our sense of the human interest of the story is never lost. Why is this? It is because these things are all described *only in so far as they bear upon the action*, and not in the least for themselves. If you resolve to describe a thing, you cannot describe it too carefully. But as the soul of a novel is its action, you should only describe those things which are accessory to the action. It is in determining what things *are* so accessory that real taste, science, and judgement are shown.

The reader feels that Miss Prescott describes not in accordance with any well-considered plan, but simply for the sake of describing, and of so gratifying her almost morbid love of the picturesque. There is a reason latent in every one of Balzac's tales *why* such things should appear thus, and such persons so, – a clear, well-defined reason, easily discoverable by the observing and sympathetic eye. Each separate part is conducive to the general effect; and this general effect has been studied, pondered, analysed: in the end it is produced. Balzac lays his stage, sets his scene, and introduces his puppets. He describes them once for all; this done, the story marches. He does not linger nervously about his figures, like a sculptor about his unfinished clay-model, administering a stroke here and affixing a lump there. He has done all this beforehand, in his thoughts; his figures are completed before the story begins. This latter fact is perhaps one of the most valuable in regard to Balzac. His story exists before it is told; it stands complete before his mind's eye. It was a characteristic of his mind, enriched as it was by sensual observation, to see his figures clearly and fully as with the eye of sense. So seeing them, the desire was irresistible to present them to the reader. How clearly he saw them we may judge from the minuteness of his presentations. It was clearly done because it was *scientifically* done. That word resumes our lesson. He set down things in black and white, not, as Miss Prescott seems vaguely to aim at doing, in red, blue, and green, – in prose, scientifically, as they stood. He aimed at local colour; that is, at giving the facts of things. To determine these facts required labour, foresight, reflection; but Balzac shrank from no labour of eye or brain, provided he could adequately cover the framework of his story . . .

If Miss Prescott would only take such good old English words as we possess, words instinct with the meaning of centuries, and, having fully resolved upon that which she wished to convey, cast her intention in those familiar terms which long use has invested with almost absolute force of expression, then she would describe things in a manner which could not fail to arouse the sympathy, the interest, the dormant memories of the reader. What is the possible bearing of such phrases as 'vermeil ardency', or 'a tang of colour'? of such childish attempts at alliteration – the most frequent bugbear of Miss Prescott's readers – as 'studded with starry sprinkle and spatter of splendour', and the following sentence, in which, speaking of the leaves of the blackberry-vine, she tells us that they are 'damasked with deepening layer and spilth of colour, brinded and barred and blotted beneath the dripping fingers of October, nipped by nest-lining bees', – and, lastly, 'suffused through all their veins with the shining soul of the mild and mellow season'?

This is nothing but 'words, words, words, Horatio!' They express nothing; they only seem to express. The true test of the worth of a prose description – to simplify matters we leave poetry quite out of the question – is one's ability to resolve it back into its original elements. You construct your description from a chosen object; can you, conversely, from your description construct that object? We defy any one to represent the 'fine scarlet of the blackberry vine', and 'the gilded bronze of beeches', – fair sentences by themselves, which express almost as much as we can reasonably hope to express on the subject, – under the inspiration of the rhapsody above quoted, and what follows it. Of course, where so much is attempted in the way of expression, something is sometimes expressed. But with Miss Prescott such an occasional success is apt to be what the French call a *succès manqué*. This is the fault of what our authoress must allow us to call her inveterate bad taste; for whenever she has said a good thing, she invariably spoils it by trying to make it better: to let well enough alone is indeed in all respects the great lesson which experience has in store for her. It is sufficiently felicitous, for instance, as such things go, to call the chandelier of a theatre 'a basket of light'. There stands the simple successful image. But Miss Prescott immediately tacks on the assertion that it 'pours down on all its brimming burden of lustre'. It would be bad taste again, if it were not such bad physiology, to speak of Azarian's flaccid hair being 'drenched with some penetrating perfume, an Oriental water that stung the brain to vigour'. The idea that a man's intellectual mood is at the mercy of his *pommade* is one which we recommend to the serious consideration of barbers. The reader will observe that Azarian's hair is *drenched*: an instance of the habitual intensity of Miss Prescott's style. The word *intensity* expresses better than any other its various shortcomings, or rather excesses. The only intensity worth anything in writing is intensity of thought. To endeavour to fortify flimsy conceptions by the constant use of verbal superlatives is like painting the cheeks and pencilling the eyebrows of a corpse.

3

Wilhelm Meister: Apprenticeship and Travels. From the German of Goethe *by Thomas Carlyle, 1865*. North American Review, *July 1865. Note the dismissal of plot and detailed superficial notation.*

THIS NEW EDITION of Goethe's great novel will give many persons the opportunity of reading a work which, although introduced to the English public forty years ago, is yet known to us chiefly by hearsay. We esteem it a matter for gratitude that it should now invite some share of attention as a novelty, if on no other ground; and we gladly take advantage of the occasion thus afforded to express our sense of its worth. We hope this republication may help to discredit the very general impression that *Wilhelm Meister* belongs to the class of the great unreadables. The sooner this impression is effaced, the better for those who labour under it. Something will have been gained, at least, if on experiment it should pass from a mere prejudice into a responsible conviction; and a great deal more will have been gained, if it is completely reversed.

To read *Wilhelm Meister* for the first time is an enviable and almost a unique sensation. Few other books, to use an expression which Goethe's admirers will understand, so steadily and gradually *dawn* upon the intelligence. In few other works is so profound a meaning enveloped in so common a form. The slow, irresistible action of this latent significance is an almost awful phenomenon, and one which we may vainly seek in those imaginative works in which the form of the narrative bears a direct, and not, as it appears here to do, an inverse, relation to its final import; or in which the manner appeals from the outset to the reader's sympathy. Whatever may be the lesson which Goethe proposes to teach us, however profound or however sublime, his means invariably remain homely and prosaic. In no book is the intention of elegance, the principle of selection, less apparent. He introduces us to the shabbiest company, in order to enrich us with knowledge, he leads us to the fairest goals by the longest and roughest roads. It is to this fact, doubtless, that the work owes its reputation of tediousness; but it justifies the reputation only when, behind the offensive detail, the patient reader fails to discover, not a glittering, but a steadily shining generality. Frequently the reader is unable to find any justification for certain wearisome *minutiae*; and, indeed, many of the incidents are so 'flat', that the reader who comes to his task with a vague inherited sense of Goethe's greatness is constrained, for very pity, to supply them with a hidden meaning. It would not, therefore, be difficult to demonstrate that the great worth of *Wilhelm Meister* is a vast and hollow delusion, upheld by a host of interested dupes. The book is, indeed, so destitute of the quality of cleverness, that it would be comparatively easy for a clever man to make out any given case whatsoever against it; do anything with it, in short, except understand it. The man who is only clever may do much; but he may not do this. It is perhaps one of the most valuable properties of *Wilhelm Meister* that it does not react against this kind of manipulation. We gladly admit, nay, we assert, that, unless seriously read, the book must be inexpressibly dull. It was written, not to entertain, but to edify. It has no factitious qualities, as we may call them; none of those innumerable little arts and graces by which the modern novel continually and tacitly deprecates criticism. It stands on its own bottom, and freely takes for granted that the reader cannot but be interested. It exhibits, indeed, a sublime indifference to the reader, – the indifference of humanity in the aggregate to the individual observer. The author, calmly and steadily guided by his purpose, has none of that preoccupation of *success* which so detracts from the grandeur of most writers at the present day, and leads us at times to decide sweepingly that all our contemporaries are of the second class.

Of plot there is in this book properly none. We have Goethe's own assertion that the work contains no central point. It contains, however, a central figure, that of the hero. By him, through him, the tale is unfolded. It consists of the various adventures of a burgher youth, who sets out on his journey through life in quest, to speak generally, of happiness, – that happiness which, as he is never weary of repeating, can be found only in the subject's perfect harmony with himself. This is certainly a noble idea. Whatever pernicious conclusions may be begotten upon it, let us freely admit that at the outset, in its virginity, it is beautiful. Meister conceives that he can best satisfy his nature by connecting himself with the theatre, the home, as he believes, potentially at least, of all noble aims and lessons. The history of this connection, which is given at great length, is to our mind the most interesting part of the whole work; and for these reasons: that those occasional discussions by which the action is so frequently retarded or advanced (as you choose to consider it), and of which, in spite of their frequency, we would not forfeit a single one, are here more directly suggestive than in subsequent chapters; and that the characters are more positive. The 'Apprenticeship' is, in the first half, more of a story, or, to state it scientifically, more dramatic than in the last. If Goethe is great as a critic, he is at least equally great as a poet; and if *Wilhelm Meister* contains pages of disquisition which cannot be too deeply studied, it likewise contains men and women who cannot be forgotten. Meister's companions bear no comparison with the ingenious puppets produced by the great turning-lathe of our modern fancy.

There is the same difference between them and the figures of last month's successful novel, as there is between a portrait by Velasquez and a photograph by Brady. Which of these creations will live longest in your memory? Goethe's persons are not lifelike; that is the mark of our fashionable photographic heroes and heroines: they are life itself. It was a solid criticism of certain modern works of art, that we recently heard applied to a particular novelist: 'He tells you everything except the very thing you want to know.' We know concerning Philena, Aurelia, Theresa, Serlo, and Werner none of those things of which the clever story-teller of the present day would have made hot haste to inform us; we know neither their costume, nor their stature, nor the indispensable colour of their eyes; and yet, for all that, they *live*, – and assuredly a figure cannot do more than that.

The women in *Wilhelm Meister* are, to our mind, truer even than the men. The three female names above mentioned stand for three persons, which abide in our memory with so unquestioned a right of presence that it is hard to believe that we have not actually known them. Is there in the whole range of fiction a more natural representation of a light-hearted coquette than that of the actress Philena, – she who, at the outset of an excursion into the country, proposes that a law be passed prohibiting the discussion of inanimate objects? Where, too, is there as perfect an example of an irretrievable sentimentalist as her comrade Aurelia, she who, as herself declares, bears hard upon all things, as all things bear hard upon her, and who literally dies for the sake of poetic consistency? What an air of solid truth, again, invests the practical, sensible, reasonable Theresa!

Wilhelm's purpose being exclusively one of self-culture, he is an untiring observer. He listens to every man, woman, and child, for he knows that from each something may be learned. As a character, he is vague and shadowy, and the results of his experience are generally left to the reader's inference. Indeed, as his lessons are mostly gathered from conversations for which he furnishes the original motive, the reader may place himself in the hero's position of an eminently respectful auditor, and judge of the latter's impressions by his own.

Although incidentally dramatic, therefore, it will be seen that, as a whole, *Wilhelm Meister* is anything but a novel, as we have grown to understand the word. As a whole, it has, in fact, no very definite character; and, were we not vaguely convinced that its greatness as a work of art resides in this very absence of form, we should say that, as a work of art, it is lamentably defective. A modern novelist, taking the same subject in hand, would restrict himself to showing the sensations of his hero during the process of education; that is, his hero would be the broad end, and the aggregate of circumstances the narrow end, of the glass through which we were invited to look; and we should so have a comedy or a tragedy, as the case might be. But Goethe, taking a single individual as a pretext for looking into the world, becomes so absorbed in the spectacle before him, that, while still clinging to his hero as a pretext, he quite forgets him as a subject. It may be here objected, that the true artist never forgets either himself or anything else. However that may be, each reader becomes his own Wilhelm Meister, an apprentice, a traveller, on his own account; and as his understanding is large or small, will Wilhelm and the whole work be real or the contrary. It is, indeed, to the understanding exclusively, and never, except in the episode of Mignon, to the imagination, that the author appeals. For what, as we read on, strikes us as his dominant quality? His love of the real. 'It will astonish many persons,' says a French critic, 'to learn that Goethe was a great scorner of what we call the ideal. Reality, religiously studied, was always his muse and his inspiration.'

The bearing of *Wilhelm Meister* is eminently practical. It might almost be called a treatise on moral economy, – a work intended to show how the experience of life may least be wasted, and best be turned to account. This fact gives it a seriousness which is almost sublime. To Goethe, nothing was vague, nothing empty, nothing trivial, – we had almost said, nothing false. Was there ever a book so dispassionate, or, as some persons prefer to call it, cold-blooded? In reading it, we learn the meaning of the traditional phrase about the author's calmness. This calmness seems nearly identical with the extraordinary activity of his mind, as they must both indeed have been the result of a deep sense of intellectual power. It is hard to say which is the truer, that his mind is without haste or without rest. In the pages before us there is not a ray of humour, and hardly a flash of wit; or if they exist, they are lost in the luminous atmosphere of justice which fills the book. These things imply some degree of passion; and Goethe's plan was *non flere, non indignari, sed intelligere.*

We do not know that in what we have said there is much to lead those who are strangers to this work to apply themselves to the perusal of it. We are well aware that our remarks are lamentably disproportionate to the importance of our subject. To attempt to throw a general light upon it in the limits here prescribed would be like striking a match to show off the *Transfiguration*. We would therefore explicitly recommend its perusal to all such persons, especially young persons, as feel that it behooves them to attach a meaning to life. Even if it settles nothing in their minds, it will be a most valuable experience to have read it. It is worth reading, if only to differ with it. If it is a priceless book to love, it is almost as important a one to hate; and whether there is more in it of truth or of error, it is at all events *great*. Is not this by itself sufficient? *Wilhelm Meister* may not have much else that other books have, but it has this, that it is the product of a great mind. There are scores of good books written every day; but this one is a specimen of the grand manner.

4

✶

Essays in Criticism *by Matthew Arnold, 1865.* North
American Review, *July 1865. Arnold is proposed as a model
for the modern critic.*

MR ARNOLD'S *Essays in Criticism* come to American readers with a
reputation already made, – the reputation of a charming style, a great
deal of excellent feeling, and an almost equal amount of questionable
reasoning. It is for us either to confirm the verdict passed in the
author's own country, or to judge his work afresh. It is often the
fortune of English writers to find mitigation of sentence in the United
States.

The Essays contained in this volume are on purely literary subjects; which is for us, by itself, a strong recommendation. English
literature, especially contemporary literature, is, compared with that
of France and Germany, very poor in collections of this sort. A great
deal of criticism is written, but little of it is kept; little of it is deemed
to contain any permanent application. Mr Arnold will doubtless find
in this fact – if indeed he has not already signalized it – but another
proof of the inferiority of the English to the Continental school of
criticism, and point to it as a baleful effect of the narrow practical
spirit which animates, or, as he would probably say, paralyses, the
former. But not only is his book attractive as a whole, from its
exclusively literary character; the subject of each essay is moreover
particularly interesting. The first paper is on the function of Criticism
at the present time; a question, if not more important, perhaps more
directly pertinent here than in England. The second, discussing the
literary influence of Academies, contains a great deal of valuable
observation and reflection in a small compass and under an inadequate title. The other essays are upon the two De Guérins,

Heinrich Heine, Pagan and Mediaeval Religious Sentiment, Joubert, Spinoza, and Marcus Aurelius. The first two articles are, to our mind, much the best; the next in order of excellence is the paper on Joubert; while the others, with the exception, perhaps, of that on Spinoza, are of about equal merit.

Mr Arnold's style has been praised at once too much and too little. Its resources are decidedly limited; but if the word had not become so cheap, we should nevertheless call it fascinating. This quality implies no especial force; it rests in this case on the fact that, whether or not you agree with the matter beneath it, the manner inspires you with a personal affection for the author. It expresses great sensibility, and at the same time great good-nature; it indicates a mind both susceptible and healthy. With the former element alone it would savour of affectation; with the latter, it would be coarse. As it stands, it represents a spirit both sensitive and generous. We can best describe it, perhaps, by the word sympathetic. It exhibits frankly, and without detriment to its national character, a decided French influence. Mr Arnold is too wise to attempt to write French English; he probably knows that a language can only be indirectly enriched; but as nationality is eminently a matter of form, he knows too that he can really violate nothing so long as he adheres to the English letter.

His Preface is a striking example of the intelligent amiability which animates his style. His two leading Essays were, on their first appearance, made the subject of much violent contention, their moral being deemed little else than a wholesale schooling of the English press by the French programme. Nothing could have better proved the justice of Mr Arnold's remarks upon the 'provincial' character of the English critical method, than the reception which they provoked. He now acknowledges this reception in a short introduction, which admirably reconciles smoothness of temper with sharpness of wit. The taste of this performance has been questioned; but wherever it may err, it is assuredly not in being provincial; it is essentially civil. Mr Arnold's amiability is, in our eye, a strong proof of his wisdom. If he were a few degrees more short-sighted, he might have less equanimity at his command. Those who sympathize with him warmly will probably like him best as he is; but with such as are only half his friends, this freedom from party passion, from what is after all but a lawful professional emotion, will argue against his sincerity. For ourselves, we doubt not that Mr Arnold possesses thoroughly what the French call the courage of his opinions. When you lay down a proposition which is forthwith controverted, it is of course optional with you to take up the cudgels in its defence. If you are deeply convinced of its truth, you will perhaps be content to leave it to take care of itself; or, at all events, you will not go out of your way to push its fortunes; for you will reflect that in the long run an opinion often borrows credit from the forbearance of its patrons. In the long run, we say; it will meanwhile cost you an occasional pang to see your cherished theory turned into a football by the critics. A football is not, as such, a very respectable object, and the more numerous the players, the more ridiculous it becomes. Unless, therefore, you are very confident of your ability to rescue it from the chaos of kicks, you will best consult its interests by not mingling in the game. Such has been Mr Arnold's choice. His opponents say that he is too much of a poet to be a critic; he is certainly too much of a poet to be a disputant. In the Preface in question he has abstained from reiterating any of the views put forth in the two offensive Essays; he has simply taken a delicate literary vengeance upon his adversaries.

For Mr Arnold's critical feeling and observation, used independently of his judgement, we profess a keen relish. He has these qualities, at any rate, of a good critic, whether or not he have the others – the science and the logic. It is hard to say whether the literary critic is more called upon to understand or to feel. It is certain that he will accomplish little unless he can feel acutely; although it is perhaps equally certain that he will become weak the moment that he begins to 'work', as we may say, his natural sensibilities. The best critic is probably he who leaves his feelings out of account, and relies upon reason for success. If he actually possesses delicacy of feeling, his work will be delicate without detriment to its solidity. The complaint of Mr Arnold's critics is that his arguments are too sentimental. Whether this complaint is well founded, we shall hereafter inquire; let us determine first what sentiment has done for him. It has given him, in our opinion, his greatest charm and his greatest worth. Hundreds of other critics have stronger heads; few, in England at least, have more delicate perceptions. We regret that we have not the space to confirm this assertion by extracts. We must refer the reader to the book itself, where he will find on every page an illustration of our meaning. He will find one, first of all, in the apostrophe to the University of Oxford, at the close of the Preface – 'home of lost causes and forsaken beliefs and unpopular names and impossible loyalties'. This is doubtless nothing but sentiment, but it seizes a shade of truth, and conveys it with a directness which is not at the command of logical demonstration. Such a process might readily prove, with the aid of a host of facts, that the University is actually the abode of much retarding conservatism; a fine critical instinct alone, and the measure of audacity which accompanies such an instinct, could succeed in placing her on the side of progress by boldly saluting her as the Queen of Romance: romance being the deadly enemy of the commonplace; the commonplace being the fast ally of Philistinism, and Philistinism the heaviest drag upon the march of civilization. Mr Arnold is very fond of quoting Goethe's eulogy upon Schiller, to the effect that his friend's greatest glory was to have left so far behind him *was uns alle bändigt, das Gemeine*, that bane of mankind, the common. Exactly how much the inscrutable Goethe made of this fact, it is hard at this day to determine; but it will seem to many readers that Mr Arnold makes too much of it. Perhaps he does, for himself; but for the public in general he decidedly does not. One of the chief duties of criticism is to exalt the importance of the ideal; and Goethe's speech has a long career in prospect before we can say with the vulgar that it is 'played out'. Its repeated occurrence in Mr Arnold's pages is but another instance of poetic feeling subserving the ends of criticism. The famous comment upon the girl Wragg, over which the author's opponents made so merry, we likewise owe – we do not hesitate to declare it – to this same poetic feeling. Why cast discredit upon so valuable an instrument of truth? Why not wait at least until it is used in the service of error? The worst that can be said of the paragraph in question is, that it is a great ado about nothing. All thanks, say we, to the critic who will pick up such nothings as these; for if he neglects them, they are blindly trodden under foot. They may not be especially valuable, but they are for that very reason the critic's particular care. Great truths take care of themselves; great truths are carried aloft by philosophers and poets; the critic deals in contributions to truth. Another illustration of the nicety of Mr Arnold's feeling is furnished by his remarks upon the quality of *distinction* as exhibited in Maurice and Eugénie de Guérin, 'that quality which at last inexorably corrects the world's blunders and fixes the world's ideals, [which] procures that the popular poet shall not pass for a Pindar, the popular historian for a Tacitus, nor the popular preacher for a Bossuet.' Another is offered by his incidental remarks upon Coleridge, in the article on Joubert; another, by the remarkable felicity with which he has translated Maurice de Guérin's *Centaur*; and another, by the whole body of citations with which, in his second Essay, he fortifies his proposition that the establishment in England of an authority answering to the French Academy would have arrested certain evil tendencies of English literature – for to nothing more offensive than this, as far as we can see, does his argument amount.

In the first and most important of his Essays Mr Arnold puts forth his views upon the actual duty of criticism. They may be summed up as follows. Criticism has no concern with the practical; its function is simply to get at the best thought which is current – to see things in themselves as they are – to be disinterested. Criticism can be disinterested, says Mr Arnold,

'by keeping from practice; by resolutely following the law of its own nature, which is to be a free play of the mind on all subjects which it touches, by steadily refusing to lend itself to any of those ulterior political, practical considerations about ideas which plenty of people will be sure to attach to them, which perhaps ought often to be attached to them, which in this country, at any rate, are certain to be attached to them, but which criticism has really nothing to do with. Its business is simply to know the best that is known and thought in the world, and, by in its turn making this known, to create a current of true and fresh ideas. Its business is to do this with inflexible honesty, with due ability; but its business is to do no more, and to leave alone all questions of practical consequences and applications – questions which will never fail to have due prominence given to them.'

We used just now a word of which Mr Arnold is very fond – a word of which the general reader may require an explanation, but which, when explained, he will be likely to find indispensable; we mean the word *Philistine*. The term is of German origin, and has no English synonyme. 'At Soli,' remarks Mr Arnold, 'I imagined they did not talk of solecisms; and here, at the very head-quarters of Goliath, nobody talks of Philistinism.' The word *epicier*, used by Mr

Arnold as a French synonyme, is not so good as *bourgeois*, and to those who know that *bourgeois* means a citizen, and who reflect that a citizen is a person seriously interested in the maintenance of order, the German term may now assume a more special significance. An English review briefly defines it by saying that 'it applies to the fat-headed respectable public in general'. This definition must satisfy us here. The Philistine portion of the English press, by which we mean the considerably larger portion, received Mr Arnold's novel programme of criticism with the uncompromising disapprobation which was to be expected from a literary body, the principle of whose influence, or indeed of whose being, is its subservience, through its various members, to certain political and religious interests. Mr Arnold's general theory was offensive enough; but the conclusions drawn by him from the fact that English practice has been so long and so directly at variance with it, were such as to excite the strongest animosity. Chief among these was the conclusion that this fact has retarded the development and vulgarized the character of the English mind, as compared with the French and the German mind. This rational inference may be nothing but a poet's flight; but for ourselves, we assent to it. It reaches us too. The facts collected by Mr Arnold on this point have long wanted a voice. It has long seemed to us that, as a nation, the English are singularly incapable of large, of high, of general views. They are indifferent to pure truth, to *la verité vraie*. Their views are almost exclusively practical, and it is in the nature of practical views to be narrow. They seldom indeed admit a fact but on compulsion; they demand of an idea some better recommendation, some longer pedigree, than that it is true. That this lack of spontaneity in the English intellect is caused by the tendency of English criticism, or that it is to be corrected by a diversion, or even by a complete reversion, of this tendency, neither Mr Arnold nor ourselves suppose, nor do we look upon such a result as desirable. The part which Mr Arnold assigns to his reformed method of criticism is a purely tributary part. Its indirect result will be to quicken the naturally irrational action of the English mind; its direct result will be to furnish that mind with a larger stock of ideas than it has enjoyed under the time-honoured *régime* of Whig and Tory, High-Church and Low-Church organs.

We may here remark, that Mr Arnold's statement of his principles is open to some misinterpretation – an accident against which he has, perhaps, not sufficiently guarded it. For many persons the word *practical* is almost identical with the word *useful*, against which, on the other hand, they erect the word *ornamental*. Persons who are fond of regarding these two terms as irreconcilable, will have little patience with Mr Arnold's scheme of criticism. They will look upon it as an organized preference of unprofitable speculation to common sense. But the great beauty of the critical movement advocated by Mr Arnold is that in either direction its range of action is unlimited. It deals with plain facts as well as with the most exalted fancies; but it deals with them only for the sake of the truth which is in them, and not for *your* sake, reader, and that of your party. It takes *high ground*, which is the ground of theory. It does not busy itself with consequences, which are all in all to you. Do not suppose that it for this reason pretends to ignore or to undervalue consequences; on the contrary, it is because it knows that consequences are inevitable that it leaves them alone. It cannot do two things at once; it cannot serve two masters. Its business is to make truth generally accessible, and not to apply it. It is only on condition of having its hands free, that it can make truth generally accessible. We said just now that its duty was, among other things, to exalt, if possible, the importance of the ideal. We should perhaps have said the intellectual; that is, of the principle of understanding things. Its business is to urge the claims of all things to be understood. If this is its function in England, as Mr Arnold represents, it seems to us that it is doubly its function in this country. Here is no lack of votaries of the practical, of experimentalists, of empirics. The tendencies of our civilization are certainly not such as foster a preponderance of morbid speculation. Our national genius inclines yearly more and more to resolve itself into a vast machine for sifting, in all things, the wheat from the chaff. American society is so shrewd, that we may safely allow it to make application of the truths of the study. Only let us keep it supplied with the truths of the study, and not with the half-truths of the forum. Let criticism take the stream of truth at its source, and then practice can take it half-way down. When criticism takes it half-way down, practice will come poorly off.

If we have not touched upon the faults of Mr Arnold's volume, it is because they are faults of detail, and because, when, as a whole, a book commands our assent, we do not incline to quarrel with its parts. Some of the parts in these Essays are weak, others are strong; but the impression which they all combine to leave is one of such beauty as to make us forget, not only their particular faults, but their particular merits. If we were asked what is the particular merit of a given essay, we should reply that it is a merit much less common at the present day than is generally supposed – the merit which pre-eminently characterizes Mr Arnold's poems, the merit, namely, of having a *subject*. Each essay is *about* something. If a literary work now-a-days start with a certain topic, that is all that is required of it; and yet it is a work of art only on condition of ending with that topic, on condition of being written, not from it, but to it. If the average modern essay or poem were to wear its title at the close, and not at the beginning, we wonder in how many cases the reader would fail to be surprised by it. A book or an article is looked upon as a kind of Staubbach waterfall, discharging itself into infinite space. If we were questioned as to the merit of Mr Arnold's book as a whole, we should say that it lay in the fact that the author takes high ground. The manner of his Essays is a model of what criticisms should be. The foremost English critical journal, the Saturday Review, recently disposed of a famous writer by saying, in a parenthesis, that he had done nothing but write nonsense all his life. Mr Arnold does not pass judgment in parenthesis. He is too much of an artist to use leading propositions for merely literary purposes. The consequence is, that he says a few things in such a way as that almost in spite of ourselves we remember them, instead of a number of things which we cannot for the life of us remember. There are many things which we wish he had said better. It is to be regretted, for instance, that, when Heine is for once in a way seriously spoken of, he should not be spoken of more as the great poet which he is, and which even in New England he will one day be admitted to be, than with reference to the great moralist which he is not, and which he never claimed to be. But here, as in other places, Mr Arnold's excellent spirit reconciles us with his short-comings. If he has not spoken of Heine exhaustively, he has at all events spoken of him seriously, which for an Englishman is a good deal. Mr Arnold's supreme virtue is that he speaks of all things seriously, or, in other words, that he is not offensively clever. The writers who are willing to resign themselves to this obscure distinction are in our opinion the only writers who understand their time. That Mr Arnold thoroughly understands his time we do not mean to say, for this is the privilege of a very select few; but he is, at any rate, profoundly conscious of his time. This fact was clearly apparent in his poems, and it is even more apparent in these Essays. It gives them a peculiar character of melancholy — that melancholy which arises from the spectacle of the old-fashioned instinct of enthusiasm in conflict (or at all events in contact) with the modern desire to be fair — the melancholy of an age which not only has lost its *naïveté*, but which knows it has lost it.

The American publishers have enriched this volume with the author's Lectures on Homer, and with his French Eton. The Lectures demand a notice apart; we can only say here that they possess all the habitual charm of Mr Arnold's style. This same charm will also lend an interest to his discussion of a question which bears but remotely upon the subject of education in this country.

5

Walt Whitman's Drum-Taps, *1865. Nation, 16 November*
1865. Later James came to admire 'the good Walt' for his
compassionate pacifist patriotism; and Edith Wharton records
an evening on which they agreed that he was the 'greatest of
American poets' and James read aloud from Leaves of Grass
with great feeling.

IT HAS BEEN a melancholy task to read this book; and it is a still
more melancholy one to write about it. Perhaps since the day of Mr
Tupper's 'Philosophy' there has been no more difficult reading of the
poetic sort. It exhibits the effort of an essentially prosaic mind to lift
itself, by a prolonged muscular strain, into poetry. Like hundreds of
other good patriots, during the last four years, Mr Walt Whitman
has imagined that a certain amount of violent sympathy with the
great deeds and sufferings of our soldiers, and of admiration for our
national energy, together with a ready command of picturesque
language, are sufficient inspiration for a poet. If this were the case, we
had been a nation of poets. The constant developments of the war
moved us continually to strong feeling and to strong expression of it.
But in those cases in which these expressions were written out and
printed with all due regard to prosody, they failed to make poetry, as
any one may see by consulting now in cold blood the back volumes of
the *Rebellion Record. Of course* the city of Manhattan, as Mr
Whitman delights to call it, when regiments poured through it in the
first months of the war, and its own sole god, to borrow the words of
a real poet, ceased for a while to be the millionaire, was a noble
spectacle, and a poetical statement to this effect is possible. *Of course*
the tumult of a battle is grand, the results of a battle tragic, and the
untimely deaths of young men a theme for elegies. But he is not a poet

43

who merely reiterates these plain facts *ore rotundo*. He only sings them worthily who views them from a height. Every tragic event collects about it a number of persons who delight to dwell upon its superficial points – of minds which are bullied by the *accidents* of the affair. The temper of such minds seems to us to be the reverse of the poetic temper; for the poet, although he incidentally masters, grasps, and uses the superficial traits of his theme, is really a poet only in so far as he extracts its latent meaning and holds it up to common eyes. And yet from such minds most of our war-verses have come, and Mr Whitman's utterances, much as the assertion may surprise his friends, are in this respect no exception to general fashion. They are an exception, however, in that they openly pretend to be something better; and this it is that makes them melancholy reading. Mr Whitman is very fond of blowing his own trumpet, and he has made very explicit claims for his book. 'Shut not your doors,' he exclaims at the outset –

'Shut not your doors to me, proud libraries,
For that which was lacking among you all, yet needed most,
    I bring;
A book I have made for your dear sake, O soldiers,
And for you, O soul of man, and you, love of comrades;
The words of my book nothing, the life of it everything;
A book separate, not link'd with the rest, nor felt by the intellect;
But you will feel every word, O Libertad! arm'd Libertad!
It shall pass by the intellect to swim the sea, the air,
With joy with you, O soul of man.'

These are great pretensions, but it seems to us that the following are even greater:

'From Paumanok starting, I fly like a bird,
Around and around to soar, to sing the idea of all;
To the north betaking myself, to sing their arctic songs,
To Kanada, 'till I absorb Kanada in myself – to Michigan then,
To Wisconsin, Iowa, Minnesota, to sing their songs (they are
    inimitable);
Then to Ohio and Indiana, to sing theirs – to Missouri and
    Kansas and Arkansas to sing theirs,

44

To Tennessee and Kentucky – to the Carolinas and Georgia, to
   sing theirs,
To Texas, and so along up toward California, to roam accepted
   everywhere;
To sing first (to the tap of the war-drum, if need be)
The idea of all – of the western world, one and inseparable,
And then the song of each member of these States.'

Mr Whitman's primary purpose is to celebrate the greatness of our
armies; his secondary purpose is to celebrate the greatness of the city
of New York. He pursues these objects through a hundred pages of
matter which remind us irresistibly of the story of the college
professor who, on a ventursome youth's bringing him a theme done
in blank verse, reminded him that it was not customary in writing
prose to begin each line with a capital. The frequent capitals are the
only marks of verse in Mr Whitman's writing. There is, fortunately,
but one attempt at rhyme. We say fortunately, for if the inequality of
Mr Whitman's lines were self-registering, as it would be in the case of
an anticipated syllable at their close, the effect would be painful in
the extreme. As the case stands, each line starts off by itself, in
resolute independence of its companions, without a visible goal. But
if Mr Whitman does not write verse, he does not write ordinary
prose. The reader has seen that liberty is 'libertad'. In like manner,
comrade is 'camerado', Americans are 'Americanos', a pavement is a
'trottoir', and Mr Whitman himself is a 'chansonnier'. If there is one
thing that Mr Whitman is not, it is this, for Béranger was a
chansonnier. To appreciate the force of our conjunction, the reader
should compare his military lyrics with Mr Whitman's declamations.
Our author's novelty, however, is not in his words, but in the form of
his writing. As we have said, it begins for all the world like verse and
turns out to be arrant prose. It is more like Mr Tupper's proverbs
than anything we have met. But what if, in form, it *is* prose? it may be
asked. Very good poetry has come out of prose before this. To this we
would reply that it must first have gone into it. Prose, in order to be
good poetry, must first be good prose. As a general principle, we
know of no circumstance more likely to impugn a writer's earnestness than the adoption of an anomalous style. He must have something very original to say if none of the old vehicles will carry his

thoughts. Of course he *may* be surprisingly original. Still, presumption is against him. If on examination the matter of his discourse proves very valuable, it justifies, or at any rate excuses, his literary innovation.

But if, on the other hand, it is of a common quality, with nothing new about it but its manners, the public will judge the writer harshly. The most that can be said of Mr Whitman's vaticinations is, that, cast in a fluent and familiar manner, the average substance of them might escape unchallenged. But we have seen that Mr Whitman prides himself especially on the substance – the life – of his poetry. It may be rough, it may be grim, it may be clumsy – such we take to be the author's argument – but it is sincere, it is sublime, it appeals to the soul of man, it is the voice of a people. He tells us, in the lines quoted, that the words of his book are nothing. To our perception they are everything, and very little at that. A great deal of verse that is nothing but words has, during the war, been sympathetically sighed over and cut out of newspaper corners, because it has possessed a certain simple melody. But Mr Whitman's verse, we are confident, would have failed even of this triumph, for the simple reason that no triumph, however small, is won but through the exercise of art, and that this volume is an offence against art. It is not enough to be grim and rough and careless; common sense is also necessary, for it is by common sense that we are judged. There exists in even the commonest minds, in literary matters, a certain precise instinct of conservatism, which is very shrewd in detecting wanton eccentricities. To this instinct Mr Whitman's attitude seems monstrous. It is monstrous because it pretends to persuade the soul while it slights the intellect; because it pretends to gratify the feelings while it outrages the taste. The point is that it does this *on theory*, wilfully, consciously, arrogantly. It is the little nursery game of 'open your mouth and shut your eyes'. Our hearts are often touched through a compromise with the artistic sense, but never in direct violation of it. Mr Whitman sits down at the outset and counts out the intelligence. This were indeed a wise precaution on his part if the intelligence were only submissive! But when she is deliberately insulted, she takes her revenge by simply standing erect and open-eyed. This is assuredly the best she can do. And if she could find a voice she would probably address Mr Whitman as follows: 'You came to woo my sister, the human soul. Instead of giving me a kick as you approach, you should either greet me courteously, or, at least, steal in unobserved. But now you have me on your hands. Your chances are poor. What the human heart desires above all is sincerity, and you do not appear to me sincere. For a lover you talk entirely too much about yourself. In one place you threaten to absorb Kanada. In another you call upon the city of New York to incarnate you, as you have incarnated it. In another you inform us that neither youth pertains to you nor "delicatesse", that you are awkward in the parlour, that you do not dance, and that you have neither bearing, beauty, knowledge, nor fortune. In another place, by an allusion to your "little songs", you seem to identify yourself with the third person of the Trinity. For a poet who claims to sing "the idea of all", this is tolerably egotistical. We look in vain, however, through your book for a single idea. We find nothing but flashy imitations of ideas. We find a medley of extravagances and commonplaces. We find art, measure, grace, sense sneered at on every page, and nothing positive given us in their stead. To be positive one must have something to say; to be positive requires reason, labour, and art; and art requires, above all things, a suppression of one's self, a subordination of one's self to an idea. This will never do for you, whose plan is to adapt the scheme of the universe to your own limitations. You cannot entertain and exhibit ideas; but, as we have seen, you are prepared to incarnate them. It is for this reason, doubtless, that when once you have planted yourself squarely before the public, and in view of the great service you have done to the ideal, have become, as you say, "accepted everywhere", you can afford to deal exclusively in words. What would be bald nonsense and dreary platitudes in any one else becomes sublimity in you. But all this is a mistake. To become adopted as a national poet, it is not enough to discard everything in particular and to accept everything in general, to amass crudity upon crudity, to discharge the undigested contents of your blotting-book into the lap of the public. You must respect the public which you address; for it has taste, if you have not. It delights in the grand, the heroic, and the masculine; but it delights to see these conceptions cast into worthy form. It is indifferent to brute sublimity. It will never do for you to thrust your hands into your pockets and cry out that, as the research of form is an intolerable bore, the shortest and most economical way for the public to embrace its idols – for the nation to realize its genius – is in your own person. This democratic, liberty-loving, American populace, this stern and war-tried people, is a great civilizer. It is devoted to refinement. If it has sustained a monstrous war, and practised human nature's best in so many ways for the last five years, it is not to put up with spurious poetry afterwards. To sing aright our battles and our glories it is not enough to have served in a hospital (however praiseworthy the task in itself), to be aggressively careless, inelegant, and ignorant, and to be constantly preoccupied with yourself. It is not enough to be rude, lugubrious, and grim. You must also be serious. You must forget yourself in your ideas. Your personal qualities – the vigour of your temperament, the manly independence of your nature, the tenderness of your heart – these facts are impertinent. You must be *possessed*, and you must strive to possess your possession. If in your striving you break into divine eloquence, then you are a poet. If the idea which possesses you is the idea of your country's greatness, then you are a national poet; and not otherwise.'

6

Our Mutual Friend, *by Charles Dickens, 1865.* Nation, *21
December 1865. In* A Small Boy and Others *James says that
Dickens 'entered so early into the blood and bone of our
intelligence' that it is now (1913) almost impossible to re-read
him or arrive at 'detached appraisement'. This feeling about
the influence of Dickens on childhood has perhaps only recently disappeared. But the younger James was writing as one
who saw 'realism' as his vocation. Note that the interesting
disapproval of Jenny Wren did not prevent him from taking a
hint for Rose Muniment in* The Princess Casamassima.

OUR MUTUAL FRIEND is, to our perception, the poorest of Mr
Dickens's works. And it is poor with the poverty not of momentary
embarrassment, but of permanent exhaustion. It is wanting in
inspiration. For the last ten years it has seemed to us that Mr Dickens
has been unmistakably forcing himself. *Bleak House* was forced;
Little Dorrit was laboured; the present work is dug out as with a
spade and pick-axe. Of course – to anticipate the usual argument –
who but Dickens could have written it? Who, indeed? Who else
would have established a lady in business in a novel on the admirably
solid basis of her always putting on gloves and tieing a handkerchief
round her head in moments of grief, and of her habitually addressing
her family with 'Peace! hold!' It is needless to say that Mrs Reginald
Wilfer is first and last the occasion of considerable true humour.
When, after conducting her daughter to Mrs Boffin's carriage, in
sight of all the envious neighbours, she is described as enjoying her
triumph during the next quarter of an hour by airing herself on the
door-step 'in a kind of splendidly serene trance', we laugh with as
uncritical a laugh as could be desired of us. We pay the same tribute

to her assertions, as she narrates the glories of the society she enjoyed at her father's table, that she has known as many as three copper-plate engravers exchanging the most exquisite sallies and retorts there at one time. But when to these we have added a dozen more happy examples of the humour which was exhaled from every line of Mr Dickens's earlier writings, we shall have closed the list of the merits of the work before us. To say that the conduct of the story, with all its complications, betrays a long-practised hand, is to pay no compliment worthy the author. If this were, indeed, a compliment, we should be inclined to carry it further, and congratulate him on his success in what we should call the manufacture of fiction; for in so doing we should express a feeling that has attended us throughout the book. Seldom, we reflected, had we read a book so intensely *written*, so little seen, known, or felt.

In all Mr Dickens's works the fantastic has been his great resource; and while his fancy was lively and vigorous it accomplished great things. But the fantastic, when the fancy is dead, is a very poor business. The movement of Mr Dickens's fancy in Mrs Wilfer and Mr Boffin and Lady Tippins, and the Lammles and Miss Wren, and even in Eugene Wrayburn, is, to our mind, a movement lifeless, forced, mechanical. It is the letter of his old humour without the spirit. It is hardly too much to say that every character here put before us is a mere bundle of eccentricities, animated by no principle of nature whatever. In former days there reigned in Mr Dickens's extravagances a comparative consistency; they were exaggerated statements of types that really existed. We had, perhaps, never known a Newman Noggs, nor a Pecksniff, nor a Micawber; but we had known persons of whom these figures were but the strictly logical consummation. But among the grotesque creatures who occupy the pages before us, there is not one whom we can refer to as an existing type. In all Mr Dickens's stories, indeed, the reader has been called upon, and has willingly consented, to accept a certain number of figures or creatures of pure fancy, for this was the author's poetry. He was, moreover, always repaid for his concession by a peculiar beauty or power in these exceptional characters. But he is now expected to make the same concession with a very inadequate reward. What do we get in return for accepting Miss Jenny Wren as a possible person? This young lady is the type of a certain class of characters of which Mr Dickens has made a specialty, and with which he has been accustomed to draw alternate smiles and tears, according as he pressed one spring or another. But this is very cheap merriment and very cheap pathos. Miss Jenny Wren is a poor little dwarf, afflicted, as she constantly reiterates, with a 'bad back' and 'queer legs', who makes doll's dresses, and is for ever pricking at those with whom she converses, in the air, with her needle, and assuring them that she knows their 'tricks and their manners'. Like all Mr Dickens's pathetic characters, she is a little monster; she is deformed, unhealthy, unnatural; she belongs to the troop of hunchbacks, imbeciles, and precocious children who have carried on the sentimental business in all Mr Dickens's novels; the little Nells, the Smikes, the Paul Dombeys.

Mr Dickens goes as far out of the way for his wicked people as he does for his good ones. Rogue Riderhood, indeed, in the present story, is villanous with a sufficiently natural villany; he belongs to that quarter of society in which the author is most at his ease. But was there ever such wickedness as that of the Lammles and Mr Fledgeby? Not that people have not been as mischievous as they; but was any one ever mischievous in that singular fashion? Did a couple of elegant swindlers ever take such particular pains to be aggressively inhuman? – for we can find no other word for the gratuitous distortions to which they are subjected. The word *humanity* strikes us as strangely discordant, in the midst of these pages; for, let us boldly declare it, there is no humanity here. Humanity is nearer home than the Boffins, and the Lammles, and the Wilfers, and the Veneerings. It is in what men have in common with each other, and not in what they have in distinction. The people just named have nothing in common with each other, except the fact that they have nothing in common with mankind at large. What a world were this world if the world of *Our Mutual Friend* were an honest reflection of it! But a community of eccentrics is impossible. Rules alone are consistent with each other; exceptions are inconsistent. Society is maintained by natural sense and natural feeling. We cannot conceive a society in which these principles are not in some manner represented. Where in these pages are the depositaries of that intelligence without which the movement of life would cease? Who represents nature? Accepting half of Mr Dickens's persons as intentionally grotesque, where are those exemplars of sound humanity who should afford us the proper measure of their companions' variations? We ought not, in justice to the author, to seek them among his weaker – that is, his mere conventional – characters; in John Harmon, Lizzie Hexam, or Mortimer Lightwood; but we assuredly cannot find them among his stronger – that is, his artificial creations. Suppose we take Eugene Wrayburn and Bradley Headstone. They occupy a half-way position between the habitual probable of nature and the habitual impossible of Mr Dickens. A large portion of the story rests upon the enmity borne by Headstone to Wrayburn, both being in love with the same woman. Wrayburn is a gentleman, and Headstone is one of the people. Wrayburn is well-bred, careless, elegant, sceptical, and idle: Headstone is a high-tempered, hard-working, ambitious young schoolmaster. There lay in the opposition of these two characters a very good story. But the prime requisite was that they should *be* characters: Mr Dickens, according to his usual plan, has made them simply figures, and between them the story that was to be, the story that should have been, has evaporated. Wrayburn lounges about with his hands in his pockets, smoking a cigar, and talking nonsense. Headstone strides about, clenching his fists and biting his lips and grasping his stick. There is one scene in which Wrayburn chaffs the schoolmaster with easy insolence, while the latter writhes impotently under his well-bred sarcasm. This scene is very clever, but it is very insufficient. If the majority of readers were not so very timid in the use of words we should call it vulgar. By this we do not mean to indicate the conventional impropriety of two gentlemen exchanging lively personalities; we mean to emphasize the essentially small character of these personalities. In other words, the moment, dramatically, is great, while the author's conception is weak. The friction of two *men*, of two characters, of two passions, produces stronger sparks than Wrayburn's boyish repartees and Headstone's melodramatic commonplaces. Such scenes as this are useful in fixing the limits of Mr Dickens's insight. Insight is, perhaps, too strong a word; for we are convinced that it is one of the chief conditions of his genius not to see beneath the surface of things. If we might hazard a definition of his literary character, we should, accordingly, call him the greatest of superficial novelists. We are aware that this definition confines him to an inferior rank in the department of letters which he adorns; but we accept this consequence of our proposition. It were, in our opinion, an offence against humanity to place Mr Dickens among the greatest novelists. For, to repeat what we have already intimated, he has created nothing but figure. He has added nothing to our understanding of human character. He is master of but two alternatives; he reconciles us to what is commonplace, and he reconciles us to what is odd. The value of the former service is questionable; and the manner in which Mr Dickens performs it sometimes conveys a certain impression of charlatanism. The value of the latter service is incontestable, and here Mr Dickens is an honest, an admirable artist. But what is the condition of the truly great novelist? For him there are no alternatives, for him there are no oddities, for him there is nothing outside of humanity. He cannot shirk it; it imposes itself upon him. For him alone, therefore, there is a true and a false; for him alone it is possible to be right, because it is possible to be wrong. Mr Dickens is a great observer and a great humorist, but he is nothing of a philosopher. Some people may hereupon say, so much the better; we say, so much the worse. For a novelist very soon has need of a little philosophy. In treating of Micawber, and Boffin, and Pickwick, *et hoc genus omne*, he can, indeed, dispense with it, for this – we say it with all deference – is not serious writing. But when he comes to tell the story of a passion, a story like that of Headstone and Wrayburn, he becomes a moralist as well as an artist. He must know *man* as well as *men*, and to know man is to be a philosopher. The writer who knows men alone, if he have Mr Dickens's humour and fancy, will give us figures and pictures for which we cannot be too grateful, for he will enlarge our knowledge of the world. But when he introduces men and women whose interest is preconceived to lie not in the poverty, the weakness, the drollery of their natures, but in their complete and unconscious subjection to ordinary and healthy human emotions, all his humour, all his fancy, will avail him nothing if, out of the fulness of his sympathy, he is unable to prosecute those generalizations in which alone consists the real greatness of a work of art. This may sound like very subtle talk about a very simple matter; it is rather very simple talk about a very subtle matter. A story based upon those elementary passions in which alone we seek the true and final manifestation of character must be told in a spirit of intellectual superiority to those passions. That is, the author must understand what he is talking about. The perusal of a story so told is one of the most elevating experiences within the reach of the human mind. The perusal of a story which is not so told is infinitely depressing and unprofitable.

7

The Belton Estate, *by Anthony Trollope, 1866. Nation, 4 January 1866. Compare this review with No. 23.*

HERE, in the natural order of events, is a new novel by Mr Trollope. This time it is Miss Clara Amedroz who is agitated by conflicting thoughts. Like most of Mr Trollope's recent heroines, she is no longer in the first blush of youth; and her story, like most of Mr Trollope's recent stories, is that of a woman standing irresolute between a better lover and a worse. She first rejects the better for the worse, and then rejects the worse for the better. This latter movement is final, and Captain Aylmer, like Crosbie, in *The Small House at Allington*, has to put up with a red-nosed Lady Emily. The reader will surmise that we are not in *The Belton Estate* introduced to very new ground. The book is, nevertheless, to our mind, more readable than many of its predecessors. It is comparatively short, and has the advantage of being a single story, unencumbered by any subordinate or co-ordinate plot. The interest of Mr Trollope's main narrative is usually so far from being intense that repeated interruption on behalf of the actors charged with the more strictly humorous business is often very near proving altogether fatal. To become involved in one of his love stories is very like sinking into a gentle slumber; and it is well known that when you are aroused from your slumber to see something which your well-meaning intruder considers very entertaining, it is a difficult matter to woo it back again. In the tale before us we slumber on gently to the end. There is no heroine but Miss Clara Amedroz, and no heroes but her two suitors. The lady loves amiss, but discovers it in time, and invests her affections more safely. Such, in strictness, is the substance of the tale; but it is filled out as Mr Trollope alone knows how to fill out the primitive meagreness of his dramatic skeletons. The three persons whom we have mentioned are each a character in a way, and their sayings and doings, their comings and goings, are registered to the letter and timed to the minute. They write a number of letters, which are duly transcribed; they make frequent railway journeys by the down-train from London; they have cups of tea in their bed-rooms; and they do, in short, in the novel very much as the reader is doing out of it. We do not make these remarks in a tone of complaint. Mr Trollope has been long enough before the public to have enabled it to take his measure. We do not open his books with the expectation of being thrilled, or convinced, or deeply moved in any way, and, accordingly, when we find one to be as flat as a Dutch landscape, we remind ourselves that we have wittingly travelled into Holland, and that we have no right to abuse the scenery for being in character. We reflect, moreover, that there are a vast number of excellent Dutchmen for whom this low-lying horizon has infinite charms. If we are passionate and egotistical, we turn our back upon them for a nation of irreclaimable dullards; but if we are critical and disinterested, we endeavour to view the prospect from a Dutch stand-point.

Looking at *The Belton Estate*, then, from Mr Trollope's own point of view, it is a very pleasing tale. It contains not a word against nature. It relates, with great knowledge, humour, and grace of style, the history of the affections of a charming young lady. No unlawful devices are resorted to in order to interest us. People and things are painted as they stand. Miss Clara Amedroz is charming only as two-thirds of her sex are charming — by the sweetness of her face and figure, the propriety of her manners, and the amiability of her disposition. Represented thus, without perversion or exaggeration, she engages our sympathy as one whom we can understand, from having known a hundred women exactly like her. Will Belton, the lover whom she finally accepts, is still more vividly natural. Even the critic, who judges the book strictly from a reader's stand-point, must admit that Mr Trollope has drawn few better figures than this, or even (what is more to the purpose) that, as a representation, he is an approach to ideal excellence. The author understands him well in the life, and the reader understands him well in the book. As soon as he begins to talk we begin to know and to like him, as we know and like such men in the flesh after half an hour of their society. It is true that for many of us half an hour of their society is sufficient, and that here Will Belton is kept before us for days and weeks. No better reason for this is needed than the presumption that the author does not tire of such men so rapidly as we: men healthy, hearty, and shrewd, but men, as we take the liberty of declaring, utterly without mind. Mr Trollope is simply unable to depict a *mind* in any liberal sense of the word. He tried it in John Grey in *Can You Forgive Her?* but most readers will agree that he failed to express very vividly this gentleman's scholarly intelligence. Will Belton is an enterprising young squire, with a head large enough for a hundred prejudices, but too small for a single opinion, and a heart competent – on the condition, however, as it seems to us, of considerable generous self-contraction on her part – to embrace Miss Amedroz.

The other lover, Captain Aylmer, is not as successful a figure as his rival, but he is yet a very fair likeness of a man who probably abounds in the ranks of that society from which Mr Trollope recruits his characters, and who occurs, we venture to believe, in that society alone. Not that there are not in all the walks of life weak and passionless men who allow their mothers to bully their affianced wives, and who are utterly incompetent to entertain an idea. But in no other society than that to which Captain Aylmer belongs do such frigidity and such stupidity stand so little in the way of social success. They seem in his case, indeed, to be a passport to it. His prospects depend upon his being respectable, and his being respectable depends, apparently, on his being contemptible. We do not suppose, however, that Mr Trollope likes him any better than we. In fact, Mr Trollope never fails to betray his antipathy for mean people and mean actions. And antipathetic to his tastes as is Captain Aylmer's nature, it is the more creditable to him that he has described it so coolly, critically, and temperately. Mr Trollope is never guilty of an excess in any direction, and the vice of his villain is of so mild a quality that it is powerless to prejudice him against his even milder virtues. These seem to us insufficient to account for Clara's passion, for we are bound to believe that for her it was a passion. As far as the reader sees, Captain Aylmer has done nothing to excite it and everything to quench it, and, indeed, we are quite taken by surprise when, after her aunt's death, she answers his proposal with so emphatic an affirmative. It is a pleasant surprise, however, to find any of Mr Trollope's people doing a thing contrary to common sense. Nothing can be better – always from the Dutch point of view – than the management of the reaction in both parties against their engagement; but to base the rupture of a marriage engagement upon an indisposition on the part of the gentleman's mother that the lady shall maintain an acquaintance of long standing with another lady whose past history is discovered to offer a certain little vantage-point for scandal, is, even from the Dutch point of view, an unwarrantable piece of puerility. But the shabbiness of grand society – and especially the secret meannesses, parsimonies, and cruelties of the exemplary British matron – have as great an attraction for Mr Trollope as they had for Thackeray; and the account of Clara's visit to the home of her intended, the description of the magnificent bullying of Lady Aylmer, and the picture of Miss Aylmer – 'as ignorant, weak, and stupid a poor woman as you shall find anywhere in Europe' – make a sketch almost as relentless as the satire of *Vanity Fair* or the *Newcomes*. There are several other passages equally clever, notably the chapter in which Belton delivers up Miss Amedroz to her lover's care at the hotel in London; and in which, secure in his expression elsewhere of Belton's superiority to Aylmer, the author feels that he can afford to make him still more delicately natural than he has made him already by contrasting him, *pro tempore*, very disadvantageously with his rival, and causing him to lose his temper and make a fool of himself.

Such praise as this we may freely bestow on the work before us, because, qualified by the important stricture which we have kept in reserve, we feel that it will not seem excessive. Our great objection to *The Belton Estate* is that, as we read it, we seemed to be reading a work written for children; a work prepared for minds unable to think; a work below the apprehension of the average man and woman, or, at the very most, on a level with it, and in no particular above it. *The Belton Estate* is a *stupid* book; and in a much deeper sense than that of being simply dull, for a dull book is always a book that might have been lively. A dull book is a failure. Mr Trollope's story is stupid and a success. It is essentially, organically, consistently stupid; stupid in direct proportion to its strength. It is without a single idea. It is utterly incompetent to the primary functions of a book, of whatever nature, namely – to suggest thought. In a certain way, indeed, it suggests thought; but this is only on the ruins of its own existence as a book. It acts as the occasion, not as the cause, of thought. It indicates the manner in which a novel should *not*, on any account, be written. That it should deal exclusively with dull, flat, commonplace people was to be expected; and this need not be a fault; but it deals with such people as one of themselves; and this is what Lady Aylmer would call a 'damning' fault. Mr Trollope is a good observer; but he is literally nothing else. He is apparently as incapable of disengaging an idea as of drawing an inference. All his incidents are, if we may so express it, *empirical*. He has seen and heard every act and every speech that appears in his pages. That minds like his should exist, and exist in plenty, is neither to be wondered at nor to be deplored; but that such a mind as his should devote itself to writing novels, and that these novels should be successful, appears to us an extraordinary fact.

8

From a review of Notes sur l'Angleterre, *by Hippolyte Taine,*
1872. Nation, *25 January 1872. This and the following have*
the special interest that James was at the time valuing both
English and French civilization from the outside for himself. As
to French happiness: the Franco-Prussian War had just ended
in national disaster.

. . . UPON education there is a very interesting chapter, especially in
its remarks on the public schools and on Oxford. English children
seem to him essentially different from French – the grand distinction
being that, as regards boys especially, there is no definite line of
division, as in France, between the moral life of the child and that of
the grown man. 'School and society are on a level, without intermedi-
ate wall or moat: one prepares for the other and leads into it, and the
boy enters life not from a forcing-house and special atmosphere . . .
The French collegian is *ennuyé*, embittered, over-refined, precocious
– too precocious; he is kept in a cage, and his imagination ferments.'
The relation between English parents and children puzzles him, as it
does most foreigners. The apparently reckless multiplication of
offspring, the necessity not only of sons but of daughters shifting for
themselves, the want of sentimental confidence between mothers and
sons, are all at variance with French tradition. As to French habits
under this last head, he mentions some facts which the unregenerate
Anglo-Saxon mind hardly knows whether to pronounce very nice or
(as Charles Lamb says) very nasty. He closes his account of Oxford
with a reflection which admits us vividly into a certain bitter and, as it
were, tragical phase of an intelligent Frenchman's consciousness –
words which suggest afresh what so frequently occurs to students of

French literature, that the rays of the sun of 'glory' must, after all, be rather chilling ones:

I visit [at Oxford] two or three of the professors' residences; some recalling old French *hôtels*, others modern and delightful, all with gardens and flowers, outlooks noble or graceful. In the very oldest, beneath the portraits of former occupants, are gathered all the elements of modern comfort. I compare them to those of our *savants* – denlike lodgings in some third story, in a great city, or to the gloomy quarters of the Sorbonne, and I think of the meagre, colorless aspect of our Collége de France. Poor French! poor, indeed, living here and there as we can! We are of yesterday; we have been ruined from father to son by Louis XIV, Louis XV, by the Revolution, by the Empire. We had pulled down, and had to make over all things anew. Here the generation that follows never breaks with the generation that precedes; institutions are reformed by superposition, and the present, resting on the past, continues it.

Both the interest of M. Taine's work and the rigour of his method reach their climax in his chapter on 'The English Mind'. He has collected here a number of suggestive facts – such facts as a society rarely disengages by any spontaneous attempt at self-analysis, and for which it is generally indebted to the fresher vision of an alien. His main impression is that the characteristic English mind is indifferent and even hostile to ideas, and finds its almost exclusive pabulum in facts. The inside of an English head is like one of Murray's guide-books, crammed with facts, figures, statistics, maps, bits of historical information, useful-moral admonitions; it lacks *vues d'ensemble*, spontaneity of thought, the general harmonizing action of a sense of style and form. Society furnishes the young Englishman when he enters it with ready-made moulds (*cadres*) of thought; the religion is reasonable, the constitution excellent; the great lines of belief are distinctly traced. The author says elsewhere, we remember, that the Englishman who begins life finds on all things ready-made answers; the young Frenchman nothing but ready-made doubts. To theories, inferences, conclusions, to the more or less irresponsible play of conjecture, opinion, and invention, the Englishman turns the cold shoulder. His power of conclusion strikes the author as strangely unproportioned to his rate of information. M. Taine cites as an example a letter in Carlyle's *Life of Sterling*, written by Sterling from the West Indies to his mother immediately after a fierce tornado had ravaged his estate and almost destroyed his house. The writer is an author, a poet, a man of fancy, but he confines himself to a naked statement of facts; he accumulates details, he draws a diagram, he suggests Gulliver and Robinson Crusoe. The point with M. Taine is that he makes no phrases, no attempt to embroider, generalize, or round off his picture. And this love of facts is the more striking, as it includes the taste for moral as well as material facts. M. Taine mentions two letters shown him by an English lady, from two young friends recently married, each considering herself the happiest woman in the world. One of these ladies gives an exhaustive account of her material circumstances – of her husband's appearance, manners, temper, of their house, their neighbours, their expenditure, their whole external economy. The other traces, in equal detail, the moral history of her courtship and honeymoon, and reveals a singular aptitude for psychological observation. The clearness, directness, and simplicity of each letter is the same; each is a string of special facts, without a hint of general reflection or conception.

M. Taine touches further upon the comparative paucity in English speech of abstract words and general terms. Nothing is more natural in French than such a formula as *le vrai, le beau et le bien*; nothing is less a matter of course in English than to allude to the True, the Beautiful, and the Good. M. Taine, we suppose, pretends here to be dealing only with those straws which show how the wind blows, so that we may suggest a case even more in point – the common currency in French speech of the term *la femme*, as compared with its English analogue. For twenty times that this agreeable entity figures in an average French conversation, it puts in but the shadow of an appearance in an English one. M. Taine's theory may be infinitely fortified by special examples, and Americans, as a general thing, if they are not sensibly more furnished with the conceptive turn of mind, as we may roughly term it, than the English, are sufficiently less oppressed by that indefinable social proscription which, in England, weighs upon the jauntily-theorizing tendency, to feel a certain kindly fellowship with our author in his effort to establish his distinction. There is that in the walk and conversation of the average self-respecting Briton which denotes the belief that it is a sign of inferior, or at best of foreign, breeding to indulge, in the glow of conversational confidence, the occasional impulse to extemporize a picturesque formula, or to harmonize fact with fact by the plastic solvent of an 'idea'. This idiosyncrasy, definitely stated, however, belongs to that class of allegations which immediately evokes as large a body of contradictory as of confirmatory testimony; and to our minds a juster, or at least a simpler, expression of the prime intellectual difference between the English and French is to be found in their unequal apportionment of the sense of form and shape. The French possess that lively aesthetic conscience which, on the whole, is such a simplifier. Upon this point our author also touches: 'In our magazines an article, even on science or on political economy, should have an exordium, a peroration, an architecture; there occur few in the *Revue des Deux Mondes* which are not preceded by a sort of porch of general ideas.' That quality of the English mind on which M. Taine most insists – its imaginative force – might seem in some degree to undermine this charge of the want of intellectual agility; but in English imaginations it is the moral leaven that works most strongly; their home is the realm of psychology, and their fondest exercise not the elaboration of theories, but the exposition of the facts of human character, the mysteries and secrets of conscience and the innumerable incidents of life. The English genius for psychological observation has no correlative in France. Its vast range is indicated, in M. Taine's opinion, by that delicate scrutiny of the childish mind effected by so many English-writing novelists – Dickens, George Eliot, the author of the *Wide, Wide World.* We may say, on the other hand, however, that the enquiry has perhaps been pushed at one end to its undue curtailment at the other. If there are no David Copperfields nor Tom Tullivers in French literature, there are no Madame Bovarys, Jacques, nor Mauprats in English.

It is in fiction and in painting that this characteristic comes out most strongly; and upon the English school of art M. Taine has several very interesting pages. The absence of form, of the sense of design and of beauty, and the rich suggestiveness on the moral and sentimental line, seem to him here equally conspicuous. He professes a deep though restricted relish for Wilkie and Mulready, Landseer and Leslie:

'It is impossible to be more expressive, to expend more effort to address the mind through the senses, to illustrate an idea or a truth, to collect into a surface of twelve square inches a closer group of psychological observations. What patient and penetrating critics! What connoisseurs of man! . . . I find here and there masterpieces of this kind – that of Johnston, for example – "Lord and Lady Russell receiving the Sacrament". Lord Russell is about to ascend the scaffold; his wife looks at him full in the face to learn if he is reconciled with God. This intense gaze of the wife and Christian is admirable; she is satisfied now of her husband's salvation. What a pity that it should have been painted instead of being written!'

The reader who remembers the work in question (at Kensington) will agree that it is a singularly characteristic mixture of sentimental delicacy and pictorial ineffectiveness. We refer him to the author's remarks on the further idiosyncrasies of English art and on Mr Ruskin's theories. They will yield some of the elements of that critical corrective without which Ruskin is so erratic, and with which he is so profitable, a monitor. The art in which the English have best succeeded is that of poetry; the deep impressibility of the moral *ego* feeds the sources of their verse with unequalled generosity:

'No poetry equals theirs, speaks so strongly and distinctly to the soul, moves it more to the depths, carries in its diction a heavier burden of meaning, reflects better the shocks and the strivings of our inward being, grasps the mind more potently and effectively, and draws from the innermost chords of personality sounds so magnificent and so searching.'

The reader will be surprised after this handsome compliment to find M. Taine citing *Aurora Leigh* with infinite admiration as a representative English poem. This choice is a capital example of that want of *initiation* which his history so constantly betrays, of his insensibility to the colour and mystery, as we may say, of English diction, and of his consequent failure to apprehend the native code of aesthetics and do justice to a whole great province of the English mind. This province he has hardly visited; he might have gathered there on the outskirts many a Tennysonian, a Wordsworthian, or even a Byronic lyric, telling more in its twenty lines of the real genius of English verse than Mrs Browning in her twenty thousand. Mrs Browning, however, was certainly a poet of English temper, and we have no desire to cut the ground from under the feet of genuine admiration.

M. Taine, reviewing his impressions, briefly concludes that the English are better off than the French in three main points: the stability and liberality of their political system; the morality and healthy tone of their religion; the extent of their acquired wealth, and their greater ease in acquiring and producing. Against these advantages he places in France: the better climate; the more equal distribution of property; and the *vie de famille et de société*. You have in France the immense advantage that –

'In talk, you can say anything – go to the end of your story or your theory. Fiction, criticism, art, philosophy, and general curiosity are not shackled, as on the other side of the Channel, by religion, morality, and the official proprieties ... These differences make the English stronger, the French happier.'

A very obvious remark is that if, just now, the French can manage to be happy, we can but wonder and admire. But, in fact, French optimism has been pretty rudely tested through the whole course of French history. The 'spirit of conversation' apparently holds its own. May it still stand firm and continue to produce talents as vigorous, as living, as national as that of M. Taine!

9

*History of English Literature, by H. A. Taine. Translated by
H. Van Laun, 1871. Atlantic Monthly, April 1872.*

WE HESITATE to express perfect satisfaction at the appearance of an
English version of M. Taine's massive essay. On the one hand, the
performance is no more than a proper compliment to a highly
complimentary work; but, on the other, it involves so effective a
violation of the spirit of that work and so rude a displacement of its
stand-point, as to interfere with a just comprehension of it. M. Taine
himself, however, stands sponsor in a short Preface, and the liberal
reception of the two volumes seems to indicate that English readers
are not sensible of having unduly lost by the transfer. The English
version may fairly demand success on its own merits, being careful,
exact, and spirited. It errs, we think, on the side of a too literal
exactness, through which it frequently ceases to be idiomatic. 'He
tore from his vitals, . . .' for instance, 'the idea which he had
conceived', would render M. Taine's figure better than 'he tore from
his *entrails*'. And it is surely in strong contradiction to the author's
portrait of Lord Macaulay to translate his allusion to the great
historian's *physionomie animée et pensante* by 'an animated and
pensive face'. No one, we fancy, not even M. Taine, ever accused
Lord Macaulay of being pensive.

M. Taine's work is a history of our literature only in a partial sense
of the term. 'Just as astronomy,' he says, 'is at bottom a problem in
mechanics, and physiology a problem in chemistry, so history at
bottom is a problem in psychology.' His aim has been 'to establish
the psychology of a people'. A happier title for his work, therefore,
save for its amplitude, would be, 'A Comparative Survey of the
English Mind in the leading Works of its Literature'. It is a picture of

the English intellect, with literary examples and allusions in evidence, and not a record of works nor an accumulation of facts. To philological or biographical research it makes no claim. In this direction it is altogether incomplete. Various important works are unmentioned, common tradition as to facts is implicitly accepted, and dates, references, and minor detail conspicuous by their absence. The work is wholly critical and pictorial, and involves no larger information than the perusal of a vast body of common documents. Its purpose is to discover in the strongest features of the strongest works the temper of the race and time; which involves a considerable neglect not only of works, but of features. But what is mainly to the point with the English reader (as it is of course excessively obvious in the English version) is that M. Taine writes from an avowedly foreign stand-point. The unit of comparison is throughout assumed to be the French mind. The author's undertaking strikes us, therefore, constantly as an *excursion*. It is not as if he and our English tongue were old friends, as if through a taste early formed and long indulged he had gradually been won to the pious project of paying his debt and embodying his impressions; but as if rather, on reaching his intellectual majority and coming into a handsome property of doctrine and dogma, he had cast about him for a field to conquer, a likely subject for experiment, and, measuring the vast capacity of our English record of expression, he had made a deliberate and immediate choice. We may fancy him declaring, too, that he would do the thing handsomely; devote five or six years to it, and spend five or six months in the country. He has performed his task with a vigour proportionate to this sturdy resolve; but in the nature of the case his treatment of the subject lacks that indefinable quality of spiritual initiation which is the tardy consummate fruit of a wasteful, purposeless, passionate sympathy. His opinions are prompted, not by a sentiment, but by a design. He remains an interpreter of the English mind to the mind of another race; and only remotely, therefore – only by allowance and assistance – an interpreter of the English mind to itself. A greater fault than any of his special errors of judgment is a certain reduced, contracted, and limited air in the whole field. He has made his subject as definite as his method.

M. Taine is fairly well known by this time as a man with a method, the apostle of a theory – the theory that 'vice and virtue are products, like vitriol and sugar', and that art, literature, and conduct are the result of forces which differ from those of the physical world only in being less easily ascertainable. His three main factors – they have lately been reiterated to satiety – are the race, the medium, and the time. Between them they shape the phenomena of history. We have not the purpose of discussing this doctrine; it opens up a dispute as ancient as history itself – the quarrel between the minds which cling to the supernatural and the minds which dismiss it. M. Taine's originality is not in his holding of these principles, but in his lively disposition to apply them, or, rather, in the very temper and terms in which he applies them. No real observer but perceives that a group of works is more or less the product of a 'situation', and that as he himself is forever conscious of the attrition of infinite waves of circumstance, so the cause to which, by genius as by 'fate', he contributes, is a larger deposit in a more general current. Observers differ, first, as to whether there are elements in the deposit which cannot be found in the current; second, as to the variety and complexity of the elements: maintaining, on the one side, that fairly to enumerate them and establish their mutual relations the vision of science is as yet too dim; and, on the other, that a complete analysis is at last decently possible, and with it a complete explanation. M. Taine is an observer of the latter class; in his own sole person indeed he almost includes it. He pays in his Preface a handsome tribute to the great service rendered by Sainte-Beuve to the new criticism. Now Sainte-Beuve is, to our sense, the better apostle of the two. In purpose the least doctrinal of critics, it was by his very horror of dogmas, moulds, and formulas, that he so effectively contributed to the science of literary interpretation. The truly devout patience with which he kept his final conclusion in abeyance until after an exhaustive survey of the facts, after perpetual returns and ever-deferred farewells to them, is his living testimony to the importance of the facts. Just as he could never reconcile himself to saying his last word on book or author, so he never pretended to have devised a method which should be a key to truth. The truth for M. Taine lies stored up, as one may say, in great lumps and blocks, to be released and detached by a few lively hammer-blows; while for Sainte-Beuve it was a diffused and imponderable essence, as vague as the carbon in the air which nourishes vegetation, and, like it, to be disengaged by patient chemistry. His only method was fairly to dissolve his attention in the sea of circumstance surrounding the object of his study, and we cannot but think his frank provisional empiricism more truly scientific than M. Taine's premature philosophy. In fact, M. Taine plays fast and loose with his theory, and is mainly successful in so far as he is inconsequent to it. There is a constantly visible hiatus between his formula and his application of it. It serves as his badge and motto, but his best strokes are prompted by the independent personal impression. The larger conditions of his subject loom vaguely in the background, like a richly figured tapestry of good regulation pattern, gleaming here and there in the author's fitful glance, and serving a picturesque purpose decidedly more than a scientific one. This is especially noticeable in the early chapters of the present work, where the changes are rung to excess upon a note of rather slender strain – the common 'Gothic' properties of history and fiction – Norse blood, gloomy climate, ferocious manners, considered as shaping forces. The same remark applies, we imagine, to the author's volumes on Italy, where a thin soil of historical evidence is often made to produce some most luxuriant flowers of deduction. The historical position is vague, light, and often insecure, and the author's passage from the general conditions to the particular case is apt to be a flying leap of fancy, which, though admirable writing, is rather imperfect science.

We of course lack space to discuss his work in its parts. His portrayal of authors and works is always an attempt to fix the leading or motive faculty, and through his neglect of familiar details and his amplification of the intellectual essence which is the object of his search, his figures often seem out of drawing to English eyes. He distorts the outline, confounds the light and shade, and alters the colouring. His judgments are sometimes very happy and sometimes very erroneous. He proposes some very wise amendments to critical tradition; in other cases he enforces the common verdict with admirable point and vigour. For Spenser, for instance, we doubt whether the case has ever been stated with a more sympathetic and penetrating eloquence. His errors and misjudgments arise partly from his being so thoroughly a stranger to what we may call the intellectual climate of our literature, and partly from his passionate desire to simplify his conception and reduce it to the limits, not merely of the distinctly knowable, but of the symmetrically and neatly presentable. The leading trait of his mind, and its great defect, is an inordinate haste to conclude, combined with a passion for a sort of largely pictorial and splendidly comprehensive expression. A glance at the list of his works will show how actively he has kept terms with each of these tendencies. He is, to our sense, far from being a man of perceptions; the bent of his genius seems to be to generate ideas and images on two distinct lines. For ourselves, on the whole, we prefer his images. These are immensely rich and vivid, and on this side the author is a great artist. His constant effort is to reconcile and harmonize these two groups, and make them illumine and vivify each other. Where he succeeds his success is admirable, and the reader feels that he has rarely seen a truth so completely presented. Where he fails the violence of his diction only serves to emphasize the inadequacy of his conception. M. Taine's great strength is to be found close to his eminent fallibility as a critic – in his magnificent power of eloquent and vivid statement and presentation. His style is admirable; we know of none that is at once more splendid and more definite, that has at once more structure and more colour. Just as his natural preference is evidently for energy and vehemence in talent, his own movement is toward a sort of monstrous cumulative violence of expression; to clinch, to strike, to hit hard, to hit again, till the idea rings and resounds, to force colour *à l'outrance* and make proportion massive, is his notion of complete utterance. This is productive of many effects splendid in themselves, but it is fatal to truth in so far as truth resides in fine shades and degrees.

In this intense constructive glow, M. Taine quite forgets his subject and his starting-point; the impetus of his rhetoric, the effort to complete his picture and reach forward to the strongest word and the largest phrase, altogether absorbs him. For ourselves, we confess that, as we read, we cease to hold him at all rigidly to his premises, and content ourselves with simply enjoying the superb movement of his imagination, thankful when it lights his topic at all truly, and mainly conscious of its radiance as colour, heat, and force. Thus, while as a gallery of portraits the work demands constant revision and correction, as a sort of enormous *tableau vivant*, ingeniously and artificially combined, it is extremely rich and various. A phrase of very frequent occurrence with M. Taine, and very wholesome in its frequency, is *la grande invention*; his own tendency is to practise it. In effort and inclination, however, he is nothing if not impartial; and there is something almost touching in the sympathetic breadth of his admiration for a tone of genius so foreign to French tradition as the great Scriptural inspiration of Bunyan and of Milton. To passionate vigour he always does justice. On the other hand, when he deals with a subject simply because it stands in his path, he is far less satisfactory. His estimate of Swift is a striking example of his tendency to overcharge his portrait and make a picture at all hazards. Swift was a bitter and incisive genius, but he had neither the volume nor the force implied in M. Taine's report of him. We might add a hundred instances of the fatally defective perception of 'values', as the painters say, produced by the author's foreign stand-point. M. Taine expresses altogether the 'Continental' view of Byron, between which and the English view there is much the same difference as between the estimate Byron courted and the estimate he feared. A hundred special points may be conceded; but few modern Englishmen are prepared to accept him, as a whole, as the consistently massive phenomenon described by M. Taine. Touching the later poets, the author is extremely incomplete and fallacious; he pretends, indeed, merely to sketch general tendencies. On Wordsworth, however, he has some pertinent remarks from that protesting man-of-the-world point of view to which the great frugal bard drives most Englishmen for desperate refuge, let alone an epigrammatic Frenchman. We are tempted to say that a Frenchman who should have twisted himself into a relish for Wordsworth would almost have forfeited our respect. On Thackeray and Dickens he has two chapters of great suggestiveness to those who know the authors, but on the whole of excessively contracted outline. Of course, one cannot pronounce upon important literary figures, of whatever dimensions, without a certain work of elimination; but a valid charge against M. Taine is that, whereas your distinctly sensitive critic finds this process to be an effort, M. Taine has the air of finding it a relief. A compromise is perfectly legitimate so long as it is not offered as a synthesis.

With all abatements, and especially in spite of one most important abatement, M. Taine's work remains a very admirable performance. As a philosophical effort it is decidedly a failure; as the application of a theory it is ineffective; but it is a great literary achievement. The fruit of an extremely powerful, vivacious, and observant mind, it is rich in suggestive sidelights and forcible aids to opinion. With a great many errors of detail, as a broad expression of the general essence of the English genius it seems to us equally eloquent and just. M. Taine has felt this genius with an intensity and conceived it with a lucidity which, in themselves, form a great intellectual feat. Even under this head the work is not conclusive in the sense in which the author tenders it, but it is largely and vividly contributive, and we shall wait till we have done better ourselves before we judge it too harshly. It is, in other words, very entertaining provisional criticism and very perfect final art. It is, indeed, a more significant testimony to the French genius than to the English, and bears more directly upon the author's native literature than on our own. In its powerful, though arbitrary, unity of composition, in its sustained aesthetic temper, its brilliancy, variety, and symmetry, it is a really monumental accession to a literature which, whatever its limitations in the reach of its ideas, is a splendid series of masterly compositions.

IO

---------- ✤ ----------

*On the critic and the artist's intention, from a letter to Charles
Eliot Norton, November 1872 (HJL, vol. 1, 310).*

... YOU SAY the inventor of a work of art is always right. In a certain
sense; but the critic is always right too; that is the impression of an
intelligent observer has always an element of truth and value. I
should be sorry never to write anything which mightn't suggest a
question of its being right or wrong, at points ...

II

-------------- ⚘ --------------

*Middlemarch. A Study of Provincial Life, by George Eliot,
1872. Galaxy, March 1873. James criticized this review in a
letter to William James in January 1873: 'I admired and
relished* Middlemarch *hugely, and yet I am afraid you will
think I have spoken of it stingily . . . I don't make perhaps, a
sufficiently succinct statement of its rare intellectual power.
This is amazing.'* (HJL, *vol. 1, 323–4); but in March 1873,
while humorously admitting to Grace Norton that 'a marvellous* mind *throbs through every page . . . It raises the standard
of what is to be expected of women,' he returns to the probable
root of his reservations: 'To produce some little exemplary
works of art is my narrow and lowly dream. They are to have
less "brain" than* Middlemarch; *but (I boldly proclaim it) they
are to have more* form' (HJL, *vol. 1, 351).*

MIDDLEMARCH is at once one of the strongest and one of the
weakest of English novels. Its predecessors as they appeared might
have been described in the same terms; *Romola*, is especially a rare
masterpiece, but the least *entraînant* of masterpieces. *Romola* sins by
excess of analysis; there is too much description and too little drama;
too much reflection (all certainly of a highly imaginative sort) and
too little creation. Movement lingers in the story, and with it
attention stands still in the reader. The error in *Middlemarch* is not
precisely of a similar kind, but it is equally detrimental to the total
aspect of the work. We can well remember how keenly we wondered,
while its earlier chapters unfolded themselves, what turn in the way
of form the story would take – that of an organized, moulded,
balanced composition, gratifying the reader with a sense of design
and construction, or a mere chain of episodes, broken into accidental

lengths and unconscious of the influence of a plan. We expected the actual result, but for the sake of English imaginative literature which, in this line is rarely in need of examples, we hoped for the other. If it had come we should have had the pleasure of reading, what certainly would have seemed to us in the immediate glow of attention, the first of English novels. But that pleasure has still to hover between prospect and retrospect. *Middlemarch* is a treasure-house of details, but it is an indifferent whole.

Our objection may seem shallow and pedantic, and may even be represented as a complaint that we have had the less given us rather than the more. Certainly the greatest minds have the defects of their qualities, and as George Eliot's mind is preëminently contemplative and analytic, nothing is more natural than that her manner should be discursive and expansive. 'Concentration' would doubtless have deprived us of many of the best things in the book – of Peter Featherstone's grotesquely expectant legatees, of Lydgate's medical rivals, and of Mary Garth's delightful family. The author's purpose was to be a generous rural historian, and this very redundancy of touch, born of abundant reminiscence, is one of the greatest charms of her work. It is as if her memory was crowded with antique figures, to whom for very tenderness she must grant an appearance. Her novel is a picture – vast, swarming, deep-coloured, crowded with episodes, with vivid images, with lurking master-strokes, with brilliant passages of expression; and as such we may freely accept it and enjoy it. It is not compact, doubtless; but when was a panorama compact? And yet, nominally, *Middlemarch* has a definite subject – the subject indicated in the eloquent preface. An ardent young girl was to have been the central figure, a young girl framed for a larger moral life than circumstance often affords, yearning for a motive for sustained spiritual effort and only wasting her ardour and soiling her wings against the meanness of opportunity. The author, in other words, proposed to depict the career of an obscure St Theresa. Her success has been great, in spite of serious drawbacks. Dorothea Brooke is a genuine creation, and a most remarkable one when we consider the delicate material in which she is wrought. George Eliot's men are generally so much better than the usual trowsered offspring of the female fancy, that their merits have perhaps overshadowed those of her women. Yet her heroines have always been of an

exquisite quality, and Dorothea is only that perfect flower of conception of which her predecessors were the less unfolded blossoms. An
indefinable moral elevation is the sign of these admirable creatures;
and of the representation of this quality in its superior degrees the
author seems to have in English fiction a monopoly. To render the
expression of a soul requires a cunning hand; but we seem to look
straight into the unfathomable eyes of the beautiful spirit of
Dorothea Brooke. She exhales a sort of aroma of spiritual sweetness,
and we believe in her as in a woman we might providentially meet
some fine day when we should find ourselves doubting of the
immortality of the soul. By what unerring mechanism this effect is
produced – whether by fine strokes or broad ones, by description or
by narration, we can hardly say; it is certainly the great achievement
of the book. Dorothea's career is, however, but an episode, and
though doubtless in intention, not distinctly enough in fact, the
central one. The history of Lydgate's *menage*, which shares honours
with it, seems rather to the reader to carry off the lion's share. This is
certainly a very interesting story, but on the whole it yields in dignity
to the record of Dorothea's unresonant woes. The 'love-problem', as
the author calls it, of Mary Garth, is placed on a rather higher level
than the reader willingly grants it. To the end we care less about Fred
Vincy than appears to be expected of us. In so far as the writer's
design has been to reproduce the total sum of life in an English village
forty years ago, this common-place young gentleman, with his
somewhat meagre tribulations and his rather neutral egotism, has his
proper place in the picture; but the author narrates his fortunes with
a fulness of detail which the reader often finds irritating. The reader
indeed is sometimes tempted to complain of a tendency which we are
at loss exactly to express – a tendency to make light of the serious
elements of the story and to sacrifice them to the more trivial ones. Is
it an unconscious instinct or is it a deliberate plan? With its abundant
and massive ingredients *Middlemarch* ought somehow to have
depicted a weightier drama. Dorothea was altogether too superb a
heroine to be wasted; yet she plays a narrower part than the
imagination of the reader demands. She is of more consequence than
the action of which she is the nominal centre. She marries enthusiasti-
cally a man whom she fancies a great thinker, and who turns out to
be but an arid pedant. Here, indeed, is a disappointment with much

of the dignity of tragedy; but the situation seems to us never to expand to its full capacity. It is analysed with extraordinary penetration, but one may say of it, as of most of the situations in the book, that it is treated with too much refinement and too little breadth. It revolves too constantly on the same pivot; it abounds in fine shades, but it lacks, we think, the great dramatic *chiaroscuro*. Mr Casaubon, Dorothea's husband (of whom more anon) embittered, on his side, by matrimonial disappointment, takes refuge in vain jealousy of his wife's relations with an interesting young cousin of his own and registers this sentiment in a codicil to his will, making the forfeiture of his property the penalty of his widow's marriage with this gentleman. Mr Casaubon's death befalls about the middle of the story, and from this point to the close our interest in Dorothea is restricted to the question, will she or will she not marry Will Ladislaw? The question is relatively trivial and the implied struggle slightly factitious. The author has depicted the struggle with a sort of elaborate solemnity which in the interviews related in the two last books tends to become almost ludicrously excessive.

The dramatic current stagnates; it runs between hero and heroine almost a game of hair-splitting. Our dissatisfaction here is provoked in a great measure by the insubstantial character of the hero. The figure of Will Ladislaw is a beautiful attempt, with many finely-completed points; but on the whole it seems to us a failure. It is the only eminent failure in the book, and its defects are therefore the more striking. It lacks sharpness of outline and depth of colour; we have not found ourselves believing in Ladislaw as we believe in Dorothea, in Mary Garth, in Rosamond, in Lydgate, in Mr Brooke and Mr Casaubon. He is meant, indeed, to be a light creature (with a large capacity for gravity, for he finally gets into Parliament), and a light creature certainly should not be heavily drawn. The author, who is evidently very fond of him, has found for him here and there some charming and eloquent touches; but in spite of these he remains vague and impalpable to the end. He is, we may say, the one figure which a masculine intellect of the same power as George Eliot's would not have conceived with the same complacency; he is, in short, roughly speaking, a woman's man. It strikes us as an oddity in the author's scheme that she should have chosen just this figure of Ladislaw as the creature in whom Dorothea was to find her spiritual compensations. He is really, after all, not the ideal foil to Mr Casaubon which her soul must have imperiously demanded, and if the author of the 'Key to all Mythologies' sinned by lack of order, Ladislaw too has not the concentrated fervour essential in the man chosen by so nobly strenuous a heroine. The impression once given that he is a *dilettante* is never properly removed, and there is slender poetic justice in Dorothea's marrying a *dilettante*. We are doubtless less content with Ladislaw, on account of the noble, almost sculptural, relief of the neighbouring figure of Lydgate, the real hero of the story. It is an illustration of the generous scale of the author's picture and of the conscious power of her imagination that she has given us a hero and heroine of broadly distinct interests – erected, as it were, two suns in her firmament, each with its independent solar system. Lydgate is so richly successful a figure that we have regretted strongly at moments, for immediate interests' sake, that the current of his fortunes should not mingle more freely with the occasionally thin-flowing stream of Dorothea's. Toward the close, these two fine characters are brought into momentary contact so effectively as to suggest a wealth of dramatic possibility between them; but if this train had been followed we should have lost Rosamond Vincy – a rare psychological study. Lydgate is a really complete portrait of a *man*, which seems to us high praise. It is striking evidence of the altogether superior quality of George Eliot's imagination that, though elaborately represented, Lydgate should be treated so little from what we may roughly (and we trust without offence) call the sexual point of view. Perception charged with feeling has constantly guided the author's hand, and yet her strokes remain as firm, her curves as free, her whole manner as serenely impersonal, as if, on a small scale, she were emulating the creative wisdom itself. Several English romancers – notably Fielding, Thackeray, and Charles Reade – have won great praise for their figures of women: but they owe it, in reversed conditions, to a meaner sort of art, it seems to us, than George Eliot has used in the case of Lydgate; to an indefinable appeal to masculine prejudice – to a sort of titillation of the masculine sense of difference. George Eliot's manner is more philosophic – more broadly intelligent, and yet her result is as concrete or, if you please, as picturesque. We have no space to dwell on Lydgate's character; we can but repeat that he is a vividly consistent, manly figure – powerful, ambitious, sagacious, with the maximum rather than the minimum of egotism, strenuous, generous, fallible, and altogether human. A work of the liberal scope of *Middlemarch* contains a multitude of artistic intentions, some of the finest of which become clear only in the meditative after-taste of perusal. This is the case with the balanced contrast between the two histories of Lydgate and Dorothea. Each is a tale of matrimonial infelicity, but the conditions in each are so different and the circumstances so broadly opposed that the mind passes from one to the other with that supreme sense of the vastness and variety of human life, under aspects apparently similar, which it belongs only to the greatest novels to produce. The most perfectly successful passages in the book are perhaps those painful fireside scenes between Lydgate and his miserable little wife. The author's rare psychological penetration is lavished upon this veritably mulish domestic flower. There is nothing more powerfully real than these scenes in all English fiction, and nothing certainly more *intelligent*. Their impressiveness, and (as regards Lydgate) their pathos, is deepened by the constantly low key in which they are pitched. It is a tragedy based on unpaid butchers' bills, and the urgent need for small economies. The author has desired to be strictly real and to adhere to the facts of the common lot, and she has given us a powerful version of that typical human drama, the struggles of an ambitious soul with sordid disappointments and vulgar embarrassments. As to her catastrophe we hesitate to pronounce (for Lydgate's ultimate assent to his wife's worldly programme is nothing less than a catastrophe). We almost believe that some terrific explosion would have been more probable than his twenty years of smothered aspiration. Rosamond deserves almost to rank with Tito in *Romola* as a study of a gracefully vicious, or at least of a practically baleful nature. There is one point, however, of which we question the consistency. The author insists on her instincts of coquetry, which seems to us a discordant note. They would have made her better or worse – more generous or more reckless; in either case more manageable. As it is, Rosamond represents, in a measure, the fatality of British decorum.

In reading, we have marked innumerable passages for quotation and comment; but we lack space and the work is so ample that half a dozen extracts would be an ineffective illustration. There would be a great deal to say on the broad array of secondary figures, Mr Casaubon, Mr Brooke, Mr Bulstrode, Mr Farebrother, Caleb Garth, Mrs Cadwallader, Celia Brooke. Mr Casaubon is an excellent invention; as a dusky *repoussoir* to the luminous figure of his wife he could not have been better imagined. There is indeed something very noble in the way in which the author has apprehended his character. To depict hollow pretentiousness and mouldy egotism with so little of narrow sarcasm and so much of philosophic sympathy, is to be a rare moralist as well as a rare story-teller. The whole portrait of Mr Casaubon has an admirably sustained greyness of tone in which the shadows are never carried to the vulgar black of coarser artists. Every stroke contributes to the unwholesome, helplessly sinister expression. Here and there perhaps (as in his habitual diction), there is a hint of exaggeration; but we confess we like fancy to be fanciful. Mr Brooke and Mr Garth are in their different lines supremely genial creations; they are drawn with the touch of a Dickens chastened and intellectualized. Mrs Cadwallader is, in another walk of life, a match for Mrs Poyser, and Celia Brooke is as pretty a fool as any of Miss Austen's. Mr Farebrother and his delightful 'womankind' belong to a large group of figures begotten of the super-abundance of the author's creative instinct. At times they seem to encumber the stage and to produce a rather ponderous mass of dialogue; but they add to the reader's impression of having walked in the Middlemarch lanes and listened to the Middlemarch accent. To but one of these accessory episodes – that of Mr Bulstrode, with its multiplex ramifications – do we take exception. It has a slightly artificial cast, a melodramatic tinge, unfriendly to the richly natural colouring of the whole. Bulstrode himself – with the history of whose troubled conscience the author has taken great pains – is, to our sense, too diffusely treated; he never grasps the reader's attention. But the touch of genius is never idle or vain. The obscure figure of Bulstrode's comely wife emerges at the needful moment, under a few light strokes, into the happiest reality.

All these people, solid and vivid in their varying degrees, are members of a deeply human little world, the full reflection of whose antique image is the great merit of these volumes. How bravely rounded a little world the author has made it – with how dense an atmosphere of interest and passions and loves and enmities and strivings and failings, and how motley a group of great folk and small, all after their kind, she has filled it, the reader must learn for himself. No writer seems to us to have drawn from a richer stock of those long-cherished memories which one's later philosophy makes doubly tender. There are few figures in the book which do not seem to have grown mellow in the author's mind. English readers may fancy they enjoy the 'atmosphere' of *Middlemarch*; but we maintain that to relish its inner essence we must – for reasons too numerous to detail – be an American. The author has commissioned herself to be real, her native tendency being that of an idealist, and the intellectual result is a very fertilizing mixture. The constant presence of thought, of generalizing instinct, of *brain*, in a word, behind her observation, gives the latter its great value and her whole manner its high superiority. It denotes a mind in which imagination is illumined by faculties rarely found in fellowship with it. In this respect – in that broad reach of vision which would make the worthy historian of solemn fact as well as wanton fiction – George Eliot seems to us among English romancers to stand alone. Fielding approaches her, but to our mind, she surpasses Fielding. Fielding was didactic – the author of *Middlemarch* is really philosophic. These great qualities imply corresponding perils. The first is the loss of simplicity. George Eliot lost hers some time since; it lies buried (in a splendid mausoleum) in *Romola*. Many of the discursive portions of *Middlemarch* are, as we may say, too clever by half. The author wishes to say too many things, and to say them too well; to recommend herself to a scientific audience. Her style, rich and flexible as it is, is apt to betray her on these transcendental flights; we find, in our copy, a dozen passages marked 'obscure'. *Silas Marner* has a delightful tinge of Goldsmith – we may almost call it; *Middlemarch* is too often an echo of Messrs Darwin and Huxley. In spite of these faults – which it seems graceless to indicate with this crude rapidity – it remains a very splendid performance. It sets a limit, we think, to the development of the old-fashioned English novel. Its diffuseness, on which we have touched, makes it too copious a dose of pure fiction. If we write novels so, how shall we write History? But it is nevertheless a contribution of the first importance to the rich imaginative department of our literature.

12

From a review of Frühlingsfluthen, Ein König Lear des Dorfes, *von Iwan Turgeniew, 1873.* North American Review, *April 1874. This review develops into a longish general essay which was reprinted in* French Poets and Novelists, *1878. The two works occasioning it are known to us (on the whole) as 'Spring Torrents' and 'A King Lear of the Steppes'. 'Hélène' is* On the Eve. *See No. 40 for a slightly fuller view of Turgenev. It is a pity that James never wrote one of his best critical surveys on his favourite novelist.*

HE BELONGS to the limited class of very careful writers. It is to be admitted at the outset that he is a zealous genius, rather than an abundant one. His line is narrow observation. He has not the faculty of rapid, passionate, almost reckless improvisation – that of Walter Scott, of Dickens, of George Sand. This is an immense charm in a story-teller; on the whole, to our sense, the greatest. Turgenieff lacks it; he charms us in other ways. To describe him in the fewest terms, he is a story-teller who has taken notes. This must have been a life-long habit. His tales are a magazine of small facts, of anecdotes, of descriptive traits, taken, as the phrase is, *sur le vif*. If we are not mistaken, he notes down an idiosyncracy of character, a fragment of talk, an attitude, a feature, a gesture, and keeps it, if need be, for twenty years, till just the moment for using it comes, just the spot for placing it. 'Stachoff spoke French tolerably, and as he led a quiet sort of life, passed for a philosopher. Even as an ensign, he was fond of disputing warmly whether, for instance, a man in his life might visit every point of the globe, or whether he might learn what goes on at the bottom of the sea, and was always of the opinion that it was impossible.' The writer of this description may sometimes be erratic, but he is never vague. He has a passion for distinctness, for bringing his characterization to a point, for giving you an example of his meaning. He often, indeed, strikes us as loving details for their own sake, as a bibliomaniac loves the books he never reads. His figures are all portraits; they have each something special, something peculiar, something that none of their neighbours have, and that rescues them from the limbo of the gracefully general. We remember, in one of his stories, a gentleman who makes a momentary appearance as host at a dinner-party, and after being described as having such and such a face, clothes, and manners, has our impression of his personality completed by the statement that the soup at his table was filled with little paste figures, representing hearts, triangles, and trumpets. In the author's conception, there is a secret affinity between the character of this worthy man and the contortions of his vermicelli. This habit of specializing people by vivid oddities was the gulf over which Dickens danced the tight-rope with such agility. But Dickens, as we say, was an improvisatore; the practice, for him, was a lawless revel of the imagination. Turgenieff, on the other hand, always proceeds by book . . .

He seems to us to care for more things in life, to be solicited on more sides, than any novelist save George Eliot. Walter Scott cares for adventure and bravery and honour and ballad-figures and the humour of Scotch peasants; Dickens cares, on an immense, far-reaching scale, for picturesqueness; George Sand cares for love and mineralogy. But these writers care also, greatly, and indeed almost supremely, for their fable, for its twists and turns and surprises, for the work they have in hand of amusing the reader. Even George Eliot, who cares for so many other things besides, has a weakness for making a rounded plot, and often swells out her tales with mechanical episodes, in the midst of which their moral unity quite evaporates. The Bulstrode-Raffles episode in *Middlemarch*, and the whole fable of *Felix Holt*, are striking cases in point. M. Turgenieff lacks, as regards form, as we have said, this immense charm of absorbed inventiveness; but in the way of substance there is literally almost nothing he does not care for. Every class of society, every type of character, every degree of fortune, every phase of manners, passes through his hands; his imagination claims its property equally, in town and country, among rich and poor, among wise people and idiots, *dilettanti* and peasants, the tragic and the joyous, the probable and the grotesque. He has an eye for all our passions, and a deeply sympathetic sense of the wonderful complexity of our souls. He relates in 'Mumu' the history of a deaf-and-dumb serf and a lap-dog, and he portrays in 'A Strange Story' an extraordinary case of religious fanaticism. He has a passion for shifting his point of view, but his object is constantly the same – that of finding an incident, a person, a situation, *morally* interesting. This is his great merit, and the underlying harmony of his apparently excessive attention to detail. He believes in the intrinsic value of 'subject' in art; he holds that there are trivial subjects and serious ones, that the latter are much the best, and that their superiority resides in their giving us absolutely a greater amount of information about the human mind. Deep into the mind he is always attempting to look, though he often applies his eye to very dusky apertures. There is perhaps no better evidence of his minutely psychological attitude than the considerable part played in his tales by simpletons and weak-minded persons. There are few novelists who have not been charmed by the quaintness and picturesqueness of mental invalids; but M. Turgenieff is attracted by something more – by the opportunity of watching the machinery of character, as it were, through a broken window-pane. One might collect from his various tales a perfect regiment of incapables, of the stragglers on life's march. Almost always, in the background of his groups of well-to-do persons there lurks some grotesque, under-witted poor relation, who seems to hover about as a vague memento, in his scheme, of the instability both of fortune and of human cleverness. Such, for instance, is Uvar Ivanovitsch, who figures as a kind of inarticulate chorus in the tragedy of 'Hélène'. He sits about, looking very wise and opening and closing his fingers, and in his person, in this attitude, the drama capriciously takes leave of us . . .

13

On the eighteenth century, from a review of Correspondance Inédite de la Comtesse de Sabran et du Chevalier du Boufflers, *1875.* Galaxy, *October 1875.*

. . . AS REGARDS the eighteenth century, it is rather late in the day, perhaps, to talk about that; but so long as we read the books of the time, so long will our sense of its perplexing confusion of qualities retain a certain freshness. No other age appeals at once so much and so little to our sympathies, or provokes such alternations of curiosity and repugnance. It is near enough to us to seem to partake of many of our current feelings, and yet it is divided from us by an impassable gulf. For many persons it will always have in some ways an indefin-able charm – a charm that they will entertain themselves in looking for even in the faded and mouldering traces of its material envelope – its costumes, its habits, its scenic properties. There are few imagina-tions possessed of a desultory culture that are not able to summon at will the dim vision of a high saloon, panelled in some pale colour, with oval medallions over the doors, with a polished, uncarpeted floor, with thin-legged chairs and tables, with Chinese screens, with a great glass door looking out upon a terrace where clipped shrubs are standing in square green boxes. It is peopled with men and women whose style of dress inspires both admiration and mistrust. There is a sort of noble amplitude in the cut of their garments and a richness of texture in the stuff; breeches and stockings set off the manly figure, and the stiffly-pointed waists of the women serve as a stem to the flower-like exuberance of dazzling bosoms. As we glance from face to face the human creature seems to be in an expansive mood; we receive a lively impression of vigour of temperament, of sentimental fermentation, of moral curiosity. The men are full of natural

gallantry and the women of natural charm, and of forms and traditions they seem to take and leave very much what they choose. It is
very true that they by no means always gain by minute inspection.
An acute sense of untidiness is brought home to us as we move from
group to group. Their velvets and brocades are admirable, but they
are worn with rather too bold a confidence in their intrinsic merit,
and we arrive at the conviction that powder and pomatum are not a
happy combination in a lady's tresses, and that there are few things
less attractive than soiled satin and tarnished embroidery. In the
same way we gather an uneasy impression of moral cynicism; we
overhear various phrases which make us wonder whither our steps
have strayed. And yet, as we retreat, we cast over the threshold a look
that is on the whole a friendly one; we say to ourselves that after all
these people are singularly human. They care intensely for the things
of the mind and the heart, and though they often make a very foolish
use of them they strike here and there a light by whose aid we are now
reading certain psychological mysteries. They have the psychological
passion, and if they expose themselves in morbid researches it is
because they wish to learn by example as well as precept and are not
afraid to pay for their knowledge. 'The French age *par excellence*,' an
acute French critic has said, 'it has both our defects and our qualities.
Better in its intelligence than in its behaviour, more reasoning than
philosophical, more moralistic than moral, it has offered the world
lessons rather than examples, and examples rather than models. It
will be ever a bad sign in France when we make too much of it or too
little; but it would be in especial a fatal day were we to borrow its
frivolity and its corruption and leave aside its noble instincts and its
faculty of enthusiasm.' A part of our kindness for the eighteenth
century rests on the fact that it paid so completely the price of both
corruptions and enthusiasms. As we move to and fro in it we see
something that our companions do not see – we see the sequel, the
consummation, the last act of the drama. The French Revolution
rounds off the spectacle and renders it a picturesque service which
has also something besides picturesqueness. It casts backward a sort
of supernatural light, in the midst of which, at times, we seem to see a
stage full of actors performing fantastic antics for our entertainment.
But retroactively, too, it seems to exonerate the generations that
preceded it, to make them irresponsible and give them the right to say

that, since the penalty was to be exorbitant, a little pleasure more or less would not signify. There is nothing in all history which, to borrow a term from the painters, 'composes' better than the opposition, from 1600 to 1800, of the audacity of the game and the certainty of the reckoning. We all know the idiom which speaks of such reckonings as 'paying the piper'. The piper here is the People. We see the great body of society executing its many-figured dance on its vast polished parquet; and in a dusky corner, behind the door, we see the lean, gaunt, ragged Orpheus filling his hollow reed with tunes in which every breath is an agony.

14

ON THE CONTRARY ESSAYS

From 'Honoré de Balzac', Galaxy, December 1875.

. . . SPEAKING generally, it may be said that he had little belief in virtue and still less admiration for it. He is so large and various that you find all kinds of contradictory things in him; he has that sign of the few supreme geniuses that, if you look long enough he offers you a specimen of every possible mode of feeling. He has represented virtue, innocence and purity in the most vivid forms. César Birotteau, Eugénie Grandet, Mlle Cormon, Mme Graslin, Mme Claës, Mme de Mortsauf, Popinot, Genestas, the Cousin Pons, Schmucke, Chesnel, Joseph Bridau, Mme Hulot – these and many others are not only admirably good people, but they are admirably successful figures. They live and move, they produce an illusion, for all their goodness, quite as much as their baser companions – Mme Vauquer, Mme Marneffe, Vautrin, Philippe Bridau, Mme de Rochefide. Balzac had evidently an immense kindliness, a salubrious good nature which enabled him to feel the charm of all artless and helpless manifestations of life. That robustness of temperament and those high animal spirits which carried him into such fantastic explorations of man's carnal nature as the *Physiologie du Mariage* and the *Contes Drôlatiques* – that lusty natural humour which was not humour in our English sense, but a relish, sentimentally more dry but intellectually more keen, of all grotesqueness and quaintness and uncleanness, and which, when it felt itself flagging, had still the vigour to keep itself up a while as what the French call the 'humoristic' – to emulate Rabelais, to torture words, to string together names, to be pedantically jovial and archaically hilarious – all this helped Balzac to appreciate the simple and the primitive with an intensity subordinate only to his enjoyment of corruption and sophistication. We do wrong indeed to say subordinate; Balzac was here as strong and as frank as he was anywhere. We are almost inclined to say that his profoundly simple people are his best – that in proportion to the labour expended upon them they are most lifelike. Such a figure as 'big Nanon', the great, strapping, devoted maidservant in *Eugénie Grandet*, may stand as an example. (Balzac is full, by the way, of good servants; from Silvie and Christophe in *Le Père Goriot* to Chesnel the notary, whose absolutely canine fidelity deprives him even of the independence of a domestic, in *Le Cabinet des Antiques*.) What he represents best is extremely simple virtue, and vice simple or complex, as you please. In superior virtue, intellectual virtue, he fails; when his superior people begin to reason they are lost – they become prigs and hypocrites, or worse. Madame de Mortsauf, who is intended to be at once the purest and cleverest of his good women, is a kind of fantastic monster; she is perhaps only equalled by the exemplary Madame de l'Estorade, who (in *Le Député d'Arcis*) writes to a lady with whom she is but scantily acquainted a series of *pros* and *cons* on the question whether 'it will be given' (as she phrases it) to a certain gentleman to make her 'manquer à ses devoirs'. This gentleman has snatched her little girl from under a horse's hoofs, and for a while afterward has greatly annoyed her by his importunate presence on her walks and drives. She immediately assumes that he has an eye to her 'devoirs'. Suddenly, however, he disappears, and it occurs to her that he is 'sacrificing his fancy to the fear of spoiling his fine action'. At this attractive thought her 'devoirs' begin to totter, and she ingenuously exclaims, 'But on this footing he would really be a man to reckon with, and, my dear M. de l'Estorade, you would have decidedly to look out!' And yet Madame de l'Estorade is given us as a model of the all-gracious wife and mother; she figures in the *Deux Jeunes Mariées* as the foil of the luxurious, passionate and pedantic Louise de Chaulieu – the young lady who, on issuing from the convent where she has got her education, writes to her friend that she is the possessor of a 'virginité savante'.

There are two writers in Balzac – the spontaneous one and the reflective one – the former of which is much the more delightful, while the latter is the more extraordinary. It was the reflective observer that aimed at colossal completeness and equipped himself with a universal philosophy: and it was of this one we spoke when we said just now that Balzac had little belief in virtue. Balzac's beliefs, it must be confessed, are delicate ground; from certain points of view, perhaps, the less said about them the better. His sincere, personal beliefs may be reduced to a very compact formula; he believed that it was possible to write magnificent novels, and that he was the man to do it. He believed, otherwise stated, that human life was infinitely dramatic and picturesque, and that he possessed an incomparable analytic perception of the fact. His other convictions were all derived from this and humbly danced attendance upon it; for if being a man of genius means being identical with one's productive faculty, never was there such a genius as Balzac's. A monarchical society is unquestionably more picturesque, more available for the novelist than any other, as the others have as yet exhibited themselves; and therefore Balzac was with glee, with gusto, with imagination, a monarchist. Of what is to be properly called religious feeling we do not remember a suggestion in all his many pages; on the other hand, the reader constantly encounters the handsomest compliments to the Catholic Church as a social *régime*. A hierarchy is as much more picturesque than a 'congregational society' as a mountain is than a plain. Bishops, abbés, priests, Jesuits, are invaluable figures in fiction, and the morality of the Catholic Church allows of an infinite *chiaroscuro*. In *La Fille aux Yeux d'Or* there is a portrait of a priest who becomes preceptor to the youthful hero. 'This priest, vicious but politic, sceptical but learned, perfidious but amiable, feeble in aspect, but as strong in body as in head, was so truly useful to his pupil, so complaisant to his vices, so good a calculator of every sort of force, so deep when it was necessary to play some human trick, so young at table, at the gaming house, at – I don't know where – that the only thing the grateful Henry de Marsay could feel soft-hearted over in 1814 was the portrait of his dear bishop – the single object of personal property he was able to inherit from this prelate, an admirable type of the men whose genius will save the Catholic Apostolic and Roman Church.' It is hardly an exaggeration to say that we here come as near as we do at any point to Balzac's religious feeling. The reader will see that it is simply a lively assent to that great worldly force of the Catholic Church, the art of using all sorts of servants and all sorts of means. Balzac was willing to accept any morality that was curious and unexpected, and he found himself as a matter of course more in sympathy with a theory of conduct which takes account of circumstances and recognizes the merits of duplicity, than with the comparatively colourless idea that virtue is nothing if not uncompromising. Like all persons who have looked a great deal at human life, he had been greatly struck with most people's selfishness, and this quality seemed to him the most general in mankind. Selfishness may go to dangerous lengths, but Balzac believed that it may somehow be regulated and even chastened by a strong throne and a brilliant court, with MM. de Rastignac and de Trailles as supports of the one and Mesdames de Maufrigneuse and d'Espard as ornaments of the other, and by a clever and impressive Church, with plenty of bishops of the pattern of the one from whose history a leaf has just been given. If we add to this that he had a great fancy for 'electricity' and animal magnetism, we have touched upon the most salient points of Balzac's philosophy. This makes, it is true, rather a bald statement of a matter which at times seems much more considerable; but it may be maintained that an exact analysis of his heterogeneous opinions will leave no more palpable deposit. His imagination was so fertile, the movement of his mind so constant, his curiosity and ingenuity so unlimited, the energy of his phrase so striking, he raises such a cloud of dust about him as he goes, that the reader to whom he is new has a sense of his opening up gulfs and vistas of thought and pouring forth flashes and volleys of wisdom. But from the moment he ceases to be a simple dramatist Balzac is an arrant charlatan. It is probable that no equally vigorous mind was ever at pains to concoct such elaborate messes of folly. They spread themselves over page after page, in a close, dense verbal tissue, which the reader scans in vain for some little flower of available truth. It all rings false – it is all mere flatulent pretension. It may be said that from the moment he attempts to deal with an abstraction the presumption is always dead against him. About what the discriminating reader thus brutally dubs his charlatanism, as about everything else in Balzac, there would be very much more to say than this small compass admits of. (Let not the discriminating reader, by the way, repent of his brutality; Balzac himself was brutal, and must be handled with his own weapons. It would be absurd to write of him in semi-tones and innuendoes; he never used them himself.) The chief point is that he himself was his most perfect dupe; he believed in his own magnificent rubbish, and if he made it up, as the phrase is, as he went along, his credulity kept pace with his invention. This was, briefly speaking, because he was morally and intellectually so superficial. He paid himself, as the French say, with shallower conceits than ever before passed muster with a strong man. The moral, the intellectual atmosphere of his genius is extraordinarily gross and turbid; it is no wonder that the flower of truth does not bloom in it, nor any natural flower whatever. The difference in this respect between Balzac and the other great novelists is extremely striking. When we approach Thackeray and George Eliot, George Sand and Turgenieff, it is into the conscience and the mind that we enter, and we think of these writers primarily as great consciences and great minds. When we approach Balzac we seem to enter into a great temperament – a prodigious nature. He strikes us half the time as an extraordinary physical phenomenon. His robust imagination seems a sort of physical faculty and impresses us more with its sensible mass and quantity than with its lightness or fineness.

This brings us back to what was said just now touching his disbelief in virtue and his homage to the selfish passions. He had no natural sense of morality, and this we cannot help thinking a serious fault in a novelist. Be the morality false or true, the writer's deference to it greets us as a kind of essential perfume. We find such a perfume in Shakespeare; we find it, in spite of his so-called cynicism, in Thackeray; we find it, potently, in George Eliot, in George Sand, in Turgenieff. They care for moral questions; they are haunted by a moral ideal. This southern slope of the mind, as we may call it, was very barren in Balzac, and it is partly possible to account for its barrenness. Large as Balzac is, he is all of one piece and he hangs perfectly together. He pays for his merits and he sanctifies his defects. He had a sense of this present terrestrial life which has never been surpassed, and which in his genius overshadowed everything else. There are many men who are not especially occupied with the idea of another world, but we believe there has never been a man so completely detached from it as Balzac. This world of our senses, of our purse, of our name, of our *blason* (or the absence of it) – this palpable world of houses and clothes, of seven per cents and multiform human faces, pressed upon his imagination with an unprecedented urgency. It certainly is real enough to most of us, but to Balzac it was ideally real – charmingly, absorbingly, absolutely real. There is nothing in all imaginative literature that in the least resembles his mighty passion for *things* – for material objects, for furniture, upholstery, bricks and mortar. The world that contained these things filled his consciousness, and *being*, at its intensest, meant simply being thoroughly at home among them. Balzac possessed indeed a lively interest in the supernatural: *La Peau de Chagrin*, *Louis Lambert*, *Séraphita*, are a powerful expression of it. But it was a matter of adventurous fancy, like the same quality in Edgar Poe; it was perfectly cold, and had nothing to do with his moral life. To get on in this world, to succeed, to live greatly in all one's senses, to have plenty of *things* – this was Balzac's infinite; it was here that his heart expanded. It was natural, therefore, that the life of mankind should seem to him above all an eager striving along this line – a multi-tudinous greed for personal enjoyment. The master-passion among these passions – the passion of the miser – he has depicted as no one else has begun to do. Wherever we look, in the *Comédie Humaine*, we see a miser, and he – or she – is sure to be a marvel of portraiture. In the struggle and the scramble it is not the sweetest qualities that come uppermost, and Balzac, watching the spectacle, takes little account of these. It is strength and cunning that are most visible – the power to climb the ladder, to wriggle to the top of the heap, to clutch the money-bag. In human nature, viewed in relation to this end, it is force only that is desirable, and a feeling is fine only in so far as it is a profitable practical force. Strength of purpose seems the supremely admirable thing, and the spectator lingers over all eminent exhibi-tions of it. It may show itself in two great ways – in vehemence and in astuteness, in eagerness and in patience. Balzac has a vast relish for both, but on the whole he prefers the latter form as being the more dramatic. It admits of duplicity, and there are few human ac-complishments that Balzac professes so explicit a respect for as this. He scatters it freely among his dear 'gens d'église', and his women are all compounded of it. If he had been asked what was, for human purposes, the faculty he valued most highly, he would have said the power of dissimulation. He regards it as a sign of all superior people, and he says somewhere that nothing forms the character so finely as having had to exercise it in one's youth, in the bosom of one's family. In this attitude of Balzac's there is an element of affectation and of pedantry; he praises duplicity because it is original and audacious to do so. But he praises it also because it has for him the highest recommendation that anything can have – it is picturesque. Duplicity is more picturesque than honesty – just as the line of beauty is the curve and not the straight line. In place of a moral judgment of conduct, accordingly, Balzac usually gives us an aesthetic judgement. A magnificent action with him is not an action which is remarkable for its high motive, but an action with a great force of will or of desire behind it, which throws it into striking and monumental relief. It may be a magnificent sacrifice, a magnificent devotion, a magnificent act of faith; but the presumption is that it will be a magnificent lie, a magnificent murder, or a magnificent adultery.

15

---------- ❧ ----------

Turgenev and James on Flaubert, from a letter to William James, February 1876 (HJL, vol. 2, 26–7).

... [TURGENEV] also talked much about Flaubert, with regard to whom he thinks that the great trouble is that he has never known a decent woman – or even a woman who was a little interesting. He has passed his life exclusively *'avec des courtisanes et des rien-du-tout'*. In poor old Flaubert there is something almost tragic: his big intellectual temperament, machinery, etc., and vainly colossal attempts to press out the least little drop of *passion*. So much talent, and so much naïveté and honesty, and yet so much dryness and coldness ...

16

On Madame Bovary *from 'Charles de Bernard and Gustave Flaubert: The Minor French Novelists', Galaxy, February 1876. After dismissing* L'Éducation Sentimentale *as 'elaborately and massively dreary' by comparison, James goes on to discuss the Goncourts (see No. 31). No. 49 is his final estimate of Flaubert.*

. . . IN TAINE's elaborate satire, *The Opinions of M. Graindorge*, there is a report of a conversation at a dinner party between an English spinster of didactic habits and a decidedly audacious Frenchman. He begs to recommend to her a work which he has lately been reading and which cannot fail to win the approval of all persons interested in the propagation of virtue. The lady lends a sympathetic ear, and he gives a rapid sketch of the tale – the history of a wicked woman who goes from one abomination to another, until at last the judgment of heaven descends upon her, and, blighted and blasted, she perishes miserably. The lady grasps her pencil and note-book and begs for the name of the edifying volume, and the gentleman leans across the dinner table and answers with a smile – '*Madame Bovary; or, The Consequences of Misconduct.*' This is a very pretty epigram, but it is more than an epigram. It may be very seriously maintained that M. Flaubert's masterpiece is the pearl of 'Sunday reading'. Practically M. Flaubert is a potent moralist; whether, when he wrote his book, he was so theoretically is a matter best known to himself. Every out-and-out realist who provokes curious meditation may claim that he is a moralist, for that, after all, is the most that the moralists can do for us. They sow the seeds of virtue; they can hardly pretend to raise the crop. Excellence in this matter consists in the tale and the moral hanging well together, and this they are certainly more likely to do when there has been a definite intention – that intention of which artists who cultivate 'art for art' are usually so extremely mistrustful; exhibiting thereby, surely, a most injurious disbelief in the illimitable alchemy of art. We may say on the whole doubtless that the highly didactic character of *Madame Bovary* is an accident, inasmuch as the works that have followed it, both from its author's and from other hands, have been things to read much less for meditation's than for sensation's sake. M. Flaubert's theory as a novelist, briefly expressed, is t begin on the outside. Human life, he says, is before all things a spectacle, a thing to be looked at, seen, apprehended, enjoyed with the eyes. What our eyes show us is all that we are sure of; so with this we will, at any rate, begin. As this is infinitely curious and entertaining, if we know how to look at it, and as such looking consumes a great deal of time and space, it is very possible that with this also we may end. We admit nevertheless that there is something else, beneath and behind, that belongs to the realm of vagueness and uncertainty, and into this we must occasionally dip. It crops up sometimes irrepressibly, and of course we don't positively count it out. On the whole, we will leave it to take care of itself, and let it come off as it may. If we propose to represent the pictorial side of life, of course we must do it thoroughly well – we must be complete. There must be no botching, no bungling, no scamping; it must be a very serious matter. We will 'render' things – anything, everything, from a chimney-pot to the shoulders of a duchess – as painters render them. We believe there is a certain particular phrase, better than any other, for everything in the world, and the thoroughly accomplished writer ends by finding it. We care only for what *is* – we know nothing about what ought to be. Human life is interesting, because we are in it and of it; all kinds of curious things are taking place in it (we don't analyse the curious – for artists it is an ultimate fact); we select as many of them as possible. Some of the most curious are the most disagreeable, but the chance for 'rendering' in the disagreeable is as great as anywhere else (some people think even greater), and moreover the disagreeable is extremely characteristic. The real is the most satisfactory thing in the world, and if once we fairly get into it, nothing shall frighten us back.

Some such words as these may stand as a rough sketch of the sort of intellectual conviction under which *Madame Bovary* was written.

The theory in this case at least was applied with brilliant success; it produced a masterpiece. Realism seems to me with *Madame Bovary* to have said its last word. I doubt whether the same process will ever produce anything better. In M. Flaubert's own hands it has distinctly failed to do so. *L'Education Sentimentale* is in comparison mechanical and inanimate. The great good fortune of *Madame Bovary* is that here the theory seems to have been invented after the fact. The author began to describe because he had laid up a great fund of disinterested observations; he had been looking at things for years, for his own edification, in that particular way. The imitative talents in the same line, those whose highest ambition is to 'do' their Balzac or their Flaubert, give us the sense of looking at the world only with the most mercenary motives – of going about to stare at things only for the sake of their forthcoming novel. M. Flaubert knew what he was describing – knew it extraordinarily well. One can hardly congratulate him on his knowledge; anything drearier, more sordid, more vulgar, and sterile, and desolate than the greater part of the subject-matter of the book it would be impossible to conceive. 'Moeurs de Province', the sub-title runs, and the work is the most striking possible example of that remarkable passion which possesses most Frenchmen of talent for making out their provincial life to be the most hideous thing on earth. Emma Bovary is the daughter of a small farmer, who has been able to send her to boarding-school, and to give her something of an 'elegant' education. She is pretty and graceful, and she marries a small country doctor – the kindest, simplest, and stupidest of husbands. He takes her to live in a squalid little country town, called Yonville-l'Abbaye, near Rouen; she is luxurious and sentimental; she wastes away with *ennui*, and loneliness, and hatred of her narrow lot and absent opportunities, and on the very first chance she takes a lover. With him she is happy for a few months, and then he deserts her brutally and cynically. She falls violently ill, and comes near dying; then she gets well, and takes another lover of a different kind. All the world – the very little world of Yonville-l'Abbaye – sees and knows and gossips; her husband alone neither sees or suspects. Meanwhile she has been spending money remorselessly and insanely; she has made promissory notes, and she is smothered in debt. She has undermined the ground beneath her husband's feet; her second lover leaves her; she is ruined, dishonoured, utterly at bay. She goes back as a beggar to her first lover, and he refuses to give her a sou. She tries to sell herself and fails; then, in impatience and desperation, she collapses. She takes poison and dies horribly, and the bailiffs come down on her husband, who is still heroically ignorant. At last he learns, and it is too much for him; he loses all courage, and dies one day on his garden bench, leaving twelve francs fifty centimes to his little girl, who is sent to get her living in a cotton mill. The tale is a tragedy, unillumined and unredeemed, and it might seem, on this rapid and imperfect showing, to be rather a vulgar tragedy. Women who get into trouble with the extreme facility of Mme Bovary, and by the same method, are unfortunately not rare, and the better opinion seems to be that they deserve but a limited degree of sympathy. The history of M. Flaubert's heroine is nevertheless full of substance and meaning. In spite of the elaborate system of portraiture to which she is subjected, in spite of being minutely described in all her attitudes and all her moods, from the hem of her garment to the texture of her finger-nails, she remains a living creature, and as a living creature she interests us. The only thing that poor Charles Bovary, after her death, can find to say to her lovers is, 'It's the fault of fatality.' And in fact, as we enter into the situation, it is. M. Flaubert gives his readers the impression of having known few kinds of women, but he has evidently known intimately this particular kind. We see the process of her history; we see how it marches from step to step to its horrible termination, and we do not perceive how it could well have done otherwise. It is a case of the passion for luxury, for elegance, for the world's most agreeable and comfortable things, of an intense and complex imagination, corrupt almost in the germ, and finding corruption, and feeding on it, in the most unlikely and unfavouring places – it is a case of all this being pressed back upon itself with a force which makes an explosion inevitable. Mme Bovary has an insatiable hunger for pleasure, and she lives amid dreariness; she is ignorant, vain, naturally depraved; of the things she dreams about not an intimation ever reaches her; so she makes her *trouée*, as the French say, bores her opening, scrapes and scratches her way out into the light where she can. The reader may protest against a heroine who is 'naturally depraved'. You are welcome, he may say, to make of a heroine what you please, to carry her where you please; but in mercy don't set us down to a young lady of whom, on the first page, there is nothing better to be said than that. But all this is a question of degree. Mme Bovary is typical, like all powerfully conceived figures in fiction. There are a great many potential Mme Bovarys, a great many young women, vain, ignorant, leading dreary, vulgar, intolerable lives, and possessed of irritable nerves and of a high natural appreciation of luxury, of admiration, of agreeable sensations, of what they consider the natural rights of pretty women, who are more or less launched upon the rapid slope which she descended to the bottom. The gentleman who recommended her history to the English lady at M. Taine's dinner party would say that her history was in intention a solemn warning to such young women not to allow themselves to think too much about the things they cannot have. Does M. Flaubert in this case complete his intention? does he suggest an alternative – a remedy? plenty of plain sewing, serious reading, general housework? M. Flaubert keeps well out of the province of remedies; he simply relates his facts, in all their elaborate horror. The accumulation of detail is so immense, the vividness of portraiture of people, of things, of places, of times and hours, is so poignant and convincing, that one is dragged into the very current and tissue of the story; the reader seems to have lived in it all, more than in any novel I can recall. At the end the intensity of illusion becomes horrible; overwhelmed with disgust and pity, the reader closes the book.

Besides being the history of the most miserable of women, *Madame Bovary* is also an elaborate picture of small *bourgeois* rural life. Anything, in this direction, more remorseless and complete it would be hard to conceive. Into all that makes life ignoble, and vulgar, and sterile M. Flaubert has entered with an extraordinary penetration. The dulness and flatness of it all suffocate us; the pettiness and ugliness sicken us. Every one in the book is either stupid or mean, but against the shabby-coloured background two figures stand out in salient relief. One is Charles Bovary, the husband of the heroine; the other is M. Homais, the village apothecary. Bovary is introduced to us in his childhood, at school, and we see him afterward at college and during his first marriage – a union with a widow of meagre charms, twenty years older than himself. He is the only good person of the book, but he is stupidly, helplessly good. At school 'he had for correspondent a wholesale hardware merchant of the Rue Ganterie, who used to fetch him away once a month, on a Sunday, send him to walk in the harbour and look at the boats, and then bring him back to college by seven o'clock, before supper. Every Thursday evening he wrote a long letter to his mother, with red ink and three wafers; then he went over his copy books, or else read an old volume of *Anacharsis* which was knocking about the class room. In our walks he used to talk with the servant, who was from the country like himself.' Charles Bovary is one of the persons whose merits and defects and whole earthly fortune are summed up in those only two words we can say about them, 'poor fellow'. In Homais, the apothecary, M. Flaubert has really added to our knowledge of human nature – at least as human nature is modified by French social conditions. To American readers, fortunately, this figure represents nothing familiar; we do not as yet possess any such mellow perfection of charlatanism. The apothecary is that unwholesome compound, a Philistine radical – a *père de famille*, a free-thinker, a rapacious shopkeeper, a stern moralist, an ardent democrat, and an abject snob. He is a complete creation; he is taken, as the French say, *sur le vif*, and his talk, his accent, his pompous vocabulary, his attitudes, his vanities, his windy vacuity, are inimitably rendered. Except her two lovers. M. Homais is Mme Bovary's sole male acquaintance, and her only social recreation is to spend the evening with his wife and her own husband in his book-shop. Her life has known, in this line, but two other events. Once she has been at a ball at the house of a neighbouring nobleman, for whom her husband had lanced an abscess in his cheek, and who sends the invitation as part payment – a fatal ball, which has opened her eyes to her own deprivations and intolerably quickened her desires; and once she has been to the theatre at Rouen. Both of these episodes are admirably put before us, and they play a substantial part in the tale. The book is full of expressive episodes; the most successful in its hideous relief and reality is the long account of the operation performed by Charles Bovary upon the club-foot of the ostler at the inn, an operation superfluous, ridiculous, abjectly unskilful and clumsy, and which results in the amputation of the poor fellow's whole leg after he has lain groaning under the reader's eyes and nose for a dozen pages, amid the flies and dirt, the brooms and pails, the comings and goings of his squalid corner of the tavern. The reader asks himself the meaning of this elaborate presentation of the most repulsive of incidents, and feels inclined at first to charge it to a sort of artistic bravado on the author's part – a desire to complete his theory of realism by applying his resources to the simply disgusting. But he presently sees that the whole episode has a kind of metaphysical value. It completes the general picture; it characterizes the daily life of a community in which such incidents assumed the importance of leading events, and it gives the final touch to our sense of poor Charles Bovary's bungling mediocrity. Everything in the book is ugly: turning over its pages, my eyes fall upon only this one little passage in which an agreeable 'effect' is rendered. It treats of Bovary's visits to Emma, at her father's farm, before their marriage, and is a happy instance of the way in which this author's style arrests itself at every step in a picture. 'Once, when it was thawing, the bark of the trees was reeking in the yard, the snow was melting on the roofs of the outbuildings. She was upon the threshold; she went in and fetched her umbrella and opened it. The umbrella, of dove-coloured silk, with the sun coming through it, lighted up her white complexion with changing reflections. Beneath it she smiled in the soft warmth, and he heard the water-drops fall one by one upon the stretched silk' . . .

17

. . . THE CRUDITY of sentiment of the advocates of 'art for art' is
often a striking example of the fact that a great deal of what is called
culture may fail to dissipate a well-seated provincialism of spirit.
They talk of morality as Miss Edgeworth's infantine heroes and
heroines talk of 'physic' – they allude to its being put into and kept
out of a work of art, put into and kept out of one's appreciation of the
same, as if it were a coloured fluid kept in a big-labelled bottle in
some mysterious intellectual closet. It is in reality simply a part of the
essential richness of inspiration – it has nothing to do with the artistic
process and it has everything to do with the artistic effect. The more a
work of art feels it at its source, the richer it is; the less it feels it, the
poorer it is. People of a large taste prefer rich works to poor ones and
they are not inclined to assent to the assumption that the process is
the whole work. We are safe in believing that all this is comfortably
clear to most of those who have, in any degree, been initiated into art
by production. For them the subject is as much a part of their work as
their hunger is a part of their dinner . . .

18

———— ✢ ————

'Daniel Deronda: A Conversation', Atlantic Monthly, Decem-
ber 1876. Earlier James had looked forward to 'almost a year'
of the 'lateral extension into another multitudinous world'
afforded by the serialization of Daniel Deronda. Later, in The
Middle Years *(1917), remembering a rather embarrassing*
meeting with George Eliot he wrote, 'I was to become, I was to
remain . . . even a very Derondist of Derondists, for my own
wanton joy: which amounts to saying that I found the figured
tapestry always *vivid enough to brave no matter what*
complication of the stitch.'

THEODORA, one day early in the autumn, sat on her verandah with a
piece of embroidery, the design of which she made up as she
proceeded, being careful, however, to have a Japanese screen before
her, to keep her inspiration at the proper altitude. Pulcheria, who
was paying her a visit, sat near her with a closed book, in a paper
cover, in her lap. Pulcheria was playing with the pug-dog, rather idly,
but Theodora was stitching, steadily and meditatively. 'Well,' said
Theodora, at last, 'I wonder what he accomplished in the East.'
Pulcheria took the little dog into her lap and made him sit on the
book. 'Oh,' she replied, 'they had tea-parties at Jerusalem — exclusively of ladies — and he sat in the midst and stirred his tea and made
high-toned remarks. And then Mirah sang a little, just a little, on
account of her voice being so weak. Sit still, Fido,' she continued,
addressing the little dog, 'and keep your nose out of my face. But it's a
nice little nose, all the same,' she pursued, 'a nice little short snub
nose and not a horrid big Jewish nose. Oh, my dear, when I think
what a collection of noses there must have been at that wedding!' At
this moment Constantius steps upon the verandah from within, hat

and stick in hand and his shoes a trifle dusty. He has some distance to come before he reaches the place where the ladies are sitting, and this gives Pulcheria time to murmur, 'Talk of snub noses!' Constantius is presented by Theodora to Pulcheria, and he sits down and exclaims upon the admirable blueness of the sea, which lies in a straight band across the green of the little lawn; comments too upon the pleasure of having one side of one's verandah in the shade. Soon Fido, the little dog, still restless, jumps off Pulcheria's lap and reveals the book, which lies title upward. 'Oh,' says Constantius, 'you have been finishing *Daniel Deronda*?' Then follows a conversation which it will be more convenient to present in another form.

Theodora. Yes, Pulcheria has been reading aloud the last chapters to me. They are wonderfully beautiful.

Constantius (after a moment's hesitation). Yes, they are very beautiful. I am sure you read well, Pulcheria, to give the fine passages their full value.

Theodora. She reads well when she chooses, but I am sorry to say that in some of the fine passages of this last book she took quite a false tone. I couldn't have read them aloud myself; I should have broken down. But Pulcheria – would you really believe it? – when she couldn't go on it was not for tears, but for – the contrary.

Constantius. For smiles? Did you really find it comical? One of my objections to *Daniel Deronda* is the absence of those delightfully humorous passages which enlivened the author's former works.

Pulcheria. Oh, I think there are some places as amusing as anything in *Adam Bede* or *The Mill on the Floss*: for instance where, at the last, Deronda wipes Gwendolen's tears and Gwendolen wipes his.

Constantius. Yes, I know what you mean. I can understand that situation presenting a slightly ridiculous image; that is, if the current of the story don't swiftly carry you past.

Pulcheria. What do you mean by the current of the story? I never read a story with less current. It is not a river; it is a series of lakes. I once read of a group of little uneven ponds resembling, from a bird's-eye view, a looking-glass which had fallen upon the floor and broken, and was lying in fragments. That is what *Daniel Deronda* would look like, on a bird's-eye view.

Theodora. Pulcheria found that comparison in a French novel. She is always reading French novels.

Constantius. Ah, there are some very good ones.

Pulcheria (perversely). I don't know; I think there are some very poor ones.

Constantius. The comparison is not bad, at any rate. I know what you mean by *Daniel Deronda* lacking current. It has almost as little as *Romola*.

Pulcheria. Oh, *Romola* is unpardonably slow; it is a kind of literary tortoise.

Constantius. Yes, I know what you mean by that. But I am afraid you are not friendly to our great novelist.

Theodora. She likes Balzac and George Sand and other impure writers.

Constantius. Well, I must say I understand that.

Pulcheria. My favourite novelist is Thackeray, and I am extremely fond of Miss Austen.

Constantius. I understand that too. You read over *The Newcomes* and *Pride and Prejudice*.

Pulcheria. No, I don't read them over now; I think them over. I have been making visits for a long time past to a series of friends, and I have spent the last six months in reading *Daniel Deronda* aloud. Fortune would have it that I should always arrive by the same train as the new number. I am accounted a frivolous, idle creature; I am not a disciple in the new school of embroidery, like Theodora; so I was immediately pushed into a chair and the book thrust into my hand, that I might lift up my voice and make peace between all the impatiences that were snatching at it. So I may claim at least that I have read every word of the work. I never skipped.

Theodora. I should hope not, indeed!

Constantius. And do you mean that you really didn't enjoy it?

Pulcheria. I found it protracted, pretentious, pedantic.

Constantius. I see; I can understand that.

Theodora. Oh, you understand too much! This is the twentieth time you have used that formula.

Constantius. What will you have? You know I must try to understand; it's my trade.

Theodora. He means he writes reviews. Trying *not* to understand is what I call that trade!

Constantius. Say then I take it the wrong way; that is why it has never made my fortune. But I do try to understand; it is my – my – (He pauses.)

Theodora. I know what you want to say. Your strong side.

Pulcheria. And what is his weak side?

Theodora. He writes novels.

Constantius. I have written one. You can't call that a side. It's a little facet, at the most.

Pulcheria. You talk as if you were a diamond. I should like to read it – not aloud!

Constantius. You can't read it softly enough. But you, Theodora, you didn't find our book too 'protracted'?

Theodora. I should have liked it to continue indefinitely, to keep coming out always, to be one of the regular things of life.

Pulcheria. Oh, come here, little dog! To think that *Daniel Deronda* might be perpetual when you, little short-nosed darling, can't last at the most more than nine or ten years!

Theodora. A book like *Daniel Deronda* becomes part of one's life; one lives in it, or alongside of it. I don't hesitate to say that I have been living in this one for the last eight months. It is such a complete world George Eliot builds up; it is so vast, so much-embracing! It has such a firm earth and such an ethereal sky. You can turn into it and lose yourself in it.

Pulcheria. Oh, easily, and die of cold and starvation!

Theodora. I have been very near to poor Gwendolen and very near to that sweet Mirah. And the dear little Meyricks also; I know them intimately well.

Pulcheria. The Meyricks, I grant you, are the best thing in the book.

Theodora. They are a delicious family; I wish they lived in Boston. I consider Herr Klesmer almost Shakespearean, and his wife is almost as good. I have been near to poor grand Mordecai –

Pulcheria. Oh, reflect, my dear; not too near!

Theodora. And as for Deronda himself I freely confess that I am consumed with a hopeless passion for him. He is the most irresistible man in the literature of fiction.

Pulcheria. He is not a man at all.

Theodora. I remember nothing more beautiful than the description of his childhood, and that picture of his lying on the grass in the abbey cloister, a beautiful seraph-faced boy, with a lovely voice, reading history and asking his Scotch tutor why the Popes had so many nephews. He must have been delightfully handsome.

Pulcheria. Never, my dear, with that nose! I am sure he had a nose, and I hold that the author has shown great pusillanimity in her treatment of it. She has quite shirked it. The picture you speak of is very pretty, but a picture is not a person. And why is he always grasping his coat-collar, as if he wished to hang himself up? The author had an uncomfortable feeling that she must make him do something real, something visible and sensible, and she hit upon that clumsy figure. I don't see what you mean by saying you have been *near* those people; that is just what one is not. They produce no illusion. They are described and analysed to death, but we don't see them nor hear them nor touch them. Deronda clutches his coat-collar, Mirah crosses her feet, Mordecai talks like the Bible; but that doesn't make real figures of them. They have no existence outside of the author's study.

Theodora. If you mean that they are nobly imaginative I quite agree with you; and if they say nothing to your own imagination the fault is yours, not theirs.

Pulcheria. Pray don't say they are Shakespearean again. Shakespeare went to work another way.

Constantius. I think you are both in a measure right; there is a distinction to be drawn. There are in *Daniel Deronda* the figures based upon observation and the figures based upon invention. This distinction, I know, is rather a rough one. There are no figures in any novel that are pure observation, and none that are pure invention. But either element may preponderate, and in those cases in which invention has preponderated George Eliot seems to me to have achieved at the best but so many brilliant failures.

Theodora. And are *you* turning severe? I thought you admired her so much.

Constantius. I defy any one to admire her more, but one must discriminate. Speaking brutally, I consider *Daniel Deronda* the weakest of her books. It strikes me as very sensibly inferior to *Middlemarch*. I have an immense opinion of *Middlemarch*.

Pulcheria. Not having been obliged by circumstances to read *Middlemarch* to other people, I didn't read it at all. I couldn't read it to myself. I tried, but I broke down. I appreciated Rosamond, but I couldn't believe in Dorothea.

Theodora (very gravely). So much the worse for you, Pulcheria. I have enjoyed *Daniel Deronda because* I had enjoyed *Middlemarch*. Why should you throw *Middlemarch* up against her? It seems to me that if a book is fine it is fine. I have enjoyed *Deronda* deeply, from beginning to end.

Constantius. I assure you, so have I. I can read nothing of George Eliot's without enjoyment. I even enjoy her poetry, though I don't approve of it. In whatever she writes I enjoy her intelligence; it has space and air, like a fine landscape. The intellectual brilliancy of *Daniel Deronda* strikes me as very great, in excess of anything the author has done. In the first couple of numbers of the book this ravished me. I delighted in its deep, rich English tone, in which so many notes seemed melted together.

Pulcheria. The tone is not English, it is German.

Constantius. I understand that – if Theodora will allow me to say so. Little by little I began to feel that I cared less for certain notes than for others. I say it under my breath – I began to feel an occasional temptation to skip. Roughly speaking, all the Jewish burden of the story tended to weary me; it is this part that produces the poor illusion which I agree with Pulcheria in finding. Gwendolen and Grandcourt are admirable – Gwendolen is a masterpiece. She is known, felt and presented, psychologically, altogether in the grand manner. Beside her and beside her husband – a consummate picture of English brutality refined and distilled (for Grandcourt is before all things brutal), Deronda, Mordecai and Mirah are hardly more than shadows. They and their fortunes are all improvisation. I don't say anything against improvisation. When it succeeds it has a surpassing charm. But it must succeed. With George Eliot it seems to me to succeed, but a little less than one would expect of her talent. The story of Deronda's life, his mother's story, Mirah's story, are quite the sort of thing one finds in George Sand. But they are really not so good as they would be in George Sand. George Sand would have carried it off with a lighter hand.

Theodora. Oh, Constantius, how can you compare George Eliot's novels to that woman's? It is sunlight and moonshine.

Pulcheria. I really think the two writers are very much alike. They are both very voluble, both addicted to moralizing and philosophizing *à tout bout de champ*, both inartistic.

Constantius. I see what you mean. But George Eliot is solid, and George Sand is liquid. When occasionally George Eliot liquefies – as in the history of Deronda's birth, and in that of Mirah – it is not to so crystalline a clearness as the author of *Consuelo* and *André*. Take Mirah's long narrative of her adventures, when she unfolds them to Mrs Meyrick. It is arranged, it is artificial, *ancien jeu*, quite in the George Sand manner. But George Sand would have done it better. The false tone would have remained, but it would have been more persuasive. It would have been a fib, but the fib would have been neater.

Theodora. I don't think fibbing neatly a merit, and I don't see what is to be gained by such comparisons. George Eliot is pure and George Sand is impure; how can you compare them? As for the Jewish element in Deronda, I think it a very fine idea; it's a noble subject. Wilkie Collins and Miss Braddon would not have thought of it, but that does not condemn it. It shows a large conception of what one may do in a novel. I heard you say, the other day, that most novels were so trivial – that they had no general ideas. Here is a general idea, the idea interpreted by Deronda. I have never disliked the Jews as some people do; I am not like Pulcheria, who sees a Jew in every bush. I wish there were one; I would cultivate shrubbery. I have known too many clever and charming Jews; I have known none that were not clever.

Pulcheria. Clever, but not charming.

Constantius. I quite agree with you as to Deronda's going in for the Jews and turning out a Jew himself being a fine subject, and this quite apart from the fact of whether such a thing as a Jewish revival be at all a possibility. If it be a possibility, so much the better – so much the better for the subject, I mean.

Pulcheria. A la bonne heure!

Constantius. I rather suspect it is not a possibility; that the Jews in general take themselves much less seriously than that. They have other fish to fry. George Eliot takes them as a person outside of Judaism – aesthetically. I don't believe that is the way they take themselves.

Pulcheria. They have the less excuse then for keeping themselves so dirty.

Theodora. George Eliot must have known some delightful Jews.

Constantius. Very likely; but I shouldn't wonder if the most delightful of them had smiled a trifle, here and there, over her book. But that makes nothing, as Herr Klesmer would say. The subject is a noble one. The idea of depicting a nature able to feel and worthy to feel the sort of inspiration that takes possession of Deronda, of depicting it sympathetically, minutely and intimately – such an idea has great elevation. There is something very fascinating in the mission that Deronda takes upon himself. I don't quite know what it means, I don't understand more than half of Mordecai's rhapsodies, and I don't perceive exactly what practical steps could be taken. Deronda could go about and talk with clever Jews – not an unpleasant life.

Pulcheria. All that seems to me so unreal that when at the end the author finds herself confronted with the necessity of making him start for the East by the train, and announces that Sir Hugo and Lady Mallinger have given his wife 'a complete Eastern outfit', I descend to the ground with a ludicrous jump.

Constantius. Unreal, if you please; that is no objection to it; it greatly tickles my imagination. I like extremely the idea of Mordecai believing, without ground of belief, that if he only wait, a young man on whom nature and society have centred all their gifts will come to him and receive from his hands the precious vessel of his hopes. It is romantic, but it is not vulgar romance; it is finely romantic. And there is something very fine in the author's own feeling about Deronda. He is a very liberal creation. He is, I think, a failure – a brilliant failure; if he had been a success I should call him a splendid creation. The author meant to do things very handsomely for him; she meant apparently to make a faultless human being.

Pulcheria. She made a dreadful prig.

Constantius. He *is* rather priggish, and one wonders that so clever a woman as George Eliot shouldn't see it.

Pulcheria. He has no blood in his body. His attitude at moments is like that of a high-priest in a *tableau vivant*.

Theodora. Pulcheria likes the little gentlemen in the French novels who take good care of their attitudes, which are always the same attitude, the attitude of 'conquest' – of a conquest that tickles their vanity. Deronda has a contour that cuts straight through the middle of all that. He is made of a stuff that isn't dreamt of in their philosophy.

Pulcheria. Pulcheria likes very much a novel which she read three or four years ago, but which she has not forgotten. It was by Ivan Turgenieff, and it was called *On the Eve*. Theodora has read it, I know, because she admires Turgenieff, and Constantius has read it, I suppose, because he has read everything.

Constantius. If I had no reason but that for my reading, it would be small. But Turgenieff is my man.

Pulcheria. You were just now praising George Eliot's general ideas. The tale of which I speak contains in the portrait of the hero very much such a general idea as you find in the portrait of Deronda. Don't you remember the young Bulgarian student, Inssaroff, who gives himself the mission of rescuing his country from its subjection to the Turks? Poor man, if he had foreseen the horrible summer of 1876! His character is the picture of a race-passion of patriotic hopes and dreams. But what a difference in the vividness of the two figures. Inssaroff is a man; he stands up on his feet; we see him, hear him, touch him. And it has taken the author but a couple of hundred pages – not eight volumes – to do it.

Theodora. I don't remember Inssaroff at all, but I perfectly remember the heroine, Helena. She is certainly most remarkable, but, remarkable as she is, I should never dream of calling her as wonderful as Gwendolen.

Constantius. Turgenieff is a magician, which I don't think I should call George Eliot. One is a poet, the other is a philosopher. One cares for the aspect of things and the other cares for the reason of things. George Eliot, in embarking with Deronda, took aboard, as it were, a far heavier cargo than Turgenieff with his Inssaroff. She proposed, consciously, to strike more notes.

Pulcheria. Oh, consciously, yes!

Constantius. George Eliot wished to show the possible picturesqueness – the romance, as it were – of a high moral tone. Deronda is a moralist, a moralist with a rich complexion.

Theodora. It is a most beautiful nature. I don't know anywhere a more complete, a more deeply analysed portrait of a great nature. We praise novelists for wandering and creeping so into the small corners of the mind. That is what we praise Balzac for when he gets down upon all fours to crawl through *Le Père Goriot* or *Les Parents Pauvres*. But I must say I think it a finer thing to unlock with as firm a hand as George Eliot some of the greater chambers of human character. Deronda is in a manner an ideal character, if you will, but he seems to me triumphantly married to reality. There are some admirable things said about him; nothing can be finer than those pages of description of his moral temperament in the fourth book – his elevated way of looking at things, his impartiality, his universal sympathy, and at the same time his fear of their turning into mere irresponsible indifference. I remember some of it verbally: 'He was ceasing to care for knowledge – he had no ambition for practice – unless they could be gathered up into one current with his emotions.'

Pulcheria. Oh, there is plenty about his emotions. Everything about him is 'emotive'. That bad word occurs on every fifth page.

Theodora. I don't see that it is a bad word.

Pulcheria. It may be good German, but it is poor English.

Theodora. It is not German at all; it is Latin. So, my dear!

Pulcheria. As I say, then, it is not English.

Theodora. This is the first time I ever heard that George Eliot's style was bad!

Constantius. It is admirable; it has the most delightful and the most intellectually comfortable suggestions. But it is occasionally a little too long-sleeved, as I may say. It is sometimes too loose a fit for the thought, a little baggy.

Theodora. And the advice he gives Gwendolen, the things he says to her, they are the very essence of wisdom, of warm human wisdom, knowing life and feeling it. 'Keep your fear as a safeguard, it may make consequences passionately present to you.' What can be better than that?

Pulcheria. Nothing, perhaps. But what can be drearier than a novel in which the function of the hero – young, handsome and brilliant – is to give didactic advice, in a proverbial form, to the young, beautiful and brilliant heroine?

Constantius. That is not putting it quite fairly. The function of Deronda is to make Gwendolen fall in love with him, to say nothing of falling in love himself with Mirah.

Pulcheria. Yes, the less said about that the better. All we know about Mirah is that she has delicate rings of hair, sits with her feet crossed, and talks like an article in a new magazine.

Constantius. Deronda's function of adviser to Gwendolen does not strike me as so ridiculous. He is not nearly so ridiculous as if he were lovesick. It is a very interesting situation – that of a man with whom a beautiful woman in trouble falls in love and yet whose affections are so preoccupied that the most he can do for her in return is to enter kindly and sympathetically into her position, pity her and talk to her. George Eliot always gives us something that is strikingly and ironically characteristic of human life; and what savours more of the essential crookedness of our fate than the sad cross-purposes of these two young people? Poor Gwendolen's falling in love with Deronda is part of her own luckless history, not of his.

Theodora. I do think he takes it to himself rather too little. No man had ever so little vanity.

Pulcheria. It is very inconsistent, therefore, as well as being extremely impertinent and ill-mannered, his buying back and sending to her her necklace at Leubronn.

Constantius. Oh, you must concede that; without it there would have been no story. A man writing of him, however, would certainly have made him more peccable. As George Eliot lets herself go, in that quarter, she becomes delightfully, almost touchingly, feminine. It is like her making Romola go to housekeeping with Tessa, after Tito Melema's death; like her making Dorothea marry Will Ladislaw. If Dorothea had married any one after her misadventure with Casaubon, she would have married a trooper.

Theodora. Perhaps some day Gwendolen will marry Rex.

Pulcheria. Pray, who is Rex?

Theodora. Why, Pulcheria, how can you forget?

Pulcheria. Nay, how can I remember? But I recall such a name in the dim antiquity of the first or second book. Yes, and then he is pushed to the front again at the last, just in time not to miss the falling of the curtain. Gwendolen will certainly not have the audacity to marry any one we know so little about.

Constantius. I have been wanting to say that there seems to me to be two very distinct elements in George Eliot – a spontaneous one and an artificial one. There is what she is by inspiration and what she is because it is expected of her. These two heads have been very perceptible in her recent writings; they are much less noticeable in her early ones.

Theodora. You mean that she is too scientific? So long as she remains the great literary genius that she is, how can she be too scientific? She is simply permeated with the highest culture of the age.

Pulcheria. She talks too much about the 'dynamic quality' of people's eyes. When she uses such a phrase as that in the first sentence in her book she is not a great literary genius, because she shows a want of tact. There can't be a worse limitation.

Constantius. The 'dynamic quality' of Gwendolen's glance has made the tour of the world.

Theodora. It shows a very low level of culture on the world's part to be agitated by a term perfectly familiar to all decently-educated people.

Pulcheria. I don't pretend to be decently educated; pray tell me what it means.

Constantius (promptly). I think Pulcheria has hit it in speaking of a want of tact. In the manner of the book, throughout, there is something that one may call a want of tact. The epigraphs in verse are a want of tact; they are sometimes, I think, a trifle more pretentious than really pregnant; the importunity of the moral reflections is a want of tact; the very diffuseness is a want of tact. But it comes back to what I said just now about one's sense of the author writing under a sort of external pressure. I began to notice it in *Felix Holt*; I don't think I had before. She strikes me as a person who certainly has naturally a taste for general considerations, but who has fallen upon an age and a circle which have compelled her to give them an exaggerated attention. She does not strike me as naturally a critic, less still as naturally a sceptic; her spontaneous part is to observe life and to feel it, to feel it with admirable depth. Contemplation, sympathy and faith – something like that, I should say, would have been her natural scale. If she had fallen upon an age of enthusiastic assent to old articles of faith, it seems to me possible that she would have had a more perfect, a more consistent and graceful development, than she has actually had. If she had cast herself into such a current – her genius being equal – it might have carried her to splendid distances. But she has chosen to go into criticism, and to the critics she addresses her work; I mean the critics of the universe. Instead of feeling life itself, it is 'views' upon life that she tries to feel.

Pulcheria. She is the victim of a first-class education. I am so glad!

Constantius. Thanks to her admirable intellect she philosophizes very sufficiently; but meanwhile she has given a chill to her genius. She has come near spoiling an artist.

Pulcheria. She has quite spoiled one. Or rather I shouldn't say that, because there was no artist to spoil. I maintain that she is not an artist. An artist could never have put a story together so monstrously ill. She has no sense of form.

Theodora. Pray, what could be more artistic than the way that Deronda's paternity is concealed till almost the end, and the way we are made to suppose Sir Hugo is his father?

Pulcheria. And Mirah his sister. How does that fit together? I was as little made to suppose he was not a Jew as I cared when I found out he was. And his mother popping up through a trap-door and popping down again, at the last, in that scrambling fashion! His mother is very bad.

Constantius. I think Deronda's mother is one of the unvivified characters; she belongs to the cold half of the book. All the Jewish part is at bottom cold; that is my only objection. I have enjoyed it because my fancy often warms cold things; but beside Gwendolen's history it is like the empty half of the lunar disk beside the full one. It is admirably studied, it is imagined, it is understood, but it is not embodied. One feels this strongly in just those scenes between Deronda and his mother; one feels that one has been appealed to on rather an artificial ground of interest. To make Deronda's reversion to his native faith more dramatic and profound, the author has given him a mother who on very arbitrary grounds, apparently, has separated herself from this same faith and who has been kept waiting in the wing, as it were, for many acts, to come on and make her speech and say so. This moral situation of hers we are invited retrospectively to appreciate. But we hardly care to do so.

Pulcheria. I don't *see* the princess, in spite of her flame-coloured robe. Why should an actress and prima-donna care so much about religious matters?

Theodora. It was not only that; it was the Jewish race she hated, Jewish manners and looks. You, my dear, ought to understand that.

Pulcheria. I do, but I am not a Jewish actress of genius; I am not what Rachel was. If I were I should have other things to think about.

Constantius. Think now a little about poor Gwendolen.

Pulcheria. I don't care to think about her. She was a second-rate English girl who got into a flutter about a lord.

Theodora. I don't see that she is worse than if she were a first-rate American girl who should get into exactly the same flutter.

Pulcheria. It wouldn't be the same flutter at all; it wouldn't be any flutter. She wouldn't be afraid of the lord, though she might be amused at him.

Theodora. I am sure I don't perceive whom Gwendolen was afraid of. She was afraid of her misdeed – her broken promise – after she had committed it, and through that fear she was afraid of her husband. Well she might be! I can imagine nothing more vivid than the sense we get of his absolutely clammy selfishness.

Pulcheria. She was not afraid of Deronda when, immediately after her marriage and without any but the most casual acquaintance with him, she begins to hover about him at the Mallingers' and to drop little confidences about her conjugal woes. That seems to me very indelicate; ask any woman.

Constantius. The very purpose of the author is to give us an idea of the sort of confidence that *Deronda* inspired – its irresistible potency.

Pulcheria. A lay father-confessor – horrid!

Constantius. And to give us an idea also of the acuteness of Gwendolen's depression, of her haunting sense of impending trouble.

Theodora. It must be remembered that Gwendolen was in love with Deronda from the first, long before she knew it. She didn't know it, poor girl, but that was it.

Pulcheria. That makes the matter worse. It is very disagreeable to see her hovering and rustling about a man who is indifferent to her.

Theodora. He was not indifferent to her, since he sent her back her necklace.

Pulcheria. Of all the delicate attention to a charming girl that I ever heard of, that little pecuniary transaction is the most felicitous.

Constantius. You must remember that he had been *en rapport* with her at the gaming-table. She had been playing in defiance of his observation, and he, continuing to observe her, had been in a measure responsible for her loss. There was a tacit consciousness of this between them. You may contest the possibility of tacit consciousness going so far, but that is not a serious objection. You may point out two or three weak spots in detail; the fact remains that Gwendolen's whole history is vividly told. And see how the girl is known, inside out, how thoroughly she is felt and understood. It is the most *intelligent* thing in all George Eliot's writing, and that is saying much. It is so deep, so true, so complete, it holds such a wealth of psychological detail, it is more than masterly.

Theodora. I don't know where the perception of character has sailed closer to the wind.

Pulcheria. The portrait may be admirable, but it has one little fault. You don't care a straw for the original. Gwendolen is not an interesting girl, and when the author tries to invest her with a deep tragic interest she does so at the expense of consistency. She has made her at the outset too light, too flimsy; tragedy has no hold on such a girl.

Theodora. You are hard to satisfy. You said this morning that Dorothea was too heavy, and now you find Gwendolen too light. George Eliot wished to give us the perfect counterpart of Dorothea. Having made one portrait she was worthy to make the other.

Pulcheria. She has committed the fatal error of making Gwendolen vulgarly, pettily, drily selfish. She was *personally* selfish.

Theodora. I know nothing more personal than selfishness.

Pulcheria. I am selfish, but I don't go about with my chin out like that; at least I hope I don't. She was an odious young woman, and one can't care what becomes of her. When her marriage turned out ill she would have become still more hard and positive; to make her soft and appealing is very bad logic. The second Gwendolen doesn't belong to the first.

Constantius. She is perhaps at the first a little childish for the weight of interest she has to carry, a little too much after the pattern of the unconscientious young ladies of Miss Yonge and Miss Sewell.

Theodora. Since when is it forbidden to make one's heroine young? Gwendolen is a perfect picture of youthfulness – its eagerness, its presumption, its preoccupation with itself, its vanity and silliness, its sense of its own absoluteness. But she is extremely intelligent and clever, and therefore tragedy *can* have a hold upon her. Her conscience doesn't make the tragedy; that is an old story and, I think, a secondary form of suffering. It is the tragedy that makes her conscience, which then reacts upon it; and I can think of nothing more powerful than the way in which the growth of her conscience is traced, nothing more touching than the picture of its helpless maturity.

Constantius. That is perfectly true. Gwendolen's history is admirably typical – as most things are with George Eliot: it is the very stuff that human life is made of. What is it made of but the discovery by each of us that we are at the best but a rather ridiculous fifth wheel to the coach, after we have sat cracking our whip and believing that we are at least the coachman in person? We think we are the main hoop to the barrel, and we turn out to be but a very incidental splinter in one of the staves. The universe forcing itself with a slow, inexorable pressure into a narrow, complacent, and yet after all extremely sensitive mind, and making it ache with the pain of the process – that is Gwendolen's story. And it becomes completely characteristic in that her supreme perception of the fact that the world is whirling past her is in the disappointment not of a base but of an exalted passion. The very chance to embrace what the author is so fond of calling a 'larger life' seems refused to her. She is punished for being narrow, and she is not allowed a chance to expand. Her finding Deronda pre-engaged to go to the East and stir up the race-feeling of the Jews strikes me as a wonderfully happy invention. The irony of the situation, for poor Gwendolen, is almost grotesque, and it makes one wonder whether the whole heavy structure of the Jewish question in the story was not built up by the author for the express purpose of giving its proper force to this particular stroke.

Theodora. George Eliot's intentions are extremely complex. The mass is for each detail and each detail is for the mass.

Pulcheria. She is very fond of deaths by drowning. Maggie Tulliver and her brother are drowned, Tito Melema is drowned, Mr Grand-court is drowned. It is extremely unlikely that Grandcourt should not have known how to swim.

Constantius. He did, of course, but he had a cramp. It served him right. I can't imagine a more consummate representation of the most detestable kind of Englishman – the Englishman who thinks it low to articulate. And in Grandcourt the type and the individual are so happily met: the type with its sense of the proprieties and the individual with his absence of all sense. He is the apotheosis of dryness, a human expression of the simple idea of the perpendicular.

Theodora. Mr Casaubon, in *Middlemarch*, was very dry too; and yet what a genius it is that can give us two disagreeable husbands who are so utterly different!

Pulcheria. You must count the two disagreeable wives too – Rosamond Vincy and Gwendolen. They are very much alike. I know the author didn't mean it; it proves how common a type the worldly, *pincée*, selfish young woman seemed to her. They are both disagree-able; you can't get over that.

Constantius. There is something in that, perhaps. I think, at any rate, that the secondary people here are less delightful than in *Middlemarch*; there is nothing so good as Mary Garth and her father, or the little old lady who steals sugar, or the parson who is in love with Mary, or the country relatives of old Mr Featherstone. Rex Gascoigne is not so good as Fred Vincy.

Theodora. Mr Gascoigne is admirable, and Mrs Davilow is charming.

Pulcheria. And you must not forget that you think Herr Klesmer 'Shakespearean'. Wouldn't 'Wagnerian' be high enough praise?

Constantius. Yes, one must make an exception with regard to the Klesmers and the Meyricks. They are delightful, and as for Klesmer himself, and Hans Meyrick, Theodora may maintain her epithet. Shakespearean characters are characters that are born of the *over-flow* of observation – characters that make the drama seem multitud-inous, like life. Klesmer comes in with a sort of Shakespearean 'value', as a painter would say, and so, in a different tone, does Hans Meyrick. They spring from a much-peopled mind.

Theodora. I think Gwendolen's confrontation with Klesmer one of the finest things in the book.

Constantius. It is like everything in George Eliot; it will bear thinking of.

Pulcheria. All that is very fine, but you cannot persuade me that *Deronda* is not a very ponderous and ill-made story. It has nothing that one can call a subject. A silly young girl and a solemn, sapient young man who doesn't fall in love with her! That is the *donnée* of eight monthly volumes. I call it very flat. Is that what the exquisite art of Thackeray and Miss Austen and Hawthorne has come to? I would as soon read a German novel outright.

Theodora. There is something higher than form – there is spirit.

Constantius. I am afraid Pulcheria is sadly aesthetic. She had better confine herself to Mérimée.

Pulcheria. I shall certainly to-day read over *La Double Méprise*.

Theodora. Oh, my dear, *y pensez-vous?*

Constantius. Yes, I think there is little art in *Deronda*, but I think there is a vast amount of life. In life without art you can find your account; but art without life is a poor affair. The book is full of the world.

Theodora. It is full of beauty and knowledge, and that is quite art enough for me.

Pulcheria (to the little dog). We are silenced, darling, but we are not convinced, are we? (The pug begins to bark.) No, we are not even silenced. It's a young woman with two bandboxes.

Theodora. Oh, it must be our muslins.

Constantius (rising to go). I see what you mean!

19

From 'George Sand', Galaxy, July 1877. James continued to write about George Sand but he retained his opinion of her lack of credibility. 'Her novels to-day have turned rather pale and faint,' he wrote in 1897; her 'brightness and vagueness' is 'no drawback when she is on the ground of her own life, to which she is tied by a certain number of tangible threads; but to embark on one of her confessed fictions is to have – after all that has come and gone, in our time, in the trick of persuasion – a little too much the feeling of going up in a balloon. We are borne by a fresh cool current and the car delightfully dangles; but as we peep over the sides we see things – as we usually know them – at a dreadful drop beneath.' George Sand had become old-fashioned for James.

... WHAT WE have called briefly and crudely her want of veracity requires some explanation. It is doubtless a condition of her serene volubility; but if this latter is a great literary gift, its value is impaired by our sense that it rests to a certain extent upon a weakness. There is something very liberal and universal in George Sand's genius, as well as very masculine; but our final impression of her always is that she is a woman and a Frenchwoman. Women, we are told, do not value the truth for its own sake, but only for some personal use they make of it. My present criticism involves an assent to this somewhat cynical dogma. Add to this that woman, if she happens to be French, has an extraordinary taste for investing objects with a graceful drapery of her own contrivance, and it will be found that George Sand's cast of mind includes both the generic and the specific idiosyncrasy. We have more than once heard her readers say (whether it was professed fact or admitted fiction that they had in hand), 'It is all very well, but I can't believe a word of it!' There is something very peculiar in this inability to believe George Sand even in that relative sense in which we apply the term to novelists at large. We believe Balzac, we believe Gustave Flaubert, we believe Dickens and Thackeray and Miss Austen. Dickens is far more incredible than George Sand, and yet he produces much more illusion. In spite of her plausibility, the author of *Consuelo* always appears to be telling a fairy-tale. We say in spite of her plausibility, but we might rather say that her excessive plausibility is the reason of our want of faith. The narrative is too smooth, too fluent; the narrator has a virtuous independence that the Muse of history herself might envy her. The effect it produces is that of a witness who is eager to tell more than is asked him, the worth of whose testimony is impaired by its importunity. The thing is beautifully done, but you feel that rigid truth has come off as it could; the author has not a high standard of exactitude; she never allows facts to make her uncomfortable. *L'Histoire de ma Vie* is full of charming recollections and impressions of Madame Sand's early years, of delightful narrative, of generous and elevated sentiment; but we have constantly the feeling that it is what children call 'made up'. If the fictitious quality in our writer's reminiscences is very sensible, of course the fictitious quality in her fictions is still more so; and it must be said that in spite of its odd mixture of the didactic and the irresponsible, *L'Histoire de ma Vie* sails nearer to the shore than its professedly romantic companions . . .

We have given, however, no full enumeration of the author's romances, and it seems needless to do so. We have lately been trying to read them over, and we frankly confess that we have found it impossible. They are excellent reading for once, but they lack that quality which makes things classical – makes them impose themselves. It has been said that what makes a book a classic is its style. We should modify this, and instead of style say *form*. Madame Sand's novels have plenty of style, but they have no form. Balzac's have not a shred of style, but they have a great deal of form. Posterity doubtless will make a selection from each list, but the few volumes of Balzac it preserves will remain with it much longer, we suspect, than those which it borrows from his great contemporary. We cannot easily imagine posterity travelling with *Valentine* or *Mauprat*, *Consuelo* or the *Marquis de Villemer* in its trunk. At the same time we can imagine that if these admirable tales fall out of fashion, such of our descendants as stray upon them in the dusty corners of old libraries will sit down on the bookcase ladder with the open volume and turn it over with surprise and enchantment. What a beautiful mind! they will say; what an extraordinary style! Why have we not known more about these things? And as, when that time comes, we suppose the world will be given over to a 'realism' that we have not as yet begun faintly to foreshadow, George Sand's novels will have, for the children of the twenty-first century, something of the same charm which Spenser's '*Fairy Queen*' has for those of the nineteenth. For a critic of to-day to pick and choose among them seems almost pedantic; they all belong quite to the same intellectual family. They are the easy writing which makes hard reading.

20

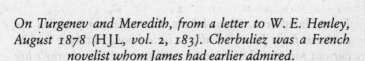

*On Turgenev and Meredith, from a letter to W. E. Henley,
August 1878 (HJL, vol. 2, 183). Cherbuliez was a French
novelist whom James had earlier admired.*

. . . GEORGE MEREDITH strikes me as a capital example of the sort
of writer that Turgenieff is most absolutely opposite to – the
*un*realists – the *literary* story-tellers. T. doesn't care a straw for an
epigram or a phrase – his inspiration is not a whit literary, but purely
and simply, human, moral. G. M. cares, I should say, enormously for
epigrams and phrases. He's a mannerist, a *coquette*, in a word: like
that pitiful prostitute, Victor Cherbuliez. Turgenieff hasn't a gram of
coquetry! . . .

21

————— ⚜ —————

From Hawthorne, 1879. *I have been able to reprint all the criticism from James's brilliant little book, but have had to cut out most of the charming treatment of Hawthorne's life (1804–64) including accounts of the 'Transcendentalist ... Abolitionist ... Fourierite' community at Brook Farm which Hawthorne was 'at ... without being of' and on which* The Blithedale Romance *is based; of the Concord of Emerson and Thoreau; and of Hawthorne's experience as American Consul at Liverpool. Hawthorne caused a mild disturbance in America at the time because it was thought to undervalue American society – by W. D. Howells among others. But this was often a complaint against the expatriate James in the 1880s.*
G. P. Lathrop, Hawthorne's son-in-law, had published his A study of Hawthorne *in 1876.*

[INTRODUCTION]

IT WILL be necessary, for several reasons, to give this short sketch the form rather of a critical essay than of a biography. The data for a life of Nathaniel Hawthorne are the reverse of copious, and even if they were abundant they would serve but in a limited measure the purpose of the biographer. Hawthorne's career was probably as tranquil and uneventful a one as ever fell to the lot of a man of letters; it was almost strikingly deficient in incident, in what may be called the dramatic quality. Few men of equal genius and of equal eminence can have led on the whole a simpler life. His six volumes of Note-Books illustrate this simplicity; they are a sort of monument to an unagitated fortune. Hawthorne's career had few vicissitudes or variations; it was passed for the most part in a small and homogeneous society, in a provincial, rural community; it had few perceptible points of contact with what is called the world, with public events, with the manners of his time, even with the life of his neighbours. Its literary incidents are not numerous. He produced, in quantity, but little. His works consist of four novels and the fragment of another, five volumes of short tales, a collection of sketches, and a couple of story-books for children. And yet some account of the man and the writer is well worth giving. Whatever may have been Hawthorne's private lot, he has the importance of being the most beautiful and most eminent representative of a literature. The importance of the literature may be questioned, but at any rate, in the field of letters, Hawthorne is the most valuable example of the American genius. That genius has not, as a whole, been literary; but Hawthorne was on his limited scale a master of expression. He is the writer to whom his countrymen most confidently point when they wish to make a claim to have enriched the mother-tongue, and, judging from present appearances, he will long occupy this honourable position. If there is something very fortunate for him in the way that he borrows an added relief from the absence of competitors in his own line and from the general flatness of the literary field that surrounds him, there is also, to a spectator, something almost touching in his situation. He was so modest and delicate a genius that we may fancy him appealing from the lonely honour of a representative attitude – perceiving a painful incongruity between his imponderable literary baggage and the large conditions of American life. Hawthorne on the one side is so subtle and slender and unpretending, and the American world on the other is so vast and various and substantial, that it might seem to the author of *The Scarlet Letter* and the *Mosses from an Old Manse*, that we render him a poor service in contrasting his proportions with those of a great civilization. But our author must accept the awkward as well as the graceful side of his fame; for he has the advantage of pointing a valuable moral. This moral is that the flower of art blooms only where the soil is deep, that it takes a great deal of history to produce a little literature, that it needs a complex social machinery to set a writer in motion. American civilization has hitherto had other things to do than to produce flowers, and before giving birth to writers it has wisely occupied itself with providing something for them to write about. Three or four beautiful talents of trans-Atlantic growth are the sum of what the world usually recognizes, and in this modest nosegay the genius of Hawthorne is admitted to have the rarest and sweetest fragrance.

His very simplicity has been in his favour; it has helped him to appear complete and homogeneous. To talk of his being national would be to force the note and make a mistake of proportion; but he is, in spite of the absence of the realistic quality, intensely and vividly local. Out of the soil of New England he sprang – in a crevice of that immitigable granite he sprouted and bloomed. Half of the interest that he possesses for an American reader with any turn for analysis must reside in his latent New England savour; and I think it no more than just to say that whatever entertainment he may yield to those who know him at a distance, it is an almost indispensable condition of properly appreciating him to have received a personal impression of the manners, the morals, indeed of the very climate, of the great region of which the remarkable city of Boston is the metropolis. The cold, bright air of New England seems to blow through his pages, and these, in the opinion of many people, are the medium in which it is most agreeable to make the acquaintance of that tonic atmosphere. As to whether it is worth while to seek to know something of New England in order to extract a more intimate quality from *The House of Seven Gables* and *The Blithedale Romance*, I need not pronounce; but it is certain that a considerable observation of the society to which these productions were more directly addressed is a capital preparation for enjoying them. I have alluded to the absence in Hawthorne of that quality of realism which is now so much in fashion, an absence in regard to which there will of course be more to say; and yet I think I am not fanciful in saying that he testifies to the sentiments of the society in which he flourished almost as pertinently (proportions observed) as Balzac and some of his descendants – MM. Flaubert and Zola – testify to the manners and morals of the French people. He was not a man with a literary theory; he was guiltless of a system, and I am not sure that he had ever heard of Realism, this remarkable compound having (although it was invented some time earlier) come into general use only since his death. He had certainly not proposed to himself to give an account of the social idiosyncrasies of his fellow-citizens, for his touch on such points is always light and vague, he has none of the apparatus of an historian, and his shadowy style of portraiture never suggests a rigid standard of accuracy. Nevertheless he virtually offers the most vivid reflection of New England life that has found its way into literature. His value in this respect is not diminished by the fact that he has not attempted to portray the usual Yankee of comedy, and that he has been almost culpably indifferent to his opportunities for commemorating the variations of colloquial English that may be observed in the New World.

[AS A YOUNG MAN]

He was poor, he was solitary, and he undertook to devote himself to literature in a community in which the interest in literature was as yet of the smallest. It is not too much to say that even to the present day it is a considerable discomfort in the United States not to be 'in business'. The young man who attempts to launch himself in a career that does not belong to the so-called practical order; the young man who has not, in a word, an office in the business-quarter of the town, with his name painted on the door, has but a limited place in the social system, finds no particular bough to perch upon. He is not looked at askance, he is not regarded as an idler; literature and the arts have always been held in extreme honour in the American world, and those who practise them are received on easier terms than in other countries. If the tone of the American world is in some respects provincial, it is in none more so than in this matter of the exaggerated homage rendered to authorship. The gentleman or the lady who has written a book is in many circles the object of an admiration too indiscriminating to operate as an encouragement to good writing. There is no reason to suppose that this was less the case fifty years ago; but fifty years ago, greatly more than now, the literary man must have lacked the comfort and inspiration of belonging to a class. The best things come, as a general thing, from the talents that are members of a group; every man works better when he has companions working in the same line, and yielding the stimulus of suggestion, comparison, emulation. Great things of course have been done by solitary workers; but they have usually been done with double the pains they would have cost if they had been produced in more genial circumstances. The solitary worker loses the profit of example and discussion; he is apt to make awkward experiments; he is in the nature of the case more or less of an empiric. The empiric may, as I say, be treated by the world as an expert; but the drawbacks and discomforts of empiricism remain to him, and are in fact increased by the suspicion that is mingled with his gratitude, of a want in the public taste of a sense of the proportions of things. Poor Hawthorne, beginning to write subtle short tales at Salem, was empirical enough; he was one of, at most, some dozen Americans who had taken up literature as a profession. The profession in the United States is still very young, and of diminutive stature; but in the year 1830 its head could hardly have been seen above ground. It strikes the observer of to-day that Hawthorne showed great courage in entering a field in which the honours and emoluments were so scanty as the profits of authorship must have been at that time. I have said that in the United States at present authorship is a pedestal, and literature is the fashion; but Hawthorne's history is a proof that it was possible, fifty years ago, to write a great many little masterpieces without becoming known. He begins the preface to the *Twice-Told Tales* by remarking that he was 'for many years the obscurest man of letters in America'. When once this work obtained recognition, the recognition left little to be desired. Hawthorne never, I believe, made large sums of money by his writings, and the early profits of these charming sketches could not have been considerable; for many of them, indeed, as they appeared in journals and magazines, he had never been paid at all; but the honour, when once it dawned – and it dawned tolerably early in the author's career – was never thereafter wanting . . .

Hawthorne, however, was an inveterate observer of small things, and he found a field for fancy among the most trivial accidents. There could be no better example of this happy faculty than the little paper entitled 'Night Sketches', included among the *Twice-Told Tales*. This small dissertation is about nothing at all, and to call attention to it is almost to overrate its importance. This fact is equally true, indeed, of a great many of its companions, which give even the most appreciative critic a singular feeling of his own indiscretion – almost of his own cruelty. They are so light, so slight, so tenderly trivial, that simply to mention them is to put them in a false position. The author's claim for them is barely audible, even to the most acute listener. They are things to take or to leave – to enjoy, but not to talk about. Not to read them would be to do them an injustice (to read them is essentially to relish them), but to bring the machinery of criticism to bear upon them would be to do them a still greater wrong. I must remember, however, that to carry this principle too far would be to endanger the general validity of the present little work – a consummation which it can only be my desire to avert. Therefore it is that I think it permissible to remark that in Hawthorne, the whole class of little descriptive effusions directed upon common things, to which these just-mentioned Night Sketches belong, have a greater charm than there is any warrant for in their substance. The charm is made up of the spontaneity, the personal quality, of the fancy that plays through them, its mingled simplicity and subtlety, its purity and its *bonhomie*. The Night Sketches are simply the light, familiar record of a walk under an umbrella, at the end of a long, dull, rainy day, through the sloppy, ill-paved streets of a country town, where the rare gas-lamps twinkle in the large puddles, and the blue jars in the druggist's window shine through the vulgar drizzle. One would say that the inspiration of such a theme could have had no great force, and such doubtless was the case; but out of the Salem puddles, nevertheless, springs, flower-like, a charming and natural piece of prose.

I have said that Hawthorne was an observer of small things, and indeed he appears to have thought nothing too trivial to be sugges-tive. His Note-Books give us the measure of his perception of common and casual things, and of his habit of converting them into *memoranda*. These Note-Books, by the way – this seems as good a place as any other to say it – are a very singular series of volumes; I doubt whether there is anything exactly corresponding to them in the whole body of literature. They were published – in six volumes, issued at intervals – some years after Hawthorne's death, and no person attempting to write an account of the romancer could afford to regret that they should have been given to the world. There is a point of view from which this may be regretted; but the attitude of the biographer is to desire as many documents as possible. I am thankful, then, as a biographer, for the Note-Books, but I am obliged to confess that, though I have just re-read them carefully, I am still at a loss to perceive how they came to be written – what was Hawthorne's purpose in carrying on for so many years this minute and often trivial chronicle. For a person desiring information about him at any cost, it is valuable; it sheds a vivid light upon his character, his habits, the nature of his mind. But we find ourselves wondering what was its value to Hawthorne himself. It is in a very partial degree a register of impressions, and in a still smaller sense a record of emotions. Outward objects play much the larger part in it; opinions, convictions, ideas pure and simple, are almost absent. He rarely takes his Note-Book into his confidence or commits to its pages any reflections that might be adapted for publicity; the simplest way to describe the tone of these extremely objective journals is to say that they read like a series of very pleasant, though rather dullish and decidedly formal, letters, addressed to himself by a man who, having suspicions that they might be opened in the post, should have determined to insert nothing compromising. They contain much that is too futile for things intended for publicity; whereas, on the other hand, as a receptacle of private impressions and opinions, they are curiously cold and empty. They widen, as I have said, our glimpse of Hawthorne's mind (I do not say that they elevate our estimate of it), but they do so by what they fail to contain, as much as by what we find in them. Our business for the moment, however, is not with the light that they throw upon his intellect, but with the information they offer about his habits and his social circumstances . . .

We are struck with the large number of elements that were absent from them, and the coldness, the thinness, the blankness, to repeat my epithet, present themselves so vividly that our foremost feeling is that of compassion for a romancer looking for subjects in such a field. It takes so many things, as Hawthorne must have felt later in life, when he made the acquaintance of the denser, richer, warmer European spectacle – it takes such an accumulation of history and custom, such a complexity of manners and types, to form a fund of suggestion for a novelist. If Hawthorne had been a young Englishman, or a young Frenchman of the same degree of genius, the same cast of mind, the same habits, his consciousness of the world around him would have been a very different affair; however obscure, however reserved, his own personal life, his sense of the life of his fellow-mortals would have been almost infinitely more various. The negative side of the spectacle on which Hawthorne looked out, in his contemplative saunterings and reveries, might, indeed, with a little ingenuity, be made almost ludicrous; one might enumerate the items of high civilization, as it exists in other countries, which are absent from the texture of American life, until it should become a wonder to know what was left. No State, in the European sense of the word, and indeed barely a specific national name. No sovereign, no court, no personal loyalty, no aristocracy, no church, no clergy, no army, no diplomatic service, no country gentlemen, no palaces, no castles, nor manors, nor old country-houses, nor parsonages, nor thatched cottages nor ivied ruins; no cathedrals, nor abbeys, nor little Norman churches; no great Universities nor public schools – no Oxford, nor Eton, nor Harrow; no literature, no novels, no museums, no pictures, no political society, no sporting class – no Epsom nor Ascot! Some such list as that might be drawn up of the absent things in American life – especially in the American life of forty years ago, the effect of which, upon an English or a French imagination, would probably as a general thing be appalling. The natural remark, in the almost lurid light of such an indictment, would be that if these things are left out, everything is left out. The American knows that a good deal remains; what it is that remains – that is his secret, his joke, as one may say. It would be cruel, in this terrible denudation, to deny him the consolation of his national gift, that 'American humour' of which of late years we have heard so much.

[EARLY WRITINGS]

... As for the *Twice-Told Tales* themselves, they are an old story now; every one knows them a little, and those who admire them particularly have read them a great many times. The writer of this sketch belongs to the latter class, and he has been trying to forget his familiarity with them, and ask himself what impression they would have made upon him at the time they appeared, in the first bloom of their freshness, and before the particular Hawthorne-quality, as it may be called, had become an established, a recognized and valued, fact. Certainly, I am inclined to think, if one had encountered these delicate, dusky flowers in the blossomless garden of American journalism, one would have plucked them with a very tender hand;

one would have felt that here was something essentially fresh and new; here, in no extraordinary force or abundance, but in a degree distinctly appreciable, was an original element in literature. When I think of it, I almost envy Hawthorne's earliest readers; the sensation of opening upon *The Great Carbuncle*, *The Seven Vagabonds*, or *The Threefold Destiny* in an American annual of forty years ago, must have been highly agreeable.

Among these shorter things (it is better to speak of the whole collection, including the *Snow Image*, and the *Mosses from an Old Manse* at once) there are three sorts of tales, each one of which has an original stamp. There are, to begin with, the stories of fantasy and allegory – those among which the three I have just mentioned would be numbered, and which on the whole, are the most original. This is the group to which such little masterpieces as *Malvin's Burial*, *Rappaccini's Daughter*, and *Young Goodman Brown* also belong – these two last perhaps representing the highest point that Hawthorne reached in this direction. Then there are the little tales of New England history, which are scarcely less admirable, and of which *The Grey Champion*, *The Maypole of Merry Mount*, and the four beautiful *Legends of the Province House*, as they are called, are the most successful specimens. Lastly come the slender sketches of actual scenes and of the objects and manners about him, by means of which, more particularly, he endeavoured 'to open an intercourse with the world', and which, in spite of their slenderness, have an infinite grace and charm. Among these things *A Rill from the Town Pump*, *The Village Uncle*, *The Toll-Gatherer's Day*, the *Chippings with a Chisel*, may most naturally be mentioned. As we turn over these volumes we feel that the pieces that spring most directly from his fancy, consti-tute, as I have said (putting his four novels aside), his most substan-tial claim to our attention. It would be a mistake to insist too much upon them; Hawthorne was himself the first to recognize that. 'These fitful sketches,' he says in the preface to the *Mosses from an Old Manse*, 'with so little of external life about them, yet claiming no profundity of purpose – so reserved even while they sometimes seem so frank – often but half in earnest, and never, even when most so, expressing satisfactorily the thoughts which they profess to image – such trifles, I truly feel, afford no solid basis for a literary reputation.' This is very becomingly uttered; but it may be said, partly in answer to it, and partly in confirmation, that the valuable element in these things was not what Hawthorne put into them consciously, but what passed into them without his being able to measure it – the element of simple genius, the quality of imagination. This is the real charm of Hawthorne's writing – this purity and spontaneity and naturalness of fancy. For the rest, it is interesting to see how it borrowed a particular colour from the other faculties that lay near it – how the imagination, in this capital son of the old Puritans, reflected the hue of the more purely moral part, of the dusky, overshadowed conscience. The conscience, by no fault of its own, in every genuine offshoot of that sombre lineage, lay under the shadow of the sense of *sin*. This darkening cloud was no essential part of the nature of the individual; it stood fixed in the general moral heaven under which he grew up and looked at life. It projected from above, from outside, a black patch over his spirit, and it was for him to do what he could with the black patch. There were all sorts of possible ways of dealing with it; they depended upon the personal temperament. Some natures would let it lie as it fell, and contrive to be tolerably comfortable beneath it. Others would groan and sweat and suffer; but the dusky blight would remain, and their lives would be lives of misery. Here and there an individual, irritated beyond endurance, would throw it off in anger, plunging probably into what would be deemed deeper abysses of depravity. Hawthorne's way was the best, for he contrived, by an exquisite process, best known to himself, to transmute this heavy moral burden into the very substance of the imagination, to make it evaporate in the light and charming fumes of artistic production. But Hawthorne, of course, was exceptionally fortunate; he had his genius to help him. Nothing is more curious and interesting than this almost exclusively *imported* character of the sense of sin in Hawthorne's mind; it seems to exist there merely for an artistic or literary purpose. He had ample cognizance of the Puritan conscience; it was his natural heritage; it was reproduced in him; looking into his soul, he found it there. But his relation to it was only, as one may say, intellectual; it was not moral and theological. He played with it and used it as a pigment; he treated it, as the metaphysicians say, objectively. He was not discomposed, disturbed, haunted by it, in the manner of its usual and regular victims, who had not the little postern door of fancy to slip through, to the other side of the wall. It was, indeed, to his imaginative vision, the great fact of man's nature; the light element that had been mingled with his own composition always clung to this rugged prominence of moral responsibility, like the mist that hovers about the mountain. It was a necessary condition for a man of Hawthorne's stock that if his imagination should take licence to amuse itself, it should at least select this grim precinct of the Puritan morality for its play-ground. He speaks of the dark disapproval with which his old ancestors, in the case of their coming to life, would see him trifling himself away as a story-teller. But how far more darkly would they have frowned could they have understood that he had converted the very principle of their own being into one of his toys!

It will be seen that I am far from being struck with the justice of that view of the author of the *Twice-Told Tales*, which is so happily expressed by the French critic to whom I alluded at an earlier stage of this essay. To speak of Hawthorne, as M. Emile Montégut does, as a *romancier pessimiste*, seems to me very much beside the mark. He is no more a pessimist than an optimist, though he is certainly not much of either. He does not pretend to conclude, or to have a philosophy of human nature; indeed, I should even say that at bottom he does not take human nature as hard as he may seem to do. 'His bitterness,' says M. Montégut, 'is without abatement, and his bad opinion of man is without compensation . . . His little tales have the air of confessions which the soul makes to itself; they are so many little slaps which the author applies to our face.' This, it seems to me, is to exaggerate almost immeasurably the reach of Hawthorne's relish of gloomy subjects. What pleased him in such subjects was their picturesqueness, their rich duskiness of colour, their chiaroscuro; but they were not the expression of a hopeless, or even of a predominantly melancholy, feeling about the human soul. Such at least is my own impression. He is to a considerable degree ironical – this is part of his charm – part even, one may say, of his brightness; but he is neither bitter nor cynical – he is rarely even what I should call tragical. There have certainly been story-tellers of a gayer and lighter spirit; there have been observers more humorous, more hilarious – though on the whole Hawthorne's observation has a smile in it oftener than may at first appear; but there has rarely been an observer more serene, less agitated by what he sees and less disposed to call things deeply into question. As I have already intimated, his Note-Books are full of this simple and almost childlike serenity. That dusky pre-occupation with the misery of human life and the wickedness of the human heart which such a critic as M. Emile Montégut talks about, is totally absent from them; and if we may suppose a person to have read these Diaries before looking into the tales, we may be sure that such a reader would be greatly surprised to hear the author described as a disappointed, disdainful genius. 'This marked love of cases of conscience,' says M. Montégut, 'this taciturn, scornful cast of mind, this habit of seeing sin everywhere and hell always gaping open, this dusky gaze bent always upon a damned world and a nature draped in mourning, these lonely conversations of the imagination with the conscience, this pitiless analysis resulting from a perpetual examination of one's self, and from the tortures of a heart closed before men and open to God – all these elements of the Puritan character have passed into Mr Hawthorne, or to speak more justly, have *filtered* into him, through a long succession of generations.' This is a very pretty and very vivid account of Hawthorne, superficially considered; and it is just such a view of the case as would commend itself most easily and most naturally to a hasty critic. It is all true indeed, with a difference; Hawthorne was all that M. Montégut says, *minus* the conviction. The old Puritan moral sense, the consciousness of sin and hell, of the fearful nature of our responsibilities and the savage character of our Taskmaster – these things had been lodged in the mind of a man of Fancy, whose fancy had straightway begun to take liberties and play tricks with them – to judge them (Heaven forgive him!) from the poetic and aesthetic point of view, the point of view of entertainment and irony. This absence of conviction makes the difference; but the difference is great.

Hawthorne was a man of fancy, and I suppose that in speaking of him it is inevitable that we should feel ourselves confronted with the familiar problem of the difference between the fancy and the imagination. Of the larger and more potent faculty he certainly possessed a liberal share; no one can read *The House of the Seven Gables* without feeling it to be a deeply imaginative work. But I am often struck, especially in the shorter tales, of which I am now chiefly speaking, with a kind of small ingenuity, a taste for conceits and analogies, which bears more particularly what is called the fanciful stamp. The finer of the shorter tales are redolent of a rich imagination.

'Had Goodman Brown fallen asleep in the forest and only dreamed a wild dream of witch-meeting? Be it so, if you will; but, alas, it was a dream of evil omen for young Goodman Brown! a stern, a sad, a darkly meditative, a distrustful, if not a desperate, man, did he become from the night of that fearful dream. On the Sabbath-day, when the congregation were singing a holy psalm, he could not listen, because an anthem of sin rushed loudly upon his ear and drowned all the blessed strain. When the minister spoke from the pulpit, with power and fervid eloquence, and with his hand on the open Bible of the sacred truth of our religion, and of saint-like lives and triumphant deaths, and of future bliss or misery unutterable, then did Goodman Brown grow pale, dreading lest the roof should thunder down upon the gray blasphemer and his hearers. Often, awaking suddenly at midnight, he shrank from the bosom of Faith; and at morning or eventide, when the family knelt down at prayer, he scowled and muttered to himself, and gazed sternly at his wife, and turned away. And when he had lived long, and was borne to his grave a hoary corpse, followed by Faith, an aged woman, and children, and grandchildren, a goodly procession, besides neighbours not a few, they carved no hopeful verse upon his tombstone, for his dying hour was gloom.'

There is imagination in that, and in many another passage that I might quote; but as a general thing I should characterize the more metaphysical of our author's short stories as graceful and felicitous conceits. They seem to me to be qualified in this manner by the very fact that they belong to the province of allegory. Hawthorne, in his metaphysical moods, is nothing if not allegorical, and allegory, to my sense, is quite one of the lighter exercises of the imagination. Many excellent judges, I know, have a great stomach for it; they delight in symbols and correspondences, in seeing a story told as if it were another and a very different story. I frankly confess that I have as a general thing but little enjoyment of it and that it has never seemed to me to be, as it were, a first-rate literary form. It has produced assuredly some first-rate works; and Hawthorne in his younger years had been a great reader and devotee of Bunyan and Spenser, the great masters of allegory. But it is apt to spoil two good things – a story and a moral, a meaning and a form; and the taste for it is responsible for a large part of the forcible feeble writing that has been inflicted upon the world. The only cases in which it is endurable is when it is extremely spontaneous, when the analogy presents itself with eager promptitude. When it shows signs of having been groped and fumbled for, the needful illusion is of course absent and the failure complete. Then the machinery alone is visible, and the end to which it operates becomes a matter of indifference. There was but little literary criticism in the United States at the time Hawthorne's earlier works were published; but among the reviewers Edgar Poe perhaps held the scales the highest. He at any rate rattled them loudest, and pretended, more than any one else, to conduct the weighing-process on scientific principles. Very remarkable was this process of Edgar Poe's, and very extraordinary were his principles; but he had the advantage of being a man of genius, and his intelligence was frequently great. His collection of critical sketches of the American writers flourishing in what M. Taine would call his *milieu* and *moment*, is very curious and interesting reading, and it has one quality which ought to keep it from ever being completely forgotten. It is probably the most complete and exquisite specimen of *provincialism* ever prepared for the edification of men. Poe's judgments are pretentious, spiteful, vulgar; but they contain a great deal of sense and discrimination as well, and here and there, sometimes at frequent intervals, we find a phrase of happy insight imbedded in a patch of the most fatuous pedantry. He wrote a chapter upon Hawthorne, and spoke of him on the whole very kindly; and his estimate is of sufficient value to make it noticeable that he should express lively disapproval of the large part allotted to allegory in his tales – in defence of which, he says, 'however, or for whatever object employed, there is scarcely one respectable word to be said . . . The deepest emotion,' he goes on, 'aroused within us by the happiest allegory *as* allegory, is a very, *very* imperfectly satisfied sense of the writer's ingenuity in overcoming a difficulty we should have preferred his not having attempted to overcome . . . One thing is clear, that if allegory ever establishes a fact, it is by dint of overturning a fiction'; and Poe has furthermore the courage to remark that the *Pilgrim's Progress* is a 'ludicrously overrated book'. Certainly, as a general thing, we are struck with the ingenuity and felicity of Hawthorne's analogies and correspondences; the idea appears to have made itself at home in them easily. Nothing could be better in this respect than *The Snow-Image* (a little masterpiece), or *The Great Carbuncle*, or *Doctor Heidegger's Experiment*, or *Rappaccini's Daughter*. But in such things as *The Birth-Mark* and *The Bosom-Serpent*, we are struck with something stiff and mechanical, slightly incongruous, as if the kernel had not assimilated its envelope. But these are matters of light impression, and there would be a want of tact in pretending to discriminate too closely among things which all, in one way or another, have a charm. The charm — the great charm — is that they are glimpses of a great field, of the whole deep mystery of man's soul and conscience. They are moral, and their interest is moral; they deal with something more than the mere accidents and conventionalities, the surface occurrences of life. The fine thing in Hawthorne is that he cared for the deeper psychology, and that, in his way, he tried to become familiar with it. This natural, yet fanciful familiarity with it, this air, on the author's part, of being a confirmed *habitué* of a region of mysteries and subtleties, constitutes the originality of his tales. And then they have the further merit of seeming, for what they are, to spring up so freely and lightly. The author has all the ease, indeed, of a regular dweller in the moral, psychological realm; he goes to and fro in it, as a man who knows his way. His tread is a light and modest one, but he keeps the key in his pocket.

His little historical stories all seem to me admirable; they are so good that you may re-read them many times. They are not numerous, and they are very short; but they are full of a vivid and delightful sense of the New England past; they have, moreover, the distinction, little tales of a dozen and fifteen pages as they are, of being the only successful attempts at historical fiction that have been made in the United States. Hawthorne was at home in the early New England history; he had thumbed its records and he had breathed its air, in whatever odd receptacles this somewhat pungent compound still lurked. He was fond of it, and he was proud of it, as any New Englander must be, measuring the part of that handful of half-starved fanatics who formed his earliest precursors, in laying the foundations of a mighty empire. Hungry for the picturesque as he always was, and not finding any very copious provision of it around him, he turned back into the two preceding centuries, with the earnest determination that the primitive annals of Massachusetts should at least *appear* picturesque. His fancy, which was always alive, played a little with the somewhat meagre and angular facts of the colonial period and forthwith converted a great many of them into impressive legends and pictures. There is a little infusion of colour, a little vagueness about certain details, but it is very gracefully and discreetly done, and realities are kept in view sufficiently to make us feel that if we are reading romance, it is romance that rather supplements than contradicts history. The early annals of New England were not fertile in legend, but Hawthorne laid his hands upon everything that would serve his purpose, and in two or three cases his version of the story has a great deal of beauty. *The Grey Champion* is a sketch of less than eight pages, but the little figures stand up in the tale as stoutly, at the least, as if they were propped up on half-a-dozen chapters by a dryer annalist, and the whole thing has the merit of those cabinet pictures in which the artist has been able to make his persons look the size of life. Hawthorne, to say it again, was not in the least a realist – he was not to my mind enough of one; but there is no genuine lover of the good city of Boston but will feel grateful to him for his courage in attempting to recount the 'traditions' of Washington Street, the main thoroughfare of the Puritan capital. The four *Legends of the Province House* are certain shadowy stories which he professes to have gathered in an ancient tavern lurking behind the modern shop-fronts of this part of the city. The Province House disappeared some years ago, but while it stood it was pointed to as the residence of the Royal Governors of Massachusetts before the Revolution. I have no recollection of it, but it cannot have been, even from Hawthorne's account of it, which is as pictorial as he ventures to make it, a very imposing piece of antiquity. The writer's charming touch, however, throws a rich brown tone over its rather shallow venerableness; and we are beguiled into believing, for instance, at the close of *Howe's Masquerade* (a story of a strange occurrence at an entertainment given by Sir William Howe, the last of the Royal Governors, during the siege of Boston by Washington), that 'superstition, among other legends of this mansion, repeats the wondrous tale that on the anniversary night of Britain's discomfiture the ghosts of the ancient governors of Massachusetts still glide through the Province House. And last of all comes a figure shrouded in a military cloak, tossing his clenched hands into the air and stamping his iron-shod boots upon the freestone steps, with a semblance of feverish despair, but without the sound of a foottramp.' Hawthorne had, as regards the two earlier centuries of New England life, that faculty which is called now-a-days the historic consciousness. He never sought to exhibit it on a large scale; he exhibited it indeed on a scale so minute that we must not linger too much upon it. His vision of the past was filled with definite images – images none the less definite that they were concerned with events as shadowy as this dramatic passing away of the last of King George's representatives in his long loyal but finally alienated colony . . .

[THE THREE AMERICAN NOVELS]

The prospect of official station and emolument which Hawthorne mentions in one of those paragraphs from his Journals which I have just quoted, as having offered itself and then passed away, was at last, in the event, confirmed by his receiving from the administration of President Polk the gift of a place in the Custom-house of his native town. The office was a modest one, and 'official station' may perhaps appear a magniloquent formula for the functions sketched in the admirable Introduction to *The Scarlet Letter*. Hawthorne's duties were those of Surveyor of the port of Salem, and they had a salary attached, which was the important part; as his biographer tells us that he had received almost nothing for the contributions to the *Democratic Review*. He bade farewell to his ex-parsonage and went back to Salem in 1846, and the immediate effect of his ameliorated fortune was to make him stop writing. None of his Journals of the period from his going to Salem to 1850 have been published; from which I infer that he even ceased to journalize. *The Scarlet Letter* was not written till 1849. In the delightful prologue to that work, entitled *The Custom-house*, he embodies some of the impressions gathered during these years of comparative leisure (I say of leisure because he does not intimate in this sketch of his occupations that his duties were onerous). He intimates, however, that they were not interesting, and that it was a very good thing for him, mentally and morally, when his term of service expired – or rather when he was removed from office by the operation of that wonderful 'rotatory' system which his countrymen had invented for the administration of their affairs. This sketch of the Custom-house is, as simple writing, one of the most perfect of Hawthorne's compositions, and one of the most gracefully and humorously autobiographic. It would be interesting to examine it in detail, but I prefer to use my space for making some remarks upon the work which was the ultimate result of this period of Hawthorne's residence in his native town; and I shall, for con- venience' sake, say directly afterwards what I have to say about the two companions of *The Scarlet Letter* – *The House of the Seven Gables* and *The Blithedale Romance*. I quoted some passages from the prologue to the first of these novels in the early pages of this essay. There is another passage, however, which bears particularly upon this phase of Hawthorne's career, and which is so happily expressed as to make it a pleasure to transcribe it – the passage in which he says that 'for myself, during the whole of my Custom-house experience, moonlight and sunshine, and the glow of the fire-light, were just alike in my regard, and neither of them was of one whit more avail than the twinkle of a tallow candle. An entire class of susceptibilities, and a gift connected with them – of no great richness or value, but the best I had – was gone from me.' He goes on to say that he believes that he might have done something if he could have made up his mind to convert the very substance of the commonplace that surrounded him into matter of literature.

'I might, for instance, have contented myself with writing out the narratives of a veteran shipmaster, one of the inspectors, whom I should be most ungrateful not to mention; since scarcely a day passed that he did not stir me to laughter and admiration by his marvellous gift as a story-teller . . . Or I might readily have found a more serious task. It was a folly, with the materiality of this daily life pressing so intrusively upon me, to attempt to fling myself back into another age; or to insist on creating a semblance of a world out of airy matter . . . This wiser effort would have been, to diffuse thought and imagination through the opaque substance of to-day, and thus make it a bright transparency . . . to seek resolutely the true and indestruc- tible value that lay hidden in the petty and wearisome incidents and ordinary characters with which I was now conversant. The fault was mine. The page of life that was spread out before me was dull and commonplace, only because I had not fathomed its deeper import. A better book than I shall ever write was there . . . These perceptions came too late . . . I had ceased to be a writer of tolerably poor tales and essays, and had become a tolerably good Surveyor of the Customs. That was all. But, nevertheless, it is anything but agreeable to be haunted by a suspicion that one's intellect is dwindling away, or exhaling, without your consciousness, like ether out of phial; so that at every glance you find a smaller and less volatile residuum.'

As, however, it was with what was left of his intellect after three years' evaporation, that Hawthorne wrote *The Scarlet Letter*, there is little reason to complain of the injury he suffered in his Surveyorship.

His publisher, Mr Fields, in a volume entitled *Yesterdays with Authors*, has related the circumstances in which Hawthorne's masterpiece came into the world. 'In the winter of 1849, after he had been ejected from the Custom-house, I went down to Salem to see him and inquire after his health, for we heard he had been suffering from illness. He was then living in a modest wooden house ... I found him alone in a chamber over the sitting-room of the dwelling, and as the day was cold he was hovering near a stove. We fell into talk about his future prospects, and he was, as I feared I should find him, in a very desponding mood.' His visitor urged him to bethink himself of publishing something, and Hawthorne replied by calling his attention to the small popularity his published productions had yet acquired, and declaring that he had done nothing and had no spirit for doing anything. The narrator of the incident urged upon him the necessity of a more hopeful view of his situation, and proceeded to take leave. He had not reached the street, however, when Hawthorne hurried to overtake him, and, placing a roll of MS in his hand, bade him take it to Boston, read it, and pronounce upon it. 'It is either very good or very bad,' said the author; 'I don't know which.' 'On my way back to Boston,' says Mr Fields, 'I read the germ of *The Scarlet Letter*; before I slept that night I wrote him a note all aglow with admiration of the marvellous story he had put into my hands, and told him that I would come again to Salem the next day and arrange for its publication. I went on in such an amazing state of excitement, when we met again in the little house, that he would not believe I was really in earnest. He seemed to think I was beside myself, and laughed sadly at my enthusiasm.' Hawthorne, however, went on with the book and finished it, but it appeared only a year later. His biographer quotes a passage from a letter which he wrote in February, 1850, to his friend Horatio Bridge. 'I finished my book only yesterday; one end being in the press at Boston, while the other was in my head here at Salem, so that, as you see, my story is at least fourteen miles long . . . My book, the publisher tells me, will not be out before April. He speaks of it in tremendous terms of appro-bation, so does Mrs Hawthorne, to whom I read the conclusion last night. It broke her heart, and sent her to bed with a grievous headache – which I look upon as a triumphant success. Judging from the effect upon her and the publisher, I may calculate on what bowlers call a ten-strike. But I don't make any such calculation.' And Mr Lathrop calls attention, in regard to this passage, to an allusion in the English Note-Books (September 14, 1855). 'Speaking of Thackeray, I cannot but wonder at his coolness in respect to his own pathos, and compare it to my emotions when I read the last scene of *The Scarlet Letter* to my wife, just after writing it – tried to read it rather, for my voice swelled and heaved as if I were tossed up and down on an ocean as it subsides after a storm. But I was in a very nervous state then, having gone through a great diversity of emotion while writing it, for many months.'

The work has the tone of the circumstances in which it was produced. If Hawthorne was in a sombre mood, and if his future was painfully vague, *The Scarlet Letter* contains little enough of gaiety or of hopefulness. It is densely dark, with a single spot of vivid colour in it; and it will probably long remain the most consistently gloomy of English novels of the first order. But I just now called it the author's masterpiece, and I imagine it will continue to be, for other gener-ations than ours, his most substantial title to fame. The subject had probably lain a long time in his mind, as his subjects were apt to do; so that he appears completely to possess it, to know it and feel it. It is simpler and more complete than his other novels; it achieves more perfectly what it attempts, and it has about it that charm, very hard to express, which we find in an artist's work the first time he has touched his highest mark – a sort of straightness and naturalness of execution, an unconsciousness of his public, and freshness of interest in his theme. It was a great success, and he immediately found himself famous. The writer of these lines, who was a child at the time, remembers dimly the sensation the book produced, and the little shudder with which people alluded to it, as if a peculiar horror were mixed with its attractions. He was too young to read it himself, but its title, upon which he fixed his eyes as the book lay upon the table, had a mysterious charm. He had a vague belief indeed that the 'letter' in question was one of the documents that come by the post, and it was a source of perpetual wonderment to him that it should be of such an unaccustomed hue. Of course it was difficult to explain to a child the significance of poor Hester Prynne's blood-coloured A. But the mystery was at last partly dispelled by his being taken to see a collection of pictures (the annual exhibition of the National Academy), where he encountered a representation of a pale, hand-some woman, in a quaint black dress and a white coif, holding between her knees an elfish-looking little girl, fantastically dressed and crowned with flowers. Embroidered on the woman's breast was a great crimson A, over which the child's fingers, as she glanced strangely out of the picture, were maliciously playing. I was told that this was Hester Prynne and little Pearl, and that when I grew older I might read their interesting history. But the picture remained vividly imprinted on my mind; I had been vaguely frightened and made uneasy by it; and when, years afterwards, I first read the novel, I seemed to myself to have read it before, and to be familiar with its two strange heroines. I mention this incident simply as an indication of the degree to which the success of *The Scarlet Letter* had made the book what is called an actuality. Hawthorne himself was very modest about it; he wrote to his publisher, when there was a question of his undertaking another novel, that what had given the history of Hester Prynne its 'vogue' was simply the introductory chapter. In fact, the publication of *The Scarlet Letter* was in the United States a literary event of the first importance. The book was the finest piece of imaginative writing yet put forth in the country. There was a consciousness of this in the welcome that was given it – a satisfaction in the idea of America having produced a novel that belonged to literature, and to the forefront of it. Something might at last be sent to Europe as exquisite in quality as anything that had been received, and the best of it was that the thing was absolutely American; it belonged to the soil, to the air; it came out of the very heart of New England.

It is beautiful, admirable, extraordinary; it has in the highest degree that merit which I have spoken of as the mark of Hawthorne's best things – an indefinable purity and lightness of conception, a quality which in a work of art affects one in the same way as the absence of grossness does in a human being. His fancy, as I just now said, had evidently brooded over the subject for a long time; the situation to be represented had disclosed itself to him in all its phases. When I say in all its phases, the sentence demands modification; for it is to be remembered that if Hawthorne laid his hand upon the well-worn theme, upon the familiar combination of the wife, the lover, and the husband, it was after all but to one period of the history of these three persons that he attached himself. The situation is the situation after the woman's fault has been committed, and the current of expiation and repentance has set in. In spite of the relation between Hester Prynne and Arthur Dimmesdale, no story of love was surely ever less of a 'love story'. To Hawthorne's imagination the fact that these two persons had loved each other too well was of an interest comparatively vulgar; what appealed to him was the idea of their moral situation in the long years that were to follow. The story indeed is in a secondary degree that of Hester Prynne; she becomes, really, after the first scene, an accessory figure; it is not upon her the *dénouement* depends. It is upon her guilty lover that the author projects most frequently the cold, thin rays of his fitfully-moving lantern, which makes here and there a little luminous circle, on the edge of which hovers the livid and sinister figure of the injured and retributive husband. The story goes on for the most part between the lover and the husband – the tormented young Puritan minister, who carries the secret of his own lapse from pastoral purity locked up beneath an exterior that commends itself to the reverence of his flock, while he sees the softer partner of his guilt standing in the full glare of exposure and humbling herself to the misery of atonement – between this more wretched and pitiable culprit, to whom dishonour would come as a comfort and the pillory as a relief, and the older, keener, wiser man, who, to obtain satisfaction for the wrong he has suffered, devises the infernally ingenious plan of conjoining himself with his wronger, living with him, living upon him, and while he pretends to minister to his hidden ailment and to sympathize with his pain, revels in his unsuspected knowledge of these things and stimulates them by malignant arts. The attitude of Roger Chillingworth, and the means he takes to compensate himself – these are the highly original elements in the situation that Hawthorne so ingeniously treats. None of his works are so impregnated with that after-sense of the old Puritan consciousness of life to which allusion has so often been made. If, as M. Montégut says, the qualities of his ancestors *filtered* down through generations into his composition, *The Scarlet Letter* was, as it were, the vessel that gathered up the last of the precious drops. And I say this not because the story happens to be of so-called historical cast, to be told of the early days of Massachusetts and of people in steeple-crowned hats and sad coloured garments. The historical colouring is rather weak than otherwise; there is little elaboration of detail, of the modern realism of research; and the author has made no great point of causing his figures to speak the English of their period. Nevertheless, the book is full of the moral presence of the race that invented Hester's penance – diluted and complicated with other things, but still perfectly recognizable. Puritanism, in a word, is there, not only objectively, as Hawthorne tried to place it there, but subjectively as well. Not, I mean, in his judgment of his characters, in any harshness of prejudice, or in the obtrusion of a moral lesson; but in the very quality of his own vision, in the tone of the picture, in a certain coldness and exclusiveness of treatment.

The faults of the book are, to my sense, a want of reality and an abuse of the fanciful element – of a certain superficial symbolism. The people strike me not as characters, but as representatives, very picturesquely arranged, of a single state of mind; and the interest of the story lies, not in them, but in the situation, which is insistently kept before us, with little progression, though with a great deal, as I have said, of a certain stable variation; and to which they, out of their reality, contribute little that helps it to live and move. I was made to feel this want of reality, this over-ingenuity, of *The Scarlet Letter*, by chancing not long since upon a novel which was read fifty years ago much more than to-day, but which is still worth reading – the story of *Adam Blair*, by John Gibson Lockhart. This interesting and powerful little tale has a great deal of analogy with Hawthorne's novel – quite enough, at least, to suggest a comparison between them; and the comparison is a very interesting one to make, for it speedily leads us to larger considerations than simple resemblances and divergences of plot.

Adam Blair, like Arthur Dimmesdale, is a Calvinistic minister who becomes the lover of a married woman, is overwhelmed with remorse at his misdeed, and makes a public confession of it; then expiates it by resigning his pastoral office and becoming a humble tiller of the soil, as his father had been. The two stories are of about the same length, and each is the masterpiece (putting aside of course, as far as Lockhart is concerned, the *Life of Scott*) of the author. They deal alike with the manners of a rigidly theological society, and even in certain details they correspond. In each of them, between the guilty pair, there is a charming little girl; though I hasten to say that Sarah Blair (who is not the daughter of the heroine but the legitimate offspring of the hero, a widower) is far from being as brilliant and graceful an apparition as the admirable little Pearl of *The Scarlet Letter*. The main difference between the two tales is the fact that in the American story the husband plays an all-important part, and in the Scottish plays almost none at all. *Adam Blair* is the history of the passion, and *The Scarlet Letter* the history of its sequel; but nevertheless, if one has read the two books at a short interval, it is impossible to avoid confronting them. I confess that a large portion of the interest of *Adam Blair*, to my mind, when once I had perceived that it would repeat in a great measure the situation of *The Scarlet Letter*, lay in noting its difference of tone. It threw into relief the passionless quality of Hawthorne's novel, its element of cold and ingenious fantasy, its elaborate imaginative delicacy. These things do not precisely constitute a weakness in *The Scarlet Letter*; indeed, in a certain way they constitute a great strength; but the absence of a certain something warm and straightforward, a trifle more grossly human and vulgarly natural, which one finds in *Adam Blair*, will always make Hawthorne's tale less touching to a large number of even very intelligent readers, than a love-story told with the robust, synthetic pathos which served Lockhart so well. His novel is not of the first rank (I should call it an excellent second-rate one), but it borrows a charm from the fact that his vigorous, but not strongly imaginative, mind was impregnated with the reality of his subject. He did not always succeed in rendering this reality; the expression is sometimes awkward and poor. But the reader feels that his vision was clear, and his feeling about the matter very strong and rich. Hawthorne's imagination, on the other hand, plays with his theme so incessantly, leads it such a dance through the moonlighted air of his intellect, that the thing cools off, as it were, hardens and stiffens, and, producing effects much more exquisite, leaves the reader with a sense of having handled a splendid piece of silversmith's work. Lockhart, by means much more vulgar, produces at moments a great illusion, and satisfies our inevitable desire for something, in the people in whom it is sought to interest us, that shall be of the same pitch and the same continuity with ourselves. Above all, it is interesting to see how the same subject appears to two men of a thoroughly different cast of mind and of a different race. Lockhart was struck with the warmth of the subject that offered itself to him, and Hawthorne with its coldness; the one with its glow, its sentimental interest – the other with its shadow, its moral interest. Lockhart's story is as decent, as severely draped, as *The Scarlet Letter*; but the author has a more vivid sense than appears to have imposed itself upon Hawthorne, of some of the incidents of the situation he describes; his tempted man and tempting woman are more actual and personal; his heroine in especial, though not in the least a delicate or a subtle conception, has a sort of credible, visible, palpable property, a vulgar roundness and relief, which are lacking to the dim and chastened image of Hester Prynne. But I am going too far; I am comparing simplicity with subtlety, the usual with the refined. Each man wrote as his turn of mind impelled him, but each expressed something more than himself. Lockhart was a dense, substantial Briton, with a taste for the concrete, and Hawthorne was a thin New Englander, with a miasmatic conscience.

In *The Scarlet Letter* there is a great deal of symbolism; there is, I think, too much. It is overdone at times, and becomes mechanical; it ceases to be impressive, and grazes triviality. The idea of the mystic *A* which the young minister finds imprinted upon his breast and eating into his flesh, in sympathy with the embroidered badge that Hester is condemned to wear, appears to me to be a case in point. This suggestion should, I think, have been just made and dropped; to insist upon it and return to it, is to exaggerate the weak side of the subject. Hawthorne returns to it constantly, plays with it, and seems charmed by it; until at last the reader feels tempted to declare that his enjoyment of it is puerile. In the admirable scene, so superbly conceived and beautifully executed, in which Mr Dimmesdale, in the stillness of the night, in the middle of the sleeping town, feels impelled to go and stand upon the scaffold where his mistress had formerly enacted her dreadful penance, and then, seeing Hester pass along the street, from watching at a sick-bed, with little Pearl at her side, calls them both to come and stand there beside him – in this masterly episode the effect is almost spoiled by the introduction of one of these superficial conceits. What leads up to it is very fine – so fine that I cannot do better than quote it as a specimen of one of the striking pages of the book.

'But before Mr Dimmesdale had done speaking, a light gleamed far and wide over all the muffled sky. It was doubtless caused by one of those meteors which the night-watcher may so often observe burning out to waste in the vacant regions of the atmosphere. So powerful was its radiance that it thoroughly illuminated the dense medium of cloud, betwixt the sky and earth. The great vault brightened, like the dome of an immense lamp. It showed the familiar scene of the street with the distinctness of mid-day, but also with the awfulness that is always imparted to familiar objects by an unaccustomed light. The wooden houses, with their jutting stories and quaint gable-peaks; the doorsteps and thresholds, with the early grass springing up about them; the garden-plots, black with freshly-turned earth; the wheel-track, little worn, and, even in the market-place, margined with green on either side – all were visible, but with a singularity of aspect that seemed to give another moral interpretation to the things of this world than they had ever borne before. And there stood the minister, with his hand over his heart; and Hester Prynne, with the embroidered letter glimmering on her bosom; and little Pearl, herself a symbol, and the connecting-link between these two. They stood in the noon of that strange and solemn splendour, as if it were the light that is to reveal all secrets, and the daybreak that shall unite all that belong to one another.'

That is imaginative, impressive, poetic; but when, almost immediately afterwards, the author goes on to say that 'the minister looking upward to the zenith, beheld there the appearance of an immense letter – the letter A – marked out in lines of dull red light,' we feel that he goes too far and is in danger of crossing the line that separates the sublime from its intimate neighbour. We are tempted to say that this is not moral tragedy, but physical comedy. In the same way, too much is made of the intimation that Hester's badge had a scorching property, and that if one touched it one would immediately withdraw one's hand. Hawthorne is perpetually looking for images which shall place themselves in picturesque correspondence with the spiritual facts with which he is concerned, and of course the search is of the very essence of poetry. But in such a process discretion is everything, and when the image becomes importunate it is in danger of seeming to stand for nothing more serious than itself. When Hester meets the minister by appointment in the forest, and sits talking with him while little Pearl wanders away and plays by the edge of the brook, the child is represented as at last making her way over to the other side of the woodland stream, and disporting herself there in a manner which makes her mother feel herself, 'in some indistinct and tantalizing manner, estranged from Pearl; as if the child, in her lonely ramble through the forest, had strayed out of the sphere in which she and her mother dwelt together, and was now vainly seeking to return to it.' And Hawthorne devotes a chapter to this idea of the child's having, by putting the brook between Hester and herself, established a kind of spiritual gulf, on the verge of which her little fantastic person innocently mocks at her mother's sense of bereavement. This conception belongs, one would say, quite to the lighter order of a story-teller's devices, and the reader hardly goes with Hawthorne in the large development he gives to it. He hardly goes with him either, I think, in his extreme predilection for a small number of vague ideas which are represented by such terms as 'sphere' and 'sympathies'. Hawthorne makes too liberal a use of these two substantives; it is the solitary defect of his style; and it counts as a defect partly because the words in question are a sort of specialty with certain writers immeasurably inferior to himself.

I had not meant, however, to expatiate upon his defects, which are of the slenderest and most venial kind. *The Scarlet Letter* has the beauty and harmony of all original and complete conceptions, and its weaker spots, whatever they are, are not of its essence; they are mere light flaws and inequalities of surface. One can often return to it; it supports familiarity and has the inexhaustible charm and mystery of great works of art. It is admirably written. Hawthorne afterwards polished his style to a still higher degree, but in his later productions — it is almost always the case in a writer's later productions — there is a touch of mannerism. In *The Scarlet Letter* there is a high degree of polish, and at the same time a charming freshness; his phrase is less conscious of itself. His biographer very justly calls attention to the fact that his style was excellent from the beginning; that he appeared to have passed through no phase of learning how to write, but was in possession of his means from the first of his handling a pen. His early tales, perhaps, were not of a character to subject his faculty of expression to a very severe test, but a man who had not Hawthorne's natural sense of language would certainly have contrived to write them less well. This natural sense of language – this turn for saying things lightly and yet touchingly, picturesquely yet simply, and for infusing a gently colloquial tone into matter of the most unfamiliar import, he had evidently cultivated with great assiduity. I have spoken of the anomalous character of his Note-Books – of his going to such pains often to make a record of incidents which either were not worth remembering or could be easily remembered without its aid. But it helps us to understand the Note-Books if we regard them as a literary exercise. They were compositions, as school boys say, in which the subject was only the pretext, and the main point was to write a certain amount of excellent English. Hawthorne must at least have written a great many of these things for practice, and he must often have said to himself that it was better practice to write about trifles, because it was a greater tax upon one's skill to make them interesting. And his theory was just, for he has almost always made his trifles interesting. In his novels his art of saying things well is very positively tested, for here he treats of those matters among which it is very easy for a blundering writer to go wrong – the subtleties and mysteries of life, the moral and spiritual maze. In such a passage as one I have marked for quotation from *The Scarlet Letter* there is the stamp of the genius of style.

'Hester Prynne, gazing steadfastly at the clergyman, felt a dreary influence come over her, but wherefore or whence she knew not, unless that he seemed so remote from her own sphere and utterly beyond her reach. One glance of recognition she had imagined must needs pass between them. She thought of the dim forest with its little dell of solitude, and love, and anguish, and the mossy tree-trunk, where, sitting hand in hand, they had mingled their sad and passionate talk with the melancholy murmur of the brook. How deeply had they known each other then! And was this the man? She hardly knew him now! He, moving proudly past, enveloped as it were in the rich music, with the procession of majestic and venerable fathers; he, so unattainable in his worldly position, and still more so in that far vista in his unsympathising thoughts, through which she now beheld him! Her spirit sank with the idea that all must have been a delusion, and that vividly as she had dreamed it, there could be no real bond betwixt the clergyman and herself. And thus much of woman there was in Hester, that she could scarcely forgive him – least of all now, when the heavy footstep of their approaching fate might be heard, nearer, nearer, nearer! – for being able to withdraw himself so completely from their mutual world, while she groped darkly, and stretched forth her cold hands, and found him not!'

The House of the Seven Gables was written at Lenox, among the mountains of Massachusetts, a village nestling, rather loosely, in one of the loveliest corners of New England, to which Hawthorne had betaken himself after the success of *The Scarlet Letter* became conspicuous, in the summer of 1850, and where he occupied for two years an uncomfortable little red house which is now pointed out to the inquiring stranger. The inquiring stranger is now a frequent figure at Lenox, for the place has suffered the process of lionization. It has become a prosperous watering-place, or at least (as there are no waters), as they say in America, a summer-resort. It is a brilliant and generous landscape, and thirty years ago a man of fancy, desiring to apply himself, might have found both inspiration and tranquillity there. Hawthorne found so much of both that he wrote more during his two years of residence at Lenox than at any period of his career. He began with *The House of the Seven Gables*, which was finished in the early part of 1851. This is the longest of his three American novels, it is the most elaborate, and in the judgment of some persons it is the finest. It is a rich, delightful, imaginative work, larger and more various than its companions, and full of all sorts of deep intentions, of interwoven threads of suggestion. But it is not so rounded and complete as *The Scarlet Letter*; it has always seemed to me more like a prologue to a great novel than a great novel itself. I think this is partly owing to the fact that the subject, the *donnée*, as the French say, of the story, does not quite fill it out, and that we get at the same time an impression of certain complicated purposes on the author's part, which seem to reach beyond it. I call it larger and more various than its companions, and it has indeed a greater richness of tone and density of detail. The colour, so to speak, of *The House of the Seven Gables* is admirable. But the story has a sort of expansive quality which never wholly fructifies, and as I lately laid it down, after reading it for the third time, I had a sense of having interested myself in a magnificent fragment. Yet the book has a great fascination, and of all of those of its author's productions which I have read over while writing this sketch, it is perhaps the one that has gained most by re-perusal. If it be true of the others that the pure, natural quality of the imaginative strain is their great merit, this is at least as true of *The House of the Seven Gables*, the charm of which is in a peculiar degree of the kind that we fail to reduce to its grounds — like that of the sweetness of a piece of music, or the softness of fine September weather. It is vague, indefinable, ineffable; but it is the sort of thing we must always point to in justification of the high claim that we make for Hawthorne. In this case of course its vagueness is a drawback, for it is difficult to point to ethereal beauties; and if the reader whom we have wished to inoculate with our admiration inform us after looking a while that he perceives nothing in particular, we can only reply that, in effect, the object is a delicate one.

The House of the Seven Gables comes nearer being a picture of contemporary American life than either of its companions; but on this ground it would be a mistake to make a large claim for it. It cannot be too often repeated that Hawthorne was not a realist. He had a high sense of reality — his Note-Books super-abundantly testify to it; and fond as he was of jotting down the items that make it up, he never attempted to render exactly or closely the actual facts of the society that surrounded him. I have said — I began by saying — that his pages were full of its spirit, and of a certain reflected light that springs from it; but I was careful to add that the reader must look for his local and national quality between the lines of his writing and in the *indirect* testimony of his tone, his accent, his temper, of his very omissions and suppressions. *The House of the Seven Gables* has, however, more literal actuality than the others, and if it were not too fanciful an account of it, I should say that it renders, to an initiated reader, the impression of a summer afternoon in an elm-shadowed New England town. It leaves upon the mind a vague correspondence to some such reminiscence, and in stirring up the association it renders it delightful. The comparison is to the honour of the New England town, which gains in it more than it bestows. The shadows of the elms, in *The House of the Seven Gables*, are exceptionally dense and cool; the summer afternoon is peculiarly still and beauti-ful; the atmosphere has a delicious warmth, and the long daylight seems to pause and rest. But the mild provincial quality is there, the mixture of shabbiness and freshness, the paucity of ingredients. The end of an old race – this is the situation that Hawthorne has depicted, and he has been admirably inspired in the choice of the figures in whom he seeks to interest us. They are all figures rather than characters – they are all pictures rather than persons. But if their reality is light and vague, it is sufficient, and it is in harmony with the low relief and dimness of outline of the objects that surround them. They are all types, to the author's mind, of something general, of something that is bound up with the history, at large, of families and individuals, and each of them is the centre of a cluster of those ingenious and meditative musings, rather melancholy, as a general thing, than joyous, which melt into the current and texture of the story and give it a kind of moral richness. A grotesque old spinster, simple, childish, penniless, very humble at heart, but rigidly conscious of her pedigree; an amiable bachelor, of an epicurean temperament and an enfeebled intellect, who has passed twenty years of his life in penal confinement for a crime of which he was unjustly pronounced guilty; a sweet-natured and bright-faced young girl from the country, a poor relation of these two ancient decrepitudes, with whose moral mustiness her modern freshness and soundness are contrasted; a young man still more modern, holding the latest opinions, who has sought his fortune up and down the world, and, though he has not found it, takes a genial and enthusiastic view of the future: these, with two or three remarkable accessory figures, are the persons concerned in the little drama. The drama is a small one, but as Hawthorne does not put it before us for its own superficial sake, for the dry facts of the case, but for something in it which he holds to be symbolic and of large application, something that points a moral and that it behoves us to remember, the scenes in the rusty wooden house whose gables give its name to the story, have something of the dignity both of history and of tragedy. Miss Hephzibah Pyncheon, dragging out a disappointed life in her paternal dwelling, finds herself obliged in her old age to open a little shop for the sale of penny toys and gingerbread. This is the central incident of the tale, and, as Hawthorne relates it, it is an incident of the most impressive magnitude and most touching interest. Her dishonoured and vague-minded brother is released from prison at the same moment, and returns to the ancestral roof to deepen her perplexities. But, on the other hand, to alleviate them, and to introduce a breath of the air of the outer world into this long unventilated interior, the little country cousin also arrives, and proves the good angel of the feebly distracted household. All this episode is exquisite – admirably conceived, and executed with a kind of humorous tenderness, an equal sense of everything in it that is picturesque, touching, ridiculous, worthy of the highest praise. Hephzibah Pyncheon, with her near-sighted scowl, her rusty joints, her antique turban, her map of a great territory to the eastward which ought to have belonged to her family, her vain terrors and scruples and resentments, the inaptitude and repugnance of an ancient gentlewoman to the vulgar little commerce which a cruel fate has compelled her to engage in – Hephzibah Pyncheon is a masterly picture. I repeat that she is a picture, as her companions are pictures; she is a charming piece of descriptive writing, rather than a dramatic exhibition. But she is described, like her companions too, so subtly and lovingly that we enter into her virginal old heart and stand with her behind her abominable little counter. Clifford Pyncheon is a still more remarkable conception, though he is perhaps not so vividly depicted. It was a figure needing a much more subtle touch, however, and it was of the essence of his character to be vague and unemphasized. Nothing can be more charming than the manner in which the soft, bright, active presence of Phoebe Pyncheon is indicated, or than the account of her relations with the poor dimly sentient kinsman for whom her light-handed sisterly offices, in the evening of a melancholy life, are a revelation of lost possibilities of happiness. 'In her aspect,' Hawthorne says of the young girl, 'there was a familiar gladness, and a holiness that you could play with, and yet reverence it as much as ever. She was like a prayer offered up in the homeliest beauty of one's mother-tongue. Fresh was Phoebe, moreover, and airy, and sweet in her apparel; as if nothing that she wore – neither her gown, nor her small straw bonnet, nor her little kerchief, any more than her snowy stockings – had ever been put on before; or if worn, were all the fresher for it, and with a fragrance as if they had lain among the rose-buds.' Of the influence of her maidenly salubrity upon poor Clifford, Hawthorne gives the prettiest description, and then, breaking off suddenly, renounces the attempt in language which, while pleading its inadequacy, conveys an exquisite satisfaction to the reader. I quote the passage for the sake of its extreme felicity, and of the charming image with which it concludes.

'But we strive in vain to put the idea into words. No adequate expression of the beauty and profound pathos with which it impresses us is attainable. This being, made only for happiness, and heretofore so miserably failing to be happy – his tendencies so hideously thwarted that some unknown time ago, the delicate springs of his character, never morally or intellectually strong, had given way, and he was now imbecile – this poor forlorn voyager from the Islands of the Blest, in a frail bark, on a tempestuous sea, had been flung by the last mountain-wave of his shipwreck, into a quiet harbour. There, as he lay more than half lifeless on the strand, the fragrance of an earthly rose-bud had come to his nostrils, and, as odours will, had summoned up reminiscences or visions of all the living and breathing beauty amid which he should have had his home. With his native susceptibility of happy influences, he inhales the slight ethereal rapture into his soul, and expires!'

I have not mentioned the personage in *The House of the Seven Gables* upon whom Hawthorne evidently bestowed most pains, and whose portrait is the most elaborate in the book; partly because he is, in spite of the space he occupies, an accessory figure, and partly because, even more than the others, he is what I have called a picture rather than a character. Judge Pyncheon is an ironical portrait, very richly and broadly executed, very sagaciously composed and rendered – the portrait of a superb, full-blown hypocrite, a large-based, full-nurtured Pharisee, bland, urbane, impressive, diffusing about him a 'sultry' warmth of benevolence, as the author calls it again and again, and basking in the noontide of prosperity and the consideration of society; but in reality hard, gross, and ignoble. Judge Pyncheon is an elaborate piece of description, made up of a hundred admirable touches, in which satire is always winged with fancy, and fancy is linked with a deep sense of reality. It is difficult to say whether Hawthorne followed a model in describing Judge Pyncheon; but it is tolerably obvious that the picture is an impression – a copious impression – of an individual. It has evidently a definite starting-point in fact, and the author is able to draw, freely and confidently, after the image established in his mind. Holgrave, the modern young man, who has been a Jack-of-all-trades and is at the period of the story a daguerreotypist, is an attempt to render a kind of national type – that of the young citizen of the United States whose fortune is simply in his lively intelligence, and who stands naked, as it were, unbiased and unencumbered alike, in the centre of the far-stretching level of American life. Holgrave is intended as a contrast; his lack of traditions, his democratic stamp, his condensed experience, are opposed to the desiccated prejudices and exhausted vitality of the race of which poor feebly-scowling, rusty-jointed Hephzibah is the most heroic representative. It is perhaps a pity that Hawthorne should not have proposed to himself to give the old Pyncheon-qualities some embodiment which would help them to balance more fairly with the elastic properties of the young daguerreotypist – should not have painted a lusty conservative to match his strenuous radical. As it is, the mustiness and mouldiness of the tenants of the House of the Seven Gables crumble away rather too easily. Evidently, however, what Hawthorne designed to represent was not the struggle between an old society and a new, for in this case he would have given the old one a better chance; but simply, as I have said, the shrinkage and extinction of a family. This appealed to his imagination; and the idea of long perpetuation and survival always appears to have filled him with a kind of horror and disapproval. Conservative, in a certain degree, as he was himself, and fond of retrospect and quietude and the mellowing influences of time, it is singular how often one encounters in his writings some expression of mistrust of old houses, old institutions, long lines of descent. He was disposed apparently to allow a very moderate measure in these respects, and he condemns the dwelling of the Pyncheons to disappear from the face of the earth because it has been standing a couple of hundred years. In this he was an American of Americans; or rather he was more American than many of his countrymen, who, though they are accustomed to work for the short run rather than the long, have often a lurking esteem for things that show the marks of having lasted. I will add that Holgrave is one of the few figures, among those which Hawthorne created, with regard to which the absence of the realistic mode of treatment is felt as a loss. Holgrave is not sharply enough characterized; he lacks features; he is not an individual, but a type. But my last word about this admirable novel must not be a restrictive one. It is a large and generous production, pervaded with that vague hum, that indefinable echo, of the whole multitudinous life of man, which is the real sign of a great work of fiction.

After the publication of *The House of the Seven Gables*, which brought him great honour, and, I believe, a tolerable share of a more ponderable substance, he composed a couple of little volumes for children – *The Wonder-Book*, and a small collection of stories entitled *Tanglewood Tales*. They are not among his most serious literary titles, but if I may trust my own early impression of them, they are among the most charming literary services that have been rendered to children in an age (and especially in a country) in which the exactions of the infant mind have exerted much too palpable an influence upon literature. Hawthorne's stories are the old Greek myths, made more vivid to the childish imagination by an infusion of details which both deepen and explain their marvels. I have been careful not to read them over, for I should be very sorry to risk disturbing in any degree a recollection of them that has been at rest since the appreciative period of life to which they are addressed. They seem at that period enchanting, and the ideal of happiness of many American children is to lie upon the carpet and lose themselves in *The Wonder-Book*. It is in its pages that they first make the acquaintance of the heroes and heroines of the antique mythology, and something of the nursery fairy-tale quality of interest which Hawthorne imparts to them always remains.

I have said that Lenox was a very pretty place, and that he was able to work there Hawthorne proved by composing *The House of the Seven Gables* with a good deal of rapidity. But at the close of the year in which this novel was published he wrote to a friend (Mr Fields, his publisher,) that 'to tell you a secret I am sick to death of Berkshire, and hate to think of spending another winter here . . . The air and climate do not agree with my health at all, and for the first time since I was a boy I have felt languid and dispirited . . . O that Providence would build me the merest little shanty, and mark me out a rood or two of garden ground, near the sea-coast!' He was at this time for a while out of health; and it is proper to remember that though the Massachusetts Berkshire, with its mountains and lakes, was charming during the ardent American summer, there was a reverse to the medal, consisting of December snows prolonged into April and May. Providence failed to provide him with a cottage by the sea; but he betook himself for the winter of 1852 to the little town of West Newton, near Boston, where he brought into the world *The Blithedale Romance*.

This work, as I have said, would not have been written if Hawthorne had not spent a year at Brook Farm, and though it is in no sense of the word an account of the manners or the inmates of that establishment, it will preserve the memory of the ingenious community at West Roxbury for a generation unconscious of other reminders. I hardly know what to say about it save that it is very charming; this vague, unanalytic epithet is the first that comes to one's pen in treating of Hawthorne's novels, for their extreme amenity of form invariably suggests it; but if on the one hand it claims to be uttered, on the other it frankly confesses its inconclusiveness. Perhaps, however, in this case, it fills out the measure of appreciation more completely than in others, for *The Blithedale Romance* is the lightest, the brightest, the liveliest, of this company of unhumorous fictions.

The story is told from a more joyous point of view – from a point of view comparatively humorous – and a number of objects and incidents touched with the light of the profane world – the vulgar, many-coloured world of actuality, as distinguished from the crepuscular realm of the writer's own reveries – are mingled with its course. The book indeed is a mixture of elements, and it leaves in the memory an impression analogous to that of an April day – an alternation of brightness and shadow, of broken sun-patches and sprinkling clouds. Its dénouement is tragical – there is indeed nothing so tragical in all Hawthorne, unless it be the murder of Miriam's persecutor by Donatello, in *Transformation*, as the suicide of Zenobia; and yet on the whole the effect on the novel is to make one think more agreeably of life. The standpoint of the narrator has the advantage of being a concrete one; he is no longer, as in the preceding tales, a disembodied spirit, imprisoned in the haunted chamber of his own contemplations, but a particular man, with a certain human grossness.

Of Miles Coverdale I have already spoken, and of its being natural to assume that in so far as we may measure this lightly indicated identity of his, it has a great deal in common with that of his creator. Coverdale is a picture of the contemplative, observant, analytic nature, nursing its fancies, and yet, thanks to an element of strong good sense, not bringing them up to be spoiled children; having little at stake in life, at any given moment, and yet indulging, in imagination, in a good many adventures; a portrait of a man, in a word, whose passions are slender, whose imagination is active, and whose happiness lies, not in doing, but in perceiving – half a poet, half a critic, and all a spectator. He is contrasted, excellently, with the figure of Hollingsworth, the heavily treading Reformer, whose attitude with regard to the world is that of the hammer to the anvil, and who has no patience with his friend's indifferences and neutralities. Coverdale is a gentle sceptic, a mild cynic; he would agree that life is a little worth living – or worth living a little; but would remark that, unfortunately, to live little enough, we have to live a great deal. He confesses to a want of earnestness, but in reality he is evidently an excellent fellow, to whom one might look, not for any personal performance on a great scale, but for a good deal of generosity of detail. 'As Hollingsworth once told me, I lack a purpose,' he writes, at the close of his story. 'How strange! He was ruined, morally, by an overplus of the same ingredient the want of which, I occasionally suspect, has rendered my own life all an emptiness. I by no means wish to die. Yet were there any cause in this whole chaos of human struggle, worth a sane man's dying for, and which my death would benefit, then – provided, however, the effort did not involve an unreasonable amount of trouble – methinks I might be bold to offer up my life. If Kossuth, for example, would pitch the battle-field of Hungarian rights within an easy ride of my abode, and choose a mild sunny morning, after breakfast, for the conflict, Miles Coverdale would gladly be his man, for one brave rush upon the levelled bayonets. Further than that I should be loth to pledge myself.'

The finest thing in *The Blithedale Romance* is the character of Zenobia, which I have said elesewhere strikes me as the nearest approach that Hawthorne has made to the complete creation of a *person*. She is more concrete than Hester or Miriam, or Hilda or Phoebe; she is a more definite image, produced by a greater multiplicity of touches. It is idle to inquire too closely whether Hawthorne had Margaret Fuller in his mind in constructing the figure of this brilliant specimen of the strong-minded class and endowing her with the genius of conversation; or, on the assumption that such was the case, to compare the image at all strictly with the model. There is no strictness in the representation by novelists of persons who have struck them in life, and there can in the nature of things be none. From the moment the imagination takes a hand in the game, the inevitable tendency is to divergence, to following what may be called new scents. The original gives hints, but the writer does what he likes with them, and imports new elements into the picture. If there is this amount of reason for referring the wayward heroine of Blithedale to Hawthorne's impression of the most distinguished woman of her day in Boston, that Margaret Fuller was the only literary lady of eminence whom there is any sign of his having known, that she was proud, passionate, and eloquent, that she was much connected with the little world of Transcendentalism out of which the experiment of Brook Farm sprung, and that she had a miserable end and a watery grave – if these are facts to be noted on one side, I say; on the other, the beautiful and sumptuous Zenobia, with her rich and picturesque temperament and physical aspects, offers many points of divergence from the plain and strenuous invalid who represented feminine culture in the suburbs of the New England metropolis. This picturesqueness of Zenobia is very happily indicated and maintained; she is a woman, in all the force of the term, and there is something very vivid and powerful in her large expression of womanly gifts and weaknesses. Hollingsworth is, I think, less successful, though there is much reality in the conception of the type to which he belongs – the strong-willed, narrow-hearted apostle of a special form of redemption for society. There is nothing better in all Hawthorne than the scene between him and Coverdale, when the two men are at work together in the field (piling stones on a dyke), and he gives it to his companion to choose whether he will be with him or against him. It is a pity, perhaps, to have represented him as having begun life as a blacksmith, for one grudges him the advantage of so logical a reason for his roughness and hardness.

'Hollingsworth scarcely said a word, unless when repeatedly and pertinaciously addressed. Then indeed he would glare upon us from the thick shrubbery of his meditations, like a tiger out of a jungle, make the briefest reply possible, and betake himself back into the solitude of his heart and mind . . . His heart, I imagine, was never really interested in our socialist scheme, but was for ever busy with his strange, and as most people thought, impracticable plan for the reformation of criminals through an appeal to their higher instincts. Much as I liked Hollingsworth, it cost me many a groan to tolerate him on this point. He ought to have commenced his investigation of the subject by committing some huge sin in his proper person, and examining the condition of his higher instincts afterwards.'

The most touching element in the novel is the history of the grasp that this barbarous fanatic has laid upon the fastidious and high-tempered Zenobia, who, disliking him and shrinking from him at a hundred points, is drawn into the gulf of his omnivorous egotism. The portion of the story that strikes me as least felicitous is that which deals with Priscilla and with her mysterious relation to Zenobia – with her mesmeric gifts, her clairvoyance, her identity with the Veiled Lady, her divided subjection to Hollingsworth and Westervelt, and her numerous other graceful but fantastic properties – her Sibylline attributes, as the author calls them. Hawthorne is rather too fond of Sibylline attributes – a taste of the same order as his disposition, to which I have already alluded, to talk about spheres and sympathies. As the action advances, in *The Blithedale Romance*, we get too much out of reality, and cease to feel beneath our feet the firm ground of an appeal to our own vision of the world, our observation. I should have liked to see the story concern itself more with the little community in which its earlier scenes are laid, and avail itself of so excellent an opportunity for describing unhackneyed specimens of human nature. I have already spoken of the absence of satire in the novel, of its not aiming in the least at satire, and of its offering no grounds for complaint as an invidious picture. Indeed the brethren of Brook Farm should have held themselves slighted rather than misrepresented, and have regretted that the admirable genius who for a while was numbered among them should have treated their institution mainly as a perch for starting upon an imaginative flight. But when all is said about a certain want of substance and cohesion in the latter portions of *The Blithedale Romance*, the book is still a delightful and beautiful one. Zenobia and Hollingsworth live in the memory, and even Priscilla and Coverdale, who linger there less importunately, have a great deal that touches us and that we believe in. I said just now that Priscilla was infelicitous; but immediately afterwards I open the volume at a page in which the author describes some of the out-of-door amusements at Blithedale, and speaks of a foot-race across the grass, in which some of the slim young girls of the society joined. 'Priscilla's peculiar charm in a foot-race was the weakness and irregularity with which she ran. Growing up without exercise, except to her poor little fingers, she had never yet acquired the perfect use of her legs. Setting buoyantly forth therefore, as if no rival less swift than Atalanta could compete with her, she ran falteringly, and often tumbled on the grass. Such an incident – though it seems too slight to think of – was a thing to laugh at, but which brought the water into one's eyes, and lingered in the memory after far greater joys and sorrows were wept out of it, as antiquated trash. Priscilla's life, as I beheld it, was full of trifles that affected me in just this way.' That seems to me exquisite, and the book is full of touches as deep and delicate . . .

[THE LATER WORK]

Out of his mingled sensations, his pleasure and his weariness, his discomforts and his reveries [in Italy] there sprang another beautiful work. During the summer of 1858, he hired a picturesque old villa on the hill of Bellosguardo, near Florence, a curious structure with a crenelated tower, which, after having in the course of its career suffered many vicissitudes and played many parts, now finds its most vivid identity in being pointed out to strangers as the sometime residence of the celebrated American romancer. Hawthorne took a fancy to the place, as well he might, for it is one of the loveliest spots on earth, and the great view that stretched itself before him contains every element of beauty. Florence lay at his feet with her memories and treasures; the olive-covered hills bloomed around him, studded with villas as picturesque as his own; the Apennines, perfect in form and colour, disposed themselves opposite, and in the distance, along its fertile valley, the Arno wandered to Pisa and the sea. Soon after coming hither he wrote to a friend in a strain of high satisfaction:

'It is pleasant to feel at last that I am really away from America – a satisfaction that I never really enjoyed as long as I stayed in Liverpool, where it seemed to be that the quintessence of nasal and hand-shaking Yankeedom was gradually filtered and sublimated through my consulate, on the way outward and homeward. I first got acquainted with my own countrymen there. At Rome too it was not much better. But here in Florence, and in the summer-time, and in this secluded villa, I have escaped out of all my old tracks, and am really remote. I like my present residence immensely. The house stands on a hill, overlooking Florence, and is big enough to quarter a regiment, insomuch that each member of the family, including servants, has a separate suite of apartments, and there are vast wildernesses of upper rooms into which we have never yet sent exploring expeditions. At one end of the house there is a moss-grown tower, haunted by owls and by the ghost of a monk who was confined there in the thirteenth century, previous to being burnt at the stake in the principal square of Florence. I hire this villa, tower and all, at twenty-eight dollars a month; but I mean to take it away bodily and clap it into a romance, which I have in my head, ready to be written out.'

This romance was *Transformation*, which he wrote out during the following winter in Rome, and re-wrote during the several months that he spent in England, chiefly at Leamington, before returning to America. The Villa Montauto figures, in fact, in this tale as the castle of Monte-Beni, the patrimonial dwelling of the hero. 'I take some credit to myself,' he wrote to the same friend, on returning to Rome, 'for having sternly shut myself up for an hour or two every day, and come to close grips with a romance which I have been trying to tear out of my mind.' And later in the same winter he says – 'I shall go home, I fear, with a heavy heart, not expecting to be very well contented there . . . If I were but a hundred times richer than I am, how very comfortable I could be! I consider it a great piece of good fortune that I have had experience of the discomforts and miseries of Italy, and did not go directly home from England. Anything will seem like a Paradise after a Roman winter.' But he got away at last, late in the spring, carrying his novel with him, and the book was published, after, as I say, he had worked it over, mainly during some weeks that he passed at the little watering-place of Redcar, on the Yorkshire coast, in February of the following year. It was issued primarily in England; the American edition immediately followed. It is an odd fact that in the two countries the book came out under different titles. The title that the author had bestowed upon it did not satisfy the English publishers, who requested him to provide it with another; so that it is only in America that the work bears the name of *The Marble Faun*. Hawthorne's choice of this appellation is, by the way, rather singular, for it completely fails to characterize the story, the subject

of which is the living faun, the faun of flesh and blood, the unfortunate Donatello. His marble counterpart is mentioned only in the
opening chapter. On the other hand Hawthorne complained that
Transformation 'gives one the idea of Harlequin in a pantomime'.
Under either name, however, the book was a great success, and it has
probably become the most popular of Hawthorne's four novels. It is
part of the intellectual equipment of the Anglo-Saxon visitor to
Rome, and is read by every English-speaking traveller who arrives
there, who has been there, or who expects to go.

It has a great deal of beauty, of interest and grace; but it has to my
sense a slighter value than its companions, and I am far from
regarding it as the masterpiece of the author, a position to which we
sometimes hear it assigned. The subject is admirable, and so are
many of the details; but the whole thing is less simple and complete
than either of the three tales of American life, and Hawthorne
forfeited a precious advantage in ceasing to tread his native soil. Half
the virtue of *The Scarlet Letter* and *The House of the Seven Gables* is
in their local quality; they are impregnated with the New England
air. It is very true that Hawthorne had no pretension to pourtray
actualities and to cultivate that literal exactitude which is now the
fashion. Had this been the case, he would probably have made a still
graver mistake in transporting the scene of his story to a country
which he knew only superficially. His tales all go on more or less 'in
the vague', as the French say, and of course the vague may as well be
placed in Tuscany as in Massachusetts. It may also very well be urged
in Hawthorne's favour here, that in *Transformation* he has attempted to deal with actualities more than he did in either of his
earlier novels. He has described the streets and monuments of Rome
with a closeness which forms no part of his reference to those of
Boston and Salem. But for all this he incurs that penalty of seeming
factitious and unauthoritative, which is always the result of an
artist's attempt to project himself into an atmosphere in which he has
not a transmitted and inherited property. An English or a German
writer (I put poets aside) may love Italy well enough, and know her
well enough, to write delightful fictions about her; the thing has often
been done. But the productions in question will, as novels, always
have about them something second-rate and imperfect. There is in
Transformation enough beautiful perception of the interesting

character of Rome, enough rich and eloquent expression of it, to save the book, if the book could be saved; but the style, what the French call the *genre*, is an inferior one, and the thing remains a charming romance with intrinsic weaknesses.

Allowing for this, however, some of the finest pages in all Hawthorne are to be found in it. The subject, as I have said, is a particularly happy one, and there is a great deal of interest in the simple combination and opposition of the four actors. It is noticeable that in spite of the considerable length of the story, there are no accessory figures; Donatello and Miriam, Kenyon and Hilda, exclusively occupy the scene. This is the more noticeable as the scene is very large, and the great Roman background is constantly presented to us. The relations of these four people are full of that moral picturesqueness which Hawthorne was always looking for; he found it in perfection in the history of Donatello. As I have said, the novel is the most popular of his works, and every one will remember the figure of the simple, joyous, sensuous young Italian, who is not so much a man as a child, and not so much a child as a charming, innocent animal, and how he is brought to self-knowledge and to a miserable conscious manhood, by the commission of a crime. Donatello is rather vague and impalpable; he says too little in the book, shows himself too little, and falls short, I think, of being a creation. But he is enough of a creation to make us enter into the situation, and the whole history of his rise, or fall, whichever one chooses to call it – his tasting of the tree of knowledge and finding existence complicated with a regret – is unfolded with a thousand ingenious and exquisite touches. Of course, to make the interest complete, there is a woman in the affair, and Hawthorne has done few things more beautiful than the picture of the unequal complicity of guilt between his immature and dimly-puzzled hero, with his clinging, unquestioning, unexacting devotion, and the dark, powerful, more widely-seeing feminine nature of Miriam. Deeply touching is the representation of the manner in which these two essentially different persons – the woman intelligent, passionate, acquainted with life, and with a tragic element in her own career; the youth ignorant, gentle, unworldly, brightly and harmlessly natural – are equalized and bound together by their common secret, which insulates them, morally, from the rest of mankind. The character of Hilda has always struck me as an admirable invention – one of those things that mark the man of genius. It needed a man of genius and of Hawthorne's imaginative delicacy, to feel the propriety of such a figure as Hilda's and to perceive the relief it would both give and borrow. This pure and somewhat rigid New England girl, following the vocation of a copyist of pictures in Rome, unacquainted with evil and untouched by impurity, has been accidentally the witness, unknown and unsuspected, of the dark deed by which her friends, Miriam and Donatello, are knit together. This is *her* revelation of evil, her loss of perfect innocence. She has done no wrong, and yet wrong-doing has become a part of her experience, and she carries the weight of her detested knowledge upon the heart. She carries it a long time, saddened and oppressed by it, till at last she can bear it no longer. If I have called the whole idea of the presence and effect of Hilda in the story a trait of genius, the purest touch of inspiration is the episode in which the poor girl deposits her burden. She has passed the whole lonely summer in Rome, and one day, at the end of it, finding herself in St Peter's, she enters a confessional, strenuous daughter of the Puritans as she is, and pours out her dark knowledge into the bosom of the Church – then comes away with her conscience lightened, not a whit the less a Puritan than before. If the book contained nothing else noteworthy but this admirable scene, and the pages describing the murder committed by Donatello under Miriam's eyes, and the ecstatic wandering, afterwards, of the guilty couple, through the 'blood-stained streets of Rome', it would still deserve to rank high among the imaginative productions of our day.

Like all of Hawthorne's things, it contains a great many light threads of symbolism, which shimmer in the texture of the tale, but which are apt to break and remain in our fingers if we attempt to handle them. These things are part of Hawthorne's very manner – almost, as one might say, of his vocabulary; they belong much more to the surface of his work than to its stronger interest. The fault of *Transformation* is that the element of the unreal is pushed too far, and that the book is neither positively of one category nor of another. His 'moonshiny romance', he calls it in a letter; and, in truth, the lunar element is a little too pervasive. The action wavers between the streets of Rome, whose literal features the author perpetually sketches, and a vague realm of fancy, in which quite a different verisimilitude prevails. This is the trouble with Donatello himself. His companions are intended to be real – if they fail to be so, it is not for want of intention; whereas he is intended to be real or not, as you please. He is of a different substance from them; it is as if a painter, in composing a picture, should try to give you an impression of one of his figures by a strain of music. The idea of the modern faun was a charming one; but I think it a pity that the author should not have made him more definitely modern, without reverting so much to his mythological properties and antecedents, which are very gracefully touched upon, but which belong to the region of picturesque conceits, much more than to that of real psychology. Among the young Italians of to-day there are still plenty of models for such an image as Hawthorne appears to have wished to present in the easy and natural Donatello. And since I am speaking critically, I may go on to say that the art of narration, in *Transformation*, seems to me more at fault than in the author's other novels. The story struggles and wanders, is dropped and taken up again, and towards the close lapses into an almost fatal vagueness . . .

He began at this time [in his last four years] two novels, neither of which he lived to finish, but both of which were published, as fragments, after his death. The shorter of these fragments, to which he had given the name of *The Dolliver Romance*, is so very brief that little can be said of it. The author strikes, with all his usual sweetness, the opening notes of a story of New England life, and the few pages which have been given to the world contain a charming picture of an old man and a child.

The other rough sketch – it is hardly more – is in a manner complete; it was unfortunately deemed complete enough to be brought out in a magazine as a serial novel. This was to do it a great wrong, and I do not go too far in saying that poor Hawthorne would probably not have enjoyed the very bright light that has been projected upon this essentially crude piece of work. I am at a loss to know how to speak of *Septimius Felton, or the Elixir of Life*; I have purposely reserved but a small space for doing so, for the part of discretion seems to be to pass it by lightly. I differ therefore widely from the author's biographer and son-in-law in thinking it a work of the greatest weight and value, offering striking analogies with Goethe's *Faust*; and still more widely from a critic whom Mr

Lathrop quotes, who regards a certain portion of it as 'one of the very greatest triumphs in all literature'. It seems to me almost cruel to pitch in this exalted key one's estimate of the rough first draught of a tale in regard to which the author's premature death operates, virtually, as a complete renunciation of pretensions. It is plain to any reader that *Septimius Felton*, as it stands, with its roughness, its gaps, its mere allusiveness and slightness of treatment, gives us but a very partial measure of Hawthorne's full intention; and it is equally easy to believe that this intention was much finer than anything we find in the book. Even if we possessed the novel in its complete form, however, I incline to think that we should regard it as very much the weakest of Hawthorne's productions. The idea itself seems a failure, and the best that might have come of it would have been very much below *The Scarlet Letter* or *The House of the Seven Gables*. The appeal to our interest is not felicitously made, and the fancy of a potion, to assure eternity of existence, being made from the flowers which spring from the grave of a man whom the distiller of the potion has deprived of life, though it might figure with advantage in a short story of the pattern of the *Twice-Told Tales*, appears too slender to carry the weight of a novel. Indeed, this whole matter of elixirs and potions belongs to the fairy-tale period of taste, and the idea of a young man enabling himself to live forever by concocting and imbibing a magic draught, has the misfortune of not appealing to our sense of reality or even to our sympathy. The weakness of *Septimius Felton* is that the reader cannot take the hero seriously — a fact of which there can be no better proof than the element of the ridiculous which inevitably mingles itself in the scene in which he entertains his lady-love with a prophetic sketch of his occupations during the successive centuries of his earthly immortality. I suppose the answer to my criticism is that this is allegorical, symbolic, ideal; but we feel that it symbolizes nothing substantial, and that the truth — whatever it may be — that it illustrates, is as moonshiny, to use Hawthorne's own expression, as the allegory itself. Another fault of the story is that a great historical event — the war of the Revolution — is introduced in the first few pages, in order to supply the hero with a pretext for killing the young man from whose grave the flower of immortality is to sprout, and then drops out of the narrative altogether, not even forming a background to the sequel. It seems to me that Hawthorne should either have invented some other occasion for the death of his young officer, or else, having struck the note of the great public agitation which overhung his little group of characters, have been careful to sound it through the rest of his tale. I do wrong, however, to insist upon these things, for I fall thereby into the error of treating the work as if it had been cast into its ultimate form and acknowledged by the author. To avoid this error I shall make no other criticism of details, but content myself with saying that the idea and intention of the book appear, relatively speaking, feeble, and that even had it been finished it would have occupied a very different place in the public esteem from the writer's masterpieces . . .

He was a beautiful, natural, original genius, and his life had been singularly exempt from worldly preoccupations and vulgar efforts. It had been as pure, as simple, as unsophisticated, as his work. He had lived primarily in his domestic affections, which were of the tenderest kind; and then – without eagerness, without pretension, but with a great deal of quiet devotion – in his charming art. His work will remain; it is too original and exquisite to pass away; among the men of imagination he will always have his niche. No one has had just that vision of life, and no one has had a literary form that more successfully expressed his vision. He was not a moralist, and he was not simply a poet. The moralists are weightier, denser, richer, in a sense; the poets are more purely inconclusive and irresponsible. He combined in a singular degree the spontaneity of the imagination with a haunting care for moral problems. Man's conscience was his theme, but he saw it in the light of a creative fancy which added, out of its own substance, an interest, and, I may almost say, an importance.

22

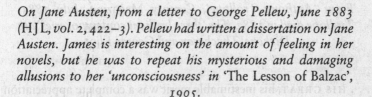

On Jane Austen, from a letter to George Pellew, June 1883 (HJL, vol. 2, 422–3). Pellew had written a dissertation on Jane Austen. James is interesting on the amount of feeling in her novels, but he was to repeat his mysterious and damaging allusions to her 'unconsciousness' in 'The Lesson of Balzac', 1905.

. . . I COULD have found it in me to speak more of her genius – of the extraordinary vividness with which she saw what she did see, and of her narrow unconscious perfection of form. But you point out very well all that she didn't see, and especially what I remember not to have seen indicated before, the want of moral illumination on the part of her heroines, who had undoubtedly small and second-rate minds and were perfect little she-Philistines. But I think that is partly what makes them interesting today. All that there was of them was feeling – a sort of simple undistracted concentrated feeling which we scarcely find any more. In of course an infinitely less explicit way, Emma Woodhouse and Anne Eliot give us as great an impression of 'passion' – that celebrated quality – as the ladies of G. Sand and Balzac. Their small gentility and front parlour existence doesn't suppress it, but only modifies the outward form of it. You do very well when you allude to the narrowness of Miss Austen's social horizon – of the young Martin in *Emma* being kept at a distance, etc; all that is excellent. Also in what you say of her apparent want of consciousness of nature.

23

———— ✤ ————

From 'Anthony Trollope', Century Magazine, July 1883.
Trollope died in 1882. The 'three brilliant contemporaries' are
Dickens, Thackeray and George Eliot.

... HIS GREAT, his inestimable merit was a complete appreciation of the usual. This gift is not rare in the annals of English fiction; it would naturally be found in a walk of literature in which the feminine mind has laboured so fruitfully. Women are delicate and patient observers; they hold their noses close, as it were, to the texture of life. They feel and perceive the real with a kind of personal tact, and their observations are recorded in a thousand delightful volumes. Trollope, therefore, with his eyes comfortably fixed on the familiar, the actual, was far from having invented a new category; his great distinction is that in resting there his vision took in so much of the field. And then he *felt* all daily and immediate things as well as saw them; felt them in a simple, direct, salubrious way, with their sadness, their gladness, their charm, their comicality, all their obvious and measurable meanings. He never wearied of the pre-established round of English customs – never needed a respite or a change – was content to go on indefinitely watching the life that surrounded him, and holding up his mirror to it. Into this mirror the public, at first especially, grew very fond of looking – for it saw itself reflected in all the most credible and supposable ways, with that curiosity that people feel to know how they look when they are represented, 'just as they are', by a painter who does not desire to put them into an attitude, to drape them for an effect, to arrange his light and his accessories. This exact and on the whole becoming image, projected upon a surface without a strong intrinsic tone, constitutes mainly the entertainment that Trollope offered his readers. The striking thing to the critic was that his robust and patient mind had no particular bias, his imagination no light of its own. He saw things neither pictorially and grotesquely like Dickens; nor with that combined disposition to satire and to literary form which gives such 'body', as they say of wine, to the manner of Thackeray; nor with anything of the philosophic, the transcendental cast – the desire to follow them to their remote relations – which we associate with the name of George Eliot. Trollope had his elements of fancy, of satire, of irony; but these qualities were not very highly developed, and he walked mainly by the light of his good sense, his clear, direct vision of the things that lay nearest, and his great natural kindness. There is something remarkably tender and friendly in his feeling about all human perplexities; he takes the good-natured, temperate, concili-atory view – the humorous view, perhaps, for the most part, yet without a touch of pessimistic prejudice. As he grew older, and had sometimes to go farther afield for his subjects, he acquired a savour of bitterness and reconciled himself sturdily to treating of the disagreeable. A more copious record of disagreeable matters could scarcely be imagined, for instance, than *The Way We Live Now*. But, in general, he has a wholesome mistrust of morbid analysis, an aversion to inflicting pain. He has an infinite love of detail, but his details are, for the most part, the innumerable items of the expected. When the French are disposed to pay a compliment to the English mind they are so good as to say that there is in it something remarkably *honnête*. If I might borrow this epithet without seeming to be patronizing, I should apply it to the genius of Anthony Trollope. He represents in an eminent degree this natural decorum of the English spirit, and represents it all the better that there is not in him a grain of the mawkish or the prudish. He writes, he feels, he judges like a man, talking plainly and frankly about many things, and is by no means destitute of a certain saving grace of coarseness. But he has kept the purity of his imagination and held fast to old-fashioned reverences and preferences. He thinks it a sufficient objec-tion to several topics to say simply that they are unclean. There was nothing in his theory of the story-teller's art that tended to convert the reader's or the writer's mind into a vessel for polluting things. He recognized the right of the vessel to protest, and would have regarded such a protest as conclusive. With a considerable turn for satire, though this perhaps is more evident in his early novels than in his later ones, he had as little as possible of the quality of irony. He never played with a subject, never juggled with the sympathies or the credulity of his reader, was never in the least paradoxical or mystifying. He sat down to his theme in a serious, business-like way, with his elbows on the table and his eye occasionally wandering to the clock.

To touch successively upon these points is to attempt a portrait, which I shall perhaps not altogether have failed to produce. The source of his success in describing the life that lay nearest to him, and describing it without any of those artistic perversions that come, as we have said, from a powerful imagination, from a cynical humour or from a desire to look, as George Eliot expresses it, for the suppressed transitions that unite all contrasts, the essence of this love of reality was his extreme interest in character. This is the fine and admirable quality in Trollope, this is what will preserve his best works in spite of those flatnesses which keep him from standing on quite the same level as the masters. Indeed this quality is so much one of the finest (to my mind at least), that it makes me wonder the more that the writer who had it so abundantly and so naturally should not have just that distinction which Trollope lacks, and which we find in his three brilliant contemporaries. If he was in any degree a man of genius (and I hold that he was), it was in virtue of this happy, instinctive perception of human varieties. His knowledge of the stuff we are made of, his observation of the common behaviour of men and women, was not reasoned nor acquired, not even particularly studied. All human doings deeply interested him, human life, to his mind, was a perpetual story; but he never attempted to take the so-called scientific view, the view which has lately found ingenious advocates among the countrymen and successors of Balzac. He had no airs of being able to tell you *why* people in a given situation would conduct themselves in a particular way; it was enough for him that he felt their feelings and struck the right note, because he had, as it were, a good ear. If he was a knowing psychologist he was so by grace; he was just and true without apparatus and without effort. He must have had a great taste for the moral question; he evidently believed that this is the basis of the interest of fiction. We must be careful, of course, in attributing convictions and opinions to Trollope, who, as I have said, had as little as possible of the pedantry of his art, and whose occasional chance utterances in regard to the object of the novelist and his means of achieving it are of an almost startling simplicity. But we certainly do not go too far in saying that he gave his practical testimony in favour of the idea that the interest of a work of fiction is great in proportion as the people stand on their feet. His great effort was evidently to make them stand so; if he achieved this result with as little as possible of a flourish of the hand it was nevertheless the measure of his success. If he had taken sides on the droll, bemuddled opposition between novels of character and novels of plot, I can imagine him to have said (except that he never expressed himself in epigrams), that he preferred the former class, in as much as character in itself is plot, while plot is by no means character. It is more safe indeed to believe that his great good sense would have prevented him from taking an idle controversy seriously. Character, in any sense in which we can get at it, is action, and action is plot, and any plot which hangs together, even if it pretend to interest us only in the fashion of a Chinese puzzle, plays upon our emotion, our suspense, by means of personal references. We care what happens to people only in proportion as we know what people are. Trollope's great apprehension of the real, which was what made him so interesting, came to him through his desire to satisfy us on this point – to tell us what certain people were and what they did in consequence of being so. That is the purpose of each of his tales; and if these things produce an illusion it comes from the gradual abundance of his testimony as to the temper, the tone, the passions, the habits, the moral nature, of a certain number of contemporary Britons . . .

I may take occasion to remark here upon a very curious fact – the fact that there are certain precautions in the way of producing that illusion dear to the intending novelist which Trollope not only habitually scorned to take, but really, as we may say, asking pardon for the heat of the thing, delighted wantonly to violate. He took a suicidal satisfaction in reminding the reader that the story he was telling was only, after all, a make-believe. He habitually referred to the work in hand (in the course of that work) as a novel, and to himself as a novelist, and was fond of letting the reader know that this novelist could direct the course of events according to his pleasure. Already, in *Barchester Towers*, he falls into this pernicious trick. In describing the wooing of Eleanor Bold by Mr Arabin he has occasion to say that the lady might have acted in a much more direct and natural way than the way he attributes to her. But if she had, he adds, 'where would have been my novel?' The last chapter of the same story begins with the remark, 'The end of a novel, like the end of a children's dinner party, must be made up of sweetmeats and sugar-plums.' These little slaps at credulity (we might give many more specimens) are very discouraging, but they are even more inexplicable; for they are deliberately inartistic, even judged from the point of view of that rather vague consideration of form which is the only canon we have a right to impose upon Trollope. It is impossible to imagine what a novelist takes himself to be unless he regard himself as an historian and his narrative as a history. It is only as an historian that he has the smallest *locus standi*. As a narrator of fictitious events he is nowhere; to insert into his attempt a backbone of logic, he must relate events that are assumed to be real. This assumption permeates, animates all the work of the most solid story-tellers; we need only mention (to select a single instance), the magnificent historical tone of Balzac, who would as soon have thought of admitting to the reader that he was deceiving him, as Garrick or John Kemble would have thought of pulling off his disguise in front of the footlights. Therefore, when Trollope suddenly winks at us and reminds us that he is telling us an arbitrary thing, we are startled and shocked in quite the same way as if Macaulay or Motley were to drop the historic mask and intimate that William of Orange was a myth or the Duke of Alva an invention . . .

There is perhaps little reason in it, but I find myself comparing [Trollope's] tone of allusion to many lands and many things, and whatever it brings us of easier respiration, with that narrow vision of humanity which accompanies the strenuous, serious work lately offered us in such abundance by the votaries of art for art who sit so long at their desks in Parisian *quatrièmes*. The contrast is complete, and it would be interesting, had we space to do so here, to see how far it goes. On one side a wide, good-humoured, superficial glance at a good many things; on the other a gimlet-like consideration of a few. Trollope's plan, as well as Zola's, was to describe the life that lay near him; but the two writers differ immensely as to what constitutes life and what constitutes nearness. For Trollope the emotions of a nursery-governess in Australia would take precedence of the adventures of a depraved *femme du monde* in Paris or London. They both undertake to do the same thing – to depict French and English manners; but the English writer (with his unsurpassed industry) is so occasional, so accidental, so full of the echoes of voices that are not the voice of the muse. Gustave Flaubert, Émile Zola, Alphonse Daudet, on the other hand, are nothing if not concentrated and sedentary. Trollope's realism is as instinctive, as inveterate as theirs; but nothing could mark more the difference between the French and English mind than the difference in the application, on one side and the other, of this system. We say system, though on Trollope's part it is none. He has no visible, certainly no explicit care for the literary part of the business; he writes easily, comfortably, and profusely, but his style has nothing in common either with the minute stippling of Daudet or the studied rhythms of Flaubert. He accepted all the common restrictions, and found that even within the barriers there was plenty of material. He attaches a preface to one of his novels – *The Vicar of Bullhampton* – for the express purpose of explaining why he has introduced a young woman who may, in truth, as he says, be called a 'castaway'; and in relation to this episode he remarks that it is the object of the novelist's art to entertain the young people of both sexes. Writers of the French school would, of course, protest indignantly against such a formula as this, which is the only one of the kind that I remember to have encountered in Trollope's pages. It is meagre, assuredly; but Trollope's practice was really much larger than so poor a theory. And indeed any theory was good which enabled him to produce the works which he put forth between 1856 and 1869, or later. In spite of his want of doctrinal richness I think he tells us, on the whole, more about life than the 'naturalists' in our sister republic. I say this with a full consciousness of the opportunities an artist loses in leaving so many corners unvisited, so many topics untouched, simply because I think his perception of character was naturally more just and liberal than that of the naturalists. This has been from the beginning the good fortune of our English providers of fiction, as compared with the French. They are inferior in audacity, in neatness, in acuteness, in intellectual vivacity, in the arrangement of material, in the art of characterizing visible things.

But they have been more at home in the moral world; as people say to-day they know their way about the conscience. This is the value of much of the work done by the feminine wing of the school – work which presents itself to French taste as deplorably thin and insipid. Much of it is exquisitely human, and that after all is a merit . . .

Trollope did not write for posterity; he wrote for the day, the moment; but these are just the writers whom posterity is apt to put into its pocket. So much of the life of his time is reflected in his novels that we must believe a part of the record will be saved; and the best parts of them are so sound and true and genial, that readers with an eye to that sort of entertainment will always be sure, in a certain proportion, to turn to them. Trollope will remain one of the most trustworthy, though not one of the most eloquent, of the writers who have helped the heart of man to know itself. The heart of man does not always desire this knowledge; it prefers sometimes to look at history in another way – to look at the manifestations without troubling about the motives. There are two kinds of taste in the appreciation of imaginative literature: the taste for emotions of surprise and the taste for emotions of recognition. It is the latter that Trollope gratifies, and he gratifies it the more that the medium of his own mind, through which we see what he shows us, gives a confident direction to our sympathy. His natural rightness and purity are so real that the good things he projects must be real. A race is fortunate when it has a good deal of the sort of imagination – of imaginative feeling – that had fallen to the share of Anthony Trollope; and in this possession our English race is not poor.

24

Turgenev on reviews, from 'Ivan Turgenieff', Atlantic Monthly, January 1884. This admirable commemorative essay contains James's personal reminiscences of Turgenev but little criticism.

... HE GAVE me the impression of thinking of criticism as most serious workers think of it—that it is the amusement, the exercise, the subsistence of the critic (and, so far as this goes, of immense use); but that though it may often concern other readers, it does not much concern the artist himself. In comparison with all those things which the production of a considered work forces the artist little by little to say to himself, the remarks of the critic are vague and of the moment; and yet, owing to the large publicity of the proceeding, they have a power to irritate or discourage which is quite out of proportion to their use to the person criticized. It was not, moreover (if this explanation be not more gross than the spectre it is meant to conjure away), on account of any esteem which he accorded to my own productions (I used regularly to send them to him) that I found him so agreeable, for to the best of my belief he was unable to read them. As regards one of the first that I had offered him he wrote me a little note to tell me that a distinguished friend, who was his constant companion, had read three or four chapters aloud to him the evening before and that one of them was written *de main de maître!* This gave me great pleasure, but it was my first and last pleasure of the kind. I continued, as I say, to send him my fictions, because they were the only thing I had to give; but he never alluded to the rest of the work in question, which he evidently did not finish, and never gave any sign of having read its successors. Presently I quite ceased to expect this, and saw why it was (it interested me much), that my writings could not appeal to him. He cared, more than anything else, for the air of reality, and my reality was not to the purpose. I do not think my stories struck him as quite meat for men. The manner was more apparent than the matter; they were too *tarabiscoté*, as I once heard him say of the style of a book – had on the surface too many little flowers and knots of ribbon.

25

___ ❦ ___

From 'Matthew Arnold', English Illustrated Magazine,
January 1884.

. . . THERE IS one side on which many readers will never altogether do
justice to Matthew Arnold, the side on which we see him as the
author of *St Paul and Protestantism*, and even of many portions of
Literature and Dogma. They will never cease to regret that he should
have spent so much time and ingenuity in discussing the differences –
several of which, after all, are so special, so arbitrary – between
Dissenters and Anglicans, should not rather have given these earnest
hours to the interpretation of literature. There is something dry and
dusty in the atmosphere of such discussions, which accords ill with
the fresh tone of the man of letters, the artist. It must be added that in
Mr Arnold's case they are connected with something very important,
his interest in religious ideas, his constant, characteristic sense of the
reality of religion.

The union of this element with the other parts of his mind, his love
of literature, of perfect expression, his interest in life at large,
constitutes perhaps the originality of his character as a critic, and it
certainly (to my sense) gives him that seriousness in which he has
occasionally been asserted to be wanting. Nothing can exceed the
taste, the temperance, with which he handles religious questions, and
at the same time nothing can exceed the impression he gives of really
caring for them. To his mind the religious life of humanity is the most
important thing in the spectacle humanity offers us, and he holds that
a due perception of this fact is (in connection with other lights) the
measure of the acuteness of a critic, the wisdom of a poet. He says in
his essay on Marcus Aurelius an admirable thing – 'The paramount
virtue of religion is that it has *lighted up* morality;' and such a phrase

as that shows the extent to which he feels what he speaks of. To say that this feeling, taken in combination with his love of letters, of beauty, of all liberal things, constitutes an originality is not going too far, for the religious sentiment does not always render the service of opening the mind to human life at large. Ernest Renan, in France, is, as every one knows, the great and brilliant representative of such a union; he has treated religion as he might have treated one of the fine arts. Of him it may even be said, that though he has never spoken of it but as the sovereign thing in life, yet there is in him, as an interpreter of the conscience of man, a certain dandyism, a slight fatuity, of worldly culture, of which Mr Arnold too has been accused, but from which (with the smaller assurance of an Englishman in such matters) he is much more exempt. Mr Arnold touches M. Renan on one side, as he touches Sainte-Beuve on the other (I make this double *rapprochement* because he has been spoken of more than once as the most Gallicized of English writers); and if he has gone less into the details of literature than the one, he has gone more than the other into the application of religion to questions of life. He has applied it to the current problems of English society. He has endeavoured to light up with it, to use his own phrase, some of the duskiest and most colourless of these. He has cultivated urbanity almost as successfully as M. Renan, and he has cultivated reality rather more . . .

Mr Arnold may now and then have appeared to satisfy himself with a definition not quite perfect, as when he is content to describe poetry by saying that it is a criticism of life. That surely expresses but a portion of what poetry contains – it leaves unsaid much of the essence of the matter. Literature in general is a criticism of life – prose is a criticism of life. But poetry is a criticism of life in conditions so peculiar that they are the sign by which we know poetry. Lastly, I may venture to say that our author strikes me as having, especially in his later writings, pushed to an excess some of the idiosyncracies of his delightful style – his fondness for repetition, for ringing the changes on his text, his formula – a tendency in consequence of which his expression becomes at moments slightly wordy and fatiguing . . .

These are minor blemishes, and I allude to them mainly, I confess, because I fear I may have appeared to praise too grossly. Yet I have wished to praise, to express the high appreciation of all those who in

England and America have in any degree attempted to care for literature. They owe Matthew Arnold a debt of gratitude for his admirable example, for having placed the standard of successful expression, of literary feeling and good manners, so high. They never tire of him – they read him again and again. They think the wit and humour of *Friendship's Garland* the most delicate possible, the luminosity of *Culture and Anarchy* almost dazzling, the eloquence of such a paper as the article on Lord Falkland in the *Mixed Essays* irresistible. They find him, in a word, more than any one else, the happily-proportioned, the truly distinguished man of letters. When there is a question of his efficacy, his influence, it seems to me enough to ask one's self what we should have done without him, to think how much we should have missed him, and how he has salted and seasoned our public conversation. In his absence the whole tone of discussion would have seemed more stupid, more literal. Without his irony to play over its surface, to clip it here and there of its occasional fustiness, the life of our Anglo-Saxon race would present a much greater appearance of insensibility.

26

'The Art of Fiction', Longman's Magazine, *September 1884. Walter Besant's lecture of the same title was itself a defence of the reputability of fiction – but of a provincial inadequacy which James makes pleasantly clear. For a good account of the context of the controversy see* James the Critic *by Vivien Jones (1984), pp. 124–35. For the resulting interchange of views and friendship with Stevenson see* Henry James and Robert Louis Stevenson, *ed. Janet Adam Smith (1948). The writer in the* Pall Mall Gazette *was Andrew Lang and, of course, the tales of 'Bostonian nymphs' and 'English dukes' slighted by him were James's own.*

I SHOULD not have affixed so comprehensive a title to these few remarks, necessarily wanting in any completeness upon a subject the full consideration of which would carry us far, did I not seem to discover a pretext for my temerity in the interesting pamphlet lately published under this name by Mr Walter Besant. Mr Besant's lecture at the Royal Institution – the original form of his pamphlet – appears to indicate that many persons are interested in the art of fiction, and are not indifferent to such remarks, as those who practise it may attempt to make about it. I am therefore anxious not to lose the benefit of this favourable association, and to edge in a few words under cover of the attention which Mr Besant is sure to have excited. There is something very encouraging in his having put into form certain of his ideas on the mystery of story-telling.

It is a proof of life and curiosity – curiosity on the part of the brotherhood of novelists as well as on the part of their readers. Only a short time ago it might have been supposed that the English novel was not what the French call *discutable*. It had no air of having a theory, a conviction, a consciousness of itself behind it – of being the expression of an artistic faith, the result of choice and comparison. I do not say it was necessarily the worse for that: it would take much more courage than I possess to intimate that the form of the novel as Dickens and Thackeray (for instance) saw it had any taint of incompleteness. It was, however, *naïf* (if I may help myself out with another French word); and evidently if it be destined to suffer in any way for having lost its *naïveté* it has now an idea of making sure of the corresponding advantages. During the period I have alluded to there was a comfortable, good-humoured feeling abroad that a novel is a novel, as a pudding is a pudding, and that our only business with it could be to swallow it. But within a year or two, for some reason or other, there have been signs of returning animation – the era of discussion would appear to have been to a certain extent opened. Art lives upon discussion, upon experiment, upon curiosity, upon variety of attempt, upon the exchange of views and the comparison of standpoints; and there is a presumption that those times when no one has anything particular to say about it, and has no reason to give for practice or preference, though they may be times of honour, are not times of development – are times, possibly even, a little of dulness. The successful application of any art is a delightful spectacle, but the theory too is interesting; and though there is a great deal of the latter without the former I suspect there has never been a genuine success that has not had a latent core of conviction. Discussion, suggestion, formulation, these things are fertilizing when they are frank and sincere. Mr Besant has set an excellent example in saying what he thinks, for his part, about the way in which fiction should be written, as well as about the way in which it should be published; for his view of the 'art', carried on into an appendix, covers that too. Other labourers in the same field will doubtless take up the argument, they will give it the light of their experience, and the effect will surely be to make our interest in the novel a little more what it had for some time threatened to fail to be – a serious, active, inquiring interest, under protection of which this delightful study may, in moments of confidence, venture to say a little more what it thinks of itself.

It must take itself seriously for the public to take it so. The old superstition about fiction being 'wicked' has doubtless died out in England; but the spirit of it lingers in a certain oblique regard directed toward any story which does not more or less admit that it is only a joke. Even the most jocular novel feels in some degree the weight of the proscription that was formerly directed against literary levity; the jocularity does not always succeed in passing for orthodoxy. It is still expected, though perhaps people are ashamed to say it, that a production which is after all only a 'make-believe' (for what else is a 'story'?) shall be in some degree apologetic – shall renounce the pretension of attempting really to represent life. This, of course, any sensible, wide-awake story declines to do, for it quickly perceives that the tolerance granted to it on such a condition is only an attempt to stifle it disguised in the form of generosity. The old evangelical hostility to the novel, which was as explicit as it was narrow, and which regarded it as little less favourable to our immortal part than a stage-play, was in reality far less insulting. The only reason for the existence of a novel is that it does attempt to represent life. When it relinquishes this attempt, the same attempt that we see on the canvas of the painter, it will have arrived at a very strange pass. It is not expected of the picture that it will make itself humble in order to be forgiven; and the analogy between the art of the painter and the art of the novelist is, so far as I am able to see, complete. Their inspiration is the same, their process (allowing for the different quality of the vehicle), is the same, their success is the same. They may learn from each other, they may explain and sustain each other. Their cause is the same, and the honour of one is the honour of another. The Mahometans think a picture an unholy thing, but it is a long time since any Christian did, and it is therefore the more odd that in the Christian mind the traces (dissimulated though they may be) of a suspicion of the sister art should linger to this day. The only effectual way to lay it to rest is to emphasize the analogy to which I just alluded – to insist on the fact that as the picture is reality, so the novel is history. That is the only general description (which does it justice) that we may give of the novel. But history also is allowed to represent life; it is not, any more than painting, expected to apologize. The subject-matter of fiction is stored up likewise in documents and records, and if it will not give itself away, as they say in California, it must speak with assurance, with the tone of the historian. Certain accomplished novelists have a habit of giving themselves away which must often bring tears to the eyes of people who take their fiction seriously. I was lately struck, in reading over many pages of Anthony Trollope, with his want of discretion in this particular. In a digression, a parenthesis or an aside, he concedes to the reader that he and this trusting friend are only 'making believe'. He admits that the events he narrates have not really happened, and that he can give his narrative any turn the reader may like best. Such a betrayal of a sacred office seems to me, I confess, a terrible crime; it is what I mean by the attitude of apology, and it shocks me every whit as much in Trollope as it would have shocked me in Gibbon or Macaulay. It implies that the novelist is less occupied in looking for the truth (the truth, of course I mean, that he assumes, the premises that we must grant him, whatever they may be), than the historian, and in doing so it deprives him at a stroke of all his standing-room. To represent and illustrate the past, the actions of men, is the task of either writer, and the only difference that I can see is, in proportion as he succeeds, to the honour of the novelist, consisting as it does in his having more difficulty in collecting his evidence, which is so far from being purely literary. It seems to me to give him a great character, the fact that he has at once so much in common with the philosopher and the painter; this double analogy is a magnificent heritage.

It is of all this evidently that Mr Besant is full when he insists upon the fact that fiction is one of the *fine* arts, deserving in its turn of all the honours and emoluments that have hitherto been reserved for the successful profession of music, poetry, painting, architecture. It is impossible to insist too much on so important a truth, and the place that Mr Besant demands for the work of the novelist may be represented, a trifle less abstractly, by saying that he demands not only that it shall be reputed artistic, but that it shall be reputed very artistic indeed. It is excellent that he should have struck this note, for his doing so indicates that there was need of it, that his proposition may be to many people a novelty. One rubs one's eyes at the thought; but the rest of Mr Besant's essay confirms the revelation. I suspect in truth that it would be possible to confirm it still further, and that one would not be far wrong in saying that in addition to the people to whom it has never occurred that a novel ought to be artistic, there are a great many others who, if this principle were urged upon them, would be filled with an indefinable mistrust. They would find it difficult to explain their repugnance, but it would operate strongly to put them on their guard. 'Art', in our Protestant communities, where so many things have got so strangely twisted about, is supposed in certain circles to have some vaguely injurious effect upon those who make it an important consideration, who let it weigh in the balance. It is assumed to be opposed in some mysterious manner to morality, to amusement, to instruction. When it is embodied in the work of the painter (the sculptor is another affair!) you know what it is: it stands there before you, in the honesty of pink and green and a gilt frame; you can see the worst of it at a glance, and you can be on your guard. But when it is introduced into literature it becomes more insidious – there is danger of its hurting you before you know it. Literature should be either instructive or amusing, and there is in many minds an impression that these artistic preoccupations, the search for form, contribute to neither end, interfere indeed with both. They are too frivolous to be edifying, and too serious to be diverting; and they are moreover priggish and paradoxical and superfluous. That, I think, represents the manner in which the latent thought of many people who read novels as an exercise in skipping would explain itself if it were to become articulate. They would argue, of course, that a novel ought to be 'good', but they would interpret this term in a fashion of their own, which indeed would vary considerably from one critic to another. One would say that being good means representing virtuous and aspiring characters, placed in prominent positions; another would say that it depends on a 'happy ending', on a distribution at the last of prizes, pensions, husbands, wives, babies, millions, appended paragraphs, and cheerful remarks. Another still would say that it means being full of incident and movement, so that we shall wish to jump ahead, to see who was the mysterious stranger, and if the stolen will was ever found, and shall not be distracted from this pleasure by any tiresome analysis or 'description'. But they would all agree that the 'artistic' idea would spoil some of their fun. One would hold it accountable for all the description, another would see it revealed in the absence of sympathy. Its hostility to a happy ending would be evident, and it might even in some cases render any ending at all impossible. The 'ending' of a novel is, for many persons, like that of a good dinner, a course of dessert and ices, and the artist in fiction is regarded as a sort of meddlesome doctor who forbids agreeable aftertastes. It is therefore true that this conception of Mr

Besant's of the novel as a superior form encounters not only a negative but a positive indifference. It matters little that as a work of art it should really be as little or as much of its essence to supply happy endings, sympathetic characters, and an objective tone, as if it were a work of mechanics: the association of ideas, however incongruous, might easily be too much for it if an eloquent voice were not sometimes raised to call attention to the fact that it is at once as free and as serious a branch of literature as any other.

Certainly this might sometimes be doubted in presence of the enormous number of works of fiction that appeal to the credulity of our generation, for it might easily seem that there could be no great character in a commodity so quickly and easily produced. It must be admitted that good novels are much compromised by bad ones, and that the field at large suffers discredit from overcrowding. I think, however, that this injury is only superficial, and that the superabundance of written fiction proves nothing against the principle itself. It has been vulgarized, like all other kinds of literature, like everything else to-day, and it has proved more than some kinds accessible to vulgarization. But there is as much difference as there ever was between a good novel and a bad one: the bad is swept with all the daubed canvases and spoiled marble into some unvisited limbo, or infinite rubbish-yard beneath the back-windows of the world, and the good subsists and emits its light and stimulates our desire for perfection. As I shall take the liberty of making but a single criticism of Mr Besant, whose tone is so full of the love of his art, I may as well have done with it at once. He seems to me to mistake in attempting to say so definitely beforehand what sort of an affair the good novel will be. To indicate the danger of such an error as that has been the purpose of these few pages; to suggest that certain traditions on the subject, applied *a priori*, have already had much to answer for, and that the good health of an art which undertakes so immediately to reproduce life must demand that it be perfectly free. It lives upon exercise, and the very meaning of exercise is freedom. The only obligation to which in advance we may hold a novel, without incurring the accusation of being arbitrary, is that it be interesting. That general responsibility rests upon it, but it is the only one I can think of. The ways in which it is at liberty to accomplish this result (of interesting us) strike me as innumerable, and such as can only suffer from being marked out or fenced in by prescription. They are as various as the temperament of man, and they are successful in proportion as they reveal a particular mind, different from others. A novel is in its broadest definition a personal, a direct impression of life: that, to begin with, constitutes its value, which is greater or less according to the intensity of the impression. But there will be no intensity at all, and therefore no value, unless there is freedom to feel and say. The tracing of a line to be followed, of a tone to be taken, of a form to be filled out, is a limitation of that freedom and a suppression of the very thing that we are most curious about. The form, it seems to me, is to be appreciated after the fact: then the author's choice has been made, his standard has been indicated; then we can follow lines and directions and compare tones and resemblances. Then in a word we can enjoy one of the most charming of pleasures, we can estimate quality, we can apply the test of execution. The execution belongs to the author alone; it is what is most personal to him, and we measure him by that. The advantage, the luxury, as well as the torment and responsibility of the novelist, is that there is no limit to what he may attempt as an executant – no limit to his possible experiments, efforts, discoveries, successes. Here it is especially that he works, step by step, like his brother of the brush, of whom we may always say that he has painted his picture in a manner best known to himself. His manner is his secret, not necessarily a jealous one. He cannot disclose it as a general thing if he would; he would be at a loss to teach it to others. I say this with a due recollection of having insisted on the community of method of the artist who paints a picture and the artist who writes a novel. The painter *is* able to teach the rudiments of his practice, and it is possible, from the study of good work (granted the aptitude), both to learn how to paint and to learn how to write. Yet it remains true, without injury to the *rapprochement*, that the literary artist would be obliged to say to his pupil much more than the other, 'Ah, well, you must do it as you can!' It is a question of degree, a matter of delicacy. If there are exact sciences, there are also exact arts, and the grammar of painting is so much more definite that it makes the difference.

I ought to add, however, that if Mr Besant says at the beginning of his essay that the 'laws of fiction may be laid down and taught with as much precision and exactness as the laws of harmony, perspective, and proportion,' he mitigates what might appear to be an extravagance by applying his remark to 'general' laws, and by expressing most of these rules in a manner with which it would certainly be unaccommodating to disagree. That the novelist must write from his experience, that his 'characters must be real and such as might be met with in actual life'; that 'a young lady brought up in a quiet country village should avoid descriptions of garrison life', and 'a writer whose friends and personal experiences belong to the lower middle-class should carefully avoid introducing his characters into society'; that one should enter one's notes in a common-place book; that one's figures should be clear in outline; that making them clear by some trick of speech or of carriage is a bad method, and 'describing them at length' is a worse one; that English Fiction should have a 'conscious moral purpose'; that 'it is almost impossible to estimate too highly the value of careful workmanship – that is, of style'; that 'the most important point of all is the story', that 'the story is everything': these are principles with most of which it is surely impossible not to sympathize. That remark about the lower middle-class writer and his knowing his place is perhaps rather chilling; but for the rest I should find it difficult to dissent from any one of these recommendations. At the same time, I should find it difficult positively to assent to them, with the exception, perhaps, of the injunction as to entering one's notes in a common-place book. They scarcely seem to me to have the quality that Mr Besant attributes to the rules of the novelist – the 'precision and exactness' of 'the laws of harmony, perspective, and proportion'. They are suggestive, they are even inspiring, but they are not exact, though they are doubtless as much so as the case admits of: which is a proof of that liberty of interpretation for which I just contended. For the value of these different injunctions – so beautiful and so vague – is wholly in the meaning one attaches to them. The characters, the situation, which strike one as real will be those that touch and interest one most, but the measure of reality is very difficult to fix. The reality of Don Quixote or of Mr Micawber is a very delicate shade; it is a reality so coloured by the author's vision that, vivid as it may be, one would hesitate to propose it as a model: one would expose one's self to some very embarrassing questions on the part of a pupil. It goes without saying that you will not write a good novel unless you possess the sense of reality; but it will be difficult to give you a recipe for calling that sense into being. Humanity is immense, and reality has a myriad forms; the most one can affirm is that some of the flowers of fiction have the odour of it, and others have not; as for telling you in advance how your nosegay should be composed, that is another affair. It is equally excellent and inconclusive to say that one must write from experience; to our supposititious aspirant such a declaration might savour of mockery. What kind of experience is intended, and where does it begin and end? Experience is never limited, and it is never complete; it is an immense sensibility, a kind of huge spider-web of the finest silken threads suspended in the chamber of consciousness, and catching every air-borne particle in its tissue. It is the very atmosphere of the mind; and when the mind is imaginative – much more when it happens to be that of a man of genius – it takes to itself the faintest hints of life, it converts the very pulses of the air into revelations. The young lady living in a village has only to be a damsel upon whom nothing is lost to make it quite unfair (as it seems to me) to declare to her that she shall have nothing to say about the military. Greater miracles have been seen than that, imagination assisting, she should speak the truth about some of these gentlemen. I remember an English novelist, a woman of genius, telling me that she was much commended for the impression she had managed to give in one of her tales of the nature and way of life of the French Protestant youth. She had been asked where she learned so much about this recondite being, she had been congratulated on her peculiar opportunities. These opportunities consisted in her having once, in Paris, as she ascended a staircase, passed an open door where, in the household of a *pasteur*, some of the young Protestants were seated at table round a finished meal. The glimpse made a picture; it lasted only a moment, but that moment was experience. She had got her direct personal impression, and she turned out her type. She knew what youth was, and what Protestantism; she also had the advantage of having seen what it was to be French, so that she converted these ideas into a concrete image and produced a reality. Above all, however, she was blessed with the faculty which when you give it an inch takes an ell, and which for the artist is a much greater source of strength than any accident of residence or of place in the social scale. The power to guess the unseen from the seen, to trace the implication of things, to judge the whole piece by the pattern, the condition of feeling life in general so completely that you are well on your way to knowing any particular corner of it – this cluster of gifts may almost be said to constitute experience, and they occur in country and in town, and in the most differing stages of education. If experience consists of impressions, it may be said that impressions *are* experience, just as (have we not seen it?) they are the very air we breathe. Therefore, if I should certainly say to a novice, 'Write from experience and experience only,' I should feel that this was rather a tantalizing monition if I were not careful immediately to add, 'Try to be one of the people on whom nothing is lost!'

I am far from intending by this to minimize the importance of exactness – of truth of detail. One can speak best from one's own taste, and I may therefore venture to say that the air of reality (solidity of specification) seems to me to be the supreme virtue of a novel – the merit on which all its other merits (including that conscious moral purpose of which Mr Besant speaks) helplessly and submissively depend. If it be not there they are all as nothing, and if these be there, they owe their effect to the success with which the author has produced the illusion of life. The cultivation of this success, the study of this exquisite process, form, to my taste, the beginning and the end of the art of the novelist. They are his inspiration, his despair, his reward, his torment, his delight. It is here in very truth that he competes with life; it is here that he competes with his brother the painter in *his* attempt to render the look of things, the look that conveys their meaning, to catch the colour, the relief, the expression, the surface, the substance of the human spectacle. It is in regard to this that Mr Besant is well inspired when he bids him take notes. He cannot possibly take too many, he cannot possibly take enough. All life solicits him, and to 'render' the simplest surface, to produce the most momentary illusion, is a very complicated business. His case would be easier, and the rule would be more exact, if Mr Besant had been able to tell him what notes to take. But this, I fear, he can never learn in any manual; it is the business of his life. He has to take a great many in order to select a few, he has to work them up as he can, and even the guides and philosophers who might have most to say to him must leave him alone when it comes to the application of precepts, as we leave the painter in communion with his palette. That his characters 'must be clear in outline', as Mr Besant says – he feels that down to his boots; but how he shall make them so is a secret between his good angel and himself. It would be absurdly simple if he could be taught that a great deal of 'description' would make them so, or that on the contrary the absence of description and the cultivation of dialogue, or the absence of dialogue and the multiplication of 'incident', would rescue him from his difficulties. Nothing, for instance, is more possible than that he be of a turn of mind for which this odd, literal opposition of description and dialogue, incident and description, has little meaning and light. People often talk of these things as if they had a kind of internecine distinctness, instead of melting into each other at every breath, and being intimately associated parts of one general effort to expression. I cannot imagine composition existing in a series of blocks, nor conceive, in any novel worth discussing at all, of a passage of description that is not in its intention narrative, a passage of dialogue that is not in its intention descriptive, a touch of truth of any sort that does not partake of the nature of incident, or an incident that derives its interest from any other source than the general and only source of the success of a work of art – that of being illustrative. A novel is a living thing, all one and continuous, like any other organism, and in proportion as it lives will it be found, I think, that in each of the parts there is something of each of the other parts. The critic who over the close texture of a finished work shall pretend to trace a geography of items will mark some frontiers as artificial, I fear, as any that have been known to history. There is an old-fashioned distinction between the novel of character and the novel of incident which must have cost many a smile to the intending fabulist who was keen about his work. It appears to me as little to the point as the equally celebrated distinction between the novel and the romance – to answer as little to any reality. There are bad novels and good novels, as there are bad pictures and good pictures; but that is the only distinction in which I see any meaning, and I can as little imagine speaking of a novel of character as I can imagine speaking of a picture of character. When one says picture one says of character, when one says novel one says of incident, and the terms may be transposed at will. What is character but the determination of incident? What is incident but the illustration of character? What is either a picture or a novel that is *not* of character? What else do we seek in it and find in it? It is an incident for a woman to stand up with her hand resting on a table and look out at you in a certain way; or if it be not an incident I think it will be hard to say what it is. At the same time it is an expression of character. If you say you don't see it (character in *that — allons donc!*), this is exactly what the artist who has reasons of his own for thinking he *does* see it undertakes to show you. When a young man makes up his mind that he has not faith enough after all to enter the church as he intended, that is an incident, though you may not hurry to the end of the chapter to see whether perhaps he doesn't change once more. I do not say that these are extraordinary or startling incidents. I do not pretend to estimate the degree of interest proceeding from them, for this will depend upon the skill of the painter. It sounds almost puerile to say that some incidents are intrinsically much more important than others, and I need not take this precaution after having professed my sympathy for the major ones in remarking that the only classification of the novel that I can understand is into that which has life and that which has it not.

The novel and the romance, the novel of incident and that of character — these clumsy separations appear to me to have been made by critics and readers for their own convenience, and to help them out of some of their occasional queer predicaments, but to have little reality or interest for the producer, from whose point of view it is of course that we are attempting to consider the art of fiction. The case is the same with another shadowy category which Mr Besant apparently is disposed to set up — that of the 'modern English novel'; unless indeed it be that in this matter he has fallen into an accidental confusion of standpoints. It is not quite clear whether he intends the remarks in which he alludes to it to be didactic or historical. It is as difficult to suppose a person intending to write a modern English as to suppose him writing an ancient English novel: that is a label which begs the question. One writes the novel, one paints the picture, of one's language and of one's time, and calling it modern English will not, alas! make the difficult task any easier. No more, unfortunately, will calling this or that work of one's fellow-artist a romance — unless it be, of course, simply for the pleasantness of the thing, as for instance when Hawthorne gave this heading to his story of *Blithe-dale*. The French, who have brought the theory of fiction to remarkable completeness, have but one name for the novel, and have not attempted smaller things in it, that I can see, for that. I can think of no obligation to which the 'romancer' would not be held equally with the novelist; the standard of execution is equally high for each. Of course it is of execution that we are talking – that being the only point of a novel that is open to contention. This is perhaps too often lost sight of, only to produce interminable confusions and cross-purposes. We must grant the artist his subject, his idea, his *donnée*: our criticism is applied only to what he makes of it. Naturally I do not mean that we are bound to like it or find it interesting: in case we do not our course is perfectly simple – to let it alone. We may believe that of a certain idea even the most sincere novelist can make nothing at all, and the event may perfectly justify our belief; but the failure will have been a failure to execute, and it is in the execution that the fatal weakness is recorded. If we pretend to respect the artist at all, we must allow him his freedom of choice, in the face, in particular cases, of innumerable presumptions that the choice will not fructify. Art derives a considerable part of its beneficial exercise from flying in the face of presumptions, and some of the most interesting experiments of which it is capable are hidden in the bosom of common things. Gustave Flaubert has written a story about the devotion of a servant-girl to a parrot, and the production, highly finished as it is, cannot on the whole be called a success. We are perfectly free to find it flat, but I think it might have been interesting; and I, for my part, am extremely glad he should have written it; it is a contribution to our knowledge of what can be done – or what cannot. Ivan Turgenieff has written a tale about a deaf and dumb serf and a lap-dog, and the thing is touching, loving, a little masterpiece. He struck the note of life where Gustave Flaubert missed it – he flew in the face of a presumption and achieved a victory.

Nothing, of course, will ever take the place of the good old fashion of 'liking' a work of art or not liking it: the most improved criticism will not abolish that primitive, that ultimate test. I mention this to guard myself from the accusation of intimating that the idea, the subject, of a novel or a picture, does not matter. It matters, to my sense, in the highest degree, and if I might put up a prayer it would be that artists should select none but the richest. Some, as I have already hastened to admit, are much more remunerative than others, and it would be a world happily arranged in which persons intending to treat them should be exempt from confusions and mistakes. This fortunate condition will arrive only, I fear, on the same day that critics become purged from error. Meanwhile, I repeat, we do not judge the artist with fairness unless we say to him, 'Oh, I grant you your starting-point, because if I did not I should seem to prescribe to you, and heaven forbid I should take that responsibility. If I pretend to tell you what you must not take, you will call upon me to tell you then what you must take; in which case I shall be prettily caught. Moreover, it isn't till I have accepted your data that I can begin to measure you. I have the standard, the pitch; I have no right to tamper with your flute and then criticize your music. Of course I may not care for your idea at all; I may think it silly, or stale, or unclean; in which case I wash my hands of you altogether. I may content myself with believing that you will not have succeeded in being interesting, but I shall, of course, not attempt to demonstrate it, and you will be as indifferent to me as I am to you. I needn't remind you that there are all sorts of tastes: who can know it better? Some people, for excellent reasons, don't like to read about carpenters; others, for reasons even better, don't like to read about courtesans. Many object to Americans. Others (I believe they are mainly editors and publishers) won't look at Italians. Some readers don't like quiet subjects; others don't like bustling ones. Some enjoy a complete illusion, others the consciousness of large concessions. They choose their novels accordingly, and if they don't care about your idea they won't, *a fortiori*, care about your treatment.'

So that it comes back very quickly, as I have said, to the liking: in spite of M. Zola, who reasons less powerfully than he represents, and who will not reconcile himself to this absoluteness of taste, thinking that there are certain things that people ought to like, and that they can be made to like. I am quite at a loss to imagine anything (at any rate in this matter of fiction) that people *ought* to like or to dislike. Selection will be sure to take care of itself, for it has a constant motive behind it. That motive is simply experience. As people feel life, so they will feel the art that is most closely related to it. This closeness of relation is what we should never forget in talking of the effort of the novel. Many people speak of it as a factitious, artificial form, a product of ingenuity, the business of which is to alter and arrange the things that surround us, to translate them into conventional, traditional moulds. This, however, is a view of the matter which carries us but a very short way, condemns the art to an eternal repetition of a few familiar *clichés*, cuts short its development, and leads us straight up to a dead wall. Catching the very note and trick, the strange irregular rhythm of life, that is the attempt whose strenuous force keeps Fiction upon her feet. In proportion as in what she offers us we see life *without* rearrangement do we feel that we are touching the truth; in proportion as we see it *with* rearrangement do we feel that we are being put off with a substitute, a compromise and convention. It is not uncommon to hear an extraordinary assurance of remark in regard to this matter of rearranging, which is often spoken of as if it were the last word of art. Mr Besant seems to me in danger of falling into the great error with his rather unguarded talk about 'selection'. Art is essentially selection, but it is a selection whose main care is to be typical, to be inclusive. For many people art means rose-coloured window-panes, and selection means picking a bouquet for Mrs Grundy. They will tell you glibly that artistic considerations have nothing to do with the disagreeable, with the ugly; they will rattle off shallow commonplaces about the province of art and the limits of art till you are moved to some wonder in return as to the province and the limits of ignorance. It appears to me that no one can ever have made a seriously artistic attempt without becoming conscious of an immense increase – a kind of revelation – of freedom. One perceives in that case – by the light of a heavenly ray – that the province of art is all life, all feeling, all observation, all vision. As Mr Besant so justly intimates, it is all experience. That is a sufficient answer to those who maintain that it must not touch the sad things of life, who stick into its divine unconscious bosom little prohibitory inscriptions on the end of sticks, such as we see in public gardens – 'It is forbidden to walk on the grass; it is forbidden to touch the flowers; it is not allowed to introduce dogs or to remain after dark; it is requested to keep to the right.' The young aspirant in the line of fiction whom we continue to imagine will do nothing without taste, for in that case his freedom would be of little use to him; but the first advantage of his taste will be to reveal to him the absurdity of the little sticks and tickets. If he have taste, I must add, of course he will have ingenuity, and my disrespectful reference to that quality just now was not meant to imply that it is useless in fiction. But it is only a secondary aid; the first is a capacity for receiving straight impressions.

Mr Besant has some remarks on the question of 'the story' which I shall not attempt to criticize, though they seem to me to contain a singular ambiguity, because I do not think I understand them. I cannot see what is meant by talking as if there were a part of a novel which is the story and part of it which for mystical reasons is not – unless indeed the distinction be made in a sense in which it is difficult to suppose that any one should attempt to convey anything. 'The story', if it represents anything, represents the subject, the idea, the *donnée* of the novel; and there is surely no 'school' – Mr Besant speaks of a school – which urges that a novel should be all treatment and no subject. There must assuredly be something to treat; every school is intimately conscious of that. This sense of the story being the idea, the starting-point, of the novel, is the only one that I see in which it can be spoken of as something different from its organic whole; and since in proportion as the work is successful the idea permeates and penetrates it, informs and animates it, so that every word and every punctuation-point contribute directly to the expression, in that proportion do we lose our sense of the story being a blade which may be drawn more or less out of its sheath. The story and the novel, the idea and the form, are the needle and thread, and I never heard of a guild of tailors who recommended the use of the thread without the needle, or the needle without the thread. Mr Besant is not the only critic who may be observed to have spoken as if there were certain things in life which constitute stories, and certain others which do not. I find the same odd implication in an entertaining article in the *Pall Mall Gazette*, devoted, as it happens, to Mr Besant's lecture. 'The story is the thing!' says this graceful writer, as if with a tone of opposition to some other idea. I should think it was, as every painter who, as the time for 'sending in' his picture looms in the distance, finds himself still in quest of a subject – as every belated artist not fixed about his theme will heartily agree. There are some subjects which speak to us and others which do not, but he would be a clever man who should undertake to give a rule – an index expurgatorius – by which the story and the no-story should be known apart. It is impossible (to me at least) to imagine any such rule which shall not be altogether arbitrary. The writer in the *Pall Mall* opposes the delightful (as I suppose) novel of *Margot la Balafrée* to certain tales in which 'Bostonian nymphs' appear to have 'rejected English dukes for psychological reasons'. I am not acquainted with the romance just designated, and can scarcely forgive the *Pall Mall* critic for not mentioning the name of the author, but the title appears to refer to a lady who may have received a scar in some heroic adventure. I am inconsolable at not being acquainted with this episode, but am utterly at a loss to see why it is a story when the rejection (or acceptance) of a duke is not, and why a reason, psychological or other, is not a subject when a cicatrix is. They are all particles of the multitudinous life with which the novel deals, and surely no dogma which pretends to make it lawful to touch the one and unlawful to touch the other will stand for a moment on its feet. It is the special picture that must stand or fall, according as it seem to possess truth or to lack it. Mr Besant does not, to my sense, light up the subject by intimating that a story must, under penalty of not being a story, consist of 'adventures'. Why of adventures more than of green spectacles? He mentions a category of impossible things, and among them he places 'fiction without adventure'. Why without adventure, more than without matrimony, or celibacy, or parturition, or cholera, or hydropathy, or Jansenism? This seems to me to bring the novel back to the hapless little *rôle* of being an artificial, ingenious thing – bring it down from its large, free character of an immense and exquisite correspondence with life. And what *is* adventure, when it comes to that, and by what sign is the listening pupil to recognize it? It is an adventure – an immense one – for me to write this little article; and for a Bostonian nymph to reject an English duke is an adventure only less stirring, I should say, than for an English duke to be rejected by a Bostonian nymph. I see dramas within dramas in that, and innumerable points of view. A psychological reason is, to my imagination, an object adorably pictorial; to catch the tint of its complexion – I feel as if that idea might inspire one to Titianesque efforts. There are few things more exciting to me, in short, than a psychological reason, and yet, I protest, the novel seems to me the most magnificent form of art. I have just been reading, at the same time, the delightful story of *Treasure Island*, by Mr Robert

Louis Stevenson and, in a manner less consecutive, the last tale from
M. Edmond de Goncourt, which is entitled *Chérie*. One of these
works treats of murders, mysteries, islands of dreadful renown,
hairbreadth escapes, miraculous coincidences and buried doub-
loons. The other treats of a little French girl who lived in a fine house
in Paris, and died of wounded sensibility because no one would
marry her. I call *Treasure Island* delightful, because it appears to me
to have succeeded wonderfully in what it attempts; and I venture to
bestow no epithet upon *Chérie*, which strikes me as having failed
deplorably in what it attempts – that is in tracing the development of
the moral consciousness of a child. But one of these productions
strikes me as exactly as much of a novel as the other, and as having a
'story' quite as much. The moral consciousness of a child is as much a
part of life as the islands of the Spanish Main, and the one sort of
geography seems to me to have those 'surprises' of which Mr Besant
speaks quite as much as the other. For myself (since it comes back in
the last resort, as I say, to the preference of the individual), the picture
of the child's experience has the advantage that I can at successive
steps (an immense luxury, near to the 'sensual pleasure' of which Mr
Besant's critic in the *Pall Mall* speaks) say Yes or No, as it may be, to
what the artist puts before me. I have been a child in fact, but I have
been on a quest for a buried treasure only in supposition, and it is a
simple accident that with M. de Goncourt I should have for the most
part to say No. With George Eliot, when she painted that country
with a far other intelligence, I always said Yes.

The most interesting part of Mr Besant's lecture is unfortunately
the briefest passage – his very cursory allusion to the 'conscious
moral purpose' of the novel. Here again it is not very clear whether he
be recording a fact or laying down a principle; it is a great pity that in
the latter case he should not have developed his idea. This branch of
the subject is of immense importance, and Mr Besant's few words
point to considerations of the widest reach, not to be lightly disposed
of. He will have treated the art of fiction but superficially who is not
prepared to go every inch of the way that these considerations will
carry him. It is for this reason that at the beginning of these remarks I
was careful to notify the reader that my reflections on so large a
theme have no pretension to be exhaustive. Like Mr Besant, I have
left the question of the morality of the novel till the last, and at the

last I find I have used up my space. It is a question surrounded with difficulties, as witness the very first that meets us, in the form of a definite question, on the threshold. Vagueness, in such a discussion, is fatal, and what is the meaning of your morality and your conscious moral purpose? Will you not define your terms and explain how (a novel being a picture) a picture can be either moral or immoral? You wish to paint a moral picture or carve a moral statue: will you not tell us how you would set about it? We are discussing the Art of Fiction; questions of art are questions (in the widest sense) of execution; questions of morality are quite another affair, and will you not let us see how it is that you find it so easy to mix them up? These things are so clear to Mr Besant that he has deduced from them a law which he sees embodied in English Fiction, and which is 'a truly admirable thing and a great cause for congratulation'. It is a great cause for congratulation indeed when such thorny problems become as smooth as silk. I may add that in so far as Mr Besant perceives that in point of fact English Fiction has addressed itself preponderantly to these delicate questions he will appear to many people to have made a vain discovery. They will have been positively struck, on the contrary, with the moral timidity of the usual English novelist; with his (or with her) aversion to face the difficulties with which on every side the treatment of reality bristles. He is apt to be extremely shy (whereas the picture that Mr Besant draws is a picture of boldness), and the sign of his work, for the most part, is a cautious silence on certain subjects. In the English novel (by which of course I mean the American as well), more than in any other, there is a traditional difference between that which people know and that which they agree to admit that they know, that which they see and that which they speak of, that which they feel to be a part of life and that which they allow to enter into literature. There is the great difference, in short, between what they talk of in conversation and what they talk of in print. The essence of moral energy is to survey the whole field, and I should directly reverse Mr Besant's remark and say not that the English novel has a purpose, but that it has a diffidence. To what degree a purpose in a work of art is a source of corruption I shall not attempt to inquire; the one that seems to me least dangerous is the purpose of making a perfect work. As for our novel, I may say lastly on this score that as we find it in England today it strikes me as addressed in a large degree to 'young people', and that this in itself constitutes a presumption that it will be rather shy. There are certain things which it is generally agreed not to discuss, not even to mention, before young people. That is very well, but the absence of discussion is not a symptom of the moral passion. The purpose of the English novel – 'a truly admirable thing, and a great cause for congratulation' – strikes me therefore as rather negative.

There is one point at which the moral sense and the artistic sense lie very near together; that is in the light of the very obvious truth that the deepest quality of a work of art will always be the quality of the mind of the producer. In proportion as that intelligence is fine will the novel, the picture, the statue partake of the substance of beauty and truth. To be constituted of such elements is, to my vision, to have purpose enough. No good novel will ever proceed from a superficial mind; that seems to me an axiom which, for the artist in fiction, will cover all needful moral ground: if the youthful aspirant take it to heart it will illuminate for him many of the mysteries of 'purpose'. There are many other useful things that might be said to him, but I have come to the end of my article, and can only touch them as I pass. The critic in the *Pall Mall Gazette*, whom I have already quoted, draws attention to the danger, in speaking of the art of fiction, of generalizing. The danger that he has in mind is rather, I imagine, that of particularizing, for there are some comprehensive remarks which, in addition to those embodied in Mr Besant's suggestive lecture, might without fear of misleading him be addressed to the ingenuous student. I should remind him first of the magnificence of the form that is open to him, which offers to sight so few restrictions and such innumerable opportunities. The other arts, in comparison, appear confined and hampered; the various conditions under which they are exercised are so rigid and definite. But the only condition that I can think of attaching to the composition of the novel is, as I have already said, that it be sincere. This freedom is a splendid privilege, and the first lesson of the young novelist is to learn to be worthy of it. 'Enjoy it as it deserves,' I should say to him; 'take possession of it, explore it to its utmost extent, publish it, rejoice in it. All life belongs to you, and do not listen either to those who would shut you up into corners of it and tell you that it is only here and there that art inhabits, or to those who would persuade you that this heavenly messenger wings her way outside of life altogether, breathing a superfine air, and turning away her head from the truth of things. There is no impression of life, no manner of seeing it and feeling it, to which the plan of the novelist may not offer a place; you have only to remember that talents so dissimilar as those of Alexandre Dumas and Jane Austen, Charles Dickens and Gustave Flaubert have worked in this field with equal glory. Do not think too much about optimism and pessimism; try and catch the colour of life itself. In France to-day we see a prodigious effort (that of Emile Zola, to whose solid and serious work no explorer of the capacity of the novel can allude without respect), we see an extraordinary effort vitiated by a spirit of pessimism on a narrow basis. M. Zola is magnificent, but he strikes an English reader as ignorant; he has an air of working in the dark; if he had as much light as energy, his results would be of the highest value. As for the aberrations of a shallow optimism, the ground (of English fiction especially) is strewn with their brittle particles as with broken glass. If you must indulge in conclusions, let them have the taste of a wide knowledge. Remember that your first duty is to be as complete as possible – to make as perfect a work. Be generous and delicate and pursue the prize.'

—⚜—

27

From 'The Life of George Eliot', Atlantic Monthly, May 1885.
James was reviewing George Eliot's Life by J. W. Cross.

... THE MOST interesting passage in Mr Cross's volumes is to my
sense a simple sentence in a short entry in her journal in the year
1859, just after she had finished the first volume of The Mill on the
Floss (the original title of which, by the way, had been Sister Maggie):
'We have just finished reading aloud Père Goriot, a hateful book.'
That Balzac's masterpiece should have elicited from her only this
remark, at a time, too, when her mind might have been opened to it
by her own activity of composition, is significant of so many things
that the few words are, in the whole Life, those I should have been
most sorry to lose. Of course they are not all George Eliot would have
had to say about Balzac, if some other occasion than a simple jotting
in a diary had presented itself. Still, what even a jotting may not have
said after a first perusal of Le Père Goriot is eloquent; it illuminates
the author's general attitude with regard to the novel, which, for her,
was not primarily a picture of life, capable of deriving a high value
from its form, but a moralized fable, the last word of a philosophy
endeavouring to teach by example.

This is a very noble and defensible view, and one must speak
respectfully of any theory of work which would produce such fruit as
Romola and Middlemarch. But it testifies to that side of George
Eliot's nature which was weakest – the absence of free aesthetic life (I
venture this remark in the face of a passage quoted from one of her
letters in Mr Cross's third volume); it gives the hand, as it were, to
several other instances that may be found in the same pages. 'My
function is that of the aesthetic, not the doctrinal teacher; the rousing
of the nobler emotions, which make mankind desire the social right,

not the prescribing of special measures, concerning which the artistic mind, however strongly moved by social sympathy, is often not the best judge.' That is the passage referred to in my parenthetic allusion, and it is a good general description of the manner in which George Eliot may be said to have acted on her generation; but the 'artistic mind', the possession of which it implies, existed in her with limitations remarkable in a writer whose imagination was so rich. We feel in her, always, that she proceeds from the abstract to the concrete; that her figures and situations are evolved, as the phrase is, from her moral consciousness, and are only indirectly the products of observation. They are deeply studied and massively supported, but they are not *seen*, in the irresponsible plastic way. The world was, first and foremost, for George Eliot, the moral, the intellectual world; the personal spectacle came after; and lovingly humanly as she regarded it we constantly feel that she cares for the things she finds in it only so far as they are types. The philosophic door is always open, on her stage, and we are aware that the somewhat cooling draught of ethical purpose draws across it. This constitutes half the beauty of her work; the constant reference to ideas may be an excellent source of one kind of reality – for, after all, the secret of seeing a thing well is not necessarily that you see nothing else. Her preoccupation with the universe helped to make her characters strike you as also belonging to it; it raised the roof, widened the area, of her aesthetic structure. Nothing is finer, in her genius, than the combination of her love of general truth and love of the special case; without this, indeed, we should not have heard of her as a novelist, for the passion of the special case is surely the basis of the story-teller's art. All the same, that little sign of all that Balzac failed to suggest to her showed at what perils the special case got itself considered. Such dangers increased as her activity proceeded, and many judges perhaps hold that in her ultimate work, in *Middlemarch* and *Daniel Deronda* (especially the latter), it ceased to be considered at all. Such critics assure us that Gwendolen and Grandcourt, Deronda and Myra, are not concrete images, but disembodied types, pale abstractions, signs and symbols of a 'great lesson'. I give up Deronda and Myra to the objector, but Grandcourt and Gwendolen seem to me to have a kind of superior reality; to be, in a high degree, what one demands of a figure in a novel, planted on their legs and complete.

28

❧

A Memoir of Ralph Waldo Emerson *by James Elliot Cabot,
1887,* Macmillan's Magazine, *December 1887. Emerson was a
favourite friend of the James family. Compare the account of
the 'thinness' of American civilization with that in* Hawthorne
(No. 21).

MR ELLIOT CABOT has made a very interesting contribution to a
class of books of which our literature, more than any other, offers
admirable examples: he has given us a biography intelligently and
carefully composed. These two volumes are a model of responsible
editing – I use that term because they consist largely of letters and
extracts from letters: nothing could resemble less the manner in
which the mere bookmaker strings together his frequently questionable pearls and shovels the heap into the presence of the public. Mr
Cabot has selected, compared, discriminated, steered an even course
between meagreness and redundancy, and managed to be constantly
and happily illustrative. And his work, moreover, strikes us as the
better done from the fact that it stands for one of the two things that
make an absorbing memoir a good deal more than for the other. If
these two things be the conscience of the writer and the career of his
hero, it is not difficult to see on which side the biographer of Emerson
has found himself strongest. Ralph Waldo Emerson was a man of
genius, but he led for nearly eighty years a life in which the sequence
of events had little of the rapidity, or the complexity, that a spectator
loves. There is something we miss very much as we turn these pages –
something that has a kind of accidental, inevitable presence in almost
any personal record – something that may be most definitely indicated under the name of colour. We lay down the book with a
singular impression of paleness – an impression that comes partly

from the tone of the biographer and partly from the moral complexion of his subject, but mainly from the vacancy of the page itself. That of Emerson's personal history is condensed into the single word Concord, and all the condensation in the world will not make it look rich. It presents a most continuous surface. Mr Matthew Arnold, in his *Discourses in America*, contests Emerson's complete right to the title of a man of letters; yet letters surely were the very texture of his history. Passions, alternations, affairs, adventures had absolutely no part in it. It stretched itself out in enviable quiet – a quiet in which we hear the jotting of the pencil in the notebook. It is the very life for literature (I mean for one's own, not that of another): fifty years of residence in the home of one's forefathers, pervaded by reading, by walking in the woods and the daily addition of sentence to sentence.

If the interest of Mr Cabot's pencilled portrait is incontestable and yet does not spring from variety, it owes nothing either to a source from which it might have borrowed much and which it is impossible not to regret a little that he has so completely neglected: I mean a greater reference to the social conditions in which Emerson moved, the company he lived in, the moral air he breathed. If his biographer had allowed himself a little more of the ironic touch, had put himself once in a way under the protection of Sainte-Beuve and had attempted something of a general picture, we should have felt that he only went with the occasion. I may over-estimate the latent treasures of the field, but it seems to me there was distinctly an opportunity – an opportunity to make up moreover in some degree for the white tint of Emerson's career considered simply in itself. We know a man imperfectly until we know his society, and we but half know a society until we know its manners. This is especially true of a man of letters, for manners lie very close to literature. From those of the New England world in which Emerson's character formed itself Mr Cabot almost averts his lantern, though we feel sure that there would have been delightful glimpses to be had and that he would have been in a position – that is that he has all the knowledge that would enable him – to help us to them. It is as if he could not trust himself, knowing the subject only too well. This adds to the effect of extreme discretion that we find in his volumes, but it is the cause of our not finding certain things, certain figures and scenes, evoked. What is evoked is Emerson's pure spirit, by a copious, sifted series of citations and comments. But we must read as much as possible between the lines, and the picture of the transcendental time (to mention simply one corner) has yet to be painted – the lines have yet to be bitten in. Meanwhile we are held and charmed by the image of Emerson's mind and the extreme appeal which his physiognomy makes to our art of discrimination. It is so fair, so uniform and impersonal, that its features are simply fine shades, the gradations of tone of a surface whose proper quality was of the smoothest and on which nothing was reflected with violence. It is a pleasure of the critical sense to find, with Mr Cabot's extremely intelligent help, a notation for such delicacies.

We seem to see the circumstances of our author's origin, immediate and remote, in a kind of high, vertical moral light, the brightness of a society at once very simple and very responsible. The rare singleness that was in his nature (so that he was *all* the warning moral voice, without distraction or counter-solicitation), was also in the stock he sprang from, clerical for generations, on both sides, and clerical in the Puritan sense. His ancestors had lived long (for nearly two centuries) in the same corner of New England, and during that period had preached and studied and prayed and practised. It is impossible to imagine a spirit better prepared in advance to be exactly what it was – better educated for its office in its far-away unconscious beginnings. There is an inner satisfaction in seeing so straight, although so patient, a connection between the stem and the flower, and such a proof that when life wishes to produce something exquisite in quality she takes her measures many years in advance. A conscience like Emerson's could not have been turned off, as it were, from one generation to another: a succession of attempts, a long process of refining, was required. His perfection, in his own line, comes largely from the non-interruption of the process.

As most of us are made up of ill-assorted pieces, his reader, and Mr Cabot's, envies him this transmitted unity, in which there was no mutual hustling or crowding of elements. It must have been a kind of luxury to be – that is to feel – so homogeneous, and it helps to account for his serenity, his power of acceptance, and that absence of personal passion which makes his private correspondence read like a series of beautiful circulars or expanded cards *pour prendre congé*. He had the equanimity of a result; nature had taken care of him and he had only to speak. He accepted himself as he accepted others, accepted everything; and his absence of eagerness, or in other words his modesty, was that of a man with whom it is not a question of success, who has nothing invested or at stake. The investment, the stake, was that of the race, of all the past Emersons and Bulkeleys and Waldos. There is much that makes us smile, to-day, in the commotion produced by his secession from the mild Unitarian pulpit: we wonder at a condition of opinion in which any utterance of his should appear to be wanting in superior piety – in the essence of good instruction. All that is changed: the great difference has become the infinitely small, and we admire a state of society in which scandal and schism took on no darker hue; but there is even yet a sort of drollery in the spectacle of a body of people among whom the author of *The American Scholar* and of the Address of 1838 at the Harvard Divinity College passed for profane, and who failed to see that he only gave his plea for the spiritual life the advantage of a brilliant expression. They were so provincial as to think that brilliancy came ill-recommended, and they were shocked at his ceasing to care for the prayer and the sermon. They might have perceived that he *was* the prayer and the sermon: not in the least a secularizer, but in his own subtle insinuating way a sanctifier.

Of the three periods into which his life divides itself, the first was (as in the case of most men) that of movement, experiment and selection – that of effort too and painful probation. Emerson had his message, but he was a good while looking for his form – the form which, as he himself would have said, he never completely found and of which it was rather characteristic of him that his later years (with their growing refusal to give him the *word*), wishing to attack him in his most vulnerable point, where his tenure was least complete, had in some degree the effect of despoiling him. It all sounds rather bare and stern, Mr Cabot's account of his youth and early manhood, and we get an impression of a terrible paucity of alternatives. If he would be neither a farmer nor a trader he could 'teach school'; that was the main resource and a part of the general educative process of the young New Englander who proposed to devote himself to the things of the mind. There was an advantage in the nudity, however, which was that, in Emerson's case at least, the things of the mind did get themselves admirably well considered. If it be his great distinction and his special sign that he had a more vivid conception of the moral life than any one else, it is probably not fanciful to say that he owed it in part to the limited way in which he saw our capacity for living illustrated. The plain, God-fearing, practical society which surrounded him was not fertile in variations: it had great intelligence and energy, but it moved altogether in the straightforward direction. On three occasions later – three journeys to Europe – he was introduced to a more complicated world; but his spirit, his moral taste, as it were, abode always within the undecorated walls of his youth. There he could dwell with that ripe unconsciousness of evil which is one of the most beautiful signs by which we know him. His early writings are full of quaint animadversion upon the vices of the place and time, but there is something charmingly vague, light and general in the arraignment. Almost the worst he can say is that these vices are negative and that his fellow-townsmen are not heroic. We feel that his first impressions were gathered in a community from which misery and extravagance, and either extreme, of any sort, were equally absent. What the life of New England fifty years ago offered to the observer was the common lot, in a kind of achromatic picture, without particular intensifications. It was from this table of the usual, the merely typical joys and sorrows that he proceeded to generalize – a fact that accounts in some degree for a certain inadequacy and thinness in his enumerations. But it helps to account also for his direct, intimate vision of the soul itself – not in its emotions, its contortions and perversions, but in its passive, exposed, yet healthy form. He knows the nature of man and the long tradition of its dangers; but we feel that whereas he can put his finger on the remedies, lying for the most part, as they do, in the deep recesses of virtue, of the spirit, he has only a kind of hearsay, uninformed acquaintance with the disorders. It would require some ingenuity, the reader may say too much, to trace closely this correspondence between his genius and the frugal, dutiful, happy but decidedly lean Boston of the past, where there was a great deal of will but very little fulcrum – like a ministry without an opposition.

The genius itself it seems to me impossible to contest – I mean the genius for seeing character as a real and supreme thing. Other writers have arrived at a more complete expression: Wordsworth and Goethe, for instance, give one a sense of having found their form, whereas with Emerson we never lose the sense that he is still seeking it. But no one has had so steady and constant, and above all so natural, a vision of what we require and what we are capable of in the way of aspiration and independence. With Emerson it is ever the special capacity for moral experience – always that and only that. We have the impression, somehow, that life had never bribed him to look at anything but the soul; and indeed in the world in which he grew up and lived the bribes and lures, the beguilements and prizes, were few. He was in an admirable position for showing, what he constantly endeavoured to show, that the prize was within. Any one who in New England at that time could do that was sure of success, of listeners and sympathy: most of all, of course, when it was a question of doing it with such a divine persuasiveness. Moreover, the way in which Emerson did it added to the charm – by word of mouth, face to face, with a rare, irresistible voice and a beautiful mild, modest authority. If Mr Arnold is struck with the limited degree in which he was a man of letters I suppose it is because he is more struck with his having been, as it were, a man of lectures. But the lecture surely was never more purged of its grossness – the quality in it that suggests strong light and a big brush – than as it issued from Emerson's lips; so far from being a vulgarization, it was simply the esoteric made audible, and instead of treating the few as the many, after the usual fashion of gentlemen on platforms, he treated the many as the few. There was probably no other society at that time in which he would have got so many persons to understand that; for we think the better of his audience as we read him, and wonder where else people would have had so much moral attention to give. It is to be remembered however that during the winter of 1847–48, on the occasion of his second visit to England, he found many listeners in London and in provincial cities. Mr Cabot's volumes are full of evidence of the satisfactions he offered, the delights and revelations he may be said to have promised, to a race which had to seek its entertainment, its rewards and consolations, almost exclusively in the moral world. But his own writings are fuller still; we find an instance almost wherever we open them.

'All these great and transcendent properties are ours . . . Let us find room for this great guest in our small houses . . . Where the heart is, there the muses, there the gods sojourn, and not in any geography of fame. Massachusetts,

Connecticut River, and Boston Bay, you think paltry places, and the ear loves names of foreign and classic topography. But here we are, and if we will tarry a little we may come to learn that here is best . . . The Jerseys were handsome enough ground for Washington to tread, and London streets for the feet of Milton . . . That country is fairest which is inhabited by the noblest minds.'

We feel, or suspect, that Milton is thrown in as a hint that the London streets are no such great place, and it all sounds like a sort of pleading consolation against bleakness.

The beauty of a hundred passages of this kind in Emerson's pages is that they are effective, that they do come home, that they rest upon insight and not upon ingenuity, and that if they are sometimes obscure it is never with the obscurity of paradox. We seem to see the people turning out into the snow after hearing them, glowing with a finer glow than even the climate could give and fortified for a struggle with overshoes and the east wind.

'Look to it first and only, that fashion, custom, authority, pleasure, and money, are nothing to you, are not as bandages over your eyes, that you cannot see; but live with the privilege of the immeasurable mind. Not too anxious to visit periodically all families and each family in your parish connection, when you meet one of these men or women be to them a divine man; be to them thought and virtue; let their timid aspirations find in you a friend; let their trampled instincts be genially tempted out in your atmosphere; let their doubts know that you have doubted, and their wonder feel that you have wondered.'

When we set against an exquisite passage like that, or like the familiar sentences that open the essay on History ('He that is admitted to the right of reason is made freeman of the whole estate. What Plato has thought, he may think; what a saint has felt, he may feel; what at any time has befallen any man, he can understand'); when we compare the letters, cited by Mr Cabot, to his wife from Springfield, Illinois (January 1853) we feel that his spiritual tact needed to be very just, but that if it was so it must have brought a blessing.

'Here I am in the deep mud of the prairies, misled I fear into this bog, not by a will-of-the-wisp, such as shine in bogs, but by a young New Hampshire editor, who overestimated the strength of both of us, and fancied I should glitter in the prairie and draw the prairie birds and waders. It rains and thaws incessantly, and if we step off the short street we go up to the shoulders, perhaps, in mud. My chamber is a cabin; my fellow-boarders are legislators . . . Two or three governors or ex-governors live in the house . . . I cannot command daylight and solitude for study or for more than a scrawl.'

And another extract:

'A cold, raw country this, and plenty of night-travelling and arriving at four in the morning to take the last and worst bed in the tavern. Advancing day brings mercy and favour to me, but not the sleep . . . Mercury 15° below zero . . . I find well-disposed, kindly people among these sinewy farmers of the North, but in all that is called cultivation they are only ten years old.'

He says in another letter (in 1860), 'I saw Michigan and its forests and the Wolverines pretty thoroughly'; and on another page Mr Cabot shows him as speaking of his engagements to lecture in the West as the obligation to 'wade, and freeze, and ride, and run, and suffer all manner of indignities'. This was not New England, but as regards the country districts throughout, at that time, it was a question of degree. Certainly never was the fine wine of philosophy carried to remoter or queerer corners: never was a more delicate diet offered to 'two or three governors, or ex-governors', living in a cabin. It was Mercury, shivering in a mackintosh, bearing nectar and ambrosia to the gods whom he wished those who lived in cabins to endeavour to feel that they might be.

I have hinted that the will, in the old New England society, was a clue without a labyrinth; but it had its use, nevertheless, in helping the young talent to find its mould. There were few or none ready-made: tradition was certainly not so oppressive as might have been inferred from the fact that the air swarmed with reformers and improvers. Of the patient, philosophic manner in which Emerson groped and waited, through teaching the young and preaching to the adult, for his particular vocation, Mr Cabot's first volume gives a full and orderly account. His passage from the Unitarian pulpit to the lecture-desk was a step which at this distance of time can hardly help appearing to us short, though he was long in making it, for even after ceasing to have a parish of his own he freely confounded the two, or willingly, at least, treated the pulpit as a platform. 'The young people and the mature hint at odium and the aversion of faces, to be presently encountered in society,' he writes in his journal in 1838; but in point of fact the quiet drama of his abdication was not to include the note of suffering. The Boston world might feel disapproval, but it was far too kindly to make this sentiment felt as a weight: every element of martyrdom was there but the important ones of the cause and the persecutors. Mr Cabot marks the lightness of the penalties of dissent; if they were light in somewhat later years for the transcendentalists and fruit-eaters they could press but little on a man of Emerson's distinction, to whom, all his life, people went not to carry but to ask the right word. There was no consideration to give up, he could not have been one of the dingy if he had tried; but what he did renounce in 1838 was a material profession. He was 'settled', and his indisposition to administer the communion unsettled him. He calls the whole business, in writing to Carlyle, 'a tempest in our washbowl'; but it had the effect of forcing him to seek a new source of income. His wants were few and his view of life severe, and this came to him, little by little, as he was able to extend the field in which he read his discourses. In 1835, upon his second marriage, he took up his habitation at Concord, and his life fell into the shape it was, in a general way, to keep for the next half-century. It is here that we cannot help regretting that Mr Cabot had not found it possible to treat his career a little more pictorially. Those fifty years of Concord – at least the earlier part of them – would have been a subject bringing into play many odd figures, many human incongruities: they would have abounded in illustrations of the primitive New England character, especially during the time of its queer search for something to expend itself upon. Objects and occupations have multiplied since then, and now there is no lack; but fifty years ago the expanse was wide and free, and we get the impression of a conscience gasping in the void, panting for sensations, with something of the movement of the gills of a landed fish. It would take a very fine point to sketch Emerson's benignant, patient, inscrutable countenance during the various phases of this democratic communion; but the picture, when complete, would be one of the portraits, half a revelation and half an enigma, that suggest and fascinate. Such a striking personage as old Miss Mary Emerson, our author's aunt, whose high intelligence and temper were much of an influence in his earlier years, has a kind of tormenting representative value: we want to see her from head to foot, with her frame and her background; having (for we happen to have it), an impression that she was a very remarkable specimen of the transatlantic Puritan stock, a spirit that would have dared the devil. We miss a more liberal handling, are tempted to add touches of our own, and end by convincing ourselves that Miss Mary Moody Emerson, grim intellectual virgin and daughter of a hundred ministers, with her local traditions and her combined love of empire and of speculation, would have been an inspiration for a novelist. Hardly less so the charming Mrs Ripley, Emerson's life-long friend and neighbour, most delicate and accomplished of women, devoted to Greek and to her house, studious, simple and dainty – an admirable example of the old-fashioned New England lady. It was a freak of Miss Emerson's somewhat sardonic humour to give her once a broom-stick to carry across Boston Common (under the pretext of a 'moving'), a task accepted with docility but making of the victim the most benignant witch ever equipped with that utensil.

These ladies, however, were very private persons and not in the least of the reforming tribe: there are others who would have peopled Mr Cabot's page to whom he gives no more than a mention. We must add that it is open to him to say that their features have become faint and indistinguishable to-day without more research than the question is apt to be worth: they are embalmed – in a collective way – the apprehensible part of them, in Mr Frothingham's clever *History of Transcendentalism in New England*. This must be admitted to be true of even so lively a 'factor', as we say nowadays, as the imaginative, talkative, intelligent and finally Italianized and ship-wrecked Margaret Fuller: she is now one of the dim, one of Carlyle's 'then-celebrated' at most. It seemed indeed as if Mr Cabot rather grudged her a due place in the record of the company that Emerson kept, until we came across the delightful letter he quotes toward the end of his first volume – a letter interesting both as a specimen of inimitable, imperceptible edging away, and as an illustration of the curiously generalized way, as if with an implicit protest against personalities, in which his intercourse, epistolary and other, with his friends was conducted. There is an extract from a letter to his aunt on the occasion of the death of a deeply-loved brother (his own) which reads like a passage from some fine old chastened essay on the vanity of earthly hopes: strangely unfamiliar, considering the circumstances. Courteous and humane to the furthest possible point, to the point of an almost profligate surrender of his attention, there was no familiarity in him, no personal avidity. Even his letters to his wife are courtesies, they are not familiarities. He had only one style, one manner, and he had it for everything – even for himself, in his notes, in his journals. But he had it in perfection for Miss Fuller; he retreats, smiling and flattering, on tiptoe, as if he were advancing. 'She ever seems to crave,' he says in his journal, 'something which I have not, or have not for her.' What he had was doubtless not what she craved, but the letter in question should be read to see how the modicum was administered. It is only between the lines of such a production that we read that a part of her effect upon him was to bore him; for his system was to practise a kind of universal passive hospitality – he aimed at nothing less. It was only because he was so deferential that he could be so detached; he had polished his aloofness till it reflected the image of his solicitor. And this was not because he was an 'uncommunicating egotist', though he amuses himself with saying so to Miss Fuller: egotism is the strongest of passions, and he was altogether passionless. It was because he had no personal, just as he had almost no physical wants. 'Yet I plead not guilty to the malice prepense. 'Tis imbecility, not contumacy, though perhaps somewhat more odious. It seems very just, the irony with which you ask whether you may not be trusted and promise such docility. Alas, we will all promise, but the prophet loiters.' He would not say even to himself that she bored him; he had denied himself the luxury of such easy and obvious short cuts. There is a passage in the lecture (1844) called 'Man the Reformer', in which he hovers round and round the idea that the practice of trade, in certain conditions likely to beget an underhand competition, does not draw forth the nobler parts of character, till the reader is tempted to interrupt him with, 'Say at once that it is impossible for a gentleman!'

So he remained always, reading his lectures in the winter, writing them in the summer, and at all seasons taking wood-walks and looking for hints in old books.

'Delicious summer stroll through the pastures ... On the steep park of Conantum I have the old regret – is all this beauty to perish? Shall none re-make this sun and wind; the sky-blue river; the river-blue sky; the yellow meadow, spotted with sacks and sheets of cranberry-gatherers; the red bushes; the iron-gray house, just the colour of the granite rocks; the wild orchard?'

His observation of Nature was exquisite – always the direct, irresistible impression.

'The hawking of the wild geese flying by night; the thin note of the companionable titmouse in the winter day; the fall of swarms of flies in autumn, from combats high in the air, pattering down on the leaves like rain; the angry hiss of the wood-birds; the pine throwing out its pollen for the benefit of the next century.' (*Literary Ethics.*)

I have said there was no familiarity in him, but he was familiar with woodland creatures and sounds. Certainly, too, he was on terms of free association with his books, which were numerous and dear to him; though Mr Cabot says, doubtless with justice, that his dependence on them was slight and that he was not 'intimate' with his authors. They did not feed him but they stimulated; they were not his meat but his wine – he took them in sips. But he needed them and liked them; he had volumes of notes from his reading, and he could not have produced his lectures without them. He liked literature as a thing to refer to, liked the very names of which it is full, and used them, especially in his later writings, for purposes of ornament, to dress the dish, sometimes with an unmeasured profusion. I open *The Conduct of Life* and find a dozen on the page. He mentions more authorities than is the fashion to-day. He can easily say, of course, that he follows a better one – that of his well-loved and irrepressibly allusive Montaigne. In his own bookishness there is a certain contradiction, just as there is a latent incompleteness in his whole literary side. Independence, the return to nature, the finding out and doing for one's self, was ever what he most highly recommended; and yet he is constantly reminding his readers of the conventional signs and consecrations – of what other men have done. This was partly because the independence that he had in his eye was an independence without ill-nature, without rudeness (though he likes that word), and full of gentle amiabilities, curiosities and tolerances; and partly it is a simple matter of form, a literary expedient, confessing its character – on the part of one who had never really mastered the art of composition – of continuous expression. Charming to many a reader, charming yet ever slightly droll, will remain Emerson's frequent invocation of the 'scholar': there is such a friendly vagueness and convenience in it. It is of the scholar that he expects all the heroic and uncomfortable things, the concentrations and relinquishments, that make up the noble life. We fancy this personage looking up from his book and arm-chair a little ruefully and saying, 'Ah, but why *me* always and only? Why so much of me, and is there no one else to share the responsibility?' 'Neither years nor books have yet availed to extirpate a prejudice then rooted in me [when as a boy he first saw the graduates of his college assembled at their anniversary], that a scholar is the favourite of heaven and earth, the excellency of his country, the happiest of men.'

In truth, by this term he means simply the cultivated man, the man who has had a liberal education, and there is a voluntary plainness in his use of it – speaking of such people as the rustic, or the vulgar, speak of those who have a tincture of books. This is characteristic of his humility – that humility which was nine-tenths a plain fact (for it is easy for persons who have at bottom a great fund of indifference to be humble), and the remaining tenth a literary habit. Moreover an American reader may be excused for finding in it a pleasant sign of that prestige, often so quaintly and indeed so extravagantly acknowledged, which a connection with literature carries with it among the people of the United States. There is no country in which it is more freely admitted to be a distinction – *the* distinction; or in which so many persons have become eminent for showing it even in a slight degree. Gentlemen and ladies are celebrated there on this ground who would not on the same ground, though they might on another, be celebrated anywhere else. Emerson's own tone is an echo of that, when he speaks of the scholar – not of the banker, the great merchant, the legislator, the artist – as the most distinguished figure in the society about him. It is because he has most to give up that he is appealed to for efforts and sacrifices. 'Meantime I know that a very different estimate of the scholar's profession prevails in this country,' he goes on to say in the address from which I last quoted (the *Literary Ethics*), 'and the importunity with which society presses its claim upon young men tends to pervert the views of the youth in respect to the culture of the intellect.' The manner in which that is said represents, surely, a serious mistake: with the estimate of the scholar's profession which then prevailed in New England Emerson could have had no quarrel; the ground of his lamentation was another side of the matter. It was not a question of estimate, but of accidental practice. In 1838 there were still so many things of prime material necessity to be done that reading was driven to the wall; but the reader was still thought the cleverest, for he found time as well as intelligence. Emerson's own situation sufficiently indicates it. In what other country, on sleety winter nights, would provincial and bucolic populations have gone forth in hundreds for the cold comfort of a literary discourse? The distillation anywhere else would certainly have appeared too thin, the appeal too special. But for many years the American people of the middle regions, outside of a few cities, had in the most rigorous seasons no other recreation. A gentleman, grave or gay, in a bare room, with a manuscript, before a desk, offered the reward of toil, the refreshment of pleasure, to the young, the middle-aged and the old of both sexes. The hour was brightest, doubtless, when the gentleman was gay, like Doctor Oliver Wendell Holmes. But Emerson's gravity never sapped his career, any more than it chilled the regard in which he was held among those who were particularly his own people. It was impossible to be more honoured and cherished, far and near, than he was during his long residence in Concord, or more looked upon as the principal gentleman in the place. This was conspicuous to the writer of these remarks on the occasion of the curious, sociable, cheerful public funeral made for him in 1883 by all the countryside, arriving, as for the last honours to the first citizen, in trains, in waggons, on foot, in multitudes. It was a popular manifestation, the most striking I have ever seen provoked by the death of a man of letters.

If a picture of that singular and very illustrative institution the old American lecture-system would have constituted a part of the filling-in of the ideal memoir of Emerson, I may further say, returning to the matter for a moment, that such a memoir would also have had a chapter for some of those Concord-haunting figures which are not so much interesting in themselves as interesting because for a season Emerson thought them so. And the pleasure of that would be partly that it would push us to inquire how interesting he did really think them. That is, it would bring up the question of his inner reserves and scepticisms, his secret ennuis and ironies, the way he sympathized for courtesy and then, with his delicacy and generosity, in a world after all given much to the literal, let his courtesy pass for adhesion – a question particularly attractive to those for whom he has, in general, a fascination. Many entertaining problems of that sort present themselves for such readers: there is something indefinable for them in the mixture of which he was made – his fidelity as an interpreter of the so-called transcendental spirit and his freedom from all wish for any personal share in the effect of his ideas. He drops them, sheds them, diffuses them, and we feel as if there would be a grossness in holding him to anything so temporal as a responsibility. He had the advantage, for many years, of having the question of application assumed for him by Thoreau, who took upon himself to be, in the concrete, the sort of person that Emerson's 'scholar' was in the abstract, and who paid for it by having a shorter life than that fine adumbration. The application, with Thoreau, was violent and limited (it became a matter of prosaic detail, the non-payment of taxes, the non-wearing of a necktie, the preparation of one's food one's self, the practice of a rude sincerity – all things not of the essence), so that, though he wrote some beautiful pages, which read like a translation of Emerson into the sounds of the field and forest and which no one who has ever loved nature in New England, or indeed anywhere, can fail to love, he suffers something of the *amoindrissement* of eccentricity. His master escapes that reduction altogether. I call it an advantage to have had such a pupil as Thoreau; because for a mind so much made up of reflection as Emerson's everything comes under that head which prolongs and reanimates the process – produces the return, again and yet again, on one's impressions. Thoreau must have had this moderating and even chastening effect. It did not rest, moreover, with him alone; the advantage of which I speak was not confined to Thoreau's case. In 1837 Emerson (in his journal) pronounced Mr Bronson Alcott the most extraordinary man and the highest genius of his time: the sequence of which was that for more than forty years after that he had the gentleman living but half a mile away. The opportunity for the return, as I have called it, was not wanting.

His detachment is shown in his whole attitude toward the transcendental movement – that remarkable outburst of Romanticism on Puritan ground, as Mr Cabot very well names it. Nothing can be more ingenious, more sympathetic and charming, than Emerson's account and definition of the matter in his lecture (of 1842) called 'The Transcendentalist'; and yet nothing is more apparent from his letters and journals than that he regarded any such label or banner as a mere tiresome flutter. He liked to taste but not to drink – least of all to become intoxicated. He liked to explain the transcendentalists but did not care at all to be explained by them: a doctrine 'whereof you know I am wholly guiltless,' he says to his wife in 1842, 'and which is spoken of as a known and fixed element, like salt or meal. So that I have to begin with endless disclaimers and explanations: "I am not the man you take me for."' He was never the man any one took him for, for the simple reason that no one could possibly take him for the elusive, irreducible, merely gustatory spirit for which he took himself.

'It is a sort of maxim with me never to harp on the omnipotence of limitations. Least of all do we need any suggestion of checks and measures; as if New England were anything else . . . Of so many fine people it is true that being so much they ought to be a little more, and missing that are naught. It is a sort of King Renè period; there is no doing, but rare thrilling prophecy from bands of competing minstrels.'

That is his private expression about a large part of a ferment in regard to which his public judgment was that

'That indeed constitutes a new feature in their portrait, that they are the most exacting and extortionate critics . . . These exacting children advertise us of our wants. There is no compliment, no smooth speech with them; they pay you only this one compliment of insatiable expectation; they aspire, they severely exact, and if they only stand fast in this watch-tower, and stand fast unto the end, and without end, then they are terrible friends, whereof poet and priest cannot but stand in awe; and what if they eat clouds and drink wind, they have not been without service to the race of man.'

That was saying the best for them, as he always said it for everything; but it was the sense of their being 'bands of competing minstrels' and their camp being only a 'measure and check', in a society too sparse for a synthesis, that kept him from wishing to don their uniform. This was after all but a misfitting imitation of his natural wear, and what he would have liked was to put that off – he did not wish to button it tighter. He said the best for his friends of the Dial, of Fruitlands and Brook Farm, in saying that they were fastidious and critical; but he was conscious in the next breath that what there was around them to be criticized was mainly a negative. Nothing is more perceptible to-day than that their criticism produced no fruit – that it was little else than a very decent and innocent recreation – a kind of Puritan carnival. The New England world was for much the most part very busy, but the Dial and Fruitlands and Brook Farm were the amusement of the leisure-class. Extremes meet, and as in older societies that class is known principally by its connection with castles and carriages, so at Concord it came, with Thoreau and Mr W. H. Channing, out of the cabin and the wood-lot.

Emerson was not moved to believe in their fastidiousness as a productive principle even when they directed it upon abuses which he abundantly recognized. Mr Cabot shows that he was by no means one of the professional abolitionists or philanthropists – never an enrolled 'humanitarian'.

'We talk frigidly of Reform until the walls mock us. It is that of which a man should never speak, but if he have cherished it in his bosom he should steal to it in darkness, as an Indian to his bride . . . Does he not do more to abolish slavery who works all day steadily in his own garden, than he who goes to the abolition meeting and makes a speech? He who does his own work frees a slave.'

I must add that even while I transcribe these words there comes to me the recollection of the great meeting in the Boston Music Hall, on the first day of 1863, to celebrate the signing by Mr Lincoln of the proclamation freeing the Southern slaves – of the momentousness of the occasion, the vast excited multitude, the crowded platform and the tall, spare figure of Emerson, in the midst, reading out the stanzas that were published under the name of the Boston Hymn. They are not the happiest he produced for an occasion – they do not compare with the verses on the 'embattled farmers', read at Concord in 1857, and there is a certain awkwardness in some of them. But I well remember the immense effect with which his beautiful voice pronounced the lines –

'Pay ransom to the owner
And fill the bag to the brim.
Who is the owner? The slave is owner,
And ever was. Pay *him*!'

And Mr Cabot chronicles the fact that the *gran' rifiuto* – the great backsliding of Mr Webster when he cast his vote in Congress for the Fugitive Slave Law of 1850 – was the one thing that ever moved him to heated denunciation. He felt Webster's apostasy as strongly as he had admired his genius. 'Who has not helped to praise him? Simply he was the one American of our time whom we could produce as a finished work of nature.' There is a passage in his journal (not a rough jotting, but, like most of the entries in it, a finished piece of writing), which is admirably descriptive of the wonderful orator and is moreover one of the very few portraits, or even personal sketches, yielded by Mr Cabot's selections. It shows that he could observe the human figure and 'render' it to good purpose.

'His splendid wrath, when his eyes become fire, is good to see, so intellectual it is – the wrath of the fact and the cause he espouses, and not at all personal to himself . . . These village parties must be dish-water to him, yet he shows himself just good-natured, just nonchalant enough; and he has his own way, without offending any one or losing any ground . . . His expensiveness seems necessary to him; were he too prudent a Yankee it would be a sad deduction from his magnificence. I only wish he would not truckle [to the slave-holders]. I do not care how much he spends.'

I doubtless appear to have said more than enough, yet I have passed by many of the passages I had marked for transcription from Mr Cabot's volumes. There is one, in the first, that makes us stare as we come upon it, to the effect that Emerson 'could see nothing in Shelley, Aristophanes, Don Quixote, Miss Austen, Dickens'. Mr Cabot adds that he rarely read a novel, even the famous ones (he has a point of contact here as well as, strangely enough, on two or three other sides with that distinguished moralist M. Ernest Renan, who, like Emerson, was originally a dissident priest and cannot imagine why people should write works of fiction); and thought Dante 'a man to put into a museum, but not into your house; another Zerah Colburn; a prodigy of imaginative function, executive rather than contemplative or wise'. The confession of an insensibility ranging from Shelley to Dickens and from Dante to Miss Austen and taking Don Quixote and Aristophanes on the way, is a large allowance to have to make for a man of letters, and may appear to confirm but slightly any claim of intellectual hospitality and general curiosity put forth for him. The truth was that, sparely constructed as he was and formed not wastefully, not with material left over, as it were, for a special function, there were certain chords in Emerson that did not vibrate at all. I well remember my impression of this on walking with him in the autumn of 1872 through the galleries of the Louvre and, later that winter, through those of the Vatican: his perception of the objects contained in these collections was of the most general order. I was struck with the anomaly of a man so refined and intelligent being so little spoken to by works of art. It would be more exact to say that certain chords were wholly absent; the tune was played, the tune of life and literature, altogether on those that remained. They had every wish to be equal to their office, but one feels that the number was short – that some notes could not be given. Mr Cabot makes use of a singular phrase when he says, in speaking of Hawthorne, for several years our author's neighbour at Concord and a little – a very little we gather – his companion, that Emerson was unable to read his novels – he thought them 'not worthy of him'. This is a judgment odd almost to fascination – we circle round it and turn it over and over; it contains so elusive an ambiguity. How highly he must have esteemed the man of whose genius *The House of the Seven Gables* and *The Scarlet Letter* gave imperfectly the measure, and how strange that he should not have been eager to read almost anything that such a gifted being might have let fall! It was a rare accident that made them live almost side by side so long in the same small New England town, each a fruit of a long Puritan stem, yet with such a difference of taste. Hawthorne's vision was all for the evil and sin of the world; a side of life as to which Emerson's eyes were thickly bandaged. There were points as to which the latter's conception of right could be violated, but he had no great sense of wrong – a strangely limited one, indeed, for a moralist – no sense of the dark, the foul, the base. There were certain complications in life which he never suspected. One asks one's self whether that is why he did not care for Dante and Shelley and Aristophanes and Dickens, their works containing a considerable reflection of human perversity. But that still leaves the indifference to Cervantes and Miss Austen unaccounted for.

It has not, however, been the ambition of these remarks to account for everything, and I have arrived at the end without even pointing to the grounds on which Emerson justifies the honours of biography, discussion and illustration. I have assumed his importance and continuance, and shall probably not be gainsaid by those who read him. Those who do not will hardly rub him out. Such a book as Mr Cabot's subjects a reputation to a test – leads people to look it over and hold it up to the light, to see whether it is worth keeping in use or even putting away in a cabinet. Such a revision of Emerson has no relegating consequences. The result of it is once more the impression that he serves and will not wear out, and that indeed we cannot afford to drop him. His instrument makes him precious. He did something better than any one else; he had a particular faculty, which has not been surpassed, for speaking to the soul in a voice of direction and authority. There have been many spiritual voices appealing, consoling, reassuring, exhorting, or even denouncing and terrifying, but none has had just that firmness and just that purity. It penetrates further, it seems to go back to the roots of our feelings, to where conduct and manhood begin; and moreover, to us to-day, there is something in it that says that it is connected somehow with the virtue of the world, has wrought and achieved, lived in thousands of minds, produced a mass of character and life. And there is this further sign of Emerson's singular power, that he is a striking exception to the general rule that writings live in the last resort by their form; that they owe a large part of their fortune to the art with which they have been composed. It is hardly too much, or too little, to say of Emerson's writings in general that they were not composed at all. Many and many things are beautifully said; he had felicities, inspirations, unforgettable phrases; he had frequently an exquisite eloquence.

'O my friends, there are resources in us on which we have not yet drawn. There are men who rise refreshed on hearing a threat; men to whom a crisis which intimidates and paralyses the majority – demanding not the faculties of prudence and thrift, but comprehension, immovableness, the readiness of sacrifice, come graceful and beloved as a bride . . . But these are heights that we can scarce look up to and remember without contrition and shame. Let us thank God that such things exist.'

None the less we have the impression that that search for a fashion and a manner on which he was always engaged never really came to a conclusion; it draws itself out through his later writings – it drew itself out through his later lectures, like a sort of renunciation of success. It is not on these, however, but on their predecessors, that his reputation will rest. Of course the way he spoke was the way that was on the whole most convenient to him; but he differs from most men of letters of the same degree of credit in failing to strike us as having achieved a style. This achievement is, as I say, usually the bribe or toll-money on the journey to posterity; and if Emerson goes his way, as he clearly appears to be doing, on the strength of his message alone, the case will be rare, the exception striking, and the honour great.

29

❧

'*Guy de Maupassant*', Fortnightly Review, *March 1888. In private James had referred to the 'gifted and lascivious Guy' as 'a cad – of genius' (HJL, vol. 3, 91). As to 'the unspeakable [Rider] Haggard', his 'vulgarly brutal' novels 'seem to me works in which our race and age make a very vile figure' (HJL, vol. 3, 128).*

I

THE FIRST artists, in any line, are doubtless not those whose general ideas about their art are most often on their lips – those who most abound in precept, apology, and formula and can best tell us the reasons and the philosophy of things. We know the first usually by their energetic practice, the constancy with which they apply their principles, and the serenity with which they leave us to hunt for their secret in the illustration, the concrete example. None the less it often happens that a valid artist utters his mystery, flashes upon us for a moment the light by which he works, shows us the rule by which he holds it just that he should be measured. This accident is happiest, I think, when it is soonest over; the shortest explanations of the products of genius are the best, and there is many a creator of living figures whose friends, however full of faith in his inspiration, will do well to pray for him when he sallies forth into the dim wilderness of theory. The doctrine is apt to be so much less inspired than the work, the work is often so much more intelligent than the doctrine. M. Guy de Maupassant has lately traversed with a firm and rapid step a literary crisis of this kind; he has clambered safely up the bank at the further end of the morass. If he has relieved himself in the preface to *Pierre et Jean*, the last-published of his tales, he has also rendered a service to his friends; he has not only come home in a recognizable plight, escaping gross disaster with a success which even his extreme good sense was far from making in advance a matter of course, but he has expressed in intelligible terms (that by itself is a ground of felicitation) his most general idea, his own sense of his direction. He has arranged, as it were, the light in which he wishes to sit. If it is a question of attempting, under however many disadvantages, a sketch of him, the critic's business therefore is simplified: there will be no difficulty in placing him, for he himself has chosen the spot, he has made the chalk-mark on the floor.

I may as well say at once that in dissertation M. de Maupassant does not write with his best pen; the philosopher in his composition is perceptibly inferior to the story-teller. I would rather have written half a page of *Boule de Suif* than the whole of the introduction to Flaubert's *Letters to Madame Sand*; and his little disquisition on the novel in general, attached to that particular example of it which he has just put forth, is considerably less to the point than the master-piece which it ushers in. In short, as a commentator M. de Maupassant is slightly common, while as an artist he is wonderfully rare. Of course we must, in judging a writer, take one thing with another, and if I could make up my mind that M. de Maupassant is weak in theory, it would almost make me like him better, render him more approach-able, give him the touch of softness that he lacks, and show us a human flaw. The most general quality of the author of *La Maison Tellier* and *Bel-Ami*, the impression that remains last, after the others have been accounted for, is an essential hardness—hardness of form, hardness of nature; and it would put us more at ease to find that if the fact with him (the fact of execution) is so extraordinarily definite and adequate, his explanations, after it, were a little vague and sen-timental. But I am not sure that he must even be held foolish to have noticed the race of critics: he is at any rate so much less foolish than several of that fraternity. He has said his say concisely and as if he were saying it once for all. In fine, his readers must be grateful to him for such a passage as that in which he remarks that whereas the public at large very legitimately says to a writer, 'Console me, amuse me, terrify me, make me cry, make me dream, or make me think,' what the sincere critic says is, 'Make me something fine in the form that shall suit you best, according to your temperament.' This seems to me to put into a nutshell the whole question of the different classes of fiction, concerning which there has recently been so much discourse. There are simply as many different kinds as there are persons practising the art, for if a picture, a tale, or a novel be a direct impression of life (and that surely constitutes its interest and value), the impression will vary according to the plate that takes it, the particular structure and mixture of the recipient.

I am not sure that I know what M. de Maupassant means when he says, 'The critic shall appreciate the result only according to the nature of the effort; he has no right to concern himself with tendencies.' The second clause of that observation strikes me as rather in the air, thanks to the vagueness of the last word. But our author adds to the definiteness of his contention when he goes on to say that any form of the novel is simply a vision of the world from the standpoint of a person constituted after a certain fashion, and that it is therefore absurd to say that there is, for the novelist's use, only one reality of things. This seems to me commendable, not as a flight of metaphysics, hovering over bottomless gulfs of controversy, but, on the contrary, as a just indication of the vanity of certain dogmatisms. The particular way we see the world is our particular illusion about it, says M. de Maupassant, and this illusion fits itself to our organs and senses; our receptive vessel becomes the furniture of *our* little plot of the universal consciousness.

'How childish, moreover, to believe in reality, since we each carry our own in our thought and in our organs. Our eyes, our ears, our sense of smell, of taste, differing from one person to another, create as many truths as there are men upon earth. And our minds, taking instruction from these organs, so diversely impressed, understand, analyse, judge, as if each of us belonged to a different race. Each one of us, therefore, forms for himself an illusion of the world, which is the illusion poetic, or sentimental, or joyous, or melancholy, or unclean, or dismal, according to his nature. And the writer has no other mission than to reproduce faithfully this illusion, with all the contrivances of art that he has learned and has at his command. The illusion of beauty, which is a human convention! The illusion of ugliness, which is a changing opinion! The illusion of truth, which is never immutable! The illusion of the ignoble, which attracts so many! The great artists are those who make humanity accept their particular illusion. Let us, therefore, not get angry with any one theory, since every theory is the generalized expression of a temperament asking itself questions.'

What is interesting in this is not that M. de Maupassant happens to hold that we have no universal measure of the truth, but that it is the last word on a question of art from a writer who is rich in experience and has had success in a very rare degree. It is of secondary importance that our impression should be called, or not called, an illusion; what is excellent is that our author has stated more neatly than we have lately seen it done that the value of the artist resides in the clearness with which he gives forth that impression. His particular organism constitutes a *case*, and the critic is intelligent in proportion as he apprehends and enters into that case. To quarrel with it because it is not another, which it could not possibly have been without a wholly different outfit, appears to M. de Maupassant a deplorable waste of time. If this appeal to our disinterestedness may strike some readers as chilling (through their inability to conceive of any other form than the one they like – a limitation excellent for a reader but poor for a judge), the occasion happens to be none of the best for saying so, for M. de Maupassant himself precisely presents all the symptoms of a 'case' in the most striking way, and shows us how far the consideration of them may take us. Embracing such an opportunity as this, and giving ourselves to it freely, seems to me indeed to be a course more fruitful in valid conclusions, as well as in entertainment by the way, than the more common method of establishing one's own premises. To make clear to ourselves those of the author of *Pierre et Jean* – those to which he is committed by the very nature of his mind – is an attempt that will both stimulate and repay curiosity. There is no way of looking at his work less dry, less academic, for as we proceed from one of his peculiarities to another, the whole horizon widens, yet without our leaving firm ground, and we see ourselves landed, step by step, in the most general questions – those explanations of things which reside in the race, in the society. Of course there are cases and cases, and it is the salient ones that the disinterested critic is delighted to meet.

What makes M. de Maupassant salient is two facts: the first of which is that his gifts are remarkably strong and definite, and the second that he writes directly *from* them, as it were: holds the fullest, the most uninterrupted – I scarcely know what to call it – the boldest communication with them. A case is poor when the cluster of the artist's sensibilities is small, or they themselves are wanting in keenness, or else when the personage fails to admit them – either through ignorance, or diffidence, or stupidity, or the error of a false ideal – to what may be called a legitimate share in his attempt. It is, I think, among English and American writers that this latter accident is most liable to occur; more than the French we are apt to be misled by some convention or other as to the sort of feeler we *ought* to put forth, forgetting that the best one will be the one that nature happens to have given us. We have doubtless often enough the courage of our opinions (when it befalls that we have opinions), but we have not so constantly that of our perceptions. There is a whole side of our perceptive apparatus that we in fact neglect, and there are probably many among us who would erect this tendency into a duty. M. de Maupassant neglects nothing that he possesses; he cultivates his garden with admirable energy; and if there is a flower you miss from the rich parterre, you may be sure that it could not possibly have been raised, his mind not containing the soil for it. He is plainly of the opinion that the first duty of the artist, and the thing that makes him most useful to his fellow-men, is to master his instrument, whatever it may happen to be.

His own is that of the senses, and it is through them alone, or almost alone, that life appeals to him; it is almost alone by their help that he describes it, that he produces brilliant works. They render him this great assistance because they are evidently, in his constitution, extraordinarily alive; there is scarcely a page in all his twenty volumes that does not testify to their vivacity. Nothing could be further from his thought than to disavow them and to minimize their importance. He accepts them frankly, gratefully, works them, rejoices in them. If he were told that there are many English writers who would be sorry to go with him in this, he would, I imagine, staring, say that that is about what was to have been expected of the Anglo-Saxon race, or even that many of them probably could not go with him if they would. Then he would ask how our authors can be so foolish as to sacrifice such a *moyen*, how they can afford to, and exclaim, 'They must be pretty works, those they produce, and give a fine, true, complete account of life, with such omissions, such lacunae!' M. de Maupassant's productions teach us, for instance, that his sense of smell is exceptionally acute – as acute as that of those animals of the field and forest whose subsistence and security depend upon it. It might be thought that he would, as a student of the human race, have found an abnormal development of this faculty embarrassing, scarcely knowing what to do with it, where to place it. But such an apprehension betrays an imperfect conception of his directness and resolution, as well as of his constant economy of means. Nothing whatever prevents him from representing the relations of men and women as largely governed by the scent of the parties. Human life in his pages (would this not be the most general description he would give of it?) appears for the most part as a sort of concert of odours, and his people are perpetually engaged, or he is engaged on their behalf, in sniffing up and distinguishing them, in some pleasant or painful exercise of the nostril. 'If everything in life speaks to the nostril, why on earth shouldn't we say so?' I suppose him to inquire; 'and what a proof of the empire of poor conventions and hypocrisies, *chez vous autres*, that you should pretend to describe and characterize, and yet take no note (or so little that it comes to the same thing) of that essential sign!'

Not less powerful is his visual sense, the quick, direct discrimination of his eye, which explains the singularly vivid concision of his descriptions. These are never prolonged nor analytic, have nothing of enumeration, of the quality of the observer, who counts the items to be sure he has made up the sum. His eye *selects* unerringly, unscrupulously, almost impudently – catches the particular thing in which the character of the object or the scene resides, and, by expressing it with the artful brevity of a master, leaves a convincing, original picture. If he is inveterately synthetic, he is never more so than in the way he brings this hard, short, intelligent gaze to bear. His vision of the world is for the most part a vision of ugliness, and even when it is not, there is in his easy power to generalize a certain absence of love, a sort of bird's-eye-view contempt. He has none of the superstitions of observation, none of our English indulgences, our tender and often imaginative superficialities. If he glances into a railway carriage bearing its freight into the Parisian suburbs of a summer Sunday, a dozen dreary lives map themselves out in a flash.

'There were stout ladies in farcical clothes, those middle-class goodwives of the *banlieue* who replace the distinction they don't possess by an irrelevant dignity; gentlemen weary of the office, with sallow faces and twisted bodies, and one of their shoulders a little forced up by perpetual bending at work over a table. Their anxious, joyless faces spoke moreover of domestic worries, incessant needs for money, old hopes finally shattered; for they all belonged to the army of poor threadbare devils who vegetate frugally in a mean little plaster house, with a flower-bed for a garden.' . . .

Even in a brighter picture, such as the admirable vignette of the drive of Madame Tellier and her companions, the whole thing is an impression, as painters say nowadays, in which the figures are cheap. The six women at the station clamber into a country cart and go jolting through the Norman landscape to the village.

'But presently the jerky trot of the nag shook the vehicle so terribly that the chairs began to dance, tossing up the travellers to right, to left, with movements like puppets, scared grimaces, cries of dismay suddenly interrupted by a more violent bump. They clutched the sides of the trap, their bonnets turned over on to their backs, or upon the nose or the shoulder; and the white horse continued to go, thrusting out his head and straightening the little tail, hairless like that of a rat, with which from time to time he whisked his buttocks. Joseph Rivet, with one foot stretched upon the shaft, the other leg bent under him, and his elbows very high, held the reins and emitted from his throat every moment a kind of cluck which caused the animal to prick up his ears and quicken his pace. On either side of the road the green country stretched away. The colza, in flower, produced in spots a great carpet of undulating yellow, from which there rose a strong, wholesome smell, a smell penetrating and pleasant, carried very far by the breeze. In the tall rye the cornflowers held up their little azure heads, which the women wished to pluck; but M. Rivet refused to stop. Then, in some place, a whole field looked as if it were sprinkled with blood, it was so crowded with poppies. And in the midst of the great level, taking colour in this fashion from the flowers of the soil, the trap passed on with the jog of the white horse, seeming itself to carry a nosegay of richer hues; it disappeared behind the big trees of a farm, to come out again where the foliage stopped and parade afresh through the green and yellow crops, pricked with red or blue, its blazing cartload of women, which receded in the sunshine.'

As regards the other sense, the sense *par excellence*, the sense which we scarcely mention in English fiction, and which I am not very sure I shall be allowed to mention in an English periodical, M. de Maupassant speaks for that, and of it, with extraordinary distinctness and authority. To say that it occupies the first place in his picture is to say too little; it covers in truth the whole canvas, and his work is little else but a report of its innumerable manifestations. These manifestations are not, for him, so many incidents of life; they are life itself, they represent the standing answer to any question that we may ask about it. He describes them in detail, with a familiarity and frankness which leave nothing to be added; I should say with a singular truth, if I did not consider that in regard to this article he may be taxed with a certain exaggeration. M. de Maupassant would doubtless affirm that where the empire of the sexual sense is concerned, no exaggeration is possible: nevertheless it may be said that whatever depths may be discovered by those who dig for them, the impression of the human spectacle for him who takes it as it comes has less analogy with that of the monkeys' cage than this admirable writer's account of it. I speak of the human spectacle as we Anglo-Saxons see it — as we Anglo-Saxons pretend we see it, M. de Maupassant would possibly say.

At any rate, I have perhaps touched upon this peculiarity sufficiently to explain my remark that his point of view is almost solely that of the senses. If he is a very interesting case, this makes him also an embarrassing one, embarrassing and mystifying for the moralist. I may as well admit that no writer of the day strikes me as equally so. To find M. de Maupassant a lion in the path – that may seem to some people a singular proof of want of courage; but I think the obstacle will not be made light of by those who have really taken the measure of the animal. We are accustomed to think, we of the English faith, that a cynic is a living advertisement of his errors, especially in proportion as he is a thorough-going one; and M. de Maupassant's cynicism, unrelieved as it is, will not be disposed of off-hand by a critic of a competent literary sense. Such a critic is not slow to perceive, to his no small confusion, that though, judging from usual premises, the author of Bel-Ami ought to be a warning, he somehow is not. His baseness, as it pervades him, ought to be written all over him; yet somehow there are there certain aspects – and those commanding, as the house-agents say – in which it is not in the least to be perceived. It is easy to exclaim that if he judges life only from the point of view of the senses, many are the noble and exquisite things that he must leave out. What he leaves out has no claim to get itself considered till after we have done justice to what he takes in. It is this positive side of M. de Maupassant that is most remarkable – the fact that his literary character is so complete and edifying. 'Auteur à peu près irréprochable dans un genre qui ne l'est pas,' as that excellent critic M. Jules Lemaître says of him, he disturbs us by associating a conscience and a high standard with a temper long synonymous, in our eyes, with an absence of scruples. The situation would be simpler certainly if he were a bad writer; but none the less it is possible, I think, on the whole, to circumvent him, even without attempting to prove that after all he is one.

The latter part of his introduction to *Pierre et Jean* is less felicitous than the beginning, but we learn from it – and this is interesting – that he regards the analytic fashion of telling a story, which has lately begotten in his own country some such remarkable experiments (few votaries as it has attracted among ourselves), as very much less profitable than the simple epic manner which 'avoids with care all complicated explanations, all dissertations upon motives, and confines itself to making persons and events pass before our eyes.' M. de Maupassant adds that in his view 'psychology should be hidden in a book, as it is hidden in reality under the facts of existence. The novel conceived in this manner gains interest, movement, colour, the bustle of life.' When it is a question of an artistic process, we must always mistrust very sharp distinctions, for there is surely in every method a little of every other method. It is as difficult to describe an action without glancing at its motive, its moral history, as it is to describe a motive without glancing at its practical consequence. Our history and our fiction are what we do; but it surely is not more easy to determine where what we do begins than to determine where it ends – notoriously a hopeless task. Therefore it would take a very subtle sense to draw a hard and fast line on the borderland of explanation and illustration. If psychology be hidden in life, as, according to M. de Maupassant, it should be in a book, the question immediately comes up, 'From whom is it hidden?' From some people, no doubt, but very much less from others; and all depends upon the observer, the nature of one's observation, and one's curiosity. For some people motives, reasons, relations, explanations, are a part of the very surface of the drama, with the footlights beating full upon them. For me an act, an incident, an attitude, may be a sharp, detached, isolated thing, of which I give a full account in saying that in such and such a way it came off. For you it may be hung about with implications, with relations, and conditions as necessary to help you to recognize it as the clothes of your friends are to help you know them in the street. You feel that they would seem strange to you without petticoats and trousers.

M. de Maupassant would probably urge that the right thing is to know, or to guess, how events come to pass, but to say as little about it as possible. There are matters in regard to which he feels the importance of being explicit, but that is not one of them. The contention to which I allude strikes me as rather arbitrary, so difficult is it to put one's finger upon the reason why, for instance, there should be so little mystery about what happened to Christiane Andermatt, in *Mont-Oriol*, when she went to walk on the hills with Paul Brétigny, and so much, say, about the forces that formed her for that gentleman's convenience, or those lying behind any other odd collapse that our author may have related. The rule misleads, and the best rule certainly is the tact of the individual writer, which will adapt itself to the material as the material comes to him. The cause we plead is ever pretty sure to be the cause of our idiosyncrasies, and if M. de Maupassant thinks meanly of 'explanations', it is, I suspect, that they come to him in no great affluence. His view of the conduct of man is so simple as scarcely to require them; and indeed so far as they are needed he *is*, virtually, explanatory. He deprecates reference to motives, but there is one, covering an immense ground in his horizon, as I have already hinted, to which he perpetually refers. If the sexual impulse be not a moral antecedent, it is none the less the wire that moves almost all M. de Maupassant's puppets, and as he has not hidden it, I cannot see that he has eliminated analysis or made a sacrifice to discretion. His pages are studded with that particular analysis; he is constantly peeping behind the curtain, telling us what he discovers there. The truth is that the admirable system of sim-plification which makes his tales so rapid and so concise (especially his shorter ones, for his novels in some degree, I think, suffer from it), strikes us as not in the least a conscious intellectual effort, a selective, comparative process. He tells us all he knows, all he suspects, and if these things take no account of the moral nature of man, it is because he has no window looking in that direction, and not because artistic scruples have compelled him to close it up. The very compact mansion in which he dwells presents on that side a perfectly dead wall.

This is why, if his axiom that you produce the effect of truth better by painting people from the outside than from the inside has a large utility, his example is convincing in a much higher degree. A writer is fortunate when his theory and his limitations so exactly correspond, when his curiosities may be appeased with such precision and promptitude. M. de Maupassant contends that the most that the analytic novelist can do is to put himself – his own peculiarities – into the costume of the figure analysed. This may be true, but if it applies to one manner of representing people who are not ourselves, it applies also to any other manner. It is the limitation, the difficulty of the novelist, to whatever clan or camp he may belong. M. de Maupassant is remarkably objective and impersonal, but he would go too far if he were to entertain the belief that he has kept himself out of his books. They speak of him eloquently, even if it only be to tell us how easy – how easy, given his talent of course – he has found this impersonality. Let us hasten to add that in the case of describing a character it is doubtless more difficult to convey the impression of something that is not one's self (the constant effort, however delusive at bottom, of the novelist), than in the case of describing some object more immediately visible. The operation is more delicate, but that circumstance only increases the beauty of the problem.

On the question of style our author has some excellent remarks; we may be grateful indeed for every one of them, save an odd reflection about the way to 'become original' if we happen not to be so. The recipe for this transformation, it would appear, is to sit down in front of a blazing fire, or a tree in a plain, or any object we encounter in the regular way of business, and remain there until the tree, or the fire, or the object, whatever it be, become different for us from all other specimens of the same class. I doubt whether this system would always answer, for surely the resemblance is what we wish to discover, quite as much as the difference, and the best way to preserve it is not to look for something opposed to it. Is not this indication of the road to take to become, as a writer, original touched with the same fallacy as the recommendation about eschewing analysis? It is the only *naïveté* I have encountered in M. de Maupassant's many volumes. The best originality is the most un-conscious, and the best way to describe a tree is the way in which it has struck us. 'Ah, but we don't always know how it has struck us,' the answer to that may be, 'and it takes some time and ingenuity – much fasting and prayer – to find out.' If we do not know, it probably has not struck us very much: so little indeed that our inquiry had better be relegated to that closed chamber of an artist's meditations, that sacred back kitchen, which no *a priori* rule can light up. The best thing the artist's adviser can do in such a case is to trust him and turn away, to let him fight the matter out with his conscience. And be this said with a full appreciation of the degree in which M. de Maupassant's observations on the whole question of a writer's style, at the point we have come to to-day, bear the stamp of intelligence and experience. His own style is of so excellent a tradition that the presumption is altogether in favour of what he may have to say.

He feels oppressively, discouragingly, as many another of his countrymen must have felt – for the French have worked their language as no other people have done – the penalty of coming at the end of three centuries of literature, the difficulty of dealing with an instrument of expression so worn by friction, of drawing new sounds from the old familiar pipe. 'When we read, so saturated with French writing as we are that our whole body gives us the impression of being a paste made of words, do we ever find a line, a thought, which is not familiar to us, and of which we have not had at least a confused presentiment?' And he adds that the matter is simple enough for the writer who only seeks to amuse the public by means already known; he attempts little, and he produces 'with confidence, in the candour of his mediocrity', works which answer no question and leave no trace. It is he who wants to do more than this that has less and less an easy time of it. Everything seems to him to have been done, every effect produced, every combination already made. If he be a man of genius, his trouble is lightened, for mysterious ways are revealed to him, and new combinations spring up for him even after novelty is dead. It is to the simple man of taste and talent, who has only a conscience and a will, that the situation may sometimes well appear desperate; he judges himself as he goes, and he can only go step by step over ground where every step is already a footprint.

If it be a miracle whenever there is a fresh tone, the miracle has been wrought for M. de Maupassant. Or is he simply a man of genius to whom short cuts have been disclosed in the watches of the night? At any rate he has had faith – religion has come to his aid; I mean the religion of his mother tongue, which he has loved well enough to be patient for her sake. He has arrived at the peace which passeth understanding, at a kind of conservative piety. He has taken his stand on simplicity, on a studied sobriety, being persuaded that the deepest science lies in that direction rather than in the multiplication of new terms, and on this subject he delivers himself with superlative wisdom. 'There is no need of the queer, complicated, numerous, and Chinese vocabulary which is imposed on us to-day under the name of artistic writing, to fix all the shades of thought; the right way is to distinguish with an extreme clearness all those modifications of the value of a word which come from the place it occupies. Let us have fewer nouns, verbs and adjectives of an almost imperceptible sense, and more different phrases variously constructed, ingeniously cast, full of the science of sound and rhythm. Let us have an excellent general form rather than be collectors of rare terms.' M. de Maupassant's practice does not fall below his exhortation (though I must confess that in the foregoing passage he makes use of the detestable expression 'stylist', which I have not reproduced). Nothing can exceed the masculine firmness, the quiet force of his own style, in which every phrase is a close sequence, every epithet a paying piece, and the ground is completely cleared of the vague, the ready-made and the second-best. Less than any one to-day does he beat the air; more than any one does he hit out from the shoulder.

II

He has produced a hundred short tales and only four regular novels; but if the tales desire the first place in any candid appreciation of his talent it is not simply because they are so much the more numerous: they are also more characteristic; they represent him best in his originality, and their brevity, extreme in some cases, does not prevent them from being a collection of masterpieces. (They are very unequal, and I speak of the best.) The little story is but scantily relished in England, where readers take their fiction rather by the volume than by the page, and the novelist's idea is apt to resemble one of those old-fashioned carriages which require a wide court to turn round. In America, where it is associated pre-eminently with Hawthorne's name, with Edgar Poe's, and with that of Mr Bret Harte, the short tale has had a better fortune. France, however, has been the land of its great prosperity, and M. de Maupassant had from the first the advantage of addressing a public accustomed to catch on, as the modern phrase is, quickly. In some respects, it may be said, he encountered prejudices too friendly, for he found a tradition of indecency ready made to his hand. I say indecency with plainness, though my indication would perhaps please better with another word, for we suffer in English from a lack of roundabout names for the *conte leste* – that element for which the French, with their *grivois*, their *gaillard*, their *égrillard*, their *gaudriole*, have so many convenient synonyms. It is an honoured tradition in France that the little story, in verse or in prose, should be liable to be more or less obscene (I can think only of that alternative epithet), though I hasten to add that among literary forms it does not monopolize the privilege. Our uncleanness is less producible – at any rate it is less produced.

For the last ten years our author has brought forth with regularity these condensed compositions, of which, probably, to an English reader, at a first glance, the most universal sign will be their licentiousness. They really partake of this quality, however, in a very different degree, and a second glance shows that they may be divided into numerous groups. It is not fair, I think, even to say that what they have most in common is their being extremely *lestes*. What they have most in common is their being extremely strong, and after that their being extremely brutal. A story may be obscene without being brutal, and *vice versâ*, and M. de Maupassant's contempt for those interdictions which are supposed to be made in the interest of good morals is but an incident – a very large one indeed – of his general contempt. A pessimism so great that its alliance with the love of good work, or even with the calculation of the sort of work that pays best in a country of style, is, as I have intimated, the most puzzling of anomalies (for it would seem in the light of such sentiments that nothing is worth anything), this cynical strain is the sign of such gems of narration as *La Maison Tellier*, *L'Histoire d'une Fille de Ferme*, *L'Ane*, *Le Chien*, *Mademoiselle Fifi*, *Monsieur Parent*, *L'Héritage*, *En Famille*, *Le Baptême*, *Le Père Aimable*. The author fixes a hard eye on some small spot of human life, usually some ugly, dreary, shabby, sordid one, takes up the particle, and squeezes it either till it grimaces or till it bleeds. Sometimes the grimace is very droll, sometimes the wound is very horrible; but in either case the whole thing is real, observed, noted, and represented, not an invention or a castle in the air. M. de Maupassant sees human life as a terribly ugly business relieved by the comical, but even the comedy is for the most part the comedy of misery, of avidity, of ignorance, helplessness, and grossness. When his laugh is not for these things, it is for the little *saletés* (to use one of his own favourite words) of luxurious life, which are intended to be prettier, but which can scarcely be said to brighten the picture. I like *La Bête à Maître Belhomme, La Ficelle, Le Petit Fût, Le Cas de Madame Luneau, Tribuneaux Rustique,* and many others of this category much better than his anecdotes of the mutual confidences of his little *marquises* and *baronnes.*

Not counting his novels for the moment, his tales may be divided into the three groups of those which deal with the Norman peasantry, those which deal with the *petit employé* and small shopkeeper, usually in Paris, and the miscellaneous, in which the upper walks of life are represented, and the fantastic, the whimsical, the weird, and even the supernatural, figure as well as the unexpurgated. These last things range from *Le Horla* (which is not a specimen of the author's best vein – the only occasion on which he has the weakness of imitation is when he strikes us as emulating Edgar Poe) to *Miss Harriet,* and from *Boule de Suif* (a triumph) to that almost inconceivable little growl of Anglophobia, *Découverte* – inconceivable I mean in its irresponsibility and ill-nature on the part of a man of M. de Maupassant's distinction; passing by such little perfections as *Petit Soldat, L'Abandonné, Le Collier* (the list is too long for complete enumeration), and such gross imperfections (for it once in a while befalls our author to go woefully astray), as *La Femme de Paul, Châli, Les Soeurs Rondoli.* To these might almost be added as a special category the various forms in which M. de Maupassant relates adventures in railway carriages. Numerous, to his imagination, are the pretexts for enlivening fiction afforded by first, second, and third class compartments; the accidents (which have nothing to do with the conduct of the train) that occur there constitute no inconsiderable part of our earthly transit.

It is surely by his Norman peasant that his tales will live; he knows this worthy as if he had made him, understands him down to the ground, puts him on his feet with a few of the freest, most plastic touches. M. de Maupassant does not admire him, and he is such a master of the subject that it would ill become an outsider to suggest a revision of judgment. He is a part of the contemptible furniture of the world, but on the whole, it would appear, the most grotesque part of it. His caution, his canniness, his natural astuteness, his stinginess, his general grinding sordidness, are as unmistakable as that quaint and brutish dialect in which he expresses himself, and on which our author plays like a virtuoso. It would be impossible to demonstrate with a finer sense of the humour of the thing the fatuities and densities of his ignorance, the bewilderments of his opposed appetites, the overreachings of his caution. His existence has a gay side, but it is apt to be the barbarous gaiety commemorated in *Farce Normande*, an anecdote which, like many of M. de Maupassant's anecdotes, it is easier to refer the reader to than to repeat. If it is most convenient to place *La Maison Tellier* among the tales of the peasantry, there is no doubt that it stands at the head of the list. It is absolutely unadapted to the perusal of ladies and young persons, but it shares this peculiarity with most of its fellows, so that to ignore it on that account would be to imply that we must forswear M. de Maupassant altogether, which is an incongruous and insupportable conclusion. Every good story is of course both a picture and an idea, and the more they are interfused the better the problem is solved. In *La Maison Tellier* they fit each other to perfection; the capacity for sudden innocent delights latent in natures which have lost their innocence is vividly illustrated by the singular scenes to which our acquaintance with Madame and her staff (little as it may be a thing to boast of), successively introduces us. The breadth, the freedom, and brightness of all this give the measure of the author's talent, and of that large, keen way of looking at life which sees the pathetic and the droll, the stuff of which the whole piece is made, in the queerest and humblest patterns. The tone of *La Maison Tellier* and the few compositions which closely resemble it, expresses M. de Maupassant's nearest approach to geniality. Even here, however, it is the geniality of the showman exhilarated by the success with which he feels that he makes his mannikins (and especially his womankins) caper and squeak, and who after the performance tosses them into their box with the irreverence of a practised hand. If the pages of the author of *Bel-Ami* may be searched almost in vain for a manifestation of the sentiment of respect, it is naturally not by Mme Tellier and her charges that we must look most to see it called forth; but they are among the things that please him most.

Sometimes there is a sorrow, a misery, or even a little heroism, that he handles with a certain tenderness (*Une Vie* is the capital example of this), without insisting on the poor, the ridiculous, or, as he is fond of saying, the bestial side of it. Such an attempt, admirable in its sobriety and delicacy, is the sketch, in *L'Abandonné*, of the old lady and gentleman, Mme de Cadour and M. D'Apreval, who, staying with the husband of the former at a little watering-place on the Normandy coast, take a long, hot walk on a summer's day, on a straight, white road, into the interior, to catch a clandestine glimpse of a young farmer, their illegitimate son. He has been pensioned, he is ignorant of his origin, and is a commonplace and unconciliatory rustic. They look at him, in his dirty farmyard, and no sign passes between them; then they turn away and crawl back, in melancholy silence, along the dull French road. The manner in which this dreary little occurrence is related makes it as large as a chapter of history. There is tenderness in *Miss Harriet*, which sets forth how an English old maid, fantastic, hideous, sentimental, and tract-distributing, with a smell of india-rubber, fell in love with an irresistible French painter, and drowned herself in the well because she saw him kissing the maid-servant; but the figure of the lady grazes the farcical. Is it because we know Miss Harriet (if we are not mistaken in the type the author has had in his eye) that we suspect the good spinster was not so weird and desperate, addicted though her class may be, as he says, to 'haunting all the *tables d'hôte* in Europe, to spoiling Italy, poisoning Switzerland, making the charming towns of the Mediterranean uninhabitable, carrying everywhere their queer little manias, their *mœurs de vestales pétrifiées*, their indescribable garments, and that odour of india-rubber which makes one think that at night they must be slipped into a case?' What would Miss Harriet have said to M. de Maupassant's friend, the hero of the *Découverte*, who, having married a little Anglaise because he thought she was charming when she spoke broken French, finds she is very flat as she becomes more fluent, and has nothing more urgent than to denounce her to a gentleman he meets on the steamboat, and to relieve his wrath in ejaculations of 'Sales Anglais'?

M. de Maupassant evidently knows a great deal about the army of clerks who work under government, but it is a terrible tale that he has to tell of them and of the *petit bourgeois* in general. It is true that he has treated the *petit bourgeois* in *Pierre et Jean* without holding him up to our derision, and the effort has been so fruitful, that we owe to it the work for which, on the whole, in the long list of his successes, we are most thankful. But of *Pierre et Jean,* a production neither comic nor cynical (in the degree, that is, of its predecessors), but serious and fresh, I will speak anon. In *Monsieur Parent, L'Héritage, En Famille, Une Partie de Campagne, Promenade,* and many other pitiless little pieces, the author opens the window wide to his perception of everything mean, narrow, and sordid. The subject is ever the struggle for existence in hard conditions, lighted up simply by more or less *polissonnerie.* Nothing is more striking to an Anglo-Saxon reader than the omission of all the other lights, those with which our imagination, and I think it ought to be said our observation, is familiar, and which our own works of fiction at any rate do not permit us to forget: those of which the most general description is that they spring from a certain mixture of good-humour and piety – piety, I mean, in the civil and domestic sense quite as much as in the religious. The love of sport, the sense of decorum, the necessity for action, the habit of respect, the absence of irony, the pervasiveness of childhood, the expansive tendency of the race, are a few of the qualities (the analysis might, I think, be pushed much further) which ease us off, mitigate our tension and irritation, rescue us from the nervous exasperation which is almost the commonest element of life as depicted by M. de Maupassant. No doubt there is in our literature an immense amount of conventional blinking, and it may be questioned whether pessimistic representation in M. de Maupassant's manner do not follow his particular original more closely than our perpetual quest of pleasantness (does not Mr Rider Haggard make even his African carnage pleasant?) adheres to the lines of the world we ourselves know.

Fierce indeed is the struggle for existence among even our pious and good-humoured millions, and it is attended with incidents as to which after all little testimony is to be extracted from our literature of fiction. It must never be forgotten that the optimism of that literature is partly the optimism of women and of spinsters; in other words the optimism of ignorance as well as of delicacy. It might be supposed that the French, with their mastery of the *arts d'agrément*, would have more consolations than we, but such is not the account of the matter given by the new generation of painters. To the French we seem superficial, and we are certainly open to the reproach; but none the less even to the infinite majority of readers of good faith there will be a wonderful want of correspondence between the general picture of *Bel-Ami*, of *Mont-Oriol*, of *Une Vie*, *Yvette* and *En Famille*, and our own vision of reality. It is an old impression of course that the satire of the French has a very different tone from ours; but few English readers will admit that the feeling of life is less in ours than in theirs. The feeling of life is evident, *de part et d'autre*, a very different thing. If in ours, as the novel illustrates it, there are superficialities, there are also qualities which are far from being negatives and omissions: a large imagination and (is it fatuous to say?) a large experience of the positive kind. Even those of our novelists whose manner is most ironic pity life more and hate it less than M. de Maupassant and his great initiator Flaubert. It comes back I suppose to our good-humour (which may apparently also be an artistic force); at any rate, we have reserves about our shames and our sorrows, indulgences and tolerances about our Philistinism, forbearances about our blows, and a general friendliness of conception about our possibilities, which take the cruelty from our self-derision and operate in the last resort as a sort of tribute to our freedom. There is a horrible, admirable scene in *Monsieur Parent*, which is a capital example of triumphant ugliness. The harmless gentleman who gives his name to the tale has an abominable wife, one of whose offensive attributes is a lover (unsuspected by her husband), only less impudent than herself. M. Parent comes in from a walk with his little boy, at dinner-time, to encounter suddenly in his abused, dishonoured, deserted home, convincing proof of her misbehaviour. He waits and waits dinner for her, giving her the benefit of every doubt; but when at last she enters, late in the evening, accompanied by the partner of her guilt, there is a tremendous domestic concussion. It is to the peculiar vividness of this scene that I allude, the way we hear it and see it, and its most repulsive details are evoked for us: the sordid confusion, the vulgar noise, the disordered table and ruined dinner, the shrill insolence of the wife, her brazen mendacity, the scared inferiority of the lover, the mere momentary heroics of the weak husband, the scuffle and somersault, the eminently unpoetic justice with which it all ends.

When Thackeray relates how Arthur Pendennis goes home to take pot-luck with the insolvent Newcomes at Boulogne, and how the dreadful Mrs Mackenzie receives him, and how she makes a scene, when the frugal repast is served, over the diminished mutton-bone, we feel that the notation of that order of misery goes about as far as we can bear it. But this is child's play to the history of M. and Mme Caravan and their attempt, after the death (or supposed death) of the husband's mother, to transfer to their apartment before the arrival of the other heirs certain miserable little articles of furniture belonging to the deceased, together with the frustration of the manoeuvre not only by the grim resurrection of the old woman (which is a sufficiently fantastic item), but by the shock of battle when a married daughter and her husband appear. No one gives us like M. de Maupassant the odious words exchanged on such an occasion as that: no one depicts with so just a hand the feelings of small people about small things. These feelings are very apt to be 'fury'; that word is of strikingly frequent occurrence in his pages. L'Héritage is a drama of private life in the little world of the Ministère de la Marine – a world, according to M. de Maupassant, of dreadful little jealousies and ineptitudes. Readers of a robust complexion should learn how the wretched M. Lesable was handled by his wife and her father on his failing to satisfy their just expectations, and how he comported himself in the singular situation thus prepared for him. The story is a model of narration, but it leaves our poor average humanity dangling like a beaten rag.

Where does M. de Maupassant find the great multitude of his detestable women? or where at least does he find the courage to represent them in such colours? Jeanne de Lamare, in Une Vie, receives the outrages of fate with a passive fortitude; and there is something touching in Mme Roland's âme tendre de caissière, as exhibited in Pierre et Jean. But for the most part M. de Maupassant's heroines are a mixture of extreme sensuality and extreme mendacity. They are a large element in that general disfigurement, that illusion de l'ignoble, qui attire tant d'êtres, which makes the perverse or the stupid side of things the one which strikes him first, which leads him, if he glances at a group of nurses and children sunning themselves in a

Parisian square, to notice primarily the *yeux de brute* of the nurses; or if he speaks of the longing for a taste of the country which haunts the shopkeeper fenced in behind his counter, to identify it as the *amour bête de la nature*; or if he has occasion to put the boulevards before us on a summer's evening, to seek his effect in these terms: 'The city, as hot as a stew, seemed to sweat in the suffocating night. The drains puffed their pestilential breath from their mouths of granite, and the underground kitchens poured into the streets, through their low windows, the infamous miasmas of their dish-water and old sauces.' I do not contest the truth of such indications, I only note the particular selection and their seeming to the writer the most *apropos*.

Is it because of the inadequacy of these indications when applied to the long stretch that M. de Maupassant's novels strike us as less complete, in proportion to the talent expended upon them, than his *contes* and *nouvelles*? I make this invidious distinction in spite of the fact that *Une Vie* (the first of the novels in the order of time) is a remarkably interesting experiment, and that *Pierre et Jean* is, so far as my judgment goes, a faultless production. *Bel-Ami* is full of the bustle and the crudity of life (its energy and expressiveness almost bribe one to like it), but it has the great defect that the physiological explanation of things here too visibly contracts the problem in order to meet it. The world represented is too special, too little inevitable, too much to take or to leave as we like – a world in which every man is a cad and every woman a harlot. M. de Maupassant traces the career of a finished blackguard who succeeds in life through women, and he represents him primarily as succeeding in the profession of journalism. His colleagues and his mistresses are as depraved as himself, greatly to the injury of the ironic idea, for the real force of satire would have come from seeing him engaged and victorious with natures better than his own. It may be remarked that this was the case with the nature of Mme Walter; but the reply to that is – hardly! Moreover the author's whole treatment of the episode of Mme Walter is the thing on which his admirers have least to congratulate him. The taste of it is so atrocious, that it is difficult to do justice to the way it is made to stand out. Such an instance as this pleads with irresistible eloquence, as it seems to me, the cause of that salutary diffidence or practical generosity which I mentioned on a preceding page. I know not the English or American novelist who could have written this portion of the history of *Bel-Ami* if he would. But I also find it impossible to conceive of a member of that fraternity who would have written it if he could. The subject of *Mont-Oriol* is full of queerness to the English mind. Here again the picture has much more importance than the idea, which is simply that a gentleman, if he happen to be a low animal, is liable to love a lady very much less if she presents him with a pledge of their affection. It need scarcely be said that the lady and gentleman who in M. de Maupassant's pages exemplify this interesting truth are not united in wedlock – that is with each other.

M. de Maupassant tells us that he has imbibed many of his principles from Gustave Flaubert, from the study of his works as well as, formerly, the enjoyment of his words. It is in *Une Vie* that Flaubert's influence is most directly traceable, for the thing has a marked analogy with *L'Education Sentimentale*. That is, it is the presentation of a simple piece of a life (in this case a long piece), a series of observations upon an episode *quelconque*, as the French say, with the minimum of arrangement of the given objects. It is an excellent example of the way the impression of truth may be conveyed by that form, but it would have been a still better one if in his search for the effect of dreariness (the effect of dreariness may be said to be the subject of *Une Vie*, so far as the subject is reducible) the author had not eliminated excessively. He has arranged, as I say, as little as possible; the necessity of a 'plot' has in no degree imposed itself upon him, and his effort has been to give the uncomposed, unrounded look of life, with its accidents, its broken rhythm, its queer resemblance to the famous description of 'Bradshaw' – a compound of trains that start but don't arrive, and trains that arrive but don't start. It is almost an arrangement of the history of poor Mme de Lamare to have left so many things out of it, for after all she is described in very few of the relations of life. The principal ones are there certainly; we see her as a daughter, a wife, and a mother, but there is a certain accumulation of secondary experience that marks any passage from youth to old age which is a wholly absent element in M. de Maupassant's narrative, and the suppression of which gives the thing a tinge of the arbitrary. It is in the power of this secondary experience to make a great difference, but nothing makes any difference for Jeanne de Lamare as M. de Maupassant puts her before us. Had she no other points of contact than those he describes? — no friends, no phases, no episodes, no chances, none of the miscellaneous *remplissage* of life? No doubt M. de Maupassant would say that he has had to select, that the most comprehensive enumeration is only a condensation, and that, in accordance with the very just principles enunciated in that preface to which I have perhaps too repeatedly referred, he has sacrificed what is uncharacteristic to what is characteristic. It characterizes the career of this French country lady of fifty years ago that its long grey expanse should be seen as peopled with but five or six figures. The essence of the matter is that she was deceived in almost every affection, and that essence is given if the persons who deceived her are given.

The reply is doubtless adequate, and I have only intended my criticism to suggest the degree of my interest. What it really amounts to is that if the subject of this artistic experiment had been the existence of an English lady, even a very dull one, the air of verisimilitude would have demanded that she should have been placed in a denser medium. *Une Vie* may after all be only a testimony to the fact of the melancholy void of the coast of Normandy, even within a moderate drive of a great seaport, under the Restoration and Louis Philippe. It is especially to be recommended to those who are interested in the question of what constitutes a 'story', offering as it does the most definite sequences at the same time that it has nothing that corresponds to the usual idea of a plot, and closing with an implication that finds us prepared. The picture again in this case is much more dominant than the idea, unless it be an idea that loneliness and grief are terrible. The picture, at any rate, is full of truthful touches, and the work has the merit and the charm that it is the most delicate of the author's productions and the least hard. In none other has he occupied himself so continuously with so innocent a figure as his soft, bruised heroine; in none other has he paid our poor blind human history the compliment (and this is remarkable, considering the flatness of so much of the particular subject) of finding it so little *bête*. He may think it, here, but comparatively he does not say it. He almost betrays a sense of moral things. Jeanne is absolutely passive, she has no moral spring, no active moral life, none of the edifying attributes of character (it costs her apparently as little as may be in the way of a shock, a complication of feeling, to discover, by letters, after her mother's death, that this lady has not been the virtuous woman she has supposed); but her chronicler has had to handle the immaterial forces of patience and renunciation, and this has given the book a certain purity, in spite of two or three 'physiological' passages that come in with violence – a violence the greater as we feel it to be a result of selection. It is very much a mark of M. de Maupassant that on the most striking occasion, with a single exception, on which his picture is not a picture of libertinage it is a picture of unmitigated suffering. Would he suggest that these are the only alternatives?

The exception that I here allude to is for *Pierre et Jean*, which I have left myself small space to speak of. Is it because in this masterly little novel there is a show of those immaterial forces which I just mentioned, and because Pierre Roland is one of the few instances of operative character that can be recalled from so many volumes, that many readers will place M. de Maupassant's latest production altogether at the head of his longer ones? I am not sure, inasmuch as after all the character in question is not extraordinarily distinguished, and the moral problem not presented in much complexity. The case is only relative. Perhaps it is not of importance to fix the reasons of preference in respect to a piece of writing so essentially a work of art and of talent. *Pierre et Jean* is the best of M. de Maupassant's novels mainly because M. de Maupassant has never before been so clever. It is a pleasure to see a mature talent able to renew itself, strike another note, and appear still young. This story suggests the growth of a perception that everything has not been said about the actors on the world's stage when they are represented either as helpless victims or as mere bundles of appetites. There is an air of responsibility about Pierre Roland, the person on whose behalf the tale is mainly told, which almost constitutes a pledge. An inquisitive critic may ask why in this particular case M. de Maupassant should have stuck to the *petit bourgeois*, the circumstances not being such as to typify that class more than another. There are reasons indeed which on reflection are perceptible; it was necessary that his people should be poor, and necessary even that to attenuate Madame Roland's misbehaviour she should have had the excuse of the contracted life of a shopwoman in the Rue Montmartre. Were the inquisitive critic slightly malicious as well, he might suspect the author of a fear that he should seem to give way to the *illusion du beau* if in addition to representing the little group in *Pierre et Jean* as persons of about the normal conscience he had also represented them as of the cultivated class. If they belong to the humble life this belittles and – I am still quoting the supposedly malicious critic – M. de Maupassant *must*, in one way or the other, belittle. To the English reader it will appear, I think, that Pierre and Jean are rather more of the cultivated class than two young Englishmen in the same social position. It belongs to the drama that the struggle of the elder brother – educated, proud, and acute – should be partly with the pettiness of his opportunities. The author's choice of a *milieu*, moreover, will serve to English readers as an example of how much more democratic contemporary French fiction is than that of his own country. The greater part of it – almost all the work of Zola and of Daudet, the best of Flaubert's novels, and the best of those of the brothers De Goncourt – treat of that vast, dim section of society which, lying between those luxurious walks on whose behalf there are easy presuppositions and that darkness of misery which, in addition to being picturesque, brings philanthropy also to the writer's aid, constitutes really, in extent and expressiveness, the substance of any nation. In England, where the fashion of fiction still sets mainly to the country house and the hunting-field, and yet more novels are published than anywhere else in the world, that thick twilight of mediocrity of condition has been little explored. May it yield triumphs in the years to come!

It may seem that I have claimed little for M. de Maupassant, so far as English readers are concerned with him, in saying that after publishing twenty improper volumes he has at last published a twenty-first, which is neither indecent nor cynical. It is not this circumstance that has led me to dedicate so many pages to him, but the circumstance that in producing all the others he yet remained, for those who are interested in these matters, a writer with whom it was impossible not to reckon. This is why I called him, to begin with, so many ineffectual names: a rarity, a 'case', an embarrassment, a lion in the path. He is still in the path as I conclude these observations, but I think that in making them we have discovered a legitimate way round. If he is a master of his art and it is discouraging to find what low views are compatible with mastery, there is satisfaction, on the other hand in learning on what particular condition he holds his strange success. This condition, it seems to me, is that of having totally omitted one of the items of the problem, an omission which has made the problem so much easier that it may almost be described as a short cut to a solution. The question is whether it be a fair cut. M. de Maupassant has simply skipped the whole reflective part of his men and women – that reflective part which governs conduct and produces character. He may say that he does not see it, does not know it; to which the answer is, 'So much the better for you, if you wish to describe life without it. The strings you pull are by so much the less numerous, and you can therefore pull those that remain with greater promptitude, consequently with greater firmness, with a greater air of knowledge.' Pierre Roland, I repeat, shows a capacity for reflection, but I cannot think who else does, among the thousand figures who compete with him – I mean for reflection addressed to anything higher than the gratification of an instinct. We have an impression that M. d'Apreval and Madame de Cadour reflect, as they trudge back from their mournful excursion, but that indication is not pushed very far. An aptitude for this exercise is a part of disciplined manhood, and disciplined manhood M. de Maupassant has simply not attempted to represent. I can remember no instance in which he sketches any considerable capacity for conduct, and his women betray that capacity as little as his men. I am much mistaken if he has once painted a gentleman, in the English sense of the term. His gentlemen, like Paul Brétigny and Gontran de Ravenel, are guilty of the most extraordinary deflections. For those who are conscious of this element in life, look for it and like it, the gap will appear to be immense. It will lead them to say, 'No wonder you have a contempt if that is the way you limit the field. No wonder you judge people roughly if that is the way you see them. Your work, on your premises, remains the admirable thing it is, but is your "case" not adequately explained?'

The erotic element in M. de Maupassant, about which much more might have been said, seems to me to be explained by the same limitation, and explicable in a similar way wherever else its literature occurs in excess. The carnal side of man appears the most characteristic if you look at it a great deal; and you look at it a great deal if you do not look at the other, at the side by which he reacts against his weaknesses, his defeats. The more you look at the other, the less the whole business to which French novelists have ever appeared to English readers to give a disproportionate place – the business, as I may say, of the senses – will strike you as the only typical one. Is not this the most useful reflection to make in regard to the famous question of the morality, the decency, of the novel? It is the only one, it seems to me, that will meet the case as we find the case to-day. Hard and fast rules, *a priori* restrictions, mere interdictions (you shall not speak of this, you shall not look at that), have surely served their time, and will in the nature of the case never strike an energetic talent as anything but arbitrary. A healthy, living and growing art, full of curiosity and fond of exercise, has an indefeasible mistrust of rigid prohibitions. Let us then leave this magnificent art of the novelist to itself and to its perfect freedom, in the faith that one example is as good as another, and that our fiction will always be decent enough if it be sufficiently general. Let us not be alarmed at this prodigy (though prodigies are alarming) of M. de Maupassant, who is at once so licentious and so impeccable, but gird ourselves up with the conviction that another point of view will yield another perfection.

30

❦

From 'Robert Louis Stevenson', Century Magazine, April 1888. James and Stevenson had become close literary friends. The article by William Archer was 'R. L. Stevenson, his Style and Thought', Time, November 1885. As to the end of Kidnapped, David Balfour's adventures were continued in Catriona, 1893.

... THOUGH MR STEVENSON cares greatly for his phrase, as every writer should who respects himself and his art, it takes no very attentive reading of his volumes to show that it is not what he cares for most, and that he regards an expressive style only, after all, as a means. It seems to me the fault of Mr Archer's interesting paper, that it suggests too much that the author of these volumes considers the art of expression as an end – an ingenious game of words. He finds that Mr Stevenson is not serious, that he neglects a whole side of life, that he has no perception, and no consciousness, of suffering; that he speaks as a happy but heartless pagan, living only in his senses (which the critic admits to be exquisitely fine), and that in a world full of heaviness he is not sufficiently aware of the philosophic limitations of mere technical skill. In sketching these aberrations Mr Archer himself, by the way, displays anything but ponderosity of hand. He is not the first reader, and he will not be the last, who shall have been irritated by Mr Stevenson's jauntiness. That jauntiness is an essential part of his genius; but to my sense it ceases to be irritating – it indeed becomes positively touching and constitutes an appeal to sympathy and even to tenderness – when once one has perceived what lies beneath the dancing-tune to which he mostly moves. Much as he cares for his phrase, he cares more for life, and for a certain transcendently lovable part of it. He feels, as it seems to us, and that is not given to every one. This constitutes a philosophy which Mr Archer fails to read between his lines – the respectable, desirable moral which many a reader doubtless finds that he neglects to point. He does not feel everything equally, by any manner of means; but his feelings are always his reasons. He regards them, whatever they may be, as sufficiently honourable, does not disguise them in other names or colours, and looks at whatever he meets in the brilliant candle-light that they shed. As in his extreme artistic vivacity he seems really disposed to try everything, he has tried once, by way of a change, to be inhuman, and there is a hard glitter about *Prince Otto* which seems to indicate that in this case too he has succeeded, as he has done in most of the feats that he has attempted. But *Prince Otto* is even less like his other productions than his other productions are like each other.

The part of life which he cares for most is youth, and the direct expression of the love of youth is the beginning and the end of his message. His appreciation of this delightful period amounts to a passion, and a passion, in the age in which we live, strikes us on the whole as a sufficient philosophy. It ought to satisfy Mr Archer, and there are writers who press harder than Mr Stevenson, on whose behalf no such moral motive can be alleged. Mingled with this almost equal love of a literary surface, it represents a real originality. This combination is the keynote of Mr Stevenson's faculty and the explanation of his perversities. The feeling of one's teens, and even of an earlier period (for the delights of crawling, and almost of the rattle, are embodied in *A Child's Garden of Verses*), and the feeling for happy turns – these, in the last analysis (and his sense of a happy turn is of the subtlest), are the corresponding halves of his character. If *Prince Otto* and *Doctor Jekyll* left me a clearer field for the assertion, I would say that everything he has written is a direct apology for boyhood; or rather (for it must be confessed that Mr Stevenson's tone is seldom apologetic), a direct rhapsody on the age of hetero-geneous pockets. Even members of the very numerous class who have held their breath over *Treasure Island* may shrug their shoulders at this account of the author's religion; but it is none the less a great pleasure – the highest reward of observation – to put one's hand on a rare illustration, and Mr Stevenson is certainly rare. What makes him so is the singular maturity of the expression that he has given to young sentiments: he judges them, measures them, sees them from the outside, as well as entertains them. He describes credulity with all the resources of experience, and represents a crude stage with infinite ripeness. In a word, he is an artist accomplished even to sophistication, whose constant theme is the unsophisticated. Sometimes, as in *Kidnapped*, the art is so ripe that it lifts even the subject into the general air: the execution is so serious that the idea (the idea of a boy's romantic adventures), becomes a matter of universal relations. What he prizes most in the boy's ideal is the imaginative side of it, the capacity for successful make-believe. The general freshness in which this is a part of the gloss seems to him the divinest thing in life; considerably more divine, for instance, than the passion usually regarded as the supremely tender one. The idea of making believe appeals to him much more than the idea of making love. That delightful little book of rhymes, the *Child's Garden*, commemorates from beginning to end the picturing, personifying, dramatizing faculty of infancy – the view of life from the level of the nursery-fender. The volume is a wonder for the extraordinary vividness with which it reproduces early impressions: a child might have written it if a child could see childhood from the outside, for it would seem that only a child is really near enough to the nursery floor. And what is peculiar to Mr Stevenson is that it is his own childhood he appears to delight in, and not the personal presence of little darlings. Oddly enough, there is no strong implication that he is fond of babies; he doesn't speak as a parent, or an uncle, or an educator – he speaks as a contemporary absorbed in his own game. That game is almost always a vision of dangers and triumphs, and if emotion, with him, infallibly resolves itself into memory, so memory is an evocation of throbs and thrills and suspense. He has given to the world the romance of boyhood, as others have produced that of the peerage and the police and the medical profession.

This amounts to saying that what he is most curious of in life is heroism – personal gallantry, if need be with a manner, or a banner, though he is also abundantly capable of enjoying it when it is artless. The delightful exploits of Jim Hawkins, in *Treasure Island*, are unaffectedly performed; but none the less 'the finest action is the better for a piece of purple', as the author remarks in the paper on 'The English Admirals' in *Virginibus Puerisque*, a paper of which the moral is, largely, that 'we learn to desire a grand air in our heroes; and such a knowledge of the human stage as shall make them put the dots on their own i's, and leave us in no suspense as to when they mean to be heroic.' The love of brave words as well as brave deeds – which is simply Mr Stevenson's essential love of style – is recorded in this little paper with a charming, slightly sophistical ingenuity. 'They served their guns merrily when it came to fighting, and they had the readiest ear for a bold, honourable sentiment of any class of men the world ever produced.' The author goes on to say that most men of high destinies have even high-sounding names. Alan Breck, in *Kidnapped*, is a wonderful picture of the union of courage and swagger; the little Jacobite adventurer, a figure worthy of Scott at his best, and representing the highest point that Mr Stevenson's talent has reached, shows us that a marked taste for tawdry finery – tarnished and tattered, some of it indeed, by ticklish occasions – is quite compatible with a perfectly high mettle. Alan Breck is at bottom a study of the love of glory, carried out with extreme psychological truth. When the love of glory is of an inferior order the reputation is cultivated rather than the opportunity; but when it is a pure passion the opportunity is cultivated for the sake of the reputation. Mr Stevenson's kindness for adventurers extends even to the humblest of all, the mountebank and the strolling player, or even the pedlar whom he declares that in his foreign travels he is habitually taken for, as we see in the whimsical apology for vagabonds which winds up *An Inland Voyage*. The hungry conjurer, the gymnast whose *maillot* is loose, have something of the glamour of the hero, inasmuch as they too pay with their person. 'To be even one of the outskirters of art leaves a fine stamp on a man's countenance . . . . That is the kind of thing that reconciles me to life: a ragged, tippling, incompetent old rogue, with the manners of a gentleman and the vanity of an artist, to keep up his self-respect!' What reconciles Mr Stevenson to life is the idea that in the first place it offers the widest field that we know of for odd doings, and that in the second these odd doings are the best of pegs to hang a sketch in three lines or a paradox in three pages . . . .

The novelist who leaves the extraordinary out of his account is liable to awkward confrontations, as we are compelled to reflect in this age of newspapers and of universal publicity. The next report of the next divorce case (to give an instance) shall offer us a picture of astounding combinations of circumstance and behaviour, and the annals of any energetic race are rich in curious anecdote and startling example. That interesting compilation *Vicissitudes of Families* is but a superficial record of strange accidents: the family (taken of course in the long piece), is as a general thing a catalogue of odd specimens and tangled situations, and we must remember that the most singular products are those which are not exhibited. Mr Stevenson leaves so wide a margin for the wonderful – it impinges with easy assurance upon the text – that he escapes the danger of being brought up by cases he has not allowed for. When he allows for Mr Hyde he allows for everything, and one feels moreover that even if he did not wave so gallantly the flag of the imaginative and contend that the improbable is what has most character, he would still insist that we ought to make believe. He would say we ought to make believe that the extraordinary is the best part of life even if it were not, and to do so because the finest feelings – suspense, daring, decision, passion, curiosity, gallantry, eloquence, friendship – are involved in it, and it is of infinite importance that the tradition of these precious things should not perish. He would prefer, in a word, any day in the week, Alexandre Dumas to Honoré de Balzac, and it is indeed my impression that he prefers the author of *The Three Musketeers* to any novelist except Mr George Meredith. I should go so far as to suspect that his idea of the delightful work of fiction would be the adventures of Monte Cristo related by the author of *Richard Feverel*. There is some magnanimity in his esteem for Alexandre Dumas, inasmuch as in *Kidnapped* he has put into a fable worthy of that inventor a closeness of notation with which Dumas never had anything to do. He makes us say, Let the tradition live, by all means, since it was delightful; but at the same time he is the cause of our perceiving afresh that a tradition is kept alive only by something being added to it. In this particular case – in *Doctor Jekyll* and *Kidnapped* – Mr Stevenson has added psychology.

The New Arabian Nights offer us, as the title indicates, the wonderful in the frankest, most delectable form. Partly extravagant and partly very specious, they are the result of a very happy idea, that of placing a series of adventures which are pure adventures in the setting of contemporary English life, and relating them in the placidly ingenuous tone of Scheherazade. This device is carried to perfection in *The Dynamiter*, where the manner takes on more of a kind of high-flown serenity in proportion as the incidents are more 'steep'. In this line *The Suicide Club* is Mr Stevenson's greatest success, and the first two pages of it, not to mention others, live in the memory. For reasons which I am conscious of not being able to represent as sufficient, I find something ineffaceably impressive – something really haunting – in the incident of Prince Florizel and Colonel Geraldine, who, one evening in March, are 'driven by a sharp fall of sleet into an Oyster Bar in the immediate neighbourhood of Leicester Square', and there have occasion to observe the entrance of a young man followed by a couple of commissionaires, each of whom carries a large dish of cream tarts under a cover – a young man who 'pressed these confections on every one's acceptance with exaggerated courtesy'. There is no effort at a picture here, but the imagination makes one of the lighted interior, the London sleet outside, the company that we guess, given the locality, and the strange politeness of the young man, leading on to circumstances stranger still. This is what may be called putting one in the mood for a story. But Mr Stevenson's most brilliant stroke of that kind is the opening episode of *Treasure Island*, the arrival of the brown old seaman with the sabre-cut at the 'Admiral Benbow', and the advent, not long after, of the blind sailor, with a green shade over his eyes, who comes tapping down the road, in quest of him, with his stick. *Treasure Island* is a 'boy's book' in the sense that it embodies a boy's vision of the extraordinary, but it is unique in this, and calculated to fascinate the weary mind of experience, that what we see in it is not only the ideal fable but, as part and parcel of that, as it were, the young reader himself and his state of mind: we seem to read it over his shoulder, with an arm around his neck. It is all as perfect as a well-played boy's game, and nothing can exceed the spirit and skill, the humour and the open-air feeling with which the thing is kept at the palpitating pitch. It is not only a record of queer chances, but a study of young feelings: there is a moral side in it, and the figures are not puppets with vague faces. If Jim Hawkins illustrates successful daring, he does so with a delightful rosy good-boyishness and a conscious, modest liability to error. His luck is tremendous, but it does not make him proud, and his manner is refreshingly provincial and human. So is that, even more, of the admirable John Silver, one of the most picturesque and indeed in every way most genially presented villains in the whole literature of romance. He has a singularly distinct and expressive countenance, which of course turns out to be a grimacing mask. Never was a mask more knowingly, vividly painted. *Treasure Island* will surely become – it must already have become and will remain – in its way a classic: thanks to this indescribable mixture of the prodigious and the human, of surprising coincidence and familiar feelings. The language in which Mr Stevenson has chosen to tell his story is an admirable vehicle for these feelings: with its humorous braveries and quaintnesses, its echoes of old ballads and yarns, it touches all kinds of sympathetic chords.

Is *Doctor Jekyll and Mr Hyde* a work of high philosophic intention, or simply the most ingenious and irresponsible of fictions? It has the stamp of a really imaginative production that we may take it in different ways; but I suppose it would generally be called the most serious of the author's tales. It deals with the relation of the baser parts of man to his nobler, of the capacity for evil that exists in the most generous natures; and it expresses these things in a fable which is a wonderfully happy invention. The subject is endlessly interesting, and rich in all sorts of provocation, and Mr Stevenson is to be congratulated on having touched the core of it. I may do him injustice, but it is, however, here, not the profundity of the idea which strikes me so much as the art of the presentation – the extremely successful form. There is a genuine feeling for the perpetual moral question, a fresh sense of the difficulty of being good and the brutishness of being bad; but what there is above all is a singular ability in holding the interest. I confess that that, to my sense, is the most edifying thing in the short, rapid, concentrated story, which is really a masterpiece of concision. There is something almost impertinent in the way, as I have noticed, in which Mr Stevenson achieves his best effects without the aid of the ladies, and *Doctor Jekyll* is a capital example of his heartless independence. It is usually supposed that a truly poignant impression cannot be made without them, but in the drama of Mr Hyde's fatal ascendency they remain altogether in the wing. It is very obvious – I do not say it cynically – that they must have played an important part in his development. The gruesome tone of the tale is, no doubt, deepened by their absence: it is like the late afternoon light of a foggy winter

Sunday, when even inanimate objects have a kind of wicked look. I remember few situations in the pages of mystifying fiction more to the purpose than the episode of Mr Utterson's going to Doctor Jekyll's to confer with the butler when the Doctor is locked up in his laboratory, and the old servant, whose sagacity has hitherto encountered successfully the problems of the sideboard and the pantry, confesses that this time he is utterly baffled. The way the two men, at the door of the laboratory, discuss the identity of the mysterious personage inside, who has revealed himself in two or three inhuman glimpses to Poole, has those touches of which irresistible shudders are made. The butler's theory is that his master has been murdered, and that the murderer is in the room, personating him with a sort of clumsy diabolism. 'Well, when that masked thing like a monkey jumped from among the chemicals and whipped into the cabinet, it went down my spine like ice.' That is the effect upon the reader of most of the story. I say of most rather than of all, because the ice rather melts in the sequel, and I have some difficulty in accepting the business of the powders, which seems to me too explicit and explanatory. The powders constitute the machinery of the transformation, and it will probably have struck many readers that this uncanny process would be more conceivable (so far as one may speak of the conceivable in such a case), if the author had not made it so definite.

I have left Mr Stevenson's best book to the last, as it is also the last he has given (at the present speaking) to the public – the tales comprising *The Merry Men* having already appeared; but I find that on the way I have anticipated some of the remarks that I had intended to make about it. That which is most to the point is that there are parts of it so fine as to suggest that the author's talent has taken a fresh start, various as have been the impulses in which it had already indulged, and serious the hindrances among which it is condemned to exert itself. There would have been a kind of perverse humility in his keeping up the fiction that a production so literary as *Kidnapped* is addressed to immature minds, and, though it was originally given to the world, I believe, in a 'boy's paper', the story embraces every occasion that it meets to satisfy the higher criticism. It has two weak spots, which need simply to be mentioned. The cruel and miserly uncle, in the first chapters, is rather in the tone of superseded tradition, and the tricks he plays upon his ingenuous nephew are a little like those of country conjurers. In these pages we feel that Mr Stevenson is thinking too much of what a 'boy's paper' is expected to contain. Then the history stops without ending, as it were; but I think I may add that this accident speaks for itself. Mr Stevenson has often to lay down his pen for reasons that have nothing to do with the failure of inspiration, and the last page of David Balfour's adventures is an honourable plea for indulgence. The remaining five-sixths of the book deserve to stand by *Henry Esmond* as a fictive autobiography in archaic form. The author's sense of the English idiom of the last century, and still more of the Scotch, has enabled him to give a gallant companion to Thackeray's *tour de force*. The life, the humour, the colour of the central portions of *Kidnapped* have a singular pictorial virtue: these passages read like a series of inspired footnotes on some historic page. The charm of the most romantic episode in the world, though perhaps it would be hard to say why it is the most romantic, when it was associated with so much stupidity, is over the whole business, and the forlorn hope of the Stuarts is revived for us without evoking satiety. There could be no better instance of the author's talent for seeing the familiar in the heroic, and reducing the extravagant to plausible detail, than the description of Alan Breck's defence in the cabin of the ship and the really magnificent chapters of 'The Flight in the Heather'. Mr Stevenson has in a high degree (and doubtless for good reasons of his own) what may be called the imagination of physical states, and this has enabled him to arrive at a wonderfully exact translation of the miseries of his panting Lowland hero, dragged for days and nights over hill and dale, through bog and thicket, without meat or drink or rest, at the tail of an Homeric Highlander. The great superiority of the book resides to my mind, however, in the fact that it puts two characters on their feet with admirable rectitude. I have paid my tribute to Alan Breck, and I can only repeat that he is a masterpiece. It is interesting to observe that though the man is extravagant, the author's touch exaggerates nothing: it is throughout of the most truthful, genial, ironical kind; full of penetration, but with none of the grossness of moralizing satire. The figure is a genuine study, and nothing can be more charming than the way Mr Stevenson both sees through it and admires it. Shall I say that he sees through David Balfour? This would be perhaps to underestimate the density of that medium. Beautiful, at any rate, is the expression which this unfortunate though circumspect youth gives to those qualities which combine to excite our respect and our objurgation in the Scottish character. Such a scene as the episode of the quarrel of the two men on the mountain-side is a real stroke of genius, and has the very logic and rhythm of life; a quarrel which we feel to be inevitable, though it is about nothing, or almost nothing, and which springs from exasperated nerves and the simple shock of temperaments. The author's vision of it has a profundity which goes deeper, I think, than *Doctor Jekyll*. I know of few better examples of the way genius has ever a surprise in its pocket – keeps an ace, as it were, up its sleeve. And in this case it endears itself to us by making us reflect that such a passage as the one I speak of is in fact a signal proof of what the novel can do at its best, and what nothing else can do so well. In the presence of this sort of success we perceive its immense value. It is capable of a rare transparency – it can illustrate human affairs in cases so delicate and complicated that any other vehicle would be clumsy. To those who love the art that Mr Stevenson practises he will appear, in pointing this incidental moral, not only to have won a particular triumph, but to have given a delightful pledge.

31

'The Journal of the Brothers de Goncourt', Fortnightly
Review, October 1888.

I CAN SCARCELY forbear beginning these limited remarks on an
interesting subject with a regret – the regret that I had not found the
right occasion to make them two or three years ago. This is not
because since that time the subject has become less attaching, but
precisely because it has become more so, has become so absorbing
that I am oppressively conscious of the difficulty of treating it. It was
never, I think, an easy one; inasmuch as for persons interested in
questions of literature, of art, of form, in the general question of the
observation of life for an artistic purpose, the appeal and the
solicitation of Edmond and Jules de Goncourt were essentially not
simple and soothing. The manner of this extraordinary pair, their
temper, their strenuous effort and conscious system, suggested anything but a quick solution of the problems that seemed to hum in our
ears as we read; suggested it almost as little indeed as their curious,
uncomfortable style, with its multiplied touches and pictorial ver-
bosity, was apt to evoke an immediate vision of the objects to which
it made such sacrifices of the synthetic and the rhythmic. None the
less, if one liked them well enough to persist, one ended by making
terms with them; I allude to the liking as conditional, because it
appears to be a rule of human relations that it is by no means always a
sufficient bond of sympathy for people to care for the same things:
there may be so increasing a divergence when they care for them in
different ways. The great characteristic of the way of the brothers De
Goncourt was that it was extraordinarily 'modern'; so illustrative of
feelings that had not yet found intense expression in literature that it
made at last the definite standpoint, the common ground and the

clear light for taking one's view of them. They bristled (the word is their own) with responsible professions, and took us farther into the confidence of their varied sensibility than we always felt it important to penetrate; but the formula that expressed them remained well in sight. They were historians and observers who were painters; they composed biographies, they told stories, with the palette always on their thumb.

Now, however, all that is changed and the case is infinitely more complicated. M. Edmond de Goncourt has published, at intervals of a few months, the Journal kept for twenty years by his brother and himself, and the Journal makes all the difference. The situation was comparatively manageable before, but now it strikes us as extremely embarrassing. M. Edmond de Goncourt has mixed the cards in the most extraordinary way; he has shifted his position with a carelessness of consequences of which I know no other example. Who can recall an instance of an artist's having it in his power to deprive himself of the advantage of the critical perspective in which he stands, and being eager to use that power?

That MM. de Goncourt should have so faithfully carried on their Journal is a very interesting and remarkable fact, as to which there will be much to say; but it has almost a vulgarly usual air in comparison with the circumstance that one of them has judged best to give the document to the light. If it be true that the elder and surviving brother has held a part of it back, that only adds to the judicious, responsible quality of the act. He has selected, and that indicates a plan and constitutes a presumption of sanity. There has been, so to speak, a method in M. Edmond de Goncourt's madness. I use the term madness because it so conveniently covers most of the ground. How else indeed should one express it when a man of talent defaces with his own hand not only the image of himself that public opinion has erected on the highway of literature, but also the image of a loved and lost partner who can raise no protest and offer no explanation? If instead of publishing his Journal M. de Goncourt had burned it up we should have been deprived of a very curious and entertaining book; but even with that consciousness we should have remembered that it would have been impertinent to expect him to do anything else. Barely conceivable would it have been had he withheld the copious record from the flames for the perusal of a posterity who would pass judgment on it when he himself should be dust. That would have been an act of high humility – the sacrifice of the finer part of one's reputation; but, after all, a man can commit suicide only in his life-time, and the example would have had its distinction on the part of a curious mind moved by sympathy with the curiosity of a coming age.

If I suggest that if it were possible to us to hear Jules de Goncourt's voice to-day it might convey an explanation, this perhaps represents an explanation as more possible than we see it as yet. Certainly it is difficult to see it as graceful or as conciliatory. There is scarcely any account we can give of the motive of the act that doesn't make it almost less an occasion for complacency than the act itself. (I still refer, of course, to the publication, not to the composition, of the Journal. The composition, for nervous, irritated, exasperated characters, may have been a relief – though even in this light its operation appears to have been slow and imperfect. Indeed, it occurs to one that M. Edmond de Goncourt may have felt the whimsical impulse to expose the fond remedy as ineffectual.) If the motive was not humility, not mortification, it was something else – something that we can properly appreciate only by remembering that it is not enough to be proud, and that the question inevitably comes up of what one's pride is about. If MM. de Goncourt were two almost furious *névrosés*, if the infinite vibration of their nerves and the soreness of their sentient parts were the condition on which they produced many interesting books, the fact was pathetic and the misfortune great, but the legitimacy of the whole thing was incontestable. People are made as they are made, and some are weak in one way and some in another. What passes our comprehension is the state of mind in which their weakness appears to them a source of glory or even of dolorous general interest. It may be an inevitable, or it may even for certain sorts of production be an indispensable, thing to be a *névrosé*; but in what particular juncture is it a communicable thing? M. de Goncourt not only communicates the case, but insists upon it; he has done personally what M. Maxime du Camp did a few years ago for Gustave Flaubert (in his *Souvenirs Littéraires*) when he made known to the world that the author of *Madame Bovary* had epileptic fits. The differences are great, however, for if we are disposed to question M. du Camp's right to put another person's secret into circulation, we must admit that he does so with compunction and mourning. M. de Goncourt, on the other hand, waves the banner of the infirmity that his *collaborateur* shared with him and invites all men to listen to the details. About his right, I hasten to add, so far as he speaks for himself, there is nothing dubious, and this puts us in a rare position for reading and enjoying his book. We are not accomplices and our honour is safe. People are betrayed by their friends, their enemies, their biographers, their critics, their editors, their publishers, and so far as we give ear in these cases we are not quite without guilt; but it is much plainer sailing when the burden of defence rests on the very sufferers. What would have been thought of a friend or an editor, what would have been thought even of an enemy, who should have ventured to print the Journal of MM. de Goncourt?

The reason why it must always be asked in future, with regard to any appreciation of these gentlemen, 'Was it formed before the Journal or after the Journal?' is simply that this publication has obtruded into our sense of their literary performance the disturbance of a revelation of personal character. The scale on which the disturbance presents itself is our ground for surprise, and the nature of the character exhibited our warrant for regret. The complication is simply that if to-day we wish to judge the writings of the brothers De Goncourt freely, largely, historically, the feat is almost impossible. We have to reckon with a prejudice – a prejudice of our own. And that is why a critic may be sorry to have missed the occasion of testifying to a liberal comprehension before the prejudice was engendered. Almost impossible, I say, but fortunately not altogether; for is it not the very function of criticism and the sign of its intelligence to acquit itself honourably in embarrassing conditions and track the idea with patience just in proportion as it is elusive? The good method is always to sacrifice nothing. Let us therefore not regret too much either that MM. de Goncourt did not burn their Journal if they wished their novels to be liked, or that they did not burn their novels if they wished their Journal to be forgotten. The difficult point to deal with as regards this latter production is that it is a journal of pretensions; for is it not a sound generalization to say that when we speak of pretensions we always mean pretensions exaggerated? If the Journal sets them forth, it is in the novels that we look to see them justified. If the justification is imperfect, that will not disgust us, for what does the disparity do more than help to characterize our authors? The importance of their being characterized depends largely on their talent (for people engaged in the same general effort and interested in the same questions), and of a poverty of talent even the reader most struck with the unamiable way in which, as diarists, they for the most part use their powers will surely not accuse MM. de Goncourt. They express, they represent, they give the sense of life; it is not always the life that such and such a one of their readers will find most interesting, but that is his affair and not theirs. Theirs is to vivify the picture. This art they unmistakably possess, and the Journal testifies to it still more than *Germinie Lacerteux* and *Manette Salomon*; infinitely more, I may add, than the novels published by M. Edmond de Goncourt since the death of his brother.

I do not pronounce for the moment either on the justice or the generosity of the portrait of Sainte-Beuve produced in the Journal by a thousand small touches, entries made from month to month and year to year, and taking up so much place in the whole that the representation of that figure (with the Princess Mathilde, Gavarni, Théophile Gautier, and Gustave Flaubert thrown in a little behind) may almost be said to be the main effect of the three volumes. What is incontestable is the intensity of the vision, the roundness of the conception, and the way that the innumerable little parts of the image hang together. The Sainte-Beuve of MM. de Goncourt may not be the real Sainte-Beuve, but he is a wonderfully possible and consistent personage. He is observed with detestation, but at least he is observed, and the faculty is welcome and rare. This is what we mean by talent – by having something fresh to contribute. Let us be grateful for anything at all fresh so long as our gratitude is not chilled – a case in which it has always the resource of being silent. It is obvious that this check is constantly at hand in our intercourse with MM. de Goncourt, for the simple reason that, with the greatest desire in the world to see all round, we cannot rid ourselves of the superstition that, when all is said and done, art is most in character when it most shows itself amiable. It is not amiable when it is narrow and exclusive and jealous, when it makes the deplorable confession that it has no secret for resisting exasperation. It is not the sign of a free intelligence or a rich life to be hysterical because somebody's work whom you don't like affirms itself in opposition to that of somebody else whom you do; but this condition is calculated particularly little to please when the excitement springs from a comparison more personal. It is almost a platitude to say that the artistic passion will ever most successfully assuage the popular suspicion that there is a latent cruelty in it when it succeeds in not appearing to be closely connected with egotism. The uncalculated trick played by our authors upon their reputation was to suppose that their name could bear such a strain. It is tolerably clear that it can't, and this is the mistake we should have to forgive them if we proposed to consider their productions as a whole. It doesn't cover all the ground to say that the injury of their mistake is only for themselves: it is really in some degree for those who take an interest in the art they practise. Such eccentrics, such passionate seekers, may not, in England and America, be numerous; but even if they are a modest band, their complaint is worth taking account of. No one can ever have been nearly so much interested in the work of Edmond and Jules de Goncourt as these gentlemen themselves; their deep absorption in it, defying all competition, is one of the honourable sides of their literary character. But the general brotherhood of men of letters may very well have felt humiliated by the disclosure of such wrath in celestial, that is, in analogous minds. It is, in short, rather a shock to find that artists who could make such a miniature of their Sainte-Beuve have not carried their delicacy a little further. It is always a pain to perceive that some of the qualities we prize don't imply the others.

What makes it important not to sacrifice the Journal (to speak for the present only of that) is this very illustration of the degree to which, for the indefatigable diarists, the things of literature and art are the great realities. If every genuine talent is for the critic a 'case' constituted by the special mixture of elements and faculties, it is not difficult to put one's finger on the symptoms in which that of these unanimous brothers resides. It consists in their feeling life so exclusively as a theme for descriptive pictorial prose. Their exclusiveness is, so far as I know, unprecedented; for if we have encountered men of erudition, men of science as deeply buried in learning and in physics, we have never encountered a man of letters (our authors are really one in their duality) for whom his profession was such an exhaustion of his possibilities. Their friend and countryman Flaubert doubtless gave himself up to 'art' with a few reservations, but our authors have over him exactly the superiority that the Journal gives them: it is a proof the more of their concentration, of their having drawn breath only in the world of subject and form. If they are not more representative, they are at least more convenient to refer to. Their concentration comes in part from the fact that it is the meeting of two natures, but this also would have counted in favour of expansion, of leakage. 'Collaboration' is always a mystery, and that of MM. de Goncourt was probably close beyond any other; but we have seen the process successful several times, so that the real wonder is not that in this case the parties to it should have been able to work together, to divide the task without dividing the effect, but rather that nature should have struck off a double copy of a rare original. An original is a conceivable thing, but a pair of originals who are original in exactly the same way is a phenomenon embodied so far as I know only in the authors of *Manette Salomon*. The relation borne by their feelings on the question of art and taste to their other feelings (which they assure us were very much less identical), this peculiar proportion constitutes their originality. In whom was ever the group of 'other feelings' proportionately so small? In whom else did the critical vibration (in respect to the things cared for, limited in number, even very limited, I admit) represent so nearly the totality of emotion? The occasions left for MM. de Goncourt to vibrate differently were so few that they scarcely need be counted.

The manifestation of life that most appeals to them is the manifestation of Watteau, of Lancret, of Boucher, of Fragonard; they are primarily critics of pictorial art (with sympathies restricted very much to a period) whose form of expression happens to be literary, but whose sensibility is the sensibility of the painter and the sculptor, and whose attempt, allowing for the difference of the instrument, is to do what the painter and the sculptor do. The most general stricture to be made on their work is probably that they have not allowed enough for the difference of the instrument, have persisted in the effort to render impressions that the plastic artist renders better, neglecting too much those he is unable to render. From time to time they have put forth a volume which is really an instructive instance of misapplied ingenuity. In *Madame Gervaisais*, for example, a picture of the visible, sketchable Rome of twenty-five years ago, we seem to hear the voice forced to sing in a register to which it doesn't belong, or rather (the comparison is more complete) to attempt effects of sound that are essentially not vocal. The novelist competes with the painter and the painter with the novelist, in the treatment of the aspect and figure of things; but what a happy tact each of them needs to keep his course straight, without poaching on the other's preserves! In England it is the painter who is apt to poach most, and in France the writer. However this may be, no one probably has poached more than have MM. de Goncourt.

Whether it be because there is something that touches us in pious persistence in error, or because even when it prevails there may on the part of a genuine talent be the happiest hits by the way, I will not pretend to declare; certain it is that the manner in which our authors abound in their own sense and make us feel that they would not for the world care for anything but what exactly they do care for, raises the liveliest presumption in their favour. If literature is kept alive by a passion loyal even to narrowness, MM. de Goncourt have rendered real services. They may look for it on the one side in directions too few, and on the other in regions thankless and barren; their Journal, at all events, is a signal proof of their good faith. Wonderful are such courage and patience and industry; fatigued, displeased, disappointed, they never intermit their chronicle nor falter in their task. We owe to this remarkable feat the vivid reflection of their life for twenty years, from the *coup d'état* which produced the Second Empire to the death of the younger brother on the eve of the war with Germany; the history of their numerous books, their articles, their studies, studies on the social and artistic history of France during the latter half of the last century – on Mme de Pompadour, Mme du Barry, and the other mistresses of Louis XV, on Marie Antoinette, on society and *la femme* during the Revolution and the Directory; the register, moreover, of their adventures and triumphs as collectors (collectors of the furniture, tapestries, drawings of the last century), of their observations of every kind in the direction in which their nature and their *milieu* prompt them to observe, of their talks, their visits, their dinners, their physical and intellectual states, their projects and visions, their ambitions and collapses, and, above all, of their likes and dislikes. Above all of their dislikes, perhaps I should say, for in this sort of testimony the Journal is exceedingly rich. The number of things and of people obnoxious to their taste is extremely large, especially when we consider the absence of variety, as the English reader judges variety, in their personal experience. What strikes an English reader, curious about a society in which acuteness has a high development and thankful for a picture of it, is the small surface over which the career of MM. de Goncourt is distributed. It seems all to take place in a little ring, a coterie of a dozen people. Movement, exercise, travel, other countries, play no part in it; the same persons, the same places, names, and occasions perpetually recur; there is scarcely any change of scene or any enlargement of horizon. The authors rarely go into the country, and when they do they hate it, for they find it *bête*. To the English mind that item probably describes them better than anything else. We end with the sensation of a closed room, of a want of ventilation; we long to open a window or two and let in the air of the world. The Journal of MM. de Goncourt is mainly a record of resentment and suffering, and to this circumstance they attribute many causes; but we suspect at last that the real cause is for them too the inconvenience from which we suffer as readers – simply the want of space and air.

Though the surface of the life represented is, as I have said, small, it is large enough to contain a great deal of violent reaction, an extraordinary quantity of animadversion, indignation, denunciation. Indeed, as I have intimated, the simplest way to sketch the relation of disagreement of our accomplished diarists would be to mention the handful of persons and things excepted from it. They are 'down' absolutely on Sainte-Beuve and strongly on MM. Taine and Schérer. But I am taking the wrong course. The great exceptions then, in addition to the half-dozen friends I have mentioned (the Princess, Gavarni, Théophile Gautier, Flaubert, and Paul de Saint-Victor, though the two last named with restrictions which finally become in the one case considerable and in the other very marked), are the artistic production of the reign of Louis XV and some of the literary, notably that of Diderot, which they oppose with a good deal of acrimony to that of Voltaire. They have also no quarrel with the wonderful figure of Marie Antoinette, unique in its evocation of luxury and misery, as is proved by the elaborate monograph which they published in 1858. This list may appear meagre, but I think it really exhausts their positive sympathies, so far as the Journal enlightens us. That is precisely the interesting point and the fact that arrests us, that the Journal, copious as a memorandum of the artistic life, is in so abnormally small a degree a picture of enjoyment. Such a fact suggests all sorts of reflections, and in particular an almost anxious one as to whether the passionate artistic life necessarily excludes enjoyment. I say the passionate because this makes the example better; it is only passion that gives us revelations and notes. If the artist is necessarily sensitive, does that sensitiveness form in its essence a state constantly liable to shade off into the morbid? Does this liability, moreover, increase in proportion as the effort is great and the ambition intense? MM. de Goncourt have this ground for expecting us to cite their experience in the affirmative, that it is an experience abounding in revelations. I don't mean to say that they are all, but only that they are preponderantly, revelations of suffering. In the month of March, 1859, in allusion to their occupations and projects, they make the excellent remark, the fruit of acquired wisdom, that 'In this world one must do a great deal, one must intend a great deal.' That is refreshing, that is a breath of air. But as a general thing what they commemorate as workers is the simple break-down of joy.

'Tell us,' they would probably say, 'where you will find an analysis equally close of the cheerfulness of creation, and then we will admit that our testimony is superficial. Many a record of a happy personal life, yes; but that is not to the point. The question is how many windows are opened, how many little holes are pierced, into the consciousness of the artist. Our contention would be that we have pierced more little holes than any other gimlet has achieved. Doubtless there are many people who are not curious about the consciousness of the artist who would look into our little holes – if the sense of a kind of indelicacy, even of indecency in the proceeding were not too much for them – mainly with some ulterior view of making fun of them. Of course the better economy for such people is to let us alone. But if you *are* curious (there are a few who happen to be), where will you get to the same degree as in these patient pages the particular sensation of having your curiosity stimulated and fed? Will you get it in the long biography of Scott, in that of Dickens, in the auto-biography of Trollope, in the letters of Thackeray? An intimation has reached us that in reading the letters of Thackeray you are moved, on the contrary, to wonder by what trick certain natural little betrayals of the consciousness of the artist have been conjured away. Very likely (we see you mean it) such betrayals are "natural" only when people have a sense of responsibility. This sense may very well be a fault, but it is a fault to which the world owes some valuable information. Ah! of course if you don't think our information valuable, there is no use talking.' The most convenient answer to this little address would probably be the remark that valuable information is supplied by the artist in more ways than one, and that we must look for it in his finished pieces as well as in his note-books. If we should see a flaw in this supposititious plea of our contentious friends it would be after turning back to *Germinie Lacerteux* and *Manette Salomon*. Distinguished and suggestive as these performances are, they do not illustrate the artistic view so very much more than the works of those writers whose neglect of the practice of keeping a diary of protest lays them open to the imputation of levity.

In reading the three volumes pencil in hand, I have marked page after page as strongly characteristic, but I find in turning them over that it would be difficult to quote from them without some principle of selection. The striking passages or pages range themselves under three or four heads – the observation of persons, the observation of places and things (works of art, largely), the report of conversations, and the general chapter of the subjective, which, as I have hinted, is the general chapter of the *saignant*. 'During dinner,' I read in the second volume, *'nous avons l'agacement* of hearing Sainte-Beuve, the fine talker, the fine connoisseur in letters, talk art in a muddled manner, praise Eugène Delacroix as a philosophical painter,' etc. These words, *nous avons l'agacement*, might stand as the epigraph of the Journal at large, so exact a translation would they be of the emotion apparently most frequent with the authors. On every possible and impossible occasion they have the annoyance. I hasten to add that I can easily imagine it to have been an annoyance to hear the historian of Port Royal talk, and talk badly, about Eugène Delacroix. But on whatever subject he expressed himself he seems to have been to the historians of Manette Salomon even as a red rag to a bull. The aversion they entertained for him, a plant watered by frequent intercourse and protected by punctual notes, has brought them good luck; in this sense, I mean, that they have made a more living figure of him than of any name in their work. The taste of the whole evocation is, to my mind and speaking crudely, atrocious; there is only one other case (the portrait of Madame de Païva) in which it is more difficult to imagine the justification of so great a licence. Nothing of all this is quotable by a cordial admirer of Sainte-Beuve, who, however, would resent the treachery of it even more than he does if he were not careful to remember that the scandalized reader has always the resource of opening the *Causeries du Lundi*. MM. de Goncourt write too much as if they had forgotten that. The thirty volumes of that wonderful work contain a sufficiently substantial answer to their account of the figure he cut when they dined with him as his invited guests or as fellow-members of a brilliant club. Impression for impression, we have that of the Causeries to set against that of the Journal, and it takes the larger hold of us. The reason is that it belongs to the finer part of Sainte-Beuve; whereas the picture from the Goncourt gallery (representing him, for instance, as a *petit mercier de province en partie fine*) deals only with his personal features. These are important, and they were unfortunately anything but superior; but they were not so important as MM. de Goncourt's love of art for art makes them, nor so odious surely when they were seen in conjunction with the nature of his extraordinary mind. Upon the nature of his extraordinary mind our authors throw no more light than his washerwoman or his shoemaker might have done. They may very well have said, of course, that this was not their business, and that the fault was the eminent critic's if his small and ugly sides were what showed most in his conversation. Their business, they may contend, was simply to report that conversation and its accompaniment of little, compromising personal facts as minutely and vividly as possible; to attempt to reproduce for others the image that moved before them with such infirmities, and limitations. Why for others? the reader of these volumes may well ask himself in this connection as well as in many another; so clear does it appear to him that *he* must have been out of the question of Sainte-Beuve's private relations – just as he feels that he was never included in that of Madame de Païva's or the Princess Mathilde's. We are confronted afresh with the whole subject of critical discretion, the responsibility of exposure, and the strange literary manners of our day. The Journal of MM. de Goncourt will have rendered at least the service of fortifying the blessed cause of occasional silence. If their ambition was to make Sainte-Beuve odious, it has suffered the injury that we are really more disagreeably affected by the character of the attack. That is more odious even than the want of private dignity of a demoralized investigator. And in this case the question the reader further asks is, Why even for themselves? and what superior interest was served by the elaboration week by week of this minute record of an implacable animosity? Keeping so patiently-written, so crossed and dotted and dated a register of hatred is a practice that gives the queerest account of your own nature, and indeed there are strange lights thrown throughout these pages on that of MM. de Goncourt. There is a kind of ferocity in the way the reporter that abides in them (how could they have abstained from kicking him out of doors with a 'You're very clever, but you're really a bird of night'?) pursues the decomposing *causeur* to the end, seeking effects of grotesqueness in the aspects of his person and the misery of his disease.

All this is most unholy, especially on the part of a pair of *délicats*. MM. de Goncourt, I know, profess a perfect readiness to relinquish this title in certain conditions; they consider that there is a large delicacy and a small one, and they remind us of the fact that they could never have written *Germinie Lacerteux* if they had been afraid of being called coarse. In fact they imply, I think, that for people of masculine observation the term has no relevancy at all; it is simply non-observant in its associations and exists for the convenience of the ladies – a respectable function, but one of which the importance should not be overrated. This idea is luminous, but it will probably never go far without plumping against another, namely, that there is a reality in the danger of *feeling* coarsely, that the epithet represents also a state of perception. Does it come about, the danger in question, in consequence of too prolonged a study, however disinterested, of the uglinesses and uncleannesses of life? It may occur in that fashion and it may occur in others; the point is that we recognize its ravages when we encounter them, and that they are a much more serious matter than the accident – the source of some silly reproach to our authors – of having narrated the history of an hysterical servant-girl. That is a detail (*Germinie Lacerteux* is a very brilliant experiment), whereas the catastrophe I speak of is of the very essence. We know it has taken place when we begin to notice that the artist's instrument has parted with the quality which is supposed to make it most precious – the fineness to which it owed its sureness, its exemption from mistakes. The spectator's disappointment is great, of course, in proportion as his confidence was high. The fine temper of MM. de Goncourt has inspired us with the highest; their whole attitude had been a protest against vulgarity. Mere prettiness of subject – we were aware of the very relative place they give to that; but, on the other hand, had they not mastered the whole gamut of the shades of the aristocratic sense? Was not a part of the charm of execution of *Germinie Lacerteux* the glimpse of the taper fingers that wielded the brush? It was not perhaps the brush of Vandyck, but might Vandyck not have painted the white hand that held it? It is no white hand that holds, alas, this uncontrollably querulous and systematically treacherous pen. 'Mémoires de la Vie Littéraire' is the sub-title of their Journal; but what sort of a life will posterity credit us with having led and for what sort of chroniclers will they take the two gentlemen who were assiduous attendants at the Diner Magny only to the end that they might smuggle in, as it were, the uninvited (that is, you and me who read), and entertain them at the expense of their colleagues and comrades? The Diner Magny was a club, the club is a high expression of the civilization of our time; but the way in which MM. de Goncourt interpret the institution makes them singular participants of that civilization. It is a strange performance, when one thinks of the performers – celebrated representatives of the refinement of their age. 'If this was the best society,' our grand-children may say, 'what could have been the *procédés* in that which was not so good?'

It is the firm conviction of many persons that literature is not doing well, that it is even distinctly on the wane, and that before many years it will have ceased to exist in any agreeable form, so that those living at that period will have to look far back for any happy example of it. May it not occur to us that if they look back to the phase lately embodied by MM. de Goncourt it will perhaps strike them that their loss is not cruel, since the vanished boon was, after all, so far from guaranteeing the amenities of things? May the moral not appear pointed by the authors of the Journal rather than by the *confrères* they have sacrificed? We of the English tongue move here already now in a region of uncertain light, where our proper traditions and canons cease to guide our steps. The portions of the work before us that refer to Madame de Païva, to the Princess Mathilde Bonaparte, leave us absolutely without a principle of appreciation. If it be correct according to the society in which they live, we have only to learn the lesson that we have no equivalent for some of the ideas and standards of that society. We read on one page that our authors were personal friends of Madame de Païva, her guests, her interlocutors, recipients of her confidence, partakers of her hospitality, spectators of her splendour. On the next we see her treated like the last of the last, with not only her character but her person held up to our irreverent inspection, and the declaration that 'elle s'est toute crachée', in a phrase which showed one day that she was purse-proud. Is it because the lady owed her great wealth to the favours of which she had been lavish that MM. de Goncourt hold themselves free to turn her friendship to this sort of profit? If Madame de Païva was good enough to dine, or anything else, with, she was good enough either to speak of without brutality or to speak of not at all. Does not this misdemeanour of MM. de Goncourt perhaps represent, where women are concerned, a national as well as a personal tendency – a tendency which introduces the strangest of complications into the French theory of gallantry? Our Anglo-Saxon theory has only one face, while the French appears to have two; with 'Make love to her', as it were, on one side, and 'Tue-la' on the other. The French theory, in a word, involves a great deal of killing, and the ladies who are the subject of it must often ask themselves whether they do not pay dearly for this advantage of being made love to. By 'killing' I allude to the exploits of the pen as well as to those of the directer weapons so ardently advocated by M. Dumas the younger. On what theory has M. Edmond de Goncourt handed over to publicity the whole record of his relations with the Princess Mathilde? He stays in her house for days, for weeks together, and then portrays for our entertainment her person, her clothes, her gestures, and her *salon*, repeating her words, reproducing her language, relating anecdotes at her expense, describing the freedom of speech used towards her by her *convives*, the racy expressions that passed her own lips. In one place he narrates (or is it his brother?) how the Princess was unable to resist the impulse to place a kiss upon his brow. The liberty taken is immense, and the idea of gallantry here has undergone a transmutation which lifts it quite out of measurement by any scale or scruple of ours. I repeat that the plea is surely idle that the brothers are accomplished reporters to whom an enterprising newspaper would have found it worth while to pay a high salary; for that cleverness, that intelligence, are simply the very standard by which we judge them. The betrayal of the Princess is altogether beyond us.

Would Théophile Gautier feel that he is betrayed? Probably not, for Théophile Gautier's feelings, as represented by MM. de Goncourt, were nothing if not eccentric, his judgment nothing if not perverse. His two friends say somewhere that the sign of his conversation was *l'eñormité dans le paradoxe*. He certainly then would have risen to the occasion if it were a question of maintaining that his friends had rendered a service to his reputation. This to my mind is contestable, though their intention (at least in publishing their notes on him) was evidently to do so, for the greater part of his talk, as they repeat it, owes most of its relief to its obscenity. That is not fair to a man really clever – they should have given some other examples. But what strongly strikes us, however the service to Gautier may be estimated, is that they have rendered a questionable service to themselves. He is the finest mind in their pages, he is ever the object of their sympathy and applause. That is very graceful, but it enlightens us as to their intellectual perspective, and I say this with a full recollection of all that can be urged on Gautier's behalf. He was a charming genius, he was an admirable, a delightful writer. His vision was all his own and his brush was worthy of his vision. He knew the French colour-box as well as if he had ground the pigments, and it may really be said of him that he did grind a great many of them. And yet with all this he is not one of the first, for his poverty of ideas was great. *Le sultan de l'épithète* our authors call him, but he was not the emperor of thought. To be light is not necessarily a damning limitation. Who was lighter than Charles Lamb, for instance, and yet who was wiser for our immediate needs? Gautier's defect is that he had veritably but one idea: he never got beyond the superstition that real literary greatness is to bewilder the *bourgeois*. Flaubert sat, intellectually, in the same everlasting twilight, and the misfortune is even greater for him, for his was the greater spirit.

Gautier had other misfortunes as well – the struggle that never came to success, the want of margin, of time to do the best work, the conflict, in a hand-to-mouth, hackneyed literary career, between splendid images and peculiarly sordid realities. Moreover, his paradoxes were usually genial and his pessimism was amiable – in the poetic glow of many of his verses and sketches you can scarcely tell it from optimism. All this makes us tender to his memory, but it does not blind us to the fact that MM. de Goncourt classify themselves when they show us that in the literary circle of their time they find him the most typical figure. He has the supreme importance, he looms largest and covers most ground. This leaves Gautier very much where he was, but it tickets his fastidious friends.

'Théophile Gautier, who is here for some days, talks opera-dancers,' they note in the summer of 1868. 'He describes the white satin shoe which, for each of them, is strengthened by a little cushion of silk in the places where the dancer feels that she bears and presses most; a cushion which would indicate to an expert the name of the dancer. And observe that this work is always done by the dancer herself.' I scarcely know why, but there is something singularly characteristic in this last injunction of MM. de Goncourt, or of MM. de Goncourt and Théophile Gautier combined: 'Et remarquez –!' The circumstance that a ballet-girl cobbles her shoes in a certain way has indeed an extreme significance. 'Gautier begins to rejudge *The Misanthrope*, a comedy for a Jesuit college on the return from the holidays. Ah! the pig – what a language! it *is* ill-written!' And Gautier adds that he can't say this in print; people would abuse him and it would take the bread out of his mouth. And then he falls foul of Louis XIV. 'A hog, pock-marked like a colander, and short! He was not five feet high, the great king. Always eating and – ' My quotation is nipped in the bud: an attempt to reproduce Gautier's conversation in English encounters obstacles on the threshold. In this case we must burn pastilles even to read the rest of the sketch, and we cannot translate it at all. '*Les bourgeois* – why, the most enormous things go on *chez les bourgeois*,' he remarks on another occasion. 'I have had a glimpse of a few interiors. It is the sort of thing to make you veil your face.' But again I must stop. M. Taine on this occasion courageously undertakes the defence of the *bourgeois*, of their decency, but M. Paul de Saint-Victor comes to Gautier's support with an allusion impossible even to paraphrase, which apparently leaves those gentle-men in possession of the field. The effort of our time has been, as we know, to disinter the details of history, to see the celebrities of the past, and even the obscure persons, in the small facts as well as in the big facts of their lives. In his realistic evocation of Louis XIV Gautier was in agreement with this fashion; the historic imagination operated in him by the light of the rest of his mind. But it is through the nose even more than through the eyes that it appears to have operated, and these flowers of his conversation suggest that, though he was certainly an animated talker, our wonder at such an ano-maly as that MM. de Goncourt should apparently have sacrificed almost every one else to their estimate of him is not without its reasons.

There are lights upon Flaubert's conversation which are somewhat of the same character (though not in every case) as those projected upon Gautier's. Gautier himself furnishes one of the most interesting of them when he mentions that the author of *Madame Bovary* had said to him of a new book, 'It is finished; I have a dozen more pages to write, but I have the fall of every phrase.' Flaubert had the religion of rhythm, and when he had caught the final cadence of each sentence – something that might correspond, in prose, to the rhyme – he filled in the beginning and middle. But Gautier makes the distinction that his rhythms were addressed above all to the ear (they were 'mouthers', as the author of *Le Capitaine Fracasse* happily says); whereas those that he himself sought were ocular, not intended to be read aloud. There was no style worth speaking of for Flaubert but the style that required reading aloud to give out its value; he *mouthed* his passages to himself. This was not in the least the sort of prose that MM. de Goncourt themselves cultivated. The reader of their novels will perceive that harmonies and cadences are nothing to them, and that their rhythms are, with a few rare exceptions, neither to be sounded nor to be seen. A page of *Madame Gervaisais*, for instance, is an almost impossible thing to read aloud. Perhaps this is why poor Flaubert ended by giving on their nerves when on a certain occasion he invited them to come and listen to a manuscript. They could endure the structure of his phrase no longer, and they alleviate themselves in their diary. It accounts for the great difference between their treatment of him and their treatment of Gautier: they accept the latter to the end, while with the author of *Salammbô* at a given moment they break down.

It may appear that we *have* sacrificed M M. de Goncourt's Journal, in contradiction to the spirit professed at the beginning of these remarks; so that we must not neglect to give back with the other hand something presentable as the equivalent of what we have taken away. The truth is our authors are, in a very particular degree, specialists, and the element of which, as they would say, *nous avons l'agacement* in this autobiographic publication is largely the result of a disastrous attempt, undertaken under the circumstances with a strangely good conscience, to be more general than nature intended them. Constituted in a remarkable manner for receiving impressions of the external, and resolving them into pictures in which each touch looks fidgety, but produces none the less its effect – for conveying the suggestion (in many cases, perhaps in most, the derisive or the invidious suggestion) of scenes, places, faces, figures, objects, they have not been able to deny themselves in the page directly before us the indulgence of a certain yearning for the abstract, for conceptions and ideas. In this direction they are not happy, not general and serene; they have a way of making large questions small, of thrusting in their petulance, of belittling even the religion of literature. *Je vomis mes contemporains*, one of them somewhere says, and there is always danger for them that an impression will act as an emetic. But when we meet them on their own ground, that of the perception of feature and expression, that of translation of the printed and published text of life, they are altogether admirable. It is mainly on this ground that we meet them in their novels, and the best pages of the Journal are those in which they return to it. There are, in fact, very few of these that do not contain some striking illustration of the way in which every combination of objects about them makes a picture for them, and a picture that testifies vividly to the life led in the midst of it. In the year 1853 they were legally prosecuted as authors of a so-called indecent article in a foolish little newspaper; the prosecution was puerile, and their acquittal was a matter of course. But they had to select a defender, and they called upon a barrister who had been recommended to them as 'safe'. 'In his drawing-room he had a flower-stand of which the foot consisted of a serpent in varnished wood climbing in a spiral up to a bird's nest. When I saw this flower-stand I felt a chill in my back. I guessed the sort of advocate that was to be our lot.' The object, rare or common, has on every occasion the highest importance for them; when it is common it represents and signifies, and it is ever the the thing that signifies most.

Théophile Gautier's phrase about his own talent has attained a certain celebrity ('Critics have been so good as to reason about me overmuch – I am simply a man for whom the visible world exists'), but MM. de Goncourt would have had every bit as good a right to utter it. People for whom the visible world doesn't 'exist' are people with whom they have no manner of patience, and their conception of literature is a conception of something in which such people have no part. Moreover, oddly enough, even as specialists they pay for their intensity by stopping short in certain directions; the country is a considerable part of the visible world, but their Journal is full of little expressions of annoyance and disgust with it. What they like is the things they can do something with, and they can do nothing with woods and fields, nothing with skies that are not the ceiling of crooked streets or the 'glimmering square' of windows. However, we must, of course, take men for what they have, not for what they have not, and the good faith of the two brothers is immensely fruitful when they project it upon their own little plot. What an amount of it they have needed, we exclaim as we read, to sustain them in such an attempt as *Madame Gervaisais* – an attempt to trace the conversion of a spirit from scepticism to Catholicism through contact with the old marbles and frescos, the various ecclesiastical bric-à-brac of Rome. Nothing could show less the expert, the habitual explorer of the soul than the purely pictorial plane of the demonstration. Of the attitude of the soul itself, of the combinations, the agitations, of which it was traceably the scene, there are no picture and no notation at all. When the great spiritual change takes place for their heroine, the way in which it seems to the authors most to the purpose to represent it is by a wonderful description of the confessional, at the Gesù, to which she goes for the first time to kneel. A deep Christian mystery has been wrought within her, but the account of it in the novel is that

'The confessional is beneath the mosaic of the choir, held and confined between the two supports carried by the heads of angels, with the shadow of the choir upon its brown wood, its little columns, its escutcheoned front, the hollow of its blackness detaching itself dark from the yellow marble of the pilasters, from the white marble of the wainscot. It has two steps on the side for the knees of the penitent; at the height for leaning a little square of copper trellis-work, in the middle of which the whisper of lips and the breath of sins has made a soiled, rusty circle; and above this, in a poor black frame, a meagre print, under which is stamped *Gesù muore in croce*, and the glass of which receives a sort of gleam of blood from the flickering fire of a lamp suspended in the chapel beside it.'

The weakness of such an effort as *Madame Gervaisais* is that it has so much less authority as the history of a life than as the exhibition of a palette. On the other hand, it expresses some of the aspects of the most interesting city in the world with an art altogether peculiar, an art which is too much, in places, an appeal to our patience, but which says a hundred things to us about the Rome of our senses a hundred times better than we could have said them for ourselves. At the risk of seeming to attempt to make characterization an affair of as many combined and repeated touches as MM. de Goncourt themselves, or as the cumulative Sainte-Beuve, master of aggravation, I must add that their success, even where it is great, is greatest for those readers who are submissive to description and even to enumeration. The process, I say, is an appeal to our patience, and I have already hinted that the image, the evocation, is not immediate, as it is, for instance, with Guy de Maupassant: our painters believe, above all, in shades, deal essentially with shades, have a horror of anything like rough delineation. They arrive at the exact, the particular; but it is, above all, on a second reading that we see them arrive, so that they perhaps suffer a certain injustice from those who are unwilling to give more than a first. They select, but they see so much in things that even their selection contains a multiplicity of items. The Journal, none the less, is full of aspects caught in the fact. In 1867 they make a stay in Auvergne, and their notes are perhaps precisely the more illustrative from the circumstance that they find everything odious.

'Return to Clermont. We go up and down the town. Scarcely a passer. The flat Sabbatical gloom of *la province*, to which is added here the mourning of the horrible stone of the country, the slate-stone of the Volvic, which resembles the stones of dungeons in the fifth act of popular melodramas. Here and there a *campo* which urges suicide, a little square with little pointed paving-stones and the grass of the court of a seminary growing between them, where the dogs yawn as they pass. A church, the cathedral of colliers, black without, black within, a law-court, a black temple of justice, an Odeon-theatre of the law, academically funereal, from which one drops into a public walk where the trees are so bored that they grow thin in the wide, mouldy shade. Always and everywhere the windows and doors bordered with black, like circulars conveying information of a demise. And sempiternally, on the horizon, that eternal Puy de Dôme, whose bluish cone reminds one so, grocer-fashion, of a sugar-loaf wrapped in its paper.'

A complete account of M M. de Goncourt would not close without some consideration of the whole question of, I will not say the legitimacy, but the discretion, of the attempt on the part of an artist whose vehicle is only collocations of words to be nothing if not plastic, to do the same things and achieve the same effects as the painter. Our authors offer an excellent text for a discourse on that theme, but I may not pronounce it, as I have not in these limits pretended to do more than glance in the direction of that activity in fiction on which they appear mainly to take their stand. The value of the endeavour I speak of will be differently rated according as people like to 'see' as they read, and according as in their particular case M M. de Goncourt will appear to have justified by success a manner of which it is on every occasion to be said that it was handicapped at the start. My own idea would be that they have given this manner unmistakable life. They have had an observation of their own, which is a great thing, and it has made them use language in a light of their own. They have attempted an almost impossible feat of translation, but there are not many passages they have altogether missed. Those who feel the spectacle as they feel it will always understand them enough, and any writer – even those who risk less – may be misunderstood by readers who have not that sympathy. Of course the general truth remains that if you wish to compete with the painter prose is a roundabout vehicle, and it is simpler to adopt the painter's tools. To this M M. de Goncourt would doubtless have replied that there is *no* use of words that is not an endeavour to 'render', that lines of division are arrogant and arbitrary, that the point at which the pen should give way to the brush is a matter of appreciation, that the only way to see what it can do, in certain directions of ingenuity, is to try, and that they themselves have the merit of having tried and found out. What they have found out, what they show us, is not certainly of the importance that all the irritation, all the envy and uncharitableness of their Journal would seem to announce for compositions brought forth in such throes; but the fact that they themselves make too much of their genius should not lead us to make too little. Artists will find it difficult to forgive them for introducing such a confusion between aesthetics and ill-humour. That is compromising to the cause, for it tends to make the artistic spirit synonymous with the ungenerous. When one has the better thoughts one doesn't print the worse. We have never been ignorant of the fact that talent may be considerable even when character is peevish; that is a mystery which we have had to accept. It is a poor reward for our philosophy that Providence should appoint MM. de Goncourt to insist upon the converse of the proposition during three substantial volumes.

32

'The Science of Criticism', New Review, May 1891. The ironical (?) title was changed to 'Criticism' when this was reprinted in Essays in London and Elsewhere, 1893.

IF LITERARY CRITICISM may be said to flourish among us at all, it certainly flourishes immensely, for it flows through the periodical press like a river that has burst its dikes. The quantity of it is prodigious, and it is a commodity of which, however the demand may be estimated, the supply will be sure to be in any supposable extremity the last thing to fail us. What strikes the observer above all, in such an affluence, is the unexpected proportion the discourse uttered bears to the objects discoursed of – the paucity of examples, of illustrations and productions, and the deluge of doctrine suspended in the void; the profusion of talk and the contraction of experiment, of what one may call literary conduct. This, indeed, ceases to be an anomaly as soon as we look at the conditions of contemporary journalism. Then we see that these conditions have engendered the practice of 'reviewing' – a practice that in general has nothing in common with the art of criticism. Periodical literature is a huge, open mouth which has to be fed – a vessel of immense capacity which has to be filled. It is like a regular train which starts at an advertised hour, but which is free to start only if every seat be occupied. The seats are many, the train is ponderously long, and hence the manufacture of dummies for the seasons when there are not passengers enough. A stuffed mannikin is thrust into the empty seat, where it makes a creditable figure till the end of the journey. It looks sufficiently like a passenger, and you know it is not one only when you perceive that it neither says anything nor gets out. The guard attends to it when the train is shunted, blows the cinders from its wooden face and gives a different crook to its elbow, so that it may serve for another run. In this way, in a well-conducted periodical, the blocks of *remplissage* are the dummies of criticism – the recurrent, regulated breakers in the tide of talk. They have a reason for being, and the situation is simpler when we perceive it. It helps to explain the disproportion I just mentioned, as well, in many a case, as the quality of the particular discourse. It helps us to understand that the 'organs of public opinion' must be no less copious than punctual, that publicity must maintain its high standard, that ladies and gentlemen may turn an honest penny by the free expenditure of ink. It gives us a glimpse of the high figure presumably reached by all the honest pennies accumulated in the cause, and throws us quite into a glow over the march of civilization and the way we have organized our conveniences. From this point of view it might indeed go far towards making us enthusiastic about our age. What is more calcu-lated to inspire us with a just complacency than the sight of a new and flourishing industry, a fine economy of production? The great busi-ness of reviewing has, in its roaring routine, many of the signs of blooming health, many of the features which beguile one into rendering an involuntary homage to successful enterprise.

Yet it is not to be denied that certain captious persons are to be met who are not carried away by the spectacle, who look at it much askance, who see but dimly whither it tends, and who find no aid to vision even in the great light (about itself, its spirit, and its purposes, among other things) that it might have been expected to diffuse. 'Is there any such great light at all?' we may imagine the most restless of the sceptics to inquire, 'and isn't the effect rather one of a certain kind of pretentious and unprofitable gloom?' The vulgarity, the crudity, the stupidity which this cherished combination of the off-hand review and of our wonderful system of publicity have put into circulation on so vast a scale may be represented, in such a mood, as an unprecedented invention for darkening counsel. The bewildered spirit may ask itself, without speedy answer, What is the function in the life of man of such a periodicity of platitude and irrelevance? Such a spirit will wonder how the life of man survives it, and, above all, what is much more important, how literature resists it; whether, indeed, literature does resist it and is not speedily going down beneath it. The signs of this catastrophe will not in the case we suppose be found too subtle to be pointed out – the failure of distinction, the failure of style, the failure of knowledge, the failure of thought. The case is therefore one for recognizing with dismay that we are paying a tremendous price for the diffusion of penmanship and opportunity; that the multiplication of endowments for chatter may be as fatal as an infectious disease; that literature lives essentially, in the sacred depths of its being, upon example, upon perfection wrought; that, like other sensitive organisms, it is highly susceptible of demoralization, and that nothing is better calculated than irresponsible pedagogy to make it close its ears and lips. To be puerile and untutored about it is to deprive it of air and light, and the consequence of its keeping bad company is that it loses all heart. We may, of course, continue to talk about it long after it has bored itself to death, and there is every appearance that this is mainly the way in which our descendants will hear of it. They will, however, acquiesce in its extinction.

This, I am aware, is a dismal conviction, and I do not pretend to state the case gayly. The most I can say is that there are times and places in which it strikes one as less desperate than at others. One of the places is Paris, and one of the times is some comfortable occasion of being there. The custom of rough-and-ready reviewing is, among the French, much less rooted than with us, and the dignity of criticism is, to my perception, in consequence much higher. The art is felt to be one of the most difficult, the most delicate, the most occasional; and the material on which it is exercised is subject to selection, to restriction. That is, whether or no the French are always right as to what they do notice, they strike me as infallible as to what they don't. They publish hundreds of books which are never noticed at all, and yet they are much neater bookmakers than we. It is recognized that such volumes have nothing to say to the critical sense, that they do not belong to literature, and that the possession of the critical sense is exactly what makes it impossible to read them and dreary to discuss them – places them, as a part of critical experience, out of the question. The critical sense, in France, *ne se dérange pas*, as the phrase is, for so little. No one would deny, on the other hand, that when it does set itself in motion it goes further than with us. It handles the subject in general with finer finger-tips. The bluntness of ours, as tactile implements addressed to an exquisite process, is still sometimes surprising, even after frequent exhibition. We blunder in and out of the affair as if it were a railway station – the easiest and most public of the arts. It is in reality the most complicated and the most particular. The critical sense is so far from frequent that it is absolutely rare, and the possession of the cluster of qualities that minister to it is one of the highest distinctions. It is a gift inestimably precious and beautiful; therefore, so far from thinking that it passes overmuch from hand to hand, one knows that one has only to stand by the counter an hour to see that business is done with baser coin. We have too many small school-masters; yet not only do I not question in literature the high utility of criticism, but I should be tempted to say that the part it plays may be the supremely beneficent one when it proceeds from deep sources, from the efficient combination of experience and perception. In this light one sees the critic as the real helper of the artist, a torch-bearing outrider, the interpreter, the brother. The more the tune is noted and the direction observed the more we shall enjoy the convenience of a critical literature. When one thinks of the outfit required for free work in this spirit, one is ready to pay almost any homage to the intelligence that has put it on; and when one considers the noble figure completely equipped – armed *cap-à-pie* in curiosity and sympathy – one falls in love with the apparition. It certainly represents the knight who has knelt through his long vigil and who has the piety of his office. For there is something sacrificial in his function, inasmuch as he offers himself as a general touchstone. To lend himself, to project himself and steep himself, to feel and feel till he understands, and to understand so well that he can say, to have perception at the pitch of passion and expression as embracing as the air, to be infinitely curious and incorrigibly patient, and yet plastic and inflammable and determinable, stooping to conquer and serving to direct – these are fine chances for an active mind, chances to add the idea of independent beauty to the conception of success. Just in proportion as he is sentient and restless, just in proportion as he reacts and reciprocates and penetrates, is the critic a valuable instrument; for in literature assuredly criticism *is* the critic, just as art is the artist; it being assuredly the artist who invented art and the critic who invented criticism, and not the other way round.

And it is with the kinds of criticism exactly as it is with the kinds of art – the best kind, the only kind worth speaking of, is the kind that springs from the liveliest experience. There are a hundred labels and tickets, in all this matter, that have been pasted on from the outside and appear to exist for the convenience of passers-by; but the critic who lives *in* the house, ranging through its innumerable chambers, knows nothing about the bills on the front. He only knows that the more impressions he has the more he is able to record, and that the more he is saturated, poor fellow, the more he can give out. His life, at this rate, is heroic, for it is immensely vicarious. He has to understand for others, to answer for them; he is always under arms. He knows that the whole honour of the matter, for him, besides the success in his own eyes, depends upon his being indefatigably supple, and that is a formidable order. Let me not speak, however, as if his work were a conscious grind, for the sense of effort is easily lost in the enthusiasm of curiosity. Any vocation has its hours of intensity that is so closely connected with life. That of the critic, in literature, is connected doubly, for he deals with life at second-hand as well as at first; that is, he deals with the experience of others, which he resolves into his own, and not of those invented and selected others with whom the novelist makes comfortable terms, but with the uncompromising swarm of authors, the clamorous children of history. He has to make them as vivid and as free as the novelist makes *his* puppets, and yet he has, as the phrase is, to take them as they come. We must be easy with him if the picture, even when the aim has really been to penetrate, is sometimes confused, for there are baffling and there are thankless subjects; and we make everything up to him by the peculiar purity of our esteem when the portrait is really, like the happy portraits of the other art, a text preserved by translation.

33

❧

From 'Henrik Ibsen; On the Occasion of Hedda Gabler*', New Review, June 1891. The American actress Elizabeth Robins had become a friend of James, who was much interested in the theatre at this time and who had been converted to Ibsen's plays by seeing them on the stage. Just before, in April 1891, he had described them to Gosse as 'dreary', 'tedious', 'of a grey mediocrity' and not 'dramatic, or dramas at all'. But after this article he corresponded warmly with William Archer as the translator and advocate of Ibsen; and it is often claimed with more or less conviction that his later novels show Ibsen's influence.*

... WE HAVE studied our author, it must be admitted, under difficulties, for it is impossible to read him without perceiving that merely book in hand we but half know him – he addresses himself so substantially to representation. This quickens immensely our consideration for him, since in proportion as we become conscious that he has mastered an exceedingly difficult form are we naturally reluctant, in honour, to judge him unaccompanied by its advantages, by the benefit of his full intention. Considering how much Ibsen has been talked about in England and America, he has been lamentably little seen and heard. Until *Hedda Gabler* was produced in London six weeks ago, there had been but one attempt to represent its predecessors that had consisted of more than a single performance. This circumstance has given a real importance to the undertaking of the two courageous young actresses who have brought the most recent of the author's productions to the light and who have promptly found themselves justified in their talent as well as in their energy. It was a proof of Ibsen's force that he had made us chatter about him so profusely without the aid of the theatre; but it was even more a blessing to have the aid at last. The stage is to the prose drama (and Ibsen's later manner is the very prose of prose) what the tune is to the song or the concrete case to the general law. It immediately becomes apparent that he needs the test to show his strength and the frame to show his picture. An extraordinary process of vivification takes place; the conditions seem essentially enlarged. Those of the stage in general strike us for the most part as small enough, so that the game played in them is often not more inspiring than a successful sack-race. But Ibsen reminds us that if they do not in themselves confer life they can at least receive it when the infusion is artfully attempted. Yet how much of it they were doomed to receive from *Hedda Gabler* was not to be divined till we had seen *Hedda Gabler* in the frame. The play, on perusal, left one comparatively muddled and mystified, fascinated, but – in one's intellectual sympathy – snubbed. Acted, it leads that sympathy over the straightest of roads with all the exhilaration of a superior pace. Much more, I confess, one doesn't get from it; but an hour of refreshing exercise is a reward in itself. The sense of being moved by a scientific hand as one sits in one's stall has not been spoiled for us by satiety.

Hedda Gabler then, in the frame, is exceedingly vivid and curious, and a part of its interest is in the way it lights up in general the talent of the author. It is doubtless not the most complete of Ibsen's plays, for it owes less to its subject than to its form; but it makes good his title to the possession of a real method, and in thus putting him before us as a master it exhibits at the same time his irritating, his bewildering incongruities. He is nothing, as a literary personality, if not positive; yet there are moments when his great gift seems made up of negatives, or at any rate when the total seems a contradiction of each of the parts. I premise of course that we hear him through a medium not his own, and I remember that translation is a shameless falsification of colour. Translation, however, is probably not wholly responsible for three appearances inherent in all his prose work, as we possess it, though in slightly differing degrees, and yet quite unavailing to destroy in it the expression of life; I mean of course the absence of humour, the absence of free imagination, and the absence of style. The absence of style, both in the usual and in the larger sense of the word, is extraordinary, and all the more mystifying that its place is not usurped, as it frequently is in such cases, by vulgarity. Ibsen is massively common and 'middle-class', but neither his spirit nor his manner is small. He is never trivial and never cheap, but he is in nothing more curious than in owing to a single source such distinction as he retains. His people are of inexpressive race; they give us essentially the *bourgeois* impression; even when they are furiously nervous and, like Hedda, more than sufficiently fastidious, we recognize that they live, with their remarkable creator, in a world in which selection has no great range. This is perhaps one reason why they none of them, neither the creator nor the creatures, appear to feel much impulse to *play* with the things of life. This impulse, when it breaks out, is humour, and in the scenic genius it usually breaks out in one place or another. We get the feeling, in Ibsen's plays, that such whims are too ultimate, too much a matter of luxury and leisure for the stage of feeling at which his characters have arrived. They are all too busy learning to live – humour will come in later, when they know how. A certain angular irony they frequently manifest, and some of his portraits are strongly satirical, like that, to give only two instances, of Tesman, in *Hedda Gabler* (a play indeed suffused with irrepressible irony), or that of Hialmar Ekdal, in *The Wild Duck*. But it is the ridicule without the smile, the dance without the music, a sort of sarcasm that is nearer to tears than to laughter. There is nothing very droll in the world, I think, to Dr Ibsen; and nothing is more interesting than to see how he makes up his world without a joke. Innumerable are the victories of talent, and art is a legerdemain.

It is always difficult to give an example of an absent quality, and, if the romantic is even less present in Ibsen than the comic, this is best proved by the fact that everything seems to us inveterately observed. Nothing is more puzzling to the readers of his later work than the reminder that he is the great dramatic poet of his country, or that the author of *The Pillars of Society* is also the author of *Brand* and *Peer Gynt*, compositions which, we are assured, testify to an audacious imagination and abound in complicated fantasy. In his satiric studies of contemporary life the impression that is strongest with us is that the picture is infinitely *noted*, that all the patience of the constructive pessimist is in his love of the detail of character and of conduct, in his way of accumulating the touches that illustrate them. His recurrent ugliness of surface, as it were, is a sort of proof of his fidelity to the real, in a spare, strenuous, democratic community; just as the same peculiarity is one of the sources of his charmless fascination – a touching vision of strong forces struggling with a poverty, a bare provinciality, of life. I call the fascination of Ibsen charmless (for those who feel it at all), because he holds us without bribing us; he squeezes the attention till he almost hurts it, yet with never a conciliatory stroke. He has as little as possible to say to our taste; even his large, strong form takes no account of that, gratifying it without concessions. It is the oddity of the mixture that makes him so individual – his perfect practice of a difficult and delicate art, combined with such aesthetic density. Even in such a piece as *The Lady from the Sea* (much the weakest, to my sense, of the whole series), in which he comes nearer than in others – unless indeed it be in *Hedda Gabler* – to playing with an idea from the simple instinct of sport, nothing could be less picturesque than the general effect, with every inherent incentive to have made it picturesque. The idea might have sprung from the fancy of Hawthorne, but the atmosphere is the hard light of Ibsen. One feels that the subject should have been tinted and distanced; but, in fact, one has to make an atmosphere as one reads, and one winces considerably under 'Doctor Wangel' and the pert daughters.

For readers without curiosity as to their author's point of view (and it is doubtless not a crime not to have it, though I think it is a misfortune, an open window the less), there is too much of 'Doctor Wangel' in Ibsen altogether – using the good gentleman's name for what it generally represents or connotes. It represents the ugly interior on which his curtain inexorably rises and which, to be honest, I like for the queer associations it has taught us to respect: the hideous carpet and wall-paper and curtains (one may answer for them), the conspicuous stove, the lonely centre-table, the 'lamps with green shades', as in the sumptuous first act of *The Wild Duck*, the pervasive air of small interests and standards, the sign of limited local life. It represents the very clothes, the inferior fashions, of the figures that move before us, and the shape of their hats and the tone of their conversation and the nature of their diet. But the oddest thing happens in connection with this effect – the oddest extension of sympathy or relaxation of prejudice. What happens is that we feel that whereas, if Ibsen were weak or stupid or vulgar, this parochial or suburban stamp would only be a stick to beat him with, it acts, as the case stands, and in the light of his singular masculinity, as a sort of substitute – a little clumsy, if you like – for charm. In a word, it becomes touching, so that practically the *blasé* critical mind enjoys it as a refinement. What occurs is very analogous to what occurs in our appreciation of the dramatist's remarkable art, his admirable talent for producing an intensity of interest by means incorruptibly quiet, by that almost demure preservation of the appearance of the usual in which we see him juggle with difficulty and danger and which constitutes, as it were, his only coquetry. There are people who are indifferent to these mild prodigies; there are others for whom they will always remain the most charming privilege of art.

Hedda Gabler is doubtless as suburban as any of its companions; which is indeed a fortunate circumstance, inasmuch as if it were less so we should be deprived of a singularly complete instance of a phenomenon difficult to express, but which may perhaps be described as the operation of talent without glamour. There is notoriously no glamour over the suburbs, and yet nothing could be more vivid than Dr Ibsen's account of the incalculable young woman into whom Miss Robins so artistically projects herself. To 'like' the play, as we phrase it, is doubtless therefore to give one of the fullest examples of our constitutional inability to control our affections. Several of the spectators who have liked it most will probably admit even that, with themselves, this sentiment has preceded a complete comprehension. They would perhaps have liked it better if they had understood it better – as to this they are not sure; but they at any rate liked it well enough. Well enough for what? the question may of course always be in such a case. To be absorbed, assuredly, which is the highest tribute we can pay to any picture of life, and a higher one than most pictures attempted succeed in making us pay. Ibsen is various, and *Hedda Gabler* is probably an ironical pleasantry, the artistic exercise of a mind saturated with the vision of human infirmities; saturated, above all, with a sense of the infinitude, for all its mortal savour, of *character*, finding that an endless romance and a perpetual challenge. Can there have been at the source of such a production a mere refinement of conscious power, an enjoyment of difficulty and a preconceived victory over it? We are free to imagine that in this case Dr Ibsen chose one of the last subjects that an expert might have been expected to choose, for the harmless pleasure of feeling and of showing that he was in possession of a method that could make up for its deficiencies.

The demonstration is complete and triumphant, but it does not conceal from us – on the contrary – that his drama is essentially that supposedly undramatic thing, the picture not of an action but of a condition. It is the portrait of a nature, the story of what Paul Bourget would call an *état d'âme*, and of a state of nerves as well as of soul, a state of temper, of health, of chagrin, of despair. *Hedda Gabler* is, in short, the study of an exasperated woman, and it may certainly be declared that the subject was not in advance, as a theme for scenic treatment, to be pronounced promising. There could in fact, however, be no more suggestive illustration of the folly of quarrelling with an artist over his subject. Ibsen has had only to take hold of this one in earnest to make it, against every presumption, live with an intensity of life. One can doubtless imagine other ways, but it is enough to say of this one that, put to the test, it imposes its particular spectacle. Something might have been gained, entailing perhaps a loss in another direction, by tracing the preliminary stages, showing the steps in Mrs Tesman's history which led to the spasm, as it were, on which the curtain rises and of which the breathless duration – ending in death – is the period of the piece. But a play is above everything a work of selection, and Ibsen, with his curious and beautiful passion for the unity of time (carried in him to a point which almost always implies also that of place), condemns himself to admirable rigours. We receive Hedda ripe for her catastrophe, and if we ask for antecedents and explanations we must simply find them in her character. Her motives are just her passions. What the four acts show us is these motives and that character – complicated, strange, irreconcilable, infernal – playing themselves out. We know too little why she married Tesman, we see too little why she ruins Lövborg; but we recognize that she is infinitely perverse, and Heaven knows that, as the drama mostly goes, the crevices we are called upon to stop are singularly few. That Mrs Tesman is a perfectly ill-regulated person is a matter of course, and there are doubtless spectators who would fain ask whether it would not have been better to represent in her stead a person totally different. The answer to this sagacious question seems to me to be simply that no one can possibly tell. There are many things in the world that are past finding out, and one of them is whether the subject of a work had not better have been another subject. We shall always do well to leave that matter to the author (*he* may have some secret for solving the riddle); so terrible would his revenge easily become if we were to accept a responsibility for his theme.

The distinguished thing is the firm hand that weaves the web, the deep and ingenious use made of the material. What material, indeed, the dissentient spirit may exclaim, and what 'use', worthy of the sacred name, is to be made of a wicked, diseased, disagreeable woman? That is just what Ibsen attempts to gauge, and from the moment such an attempt is resolute the case ceases to be so simple. The 'use' of Hedda Gabler is that she acts on others and that even her most disagreeable qualities have the privilege, thoroughly undeserved doubtless, but equally irresistible, of becoming a part of the history of others. And then one isn't so sure she is wicked, and by no means sure (especially when she is represented by an actress who makes the point ambiguous) that she is disagreeable. She is various and sinuous and graceful, complicated and natural; she suffers, she struggles, she is human, and by that fact exposed to a dozen interpretations, to the importunity of our suspense. Wrought with admirable closeness is the whole tissue of relations between the five people whom the author sets in motion and on whose behalf he asks of us so few concessions. That is for the most part the accomplished thing in Ibsen, the thing that converts his provincialism into artistic urbanity. He puts *us* to no expense worth speaking of – he takes all the expense himself. I mean that he thinks out our entertainment for us and shapes it of thinkable things, the passions, the idiosyncrasies, the cupidities and jealousies, the strivings and struggles, the joys and sufferings of men. The spectator's situation is different enough when what is given him is the mere dead rattle of the surface of life, into which *he* has to inject the element of thought, the 'human interest'. Ibsen kneads the soul of man like a paste, and often with a rude and indelicate hand to which the soul of man objects. Such a production as *The Pillars of Society*, with its large, dense complexity of moral cross-references and its admirable definiteness as a picture of motive and temperament (the whole canvas charged, as it were, with moral colour), such a production asks the average moral man to see too many things at once. It will never help Ibsen with the multitude that the multitude shall feel that the more they look the more intentions they shall see, for of such seeing of many intentions the multitude is but scantily desirous. It keeps indeed a positively alarmed and jealous watch in that direction; it smugly insists that intentions shall be rigidly limited . . .

34

---- ❧ ----

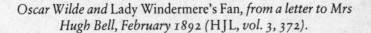

Oscar Wilde and Lady Windermere's Fan, *from a letter to Mrs Hugh Bell, February 1892 (*HJL, *vol. 3, 372).*

. . . OSCAR'S PLAY (I was there on Saturday) strikes me as a mixture that will run (I feel as if I were talking as a laundress), though infantine to my sense, both in subject and in form. As a drama it is of a candid and primitive simplicity, with a perfectly reminiscential air about it – as of things *qui ont traîné*, that one has always seen in plays. In short it doesn't, from that point of view, bear analysis or discussion. But there is so much drollery – that is, 'cheeky' paradoxical wit of dialogue, and the pit and gallery are so pleased at finding themselves clever enough to 'catch on' to four or five of the ingenious – too ingenious – *mots* in the dozen, that it makes them feel quite '*décadent*' and *raffiné* and they enjoy the sensation as a change from the stodgy. Moreover they think they are hearing the talk of the *grand monde* (poor old *grand monde*), and altogether feel privileged and modern. There is a perpetual attempt at *mots* and many of them *râter*: but those that hit are very good indeed. This will make, I think, a success – possibly a really long run (I mean through the Season) for the play. There is of course absolutely no characterization and all the people talk equally strained Oscar – but there is a 'situation' (at the end of Act III) that one has seen from the cradle, and the thing is conveniently acted. The 'impudent' speech at the end was simply inevitable mechanical Oscar – I mean the usual trick of saying the unusual – complimenting himself and his play. It was what he was there for and I can't conceive the density of those who seriously reprobate it. The tone of the virtuous journals makes me despair of our stupid humanity. Everything Oscar does is a deliberate trap for the literalist, and to see the literalist walk straight up to it, look straight at it and step straight into it, makes one freshly avert a discouraged gaze from this unspeakable animal . . .

35

Tess of the d'Urbervilles, *from letters to Robert Louis Stevenson, March 1892 and February 1893 (Henry James and Robert Louis Stevenson, ed. Janet Adam Smith, pp. 213 and 220–1). James had earlier reviewed* Far From the Madding Crowd *(1875) without enthusiasm.*

... THE GOOD little Thomas Hardy has scored a great success with *Tess of the d'Urbervilles*, which is chock-full of faults and falsity and yet has a singular beauty and charm ...

... I grant you Hardy with all my heart and even with a certain quantity of my boot-toe. I am meek and ashamed where the public clatter is deafening – so I bowed my head and let 'Tess of the D.'s' pass. But oh yes, dear Louis, she is vile. The pretence of 'sexuality' is only equalled by the absence of it, and the abomination of the language by the author's reputation for style. There are indeed some pretty smells and sights and sounds. But you have better ones in Polynesia ...

36

From a review of Correspondance de Gustave Flaubert, *1893*, Macmillan's Magazine, *March 1893. Flaubert was not a celibate, incidentally, in his relation with Louise Colet.*

... MADAME BOVARY was five years in the writing, and the *Tentation de Saint-Antoine*, which saw the light in 1874, but the consummation of an idea entertained in his boyhood. *Bouvard et Pécuchet*, the intended epos of the blatancy, the comprehensive *bêtise*, of mankind, was in like manner the working-out at the end of his days of his earliest generalization. It had literally been his life-long dream to crown his career with a panorama of human ineptitude. Everything in his literary life had been planned and plotted and prepared. One moves in it through an atmosphere of the darkest, though the most innocent, conspiracy. He was perpetually laying a train, a train of which the inflammable substance was 'style'. His great originality was that the long siege of his youth was successful. I can recall no second case in which poetic justice has interfered so gracefully. He began *Madame Bovary* from afar off, not as an amusement or a profit or a clever novel or even a work of art or a *morceau de vie*, as his successors say to-day, not even, either, as the best thing he could make it; but as a premeditated classic, a master-piece pure and simple, a thing of conscious perfection and a contribu-tion of the first magnitude to the literature of his country. There would have been every congruity in his encountering proportionate failure and the full face of that irony in things of which he was so inveterate a student. A writer of tales who should have taken the extravagance of his design for the subject of a sad 'novelette' could never have permitted himself any termination of such a story but an effective anticlimax. The masterpiece at the end of years would inevitably fall very flat and the overweening spirit be left somehow to its illusions. The solution, in fact, was very different, and as Flaubert had deliberately sown, so exactly and magnificently did he reap. The perfection of *Madame Bovary* is one of the commonplaces of criticism, the position of it one of the highest a man of letters dare dream of, the possession of it one of the glories of France. No calculation was ever better fulfilled, nor any train more successfully laid. It is a sign of the indefeasible bitterness to which Flaubert's temperament condemned him and the expression of which, so oddly, is yet as obstreperous and boyish as that of the happiness arising from animal spirits – it is a mark of his amusing pessimism that so honourable a first step should not have done more to reconcile him to life. But he was a creature of transcendent dreams and unfathomable perversities of taste, and it was in his nature to be more conscious of one broken spring in the couch of fame, more wounded by a pin-prick, more worried by an assonance, than he could ever be warmed or pacified from within. Literature and life were a single business to him, and the 'torment of style', that might occasionally intermit in one place, was sufficiently sure to break out in another. We may polish our periods till they shine again, but over the style of life our control is necessarily more limited.

To such limitations Flaubert resigned himself with the worst possible grace. He polished ferociously, but there was a side of the matter that his process could never touch. Some other process might have been of use; some patience more organized, some formula more elastic, or simply perhaps some happier trick of good-humour; at the same time it must be admitted that in his deepening vision of the imbecility of the world any remedy would have deprived him of his prime, or rather of his sole, amusement. The *bêtise* of mankind was a colossal comedy, calling aloud to heaven for an Aristophanes to match, and Flaubert's nearest approach to joy was in noting the opportunities of such an observer and feeling within himself the stirrings of such a genius. Towards the end he found himself vibrating at every turn to this ideal, and if he knew to the full the tribulation of proper speech no one ever suffered less from that of proper silence. He broke it in his letters, on a thousand queer occasions, with all the luxury of relief. He was blessed with a series of correspondents with whom he was free to leave nothing unsaid; many of them ladies, too, so that he had in their company all the inspiration of gallantry without its incidental sacrifices . . .

An incorruptible celibate and *dédaigneux des femmes* (as, in spite of the hundred and forty letters addressed to Madame Louise Colet, M. de Maupassant styles him and, in writing to Madame Sand, he confesses himself), it was his own view of his career that, as art was the only thing worth living for, he had made immense sacrifices to application – sacrificed passions, joys, affections, curiosities, and opportunities. He says that he shut his passions up in cages, and only at long intervals, for amusement, had a look at them. The *orgie de littérature*, in short, had been his sole form of excess. He knew best, of course, but his imaginations about himself (as about other matters) were, however justly, rich, and to the observer at this distance he appears truly to have been made of the very stuff of a Benedictine. He compared himself to the camel, which can neither be stopped when he is going nor moved when he is resting. He was so sedentary, so averse to physical exercise, which he speaks of somewhere as an *occupation funeste*, that his main alternative to the chair was, even by day, the bed, and so omnivorous in research that the act of composition, with him, was still more impeded by knowledge than by taste. 'I have in me,' he writes to the imperturbable Madame Sand, 'a *fond d'ecclésiastique* that people don't know' – the clerical basis of the Catholic clergy. 'We shall talk of it,' he adds, 'much better *vivâ voce* than by letter'; and we can easily imagine the thoroughness with which between the unfettered pair, when opportunity favoured, the interesting subject was treated. At another time, indeed, to the same correspondent, who had given him a glimpse of the happiness of being a grandmother, he refers with touching sincerity to the poignancy of solitude to which the 'radical absence of the feminine element' in his life had condemned him. 'Yet I was born with every capacity for tenderness. One doesn't shape one's destiny, one undergoes it. I was pusillanimous in my youth – I was *afraid* of life. We pay for everything.' Besides, it was his theory that a 'man of style' should never stoop to action. If he had been afraid of life in fact, I must add, he was preserved from the fear of it in imagination by that great 'historic start', the sensibility to the *frisson historique*, which dictates the curious and beautiful outburst, addressed to Madame Colet, when he asks why it had not been his lot to live in the age of Nero.

'How I would have talked with the Greek rhetors, travelled in the great chariots on the Roman roads, and in the evening, in the hostelries, turned in with the vagabond priests of Cybele! . . . I *have* lived, all over, in those directions; doubtless in some prior state of being. I'm sure I've been, under the Roman empire, manager of some troop of strolling players, one of the rascals who used to go to Sicily to buy women to make actresses, and who were at once professors, panders, and artists. These scoundrels have wonderful "mugs" in the comedies of Plautus, in reading which I seem to myself to remember things.'

He was an extreme admirer of Apuleius, and his florid inexperience helps doubtless somewhat to explain those extreme sophistications of taste of which *La Tentation de Saint-Antoine* is so elaborate an example. Far and strange are the refuges in which such an imagination seeks oblivion of the immediate and the ugly. His life was that of a pearl-diver, breathless in the thick element while he groped for the priceless word, and condemned to plunge again and again. He passed it in reconstructing sentences, exterminating repetitions, calculating and comparing cadences, harmonious *chutes de phrase*, and beating about the bush to deal death to the abominable assonance. Putting aside the particular ideal of style which made a pitfall of the familiar, few men surely have ever found it so difficult to deal with the members of a phrase. He loathed the smug face of facility as much as he suffered from the nightmare of toil; but if he had been marked in the cradle for literature it may be said without paradox that this was not on account of any native disposition to write, to write at least as he aspired and as he understood the term. He took long years to finish his books, and terrible months and weeks to deliver himself of his chapters and his pages. Nothing could exceed his endeavour to make them all rich and round, just as nothing could exceed the unetherized anguish in which his successive children were born. His letters, in which, inconsequently for one who had so little faith in any rigour of taste or purity of perception save his own, he takes everybody into his most intimate literary confidence, the pages of the publication before us are the record of everything that retarded him. The abyss of reading answered to the abyss of writing; with the partial exception of *Madame Bovary* every subject that he treated required a rising flood of information. There are libraries of books behind his most innocent sentences. The question of 'art' for him was so furiously the question of form, and the question of form was so intensely the question of rhythm, that from the beginning to the end of his correspondence we scarcely ever encounter a mention of any beauty but verbal beauty. He quotes Goethe fondly as to the supreme importance of the 'conception', but the conception remains for him essentially the plastic one.

There are moments when his restless passion for form strikes us as leaving the subject out of account altogether, as if he had taken it up arbitrarily, blindly, preparing himself the years of misery in which he is to denounce the grotesqueness, the insanity of his choice. Four times, with his *orgueil*, his love of magnificence, he condemned himself incongruously to the modern and familiar, groaning at every step over the horrible difficulty of reconciling 'style' in such cases with truth and dialogue with surface. He wanted to do the battle of Thermopylae, and he found himself doing *Bouvard et Pécuchet*. One of the sides by which he interests us, one of the sides that will always endear him to the student, is his extraordinary ingenuity in lifting without falsifying, finding a middle way into grandeur and edging off from the literal without forsaking truth. This way was open to him from the moment he could look down upon his theme from the position of *une blague supérieure*, as he calls it, the amused freedom of an observer as irreverent as a creator. But if subjects were made for style (as to which Flaubert had a rigid theory: the idea was good enough if the expression was), so style was made for the ear, the last court of appeal, the supreme touchstone of perfection. He was perpetually demolishing his periods in the light of his merciless *gueulades*. He tried them on every one; his *gueulades* could make him sociable. The horror, in particular, that haunted all his years was the horror of the *cliché*, the stereotyped, the thing usually said and the way it was usually said, the current phrase that passed muster. Nothing, in his view, passed muster but freshness, that which came into the world, with all the honours, for the occasion. To use the ready-made was as disgraceful as for a self-respecting cook to buy a tinned soup or a sauce in a bottle. Flaubert considered that the dispenser of such wares was indeed the grocer, and, producing his ingredients exclusively at home, he would have stabbed himself for shame like Vatel. This touches on the strange weakness of his mind, his puerile dread of the grocer, the *bourgeois*, the sentiment that in his generation and the preceding misplaced, as it were, the spirit of adventure and the sense of honour, and sterilized a whole province of French literature. That worthy citizen ought never to have kept a poet from dreaming . . .

37

On Lord Ormont and his Aminta, *and Meredith's style, from a letter to Edmund Gosse, August 1894 (HJL, vol. 3, 485–6). James seems to have liked and respected Meredith personally.*

. . . IT FILLS me with a critical rage, an artistic fury, utterly blighting in me the indispensable principle of *respect*. I have finished, at this rate, but the first volume – whereof I am moved to declare that I doubt if any equal quantity of extravagant verbiage, of airs and graces, of phrases and attitudes, of obscurities and alembications, ever *started* less their subject, ever contributed less of a statement – told the reader less of what the reader needs to know. All elaborate predicates of exposition without the ghost of a nominative to hook themselves to; and not a difficulty met, not a figure presented, not a scene constituted – not a dim shadow condensing once either into audible or into visible reality – making you hear for an instant the tap of its feet on the earth. Of course there are pretty things, but for what they are they come so much too dear, and so many of the profundities and tortuosities prove when threshed out to be only pretentious statements of the very simplest propositions . . .

There is another side, of course, which one will utter another day . . .

38

——— ❧ ———

On 'subject' from The Notebooks of Henry James *ed. F. O. Matthiessen and Kenneth B. Murdock, 1955, p. 166. The entry is for 24 October 1894.*

PLUS JE VAIS, the more intensely it comes home to me that solidity of subject, importance, emotional capacity of subject, is the only thing on which, henceforth, it is of the slightest use for me to expend myself. Everything else breaks down, collapses, turns thin, turns poor, turns wretched – betrays one miserably. Only the fine, the large, the human, the natural, the fundamental, the passionate things . . .

39

On Walter Pater, from a letter to Edmund Gosse, December 1894 (HJL, vol. 3, 492).

... I THINK he has had – will have had – the most exquisite literary fortune: i.e. to have taken it out all, wholly, exclusively, with the pen (the style, the genius) and absolutely not at all with the person. He is the mask without the face, and there isn't in his total superficies a tiny point of vantage for the newspaper to flap its wings on. You have been lively about him – but about whom *wouldn't* you be lively? I think you'd be lively about *me!* – Well, faint, pale, embarrassed, exquisite Pater! He reminds me, in the disturbed midnight of our actual literature, of one of those lucent matchboxes which you place, on going to bed, near the candle, to show you, in the darkness, where you can strike a light: he shines in the uneasy gloom – vaguely, and has a phosphorescence, not a flame. But I quite agree with you that he is not of the little day – but of the longer time ...

40

❖

'Ivan Turgeneff (1818–83)', from a Library of the World's Best Literature *ed. Charles Dudley Warner, New York, 1896.*

THERE IS perhaps no novelist of alien race who more naturally than Ivan Turgeneff inherits a niche in a Library for English readers; and this not because of any advance or concession that in his peculiar artistic independence he ever made, or could dream of making, such readers, but because it was one of the effects of his peculiar genius to give him, even in his lifetime, a special place in the regard of foreign publics. His position is in this respect singular; for it is his Russian savour that as much as anything has helped generally to domesticate him.

Born in 1818, at Orel in the heart of Russia, and dying in 1883, at Bougival near Paris, he had spent in Germany and France the latter half of his life; and had incurred in his own country in some degree the reprobation that is apt to attach to the absent – the penalty they pay for such extension or such beguilement as they may have happened to find over the border. He belonged to the class of large rural proprietors of land and of serfs; and with his ample patrimony, offered one of the few examples of literary labour achieved in high independence of the question of gain – a character that he shares with his illustrious contemporary Tolstoy, who is of a type in other respects so different. It may give us an idea of his primary situation to imagine some large Virginian or Carolinian slaveholder, during the first half of the century, inclining to 'Northern' views; and becoming (though not predominantly under pressure of these, but rather by the operation of an exquisite genius) the great American novelist – one of the great novelists of the world. Born under a social and political order sternly repressive, all Turgeneff's deep instincts, all his moral passion, placed him on the liberal side; with the consequence that early in life, after a period spent at a German university, he found himself, through the accident of a trifling public utterance, under such suspicion in high places as to be sentenced to a term of tempered exile – confinement to his own estate. It was partly under these circumstances perhaps that he gathered material for the work from the appearance of which his reputation dates – *A Sportsman's Sketches*, published in two volumes in 1852. This admirable collection of impressions of homely country life, as the old state of servitude had made it, is often spoken of as having borne to the great decree of Alexander II the relation borne by Mrs Beecher Stowe's famous novel to the emancipation of the Southern slaves. Incontestably, at any rate, Turgeneff's rustic studies sounded, like *Uncle Tom's Cabin*, a particular hour: with the difference, however, of not having at the time produced an agitation – of having rather presented the case with an art too insidious for instant recognition, an art that stirred the depths more than the surface.

The author was designated promptly enough, at any rate, for such influence as might best be exercised at a distance: he travelled, he lived abroad; early in the sixties he was settled in Germany; he acquired property at Baden-Baden, and spent there the last years of the prosperous period – in the history of the place – of which the Franco-Prussian War was to mark the violent term. He cast in his lot after that event mainly with the victims of the lost cause; setting up a fresh home in Paris – near which city he had, on the Seine, a charming alternate residence – and passing in it, and in the country, save for brief revisitations, the remainder of his days. His friendships, his attachments, in the world of art and of letters, were numerous and distinguished; he never married; he produced, as the years went on, without precipitation or frequency; and these were the years during which his reputation gradually established itself as, according to the phrase, European – a phrase denoting in this case, perhaps, a public more alert in the United States even than elsewhere.

Tolstoy, his junior by ten years, had meanwhile come to fruition; though, as in fact happened, it was not till after Turgeneff's death that the greater fame of *War and Peace* and of *Anna Karénina* began to be blown about the world. One of the last acts of the elder writer, performed on his death-bed, was to address to the other (from whom for a considerable term he had been estranged by circumstances needless to reproduce) an appeal to return to the exercise of the genius that Tolstoy had already so lamentably, so monstrously forsworn. 'I am on my death-bed; there is no possibility of my recovery. I write you expressly to tell you how happy I have been to be your contemporary, and to utter my last, my urgent prayer. Come back, my friend, to your literary labours. That gift came to you from the source from which all comes to us. Ah, how happy I should be could I think you would listen to my entreaty! My friend, great writer of our Russian land, respond to it, obey it!' These words, among the most touching surely ever addressed by one great spirit to another, throw an indirect light – perhaps I may even say a direct one – upon the nature and quality of Turgeneff's artistic temperament; so much so that I regret being without opportunity, in this place, to gather such aid for a portrait of him as might be supplied by following out the unlikeness between the pair. It would be too easy to say that Tolstoy was, from the Russian point of view, for home consumption, and Turgeneff for foreign: *War and Peace* has probably had more readers in Europe and America than *A House of Gentlefolk* or *On the Eve* or *Smoke* – a circumstance less detrimental than it may appear to my claim of our having, in the Western world, supremely adopted the author of the latter works. Turgeneff is in a peculiar degree what I may call the novelists' novelist – an artistic influence extraordinarily valuable and ineradicably established. The perusal of Tolstoy – a wonderful mass of life – is an immense event, a kind of splendid accident, for each of us: his name represents nevertheless no such eternal spell of method, no such quiet irresistibility of presentation, as shines, close to us and lighting our possible steps, in that of his precursor. Tolstoy is a reflector as vast as a natural lake; a monster harnessed to his great subject – all human life! – as an elephant might be harnessed, for purposes of traction, not to a carriage, but to a coach-house. His own case is prodigious, but his example for others dire: disciples not elephantine he can only mislead and betray.

One by one, for thirty years, with a firm, deliberate hand, with intervals and patiences and waits, Turgeneff pricked in his sharp outlines. His great external mark is probably his concision: an ideal he never threw over – it shines most perhaps even when he is least brief – and that he often applied with a rare felicity. He has masterpieces of a few pages; his perfect things are sometimes his least prolonged. He abounds in short tales, episodes clipped as by the scissors of Atropos; but for a direct translation of the whole we have still to wait – depending meanwhile upon the French and German versions, which have been, instead of the original text (thanks to the paucity among us of readers of Russian), the source of several published in English. For the novels and *A Sportsman's Sketches* we depend upon the nine volumes (1897) of Mrs Garnett. We touch her upon the remarkable side, to our vision, of the writer's fortune – the anomaly of his having constrained to intimacy even those who are shut out from the enjoyment of his medium, for whom that question is positively prevented from existing. Putting aside extrinsic intimations, it is impossible to read him without the conviction of his being, in the vividness of his own tongue, of the strong type of those made to bring home to us the happy truth of the unity, in a generous talent, of material and form – of their being inevitable faces of the same medal; the type of those, in a word, whose example deals death to the perpetual clumsy assumption that subject and style are – aesthetically speaking, or in the living work – different and separable things. We are conscious, reading him in a language not his own, of not being reached by his personal tone, his individual accent.

It is a testimony therefore to the intensity of his presence, that so much of his particular charm does reach us; that the mask turned to us has, even without his expression, still so much beauty. It is the beauty (since we must try to formulate) of the finest presentation of the familiar. His vision is of the world of character and feeling, the world of the relations life throws up at every hour and on every spot; he deals little, on the whole, in the miracles of chance – the hours and spots over the edge of time and space; his air is that of the great central region of passion and motive, of the usual, the inevitable, the intimate – the intimate for weal or woe. No theme that he ever chooses but strikes us as full; yet with all have we the sense that their animation comes from within, and is not pinned to their backs like the pricking objects used of old in the horse-races of the Roman carnival, to make the animals run. Without a patch of 'plot' to draw blood, the story he mainly tells us, the situation he mainly gives, runs as if for dear life. His first book was practically full evidence of what, if we have to specify, is finest in him – the effect, for the commonest truth, of an exquisite envelope of poetry. In this medium of feeling – full, as it were, of all the echoes and shocks of the universal danger and need – everything in him goes on; the sense of fate and folly and pity and wonder and beauty. The tenderness, the humour, the variety of *A Sportsman's Sketches* revealed on the spot an observer with a rare imagination. These faculties had attached themselves, together, to small things and to great: to the misery, the simplicity, the piety, the patience, of the unemancipated peasant; to all the natural wonderful life of earth and air and winter and summer and field and forest; to queer apparitions of country neighbours, of strange local eccentrics; to old-world practices and superstitions; to secrets gathered and types disinterred and impressions absorbed in the long, close contacts with man and nature involved in the passionate pursuit of game. Magnificent in stature and original vigour, Turgeneff, with his love of the chase, or rather perhaps of the inspiration he found in it, would have been the model of the mighty hunter, had not such an image been a little at variance with his natural mildness, the softness that often accompanies the sense of an extraordinary reach of limb and play of muscle. He was in person the model rather of the strong man at rest: massive and towering, with the voice of innocence and the smile almost of childhood. What seemed still more of a contradiction to so much of him, however, was that his work was all delicacy and fancy, penetration and compression.

If I add, in their order of succession, *Rudin*, *Fathers and Children*, *Spring Floods*, and *Virgin Soil*, to the three novels I have (also in their relation of time) named above, I shall have indicated the larger blocks of the compact monument, with a base resting deep and interstices well filled, into which that work disposes itself. The list of his minor productions is too long to draw out: I can only mention, as a few of the most striking – 'A Correspondence', 'The Wayside Inn', 'The Brigadier', 'The Dog', 'The Jew', 'Visions', 'Mumu', 'Three Meetings', 'A First Love', 'The Forsaken', 'Assia', 'The Journal of a Superfluous Man', 'The Story of Lieutenant Yergunov', 'A King Lear of the Steppe'. The first place among his novels would be difficult to assign: general opinion probably hesitates between *A House of Gentlefolk* and *Fathers and Children*. My own predilection is great for the exquisite *On the Eve*; though I admit that in such a company it draws no supremacy from being exquisite. What is less contestable is that *Virgin Soil* – published shortly before his death, and the longest of his fictions – has, although full of beauty, a minor perfection.

Character, character expressed and exposed, is in all these things what we inveterately find. Turgeneff's sense of it was the great light that artistically guided him; the simplest account of him is to say that the mere play of it constitutes in every case his sufficient drama. No one has had a closer vision, or a hand at once more ironic and more tender, for the individual figure. He sees it with its minutest signs and tricks – all its heredity of idiosyncrasies, all its particulars of weakness and strength, of ugliness and beauty, of oddity and charm; and yet it is of his essence that he sees it in the general flood of life, steeped in its relations and contacts, struggling or submerged, a hurried particle in the stream. This gives him, with his quiet method, his extraordinary breadth; dissociates his rare power to particularize from dryness or hardness, from any peril of caricature. He understands so much that we almost wonder he can express anything; and his expression is indeed wholly in absolute projection, in illustration, in giving of everything the unexplained and irresponsible specimen. He is of a spirit so human that we almost wonder at his control of his matter; of a pity so deep and so general that we almost wonder at his curiosity. The element of poetry in him is constant, and yet reality stares through it without the loss of a wrinkle. No one has more of that sign of the born novelist which resides in a respect unconditioned for the freedom and vitality, the absoluteness when summoned, of the creatures he invokes; or is more superior to the strange and second-rate policy of explaining or presenting them by reprobation or apology – of taking the short cuts and anticipating the emotions and judgments about them that should be left, at the best, to the perhaps not most intelligent reader. And yet his system, as it may summarily be called, of the mere particularized report, has a lucidity beyond the virtue of the cruder moralist.

If character, as I say, is what he gives us at every turn, I should speedily add that he offers it not in the least as a synonym, in our Western sense, of resolution and prosperity. It wears the form of the almost helpless detachment of the short-sighted individual soul; and the perfection of his exhibition of it is in truth too often but the intensity of what, for success, it just does not produce. What works in him most is the question of the will; and the most constant induction he suggests, bears upon the sad figure that principle seems mainly to make among his countrymen. He had seen – he suggests to us – its collapse in a thousand quarters; and the most general tragedy, to his view, is that of its desperate adventures and disasters, its inevitable abdication and defeat. But if the men, for the most part, let it go, it takes refuge in the other sex; many of the representatives of which, in his pages, are supremely strong – in wonderful addition, in various cases, to being otherwise admirable. This is true of such a number – the younger women, the girls, the 'heroines' in especial – that they form in themselves, on the ground of moral beauty, of the finest distinction of soul, one of the most striking groups the modern novel has given us. They are heroines to the letter, and of a heroism obscure and undecorated: it is almost they alone who have the energy to determine and to act. Elena, Lisa, Tatyana, Gemma, Marianna – we can write their names and call up their images, but I lack space to take them in turn. It is by a succession of the finest and tenderest touches that they live; and this, in all Turgenieff's work, is the process by which he persuades and succeeds.

It was his own view of his main danger that he sacrificed too much to detail; was wanting in composition, in the gift that conduces to unity of impression. But no novelist is closer and more cumulative; in none does distinction spring from a quality of truth more independent of everything but the subject, but the idea itself. This idea, this subject, moreover – a spark kindled by the innermost friction of things – is always as interesting as an unopened telegram. The genial freedom – with its exquisite delicacy – of his approach to this 'innermost' world, the world of our finer consciousness, has in short a side that I can only describe and commemorate as nobly disinterested; a side that makes too many of his rivals appear to hold us in comparison by violent means, and introduce us in comparison to vulgar things.

41

⚜

*The novel as relief; and George Gissing and the lower middle
class, from 'London Notes', Harper's Weekly, July 1897.
James's awareness of the desirable range of the novel contradicts any received idea of him as a refined snob – if that is still
necessary. For the novel as 'anodyne' compare No. 44.
The public diversion was the clamour surrounding Queen
Victoria's diamond jubilee.*

I CONTINUED last month to seek private diversion, which I found to
be more and more required as the machinery of public began to
work. Never was a better chance apparently for the great anodyne of
art. It was a supreme opportunity to test the spell of the magician, for
one felt one was saved if a fictive world would open. I knocked in this
way at a dozen doors, I read a succession of novels; with the effect
perhaps of feeling more than ever before my individual liability in
our great general debt to the novelists. The great thing to say for them
is surely that at any given moment they offer us another world,
another consciousness, an experience that, as effective as the den-
tist's ether, muffles the ache of the actual and, by helping us to an
interval, tides us over and makes us face, in the return to the
inevitable, a combination that may at least have changed. What we
get of course, in proportion as the picture lives, is simply another
actual – the actual of other people; and I no more than any one else
pretend to say *why* that should be a relief, a relief as great, I mean, as
it practically proves. We meet in this question, I think, the eternal
mystery – the mystery that sends us back simply to the queer
constitution of man and that is not in the least lighted by the plea of
'romance', the argument that relief depends wholly upon the quantity, as it were, of fable. It depends, to my sense, on the quantity of

nothing but art – in which the material, fable or fact or whatever it be, falls so into solution, is so reduced and transmuted, that I absolutely am acquainted with no receipt whatever for computing its proportion and amount.

The only amount I can compute is the force of the author, for that is directly registered in my attention, my submission. A hundred things naturally go to make it up; but he knows so much better than I what they are that I should blush to give him a glimpse of my inferior account of them. The anodyne is not the particular picture, it is our own act of surrender, and therefore most, for each reader, what he most surrenders to. This latter element would seem in turn to vary from case to case, were it not indeed that there are readers prepared, I believe, to limit their surrender in advance. With some, we gather, it declines for instance to operate save on an exhibition of 'high life'. In others again it is proof against any solicitation but that of low. In many it vibrates only to 'adventure'; in many only to Charlotte Brontë; in various groups, according to affinity, only to Jane Austen, to old Dumas, to Miss Corelli, to Dostoievsky or whomever it may be. The readers easiest to conceive, however, are probably those for whom, in the whole impression, the note of sincerity in the artist is what most matters, what most reaches and touches. That, obviously, is the relation that gives the widest range to the anodyne.

I am afraid that, profiting by my licence, I drag forward Mr George Gissing from an antiquity of several weeks . . . For this author in general, at any rate, I profess, and have professed ever since reading *The New Grub Street*, a persistent taste – a taste that triumphs even over the fact that he almost as persistently disappoints me. I fail as yet to make out why exactly it is that going so far he so sturdily refuses to go further. The whole business of distribution and composition he strikes me as having cast to the winds; but just this fact of a question about him is a part of the wonder – I use the word in the sense of enjoyment – that he excites. It is not every day in the year that we meet a novelist about whom there is a question. The circumstance alone is almost sufficient to beguile or to enthrall; and I seem to myself to have said almost everything in speaking of something that Mr Gissing 'goes far' enough to do. To go far enough to do anything is, in the conditions we live in, a lively achievement.

The Whirlpool, I crudely confess, was in a manner a grief to me, but the book has much substance, and there is no light privilege in an emotion so sustained. This emotion perhaps it is that most makes me, to the end, stick to Mr Gissing – makes me with an almost nervous clutch quite cling to him. I shall not know how to deal with him, however, if I withhold the last outrage of calling him an interesting case. He seems to me above all a case of saturation, and it is mainly his saturation that makes him interesting – I mean especially in the sense of making him singular. The interest would be greater were his art more complete; but we must take what we can get, and Mr Gissing has a way of his own. The great thing is that his saturation is with elements that, presented to us in contemporary English fiction, affect us as a product of extraordinary oddity and rarity: he reeks with the savour, he is bowed beneath the fruits, of contact with the lower, with the lowest middle-class, and that is sufficient to make him an authority – *the* authority in fact – on a region vast and unexplored.

The English novel has as a general thing kept so desperately, so nervously clear of it, whisking back compromised skirts and bumping frantically against obstacles to retreat, that we welcome as the boldest of adventurers a painter who has faced it and survived. We have had low life in plenty, for, with its sores and vices, its crimes and penalties, misery has colour enough to open the door to any quantity of artistic patronage. We have shuddered in the dens of thieves and the cells of murderers, and have dropped the inevitable tear over tortured childhood and purified sin. We have popped in at the damp cottage with my lady and heard the quaint rustic, bless his simple heart, commit himself for our amusement. We have fraternized on the other hand with the peerage and the county families, staying at fine old houses till exhausted nature has, for this source of intoxication, not a wink of sociability left. It has grown, the source in question, as stale as the sweet biscuit with pink enhancements in that familiar jar of the refreshment counter from which even the attendant young lady in black, with admirers and a social position, hesitates to extract it. We have recognized the humble, the wretched, even the wicked; also we have recognized the 'smart'. But save under the immense pressure of Dickens we have never done anything so dreadful as to recognize the vulgar. We have at the very most recognized it as the extravagant, the grotesque. The case of Dickens was absolutely special; he dealt intensely with 'lower middle', with 'lowest' middle, elements, but he escaped the predicament of showing them as vulgar by showing them only as prodigiously droll. When his people are not funny who shall dare to say what they are? The critic may draw breath as from a responsibility averted when he reflects that they almost always *are* funny. They belong to a walk of life that we may be ridiculous but never at all serious about. We may be tragic, but that is often but a form of humour. I seem to hear Mr Gissing say: 'Well, dreariness for dreariness, let us try Brondesbury and Pinner; especially as in the first place I know them so well; as in the second they are the essence of England; and as in the third they are, artistically speaking, virgin soil. Behold them glitter in the morning dew . . .'

42

On Kipling, from a letter to Grace Norton, December 1897 (HJL, vol. 4, 70). In 1891 James had written a pleasant, speculative Introduction to Mine Own People; *later he enthused about* Kim (1901).

... HIS *Ballad* future may still be big. But my view of his prose future has much shrunken in the light of one's increasingly observing how little of life he can make use of. Almost nothing civilized save steam and patriotism – and the latter only in verse, where I *hate* it so, especially mixed up with God and goodness, that that half spoils my enjoyment of his great talent. Almost nothing of the complicated soul or of the female form or of any question of *shades* – which latter constitute, to my sense, the real formative literary discipline. In his earliest time I thought he perhaps contained the seeds of an English Balzac; but I have quite given that up in proportion as he has come steadily from the less simple in subject to the more simple – from the Anglo-Indians to the natives, from the natives to the Tommies, from the Tommies to the quadrupeds, from the quadrupeds to the fish, and from the fish to the engines and screws. But he is a prodigious little success and an unqualified little happiness and a dear little chap ...

43

❖

'The Question of the Opportunities', 'American Letters',
Literature, 26 March 1898. James was always well aware of
current literary/sociological developments; and as this
example shows, what he says is relevant to times besides
his own.

ANY FRESH start of speech to-day on American literature seems to
me so inevitably a more direct and even a slightly affrighted look at
the mere numbers of the huge, homogeneous and fast-growing
population from which the flood of books issues and to which it
returns that this particular impression admonishes the observer to
pause long enough on the threshold to be sure he takes it well in.
Whatever the 'literature' already is, whatever it may be destined yet
to be, the public to which it addresses itself is of proportions that no
other single public has approached, least of all those of the periods
and societies to which we owe the comparatively small library of
books that we rank as the most precious thing in our heritage. This
question of numbers is brought home to us again and again with
force by the amazing fortune apparently open now, any year, to the
individual book – usually the lucky novel – that happens to please;
by the extraordinary career, for instance, yesterday, of *Trilby*, or,
to-day (as I hear it reported) of an historical fiction translated from
the Polish and entitled, *Quo Vadis?* It is clear enough that such a public
must be, for the observer, an immense part of the whole question of
the concatenation and quality of books, must present it in conditions
hitherto almost unobserved and of a nature probably to give an
interest of a kind so new as to suggest for the critic – even the critic
least sure of where the chase will bring him out – a delicious rest from
the oppressive *à priori*. There can be no real sport for him – if I may
use the term that fits best the critical energy – save in proportion as he

gets rid of *that*; and he can hardly fail to get rid of it just in the degree in which the conditions are vivid to his mind. They are, of course, largely those of other publics as well, in an age in which, everywhere, more people than ever before buy and sell, and read and write, and run about; but their scale, in the great common-schooled and newspapered democracy, is the largest and their pressure the greatest we see; their characteristics are magnified and multiplied. From these characteristcs no intelligent forecast of the part played in the community in question by the printed and circulated page will suffer its attention too widely to wander.

Homogeneous I call the huge American public, with a due sense of the variety of races and idioms that are more and more under contribution to build it up, for it is precisely in the great mill of the language, our predominant and triumphant English, taking so much, suffering perhaps even so much, in the process, but giving so much more, on the whole, than it has to 'put up' with, that the elements are ground into unity. Into its vast motherly lap the supreme speech manages somehow or other – with a robust indifference to trifles and shades – to see these elements poured; and just in this unique situation of the tongue itself we may surely find, if we attend, the interest of the drama and the excitement of the question. It is a situation that strikes me as presenting to the critic some of the strain and stress – those of suspense, of life, movement, change, the multiplication of possibilities, surprise, disappointments (emotions, whatever they may be, of the truth-hunter) – that the critic likes most to encounter. What may be, from point to point, noted as charming, or even as alarming, consequences? What forms, what colours, what sounds may the language take on or throw off in accommodating itself to such a growth of experience; what life may it – and most of all may the literature that shall so copiously testify for it – reflect and embody? The answer to these inquiries is simply the march of the critic's drama and the bliss, when not the misery, of that spectator; but while the endless play goes on the spectator may at least so far anticipate deferred conclusions as to find a savour in the very fact that it has been reserved not for French, not for German, not for Italian to meet fate on such a scale. That consciousness is an emotion in itself and, for large views, which are the only amusing ones, a great portent; so that we can surely say to ourselves that we shall not have been called upon to supply the biggest public for nothing.

To overflow with the same confidence to others is indeed perhaps to expose ourselves to hearing it declared improbable that we have been called upon to supply it, at any rate, for literature – the moral mainly latent in literature for the million, or rather for the fast-arriving billion, finding here inevitably a tempting application. But is not our instant rejoinder to that, as inevitably, that such an application is precipitate and premature? Whether, in the conditions we consider, the supply shall achieve sufficient vitality and distinction really to be sure of itself as literature, and to communicate the certitude, is the very thing we watch and wait to discover. If the retort to that remark be in turn that all this depends on what we may take it into our heads to *call* literature, we work round to a ground of easy assent. It truly does much depend on that. But that, in its order, depends on new light – on the new light struck out by the material itself, the distinguishable symptoms of which are the justification for what I have called the critic's happy release from the cramped posture of foregone conclusions and narrow rules. There will be no real amusement if we are positively prepared to be stupid. It is assuredly true that literature for the billion will not be literature as we have hitherto known it at its best. But if the billion give the pitch of production and circulation, they do something else besides; they hang before us a wide picture of opportunities – opportunities that would be opportunities still even if, reduced to the *minimum*, they should be only those offered by the vastness of the implied habitat and the complexity of the implied history. It is impossible not to entertain with patience and curiosity the presumption that life so colossal must break into expression at points of proportionate frequency. These places, these moments will be the chances.

The first chance that, in the longer run, expression avails herself of may, of course, very well be that of breaking up into pieces and showing thereby that – as has been hitherto and in other parts of the world but imperfectly indicated – the public we somewhat loosely talk of as for literature or for anything else is really as subdivided as a chess-board, with each little square confessing only to its own *kind* of accessibility. The comparison too much sharpens and equalizes; but there are certainly, as on a map of countries, divisions and boundaries; and if these varieties become, to assist individual genius or save individual life, accentuated in American letters, we shall immediately to that tune be rewarded for our faith. It is, in other words, just from the very force of the conditions making for reaction in spots and phases that the liveliest appeal of future American production may spring – reaction, I mean, against the grossness of any view, any taste or tone, in danger of becoming so extravagantly general as to efface the really interesting thing, the traceability of the individual. Then, for all we know, we may get individual publics positively more sifted and evolved than anywhere else, shoals of fish rising to more delicate bait. That is a possibility that makes meanwhile for good humour, though I must hasten to add that it by no means exhausts the favourable list. We know what the list actually shows or what, in the past, it has mainly shown – New England quite predominantly, almost exclusively, the literary voice and dealing with little else than material supplied by herself. I have just been reading two new books that mark strikingly how the Puritan culture both used and exhausted its opportunity, how its place knows it no longer with any approach to the same intensity. Mrs Fields' *Life and Letters of Harriet Beecher Stowe* and Mr John Jay Chapman's acute and admirable *Emerson and Other Essays* (the most penetrating study, as regards his main subject, to my sense, of which that subject has been made the occasion) appear to refer to a past already left long behind, and are each, moreover, on this ground and on others, well worth returning to. The American world of to-day is a world of combinations and proportions different from those amid which Emerson and Mrs Stowe could reach right and left far enough to fill it.

The note of the difference – at least of some of it – is sharply enough struck in an equally recent volume from which I have gathered many suggestions and that exhibits a talent distinctly to come back to – Mr Owen Wister's *Lin McLean* (episodes in the career of a young 'cattle-puncher'), in which the manners of the remoter West are worked into the general context, the American air at large, by a hand of a singularly trained and modern lightness. I but glance in passing, not to lose my thread, at these things; but Mr Owen Wister's tales (an earlier strong cluster of which, *Red Men and*

White, I a year or two ago also much appreciated) give me a pretext for saying that, not inexplicably perhaps, a novelist interested in the general outlook of his trade may find the sharpest appeal of all in the idea of the chances in reserve for the work of the imagination in particular – the vision of the distinguishable poetry of things, whether expressed in such verse or (rarer phenomenon) in such prose as really does arrive at expression. I cannot but think that the American novel has in a special, far-reaching direction to sail much closer to the wind. 'Business' plays a part in the United States that other interests dispute much less showily than they sometimes dispute it in the life of European countries; in consequence of which the typical American figure is above all that 'business man' whom the novelist and the dramatist have scarce yet seriously touched, whose song has still to be sung and his picture still to be painted. He is often an obscure, but not less often an epic, hero, seamed all over with the wounds of the market and the dangers of the field, launched into action and passion by the immensity and complexity of the general struggle, a boundless ferocity of battle – driven above all by the extraordinary, the unique relation in which he for the most part stands to the life of his lawful, his immitigable womankind, the wives and daughters who float, who splash on the surface and ride the waves, his terrific link with civilization, his social substitutes and representatives, while, like a diver for shipwrecked treasure, he gasps in the depths and breathes through an air-tube.

This relation, even taken alone, contains elements that strike me as only yearning for their interpreter – elements, moreover, that would present the further merit of melting into the huge neighbouring province of the special situation of women in an order of things where to be a woman at all – certainly to be a young one – constitutes in itself a social position. The difficulty, doubtless, is that the world of affairs, as affairs are understood in the panting cities, though around us all the while, before us, behind us, beside us, and under our feet, is as special and occult a one to the outsider as the world, say, of Arctic exploration – as impenetrable save as a result of special training. Those who know it are not the men to paint it; those who might attempt it are not the men who know it. The most energetic attempt at portrayal that we have anywhere had – *L'Argent*, of Emile Zola – is precisely a warning of the difference between false and true initiation. The subject there, though so richly imagined, is all too mechanically, if prodigiously, 'got up'. Meanwhile, accordingly, the American 'business man' remains, thanks to the length and strength of the wires that move him, *the* magnificent theme *en disponibilité*. The romance of fact, indeed, has touched him in a way that quite puts to shame the romance of fiction. It gives his measure for purposes of art that it was he, essentially, who embarked in the great war of 1861–64, and who, carrying it on in the North to a triumphant conclusion, went back, since business was his standpoint, to his very 'own' with an undimmed capacity to mind it. When, in imagination, you give the type, as it exists to-day, the benefit of its great double lustre – that of these recorded antecedents and that of its preoccupied, systematic and magnanimous abasement before the other sex – you will easily feel your sense of what may be done with its overflow.

To glance at that is, at the point to which the English-speaking world has brought the matter, to remember by the same stroke that if there be no virtue in any forecast of the prospect of letters, any sounding of their deeps and shallows that fails to take account of the almost predominant hand now exercised about them by women, the precaution is doubly needful in respect to the American situation. Whether the extraordinary dimensions of the public be a promise or a threat, nothing is more unmistakable than the sex of some of the largest masses. The longest lines are feminine – feminine, it may almost be said, the principal front. Both as readers and as writers on the other side of the Atlantic women have, in fine, 'arrived' in numbers not equalled even in England, and they have succeeded in giving the pitch and marking the limits more completely than elsewhere. The public taste, as our fathers used to say, has become so largely *their* taste, their tone, their experiment, that nothing is at last more apparent than that the public cares little for anything that they cannot do. And what, after all, may the very finest opportunity of American literature be but just to show that they can do what the peoples will have ended by regarding as everything? The settlement of such a question, the ups and downs of such a process surely more than justify that sense of sport, in this direction, that I have spoken of as the privilege of the vigilant critic.

44

❧

From 'The Story-Teller at Large: Mr Henry Harland. Comedies and Errors', *Fortnightly Review, April 1898. Harland was the editor of the* Yellow Book, *and an acquaintance of James.*

. . . MR HARLAND'S method is that of the 'short story' which has of late become an object of such almost extravagant dissertation. If it has awaked to consciousness, however, it has doubtless only done what most things are doing in an age of organized talk. It took itself, in the comparatively silent years, less seriously, and there was perhaps a more general feeling that you both wrote and read your short story best when you did so in peace and patience. To turn it out, at any rate, as well as possible, by private, and almost diffident, instinct and reflection, was a part of the general virtue of the individual, the kind of virtue that shunned the high light of the public square. The public square is now the whole city, and, taking us all in, has acoustic properties so remarkable that thoughts barely whispered in a corner are heard all over the place. Therefore each of us already knows what every other of us thinks of the short story, though he knows perhaps at the same time that not every other can write it. Anything we may say about it is at best but a compendium of the current wisdom. It is a form delightful and difficult, and with one of these qualities — as, for that matter, one of them almost everywhere is — the direct reason of the other. It is an easy thing, no doubt, to do a little with, but the interest quickens at a high rate on an approximation to that liberal *more* of which we speedily learn it to be capable. The charm I find in Mr Harland's tales is that he is always trying for the more, for the extension of the picture, the full and vivid summary, and trying with an art of ingenuity, an art of a reflective order, all alive with felicities and delicacies.

Are there not two quite distinct effects to be produced by this rigour of brevity – the two that best make up for the many left unachieved as requiring a larger canvas? The one with which we are most familiar is that of the detached incident, single and sharp, as clear as a pistol-shot; the other, of rarer performance, is that of the impression, comparatively generalized – simplified, foreshortened, reduced to a particular perspective – of a complexity or a continuity. The former is an adventure comparatively safe, in which you have, for the most part, but to put one foot after the other. It is just the risks of the latter, on the contrary, that make the best of the sport. These are naturally – given the general reduced scale – immense, for nothing is less intelligible than bad foreshortening, which, if it fails to mean everything intended, means less than nothing. It is to Mr Harland's honour that he always 'goes in' for the risks. *The Friend of Man*, for instance, is an attempt as far removed as possible from the snap of the pistol-shot; it is an excellent example of the large in a small dose, the smaller form put on its mettle and trying to do – by sharp selection, composition, presentation and the sacrifice of verbiage – what the longer alone is mostly supposed capable of. It is the picture of a particular figure – eccentric, comic, pathetic, tragic – disengaged from old remembrances, encounters, accidents, exhibitions and exposures, and resolving these glimpses and patches into the unity of air and feeling that makes up a character. It is all a matter of odds and ends recovered and interpreted. The 'story' is nothing, the subject everything, and the manner in which the whole thing becomes expressive strikes me as an excellent specimen of what can be done on the minor scale when art comes in. There are, of course, particular effects that insist on space, and the thing, above all, that the short story has to renounce is the actual *pursuit* of a character. Temperaments and mixtures, the development of a nature, are shown us perforce in a tale, as they are shown us in life, only by illustration more or less copious and frequent; and the drawback is that when the tale is short the figure, before we have had time to catch up with it, gets beyond and away, dips below the horizon made by the little square of space that we have accepted . . .

45

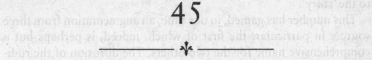

'*The Future of the Novel*', International Library of Famous Literature, *vol. XIV, 1899.*

BEGINNINGS, as we all know, are usually small things, but continuations are not always strikingly great ones, and the place occupied in the world by the prolonged prose fable has become, in our time, among the incidents of literature, the most surprising example to be named of swift and extravagant growth, a development beyond the measure of every early appearance. It is a form that has had a fortune so little to have been foretold at its cradle. The germ of the comprehensive epic was more recognizable in the first barbaric chant than that of the novel as we know it to-day in the first anecdote retailed to amuse. It arrived, in truth, the novel, late at self-consciousness; but it has done its utmost ever since to make up for lost opportunities. The flood at present swells and swells, threatening the whole field of letters, as would often seem, with submersion. It plays, in what may be called the passive consciousness of many persons, a part that directly marches with the rapid increase of the multitude able to possess itself in one way and another of the *book*. The book, in the Anglo-Saxon world, is almost everywhere, and it is in the form of the voluminous prose fable that we see it penetrate easiest and farthest. Penetration appears really to be directly aided by mere mass and bulk. There is an immense public, if public be the name, inarticulate, but abysmally absorbent, for which, at its hours of ease, the printed volume has no other association. This public – the public that subscribes, borrows, lends, that picks up in one way and another, sometimes even by purchase – grows and grows each year, and nothing is thus more apparent than that of all the recruits it brings to the book the most numerous by far are those that it brings to the 'story'.

This number has gained, in our time, an augmentation from three sources in particular, the first of which, indeed, is perhaps but a comprehensive name for the two others. The diffusion of the rudiments, the multiplication of common schools, has had more and more the effect of making readers of women and of the very young. Nothing is so striking in a survey of this field, and nothing to be so much borne in mind, as that the larger part of the great multitude that sustains the teller and the publisher of tales is constituted by boys and girls; by girls in especial, if we apply the term to the later stages of the life of the innumerable women who, under modern arrangements, increasingly fail to marry – fail, apparently, even, largely, to desire to. It is not too much to say of many of these that they live in a great measure by the immediate aid of the novel – confining the question, for the moment, to the fact of consumption alone. The literature, as it may be called for convenience, of children is an industry that occupies by itself a very considerable quarter of the scene. Great fortunes, if not great reputations, are made, we learn, by writing for schoolboys, and the period during which they consume the compound artfully prepared for them appears – as they begin earlier and continue later – to add to itself at both ends. This helps to account for the fact that public libraries, especially those that are private and money-making enterprises, put into circulation more volumes of 'stories' than of all other things together of which volumes can be made. The published statistics are extraordinary, and of a sort to engender many kinds of uneasiness. The sort of taste that used to be called 'good' has nothing to do with the matter: we are so demonstrably in presence of millions for whom taste is but an obscure, confused, immediate instinct. In the flare of railway bookstalls, in the shop-fronts of most booksellers, especially the provincial, in the advertisements of the weekly newspapers, and in fifty places besides, this testimony to the general preference triumphs, yielding a good-natured corner at most to a bunch of treatises on athletics or sport, or a patch of theology old and new.

The case is so marked, however, that illustrations easily overflow, and there is no need of forcing doors that stand wide open. What remains is the interesting oddity or mystery – the anomaly that fairly dignifies the whole circumstance with its strangeness: the wonder, in short, that men, women, and children *should* have so much attention to spare for improvisations mainly so arbitrary and frequently so loose. That, at the first blush, fairly leaves us gaping. This great fortune then, since fortune it seems, has been reserved for mere unsupported and unguaranteed history, the *inexpensive* thing, written in the air, the record of what, in any particular case, has *not* been, the account that remains responsible, at best, to 'documents' with which we are practically unable to collate it. This is the side of the whole business of fiction on which it can always be challenged, and to that degree that if the general venture had not become in such a manner the admiration of the world it might but too easily have become the derision. It has in truth, I think, never philosophically met the challenge, never found a formula to inscribe on its shield, never defended its position by any better argument than the frank, straight blow: 'Why am I not so unprofitable as to be preposterous? Because I can do *that*. There!' And it throws up from time to time some purely practical masterpiece. There is nevertheless an admirable minority of intelligent persons who care not even for the masterpieces, nor see any pressing point in them, for whom the very form itself has, equally at its best and at its worst, been ever a vanity and mockery. This class, it should be added, is beginning to be visibly augmented by a different circle altogether, the group of the formerly subject, but now estranged, the deceived and bored, those for whom the whole movement too decidedly fails to live up to its possibilities. There are people who have loved the novel, but who actually find themselves drowned in its verbiage, and for whom, even in some of its approved manifestations, it has become a terror they exert every ingenuity, every hypocrisy, to evade. The indifferent and the alienated testify, at any rate, almost as much as the omnivorous, to the reign of the great ambiguity, the enjoyment of which rests, evidently, on a primary need of the mind. The novelist can only fall back on that – on his recognition that man's constant demand for what he has to offer is simply man's general appetite for a *picture*. The novel is of all pictures the most comprehensive and the most elastic. It will stretch anywhere – it will take in absolutely anything. All it needs is a subject and a painter. But for its subject, magnificently, it has the whole human consciousness. And if we are pushed a step farther backward, and asked why the representation should be required when the object represented is itself mostly so accessible, the answer to that appears to be that man combines with his eternal desire for more experience an infinite cunning as to getting his experience as cheaply as possible. He will steal it whenever he can. He likes to live the life of others, yet is well aware of the points at which it may too intolerably resemble his own. The vivid fable, more than anything else, gives him this satisfaction on easy terms, gives him knowledge abundant yet vicarious. It enables him to select, to take and to leave; so that to feel he can afford to neglect it he must have a rare faculty, or great opportunities, for the extension of experience – by thought, by emotion, by energy – at first hand.

Yet it is doubtless not this cause alone that contributes to the contemporary deluge; other circumstances operate, and one of them is probably, in truth, if looked into, something of an abatement of the great fortune we have been called upon to admire. The high prosperity of fiction has marched, very directly, with another 'sign of the times', the demoralization, the vulgarization of literature in general, the increasing familiarity of all such methods of communication, the making itself supremely felt, as it were, of the presence of the ladies and children – by whom I mean, in other words, the reader irreflective and uncritical. If the novel, in fine, has found itself, socially speaking, at such a rate, the book *par excellence*, so on the other hand the book has in the same degree found itself a thing of small ceremony. So many ways of producing it easily have been discovered that it is by no means the occasional prodigy, for good or for evil, that it was taken for in simpler days, and has therefore suffered a proportionate discredit. Almost any variety is thrown off and taken up, handled, admired, ignored by too many people, and this, precisely, is the point at which the question of its future becomes one with that of the future of the total swarm. How are the generations to face, at all, the monstrous multiplications? Any speculation on the further development of a particular variety is subject to the reserve that the generations may at no distant day be obliged formally to decree, and to execute, great clearings of the deck, great periodical effacements and destructions. It fills, in fact, at moments the expectant ear, as we watch the progress of the ship of civilization – the huge splash that must mark the response to many an imperative, unanimous 'Overboard!' What at least is already very plain is that practically the great majority of volumes printed within a year cease to exist as the hour passes, and give up by that circumstance all claim to a career, to being accounted or provided for. In speaking of the future of the novel we must of course, therefore, be taken as limiting the inquiry to those types that have, for criticism, a present and a past. And it is only superficially that confusion seems here to reign. The fact that in England and in the United States every specimen that sees the light may look for a 'review' testifies merely to the point to which, in these countries, literary criticism has sunk. The review is in nine cases out of ten an effort of intelligence as undeveloped as the ineptitude over which it fumbles, and the critical spirit, which knows where it is concerned and where not, is not touched, is still less compromised, by the incident. There are too many reasons why newspapers must live.

So, as regards the tangible type, the end is that in its undefended, its positively exposed state, we continue to accept it, conscious even of a peculiar beauty in an appeal made from a footing so precarious. It throws itself wholly on our generosity, and very often indeed gives us, by the reception it meets, a useful measure of the quality, of the delicacy, of many minds. There is to my sense no work of literary, or of any other, art, that any human being is under the smallest positive obligation to 'like'. There is no woman – no matter of what loveliness – in the presence of whom it is anything but a man's unchallengeably *own* affair that he is 'in love' or out of it. It is not a question of manners; vast is the margin left to individual freedom; and the trap set by the artist occupies no different ground – Robert Louis Stevenson has admirably expressed the analogy – from the offer of her charms by the lady. There only remain infatuations that we envy and emulate. When we do respond to the appeal, when we *are* caught in the trap, we are held and played upon; so that how in the world can there *not* still be a future, however late in the day, for a contrivance possessed of this precious secret? The more we consider it the more we feel that the prose picture can never be at the end of its tether until it loses the sense of what it can do. It can do simply everything, and that is its strength and its life. Its plasticity, its elasticity are infinite; there is no colour, no extension it may not take from the nature of its subject or the temper of its craftsman. It has the extraordinary advantage – a piece of luck scarcely credible – that, while capable of giving an impression of the highest perfection and the rarest finish, it moves in a luxurious independence of rules and restrictions. Think as we may, there is nothing we can mention as a consideration outside itself with which it must square, nothing we can name as one of its peculiar obligations or interdictions. It must, of course, hold our attention and reward it, it must not appeal on false pretences; but these necessities, with which, obviously, disgust and displeasure interfere, are not peculiar to it – all works of art have them in common. For the rest it has so clear a field that if it perishes this will surely be by its fault – by its superficiality, in other words, or its timidity. One almost, for the very love of it, likes to think of its appearing threatened with some such fate, in order to figure the dramatic stroke of its revival under the touch of a life-giving master. The temperament of the artist can do so much for it that our desire for some exemplary felicity fairly demands even the vision of that supreme proof. If we were to linger on this vision long enough, we should doubtless, in fact, be brought to wondering – and still for very loyalty to the form itself – whether our own prospective conditions may not before too long appear to many critics to call for some such happy *coup* on the part of a great artist yet to come.

There would at least be this excuse for such a reverie: that speculation is vain unless we confine it, and that for ourselves the most convenient branch of the question is the state of the industry that makes its appeal to readers of English. From any attempt to measure the career still open to the novel in France I may be excused, in so narrow a compass, for shrinking. The French, as a result of having ridden their horse much harder than we, are at a different stage of the journey, and we have doubtless many of their stretches and baiting-places yet to traverse. But if the range grows shorter from the moment we drop to inductions drawn only from English and American material, I am not sure that the answer comes sooner. I should have at all events – a formidably large order – to plunge into the particulars of the question of the present. If the day *is* approaching when the respite of execution for almost any book is but a matter of mercy, does the English novel of commerce tend to strike us as a production more and more equipped by its high qualities for braving the danger? It would be impossible, I think, to make one's attempt at an answer to that riddle really interesting without bringing into the field many illustrations drawn from individuals – without pointing the moral with names both conspicuous and obscure. Such a freedom would carry us, here, quite too far, and would moreover only encumber the path. There is nothing to prevent our taking for granted all sorts of happy symptoms and splendid promises – so long, of course, I mean, as we keep before us the general truth that the future of fiction is intimately bound up with the future of the society that produces and consumes it. In a society with a great and diffused literary sense the talent at play can only be a less negligible thing than in a society with a literary sense barely discernible. In a world in which criticism is acute and mature such talent will find itself trained, in order successfully to assert itself, to many more kinds of precautionary expertness than in a society in which the art I have named holds an inferior place or makes a sorry figure. A community addicted to reflection and fond of ideas will try experiments with the 'story' that will be left untried in a community mainly devoted to travelling and shooting, to pushing trade and playing football. There are many judges, doubtless, who hold that experiments – queer and uncanny things at best – are not necessary to it, that its face has been, once for all, turned in one way, and that it has only to go straight before it. If that is what it is actually doing in England and America the main thing to say about its future would appear to be that this future will in very truth more and more define itself as negligible. For all the while the immense variety of life will stretch away to right and to left, and all the while there may be, on such lines, perpetuation of its great mistake of failing of intelligence. That mistake will be, ever, for the admirable art, the only one really inexcusable, because of being a mistake about, as we may say, its own soul. The form of novel that is stupid on the general question of its freedom is the single form that may, *a priori*, be unhesitatingly pronounced wrong.

The most interesting thing to-day, therefore, among ourselves is the degree in which we may count on seeing a sense of that freedom cultivated and bearing fruit. What else is this, indeed, but one of the most attaching elements in the great drama of our wide English-speaking life! As the novel is at any moment the most immediate and,

as it were, admirably *treacherous* picture of actual manners –
indirectly as well as directly, and by what it does not touch as well as
by what it does – so its present situation, where we are most
concerned with it, is exactly a reflection of our social changes and
chances, of the signs and portents that lay most traps for most
observers, and make up in general what is most 'amusing' in the
spectacle we offer. Nothing, I may say, for instance, strikes me more
as meeting this description than the predicament finally arrived at, for
the fictive energy, in consequence of our long and most respectable
tradition of making it defer supremely, in the treatment, say, of a
delicate case, to the inexperience of the young. The particular knot
the coming novelist who shall prefer not simply to beg the question,
will have here to untie may represent assuredly the essence of his
outlook. By what it shall decide to do in respect to the 'young' the
great prose fable will, from any serious point of view, practically see
itself stand or fall. What is clear is that it has, among us, veritably
never chosen – it has, mainly, always obeyed an unreasoning instinct
of avoidance in which there has often been much that was felicitous.
While society was frank, was free about the incidents and accidents
of the human constitution, the novel took the same robust ease as
society. The young then were so very young that they were not
table-high. But they began to grow, and from the moment their little
chins rested on the mahogany, Richardson and Fielding began to go
under it. There came into being a mistrust of any but the most
guarded treatment of the great relation between men and women, the
constant world-renewal, which was the conspicuous sign that whatever the prose picture of life was prepared to take upon itself, it was
not prepared to take upon itself not to be superficial. Its position
became very much: 'There are other things, don't you know? For
heaven's sake let *that* one pass!' And to this wonderful property of
letting it pass the business has been for these so many years – with the
consequences we see to-day – largely devoted. These consequences
are of many sorts, not a few altogether charming. One of them has
been that there is an immense omission in our fiction – which, though
many critics will always judge that it has vitiated the whole, others
will continue to speak of as signifying but a trifle. One can only talk
for one's self, and of the English and American novelists of whom I
am fond, I am so superlatively fond that I positively prefer to take

them as they are. I cannot so much as imagine Dickens and Scott *without* the 'love-making' left, as the phrase is, out. They were, to my perception, absolutely right – from the moment their attention to it could only be perfunctory – practically not to deal with it. In all their work it is, in spite of the number of pleasant sketches of affection gratified or crossed, the element that matters least. Why not therefore assume, it may accordingly be asked, that discriminations which have served their purpose so well in the past will continue not less successfully to meet the case? What will you have better than Scott and Dickens?

Nothing certainly *can* be, it may at least as promptly be replied, and I can imagine no more comfortable prospect than jogging along perpetually with a renewal of such blessings. The difficulty lies in the fact that two of the great conditions have changed. The novel is older, and so are the young. It would seem that everything the young can possibly do for us in the matter has been successfully done. They have kept out one thing after the other, yet there is still a certain completeness we lack, and the curious thing is that it appears to be they themselves who are making the grave discovery. 'You have kindly taken,' they seem to say to the fiction-mongers, 'our education off the hands of our parents and pastors, and that, doubtless, has been very convenient for *them*, and left them free to amuse themselves. But what, all the while, pray, if it is a question of education, have you done with your own? These are directions in which you seem dreadfully untrained, and in which *can* it be as vain as it appears to apply to you for information?' The point is whether, from the moment it is a question of averting discredit, the novel can afford to take things quite so easily as it has, for a good while, now, settled down into the way of doing. There are too many sources of interest neglected – whole categories of manners, whole corpuscular classes and provinces, museums of character and condition, unvisited; while it is on the other hand mistakenly taken for granted that safety lies in all the loose and thin material that keeps reappearing in forms at once ready-made and sadly the worse for wear. The simple themselves may finally turn against our simplifications; so that we need not, after all, be more royalist than the king or more childish than the children. It is certain that there is no real health for any art – I am not speaking, of course, of any mere industry – that does not move a step in advance of its farthest follower. It would be curious – really a great comedy – if the renewal were to spring just from the satiety of the very readers for whom the sacrifices have hitherto been supposed to be made. It bears on this that as nothing is more salient in English life to-day, to fresh eyes, than the revolution taking place in the position and outlook of women – and taking place much more deeply in the quiet than even the noise on the surface demonstrates – so we may very well yet see the female elbow itself, kept in increasing activity by the play of the pen, smash with final resonance the window all this time most superstitiously closed. The particular draught that has been most deprecated will in that case take care of the question of freshness. It is the opinion of some observers that when women do obtain a free hand they will not repay their long debt to the precautionary attitude of men by unlimited consideration for the natural delicacy of the latter.

To admit, then, that the great anodyne can ever totally fail to work, is to imply, in short, that this will only be by some grave fault in some high quarter. Man rejoices in an incomparable faculty for presently mutilating and disfiguring any plaything that has helped create for him the illusion of leisure; nevertheless, so long as life retains its power of projecting itself upon his imagination, he will find the novel work off the impression better than anything he knows. Anything better for the purpose has assuredly yet to be discovered. He will give it up only when life itself too thoroughly disagrees with him. Even then, indeed, may fiction not find a second wind, or a fiftieth, in the very portrayal of that collapse? Till the world is an unpeopled void there will be an image in the mirror. What need more immediately concern us, therefore, is the care of seeing that the image shall continue various and vivid. There is much, frankly, to be said for those who, in spite of all brave pleas, feel it to be considerably menaced, for very little reflection will help to show us how the prospect strikes them. They see the whole business too divorced on the one side from observation and perception, and on the other from the art and taste. They get too little of the first-hand impression, the effort to penetrate – that effort for which the French have the admirable expression to *fouiller* – and still less, if possible, of any science of composition, any architecture, distribution, pro-portion. It is not a trifle, though indeed it is the concomitant of an edged force, that 'mystery' should, to so many of the sharper eyes, have disappeared from the craft, and a facile flatness be, in place of it, in acclaimed possession. But these are, at the worst, even for such of the disconcerted, signs that the novelist, not that the novel, has dropped. So long as there is a subject to be treated, so long will it depend wholly on the treatment to rekindle the fire. Only the ministrant must really approach the altar; for if the novel *is* the treatment, it is the treatment that is essentially what I have called the anodyne.

—✴—

46

Women and the presentation of sex in the novel, from 'Matilde Serao', North American Review, March 1901. Matilde Serao was an Italian 'lady novelist . . . confessedly flushed with the influence of Émile Zola'. Compare No. 45.

. . . IT IS AT any rate keeping within bounds to say that the novel will surely not become less free in proportion as the condition of women becomes more easy. It is more or less in deference to their constant concern with it that we have seen it, among ourselves, pick its steps so carefully; but there are indications that the future may reserve us the surprise of having to thank the very class whose supposed sensibilities have most oppressed us for teaching it not only a longer stride, but a healthy indifference to an occasional splash. It is for instance only of quite recent years that the type of fiction commonly identified as the 'sexual' has achieved – for purposes of reference, so far as notices in newspapers may be held to constitute reference – a salience variously estimated. Now therefore, though it is early to say that all 'imaginative work' from the female hand is subject to this description, there is assuredly none markedly so subject that is *not* from the female hand. The female mind has in fact throughout the competition carried off the prize in the familiar game, known to us all from childhood's hour, of playing at 'grown-up'; finding thus its opportunity, with no small acuteness, in the more and more marked tendency of the mind of the other gender to revert, alike in the grave and the gay, to those simplicities which there would appear to be some warrant for pronouncing puerile. It is the ladies in a word who have lately done most to remind us of man's relations with himself, that is with woman. His relations with the pistol, the pirate, the police, the wild and the tame beast – are not these prevailingly what the gentlemen have given us? And does not the difference sufficiently point my moral?

47

————— ❖ —————

On the historical novel, from a letter to Sarah Orne Jewett, October 1901 (HJL, vol. 4, 208). Compare the preface in The Aspern Papers *(No. 64); also No. 73. But James did admire* Henry Esmond *and the works of Stevenson (see No. 30).*

... THE 'HISTORIC' novel is, for me, condemned ... to a fatal *cheapness*, for the simple reason that the difficulty of the job is inordinate and that a mere *escamotage*, in the interest of ease, and of the abysmal public *naiveté* becomes inevitable. You may multiply the little facts that can be got from pictures and documents, relics and prints, as much as you like — *the* real thing is almost impossible to do, and in its essence the whole effect is as nought: I mean the invention, the representation of the old CONSCIOUSNESS, the soul, the sense, the horizon, the vision of individuals in whose minds half the things that make ours, that make the modern world were non-existent. You have to *think* with your modern apparatus a man, a woman — or rather fifty — whose own thinking was intensely otherwise conditioned, you have to simplify back by an amazing *tour de force* — and even then it's all humbug ...

48

'Honoré de Balzac'. This first appeared as a critical introduction to The Two Young Brides (Deux Jeunes Mariées), *1902.*

I

STRONGER THAN ever, even than under the spell of first acquaintance and of the early time, is the sense — thanks to a renewal of intimacy and, I am tempted to say, of loyalty — that Balzac stands signally apart, that he is the first and foremost member of his craft, and that above all the Balzac-lover is in no position till he has cleared the ground by saying so. The Balzac-lover alone, for that matter, is worthy to have his word on so happy an occasion as this about the author of *La Comédie Humaine*, and it is indeed not easy to see how the amount of attention so inevitably induced could at the worst have failed to find itself turning to an act of homage. I have been deeply affected, to be frank, by the mere refreshment of memory, which has brought in its train moreover consequences critical and sentimental too numerous to figure here in their completeness. The authors and the books that have, as we say, done something for us, become part of the answer to our curiosity when our curiosity had the freshness of youth, these particular agents exist for us, with the lapse of time, as the substance itself of knowledge: they have been intellectually so swallowed, digested and assimilated that we take their general use and suggestion for granted, cease to be aware of them because they have passed out of sight. But they have passed out of sight simply by having passed into our lives. They have become a part of our personal history, a part of ourselves, very often, so far as we may have succeeded in best expressing ourselves. Endless, however, are the uses of great persons and great things, and it may easily happen in these cases that the connection, even as an 'excitement' – the form mainly of the connections of youth – is never really broken. We have largely been living on our benefactor – which is the highest acknowledgment one can make; only, thanks to a blest law that operates in the long run to rekindle excitement, we are accessible to the sense of having neglected him. Even when we may not constantly have read him over the neglect is quite an illusion, but the illusion perhaps prepares us for the finest emotion we are to have owed to the acquaintance. Without having abandoned or denied our author we yet come expressly back to him, and if not quite in tatters and in penitence like the Prodigal Son, with something at all events of the tenderness with which we revert to the parental threshold and hearthstone, if not, more fortunately, to the parental presence. The beauty of this adventure, that of seeing the dust blown off a relation that had been put away as on a shelf, almost out of reach, at the back of one's mind, consists in finding the precious object not only fresh and intact, but with its firm lacquer still further figured, gilded and enriched. It is all overscored with traces and impressions – vivid, definite, almost as valuable as itself – of the recognitions and agitations it originally produced in us. Our old – that is our young – feelings are very nearly what page after page most gives us. The case has become a case of authority *plus* association. If Balzac in himself is indubitably wanting in the sufficiently common felicity we know as charm, it is this association that may on occasion contribute the grace.

The impression then, confirmed and brightened, is of the mass and weight of the figure and of the extent of ground it occupies; a tract on which we might all of us together quite pitch our little tents, open our little booths, deal in our little wares, and not materially either diminish the area or impede the circulation of the occupant. I seem to see him in such an image moving about as Gulliver among the pigmies, and not less good-natured than Gulliver for the exercise of any function, without exception, that can illustrate his larger life. The first and the last word about the author of *Les Contes Drolatiques* is that of all novelists he is the most serious – by which I am far from meaning that in the human comedy as he shows it the comic is an absent quantity. His sense of the comic was on the scale of his extraordinary senses in general, though his expression of it suffers perhaps exceptionally from that odd want of elbow-room – the penalty somehow of his close-packed, pressed-down contents – which reminds us of some designedly beautiful thing but half-disengaged from the clay or the marble. It is the scheme and the scope that are supreme in him, applying this moreover not to mere great intention, but to the concrete form, the proved case, in which we possess them. We most of us aspire to achieve at the best but a patch here and there, to pluck a sprig or a single branch, to break ground in a corner of the great garden of life. Balzac's plan was simply to do everything that could be done. He proposed to himself to 'turn over' the great garden from north to south and from east to west; a task – immense, heroic, to this day immeasurable – that he bequeathed us the partial performance of, a prodigious ragged clod, in the twenty monstrous years representing his productive career, years of concentration and sacrifice the vision of which still makes us ache. He had indeed a striking good fortune, the only one he was to enjoy as an harrassed and exasperated worker: the great garden of life presented itself to him absolutely and exactly in the guise of the great garden of France, a subject vast and comprehensive enough, yet with definite edges and corners. This identity of his universal with his local and national vision is the particular thing we should doubtless call his greatest strength were we preparing agreeably to speak of it also as his visible weakness. Of Balzac's weaknesses, however, it takes some assurance to talk; there is always plenty of time for them; they are the last signs we know him by – such things truly as in other painters of manners often come under the head of mere exuberance of energy. So little in short do they earn the invidious name even when we feel them as defects.

What he did above all was to read the universe, as hard and as loud as he could, *into* the France of his time; his own eyes regarding his work as at once the drama of man and a mirror of the mass of social phenomena the most rounded and registered, most organized and administered, and thereby most exposed to systematic observation and portrayal, that the world had seen. There are happily other interesting societies, but these are for schemes of such an order comparatively loose and incoherent, with more extent and perhaps more variety, but with less of the great enclosed and exhibited quality, less neatness and sharpness of arrangement, fewer categories, subdivisions, juxtapositions. Balzac's France was both inspiring enough for an immense prose epic and reducible enough for a report or a chart. To allow his achievement all its dignity we should doubtless say also treatable enough for a history, since it was as a patient historian, a Benedictine of the actual, the living painter of his living time, that he regarded himself and handled his material. All painters of manners and fashions, if we will, are historians, even when they least don the uniform: Fielding, Dickens, Thackeray, George Eliot, Hawthorne among ourselves. But the great difference between the great Frenchman and the eminent others is that, with an imagination of the highest power, an unequalled intensity of vision, he saw his subject in the light of science as well, in the light of the bearing of all its parts on each other, and under pressure of a passion for exactitude, an appetite, the appetite of an ogre, for *all* the kinds of facts. We find I think in the union here suggested something like the truth about his genius, the nearest approach to a final account of him. Of imagination on one side all compact, he was on the other an insatiable reporter of the immediate, the material, the current combination, and perpetually moved by the historian's impulse to fix, preserve and explain them. One asks one's self as one reads him what concern the poet has with so much arithmetic and so much criticism, so many statistics and documents, what concern the critic and the economist have with so many passions, characters and adventures. The contradiction is always before us; it springs from the inordinate scale of the author's two faces; it explains more than anything else his eccentricities and difficulties. It accounts for his want of grace, his want of the lightness associated with an amusing literary form, his bristling surface, his closeness of texture, so rough with richness, yet so productive of the effect we have in mind when we speak of not being able to see the wood for the trees.

A thorough-paced votary, for that matter, can easily afford to declare at once that this confounding duality of character does more things still, or does at least the most important of all – introduces us without mercy (mercy for ourselves I mean) to the oddest truth we could have dreamed of meeting in such a connection. It was certainly *a priori* not to be expected we should feel it of him, but our hero is after all not in his magnificence totally an artist: which would be the strangest thing possible, one must hasten to add, were not the smallness of the practical difference so made even stranger. His endowment and his effect are each so great that the anomaly makes at the most a difference only by adding to his interest for the critic. The critic worth his salt is indiscreetly curious and wants ever to know how and why – whereby Balzac is thus a still rarer case for him, suggesting that exceptional curiosity may have exceptional rewards. The question of what makes the artist on a great scale is interesting enough; but we feel it in Balzac's company to be nothing to the question of what on an equal scale frustrates him. The scattered pieces, the *disjecta membra* of the character are here so numerous and so splendid that they prove misleading; we pile them together, and the heap assuredly is monumental; it forms an overtopping figure. The genius this figure stands for, none the less, is really such a lesson to the artist as perfection itself would be powerless to give; it carries him so much further into the special mystery. Where it carries him, at the same time, I must not in this scant space attempt to say – which would be a loss of the fine thread of my argument. I stick to our point in putting it, more concisely, that the artist of the *Comédie Humaine* is half smothered by the historian. Yet it belongs as well to the matter also to meet the question of whether the historian himself may not be an artist – in which case Balzac's catastrophe would seem to lose its excuse. The answer of course is that the reporter, however philosophic, has one law, and the originator, however substantially fed, has another; so that the two laws can with no sort of harmony or congruity make, for the finer sense, a common household. Balzac's catastrophe – so to name it once again – was in this perpetual conflict and final impossibility, an impossibility that explains his defeat on the classic side and extends so far at times as to make us think of his work as, from the point of view of beauty, a tragic waste of effort.

What it would come to, we judge, is that the irreconcilability of the two kinds of law is, more simply expressed, but the irreconcilability of two different ways of composing one's effect. The principle of composition that his free imagination would have, or certainly might have, handsomely imposed on him is perpetually dislocated by the quite opposite principle of the earnest seeker, the inquirer to a useful end, in whom nothing is free but a born antipathy to his yoke-fellow. Such a production as *Le Curé de Village*, the wonderful story of Madame Graslin, so nearly a masterpiece yet so ultimately not one, would be, in this connection, could I take due space for it, a perfect illustration. If, as I say, Madame Graslin's creator was confined by his doom to patches and pieces, no piece is finer than the first half of the book in question, the half in which the picture is determined by his unequalled power of putting people on their feet, planting them before us in their habit as they lived – a faculty nourished by observation as much as one will, but with the inner vision all the while wide-awake, the vision for which ideas are as living as facts and assume an equal intensity. This intensity, greatest indeed in the facts, has in Balzac a force all its own, to which none other in any novelist I know can be likened. His touch communicates on the spot to the object, the creature evoked, the hardness and permanence that certain substances, some sorts of stone, acquire by exposure to the air. The hardening medium, for the image soaked in it, is the air of his mind. It would take but little more to make the peopled world of fiction as we know it elsewhere affect us by contrast as a world of rather grey pulp. This mixture of the solid and the vivid is Balzac at his best, and it prevails without a break, without a note not admirably true, in *Le Curé de Village* – since I have named that instance – up to the point at which Madame Graslin moves out from Limoges to Montégnac in her ardent passion of penitence, her determination to expiate her strange and undiscovered association with a dark misdeed by living and working for others. Her drama is a particularly inward one, interesting, and in the highest degree, so long as she herself, her nature, her behaviour, her personal history and the relations in which they place her, control the picture and feed our illusion. The firmness with which the author makes them play this part, the whole constitution of the scene and of its developments from the moment we cross the threshold of her dusky stuffy old-time birth-house, is a rare delight, producing in the reader that sense of local and material immersion which is one of Balzac's supreme secrets. What characteristically befalls, however, is that the spell accompanies us but part of the way – only until, at a given moment, his attention ruthlessly transfers itself from inside to outside, from the centre of his subject to its circumference.

This is Balzac caught in the very fact of his monstrous duality, caught in his most complete self-expression. He is clearly quite unwitting that in handing over his *data* to his twin-brother the impassioned economist and surveyor, the insatiate general inquirer and reporter, he is in any sort betraying our confidence, for his good conscience at such times, the spirit of edification in him, is a lesson even to the best of us, his rich robust temperament nowhere more striking, no more marked anywhere the great push of the shoulder with which he makes his theme move, overcharged though it may be like a carrier's van. It is not therefore assuredly that he loses either sincerity or power in putting before us to the last detail such a matter as, in this case, his heroine's management of her property, her tenantry, her economic opportunities and visions, for these are cases in which he never shrinks nor relents, in which positively he stiffens and terribly towers – to remind us again of M. Taine's simplifying word about his being an artist doubled with a man of business. Balzac was indeed doubled if ever a writer was, and to that extent that we almost as often, while we read, feel ourselves thinking of him as a man of business doubled with an artist. Whichever way we turn it the oddity never fails, nor the wonder of the ease with which either character bears the burden of the other. I use the word burden because, as the fusion is never complete – witness in the book before us the fatal break of 'tone', the one unpardonable sin for the novelist – we are beset by the conviction that but for this strangest of dooms one or other of the two partners might, to our relief and to his own, have been disembarrassed. The disembarrassment, for each, by a more insidious fusion, would probably have conduced to the mastership of interest proceeding from form, or at all events to the search for it, that Balzac fails to embody. Perhaps the possibility of an artist constructed on such strong lines is one of those fine things that are not of this world, a mere dream of the fond critical spirit. Let these speculations and condonations at least pass as the amusement, as a result of the high spirits – if high spirits be the word – of the reader feeling himself again in touch. It was not of our author's difficulties – that is of his difficulty, the great one – that I proposed to speak, but of his immense clear action. Even that is not truly an impression of ease, and it is strange and striking that we are in fact so attached by his want of the unity that keeps surfaces smooth and dangers down as scarce to feel sure at any moment that we shall not come back to it with most curiosity. We are never so curious about successes as about interesting failures. The more reason therefore to speak promptly, and once for all, of the scale on which, in its own quarter of his genius, success worked itself out for him.

It is to that I *should* come back – to the infinite reach in him of the painter and the poet. We can never know what might have become of him with less importunity in his consciousness of the machinery of life, of its furniture and fittings, of all that, right and left, he causes to assail us, sometimes almost to suffocation, under the general rubric of *things*. Things, in this sense with him, are at once our delight and our despair; we pass from being inordinately beguiled and convinced by them to feeling that his universe fairly smells too much of them, that the larger ether, the diviner air, is in peril of finding among them scarce room to circulate. His landscapes, his 'local colour' – thick in his pages at a time when it was to be found in his pages almost alone – his towns, his streets, his houses, his Saumurs, Angoulêmes, Guérandes, his great prose Turner-views of the land of the Loire, his rooms, shops, interiors, details of domesticity and traffic, are a short list of the terms into which he saw the real as clamouring to be rendered and into which he rendered it with unequalled authority. It would be doubtless more to the point to make our profit of this consummation than to try to reconstruct a Balzac planted more in the open. We hardly, as the case stands, know most whether to admire in such an example as the short tale of 'La Grenadière' the exquisite feeling for 'natural objects' with which it overflows like a brimming wine-cup, the energy of perception and description which so multiplies them for beauty's sake and for the love of their beauty, or the general wealth of genius that can calculate, or at least count, so little and spend so joyously. The tale practically exists for the sake of the enchanting aspects involved – those of the embowered white house that nestles on its terraced hill above the great French river, and we can think, frankly, of no one else with an equal amount of business on his hands who would either have so put himself out for aspects or made them almost by themselves a living subject. A born son of Touraine, it must be said, he pictures his province, on every pretext and occasion, with filial passion and extraordinary breadth. The prime aspect in his scene all the while, it must be added, is the money aspect. The general money question so loads him up and weighs him down that he moves through the human comedy, from beginning to end, very much in the fashion of a camel, the ship of the desert, surmounted with a cargo. 'Things' for him are francs and centimes more than any others, and I give up as inscrutable, unfathomable, the nature, the peculiar avidity of his interest in them. It makes us wonder again and again what then is the use on Balzac's scale of the divine faculty. The imagination, as we all know, may be employed up to a certain point in inventing uses for money; but its office beyond that point is surely to make us forget that anything so odious exists. This is what Balzac never forgot; his universe goes on expressing itself for him, to its furthest reaches, on its finest sides, in the terms of the market. To say these things, however, is after all to come out where we want, to suggest his extraordinary scale and his terrible completeness. I am not sure that he does not see character too, see passion, motive, personality, as quite in the order of the 'things' we have spoken of. He makes them no less concrete and palpable, handles them no less directly and freely. It is the whole business in fine – that grand total to which he proposed to himself to do high justice – that gives him his place apart, makes him, among the novelists, the largest, weightiest presence. There are some of his obsessions – that of the material, that of the financial, that of the 'social', that of the technical, political, civil – for which I feel myself unable to judge him, judgment losing itself unexpectedly in a particular shade of pity. The way to judge him is to try to walk all round him – on which we see how remarkably far we have to go. He is the only member of his order really monumental, the sturdiest-seated mass that rises in our path.

II

We recognize none the less that the finest consequence of these re-established relations is linked with just that appearance in him, that obsession of the actual under so many heads, that makes us look at him, as we would at some rare animal in captivity, between the bars of a cage. It amounts to a sort of suffered doom, since to be solicited by the world from all quarters at once, what is that for the spirit but a denial of escape? We feel his doom to be his want of a private door, and that he felt it, though more obscurely, himself. When we speak of his want of charm therefore we perhaps so surrender the question as but to show our own poverty. If charm, to cut it short, is what he lacks, how comes it that he so touches and holds us that – above all if we be actual or possible fellow-workers – we are uncomfortably conscious of the disloyalty of almost any shade of surrender? We are lodged perhaps by our excited sensibility in a dilemma of which one of the horns is a compassion that savours of patronage; but we must resign ourselves to that by reflecting that our partiality at least takes nothing away from him. It leaves him solidly where he is and only brings us near, brings us to a view of *all* his formidable parts and properties. The conception of the *Comédie Humaine* represents them all, and represents them mostly in their felicity and their triumph – or at least the execution does: in spite of which we irresistibly find ourselves thinking of him, in reperusals, as most essentially the victim of a cruel joke. The joke is one of the jokes of fate, the fate that rode him for twenty years at so terrible a pace and with the whip so constantly applied. To have wanted to do so much, to have thought it possible, to have faced and in a manner resisted the effort, to have felt life poisoned and consumed by such a bravery of self-committal – these things form for us in him a face of trouble that, oddly enough, is not appreciably lighted by the fact of his success. It was the having wanted to do so much that was the trap, whatever possibilities of glory might accompany the good faith with which he fell into it. What accompanies *us* as we frequent him is a sense of the deepening ache of that good faith with the increase of his working consciousness, the merciless development of his huge sub-ject and of the rigour of all the conditions. We see the whole thing quite as if Destiny had said to him: 'You want to "do" France, presumptuous, magnificent, miserable man – the France of revolu-tions, revivals, restorations, of Bonapartes, Bourbons, republics, of war and peace, of blood and romanticism, of violent change and intimate continuity, the France of the first half of your century? Very well; you most distinctly *shall*, and you shall particularly let me hear, even if the great groan of your labour do fill at moments the temple of letters, how you like the job.' We must of course not appear to deny the existence of a robust joy in him, the joy of power and creation, the joy of the observer and the dreamer who finds a use for his observa-tions and his dreams as fast as they come. The *Contes Drolatiques* would by themselves sufficiently contradict us, and the savour of the *Contes Drolatiques* is not confined to these productions. His work at large tastes of the same kind of humour, and we feel him again and again, like any other great healthy producer of these matters, beguiled and carried along. He would have been, I dare say, the last not to insist that the artist has pleasures forever indescribable; he lived in short in his human comedy with the largest life we can attribute to the largest capacity. There are particular parts of his subject from which, with our sense of his enjoyment of them, we have to check the impulse to call him away – frequently as I confess in this relation that impulse arises.

The relation is with the special element of his spectacle from which he never fully detaches himself, the element, to express it succinctly, of the 'old families' and the great ladies. Balzac frankly revelled in his conception of an aristocracy – a conception that never succeeded in becoming his happiest; whether, objectively, thanks to the facts supplied him by the society he studied, or through one of the strangest deviations of taste that the literary critic is in an important connection likely to encounter. Nothing would in fact be more interesting than to attempt a general measure of the part played in the total comedy, to his imagination, by the old families; and one or two contributions to such an attempt I must not fail presently to make. I glance at them here, however, the delectable class, but as most representing on the author's part free and amused creation; by which too I am far from hinting that the amusement is at all at their expense. It is in their great ladies that the old families most shine out for him, images of strange colour and form, but 'felt' as we say, to their fingertips, and extraordinarily interesting as a mark of the high predominance – predominance of character, of cleverness, of will, of general 'personality' – that almost every scene of the Comedy attributes to women. It attributes to them in fact a recognized, an uncontested supremacy; it is through them that the hierarchy of old families most expresses itself; and it is as surrounded by them even as some magnificent indulgent pasha by his overflowing seraglio that Balzac sits most at his ease. All of which reaffirms – if it be needed – that his inspiration, and the sense of it, were even greater than his task. And yet such betrayals of spontaneity in him make for an old friend at the end of the chapter no great difference in respect to the pathos – since it amounts to that – of his genius-ridden aspect. It comes to us as we go back to him that his spirit had fairly made of itself a cage in which he was to turn round and round, always unwinding his reel, much in the manner of a criminal condemned to hard labour for life. The cage is simply the complicated but dreadfully definite French world that built itself so solidly in and roofed itself so impenetrably over him.

It is not that, caught there with him though we be, we ourselves prematurely seek an issue: we throw ourselves back, on the contrary, for the particular sense of it, into his ancient superseded comparatively *rococo* and quite patriarchal France – patriarchal in spite of social and political convulsions; into his old-time antediluvian Paris, all picturesque and all workable, full, to the fancy, of an amenity that has passed away; into his intensely differentiated sphere of *la province*, evoked in each sharpest or faintest note of its difference, described systematically as narrow and flat, and yet attaching us if only by the contagion of the author's overflowing sensibility. He feels in his vast exhibition many things, but there is nothing he feels with the communicable shocks and vibrations, the sustained fury of perception – not always a fierceness of judgment, which is another matter – that *la province* excites in him. Half our interest in him springs still from our own sense that, for all the convulsions, the revolutions and experiments that have come and gone, the order he describes is the old order that our sense of the past perversely recurs to as to something happy we have irretrievably missed. His pages bristle with the revelation of the lingering earlier world, the world in which places and people still had their queerness, their strong marks, their sharp type, and in which, as before the platitude that was to come, the observer with an appetite for the salient could by way of precaution fill his lungs. Balzac's appetite for the salient was voracious, yet he came, as it were, in time, in spite of his so often speaking as if what he sees about him is but the last desolation of the modern. His conservatism, the most entire, consistent and convinced that ever was – yet even at that much inclined to whistling in the dark as if to the tune of 'Oh how mediaeval I *am*!' – was doubtless the best point of view from which he could rake his field. But if what he sniffed from afar in that position was the extremity of change, we in turn feel both subject and painter drenched with the smell of the past. It is preserved in his work as nowhere else – not vague nor faint nor delicate, but as strong to-day as when first distilled.

It may seem odd to find a conscious melancholy in the fact that a great worker succeeded in clasping his opportunity in such an embrace, this being exactly our usual measure of the felicity of great workers. I speak, I hasten to reassert, all in the name of sympathy – without which it would have been detestable to speak at all; and the sentiment puts its hand instinctively on the thing that makes it least futile. This particular thing then is not in the least Balzac's own hold of his terrible mass of matter; it is absolutely the convolutions of the serpent he had with a magnificent courage invited to wind itself round him. We must use the common image – he had created his Frankenstein monster. It is the fellow-craftsman who can most feel for him – it being apparently possible to read him from another point of view without getting really into his presence. We undergo with him from book to book, from picture to picture, the convolutions of the serpent, we especially whose refined performances are given, as we know, but with the small common or garden snake. I stick to this to justify my image just above of his having been 'caged' by the intensity with which he saw his general matter as a whole. To see it always as a whole is our wise, our virtuous effort, the very condition, as we keep in mind, of superior art. Balzac was in this connection then wise and virtuous to the most exemplary degree; so that he doubtless ought logically but to prompt to complacent reflections. No painter ever saw his general matter nearly so much as a whole. Why is it then that we hover about him, if we are real Balzacians, not with cheerful chatter, but with a consideration deeper in its reach than any mere moralizing? The reason is largely that if you wish with absolute immaculate virtue to look at your matter as a whole and yet remain a theme for cheerful chatter, you must be careful to take some quantity that will not hug you to death. Balzac's active intention was, to vary our simile, a beast with a hundred claws, and the spectacle is in the hugging process of which, as energy against energy, the beast was capable. Its victim died of the process at fifty, and if what we see in the long gallery in which it is mirrored is not the defeat, but the admirable resistance, we none the less never lose the sense that the fighter is shut up with his fate. He has locked himself in – it is doubtless his own fault – and thrown the key away. Most of all perhaps the impression comes – the impression of the adventurer committed and anxious, but with no retreat – from the so formidably concrete nature of his plastic stuff. When we work in the open, as it were, our material is not classed and catalogued, so that we have at hand a hundred ways of being loose, superficial, disingenuous, and yet passing, to our no small profit, for remarkable. Balzac had no 'open'; he held that the great central normal fruitful country of his birth and race, overarched with its infinite social complexity, yielded a sufficiency of earth and sea and sky. We seem to see as his catastrophe that the sky, all the same, came down on him. He couldn't keep it up – in more senses than one. These are perhaps fine fancies for a critic to weave about a literary figure of whom he has undertaken to give a plain account; but I leave them so on the plea that there are relations in which, for the Balzacian, criticism simply drops out. That is not a liberty, I admit, ever to be much encouraged; critics in fact are the only people who have a right occasionally to take it. There is no such plain account of the *Comédie Humaine* as that it makes us fold up our yard-measure and put away our note-book quite as we do with some extraordinary character, some mysterious and various stranger, who brings with him his own standards and his own air. There is a kind of eminent presence that abashes even the interviewer, moves him to respect and wonder, makes him, for consideration itself, not insist. This takes of course a personage sole of his kind. But such a personage precisely is Balzac.

III

By all of which have I none the less felt it but too clear that I must not pretend in this place to take apart the pieces of his immense complicated work, to number them or group them or dispose them about. The most we can do is to pick one up here and there and wonder, as we weigh it in our hand, at its close compact substance. That is all even M. Taine could do in the longest and most penetrating study of which our author has been the subject. Every piece we handle is so full of stuff, condensed like the edibles provided for campaigns and explorations, positively so charged with distilled life, that we find ourselves dropping it, in certain states of sensibility, as we drop an object unguardedly touched that startles us by being animate. We seem really scarce to want anything to *be* so animate. It would verily take Balzac to detail Balzac, and he has had in fact Balzacians nearly enough affiliated to affront the task with courage. The *Répertoire de la Comédie Humaine* of MM. Anatole Cerfberr and Jules Christophe is a closely-printed octavo of 550 pages which constitutes in relation to his characters great and small an impeccable biographical dictionary. His votaries and expositors are so numerous that the Balzac library of comment and research must be, of its type, one of the most copious. M. de Lovenjoul has laboured all round the subject; his *Histoire des Oeuvres* alone is another crowded octavo of 400 pages; in connection with which I must mention Miss Wormeley, the devoted American translator, interpreter, worshipper, who in the course of her own studies has so often found occasion to differ from M. de Lovenjoul on matters of fact and questions of date and of appreciation. Miss Wormeley, M. Paul Bourget and many others are examples of the passionate piety that our author can inspire. As I turn over the encyclopedia of his characters I note that whereas such works usually commemorate but the ostensibly eminent of a race and time, every creature so much as named in the fictive swarm is in this case preserved to fame: so close is the implication that to have *been* named by such a dispenser of life and privilege is to be, as we say it of baronets and peers, created. He infinitely divided moreover, as we know, he subdivided, altered and multiplied his heads and categories – his *Vie Parisienne*, his *Vie de Province*, his *Vie Politique*, his *Parents Pauvres*, his *Études Philosophiques*, his *Splendeurs et Misères des Courtisanes*, his *Envers de l'Histoire Contemporaine* and all the rest; so that nominal reference to them becomes the more difficult. Yet without prejudice either to the energy of conception with which he mapped out his theme as with chalk on a huge blackboard, or to the prodigious patience with which he executed his plan, practically filling in with a wealth of illustration, from sources that to this day we fail to make out, every compartment of his table, M. de Lovenjoul draws up the list, year by year, from 1822 to 1848, of his mass of work, giving us thus the measure of the tension represented for him by almost any twelvemonth. It is wholly unequalled, considering the quality of Balzac's show, by any other eminent abundance.

I must be pardoned for coming back to it, for seeming unable to leave it; it enshrouds so interesting a mystery. How was so solidly systematic a literary attack on life to be conjoined with whatever workable minimum of needful intermission, of free observation, of personal experience? Some small possibility of personal experience and disinterested life must, at the worst, from deep within or far without, feed and fortify the strained productive machine. These things were luxuries that Balzac appears really never to have tasted on any appreciable scale. His published letters – the driest and most starved of those of any man of equal distinction – are with the exception of those to Madame de Hanska, whom he married shortly before his death, almost exclusively the audible wail of a galley-slave chained to the oar. M. Zola, in our time, among the novelists, has sacrificed to the huge plan in something of the same manner, yet with goodly modern differences that leave him a comparatively simple instance. His work assuredly has been more nearly dried up by the sacrifice than ever Balzac's was – so miraculously, given the conditions, was Balzac's to escape the anticlimax. Method and system, in the chronicle of the tribe of Rougon-Macquart, an economy in itself certainly of the rarest and most interesting, have spread so from centre to circumference that they have ended by being almost the only thing we feel. And then M. Zola has survived and triumphed in his lifetime, has continued and lasted, has piled up and, if the remark be not frivolous, enjoyed in all its *agréments* the reward for which Balzac toiled and sweated in vain. On top of which he will have had also his literary great-grandfather's heroic example to start from and profit by, the positive heritage of a *fils de famille* to enjoy, spend, save, waste. Balzac had frankly no heritage at all but his stiff subject, and by way of model not even in any direct or immediate manner that of the inner light and kindly admonition of his genius. Nothing adds more to the strangeness of his general performance than his having failed so long to find his inner light, groped for it almost ten years, missed it again and again, moved straight away from it, turned his back on it, lived in fine round about it, in a darkness still scarce penetrable, a darkness into which we peep only half to make out the dreary little waste of his numerous *oeuvres de jeunesse*. To M. Zola was vouchsafed the good fortune of settling down to the Rougon-Macquart with the happiest promptitude; it was as if time for one look about him – and I say it without disparagement to the reach of his look – had sufficiently served his purpose. Balzac moreover might have written five hundred novels without our feeling in him the faintest hint of the breath of doom, if he had only been comfortably capable of conceiving the short cut of the fashion practised by others under his eyes. As Alexandre Dumas and George Sand, illustrious contemporaries, cultivated a personal life and a disinterested consciousness by the bushel, having, for their easier duration, not too consistently known, as the true painter knows it, the obsession of the thing to be done, so Balzac was condemned by his constitution itself, by his inveterately seeing this 'thing to be done' as part and parcel, as of the very essence, of his enterprise. The latter existed for him, as the process worked and hallucination settled, in the form, and the form only, of the thing done, and not in any hocus-pocus about doing. There was no kindly convenient escape for him but the little swinging back-door of the thing *not* done. He desired – no man more – to get out of his obsession, but only at the other end, that is by boring through it. 'How then, thus deprived of the outer air almost as much as if he were gouging a passage for a railway through an Alp, *did* he live?' is the question that haunts us – with the consequence for the most part of promptly meeting its fairly tragic answer. He did *not* live – save in his imagination, or by other aid than he could find there; his imagination was all his experience; he had provably no time for the real thing. This brings us to the rich if simple truth that his imagination alone did the business, carried through both the conception and the execution – as large an effort and as proportionate a success, in all but the vulgar sense, as the faculty when equally handicapped was ever concerned in. Handicapped I say because this interesting fact about him, with the claim it makes, rests on the ground, the high distinction, that more than all the rest of us put together he went in, as we say, for detail, circumstance and specification, proposed to himself *all* the connections of every part of his matter and the full total of the parts. The whole thing, it is impossible not to keep repeating, was what he deemed treatable. One really knows in all imaginative literature no undertaking to compare with it for courage, good faith and sublimity. There, once more, was the necessity that rode him and that places him apart in our homage. It is no light thing to have been condemned to become provably sublime. And looking through, or trying to, at what is beneath and behind, we are left benevolently uncertain if the predominant quantity be audacity or innocence.

It is of course inevitable at this point to seem to hear the colder critic promptly take us up. He undertook the whole thing – oh exactly, the ponderous person! But *did* he 'do' the whole thing, if you please, any more than sundry others of fewer pretensions? The retort to this it can only be a positive joy to make, so high a note instantly sounds as an effect of the inquiry. Nothing is more interesting and amusing than to find one's self recognizing both that Balzac's pretensions were immense, portentous, and that yet, taking him – and taking *them* – altogether, they but minister in the long run to our fondness. They affect us not only as the endearing eccentricities of a person we greatly admire, but fairly as the very condition of his having become such a person. We take them thus in the first place for the very terms of his plan, and in the second for a part of that high robustness and that general richness of nature which made him in face of such a project believe in himself. One would really scarce have liked to see such a job as *La Comédie Humaine* tackled without swagger. To think of the thing really as practicable *was* swagger, and of the very rarest order. So to think assuredly implied pretensions, pretensions that risked showing as monstrous should the enterprise fail to succeed. It is for the colder critic to take the trouble to make out that of the two parties to it the body of pretension remains greater than the success. One may put it moreover at the worst for him, may recognize that it is in the matter of opinion still more than in the matter of knowledge that Balzac offers himself as universally competent. He has flights of judgment – on subjects the most special as well as the most general – that are vertiginous and on his alighting from which we greet him with a special indulgence. We can easily imagine him to respond, confessing humorously – if he had only time – to such a benevolent understanding smile as would fain hold our own eyes a moment. Then it is that he would most show us his scheme and his necessities and how in operation they all hang together. *Naturally* everything about everything, though how he had time to learn it is the last thing he has time to tell us; which matters the less, moreover, as it is not over the question of his knowledge that we sociably invite him, as it were (and remembering the two augurs behind the altar) to wink at us for a sign. His convictions it is that are his great pardonable 'swagger'; to them in particular I refer as his general operative condition, the constituted terms of his experiment, and not less as his consolation, his support, his amusement by the way. They embrace everything in the world – that is in his world of the so parti-coloured France of his age: religion, morals, politics, economics, physics, esthetics, letters, art, science, sociology, every question of faith, every branch of research. They represent thus his equipment of ideas, those ideas of which it will never do for a man who aspires to constitute a State to be deprived. He must take them with him as an ambassador extraordinary takes with him secretaries, uniforms, stars and garters, a gilded coach and a high assurance. Balzac's opinions are his gilded coach, in which he is more amused than anything else to feel himself riding, but which is indispensably concerned in getting him over the ground. What more inevitable than that they should be intensely Catholic, intensely monarchical, intensely saturated with the real genius – as between 1830 and 1848 he believed it to be – of the French character and French institutions?

Nothing is happier for us than that he should have enjoyed his outlook before the first half of the century closed. He could then still treat his subject as comparatively homogeneous. Any country could have a Revolution – every country *had* had one. A Restoration was merely what a revolution involved, and the Empire had been for the French but a revolutionary incident, in addition to being by good luck for the novelist an immensely pictorial one. He was free therefore to arrange the background of the comedy in the manner that seemed to him best to suit anything so great; in the manner at the same time prescribed according to his contention by the noblest traditions. The church, the throne, the noblesse, the bourgeoisie, the people, the peasantry, all in their order and each solidly kept in it, these were precious things, things his superabundant insistence on the price of which is what I refer to as his exuberance of opinion. It was a luxury, for more reasons than one, though one, presently to be mentioned, handsomely predominates. The meaning of that exchange of intelligences in the rear of the oracle which I have figured for him with the perceptive friend bears simply on his pleading guilty to the purport of the friend's discrimination. The point the latter makes with him – a beautiful cordial critical point – is that he truly cares for nothing in the world, thank goodness, so much as for the passions and embroilments of men and women, the free play of character and the sharp revelation of type, all the real stuff of drama and the natural food of novelists. Religion, morals, politics, economics, esthetics would be thus, as systematic matter, very well in their place, but quite secondary and subservient. Balzac's attitude is again and again that he cares for the adventures and emotions because, as his last word, he cares for the good and the greatness of the State – which is where his swagger, with a whole society on his hands, comes in. What we on our side in a thousand places gratefully feel is that he cares for his monarchical and hierarchical and ecclesiastical society because it rounds itself for his mind into the most congruous and capacious theatre for the repertory of his innumerable comedians. It has above all, for a painter abhorrent of the superficial, the inestimable benefit of the accumulated, of strong marks and fine shades, contrasts and complications. There had certainly been since 1789 dispersals and confusions enough, but the thick tradition, no more at the most than half smothered, lay under them all. So the whole of his faith and no small part of his working omniscience were neither more nor less than the historic sense which I have spoken of as the spur of his invention and which he possessed as no other novelist has done. We immediately feel that to name it in connection with him is to answer every question he suggests and to account for each of his idiosyncrasies in turn. The novel, the tale, however brief, the passage, the sentence by itself, the situation, the person, the place, the motive exposed, the speech reported – these things were in his view history, with the absoluteness and the dignity of history. This is the source both of his weight and of his wealth. What is the historic sense after all but animated, but impassioned knowledge seeking to enlarge itself? I have said that his imagination did the whole thing, no other explanation – no reckoning of the possibilities of personal saturation – meeting the mysteries of the case. Therefore his imagination achieved the miracle of absolutely resolving itself into multifarious knowledge. Since history proceeds by documents he constructed, as he needed them, the documents too – fictive sources that imitated the actual to the life. It was of course a terrible business, but at least in the light of it his claims to creatorship are justified – which is what was to be shown.

IV

It is very well even in the sketchiest attempt at a portrait of his genius to try to take particulars in their order: one peeps over the shoulder of another at the moment we get a feature into focus. The loud appeal not to be left out prevails among them all, and certainly with the excuse that each as we fix it seems to fall most into the picture. I have so indulged myself as to his general air that I find a whole list of vivid contributive marks almost left on my hands. Such a list, in any study of Balzac, is delightful for intimate edification as well as for the fine humour of the thing; we proceed from one of the items of his breathing physiognomy to the other with quite the same sense of life, the same active curiosity, with which we push our way through the thick undergrowth of one of the novels. The difficulty is really that the special point for which we at the moment observe him melts into all the other points, is swallowed up before our eyes in the formidable mass. The French apply the happiest term to certain characters when they speak of them as *entiers*, and if the word had been invented for Balzac it could scarce better have expressed him. He is 'entire' as was never a man of his craft; he moves always in his mass; wherever we find him we find him in force; whatever touch he applies he applies it with his whole apparatus. He is like an army gathered to besiege a cottage equally with a city, and living voraciously in either case on all the country about. It may well be, at any rate, that this infatuation with the idea of the social, the practical primacy of 'the sex' is the article at the top of one's list; there could certainly be no better occasion than this of a rich reissue of the *Deux Jeunes Mariées* for placing it there at a venture. Here indeed precisely we get a sharp example of the way in which, as I have just said, a capital illustration of one of his sides becomes, just as we take it up, a capital illustration of another. The correspondence of Louise de Chaulieu and Renée de Maucombe is in fact one of those cases that light up with a great golden glow all his parts at once. We needn't mean by this that such parts are themselves absolutely all golden — given the amount of tinsel for instance in his view, supereminent, transcendent here, of the old families and the great ladies. What we do convey, however, is that his creative temperament finds in such *data* as these one of its best occasions for shining out. Again we fondly recognize his splendid, his attaching swagger – that of a 'bounder' of genius and of feeling; again we see how, with opportunity, its elements may vibrate into a perfect ecstasy of creation.

Why shouldn't a man swagger, he treats us to the diversion of asking ourselves, who has created from top to toe the most brilliant, the most historic, the most insolent, above all the most detailed and discriminated of aristocracies? Balzac carried the uppermost class of his comedy, from the princes, dukes, and unspeakable duchesses down to his poor barons *de province*, about in his pocket as he might have carried a tolerably befingered pack of cards, to deal them about with a flourish of the highest authority whenever there was the chance of a game. He knew them up and down and in and out, their arms, infallibly supplied, their quarterings, pedigrees, services, inter-marriages, relationships, ramifications and other enthralling attri-butes. This indeed is comparatively simple learning; the real wonder is rather when we linger on the ground of the patrician consciousness itself, the innermost, the esoteric, the spirit, temper, tone – tone above all – of the titled and the proud. The questions multiply for every scene of the comedy; there is no one who makes us walk in such a cloud of them. The clouds elsewhere, in comparison, are at best of questions not worth asking. *Was* the patrician consciousness that figures as our author's model so splendidly fatuous as he – almost without irony, often in fact with a certain poetic sympathy – everywhere represents it? His imagination lives in it, breathes its scented air, swallows this element with the smack of the lips of the connoisseur; but I feel that we never know, even to the end, whether he be here directly historic or only quite misguidedly romantic. The romantic side of him has the extent of all the others; it represents in the oddest manner his escape from the walled and roofed structure into which he had built himself – his longing for the vaguely-felt outside and as much as might be of the rest of the globe. But it is characteristic of him that the most he could do for this relief was to bring the fantastic into the circle and fit it somehow to his conditions. Was his tone for the duchess, the marquise but the imported fantas-tic, one of those smashes of the window-pane of the real that reactions sometimes produce even in the stubborn? or are we to take it as observed, as really reported, as, for all its difference from our notion of the natural – and, quite as much, of the artificial – in another and happier strain of manners, substantially true? The whole episode, in *Les Illusions Perdues*, of Madame de Bargeton's 'chucking' Lucien de Rubempré, on reaching Paris with him, under pressure of Madame d'Espard's shockability as to his coat and trousers and other such matters, is either a magnificent lurid document or the baseless fabric of a vision. The great wonder is that, as I rejoice to put it, we can never really discover which, and that we feel as we read that we can't, and that we suffer at the hands of no other author this particular helplessness of immersion. It is *done* – we are always thrown back on that; we can't get out of it; all we can do is to say that the true itself can't be more than done and that if the false in this way equals it we must give up looking for the difference. Alone among novelists Balzac has the secret of an insistence that somehow makes the difference nought. He warms his facts into life – as witness the certainty that the episode I just cited has absolutely as much of that property as if perfect matching had been achieved. If the great ladies in question *didn't* behave, wouldn't, couldn't have behaved, like a pair of nervous snobs, why so much the worse, we say to ourselves, for the great ladies in question. We *know* them so – they owe their being to our so seeing them; whereas we never can tell ourselves how we should otherwise have known them or what quantity of being they would on a different footing have been able to put forth.

The case is the same with Louise de Chaulieu, who besides coming out of her convent school, as a quite young thing, with an amount of sophistication that would have chilled the heart of a horse-dealer, exhales – and to her familiar friend, a young person of a supposedly equal breeding – an extravagance of complacency in her 'social position' that makes us rub our eyes. Whereupon after a little the same phenomenon occurs; we swallow her bragging, against our better reason, or at any rate against our startled sense, under coercion of the total intensity. We do more than this, we cease to care for the question, which loses itself in the hot fusion of the whole picture. He has 'gone for' his subject, in the vulgar phrase, with an avidity that makes the attack of his most eminent rivals affect us as the intercourse between introduced indifferences at a dull evening party. He squeezes it till it cries out, we hardly know whether for pleasure or pain. In the case before us for example – without wandering from book to book, impossible here, I make the most of the ground already broken – he has seen at once that the state of marriage itself, sounded to its depths, is, in the connection, his real theme. He sees it of course in the conditions that exist for him, but he weighs it to the last ounce, feels it in all its dimensions, as well as in all his own, and would scorn to take refuge in any engaging side-issue. He gets, for further intensity, into the very skin of his *jeunes mariées* – into each alternately, as they are different enough; so that, to repeat again, any other mode of representing women, or of representing anybody, becomes, in juxtaposition, a thing so void of the active contortions of truth as to be comparatively wooden. He bears children with Madame de l'Estorade, knows intimately how she suffers for them, and not less intimately how her correspondent suffers, as well as enjoys, without them. Big as he is he makes himself small to be handled by her with young maternal passion and positively to handle her in turn with infantile innocence. These things are the very flourishes, the little technical amusements of his penetrating power. But it is doubtless in his hand for such a matter as the jealous passion of Louise de Chaulieu, the free play of her intelligence and the almost beautiful good faith of her egotism, that he is most individual. It is one of the neatest examples of his extraordinary leading gift, his art – which is really moreover not an art – of working the exhibition of a given character up to intensity. I say it is not an art because it acts for us rather as a hunger on the part of his nature to take on in all freedom another nature – take it by a direct process of the senses. Art is for the mass of us who have only the process of art, comparatively so stiff. The thing amounts with him to a kind of shameless personal, physical, not merely intellectual, duality – the very spirit and secret of transmigration.

49

'Gustave Flaubert'. This first appeared as an introduction to
Madame Bovary, 1902.

THE FIRST thing I find to-day and on my very threshold to say about
Gustave Flaubert is that he has been reported on by M. Émile Faguet
in the series of Les Grands Écrivains Français with such lucidity as
may almost be taken to warn off a later critic. I desire to pay at the
outset my tribute to M. Faguet's exhaustive study, which is really in
its kind a model and a monument. Never can a critic have got closer
to a subject of this order; never can the results of the approach have
been more copious or more interesting; never in short can the master
of a complex art have been more mastered in his turn, nor his art
more penetrated, by the application of an earnest curiosity. That
remark I have it at heart to make, so pre-eminently has the little
volume I refer to not left the subject where it found it. It abounds in
contributive light, and yet, I feel on reflection that it scarce wholly
dazzles another contributor away. One reason of this is that, though
I enter into everything M. Faguet has said, there are things – things
perhaps especially of the province of the artist, the fellow-craftsman
of Flaubert – that I am conscious of his not having said; another is
that inevitably there are particular possibilities of reaction in our
English-speaking consciousness that hold up a light of their own.
Therefore I venture to follow even on a field so laboured, only paying
this toll to the latest and best work because the author has made it
impossible to do less.

Flaubert's life is so almost exclusively the story of his literary
application that to speak of his five or six fictions is pretty well to
account for it all. He died in 1880 after a career of fifty-nine years
singularly little marked by changes of scene, of fortune, of attitude,

of occupation, of character, and above all, as may be said, of mind. He would be interesting to the race of novelists if only because, quite apart from the value of his work, he so personally gives us the example and the image, so presents the intellectual case. He was born a novelist, grew up, lived, died a novelist, breathing, feeling, thinking, speaking, performing every operation of life, only as that votary; and this though his production was to be small in amount and though it constituted all his diligence. It was not indeed perhaps primarily so much that he was born and lived a novelist as that he was born and lived literary, and that to be literary represented for him an almost overwhelming situation. No life was long enough, no courage great enough, no fortune kind enough to support a man under the burden of this character when once such a doom had been laid on him. His case was a doom because he felt of his vocation almost nothing but the difficulty. He had many strange sides, but this was the strangest, that if we argued from his difficulty to his work, the difficulty being registered for us in his letters and elsewhere, we should expect from the result but the smallest things. We should be prepared to find in it well-nigh a complete absence of the signs of a gift. We should regret that the unhappy man had not addressed himself to something he might have found at least comparatively easy. We should singularly miss the consecration supposedly given to a work of art by its having been conceived in joy. That is Flaubert's remarkable, his so far as I know unmatched distinction, that he has left works of an extraordinary art even the conception of which failed to help him to think in serenity. The chapter of execution, from the moment execution gets really into the shafts, is of course always and everywhere a troubled one – about which moreover too much has of late been written; but we frequently find Flaubert cursing his subjects themselves, wishing he had not chosen them, holding himself up to derision for having done so, and hating them in the very act of sitting down to them. He cared immensely for the medium, the task and the triumph involved, but was himself the last to be able to say why. He is sustained only by the rage and the habit of effort; the mere *love* of letters, let alone the love of life, appears at an early age to have deserted him. Certain passages in his correspondence make us even wonder if it be not hate that sustains him most. So, successively, his several supremely finished and crowned compositions came into the world, and we may feel sure that none others of the kind, none that were to have an equal fortune, had sprung from such adversity.

I insist upon this because his at once excited and baffled passion gives the key of his life and determines its outline. I must speak of him at least as I feel him and as in his very latest years I had the fortune occasionally to see him. I said just now, practically, that he is for many of our tribe at large *the* novelist, intent and typical, and so, gathered together and foreshortened, simplified and fixed, the lapse of time seems to show him. It has made him in his prolonged posture extraordinarily objective, made him even resemble one of his own productions, constituted him as a subject, determined him as a figure; the limit of his range, and above all of his reach, is after this fashion, no doubt, sufficiently indicated, and yet perhaps in the event without injury to his name. If our consideration of him cultivates a certain tenderness on the double ground that he suffered supremely in the cause and that there is endlessly much to be learned from him, we remember at the same time that, indirectly, the world at large possesses him not less than the *confrère*. He has fed and fertilized, has filtered through others, and so arrived at contact with that public from whom it was his theory that he was separated by a deep and impassable trench, the labour of his own spade. He is none the less more interesting, I repeat, as a failure however qualified than as a success however explained, and it is as so viewed that the unity of his career attaches and admonishes. Save in some degree by a condition of health (a liability to epileptic fits at times frequent, but never so frequent as to have been generally suspected) he was not outwardly hampered as the tribe of men of letters goes – an anxious brotherhood at the best; yet the fewest possible things appear to have ever succeeded in happening to him. The only son of an eminent provincial physician, he inherited a modest ease and no other incumbrance than, as was the case for Balzac, an over-attentive, an importunate mother; but freedom spoke to him from behind a veil, and when we have mentioned the few apparent facts of experience that make up his landmarks over and beyond his interspaced publications we shall have completed his biography. Tall, strong, striking, he caused his friends to admire in him the elder, the florid Norman type, and he seems himself, as a man of imagination, to have found some transmission of race in his stature and presence, his light-coloured salient eyes and long tawny moustache.

The central event of his life was his journey to the East in 1849 with M. Maxime Du Camp, of which the latter has left in his *Impressions Littéraires* a singularly interesting and, as we may perhaps say, slightly treacherous report, and which prepared for Flaubert a state of nostalgia that was not only never to leave him, but that was to work in him as a motive. He had during that year, and just in sufficient quantity, his revelation, the particular appropriate disclosure to which the gods at some moment treat the artist unless they happen too perversely to conspire against him: he tasted of the knowledge by which he was subsequently to measure everything, appeal from everything, find everything flat. Never probably was an impression so assimilated, so positively transmuted to a function; he lived on it to the end and we may say that in *Salammbô* and *La Tentation de Saint-Antoine* he almost died of it. He made afterwards no other journey of the least importance save a disgusted excursion to the Rigi-Kaltbad shortly before his death. The Franco-German War was of course to him for the time as the valley of the shadow itself; but this was an ordeal, unlike most of his other ordeals, shared after all with millions. He never married – he declared, toward the end, to the most comprehending of his confidants, that he had been from the first 'afraid of life'; and the friendliest element of his later time was, we judge, that admirable comfortable commerce, in her fullest maturity, with Madame George Sand, the confidant I just referred to; which has been preserved for us in the published correspondence of each. He had in Ivan Turgenieff a friend almost as valued; he spent each year a few months in Paris, where (to mention everything) he had his natural place, so far as he cared to take it, at the small literary court of the Princess Mathilde; and, lastly, he lost toward the close of his life, by no fault of his own, a considerable part of his modest fortune. It is, however, in the long security, the almost unbroken solitude of Croisset, near Rouen, that he mainly figures for us, gouging out his successive books in the wide old room, of many windows, that, with an intervening terrace, overlooked the broad Seine and the passing boats. This was virtually a monastic cell, closed to echoes and accidents; with its stillness for long periods scarce broken save by the creak of the towing-chain of the tugs across the water. When I have added that his published letters offer a view, not very refreshing, of his youthful entanglement with Madame Louise Colet – whom we name because, apparently not a shrinking person, she long ago practically named herself – I shall have catalogued his personal vicissitudes. And I may add further that the connection with Madame Colet, such as it was, rears its head for us in something like a desert of immunity from such complications.

His complications were of the spirit, of the literary vision, and though he was thoroughly profane he was yet essentially anchoretic. I perhaps miss a point, however, in not finally subjoining that he was liberally accessible to his friends during the months he regularly spent in Paris. Sensitive, passionate, perverse, not less than *immediately* sociable – for if he detested his collective contemporaries this dropped, thanks to his humanizing shyness, before the individual encounter – he was in particular and superexcellently not *banal*, and he attached men perhaps more than women, inspiring a marked, a by no means colourless shade of respect; a respect not founded, as the air of it is apt to be, on the vague presumption, but addressed almost in especial to his disparities and oddities and thereby, no doubt, none too different from affection. His friends at all events were a rich and eager *cénacle*, among whom he was on occasion, by his picturesque personality, a natural and overtopping centre; partly perhaps because he was so much and so familiarly at home. He wore, up to any hour of the afternoon, that long, colloquial dressing-gown, with trousers to match, which one has always associated with literature in France – the uniform really of freedom of talk. Freedom of talk abounded by his winter fire, for the *cénacle* was made up almost wholly of the more finely distinguished among his contemporaries; of philosophers, men of letters and men of affairs belonging to his own generation and the next. He had at the time I have in mind a small perch, far aloft, at the distant, the then almost suburban, end of the Faubourg Saint-Honoré, where on Sunday afternoons, at the very top of an endless flight of stairs, were to be encountered in a cloud of conversation and smoke most of the novelists of the general Balzac tradition. Others of a different birth and complexion were markedly not of the number, were not even conceivable as present; none of those, unless I misremember, whose fictions were at that time 'serialized' in the *Revue des Deux Mondes*.

In spite of Renan and Taine and two or three more, the contributor to the Revue would indeed at no time have found in the circle in question his foot on his native heath. One could recall if one would two or three vivid allusions to him, not of the most quotable, on the lips of the most famous of 'naturalists' – allusions to him as represented for instance by M. Victor Cherbuliez and M. Octave Feuillet. The author of these pages recalls a concise qualification of this last of his fellows on the lips of Émile Zola, which that absorbed auditor had too directly, too rashly asked for; but which is also not reproducible here. There was little else but the talk, which had extreme intensity and variety; almost nothing, as I remember, but a painted and gilded idol, of considerable size, a relic and a memento, on the chimney-piece. Flaubert was huge and diffident, but florid too and resonant, and my main remembrance is of a conception of courtesy in him, an accessibility to the human relation, that only wanted to be sure of the way taken or to take. The uncertainties of the French for the determination of intercourse have often struck me as quite matching the sharpness of their certainties, as we for the most part feel these latter, which sometimes in fact throw the indeterminate into almost touching relief. I have thought of them at such times as the people in the world one may have to go more of the way to meet than to meet any other, and this, as it were, through their being seated and embedded, provided for at home, in a manner that is all their own and that has bred them to the positive pre-acceptance of interest on their behalf. We at least of the Anglo-American race, more abroad in the world, perching everywhere, so far as grounds of intercourse are concerned, more vaguely and superficially, as well as less intelligently, are the more ready by that fact with inexpensive accommodations, rather conscious that these themselves forbear from the claim to fascinate, and advancing with the good nature that is the mantle of our obtuseness to any point whatever where entertainment may be offered us. My recollection is at any rate simplified by the fact of the presence almost always, in the little high room of the Faubourg's end, of other persons and other voices. Flaubert's own voice is clearest to me from the uneffaced sense of a winter week-day afternoon when I found him by exception alone and when something led to his reading me aloud, in support of some judgement he had thrown off, a poem of Théophile Gautier's. He cited it as an example of verse intensely and distinctively French, and French in its melancholy, which neither Goethe nor Heine nor Leopardi, neither Pushkin nor Tennyson nor, as he said, Byron, could at all have matched in *kind*. He converted me at the moment to this perception, alike by the sense of the thing and by his large utterance of it; after which it is dreadful to have to confess not only that the poem was then new to me, but that, hunt as I will in every volume of its author, I am never able to recover it. This is perhaps after all happy, causing Flaubert's own full tone, which was the note of the occasion, to linger the more unquenched. But for the rhyme in fact I could have believed him to be spouting to me something strange and sonorous of his own. The thing really rare would have been to hear him do that – hear him *gueuler*, as he liked to call it. Verse, I felt, we had always with us, and almost any idiot of goodwill could give it a value. The value of so many a passage of *Salammbô* and of *L'Éducation* was on the other hand exactly such as gained when he allowed himself, as had by the legend ever been frequent *dans l'intimité*, to 'bellow' it to its fullest effect.

One of the things that make him most exhibitional and most describable, so that if we had invented him as an illustration or a character we would exactly so have arranged him, is that he was formed intellectually of two quite distinct compartments, a sense of the real and a sense of the romantic, and that his production, for our present cognizance, thus neatly and vividly divides itself. The divisions are as marked as the sections on the back of a scarab, though their distinctness is undoubtedly but the final expression of much inward strife. M. Faguet indeed, who is admirable on this question of our author's duality, gives an account of the romanticism that found its way for him into the real and of the reality that found its way into the romantic; but he none the less strikes us as a curious splendid insect sustained on wings of a different coloration, the right a vivid red, say, and the left as frank a yellow. This duality has in its sharp operation placed *Madame Bovary* and *L'Éducation* on one side together and placed together on the other *Salammbô* and *La Tentation*. *Bouvard et Pécuchet* it can scarce be spoken of, I think, as having placed anywhere or anyhow. If it was Flaubert's way to find his subject impossible there was none he saw so much in that light as this last-named, but also none that he appears to have held so important for that very reason to pursue to the bitter end. Posterity agrees with him about the impossibility, but rather takes upon itself to break with the rest of the logic. We may perhaps, however, for symmetry, let *Bouvard et Pécuchet* figure as the tail – if scarabs ever have tails – of our analogous insect. Only in that case we should also append as the very tip the small volume of the *Trois Contes*, preponderantly of the deepest imaginative hue.

His imagination was great and splendid; in spite of which, strangely enough, his masterpiece is not his most imaginative work. *Madame Bovary*, beyond question, holds that first place, and *Madame Bovary* is concerned with the career of a country doctor's wife in a petty Norman town. The elements of the picture are of the fewest, the situation of the heroine almost of the meanest, the material for interest, considering the interest yielded, of the most unpromising; but these facts only throw into relief one of those incalculable incidents that attend the proceedings of genius. *Madame Bovary* was doomed by circumstances and causes – the freshness of comparative youth and good faith on the author's part being perhaps the chief – definitely to take its position, even though its subject was fundamentally a negation of the remote, the splendid and the strange, the stuff of his fondest and most cultivated dreams. It would have seemed very nearly to exclude the free play of the imagination, and the way this faculty on the author's part nevertheless presides is one of those accidents, manoeuvres, inspirations, we hardly know what to call them, by which masterpieces grow. He of course knew more or less what he was doing for his book in making Emma Bovary a victim of the imaginative habit, but he must have been far from designing or measuring the total effect which renders the work so general, so complete an expression of himself. His separate idiosyncrasies, his irritated sensibility to the life about him, with the power to catch it in the fact and hold it hard, and his hunger for style and history and poetry, for the rich and the rare, great reverberations, great adumbrations, are here represented together as they are not in his later writings. There is nothing of the near, of the directly observed, though there may be much of the directly perceived and the minutely detailed, either in *Salammbô* or in *Saint-Antoine*, and little enough of the extravagance of illusion in that indefinable last word of restrained evocation and cold execution *L'Éducation*

Sentimentale. M. Faguet has of course excellently noted this – that the fortune and felicity of the book were assured by the stroke that made the central figure an embodiment of helpless romanticism. Flaubert himself but narrowly escaped being such an embodiment after all, and he is thus able to express the romantic mind with extraordinary truth. As to the rest of the matter he had the luck of having been in possession from the first, having begun so early to nurse and work up his plan that, familiarity and the native air, the native soil, aiding, he had finally made out to the last lurking shade the small sordid sunny dusty village picture, its emptiness constituted and peopled. It is in the background and the accessories that the real, the real of his theme, abides; and the romantic, the romantic of his theme, accordingly occupies the front. Emma Bovary's poor adventures are a tragedy for the very reason that in a world unsuspecting, unassisting, unconsoling, she has herself to distil the rich and the rare. Ignorant, unguided, undiverted, ridden by the very nature and mixture of her consciousness, she makes of the business an inordinate failure, a failure which in its turn makes for Flaubert the most pointed, the most *told* of anecdotes.

There are many things to say about *Madame Bovary*, but an old admirer of the book would be but half-hearted – so far as they represent reserves or puzzlements – were he not to note first of all the circumstances by which it is most endeared to him. To remember it from far back is to have been present all along at a process of singular interest to a literary mind, a case indeed full of comfort and cheer. The finest of Flaubert's novels is to-day, on the French shelf of fiction, one of the first of the classics; it has attained that position, slowly but steadily, before our eyes; and we seem so to follow the evolution of the fate of a classic. We see how the thing takes place; which we rarely can, for we mostly miss either the beginning or the end, especially in the case of a consecration as complete as this. The consecrations of the past are too far behind and those of the future too far in front. That the production before us *should* have come in for the heavenly crown may be a fact to offer English and American readers a mystifying side; but it is exactly our ground and a part moreover of the total interest. The author of these remarks remembers, as with a sense of the way such things happen, that when a very young person in Paris he took up from the parental table the latest number of the periodical in which Flaubert's then duly unrecognized masterpiece was in course of publication. The moment is not historic, but it was to become in the light of history, as may be said, so unforgettable that every small feature of it yet again lives for him: it rests there like the backward end of the span. The cover of the old Revue de Paris was yellow, if I mistake not, like that of the new, and *Madame Bovary: Moeurs de Province*, on the inside of it, was already, on the spot, as a title, mysteriously arresting, inscrutably charged. I was ignorant of what had preceded and was not to know till much later what followed; but present to me still is the act of standing there before the fire, my back against the low beplushed and begarnished French chimney-piece and taking in what I might of that instalment, taking it in with so surprised an interest, and perhaps as well such a stir of faint foreknowledge, that the sunny little salon, the autumn day, the window ajar and the cheerful outside clatter of the Rue Montaigne are all now for me more or less in the story and the story more or less in them. The story, however, was at that moment having a difficult life; its fortune was all to make; its merit was so far from suspected that, as Maxime Du Camp – though verily with no excess of contrition – relates, its cloth of gold barely escaped the editorial shears. This, with much more, contributes for us to the course of things to come. The book, on its appearance as a volume, proved a shock to the high propriety of the guardians of public morals under the second Empire, and Flaubert was prosecuted as author of a work indecent to scandal. The prosecution in the event fell to the ground, but I should perhaps have mentioned this agitation as one of the very few, of any public order, in his short list. *Le Candidat* fell at the Vaudeville Theatre, several years later, with a violence indicated by its withdrawal after a performance of but two nights, the first of these marked by a deafening uproar; only if the comedy was not to recover from this accident the misprised lustre of the novel was entirely to reassert itself. It is strange enough at present – so far have we travelled since then – that *Madame Bovary* should in so comparatively recent a past have been to that extent a cause of reprobation; and suggestive above all, in such connections, as to the large unconsciousness of superior minds. The desire of the superior mind of the day – that is the governmental, official, legal – to distinguish a book with such a destiny before it is a case conceivable, but conception breaks down before its design of making the distinction purely invidious. We can imagine its knowing so little, however face to face with the object, what it had got hold of; but for it to have been so urged on by a blind inward spring to publish to posterity the extent of its ignorance, that would have been beyond imagination, beyond everything but pity.

And yet it is not after all that the place the book has taken is so overwhelmingly explained by its inherent dignity; for here comes in the curiosity of the matter. Here comes in especially its fund of admonition for alien readers. The dignity of its substance is the dignity of Madame Bovary herself as a vessel of experience – a question as to which, unmistakably, I judge, we can only depart from the consensus of French critical opinion. M. Faguet for example commends the character of the heroine as one of the most living and discriminated figures of women in all literature, praises it as a field for the display of the romantic spirit that leaves nothing to be desired. Subject to an observation I shall presently make and that bears heavily in general, I think, on Flaubert as a painter of life, subject to this restriction he is right; which is a proof that a work of art may be markedly open to objection and at the same time be rare in its kind, and that when it is perfect to this point nothing else particularly matters. *Madame Bovary* has a perfection that not only stamps it, but that makes it stand almost alone; it holds itself with such a supreme unapproachable assurance as both excites and defies judgment. For it deals not in the least, as to unapproachability, with things exalted or refined; it only confers on its sufficiently vulgar elements of exhibition a final unsurpassable form. The form is in *itself* as interesting, as active, as much of the essence of the subject as the idea, and yet so close is its fit and so inseparable its life that we catch it at no moment on any errand of its own. That verily is to *be* interesting – all round; that is to be genuine and whole. The work is a classic because the thing, such as it is, is ideally *done*, and because it shows that in such doing eternal beauty may dwell. A pretty young woman who lives, socially and morally speaking, in a hole, and who is ignorant, foolish, flimsy, unhappy, takes a pair of lovers by whom she is successively deserted; in the midst of the bewilderment of which, giving up her husband and her child, letting everything go, she sinks deeper into duplicity, debt, despair, and arrives on the spot, on the small scene itself of her poor depravities, at a pitiful tragic end. In especial she does these things while remaining absorbed in romantic intention and vision, and she remains absorbed in romantic intention and vision while fairly rolling in the dust. That is the triumph of the book as the triumph stands, that Emma interests us by the nature of her consciousness and the play of her mind, thanks to the reality and beauty with which those sources are invested. It is not only that they represent *her* state; they are so true, so observed and felt, and especially so shown, that they represent the state, actual or potential, of all persons like her, persons romantically determined. Then her setting, the medium in which she struggles, becomes in its way as important, becomes eminent with the eminence of art; the tiny world in which she revolves, the contracted cage in which she flutters, is hung out in space for her, and her companions in captivity there are as true as herself.

I have said enough to show what I mean by Flaubert's having in this picture expressed something of his intimate self, given his heroine something of his own imagination: a point precisely that brings me back to the restriction at which I just now hinted, in which M. Faguet fails to indulge and yet which is immediate for the alien reader. Our complaint is that Emma Bovary, in spite of the nature of her consciousness and in spite of her reflecting so much that of her creator, is really too small an affair. This, critically speaking, is in view both of the value and the fortune of her history, a wonderful circumstance. She associates herself with Frédéric Moreau in *L'Éducation* to suggest for us a question that can be answered, I hold, only to Flaubert's detriment. Emma taken alone would possibly not so directly press it, but in her company the hero of our author's second study of the 'real' drives it home. Why did Flaubert choose, as special conduits of the life he proposed to depict, such inferior and in the case of Frédéric such abject human specimens? I insist only in respect to the latter, the perfection of *Madame Bovary* scarce leaving one much warrant for wishing anything other. Even here, however, the general scale and size of Emma, who is small even of her sort, should be a warning to hyperbole. If I say that in the matter of Frédéric at all events the answer is inevitably detrimental I mean that it weighs heavily on our author's general credit. He wished in each case to make a picture of experience – middling experience, it is true – and of the world close to him; but if he imagined nothing better for his purpose than such a heroine and such a hero, both such limited reflectors and registers, we are forced to believe it to have been by a defect of his mind. And that sign of weakness remains even if it be objected that the images in question were addressed to his purpose better than others would have been: the purpose itself then shows as inferior. *L'Éducation Sentimentale* is a strange, an indescribable work, about which there would be many more things to say than I have space for, and all of them of the deepest interest. It is moreover, to simplify my statement, very much less satisfying a thing, less pleasing whether in its unity or its variety, than its specific predecessor. But take it as we will, for a success or a failure – M. Faguet indeed ranks it, by the measure of its quantity of intention, a failure, and I on the whole agree with him – the personage offered us as bearing the weight of the drama, and in whom we are invited to that extent to interest ourselves, leaves us mainly wondering what our entertainer could have been thinking of. He takes Frédéric Moreau on the threshold of life and conducts him to the extreme of maturity without apparently suspecting for a moment either our wonder or our protest – 'Why, why *him*?' Frédéric is positively too poor for his part, too scant for his charge; and we feel with a kind of embarrassment, certainly with a kind of compassion, that it is somehow the business of a protagonist to prevent in his designer an excessive waste of faith. When I speak of the faith in Emma Bovary as proportionately wasted I reflect on M. Faguet's judgment that she is from the point of view of deep interest richly or at least roundedly representative. Representative of what? he makes us ask even while granting all the grounds of misery and tragedy involved. The plea for her is the plea made for all the figures that live without evaporation under the painter's hand – that they are not only particular persons but types of their kind, and as valid in one light as in the other. It is Emma's 'kind' that I question for this responsibility, even if it be inquired of me why I then fail to question that of Charles Bovary, in its perfection, or that of the inimitable, the immortal Homais. If we express Emma's deficiency as the poverty of her consciousness for the typical function, it is certainly not, one must admit, that she is surpassed in this respect either by her platitudinous husband or by his friend the pretentious apothecary. The difference is none the less somehow in the fact that they are respectively studies but of their character and office, which function in each expresses adequately *all* they are. It may be, I concede, because Emma is the only woman in the book that she is taken by M. Faguet as *femininely* typical, typical in the larger illustrative way, whereas the others pass with him for images specifically conditioned. Emma is this same for myself, I plead; she is conditioned to such an excess of the specific, and the specific in her case leaves out so many even of the commoner elements of conceivable life in a woman when we are invited to see that life as pathetic, as dramatic agitation, that we challenge both the author's and the critic's scale of importances. The book is a picture of the middling as much as they like, but does Emma attain even to *that*? Hers is a narrow middling even for a little imaginative person whose 'social' significance is small. It is greater on the whole than her capacity of consciousness, taking this all round; and so, in a word, we feel her less illustrational than she might have been not only if the world had offered her more points of contact, but if she had had more of these to give it.

We meet Frédéric first, we remain with him long, as a *moyen*, a provincial bourgeois of the mid-century, educated and not without fortune, thereby with freedom, in whom the life of his day reflects itself. Yet the life of his day, on Flaubert's showing, hangs together with the poverty of Frédéric's own inward or for that matter outward life; so that, the whole thing being, for scale, intention and extension, a sort of epic of the usual (with the Revolution of 1848 introduced indeed as an episode,) it affects us as an epic without air, without wings to lift it; reminds us in fact more than anything else of a huge balloon, all of silk pieces strongly sewn together and patiently blown up, but that absolutely refuses to leave the ground. The discrimination I here make as against our author is, however, the only one inevitable in a series of remarks so brief. What it really represents – and nothing could be more curious – is that Frédéric enjoys his position not only without the aid of a single 'sympathetic' character of consequence, but even without the aid of one with whom we can directly communicate. Can we communicate with the central personage? or would we really if we could? A hundred times no, and if he himself can communicate with the people shown us as surrounding him this only proves him of their kind. Flaubert on his 'real' side was in truth an ironic painter, and ironic to a tune that makes his final accepted state, his present literary dignity and 'classic' peace, superficially anomalous. There is an explanation to which I shall immediately come; but I find myself feeling for a moment longer in presence of *L'Éducation* how much more interesting a writer may be on occasion by the given failure than by the given success. Successes pure and simple disconnect and dismiss him; failures – though I admit they must be a bit qualified – keep him in touch and in relation. Thus it is that as the work of a 'grand écrivain' *L'Éducation*, large, laboured, immensely 'written', with beautiful passages and a general emptiness, with a kind of leak in its stored sadness, moreover, by which its moral dignity escapes – thus it is that Flaubert's ill-starred novel is a curiosity for a literary museum. Thus it is also that it suggests a hundred reflections, and suggests perhaps most of them directly to the intending labourer in the same field. If in short, as I have said, Flaubert is the novelist's novelist, this performance does more than any other toward making him so.

I have to add in the same connection that I had not lost sight of Madame Arnoux, the main ornament of *L'Éducation*, in pronouncing just above on its deficiency in the sympathetic. Madame Arnoux is exactly the author's one marked attempt, here or elsewhere, to represent beauty otherwise than for the senses, beauty of character and life; and what becomes of the attempt is a matter highly significant. M. Faguet praises with justice his conception of the figure and of the relation, the relation that never bears fruit, that keeps Frédéric adoring her, through hindrance and change, from the beginning of life to the end; that keeps her, by the same constraint, forever immaculately 'good', from youth to age, though deeply moved and cruelly tempted and sorely tried. Her contacts with her adorer are not even frequent, in proportion to the field of time; her conditions of fortune, of association and occupation are almost sordid, and we see them with the march of the drama, such as it is, become more and more so; besides which – I again remember that M. Faguet excellently notes it – nothing in the nature of 'parts' is attributed to her; not only is she not presented as clever, she is scarce invested with a character at all. Almost nothing that she says is repeated, almost nothing that she does is shown. She is an image none the less beautiful and vague, an image of passion cherished and abjured, renouncing all sustenance and yet persisting in life. Only she has for real distinction the extreme drawback that she is offered us quite preponderantly through Frédéric's vision of her, that we see her practically in no other light. Now Flaubert unfortunately has not been able not so to discredit Frédéric's vision in general, his vision of everyone and everything, and in particular of his own life, that it makes a medium good enough to convey adequately a noble impression. Madame Arnoux is of course ever so much the best thing in his life – which is saying little; but his life is made up of such queer material that we find ourselves displeased at her being 'in' it on whatever terms; all the more that she seems scarcely to affect, improve or determine it. Her creator in short never had a more awkward idea than this attempt to give us the benefit of such a conception in such a way; and even though I have still something else to say about that I may as well speak of it at once as a mistake that gravely counts against him. It is but one of three, no doubt, in all his work; but I shall not, I trust, pass for extravagant if I call it the most indicative. What makes it so is its being the least superficial; the two others are, so to speak, intellectual, while this is somehow moral. It was a mistake, as I have already hinted, to propose to register in so mean a consciousness as that of such a hero so large and so mixed a quantity of life as *L'Éducation* clearly intends; and it was a mistake of the tragic sort that is a theme mainly for silence to have embarked on *Bouvard et Pécuchet* at all, not to have given it up sooner than be given up by it. But these were at the worst not wholly compromising blunders. What *was* compromising – and the great point is that it remained so, that nothing has an equal weight against it – is the unconsciousness of error in respect to the opportunity that would have counted as his finest. We feel not so much that Flaubert misses it, for that we could bear; but that he doesn't *know* he misses it is what stamps the blunder. We do not pretend to say how he might have shown us Madame Arnoux better – that was his own affair. What is ours is that he really thought he was showing her as well as he could, or as she might be shown; at which we veil our face. For once that he had a conception quite apart, apart I mean from the array of his other conceptions and more delicate than any, he 'went', as we say, and spoiled it. Let me add in all tenderness, and to make up for possibly too much insistence, that it is the only stain on his shield; let me even confess that I should not wonder if, when all is said, it is a blemish no one has ever noticed.

Perhaps no one has ever noticed either what was present to me just above as the partial makeweight there glanced at, the fact that in the midst of this general awkwardness, as I have called it, there is at the same time a danger so escaped as to entitle our author to full credit. I scarce know how to put it with little enough of the ungracious, but I think that even the true Flaubertist finds himself wondering a little that some flaw of taste, some small but unfortunate lapse by the way, *should* as a matter of fact not somehow or somewhere have waited on the demonstration of the platonic purity prevailing between this heroine and her hero – so far as we do find that image projected. It is alike difficult to indicate without offence or to ignore without unkindness a fond reader's apprehension here of a possibility of the wrong touch, the just perceptibly false note. I would not have staked my life on Flaubert's security of instinct in such a connection – as an absolutely fine and predetermined security; and yet in the event that felicity has settled, there is not so much as the lightest wrong breath (speaking of the matter in this light of tact and taste) or the shade of a crooked stroke. One exclaims at the end of the question 'Dear old Flaubert after all – !' and perhaps so risks seeming to patronize for fear of not making a point. The point made for what it is worth, at any rate, I am the more free to recover the benefit of what I mean by critical 'tenderness' in our general connection – expressing in it as I do our general respect, and my own particular, for our author's method and process and history, and my sense of the luxury of such a sentiment at such a vulgar literary time. It is a respect positive and settled and the thing that has most to do with consecrating for us that loyalty to him as the novelist of the novelist – unlike as it is even the best feeling inspired by any other member of the craft. He may stand for our operative conscience or our vicarious sacrifice; animated by a sense of literary honour, attached to an ideal of perfection, incapable of lapsing in fine from a self-respect, that enable us to sit at ease, to surrender to the age, to indulge in whatever comparative meannesses (and no meanness in art is so mean as the sneaking economic,) we may find most comfortable or profitable. May it not in truth be said that we practise our industry, so many of us, at relatively little cost just *because* poor Flaubert, producing the most expensive fictions ever written, so handsomely paid for it? It is as if this put it in our power to produce cheap and thereby sell dear; as if, so expressing it, literary honour being by his example effectively secure for the firm at large and the general concern, on its whole esthetic side, floated once for all, we find our individual attention free for literary and esthetic indifference. All the while we thus lavish our indifference the spirit of the author of *Madame Bovary*, in the cross-light of the old room above the Seine, is trying to the last admiration for the thing itself. That production puts the matter into a nutshell: *Madame Bovary*, subject to whatever qualification, is absolutely the most literary of novels, so literary that it covers us with its mantle. It shows us once for all that there is no *intrinsic* call for a debasement of the type. The mantle I speak of is wrought with surpassing fineness, and we may always, under stress of whatever charge of illiteracy, frivolity, vulgarity, flaunt it as the flag of the guild. Let us therefore frankly concede that to surround Flaubert with our consideration is the least return we can make for such a privilege. The consideration moreover is idle unless it be real, unless it be intelligent enough to measure his effort and his success. Of the effort as mere effort I have already spoken, of the desperate difficulty involved for him in making his form square with his conception; and I by no means attach general importance to these secrets of the workshop, which are but as the contortions of the fastidious muse who is the servant of the oracle. They are really rather secrets of the kitchen and contortions of the priestess of *that* tripod – they are not an upstairs matter. It is of their specially distinctive importance I am now speaking, of the light shed on them by the results before us.

They all represent the pursuit of a style, of the ideally right one for its relations, and would still be interesting if the style had not been achieved. *Madame Bovary, Salammbô, Saint-Antoine, L'Éducation* are so written and so composed (though the last-named in a minor degree) that the more we look at them the more we find in them, under this head, a beauty of intention and of effect; the more they figure in the too often dreary desert of fictional prose a class by themselves and a little living oasis. So far as that desert is of the complexion of our own English speech it supplies with remarkable rarity this particular source of refreshment. So strikingly is that the case, so scant for the most part any dream of a scheme of beauty in these connections, that a critic betrayed at artless moments into a plea for composition may find himself as blankly met as if his plea were for trigonometry. He makes inevitably his reflections, which are numerous enough; one of them being that if we turn our back so squarely, so universally to this order of considerations it is because the novel is so preponderantly cultivated among us by women, in other words by a sex ever gracefully, comfortably, enviably unconscious (it would be too much to call them even suspicious) of the requirements of form. The case is at any rate sharply enough made for us, or against us, by the circumstance that women are held to have achieved on all our ground, in spite of this weakness and others, as great results as any. The judgment is undoubtedly founded: Jane Austen was instinctive and charming, and the other recognitions — even over the heads of the ladies, some of them, from Fielding to Pater — are obvious; without, however, in the least touching my contention. For signal examples of what composition, distribution, arrangement can do, of how they intensify the life of a work of art, we have to go elsewhere; and the value of Flaubert for us is that he admirably points the moral. This is the explanation of the 'classic' fortune of *Madame Bovary* in especial, though I may add that also of Hérodias and Saint-Julien l'Hospitalier in the *Trois Contes*, as well as an aspect of these works endlessly suggestive. I spoke just now of the small field of the picture in the longest of them, the small capacity, as I called it, of the vessel; yet the way the thing is done not only triumphs over the question of value but in respect to it fairly misleads and confounds us. Where else shall we find in anything proportionately so small such an air of dignity of size? Flaubert *made* things big — it was his way, his ambition and his necessity; and I say this while remembering that in *L'Éducation* (in proportion I mean again) the effect has not been produced. The subject of *L'Éducation* is in spite of Frédéric large, but an indefinable shrinkage has overtaken it in the execution. The exception so marked, however, is single; *Salammbô* and *Saint-Antoine* are both at once very 'heavy' conceptions and very consistently and splendidly high applications of a manner.

It is in this assured manner that the lesson sits aloft, that the spell for the critical reader resides; and if the conviction under which Flaubert labours is more and more grossly discredited among us his compact mass is but the greater. He regarded the work of art as *existing* but by its expression, and defied us to name any other measure of its life that is not a stultification. He held style to be accordingly an indefeasible part of it, and found beauty, interest and distinction as dependent on it for emergence as a letter committed to the post-office is dependent on an addressed envelope. Strange enough it may well appear to us to have to apologize for such notions as eccentric. There are persons who consider that style comes of itself – we see and hear at present, I think, enough of them; and to whom he would doubtless have remarked that it goes, of itself, still faster. The thing naturally differs in fact with the nature of the imagination; the question is one of proprieties and affinities, sympathy and proportion. The sympathy of the author of *Salammbô* was all with the magnificent, his imagination for the phrase as variously noble or ignoble in itself, contributive or destructive, adapted and harmonious or casual and common. The worse among such possibilities have been multiplied by the infection of bad writing, and he denied that the better ever do anything so obliging as to come of themselves. They scarcely indeed for Flaubert 'came' at all; their arrival was determined only by fasting and prayer or by patience of pursuit, the arts of the chase, long waits and watches, figuratively speaking, among the peaks or by the waters. The production of a book was of course made inordinately slow by the fatigue of these measures; in illustration of which his letters often record that it has taken him three days* to arrive at one right sentence, tested by the pitch of his ideal of the right for the suggestion aimed at. His difficulties drew from the author, as I have mentioned, much resounding complaint; but those voices have ceased to trouble us and the final voice remains. No feature of the whole business is more edifying than the fact that he in the first place never misses style and in the second never appears to have beaten about for it. That betrayal is of course the worst

---

* It was true, delightfully true, that, extravagance in this province of his life, though apparently in no other, being Flaubert's necessity and law, he deliberated and hung fire, wrestled, retreated and returned, indulged generally in a tragi-comedy of waste; which I recall a charming expression of on the lips of Edmond de Goncourt, who quite recognized the heroic legend, but prettily qualified it: 'Il faut vous dire qu'il y avait là-dedans beaucoup de coucheries et d'école buissonière.' And he related how on the occasion of a stay with his friend under the roof of the Princess Mathilde, the friend, missed during the middle hours of a fine afternoon, was found to have undressed himself and gone to bed to think!

betrayal of all, and I think the way he has escaped it the happiest form of the peace that has finally visited him. It was truly a wonderful success to be so the devotee of the phrase and yet never its victim. Fine as he inveterately desired it should be he still never lost sight of the question Fine for what? It is always so related and associated, so properly part of something else that is in turn part of something other, part of a reference, a tone, a passage, a page, that the simple may enjoy it for its least bearing and the initiated for its greatest. That surely is to be a writer of the first order, to resemble when in the hand and however closely viewed a shapely crystal box, and yet to be seen when placed on the table and opened to contain innumerable compartments, springs and tricks. One is ornamental either way, but one is in the second way precious too.

The crystal box then figures the style of *Salammbô* and *Saint-Antoine* in a greater degree than that of *Bovary*, because, as the two former express the writer's romantic side, he had in them, while equally covering his tracks, still further to fare and still more to hunt. Beyond this allusion to their completing his duality I shall not attempt closely to characterize them; though I admit that in not insisting on them I press most lightly on the scale into which he had in his own view cast his greatest pressure. He lamented the doom that drove him so oddly, so ruefully, to choose his subjects, but he lamented it least when these subjects were most pompous and most exotic, feeling as he did that they had then after all most affinity with his special eloquence. In dealing with the near, the directly perceived, he had to keep down his tone, to make the eloquence small; though with the consequence, as we have seen, that in spite of such precautions the whole thing mostly insists on being ample. The familiar, that is, under his touch, took on character, importance, extension, one scarce knows what to call it, in order to carry the style or perhaps rather, as we may say, sit with proper ease in the vehicle, and there was accordingly a limit to its smallness; whereas in the romantic books, the preferred world of Flaubert's imagination, there was practically no need of compromise. The compromise gave him throughout endless trouble, and nothing would be more to the point than to show, had I space, why in particular it distressed him. It was obviously his strange predicament that the only spectacle open to him by experience and direct knowledge was the bourgeois, which on that ground imposed on him successively his three so intensely bourgeois themes. He was obliged to treat these themes, which he hated, because his experience left him no alternative; his only alternative was given by history, geography, philosophy, fancy, the world of erudition and of imagination, the world especially of this last. In the bourgeois sphere his ideal of expression laboured under protest; in the other, the imagined, the projected, his need for facts, for matter, and his pursuit of them, sat no less heavily. But as his style all the while required a certain exercise of pride he was on the whole more at home in the exotic than in the familiar; he escaped above all in the former connection the associations, the disparities he detested. He could be frankly noble in *Salammbô* and *Saint-Antoine*, whereas in *Bovary* and *L'Éducation* he could be but circuitously and insidiously so. He could in the one case cut his coat according to his cloth – if we mean by his cloth his predetermined tone, while in the other he had to take it already cut. Singular enough in his life the situation so constituted: the comparatively meagre human consciousness – for we must come back to that in him – struggling with the absolutely large artistic; and the large artistic half wreaking itself on the meagre human and half seeking a refuge from it, as well as a revenge against it, in something quite different.

Flaubert had in fact command of two refuges which he worked in turn. The first of these was the attitude of irony, so constant in him that *L'Éducation* bristles and hardens with it and *Bouvard et Pécuchet* – strangest of 'poetic' justices – is made as dry as sand and as heavy as lead; the second only was, by processes, by journeys the most expensive, to get away altogether. And we inevitably ask ourselves whether, eschewing the policy of flight, he might not after all have fought out his case a little more on the spot. Might he not have addressed himself to the human still otherwise than in *L'Éducation* and in *Bouvard*? When one thinks of the view of the life of his country, of the vast French community and its constituent creatures, offered in these productions, one declines to believe it could make up the *whole* vision of a man of his quality. Or when all was said and done was he absolutely and exclusively condemned to irony? The second refuge I speak of, the getting away from the human, the congruously and measurably human, altogether, perhaps becomes in the light of this possibility but an irony the more. Carthage and the

Thebaid, Salammbô, Spendius, Matho, Hannon, Saint Anthony, Hilarion, the Paternians, the Marcosians and the Carpocratians, what are all these, inviting because queer, but a confession of supreme impatience with the actual and the near, often queer enough too, no doubt, but not consolingly, not transcendently? Last remains the question whether, even if our author's immediate as distinguished from his remote view had had more reach, the particular gift we claim for him, the perfection of arrangement and form, would have had in certain directions the acquired flexibility. States of mind, states of soul, of the simpler kind, the kinds supposable in the Emma Bovarys, the Frédérics, the Bouvards and the Pécuchets, to say nothing of the Carthaginians and the Eremites – for Flaubert's eremites are eminently artless – these conditions represent, I think, his proved psychological range. And that throws us back remarkably, almost confoundingly, upon another face of the general anomaly. The 'gift' was of the greatest, a force in itself, in virtue of which he is a consummate writer; and yet there are whole sides of life to which it was never addressed and which it apparently quite failed to suspect as a field of exercise. If he never approached the complicated character in man or woman – Emma Bovary is not the least little bit complicated – or the really furnished, the finely civilized, was this because, surprisingly, he could not? *L'âme française* at all events shows in him but ill.

This undoubtedly marks a limit, but limits are for the critic familiar country, and he may mostly well feel the prospect wide enough when he finds something positively well enough done. By disposition or by obligation Flaubert selected, and though his selection was in some respects narrow he stops not too short to have left us three really 'cast' works and a fourth of several perfect parts, to say nothing of the element of perfection, of the superlative for the size, in his three *nouvelles*. What he attempted he attempted in a spirit that gives an extension to the idea of the achievable and the achieved in a literary thing, and it is by this that we contentedly gauge the matter. As success goes in this world of the approximate it may pass for success of the greatest. If I am unable to pursue the proof of my remark in *Salammbô* and *Saint-Antoine* it is because I have also had to select and have found the questions connected with their two companions more interesting. There are numerous judges, I hasten to mention, who, showing the opposite preference, lose themselves with rapture in the strange bristling archaeological picture – yet all amazingly vivified and co-ordinated – of the Carthaginian mercenaries in revolt and the sacred veil of the great goddess profaned and stolen; as well in the still more peopled panorama of the ancient sects, superstitions and mythologies that swim in the desert before the fevered eyes of the Saint. One may be able, however, at once to breathe more freely in *Bovary* than in *Salammbô* and yet to hope that there is no intention of the latter that one has missed. The great intention certainly, and little as we may be sweetly beguiled, holds us fast; which is simply the author's indomitable purpose of fully pervading his field. There are countries beyond the sea in which tracts are allowed to settlers on condition that they will really, not nominally, cultivate them. Flaubert is on his romantic ground like one of these settlers; he makes good with all his might his title to his tract, and in a way that shows how it is not only for him a question of safety but a question of honour. Honour demands that he shall set up his home and his faith there in such a way that every inch of the surface be planted or paved. He would have been ashamed merely to encamp and, after the fashion of most other adventurers, knock up a log hut among charred stumps. This was not what would have been for him taking artistic possession, it was not what would have been for him even personal honour, let alone literary; and yet the general lapse from integrity was a thing that, wherever he looked, he saw not only condoned but acclaimed and rewarded. He lived, as he felt, in an age of mean production and cheap criticism, the practical upshot of which took on for him a name that was often on his lips. He called it the hatred of literature, a hatred in the midst of which, the most literary of men, he found himself appointed to suffer. I may not, however, follow him in that direction – which would take us far; and the less that he was for himself after all, in spite of groans and imprecations, a man of resources and remedies, and that there was always his possibility of building himself in.

This he did equally in all his books – built himself into literature by means of a material put together with extraordinary art; but it leads me again to the question of what such a stiff ideal imposed on him for the element of exactitude. This element, in the romantic, was his merciless law; it was perhaps even in the romantic that – if there could indeed be degrees for him in such matters – he most despised the loose and the more-or-less. To be intensely definite and perfectly positive, to know so well what he meant that he could at every point strikingly and conclusively verify it, was the first of his needs; and if in addition to being thus synthetically final he could be strange and sad and terrible, and leave the cause of these effects inscrutable, success then had for him its highest savour. We feel the inscrutability in those memorable few words that put before us Frédéric Moreau's start upon his vain course of travel, 'Il connût alors la mélancholie des paquebots'; an image to the last degree comprehensive and embracing, but which haunts us, in its droll pathos, without our quite knowing why. But he was really never so pleased as when he could be both rare and precise about the dreadful. His own sense of all this, as I have already indicated, was that beauty comes with expression, that expression is creation, that it *makes* the reality, and only in the degree in which it *is*, exquisitely, expression; and that we move in literature through a world of different values and relations, a blest world in which we know nothing except by style, but in which also everything is saved by it, and in which the image is thus always superior to the thing itself. This quest and multiplication of the image, the image tested and warranted and consecrated for the occasion, was accordingly his high elegance, to which he too much sacrificed and to which *Salammbô* and partly *Saint-Antoine* are monstrous monuments. Old cruelties and perversities, old wonders and errors and terrors, endlessly appealed to him; they constitute the unhuman side of his work, and if we have not the bribe of curiosity, of a lively interest in method, or rather in evocation just *as* evocation, we tread our way among them, especially in *Salammbô*, with a reserve too dry for our pleasure. To my own view the curiosity and the literary interest are equal in dealing with the non-romantic books, and the world presented, the aspects and agents, are less deterrent and more amenable both to our own social and expressional terms. Style itself moreover, with all respect to Flaubert, never *totally* beguiles; since even when we are so queerly constituted as to be ninety-nine parts literary we are still a hundredth part something else. This hundredth part may, once we possess the book – or the book possesses us – make us imperfect as readers, and yet without it should we want or get the book at all? The curiosity at any rate, to repeat, is even greatest for me in *Madame Bovary*, say, for here I can measure, can more directly appreciate, the terms. The aspects and impressions being of an experience conceivable to me I am more touched by the beauty; my interest gets more of the benefit of the beauty even though this be not intrinsically greater. Which brings back our appreciation inevitably at last to the question of our author's lucidity.

I have sufficiently remarked that I speak from the point of view of his interest to a reader of his own craft, the point of view of his extraordinary technical wealth – though indeed when I think of the general power of *Madame Bovary* I find myself desiring not to narrow the ground of the lesson, not to connect the lesson, to its prejudice, with that idea of the 'technical', that question of the way a thing is done, so abhorrent, as a call upon attention, in whatever art, to the wondrous Anglo-Saxon mind. Without proposing Flaubert as the type of the newspaper novelist, or as an easy alternative to golf or the bicycle, we should do him less than justice in failing to insist that a masterpiece like *Madame Bovary* may benefit even with the simple-minded by the way it has been done. It derives from its firm roundness that sign of all rare works that there is something in it for every one. It may be read ever so attentively, ever so freely, without a suspicion of how it is written, to say nothing of put together; it may equally be read under the excitement of these perceptions alone, one of the greatest known to the reader who is fully open to them. Both readers will have been transported, which is all any can ask. Leaving the first of them, however that may be, to state the case for himself, I state it yet again for the second, if only on this final ground. The book and its companions represent for us a practical solution, Flaubert's own troubled but settled one, of the eternal dilemma of the painter of life. From the moment this rash adventurer deals with his mysterious matter at all directly his desire is not to deal with it stintedly. It at the same time remains true that from the moment he desires to produce forms in which it shall be preserved, he desires that these forms, things of *his* creation, shall not be, as testifying to his way with them, weak or ignoble. He must make them complete and beautiful, of satisfactory production, intrinsically interesting, under peril of disgrace with those who know. Those who don't know of course don't count for him, and it neither helps nor hinders him to say that every one knows about life. Every one does not – it is distinctly the case of the few; and if it were in fact the case of the many the knowledge still might exist, on the evidence around us, even in an age of unprecedented printing, without attesting itself by a multiplication of masterpieces. The question for the artist can only be of doing the artistic utmost, and thereby of *seeing* the general task. When it is seen with the intensity with which it presented itself to Flaubert a lifetime is none too much for fairly tackling it. It must either be left alone or be dealt with, and to leave it alone is a comparatively simple matter.

To deal with it is on the other hand to produce a certain number of finished works; there being no other known method; and the quantity of life depicted will depend on this array. What will this array, however, depend on, and what will condition the number of pieces of which it is composed? The 'finish', evidently, that the formula so glibly postulates and for which the novelist is thus so handsomely responsible. He has on the one side to feel his subject and on the other side to render it, and there are undoubtedly two ways in which his situation may be expressed, especially perhaps by himself. The more he feels his subject the more he *can* render it – that is the first way. The more he renders it the more he *can* feel it – that is the second way. This second way was unmistakeably Flaubert's, and if the result of it for him was a bar to abundant production he could only accept such an incident as part of the game. He probably for that matter would have challenged any easy definition of 'abundance', contested the application of it to the repetition, however frequent, of the thing not 'done'. What but the 'doing' makes the thing, he would have asked, and how can a positive result from a mere iteration of negatives, or wealth proceed from the simple addition of so many instances of penury? We should here, in closer communion with him, have got into his highly characteristic and suggestive view of the fertilization of subject by form, penetration of the sense, ever, by the expression – the latter reacting creatively on the former; a conviction in the light of which he appears to have wrought with real consistency and which borrows from him thus its high measure of credit. It would undoubtedly have suffered if his books had been things of a loose logic, whereas we refer to it not only without shame but with an encouraged confidence by their showing of a logic so close. Let the phrase, the form that the whole is at the given moment staked on, be beautiful and related, and the rest will take care of itself – such is a rough indication of Flaubert's faith; which has the importance that it was a faith sincere, active and inspiring. I hasten to add indeed that we must most of all remember how in these matters everything hangs on definitions. The 'beautiful', with our author, covered for the phrase a great deal of ground, and when every sort of propriety had been gathered in under it and every relation, in a complexity of such, protected, the idea itself, the presiding thought, ended surely by being pretty well provided for.

These, however, are subordinate notes, and the plain question, in the connection I have touched upon, is of whether we would really wish him to have written more books, say either of the type of *Bovary* or of the type of *Salammbô*, and not have written them so well. When the production of a great artist who has lived a length of years has been small there is always the regret; but there is seldom, any more than here, the conceivable remedy. For the case is doubtless predetermined by the particular kind of great artist a writer happens to be, and this even if when we come to the conflict, to the historic case, deliberation and delay may not all have been imposed by temperament. The admirable George Sand, Flaubert's beneficent friend and correspondent, is exactly the happiest example we could find of the genius constitutionally incapable of worry, the genius for whom style 'came', for whom the sought effect was ever quickly and easily struck off, the book freely and swiftly written, and who consequently is represented for us by upwards of ninety volumes. If the comparison were with this lady's great contemporary the elder Dumas the disparity would be quadrupled, but that ambiguous genius, somehow never really caught by us in the *fact* of composition, is out of our concern here: the issue is of those developments of expression which involve a style, and as Dumas never so much as once grazed one in all his long career, there was not even enough of that grace in him for a fillip of the finger-nail. Flaubert is at any rate represented by six books, so that he may on the estimate figure as poor, while Madame Sand, falling so little short of a hundred, figures as rich; and yet the fact remains that I can refer the congenial mind to him with confidence and can do nothing of the sort for it in respect to Madame Sand. She is loose and liquid and iridescent, as iridescent as we may undertake to find her; but I can imagine compositions quite without virtue – the virtue I mean, of sticking together – begotten by the impulse to emulate her. She had undoubtedly herself the benefit of her facility, but are we not left wondering to what extent *we* have it? There is too little in her, by the literary connection, for the critical mind, weary of much wandering, to rest upon. Flaubert himself wandered, wandered far, went much roundabout and sometimes lost himself by the way, but how handsomely he provided for our present repose! He found the French language inconceivably difficult to write with elegance and was confronted with the equal truths that elegance is the last thing that languages, even as they most mature, seem to concern themselves with, and that at the same time taste, asserting rights, insists on it, to the effect of showing us in a boundless circumjacent waste of effort what the absence of it may mean. He saw the less of this desert of death come back to that – that everything at all saved from it for us since the beginning had been saved by a soul of elegance within, or in other words by the last refinement of selection, by the indifference on the part of the very idiom, huge quite other than 'composing' agent, to the individual pretension. Recognizing thus that to carry through the individual pretension is at the best a battle, he adored a hard surface and detested a soft one – much more a muddled; regarded a style without rhythm and harmony as in a work of pretended beauty no style at all. He considered that the failure of complete expression so registered made of the work of pretended beauty a work of achieved barbarity. It would take us far to glance even at his fewest discriminations; but rhythm and harmony were for example most menaced in his scheme by repetition – when repetition had not a positive grace; and were above all most at the mercy of the bristling particles of which our modern tongues are mainly composed and which make of the desired surface a texture pricked through, from beneath, even to destruction, as by innumerable thorns.

On these lines production was of course slow work for him – especially as he met the difficulty, met it with an inveteracy which shows how it *can* be met; and full of interest for readers of English speech is the reflection he causes us to make as to the possibility of success at all comparable among ourselves. I have spoken of his groans and imprecations, his interminable waits and deep despairs; but what would these things have been, what would have become of him and what of his wrought residuum, had he been condemned to deal with a form of speech consisting, like ours, as to one part, of 'that' and 'which'; as to a second part, of the blest 'it', which an English sentence may repeat in three or four opposed references without in the least losing caste; as to a third face of all the 'tos' of the infinitive and the preposition; as to a fourth of our precious auxiliaries 'be' and 'do'; and as to a fifth, of whatever survives in the language for the precious art of pleasing? Whether or no the fact that the painter of 'life' among us has to contend with a medium intrinsically indocile, on certain sides, like our own, whether this drawback accounts for his having failed, in our time, to treat us, arrested and charmed, to a single case of crowned classicism, there is at any rate no doubt that we in some degree owe Flaubert's counterweight for that deficiency to *his* having, on his own ground, more happily triumphed. By which I do not mean that *Madame Bovary* is a classic because the 'thats', the 'its' and the 'tos' are made to march as Orpheus and his lute made the beasts, but because the element of order and harmony works as a symbol of everything else that is preserved for us by the history of the book. The history of the book remains the lesson and the important, the delightful thing, remains above all the drama that moves slowly to its climax. It is what we come back to for the sake of what it shows us. We see – from the present to the past indeed, never alas from the present to the future – how a classic almost inveterately grows. Unimportant, unnoticed, or, so far as noticed, contested, unrelated, alien, it has a cradle round which the fairies but scantly flock and is waited on in general by scarce a hint of significance. The significance comes by a process slow and small, the fact only that one perceptive private reader after another discovers at his convenience that the book is rare. The addition of the perceptive private readers is no quick affair, and would doubtless be a vain one did they not – while plenty of other much more remarkable books come and go – accumulate and count. They count by their quality and continuity of attention; so they have gathered for *Madame Bovary*, and so they are held. That is really once more the great circumstance. It is always in order for us to feel yet again what it is we are held by. Such is my reason, definitely, for speaking of Flaubert as the novelist's novelist. Are we not moreover – and let it pass this time as a happy hope! – pretty well all novelists now?

50

From 'Émile Zola', Atlantic Monthly, August 1903. Zola had died the previous year. It is obvious that memoirists such as the painter Jacques-Émile Blanche exaggerate James's 'contempt' for his 'vulgarity', etc. See also No. 53.

... WHAT IS at all events striking for us, critically speaking, is that, in the midst of the dishonour [the novel] has gradually harvested by triumphant vulgarity of practice, its pliancy and applicability can still plead for themselves. The curious contradiction stands forth for our relief – the circumstance that thirty years ago a young man of extraordinary brain and indomitable purpose, wishing to give the measure of these endowments in a piece of work supremely solid, conceived and sat down to Les Rougon-Macquart rather than to an equal task in physics, mathematics, politics or economics. He saw his undertaking, thanks to his patience and courage, practically to a close; so that it is exactly neither of the so-called constructive sciences that happens to have had the benefit, intellectually speaking, of one of the few most constructive achievements of our time. There then, provisionally at least, we touch bottom; we get a glimpse of the pliancy and variety, the ideal of vividness, on behalf of which our equivocal form may appeal to a strong head. In the name of what ideal on its own side, however, does the strong head yield to the appeal? What is the logic of its so deeply committing itself? Zola's case seems to tell us, as it tells us other things. The logic is in its huge freedom of adjustment to the temperament of the worker, which it carries, so to say, as no other vehicle can do. It expresses fully and directly the whole man, and big as he may be it can still be big enough for him without becoming false to its type. We see this truth made strong, from beginning to end, in Zola's work; we see the temperament, we see the whole man, with his size and all his marks, stored and packed away in the huge hold of Les Rougon-Macquart as a cargo is packed away on a ship. His personality is the thing that finally pervades and prevails, just as so often on a vessel the presence of the cargo makes itself felt for the assaulted senses. What has most come home to me in reading him over is that a scheme of fiction so conducted is in fact a capacious vessel. It can carry anything – with art and force in the stowage; nothing in this case will sink it. And it is the only form for which such a claim can be made. All others have to confess to a smaller scope – to selection, to exclusion, to the danger of distortion, explosion, combustion. The novel has nothing to fear but sailing too light. It will take aboard all we bring in good faith to the dock.

An intense vision of this truth must have been Zola's comfort from the earliest time – the years, immediately following the crash of the Empire, during which he settled himself to the tremendous task he had mapped out. No finer act of courage and confidence, I think, is recorded in the history of letters. The critic in sympathy with him returns again and again to the great wonder of it, in which something so strange is mixed with something so august. Entertained and carried out almost from the threshold of manhood, the high project, the work of a lifetime, announces beforehand its inevitable weakness and yet speaks in the same voice for its admirable, its almost unimaginable strength. The strength was in the young man's very person – in his character, his will, his passion, his fighting temper, his aggressive lips, his squared shoulders (when he 'sat up') and over-weening confidence; his weakness was in that inexperience of life from which he proposed not to suffer, from which he in fact suffered on the surface remarkably little, and from which he was never to suspect, I judge, that he had suffered at all. I may mention for the interest of it that, meeting him during his first short visit to London – made several years before his stay in England during the Dreyfus trial – I received a direct impression of him that was more informing than any previous study. I had seen him a little, in Paris, years before that, when this impression was a perceptible promise, and I was now to perceive how time had made it good. It consisted, simply stated, in his fairly bristling with the betrayal that nothing whatever had happened to him in life but to write Les Rougon-Macquart. It was even for that matter almost more as if Les Rougon-Macquart had written *him*, written him as he stood and sat, and he looked and spoke, as the long, concentrated, merciless effort had made and stamped and left him. Something very fundamental was to happen to him in due course, it is true, shaking him to his base; fate was not wholly to cheat him of an independent evolution. Recalling him from this London hour one strongly felt during the famous 'Affair' that his outbreak in connection with it was the act of a man with arrears of personal history to make up, the act of a spirit for which life, or for which at any rate freedom, had been too much postponed, treating itself at last to a luxury of experience.

I welcomed the general impression at all events – I intimately entertained it; it represented so many things, it suggested, just as it was, such a lesson. You could neither have everything nor be everything – you had to choose; you could not at once sit firm at your job and wander through space inviting initiations. The author of Les Rougon-Macquart had had all those, certainly, that this wonderful company could bring him; but I can scarce express how it was implied in him that his time had been fruitfully passed with *them* alone. His artistic evolution struck one thus as, in spite of its magnitude, singularly simple, and evidence of the simplicity seems further offered by his last production, of which we have just come into possession. *Vérité* truly does give the measure, makes the author's high maturity join hands with his youth, marks the rigid straightness of his course from point to point. He had seen his horizon and his fixed goal from the first, and no cross-scent, no new distance, no blue gap in the hills to right or to left ever tempted him to stray. *Vérité*, of which I shall have more to say, is in fact, as a moral finality and the crown of an edifice, one of the strangest possible performances. Machine-minted and made good by an immense expertness, it yet makes us ask how, for disinterested observation and perception, the writer had used so much time and so much acquisition, and how he can all along have handled so much material without some larger subjective consequence. We really rub our eyes in other words to see so great an intellectual adventure as Les Rougon-Macquart come to its end in deep desert sand. Difficult truly to read, because showing him at last almost completely a prey to the danger that had for a long time more and more dogged his steps, the danger of the mechanical all confident and triumphant, the book is nevertheless full of interest for a reader desirous to penetrate. It speaks with more distinctness of the author's temperament, tone and manner than if, like several of his volumes, it achieved or enjoyed a successful life of its own. Its heavy completeness, with all this, as of some prodigiously neat, strong and complicated scaffolding constructed by a firm of builders for the erection of a house whose foundations refuse to bear it and that is unable therefore to rise – its very betrayal of a method and a habit more than adequate, on past occasions, to similar ends, carries us back to the original rare exhibition, the grand assurance and grand patience with which the system was launched.

If it topples over, the system, by its own weight in these last applications of it, that only makes the history of its prolonged success the more curious and, speaking for myself, the spectacle of its origin more attaching. Readers of my generation will remember well the publication of *La Conquête de Plassans* and the portent, indefinable but irresistible, after perusal of the volume, conveyed in the general rubric under which it was a first instalment, Natural and Social History of a Family under the Second Empire. It squared itself there at its ease, the announcement, from the first, and we were to learn promptly enough what a fund of life it masked. It was like the mouth of a cave with a signboard hung above, or better still perhaps like the big booth at a fair with the name of the show across the flapping canvas. One strange animal after another stepped forth into the light, each in its way a monster bristling and spotted, each a curiosity of that 'natural history' in the name of which we were addressed, though it was doubtless not till the issue of *L'Assommoir* that the true type of the monstrous seemed to be reached. The enterprise, for those who had attention, was even at a distance impressive, and the nearer the critic gets to it retrospectively the more so it becomes. The pyramid had been planned and the site staked out, but the young builder stood there, in his sturdy strength, with no equipment save his two hands and, as we may say, his wheelbarrow and his trowel. His pile of material – of stone, brick and rubble or whatever – was of the smallest, but this he apparently felt as the least of his difficulties. Poor, uninstructed, unacquainted, unintroduced, he set up his subject wholly from the outside, proposing to himself wonderfully to get into it, into its depths, as he went.

If we imagine him asking himself what he knew of the 'social' life of the second Empire to start with, we imagine him also answering in all honesty: 'I have my eyes and my ears – I have all my senses: I have what I've seen and heard, what I've smelled and tasted and touched. And then I've my curiosity and my pertinacity; I've libraries, books, newspapers, witnesses, the material, from step to step, of an *enquête*. And then I've my genius – that is, my imagination, my passion, my sensibility to life. Lastly I've my method, and that will be half the battle. Best of all perhaps even, I've plentiful lack of doubt.' Of the absence in him of a doubt, indeed of his inability, once his direction taken, to entertain so much as the shadow of one, *Vérité* is a positive monument – which again represents in this way the unity of his tone and the meeting of his extremes. If we remember that his design was nothing if not architectural, that a 'majestic whole', a great balanced façade, with all its orders and parts, that a singleness of mass and a unity of effect, in fine, were before him from the first, his notion of picking up his bricks as he proceeded becomes, in operation, heroic. It is not in the least as a record of failure for him that I note this particular fact of the growth of the long series as on the whole the liveliest interest it has to offer. 'I don't know my subject, but I must live into it; I don't know life, but I must learn it as I work' – that attitude and programme represent, to my sense, a drama more intense on the worker's own part than any of the dramas he was to invent and put before us.

It was the fortune, it was in a manner the doom, of Les Rougon-Macquart to deal with things almost always in gregarious form, to be a picture of *numbers*, of classes, crowds, confusions, movements, industries – and this for a reason of which it will be interesting to attempt some account. The individual life is, if not wholly absent, reflected in coarse and common, in generalized terms; whereby we arrive precisely at the oddity just named, the circumstance that, looking out somewhere, and often woefully athirst, for the taste of fineness, we find it not in the fruits of our author's fancy, but in a different matter altogether. We get it in the very history of his effort, the image itself of his lifelong process, comparatively so personal, so spiritual even, and, through all its patience and pain, of a quality so much more distinguished than the qualities he succeeds in attributing to his figures even when he most aims at distinction. There can be no question in these narrow limits of my taking the successive volumes one by one – all the more that our sense of the exhibition is as little as possible an impression of parts and books, of particular 'plots' and persons. It produces the effect of a mass of imagery in which shades are sacrificed, the effect of character and passion in the lump or by the ton. The fullest, the most characteristic episodes affect us like a sounding chorus or procession, as with a hubbub of voices and a multitudinous tread of feet. The setter of the mass into motion, he himself, in the crowd, figures best, with whatever queer idiosyncrasies, excrescences and gaps, a being of a substance akin to our own. Taking him as we must, I repeat, for quite heroic, the interest of detail in him is the interest of his struggle at every point with his problem.

The sense for crowds and processions, for the gross and the general, was largely the *result* of this predicament, of the disproportion between his scheme and his material – though it was certainly also in part an effect of his particular turn of mind. What the reader easily discerns in him is the sturdy resolution with which breadth and energy supply the place of penetration. He rests to his utmost on his documents, devours and assimilates them, makes them yield him extraordinary appearances of life; but in his way he too improvises in the grand manner, the manner of Walter Scott and of Dumas the elder. We feel that he *has* to improvise for his moral and social world, the world as to which vision and opportunity must come, if they are to come at all, unhurried and unhustled – must take their own time, helped undoubtedly more or less by blue-books, reports and interviews, by inquiries 'on the spot', but never wholly replaced by such substitutes without a general disfigurement. Vision and opportunity reside in a personal sense and a personal history, and no short cut to them in the interest of plausible fiction has ever been discovered. The short cut, it is not too much to say, was with Zola the subject of constant ingenious experiment, and it is largely to this source, I surmise, that we owe the celebrated element of his grossness. He was *obliged* to be gross, on his system, or neglect to his cost an invaluable aid to representation, as well as one that apparently struck him as lying close at hand; and I cannot withhold my frank admiration from the courage and consistency with which he faced his need.

His general subject in the last analysis was the nature of man; in dealing with which he took up, obviously, the harp of most numerous strings. His business was to make these strings sound true, and there were none that he did not, so far as his general economy permitte., persistently try. What happened then was that many – say about half, and these, as I have noted, the most silvered, the most golden – refused to give out their music. They would only sound false, since (as with all his earnestness he must have felt) he could command them, through want of skill, of practice, of ear, to none of the right harmony. What therefore was more natural than that, still splendidly bent on producing his illusion, he should throw himself on the strings he might thump with effect, and should work them, as our phrase is, for all they were worth? The nature of man, he had plentiful warrant for holding, is an extraordinary mixture, but the great thing was to represent a sufficient part of it to show that it was solidly, palpably, commonly the nature. With this preoccupation he doubtless fell into extravagance – there was clearly so much to lead him on. The coarser side of his subject, based on the community of all the instincts, was for instance the more practicable side, a sphere the vision of which required but the general human, scarcely more than the plain physical, initiation, and dispensed thereby conveniently enough with special introductions or revelations. A free entry into this sphere was undoubtedly compatible with a youthful career as hampered right and left even as Zola's own.

He was in prompt possession thus of the range of sympathy that he *could* cultivate, though it must be added that the complete exercise of that sympathy might have encountered an obstacle that would somewhat undermine his advantage. Our friend might have found himself able, in other words, to pay to the instinctive, as I have called it, only such tribute as protesting taste (his own dose of it) permitted. Yet there it was again that fortune and his temperament served him. Taste as he knew it, taste as his own constitution supplied it, proved to have nothing to say to the matter. His own dose of the precious elixir had no perceptible regulating power. Paradoxical as the remark may sound, this accident was positively to operate as one of his greatest felicities. There are parts of his work, those dealing with romantic or poetic elements, in which the inactivity of the principle in question is sufficiently hurtful; but it surely should not be described as hurtful to such pictures as *Le Ventre de Paris*, as *L'Assommoir*, as *Germinal*. The conception on which each of these productions rests is that of a world with which taste has nothing to do, and though the act of representation may be justly held, as an artistic act, to involve its presence, the discrimination would probably have been in fact, given the particular illusion sought, more detrimental than the deficiency. There was a great outcry, as we all remember, over the rank materialism of *L'Assommoir*, but who cannot see to-day how much a milder infusion of it would have told against the close embrace of the subject aimed at? *L'Assommoir* is the nature of man – but not his finer, nobler, cleaner or more cultivated nature; it is the image of his free instincts, the better and the worse, the better struggling as they can, gasping for light and air, the worse making themselves at home in darkness, ignorance and poverty. The whole handling makes for emphasis and scale, and it is not to be measured how, as a picture of conditions, the thing would have suffered from timidity. The qualification of the painter was precisely his stoutness of stomach, and we scarce exceed in saying that to have taken in and given out again less of the infected air would, with such a resource, have meant the waste of a faculty.

I may add in this connection moreover that refinement of intention did on occasion and after a fashion of its own unmistakably preside at these experiments; making the remark in order to have done once for all with a feature of Zola's literary physiognomy that appears to have attached the gaze of many persons to the exclusion of every other. There are judges in these matters so perversely preoccupied that for them to see anywhere the 'improper' is for them straightway to cease to see anything else. The said improper, looming supremely large and casting all the varieties of the proper quite into the shade, suffers thus in their consciousness a much greater extension than it ever claimed, and this consciousness becomes, for the edification of many and the information of a few, a colossal reflector and record of it. Much may be said, in relation to some of the possibilities of the nature of man, of the nature in especial of the 'people', on the defect of our author's sense of proportion. But the sense of proportion of many of those he has scandalized would take us further yet. I recall at all events as relevant – for it comes under a very attaching general head – two occasions of long ago, two Sunday afternoons in Paris, on which I found the question of intention very curiously lighted. Several men of letters of a group in which almost every member either had arrived at renown or was well on his way to it, were assembled under the roof of the most distinguished of their number, where they exchanged free confidences on current work, on plans and ambitions, in a manner full of interest for one never previously privileged to see artistic conviction, artistic passion (at least on the literary ground) so systematic and so articulate. 'Well, I on my side,' I remember Zola's saying, 'am engaged on a book, a study of the *moeurs* of the people, for which I am making a collection of all the 'bad words', the *gros mots*, of the language, those with which the vocabulary of the people, those with which their familiar talk, bristles.' I was struck with the tone in which he made the announcement – without bravado and without apology, as an interesting idea that had come to him and that he was working, really to arrive at character and particular truth, with all his conscience; just as I was struck with the unqualified interest that his plan excited. It was *on* a plan that he was working – formidably, almost grimly, as his fatigued face showed; and the whole consideration of this interesting element partook of the general seriousness.

But there comes back to me also as a companion-piece to this another day, after some interval, on which the interest was excited by the fact that the work for love of which the brave licence had been taken was actually under the ban of the daily newspaper that had engaged to 'serialize' it. Publication had definitively ceased. The thing had run a part of its course, but it had outrun the courage of editors and the curiosity of subscribers – that stout curiosity to which it had evidently in such good faith been addressed. The chorus of contempt for the ways of such people, their pusillanimity, their superficiality, vulgarity, intellectual platitude, was the striking note on this occasion; for the journal impugned had declined to proceed and the serial, broken off, been obliged, if I am not mistaken, to seek the hospitality of other columns, secured indeed with no great difficulty. The composition so qualified for future fame was none other, as I was later to learn, than *L'Assommoir*; and my reminiscence has perhaps no greater point than in connecting itself with a matter always dear to the critical spirit, especially when the latter has not too completely elbowed out the romantic – the matter of the 'origins', the early consciousness, early steps, early tribulations, early obscurity, as so often happens, of productions finally crowned by time.

Their greatness is for the most part a thing that has originally begun so small; and this impression is particularly strong when we have been in any degree present, so to speak, at the birth. The course of the matter is apt to tend preponderantly in that case to enrich our stores of irony. In the eventual conquest of consideration by an abused book we recognize, in other terms, a drama of romantic interest, a drama often with large comic no less than with fine pathetic interweavings. It may of course be said in this particular connection that *L'Assommoir* has not been one of the literary things that creep humbly into the world. Its 'success' may be cited as almost insolently prompt, and the fact remains true if the idea of success be restricted, after the inveterate fashion, to the idea of circulation. What remains truer still, however, is that for the critical spirit circulation mostly matters not the least little bit, and it is of the success with which the history of Gervaise and Coupeau nestles in *that* capacious bosom, even as the just man sleeps in Abraham's, that I here speak . . . .

There are efforts here at stout perusal that, frankly, I have been unable to carry through, and I should verily like, in connection with the vanity of these, to dispose on the spot of the sufficiently strange phenomenon constituted by what I have called the climax [of Zola's last novels, after Les Rougon-Macquart]. It embodies in fact an immense anomaly; it casts back over Zola's prime and his middle years the queerest grey light of eclipse. Nothing moreover — nothing 'literary' — was ever so odd as in this matter the whole turn of the case, the consummation so logical yet so unexpected. Writers have grown old and withered and failed; they have grown weak and sad; they have lost heart, lost ability, yielded in one way or another — the possible ways being so numerous — to the cruelty of time. But the singular doom of this genius, and which began to multiply its symptoms ten years before his death, was to find, with life, at fifty, still rich in him, strength only to undermine all the 'authority' he had gathered. He had not grown old and he had not grown feeble; he had only grown all too wrongly insistent, setting himself to wreck, poetically, his so massive identity — to wreck it in the very waters in which he had formally arrayed his victorious fleet. (I say 'poetically' on purpose to give him the just benefit of all the beauty of his power.) The process of the disaster, so full of the effect, though so without the intention, of perversity, is difficult to trace in a few words; it may best be indicated by an example or two of its action.

The example that perhaps most comes home to me is again connected with a personal reminiscence. In the course of some talk that I had with him during his first visit to England I happened to ask him what opportunity to travel (if any) his immense application had ever left him, and whether in particular he had been able to see Italy, a country from which I had either just returned or which I was luckily – not having the Natural History of a Family on my hands – about to revisit. 'All I've done, alas,' he replied, 'was, the other year, in the course of a little journey to the south, to my own *pays* – all that has been possible was then to make a little dash as far as Genoa, a matter of only a few days.' *Le Docteur Pascal*, the conclusion of Les Rougon-Macquart, had appeared shortly before, and it further befell that I asked him what plans he had for the future, now that, still *dans la force de l'âge*, he had so cleared the ground. I shall never forget the fine promptitude of his answer – 'Oh, I shall begin at once Les Trois Villes.' 'And which cities are they to be?' The reply was finer still – 'Lourdes, Paris, Rome.'

It was splendid for confidence and cheer, but it left me, I fear, more or less gaping, and it was to give me afterwards the key, critically speaking, to many a mystery. It struck me as breathing to an almost tragic degree the fatuity of those in whom the gods stimulate that vice to their ruin. He was an honest man – he had always bristled with it at every pore; but no artistic reverse was inconceivable for an adventurer who, stating in one breath that his knowledge of Italy consisted of a few days spent at Genoa, was ready to declare in the next that he had planned, on a scale, a picture of Rome. It flooded his career, to my sense, with light; it showed how he had marched from subject to subject and had 'got up' each in turn – showing also how consummately he had reduced such getting-up to an artifice. He had success and a rare impunity behind him, but nothing would now be so interesting as to see if he could again play the trick. One would leave him, and welcome, Lourdes and Paris – he had already dealt, on a scale, with his own country and people. But was the adored Rome also to be his on such terms, the Rome he was already giving away before possessing an inch of it? One thought of one's own frequentations, saturations – a history of long years, and of how the effect of them had somehow been but to make the subject too august. Was *he* to find it easy through a visit of a month or two with 'introductions' and a Baedeker?

It was not indeed that the Baedeker and the introductions didn't show, to my sense, at that hour, as extremely suggestive; they were positively a part of the light struck out by his announcement. They defined the system on which he had brought Les Rougon-Macquart safely into port. He had had his Baedeker and his introductions for *Germinal*, for *L'Assommoir*, for *L'Argent*, for *La Débâcle*, for *Au Bonheur des Dames*; which advantages, which researches, had clearly been all the more in character for being documentary, extractive, a matter of *renseignements*, published or private, even when most mixed with personal impressions snatched, with *enquêtes sur les lieux*, with facts obtained from the best authorities, proud and happy to co-operate in so famous a connection. That was, as we say, all right, all the more that the process, to my imagination, became vivid and was wonderfully reflected back from its fruits. There *were* the fruits – so it hadn't been presumptuous. Presumption, however, was now to begin, and what omen mightn't there be in its beginning with such complacency? Well, time would show – as time in due course effectually did. *Rome*, as the second volume of The Three Cities, appeared with high punctuality a year or two later; and the interesting question, an occasion really for the moralist, was by that time not to recognize in it the mere triumph of a mechanical art, a 'receipt' applied with the skill of long practice, but to do much more than this – that is really to give a name to the particular shade of blindness that could constitute a trap for so great an artistic intelligence. The presumptuous volume, without sweetness, without antecedents, superficial and violent, has the minimum instead of the maximum of *value*; so that it betrayed or 'gave away' just in this degree the state of mind on the author's part responsible for its inflated hollowness. To put one's finger on the state of mind was to find out accordingly what was, as we say, the matter with him.

It seemed to me, I remember, that I found out as never before when, in its turn, *Fécondité* began the work of crowning the edifice. *Fécondité* is physiological, whereas *Rome* is not, whereas *Vérité* likewise is not; yet these three productions joined hands at a given moment to fit into the lock of the mystery the key of my meditation.

They came to the same thing, to the extent of permitting me to read into them together the same precious lesson. This lesson may not, barely stated, sound remarkable; yet without being in possession of it I should have ventured on none of these remarks. 'The matter with' Zola then, so far as it goes, was that, as the imagination of the artist is in the best cases not only clarified but intensified by his equal possession of Taste (deserving here if ever the old-fashioned honour of a capital) so when he has lucklessly never inherited that auxiliary blessing the imagination itself inevitably breaks down as a consequence. There is simply no limit, in fine, to the misfortune of being tasteless; it does not merely disfigure the surface and the fringe of your performance – it eats back into the very heart and enfeebles the sources of life. When you have no taste you have no discretion, which is the conscience of taste, and when you have no discretion you perpetrate books like *Rome*, which are without intellectual modesty, books like *Fécondité*, which are without a sense of the ridiculous, books like *Vérité*, which are without the finer vision of human experience . . .

Grant – and the generalization may be emphatic – that the shallow and the simple are *all* the population of his richest and most crowded pictures, and that his 'psychology', in a psychologic age, remains thereby comparatively coarse, grant this and we but get another view of the miracle. We see enough of the superficial among novelists at large, assuredly, without deriving from it, as we derive from Zola at his best, the concomitant impression of the solid. It is in general – I mean among the novelists at large – the impression of the *cheap*, which the author of Les Rougon-Macquart, honest man, never faithless for a moment to his own stiff standard, manages to spare us even in the prolonged sandstorm of *Vérité*. The Common is another matter; it is one of the forms of the superficial – pervading and consecrating all things in such a book as *Germinal* – and it only adds to the number of our critical questions. How in the world is it made, this deplorable democratic malodorous Common, so strange and so interesting? How is it taught to receive into its loins the stuff of the epic and still, in spite of that association with poetry, never depart from its nature? It is in the great lusty game he plays with the shallow and the simple that Zola's mastery resides, and we see of course that when values are small it takes innumerable items and combinations to make up the sum. In *L'Assommoir* and in *Germinal*, to some extent even in *La Débâcle*, the values are all, morally, personally, of the lowest – the highest is poor Gervaise herself, richly human in her generosities and follies – yet each is as distinct as a brass-headed nail.

What we come back to accordingly is the unprecedented case of such a combination of parts. Painters, of great schools, often of great talent, have responded liberally on canvas to the appeal of ugly things, of Spanish beggars, squalid and dusty-footed, of martyred saints or other convulsed sufferers, tortured and bleeding, of boors and louts soaking a Dutch proboscis in perpetual beer; but we had never before had to reckon with so literary a treatment of the mean and vulgar. When we others of the Anglo-Saxon race are vulgar we are, handsomely and with the best conscience in the world, vulgar all through, too vulgar to be in any degree literary, and too much so therefore to be critically reckoned with at all. The French are different – they separate their sympathies, multiply their possi-bilities, observe their shades, remain more or less outside of their worst disasters. They mostly contrive to get the *idea*, in however dead a faint, down into the lifeboat. They may lose sight of the stars, but they save in some such fashion as that their intellectual souls. Zola's own reply to all puzzlements would have been, at any rate, I take it, a straight summary of his inveterate professional habits. 'It is all very simple – I produce, roughly speaking, a volume a year, and of this time some five months go to preparation, to special study. In the other months, with all my *cadres* established, I write the book. And I can hardly say which part of the job is stiffest.'

The story was not more wonderful for him than that, nor the job more complex; which is why we must say of his whole process and its results that they constitute together perhaps the most extraordinary *imitation* of observation that we possess. Balzac appealed to 'science' and proceeded by her aid; Balzac had *cadres* enough and a tabulated world, rubrics, relationships and genealogies; but Balzac affects us in spite of everything as personally overtaken by life, as fairly hunted and run to earth by it. He strikes us as struggling and all but submerged, as beating over the scene such a pair of wings as were not soon again to be wielded by any visitor of his general air and as had not at all events attached themselves to Zola's rounded shoulders. His bequest is in consequence immeasurably more interesting, yet who shall declare that his adventure was in its greatness more successful? Zola 'pulled it off', as we say, supremely, in that he never but once found himself obliged to quit, to our vision, his magnificent treadmill of the pigeonholed and documented – the region we may qualify as that of experience by imitation. His splendid economy saw him through, he laboured to the end within sight of his notes and his charts.

The extraordinary thing, however, is that on the single occasion when, publicly – as his whole manifestation was public – life did swoop down on him, the effect of the visitation was quite perversely other than might have been looked for. His courage in the Dreyfus connection testified admirably to his ability to live for himself and out of the order of his volumes – little indeed as living at all might have seemed a question for one exposed, when his crisis was at its height and he was found guilty of 'insulting' the powers that were, to be literally torn to pieces in the precincts of the Palace of Justice. Our point is that nothing was ever so odd as that these great moments should appear to have been wasted, when all was said, for his creative intelligence. *Vérité*, as I have intimated, the production in which they might most have been reflected, is a production un-renewed and unrefreshed by them, spreads before us as somehow flatter and greyer, not richer and more relieved, by reason of them. They really arrived, I surmise, too late in the day; the imagination they might have vivified was already fatigued and spent.

I must not moreover appear to say that the power to evoke and present has not even on the dead level of *Vérité* its occasional minor revenges. There are passages, whole pages, of the old full-bodied sort, pictures that elsewhere in the series would in all likelihood have seemed abundantly convincing. Their misfortune is to have been discounted by our intensified, our finally fatal sense of the *procédé*. Quarrelling with all conventions, defiant of them in general, Zola was yet inevitably to set up his own group of them – as, for that matter, without a sufficient collection, without their aid in simplify-ing and making possible, how could he ever have seen his big ship into port? Art welcomes them, feeds upon them always; no sort of form is practicable without them. It is only a question of what particular ones we use – to wage war on certain others and to arrive at particular forms. The convention of the blameless being, the thoroughly 'scientific' creature possessed impeccably of all truth and

serving as the mouthpiece of it and of the author's highest complacencies, this character is for instance a convention inveterate and
indispensable, without whom the 'sympathetic' side of the work
could never have been achieved. Marc in *Vérité*, Pierre Froment in
Lourdes and in *Rome*, the wondrous representatives of the principle
of reproduction in *Fécondité*, the exemplary painter of *L'Oeuvre*,
sublime in his modernity and paternity, the patient Jean Macquart of
La Débâcle, whose patience is as guaranteed as the exactitude of a
well-made watch, the supremely enlightened Docteur Pascal even, as
I recall him, all amorous nepotism but all virtue too and all beauty of
life – such figures show us the reasonable and the good not merely in
the white light of the old George Sand novel and its improved
moralities, but almost in that of our childhood's nursery and school-
room, that of the moral tale of Miss Edgeworth and Mr Thomas
Day.

   Yet let not these restrictions be my last word. I had intended, under
the effect of a reperusal of *La Débâcle*, *Germinal* and *L'Assommoir*,
to make no discriminations that should not be in our hero's favour.
The long-drawn incident of the marriage of Gervaise and Cadet-
Cassis and that of the Homeric birthday feast later on in the
laundress's workshop, each treated from beginning to end and in
every item of their coarse comedy and humanity, still show the
unprecedented breadth by which they originally made us stare, still
abound in the particular kind and degree of vividness that helped
them, when they appeared, to mark a date in the portrayal of
manners. Nothing had then been so sustained and at every moment
of its grotesque and pitiful existence lived into as the nuptial day of
the Coupeau pair in especial, their fantastic processional pilgrimage
through the streets of Paris in the rain, their bedraggled exploration
of the halls of the Louvre museum, lost as in the labyrinth of Crete,
and their arrival at last, ravenous and exasperated, at the *guinguette*
where they sup at so much a head, each paying, and where we sit
down with them in the grease and the perspiration and succumb, half
in sympathy, half in shame, to their monstrous pleasantries, acerb-
ities and miseries. I have said enough of the mechanical in Zola; here
in truth is, given the elements, almost insupportably the sense of life.
That effect is equally in the historic chapter of the strike of the miners
in *Germinal*, another of those illustrative episodes, viewed as

great passages to be 'rendered', for which our author established altogether a new measure and standard of handling, a new energy and veracity, something since which the old trivialities and poverties of treatment of such aspects have become incompatible, for the novelist, with either rudimentary intelligence or rudimentary self-respect.

As for *La Débâcle*, finally, it takes its place with Tolstoi's very much more universal but very much less composed and condensed epic as an incomparably human picture of war. I have been re-reading it, I confess, with a certain timidity, the dread of perhaps impairing the deep impression received at the time of its appearance. I recall the effect it then produced on me as a really luxurious act of submission. It was early in the summer; I was in an old Italian town; the heat was oppressive, and one could but recline, in the lightest garments, in a great dim room and give one's self up. I like to think of the conditions and the emotion, which melt for me together into the memory I fear to imperil. I remember that in the glow of my admiration there was not a reserve I had ever made that I was not ready to take back. As an application of the author's system and his supreme faculty, as a triumph of what these things could do for him, how could such a performance be surpassed? The long, complex, horrific, pathetic battle, embraced, mastered, with every crash of its squadrons, every pulse of its thunder and blood resolved for us, by reflection, by communication from two of the humblest and obscurest of the military units, into immediate vision and contact, into deep human thrills of terror and pity – this bristling centre of the book was such a piece of 'doing' (to come back to our word) as could only shut our mouths. That doubtless is why a generous critic, nursing the sensation, may desire to drop for a farewell no term into the other scale. That our author was clearly great at congruous subjects – this may well be our conclusion. If the others, subjects of the private and intimate order, gave him more or less inevitably 'away', they yet left him the great distinction that the more he could be promiscuous and collective, the more even he could (to repeat my imputation) illustrate our large natural allowance of health, hearti-ness and grossness, the more he could strike us as penetrating and true. It was a distinction not easy to win and that his name is not likely soon to lose.

51

On Elizabeth Barrett Browning submerging her genius in the details of the cause of Italian freedom, from William Wetmore Story and His Friends, *1903.*

... WE ARE even perhaps slightly irritated, and end by asking ourselves if it be not because her admirable mind, otherwise splendidly exhibited, has inclined us to look in her for that saving and sacred sense of proportion, of the free and blessed *general*, that great poets, that genius and the high range of genius, give us the impression of even in emotion and passion, even in pleading a cause and calling on the gods ...

52

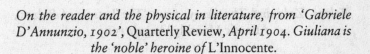

On the reader and the physical in literature, from 'Gabriele D'Annunzio, 1902', Quarterly Review, April 1904. Giuliana is the 'noble' heroine of L'Innocente.

... GIULIANA for instance affects us, beyond any figure in fiction we are likely to remember, as living and breathing under our touch and before our eyes, as a creature of organs, functions and processes, palpable, audible, pitiful physical conditions. These are facts, many of them, of an order in pursuit of which many a spectator of the 'picture of life' will instinctively desire to stop short, however great in general his professed desire to enjoy the borrowed consciousness that the picture of life gives us; and nothing, it may well be said, is more certain than that we have a right in such matters to our preference, a right to choose the kind of adventure of the imagination we like best. No obligation whatever rests on us in respect to a given kind – much light as our choice may often throw for the critic on the nature of our own intelligence. *There* at any rate, we are disposed to say of such a piece of penetration as *L'Innocente*, there is a particular dreadful adventure, as large as life, for those who can bear it. The conditions are all present; it is only the reader himself who may break down. When in general, it may be added, we see readers do so, this is truly more often because they are shocked at really finding the last consistency than because they are shocked at missing it ...

53

Balzac, Zola and Thackeray, from 'The Lesson of Balzac', Atlantic Monthly, *August 1905.*

. . . WE HAVE lately had a literary case of the same general family as the case of Balzac . . . I had occasion, not long since, after the death of Émile Zola, to attempt an appreciation of *his* extraordinary performance – his series of the *Rougon-Macquart* constituting in fact, in the library of the fiction that can hope in some degree to live, a monument to the idea of plenitude, of comprehension and variety, second only to the *Comédie Humaine*. The question presented itself, in respect to Zola's ability and Zola's career, with a different proportion and value, I quite recognize, and wearing a much less distinguished face; but it was there to be met, none the less, on the very threshold, and all the more because this was just where he himself had placed it. His idea had been, from the first, in a word, to lose no time – as if one could have experience, even the mere amount requisite for showing others as having it, *without* losing time! – and yet the degree in which he too, so handicapped, has achieved valid expression is such as still to stagger us. He had had inordinately to simplify – had had to leave out the life of the soul, practically, and confine himself to the life of the instincts, of the more immediate passions, such as can be easily and promptly caught in the fact. He had had, in a word, to confine himself almost entirely to the impulses and agitations that men and women are possessed by in common, and to take them as exhibited in mass and number, so that, being writ larger, they might likewise be more easily read. He met and solved, in this manner, his difficulty – the difficulty of knowing, and of showing, of life, only what his 'notes' would account for. But it is in the *waste*, I think, much rather – the waste of time, of passion, of curiosity, of contact – that true initiation resides; so that the most wonderful adventures of the artist's spirit are those, immensely quickening for his 'authority', that are yet not reducible to his notes. It is exactly here that we get the difference between such a solid, square, symmetrical structure as *Les Rougon-Macquart*, vitiated, in a high degree, by its mechanical side, and the monument left by Balzac – without the example of which, I surmise, Zola's work would not have existed. The mystic process of the crucible, the transformation of the material under aesthetic heat, is, in the *Comédie Humaine*, thanks to an intenser and more submissive fusion, completer, and also finer; for if the commoner and more wayside passions and conditions are, in the various episodes there, at no time gathered into so large and so thick an illustrative bunch, yet on the other hand they are shown much more freely at play in the individual case – and the individual case it is that permits of supreme fineness. It is hard to say where Zola is fine; whereas it is often, for pages together, hard to say where Balzac is, even under the weight of his too ponderous personality, not. The most fundamental and general sign of the novel, from one desperate experiment to another, is its being everywhere an effort at *representation* – this is the beginning and the end of it: wherefore it was that one could say at last, with account taken of everything, that Zola's performance, on his immense scale, was an extraordinary show of representation imitated. The imitation in places – notably and admirably, for instance, in *L'Assommoir* – breaks through into something that we take for reality; but, for the most part, the separating rift, the determining difference, holds its course straight, prevents the attempted process from becoming the sound, straight, whole thing that is given us by those who have really *bought* their information. This is where Balzac remains unshaken – in our feeling that, with all his faults of pedantry, ponderosity, pretentiousness, bad taste and charmless form, his spirit has some-how paid for its knowledge. His subject is again and again the complicated human creature or human condition; and it is with these complications as if he knew them, as Shakespeare knew them, by his charged consciousness, by the history of his soul and the direct exposure of his sensibility. This source of supply he found, forever – and one may indeed say he mostly left – sitting at his fireside; where it constituted the company with which I see him shut up and his practical intimacy with which, during such orgies and debauches of intellectual passion, might earn itself that name of high personal good fortune that I have applied.

Let me say, definitely, that I hold several of his faults to be grave, and that if there were any question of time for it I should like to speak of them; but let me add, as promptly, that they are faults, on the whole, of execution, flaws in the casting, accidents of the process: they never come back to that fault in the artist, in the novelist, that amounts most completely to a failure of dignity, the absence of saturation with his idea. When saturation fails no other presence really avails; as when, on the other hand, it operates, no failure of method fatally interferes. There is never in Balzac that damning interference which consists of the painter's not seeing, not possessing, his image; not having fixed his creature and his creature's conditions. 'Balzac aime sa Valérie,' says Taine, in his great essay – so much the finest thing ever written on our author – speaking of the way in which the awful little Madame Marneffe of *Les Parents Pauvres* is drawn, and of the long rope, for her acting herself out, that her creator's participation in her reality assures her. He has been contrasting her, as it happens, with Thackeray's Becky Sharp or rather with Thackeray's attitude toward Becky, and the marked jealousy of her freedom that Thackeray exhibits from the first. I remember reading at the time of the publication of Taine's study – though it was long, long ago – a phrase in an English review of the volume which seemed to my limited perception, even in extreme youth, to deserve the highest prize ever bestowed on critical stupidity undisguised. If Balzac loved his Valérie, said this commentator, that only showed Balzac's extraordinary taste; the truth being really, throughout, that it was just through this love of each seized identity, and of the sharpest and liveliest identities most, that Madame Marneffe's creator was able to marshal his array at all. The love, as we call it, the joy in their communicated and exhibited movement, in their standing on their feet and going of themselves and acting out their characters, was what rendered possible the saturation I speak of; what supplied him, through the inevitable gaps of his preparation and the crevices of his prison, his long prison of labour, a short cut to the knowledge he required. It was by loving them – as the terms of his subject and the nuggets of his mine – that he knew them; it was not by knowing them that he loved.

He at all events robustly loved the sense of another explored, assumed, assimilated identity – enjoyed it as the hand enjoys the glove when the glove ideally fits. My image indeed is loose; for what he liked was absolutely to get into the constituted consciousness, into all the clothes, gloves and whatever else, into the very skin and bones, of the habited, featured, coloured, articulated form of life that he desired to present. How do we know given persons, for any purpose of demonstration, unless we know their situation for themselves, unless we see it from their point of vision, that is from their point of pressing consciousness or sensation? – without our allowing for which there is no appreciation. Balzac loved his Valérie then as Thackeray did not love his Becky, or his Blanche Amory in *Pendennis*. But his prompting was not to expose her; it could only be, on the contrary – intensely aware as he was of all the lengths she might go, and paternally, maternally alarmed about them – to cover her up and protect her, in the interest of her special genius and freedom. All his impulse was to *la faire valoir*, to give her all her value, just as Thackeray's attitude was the opposite one, a desire positively to expose and desecrate poor Becky – to follow her up, catch her in the act and bring her to shame: though with a mitigation, an admiration, an inconsequence, now and then wrested from him by an instinct finer, in his mind, than the so-called 'moral' eagerness. The English writer wants to make sure, first of all, of your moral judgment; the French is willing, while it waits a little, to risk, for the sake of his subject and its interest, your spiritual salvation. Madame Marneffe, detrimental, fatal as she is, is 'exposed', so far as anything in life, or in art, may be, by the working-out of the situation and the subject themselves; so that when they have done what they would, what they logically had to, with her, we are ready to take it from them. We do not feel, very irritatedly, very lecturedly, in other words with superfluous edification, that she has been sacrificed. Who can say, on the contrary, that Blanche Amory, in *Pendennis*, with the author's lash about her little bare white back from the first – who can feel that she has *not* been sacrificed, or that her little bareness and whiteness, and all the rest of her, have been, by such a process, presented as they had a right to demand?

It all comes back, in fine, to that respect for the liberty of the subject which I should be willing to name as *the* great sign of the painter of the first order . . .

54

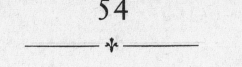

On Kipps, *from a letter to H. G. Wells, November 1905 (*HJL, *vol. 4, 379).*

... OF COURSE you know yourself how immitigably the thing is done – it is of such a brilliancy of *true* truth. I really think that you have done, at this time of day, two particular things for the first time of their doing among us. (1) You have written the first closely and intimately, the first intelligently and consistently ironic or satiric novel. In everything else there has always been the sentimental or conventional interference, the interference of which Thackeray is full. (2) You have for the very first time treated the English 'lower middle' class, etc., without the picturesque, the grotesque, the fantastic and romantic interference, of which Dickens, e.g., is so misleadingly, of which even George Eliot is so deviatingly, full. You have handled its vulgarity in so scientific and historic a spirit, and seen the whole thing all in its *own* strong light. And then the book has, throughout, such extraordinary life; everyone in it, without exception, and every piece and part of it, is so vivid and sharp and *raw*. Kipps himself is a diamond of the first water, from start to finish, exquisite and radiant; Coote is consummate, Chitterlow magnificent (the whole first evening with Chitterlow perhaps the most brilliant thing in the book – unless that glory be reserved for the way the entire matter of the *shop* is done, including the admirable image of the boss). It all in fine, from cover to cover, does you the greatest honour, and if we had any other than skin-deep criticism ... it would have immense recognition ...

55

———— ❧ ————

Introduction to The Tempest, *from* The Complete Works of William Shakespeare, *ed. Sidney Lee, 1907. James had long been fascinated by the wonder and terror of the problem of how these plays could have come from that man — according to Percy Lubbock he referred in conversation to that 'lout from Stratford'. It is still a question that we ask and ask, and one which would naturally re-pose itself with force to an artist in the process of revising and summing up his own life work in a semi-autobiographical manner. Like anyone intelligently concerned with literature, James had a lifelong relationship with Shakespeare. In 1875 he had pronounced* Henry V *unactable, but a speech from* Macbeth *as 'acting itself'; in 1896* Cymbeline *was a 'sweet jumble' in 'the high sunny air of delightful poetry', etc.; and in 1897 the 'loose, violent, straddling romance',* Richard III, *showed that 'the representation of Shakespeare is simply no longer to be borne'. Modern editors think that the first performance of* The Tempest *was in 1611.*

IF THE EFFECT of the Plays and Poems, taken in their mass, be most of all to appear often to mock our persistent ignorance of so many of the conditions of their birth, and thereby to place on the rack again our strained and aching wonder, this character has always struck me as more particularly kept up for them by *The Tempest*; the production, of the long series, in which the Questions, as the critical reader of Shakespeare must ever comprehensively and ruefully call them and more or less resignedly live with them, hover before us in their most tormenting form. It may seem no very philosophic state of mind, the merely baffled and exasperated view of one of the supreme works of all literature; though I feel, for myself, that to confess to it now and then, by way of relief, is no unworthy tribute to the work. It is not, certainly, the tribute most frequently paid, for the large body of comment and criticism of which this play alone has been the theme abounds much rather in affirmed conclusions, complacencies of conviction, full apprehensions of the meaning and triumphant pointings of the moral. The Questions, in the light of all this wisdom, convert themselves, with comparatively small difficulty, into smooth and definite answers; the innumerable dim ghosts that flit, like startled game at eventide, through the deep dusk of our speculation, with just form enough to quicken it and no other charity for us at all, bench themselves along the vista as solidly as Falstaff and as vividly as Hotspur. Everything has thus been attributed to the piece before us, and every attribution so made has been in turn brushed away; merely to glance at such a monument to the interest inspired is to recognize a battleground of opposed factions, not a little enveloped in sound and smoke. Of these copious elements, produced for the most part to the best intention, we remain accordingly conscious; so that to approach the general bone of contention, as we can but familiarly name it, for whatever purpose, we have to cross the scene of action at a mortal risk, making the fewest steps of it and trusting to the probable calm at the centre of the storm. There in fact, though there only, we find that serenity; find the subject itself intact and unconscious, seated as unwinking and inscrutable as a divinity in a temple, save for that vague flicker of derision, the only response to our interpretative heat, which adds the last beauty to its face. The divinity never relents – never, like the image of life in *The Winter's Tale*, steps down from its pedestal; it simply leaves us to stare on through the ages, with this fact indeed of having crossed the circle of fire, and so got into the real and right relation to it, for our one comfort.

The position of privilege of *The Tempest* as the latest example, to all appearance, of the author's rarer work, with its distance from us in time thereby shortened to the extent of the precious step or two, was certain to expose it, at whatever final cost, we easily see, to any amount of interpretative zeal. With its first recorded performance that of February 1613, when it was given in honour of the marriage of the Princess Elizabeth, its finished state cannot have preceded his death by more than three years, and we accordingly take it as the finest flower of his experience. Here indeed, as on so many of the Questions, judgments sharply differ, and this use of it as an ornament to the nuptials of the daughter of James I, and the young Elector Palatine may have been but a repetition of previous performances; though it is not in such a case supposable that these can have been numerous. They would antedate the play, at the most, by a year or two, and so not throw it essentially further back from us. *The Tempest* speaks to us, somehow, convincingly, as a *pièce de circonstance*, and the suggestion that it was addressed in its brevity, its rich simplicity, and its free elegance, to court-production, and above all to providing, with a string of other dramas, for the 'intellectual' splendour of a wedding-feast, is, when once entertained, not easily dislodged. A few things fail to fit, but more fit strikingly. I like therefore to think of the piece as of 1613. To refer it, as it is referred by other reckonings, to 1611 is but to thicken that impenetrability of silence in which Shakespeare's latest years enfold him. Written as it must have been on the earlier calculation, before the age of forty-seven, it has that rare value of the richly mature note of a genius who, by our present measure of growth and fulness, was still young enough to have had in him a world of life: we feel behind it the immense procession of its predecessors, while we yet stare wistfully at the plenitude and the majesty, the expression as of something broad-based and ultimate, that were not, in any but a strained sense, to borrow their warrant from the weight of years. Nothing so enlarges the wonder of the whole time-question in Shakespeare's career as the fact of this date, in easy middle life, of his time-climax; which, if we knew less, otherwise, than we do about him, might affect us as attempt, on the part of treacherous History, to pass him off as one of those monsters of precocity who, fortunately for their probable reputation, the too likely betrayal of short-windedness, are cut off in their comparative prime. The transmuted young rustic who, after a look over London, brief at the best, was ready at the age of thirty to produce *The Merchant of Venice* and *A Midsummer Night's Dream* (and this after the half-dozen splendid prelusive things that had included, at twenty-eight, *Romeo and Juliet*), had been indeed a monster of precocity – which all geniuses of the first order are not; but the day of his paying for it had neither arrived nor, however faintly, announced itself, and the fathomless strangeness of his story, the abrupt stoppage of his pulse after *The Tempest*, is not, in charity, lighted for us by a glimmer of explanation. The explanation by some interposing accident is as absent as any symptom of 'declining powers'.

His powers declined, that is – but declined merely to obey the spring we should have supposed inherent in them; and their possessor's case derives from this, I think, half the secret of its so inestimably mystifying us. He died, for a nature so organized, too lamentably soon; but who knows where we should have been with him if he had not lived long enough so to affirm, with many other mysteries, the mystery of his abrupt and complete cessation? There is that in *The Tempest*, specifically, though almost all indefinably, which seems to show us the artist consciously tasting of the first and rarest of his gifts, that of imaged creative Expression, the instant sense of some copious equivalent of thought for every grain of the grossness of reality; to show him as unresistingly aware, in the depth of his genius, that nothing like it had ever been known, or probably would ever be again known, on earth, and as so given up, more than on other occasions, to the joy of sovereign *science*. There are so many sides from which any page that shows his stamp may be looked at that a handful of reflections can hope for no coherency, in the chain of association immediately formed, unless they happen to bear upon some single truth. Such a truth then, for me, is this comparative – by which one can really but mean this superlative – artistic value of the play seen in the meagre circle of the items of our knowledge about it. Let me say that our knowledge, in the whole connection, is a quantity that shifts, surprisingly, with the measure of a felt need; appearing to some of us, on some sides, adequate, various, large, and appearing to others, on whatever side, a scant beggar's portion. We are concerned, it must be remembered, here – that is for getting *generally* near our author – not only with the number of the mustered facts, but with the kind of fact that each may strike us as being: never unmindful that such matters, when they are few, may go far for us if they be individually but ample and significant; and when they are numerous, on the other hand, may easily fall short enough to break our hearts if they be at the same time but individually small and poor. Three or four stepping-stones across a stream will serve if they are broad slabs, but it will take more than may be counted if they are only pebbles.

Beyond all gainsaying then, by many an estimate, is the penury in which even the most advantageous array of the Shakespearean facts still leaves us: strung together with whatever ingenuity they remain, for our discomfiture, as the pebbles across the stream.

To balance, for our occasion, this light scale, however, *The Tempest* affects us, taking its complexity and its perfection together, as the rarest of all examples of literary art. There may be other things as exquisite, other single exhalations of beauty reaching as high a mark and sustained there for a moment, just as there are other deep wells of poetry from which cupfuls as crystalline may, in repeated dips, be drawn; but nothing, surely, of equal length and variety lives so happily and radiantly as a whole: no poetic birth ever took place under a star appointed to blaze upon it so steadily. The felicity enjoyed is enjoyed longer and more intensely, and the art involved, completely revealed, as I suggest, to the master, holds the securest revel. The man himself, in the Plays, we directly touch, to my consciousness, positively nowhere: we are dealing too perpetually with the artist, the monster and magician of a thousand masks, not one of which we feel him drop long enough to gratify with the breath of the interval that strained attention in us which would be yet, so quickened, ready to become deeper still. Here at last the artist is, comparatively speaking, so generalized, so consummate and typical, so frankly amused with himself, that is with his art, with his power, with his theme, that it is as if he came to meet us more than his usual half-way, and as if, thereby, in meeting *him*, and touching him, we were nearer to meeting and touching the man. The man everywhere, in Shakespeare's work, is so effectually locked up and imprisoned in the artist that we but hover at the base of thick walls for a sense of him; while, in addition, the artist is so steeped in the abysmal objectivity of his characters and situations that the great billows of the medium itself play with him, to our vision, very much as, over a ship's side, in certain waters, we catch, through transparent tides, the flash of strange sea-creatures. What we are present at in this fashion is a series of incalculable plunges — the series of those that have taken effect, I mean, after the great primary plunge, made once for all, of the man into the artist: the successive plunges of the artist himself into Romeo and into Juliet, into Shylock, Hamlet, Macbeth, Coriolanus, Cleopatra, Antony, Lear, Othello, Falstaff, Hotspur;

immersions during which, though he always ultimately finds his feet, the very violence of the movements involved troubles and distracts our sight. In *The Tempest*, by the supreme felicity I speak of, is no violence; he sinks as deep as we like, but what he sinks into, beyond all else, is the lucid stillness of his style.

One can speak, in these matters, but from the impression determined by one's own inevitable standpoint; again and again, at any rate, such a masterpiece puts before me the very act of the momentous conjunction taking place for the poet, at a given hour, between his charged inspiration and his clarified experience: or, as I should perhaps better express it, between his human curiosity and his aesthetic passion. Then, if he happens to have been, all his career, with his equipment for it, more or less the victim and the slave of the former, he yields, by way of a change, to the impulse of allowing the latter, for a magnificent moment, the upper hand. The human curiosity, as I call it, is always there – with no more need of making provision for it than use in taking precautions against it; the surrender to the luxury of expertness may therefore go forward on its own conditions. I can offer no better description of *The Tempest* as fresh re-perusal lights it for me than as such a surrender, sublimely enjoyed; and I may frankly say that, under this impression of it, there is no refinement of the artistic consciousness that I do not see my way – or feel it, better, perhaps, since we but grope, at the best, in our darkness – to attribute to the author. It is a way that one follows to the end, because it is a road, I repeat, on which one least misses some glimpse of him face to face. If it be true that the thing was concocted to meet a particular demand, that of the master of the King's revels, with his prescription of date, form, tone and length, this, so far from interfering with the Poet's perception of a charming opportunity to taste for *himself*, for himself above all, and as he had almost never so tasted, not even in *A Midsummer Night's Dream*, of the quality of his mind and the virtue of his skill, would have exceedingly favoured the happy case. Innumerable one may always suppose these delicate debates and intimate understandings of an artist with himself. 'How much *taste*, in the world, may I conceive that I have? – and what a charming idea to snatch a moment for finding out! What moment could be better than this – a bridal evening before the Court, with extra candles and the handsomest company – if I can but put my hand on the right "scenario"?' We can catch, across the ages, the searching sigh and the look about; we receive the stirred breath of the ripe, amused genius; and, stretching, as I admit I do at least, for a still closer conception of the beautiful crisis, I find it pictured for me in some such presentment as that of a divine musician who, alone in his room, preludes or improvises at close of day. He sits at the harpsichord, by the open window, in the summer dusk; his hands wander over the keys. They stray far, for his motive, but at last he finds and holds it; then he lets himself go, embroidering and refining: it is the thing for the hour and his mood. The neighbours may gather in the garden, the nightingale be hushed on the bough; it is none the less a private occasion, a concert of one, both performer and auditor, who plays for his own ear, his own hand, his own innermost sense, and for the bliss and capacity of his instrument. Such are the only hours at which the artist *may*, by any measure of his own (too many things, at others, make heavily against it); and their challenge to him is irresistible if he has known, all along, too much compromise and too much sacrifice.

The face that beyond any other, however, I seem to see *The Tempest* turn to us is the side on which it so superlatively speaks of that endowment for Expression, expression as a primary force, a consuming, an independent passion, which was the greatest ever laid upon man. It is for Shakespeare's power of constitutive speech quite as if he had swum into our ken with it from another planet, gathering it up there, in its wealth, as something antecedent to the occasion and the need, and if possible quite in excess of them; something that was to make to our poor world a great flat table for receiving the glitter and clink of outpoured treasure. The idea and the motive are more often than not so smothered in it that they scarce know themselves, and the resources of such a style, the provision of images, emblems, energies of every sort, laid up in advance, affects us as the storehouse of a king before a famine or a siege – which not only, by its scale, braves depletion or exhaustion, but bursts, through mere excess of quantity or presence, out of all doors and windows. It renders the poverties and obscurities of our world, as I say, in the dazzling terms of a richer and better. It constitutes, by a miracle, more than half the author's material; so much more usually does it happen, for the painter or the poet, that life itself, in its appealing, overwhelming crudity, offers itself as the paste to be kneaded. Such a personage works in general in the very elements of experience; whereas we see Shakespeare working predominantly in the terms of expression, *all* in the terms of the artist's specific vision and genius; with a thicker cloud of images to attest his approach, at any point, than the comparatively meagre given case ever has to attest its own identity. He points for us as no one else the relation of style to meaning and of manner to motive; a matter on which, right and left, we hear such rank ineptitudes uttered. Unless it be true that these things, on either hand, are inseparable; unless it be true that the phrase, the cluster and order of terms, *is* the object and the sense, in as close a compression as that of body and soul, so that any consideration of them as distinct, from the moment style is an active, applied force, becomes a gross stupidity: unless we recognize this reality the author of *The Tempest* has no lesson for us. It is by his expression of it exactly as the expression stands that the particular thing is created, created as interesting, as beautiful, as strange, droll or terrible – as related, in short, to our understanding or our sensibility; in consequence of which we reduce it to naught when we begin to talk of either of its presented parts as matters by themselves.

All of which considerations indeed take us too far; what it is important to note being simply our Poet's high testimony to this independent, absolute value of Style, and to its need thoroughly to project and seat itself. It had been, as so seating itself, the very home of his mind, for his all too few twenty years; it had been the supreme source to him of the joy of life. It had been in fine his material, his plastic clay; since the more subtly he applied it the more secrets it had to give him, and the more these secrets might appear to him, at every point, one with the lights and shades of the human picture, one with the myriad pulses of the spirit of man. Thus it was that, as he passed from one application of it to another, tone became, for all its suggestions, more and more sovereign to him, and the subtlety of its secrets an exquisite interest. If I see him, at the last, over *The Tempest*, as the composer, at the harpsichord or the violin, extemporizing in the summer twilight, it is exactly that he is feeling there for tone and, by the same token, finding it – finding it as *The Tempest*, beyond any register of ours, immortally gives it. This surrender to the highest sincerity of virtuosity, as we nowadays call it, is to my perception *all The Tempest*; with no possible depth or delicacy in it that such an imputed character does not cover and provide for. The subject to be treated was the simple fact (if one may call anything in the matter simple) that refinement, selection, economy, the economy not of poverty, but of wealth a little weary of congestion – the very air of the lone island and the very law of the Court celebration – were here implied and imperative things. Anything was a subject, always, that offered to sight an aperture of size enough for expression and its train to pass in and deploy themselves. If they filled up all the space, none the worse; they occupied it as nothing else could do. The subjects of the Comedies are, without exception, old wives' tales – which we are not too insufferably aware of only because the iridescent veil so perverts their proportions. The subjects of the Histories are no subjects at all; each is but a row of pegs for the hanging of the cloth of gold that is to muffle them. Such a thing as *The Merchant of Venice* declines, for very shame, to be reduced to its elements of witless 'story'; such things as the two Parts of *Henry the Fourth* form no more than a straight convenient channel for the procession of evoked images that is to pour through it like a torrent. Each of these productions is none the less of incomparable splendour; by which splendour we are bewildered till we see how it comes. Then we see that every inch of it is personal tone, or in other words brooding expression raised to the highest energy. Push such energy far enough – far enough if you can! – and, being what it is, it then inevitably provides for Character. Thus we see character, in every form of which the 'story' gives the thinnest hint, marching through the pieces I have named in its habit as it lives, and so filling out the scene that nothing is missed. The 'story' in *The Tempest* is a thing of naught, for any story will provide a remote island, a shipwreck and a coincidence. Prospero and Miranda, awaiting their relatives, are, in the present case, *for* the relatives, the coincidence – just as the relatives are the coincidence for them. Ariel and Caliban, and the island-airs and island-scents, and all the rest of the charm and magic and the ineffable delicacy (a delicacy positively at its highest in the conception and execution of Caliban) are the style handed over to its last disciplined passion of curiosity; a curiosity which flowers, at this pitch, into the freshness of each of the characters.

There are judges for whom the piece is a tissue of symbols; symbols of the facts of State then apparent, of the lights of philosophic and political truth, of the 'deeper meanings of life', above all, of a high crisis in its author's career. At this most relevant of its mystic values only we may glance; the consecrated estimate of Prospero's surrender of his magic robe and staff as a figure for Shakespeare's own self-despoilment, his considered purpose, at this date, of future silence. Dr George Brandes works out in detail that analogy; the production becomes, on such a supposition, Shakespeare's 'farewell to the stage'; his retirement to Stratford, to end his days in the care of his property and in oblivion of the theatre, was a course for which his arrangements had already been made. The simplest way to put it, since I have likened him to the musician at the piano, is to say that he had decided upon the complete closing of this instrument, and that in fact he was to proceed to lock it with the sharp click that has reverberated through the ages, and to spend what remained to him of life in walking about a small, squalid country-town with his hands in his pockets and an ear for no music now but the chink of the coin they might turn over there. This is indeed in general the accepted, the imposed view of the position he had gained: this freedom to 'elect', as we say, to cease, intellectually, to exist: this ability, exercised at the zenith of his splendour, to shut down the lid, from one day to another, on the most potent aptitude for vivid reflection ever lodged in a human frame and to conduct himself thereafter, in all ease and comfort, not only as if it were not, but as if it had never been. I speak of our 'accepting' the prodigy, but by the established record we have no choice whatever; which is why it is imposed, as I say, on our bewildered credulity. With the impossibility of proving that the author of *The Tempest* did, after the date of that production, ever again press the spring of his fountain, ever again reach for the sacred key or break his heart for an hour over his inconceivable act of sacrifice, we are reduced to behaving as if we understood the strange case; so that any rubbing of our eyes, as under the obsession of a wild dream, has been held a gesture that, for common decency, must mainly take place in private. If I state that my small contribution to any renewed study of the matter can amount, accordingly, but to little more than an irresistible need to rub mine in public, I shall have done the most that the condition of our knowledge admits of. We can 'accept', but we can accept only in stupefaction – a stupefaction that, in presence of *The Tempest*, and of the intimate meaning so imputed to it, must despair of ever subsiding. These things leave us in darkness – in gross darkness about the Man; the case of which they are the warrant is so difficult to embrace. None ever appealed so sharply to some light of knowledge, and nothing could render our actual knowledge more contemptible. What manner of human being was it who *could* so, at a given moment, announce his intention of capping his divine flame with a twopenny extinguisher, and who then, the announcement made, could serenely succeed in carrying it out? Were it a question of a flame spent or burning thin, we might feel a little more possessed of matter for comprehension; the fact being, on the contrary, one can only repeat, that the value of *The Tempest* is, exquisitely, in its refinement of power, its renewed artistic freshness and roundness, its mark as of a distinction unequalled, on the whole (though I admit that we here must take subtle measures), in any predecessor. Prospero has simply waited, to cast his magic ring into the sea, till the jewel set in it shall have begun to burn as never before.

So it is then; and it puts into a nutshell the eternal mystery, the most insoluble that ever was, the complete rupture, for our understanding, between the Poet and the Man. There are moments, I admit, in this age of sound and fury, of connections, in every sense, too maddeningly multiplied, when we are willing to let it pass as a mystery, the most soothing, cooling, consoling too perhaps, that ever was. But there are others when, speaking for myself, its power to torment us intellectually seems scarcely to be borne; and we know these moments best when we hear it proclaimed that a comfortable clearness reigns. I have been for instance reading over Mr Halliwell-Phillipps, and I find him apparently of the opinion that it is all our fault if everything in our author's story, and above all in this last chapter of it, be not of a primitive simplicity. The complexity arises from our suffering our imagination to meddle with the Man at all; who is quite sufficiently presented to us on the face of the record. For critics of this writer's complexion the only facts we are urgently concerned with are the facts of the Poet, which are abundantly constituted by the Plays and the Sonnets. The Poet is *there*, and the Man is outside: the Man is for instance in such a perfectly definite circumstance as that he could never miss, after *The Tempest*, the key of his piano, as I have called it, since he could play so freely with the key of his cash-box. The supreme master of expression had made, before fifty, all the money he wanted; therefore what was there more to express? This view is admirable if you can get your mind to consent to it. It must ignore any impulse, in presence of Play or Sonnet (whatever vague stir behind either may momentarily act as provocation) to try for a lunge at the figured arras. In front of the tapestry sits the immitigably respectable person whom our little slateful of gathered and numbered items, heaven knows, does amply account for, since there is nothing in him to explain; while the undetermined figure, on the other hand – undetermined whether in the sense of respectability or of anything else – the figure who supremely interests us, remains as unseen of us as our Ariel, on the enchanted island, remains of the bewildered visitors. Mr Halliwell-Phillipps's theory, as I understand it – and I refer to it but as an advertisement of a hundred others – is that we too are but bewildered visitors, and that the state of mind of the Duke of Naples and his companions is our proper critical portion.

If our knowledge of the greatest of men consists therefore but of the neat and 'proved' addition of two or three dozen common particulars, the rebuke to a morbid and monstrous curiosity is no more than just. We know enough, by such an implication, when we admire enough, and as difficulties would appear to abound on our attempting to push further, this is an obvious lesson to us to stand as still as possible. Not difficulties – those of penetration, exploration, interpretation, those, in the word that says everything, of appreciation – are the approved field of criticism, but the very forefront of the obvious and the palpable, where we may go round and round, like holiday-makers on hobby-horses, at the turning of a crank. Differences of estimate, in this relation, come back, too clearly, let us accordingly say, to differences of view of the character of genius in general – if not, in truth, more exactly stated, to that strangest of all fallacies, the idea of the separateness of a great man's parts. His genius places itself, under this fallacy, on one side of the line and the rest of his identity on the other; the line being that, for instance, which, to Mr Halliwell-Phillipps's view, divides the author of *Hamlet* and *The Tempest* from the man of exemplary business-method whom alone we may propose to approach at all intimately. The stumbling-block here is that the boundary exists only in the vision of those able to content themselves with arbitrary marks. A mark becomes arbitrary from the moment we have no authoritative sign of where to place it, no sign of higher warrant than that it smoothes and simplifies the ground. But though smoothing and simplifying, on such terms, may, by restricting our freedom of attention and speculation, make, on behalf of our treatment of the subject, for a livelier effect of business – that business as to a zealous care for which we seem taught that our author must above all serve as our model – it will see us little further on any longer road. The fullest appreciation possible is the high tribute we must offer to greatness, and to make it worthy of its office we must surely know where we are with it. In greatness as much as in mediocrity the man is, under examination, *one*, and the elements of character melt into each other. The genius is a part of the mind, and the mind a part of the behaviour; so that, for the attitude of inquiry, without which appreciation means nothing, where does one of these provinces end and the other begin? We may take the genius first or the behaviour first, but we inevitably proceed from the one to the other; we inevitably encamp, as it were, on the high central table-land that they have in common. How are we to arrive at a relation with the object to be penetrated if we are thus forever met by a locked door flanked with a sentinel who merely invites us to take it for edifying? We take it ourselves for attaching – which is the very essence of mysteries – and profess ourselves doomed forever to hang yearningly about it. An obscurity endured, in fine, one inch further, or one hour longer, than our necessity truly holds us to, strikes us but as an artificial spectre, a muffled object with waving arms, set up to keep appreciation down.

For it is never to be forgotten that we are here in presence of the human character the most magnificently endowed, in all time, with the sense of the life of man, and with the apparatus for recording it; so that of *him*, inevitably, it goes hardest of all with us to be told that we have nothing, or next to nothing, to do with the effect in him of this gift. If it does not satisfy us that the effect was to make him write *King Lear* and *Othello*, we are verily difficult to please: so it is, meanwhile, that the case for the obscurity is argued. That is sovereign, we reply, so far as it goes; but it tells us nothing of the effect on him of being *able* to write *Lear* and *Othello*. No scrap of testimony of what this may have been is offered us; it is the quarter in which our blankness is most blank, and in which we are yet most officiously put off. It is true of the poet in general – in nine examples out of ten – that his life is mainly inward, that is events and revolutions are his great impressions and deep vibrations, and that his 'personality' is all pictured in the publication of his verse. Shakespeare, we essentially feel, is the tenth, is the millionth example; not the sleek bachelor of music, the sensitive harp set once for all in the window to catch the air, but the spirit in hungry quest of every possible experience and adventure of the spirit, and which, betimes, with the boldest of all intellectual movements, was to leap from the window into the street. We are in the street, as it were, for admiration and wonder, when the incarnation alights, and it is of no edification to shrug shoulders at the felt impulse (when made manifest) to follow, to pursue, all breathlessly to track it on its quickly-taken way. Such a quest of imaginative experience, we can only feel, has itself constituted one of the greatest observed adventures of mankind; so that no point of the history of it, however far back seized, is premature for our fond attention. Half our connection with it is our desire to 'assist' at it; so how can we fail of curiosity and sympathy? The answer to which is doubtless again that these impulses are very well, but that as the case stands they can move but in one channel. We are free to assist in the Plays themselves – to assist at whatever we like; so long, that is, as, after the fashion I have noted, we rigidly limit our inductions from them. It is put to us once more that we can make no bricks without straw, and that, rage as we may against our barrier, it none the less stubbornly exists. Granted on behalf of the vaulting spirit all that we claim for it, it still, in the street, as we say – and in spite of the effect we see it as acrobatically producing there – absolutely defies pursuit. Beyond recovery, beyond curiosity, it was to lose itself in the crowd. The crowd, for that matter, the witnesses we must take as astonished and dazzled, has, though itself surviving but in a dozen or two dim, scarce articulate ghosts, been interrogated to the last man and the last distinguishable echo. This has practically elicited nothing – nothing, that is, of a nature to gratify the indiscreetly, the morbidly inquisitive; since we find ourselves not rarely reminded that morbidity may easily become a vice. *He* was notoriously not morbid; he stuck to his

441

business – save when he so strangely gave it up; wherefore his own common sense about things in general is a model for the tone he should properly inspire. 'You speak of his career as a transcendent "adventure", as *the* conspicuously transcendent adventure – even to the sight of his contemporaries – of the mind of man; but no glimmer of any such story, of any such figure or "presence", to use your ambiguous word, as you desire to read into the situation, can be discerned in any quarter. So what is it you propose we should do? What evidence do you suggest that, with this absence of material, we should put together? We have what we have; we are not concerned with what we have not.'

In some such terms as that, one makes out, does the best attainable 'appreciation' appear to invite us to let our great personage, the mighty adventurer, slink past. He slunk past in life: that was good enough for him, the contention appears to be. Why therefore should he not slink past in immortality? One's reply can indeed only be that he evidently must; yet I profess that, even while saying so, our poor point, for which *The Tempest* once more gives occasion, strikes me as still, as always, in its desperate way, worth the making. The question, I hold, will eternally interest the student of letters and of the human understanding, and the envied privilege of our play in particular will be always to keep it before him. *How* did the faculty so radiant there contrive, in such perfection, the arrest of its divine flight? By what inscrutable process was the extinguisher applied and, when once applied, kept in its place to the end? What became of the checked torrent, as a latent, bewildered presence and energy, in the life across which the dam was constructed? What other mills did it set itself turning, or what contiguous country did it – rather indeed did it *not*, in default of these – inevitably ravage? We are referred, for an account of the matter, to recorded circumstances which are only not supremely vulgar because they are supremely dim and few; in which character they but mock, and as if all consciously, as I have said, at our unrest. The one at all large indication they give is that our hero may have died – since he died so soon – of his unnatural effort. Their quality, however, redeems them a little by having for its effect that they throw us back on the work itself with a rebellious renewal of appetite and yearning. The secret that baffles us being the secret of the Man, we know, as I have granted, that we shall never touch the

Man *directly* in the Artist. We stake our hopes thus on indirectness, which may contain possibilities; we take that very truth for our counsel of despair, try to look at it as helpful for the Criticism of the future. That of the past has been too often infantile; one has asked one's self how it *could*, on such lines, get at him. The figured tapestry, the long arras that hides him, is always there, with its immensity of surface and its proportionate underside. May it not then be but a question, for the fulness of time, of the finer weapon, the sharper point, the stronger arm, the more extended lunge?

❧

PREFACES TO THE NEW YORK EDITION

James started writing the Prefaces in 1906 and they were published with the Edition from 1907 to 1909. The Edition sold very poorly indeed and became a source of bitterness to James. But the Prefaces were an odd and influential success. In a powerful frame of mind in 1908 he wrote to W. D. Howells that he intended them to make up 'in general, a sort of plea for Criticism, for Discrimination, for Appreciation on other than infantile lines – as against the so almost universal Anglo-Saxon absence of these things . . .' And they are indeed, in a way, the last word in James's (though not Jamesian) criticism. They enjoy the peculiar freedoms of an artist writing about himself at relatively uninhibited length for an audience which can be assumed both informed and stable – an ideal public – even though he was quite realistically aware that 'ninety-nine readers in a hundred have no use whatever' for this kind of thought. There is none of the reviewer's need to explain and apologize; and there is a natural free reign given to James's frequently confessed later tendency to 're-do' in his own terms anything he read. As he notes in the preface to *The Golden Bowl* he is, in a way, recording a reading which is also a revision and finds it deeply congenial. So the tone is of a rapt fireside conversation, authoritative but intimate, and conducted under the liberating assumption that what is talked of is indeed of the highest importance. An initiated and enthusiastic reader is implied, and James often moves with fine assurance into a kind of dramatized form, a form which he had frequently used with great success in some of his happiest criticism (e.g., in '*Daniel Deronda*: A Conversation' No. 18); and also, of course, in his fictions about fiction, of which 'The Story in It' 1902, is an excellent example, not so well known or as profound as, for instance, 'The Lesson of the Master', but closer in time). ' "Why the deuce then Fleda Vetch, why a mere little flurried bundle of petticoats, why not Hamlet or Milton's Satan at once, if you're going in for a superior display of 'mind'?"' an objector demands in the preface to *The Spoils of Poynton*, and is authoritatively answered. This kind of thing is constructive and amusing and it recalls interestingly impressions of the argumentative, cultured and sparky nature of the extraordinary James family as given, for example, by Edward Emerson in 1861:

Wilky ... would say something and be instantly corrected by the little cock-sparrow Bob ... but good-naturedly defend his statement and then Henry ... would emerge from his silence in defence of Wilkie. Then Bob would be more impertinently insistent, and Mr James would advance as Moderator, and William, the eldest, join in ...

James as a critic remained a person formed by lively and educated debate amongst peers; and the conditions of the Prefaces allowed him strongly and intimately to show it. They also allowed the fullest flowering of his tendency to establish his argument by means of the logical and rigorous elaboration of metaphors and similes, earlier splendidly deployed in, e.g., 'The Art of Fiction', 1884 (No. 26, and see my introduction), but here at the very heart of the enterprise.

It is no wonder then that the Prefaces were influential. They became a quarry and source book for those interested in the discussion of prose fiction at a high level. They were used, for example, by Joseph Warren Beach in *The Method of Henry James* (1918) and most famously by Percy Lubbock, another committed 'Jamesian' and editor of the *Letters*, in *The Craft of Fiction* (1921). They provided a new and exciting vocabulary and series of exemplary methods for a pursuit which had hitherto had to rely on the excellence of its impressions and on crude and vague terms such as 'character', 'plot', 'description', 'story' and suchlike. James had remarked to Howells that '. . . it will be long before I shall want to collect them together', but it was exactly this that appealed to R. P. Blackmur when he assembled them with an introduction in 1934 under the title *The Art of the Novel*. This is certainly the single most influential volume of criticism of the novel in English yet to appear.

I have already indicated some of my reservations about the divided nature of this influence in my introduction. For a fuller account of its sometimes baleful effects see chapter 2 of Wayne C. Booth's *The*

Rhetoric of Fiction, 1961. More specifically: Blackmur was a pioneer and a fanatic for James's writing over fifty years ago, when the latter's reputation was at its lowest. As a result his work has originality and elegance coupled with a seriously damaging, but pardonable, exaggeration of the importance of his subject. In the unhappy event it has been fed into a heavy academic industry with a proneness to fall for *any* new aesthetic routines, with results which would have dismayed him. James's reputation for the formidable and arcane has been massively reinforced at the expense of the general reader; and the new language for the discussion of fiction created by the Prefaces has tended, except in the most sensitive of hands, to become a kind of jargon, often unaware of its own roots. Many critics who talk of 'centres of consciousness', 'dramatic vs. scenic' or 'selection' seem to have but the slenderest notion that they are using an apparatus devised in passionate and self-delighting consideration of a series of very special novels. Sometimes this does no harm. But often the new light given by James has been changed into a turbid mist of impressive but vague terminology, the slightly dank smell of which disturbs even the most innocent and eager and likely readers. In addition, Blackmur's most extraordinary claim makes even less sense now than it did, I imagine, in 1934. Referring to the same letter to Howells he quotes James's opinion that the Prefaces 'ought . . . to form a sort of comprehensive manual or *vade-mecum* for aspirants in our arduous profession'. This was a fine hope for James, who naturally at this time saw his own method as the best method or even the only really good one as compared, for example, with the 'large loose baggy monsters' of Tolstoy and Thackeray. But Blackmur expands it with the argument that whereas the imitators of masters such as Proust or Joyce remain mere imitators, lacking the original genius, the 'followers' of James can get, through the Prefaces, 'something of a technical mastery good for any subject, any attitude, any style'. This seems to me preposterously to misunderstand, through a pleasant excess of enthusiasm, the extremely personal nature of James's work, as well as the respectable limits of literary influence. It would take another creative writer – not just a commentator – to judge how generally useful the Prefaces are as a guide to writing. But it is easy to observe that while James does have many slight imitators there are only a few novelists of distinction who could be said to have learned from him – Edith Wharton, Ford Madox Ford and Elizabeth Bowen, for instance – and then most probably from his practice rather than his precepts. The Prefaces have naturally not become a novelist's handbook for reasons that we can appreciate while reading them. When, for example, he argues in the preface to *The Princess Casamassima* for the importance of having a strong or sensitive 'mind' at the centre of a novel, his affection for *Tom Jones* leads him to force his point into saying that Tom has so much 'life' and Fielding himself so much mind that it comes to roughly the same thing, which it clearly does not. The weakest parts of the Prefaces are when James departs from his own novels in favour of more or less binding generalization. Their real suggestiveness and use is much more subtle and specific. Therefore Blackmur's argument has served largely to add a spurious prestige to various, somewhat dubious 'arts' and 'crafts' of fiction, at some expense to the genuine achievement of the Prefaces, which is to create a great discursive example of such power, intelligence, goodwill and point as to have made the key words and concepts – 'centre of consciousness', 'point of view', 'economy' and so on, even *'ficelle'* – into potent *terms of art* for discussion of the novel. The terms are often inefficiently used, as I have remarked; but they and the fine logic behind them remain indispensable. It is for this that we have to thank Blackmur – and James.

No collection of James's criticism would, therefore, be at all complete without supplying a firm idea of the eighteen prefaces. Obviously I am unable to include them all, but as is often noticed the first five – to *Roderick Hudson* (RH), *The American* (A), *The Portrait of a Lady* (PL), *The Princess Casamassima* (PC) and *The Tragic Muse* (TM) – fortunately announce most of the leading ideas and exemplify the general manner. They lay out the intellectual ground and are incidentally (to encourage those who wish to read further) the most lush and austere. To these I add the wonderful preface to *The Wings of the Dove* (WD) which resembles that to *The Tragic Muse* in becoming, when considering what James thought failure, more specifically illuminating about the text than is elsewhere the case – which is why I have preferred it to his more celebrated and celebratory remarks on *The Ambassadors*. 'We are never as curious about successes as about interesting failures,' as he

said of Balzac. In addition, I have reprinted excerpts from most of the
other Prefaces which elaborate arguments from the first five, or
initiate others. To help and encourage the reader in finding his way
around, and in thin emulation of Blackmur, I here offer a list of a few
of the chief topics, or *leitmotivs*, with the strong proviso that they are
only a few and that they derive their importance, like real *leitmotivs*,
from their context. Most of them are inextricably interrelated to each
other and to other arguments beside, and though we do not precisely
murder in isolating them for convenience we might be conscien-
tiously aware of the demerits of dissection. The prefaces are indicated by the initials of the novels as given above; and page references
are added for further convenience.

1. *The Germ of a Subject*: A 465–7; PL 481–4, 485–7; PC
   495–7; TM 511–13; *Spoils of Poynton* 529–31; *What Maisie
   Knew* 534–5; *Ambassadors* 563–4.

2. *The Centre of Consciousness and Point of View*: RH 460–61;
   A 475–7; PL 489; PC 497–8, 504–5 and *passim*; TM 519–20;
   What Maisie Knew 533–4; WD 556–8; *Ambassadors* 564–5.

3. *Intensity and Economy of Treatment*: RH 457–8; PL 487–90,
   493–4; PC 499–501, 503–4; TM 518; *Awkward Age* 527.

4. *Composition*: TM 515–18, 526; *Spoils of Poynton* 531–2;
   Daisy Miller 545–6; WD 553–9.

5. *Plot and 'Story'*: PL 481–3, 492–4; TM 515–16; *Altar of the
   Dead* 543–4; *Ambassadors* 563–4.

6. *Representation and Meaning*: A 478; PC 501–2; TM 523;
   What Maisie Knew 523–4; WD 548–51; *Golden Bowl* 567–8.

7. *'Ficelles'*: PL 491–2; PC 498, 501–2; *Spoils of Poynton* 532;
   Ambassadors 565–6.

8. *The Scenic and the Dramatic*: TM 519–21; *Awkward Age*
   528; *What Maisie Knew* 535–6; WD 555–7.

9. *Entertaining the Reader*: PL 491, 494; PC 499; *Aspern Papers*
   538–9.

10. *The Artist and Life*: TM *passim*; *Lesson of the Master* 541–2.

To these might be added references to such *loci classici* as: *Selection*
RH 452; *Time Scheme* RH 457–60; TM 518; *Independent Characters* RH 463; PL 485–6; PC 506–8; *Unconscious Cerebration*

A 466; *Romance* A472–6; *Vitality of the Novel* PL 485; *Morality* PL 484–5; *Foreshortening Daisy Miller* 545–6; WD 561–2.

The following selections each have their own headnote. Those who wish to extend their reading will find that many editions of the novels trustingly use the relevant Preface without seeming quite to know what they are doing – thus rather dauntingly confronting the reader intent on early James fiction with what often must appear as a barrier of late James criticism. But here the fine absolutism of Blackmur is fortunately tempered by my freedom to offer an experience of the Prefaces in a much larger context – that of the many other sides of James's brilliant critical mind; which is in itself some reason for compiling this selection.

It will be noticed how often and how persuasively James uses *Shakespeare* as one of the absolute terms of his argument.

---✤---

56

Preface to Roderick Hudson. *Contrary to what James says this novel was not his 'first attempt'.* Watch and Ward *was published in the* Atlantic Monthly *in 1871, although not as a book until 1878. Presumably he thought it best left in obscurity.*

RODERICK HUDSON was begun in Florence in the spring of 1874, designed from the first for serial publication in *The Atlantic Monthly*, where it opened in January 1875 and persisted through the year. I yield to the pleasure of placing these circumstances on record, as I shall place others, and as I have yielded to the need of renewing acquaintance with the book after a quarter of a century. This revival of an all but extinct relation with an early work may often produce for an artist, I think, more kinds of interest and emotion than he shall find it easy to express, and yet will light not a little, to his eyes, that veiled face of his Muse which he is condemned for ever and all anxiously to study. The art of representation bristles with questions the very terms of which are difficult to apply and to appreciate; but whatever makes it arduous makes it, for our refreshment, infinite, causes the practice of it, with experience, to spread around us in a widening, not in a narrowing circle. Therefore it is that experience has to organize, for convenience and cheer, some system of observation – for fear, in the admirable immensity, of losing its way. We see it as pausing from time to time to consult its notes, to measure, for guidance, as many aspects and distances as possible, as many steps taken and obstacles mastered and fruits gathered and beauties enjoyed. Everything counts, nothing is superfluous in such a survey; the explorer's note-book strikes me here as endlessly receptive. This accordingly is what I mean by the contributive value – or put it simply as, to one's own sense, the beguiling charm – of the *accessory* facts in a given artistic case. This is why, as one looks back, the private history of any sincere work, however modest its pretensions, looms with its own completeness in the rich, ambiguous aesthetic air, and seems at once to borrow a dignity and to mark, so to say, a station. This is why, reading over, for revision, correction and republication, the volumes here in hand, I find myself, all attentively, in presence of some such recording scroll or engraved commemorative table – from which the 'private' character, moreover, quite insists on dropping out. These notes represent, over a considerable course, the continuity of an artist's endeavour, the growth of his whole operative consciousness and, best of all, perhaps, their own tendency to multiply, with the implication, thereby, of a memory much enriched. Addicted to 'stories' and inclined to retrospect, he fondly takes, under this backward view, his whole unfolding, his process of production, for a thrilling tale, almost for a wondrous adventure, only asking himself at what stage of remembrance the mark of the relevant will begin to fail. He frankly proposes to take this mark everywhere for granted.

Roderick Hudson was my first attempt at a novel, a long fiction with a 'complicated' subject, and I recall again the quite uplifted sense with which my idea, such as it was, permitted me at last to put quite out to sea. I had but hugged the shore on sundry previous small occasions; bumping about, to acquire skill, in the shallow waters and sandy coves of the 'short story' and master as yet of no vessel constructed to carry a sail. The subject of *Roderick* figured to me vividly this employment of canvas, and I have not forgotten, even after long years, how the blue southern sea seemed to spread immediately before me and the breath of the spice-islands to be already in the breeze. Yet it must even then have begun for me too, the ache of fear, that was to become so familiar, of being unduly tempted and led on by 'developments'; which is but the desperate discipline of the question involved in them. They are of the very essence of the novelist's process, and it is by their aid, fundamentally, that his idea takes form and lives; but they impose on him, through the principle of continuity that rides them, a proportionate anxiety. They are the very condition of interest, which languishes and drops without them; the painter's subject consisting ever, obviously, of the related state, to each other, of certain figures and things. To exhibit these relations, once they have all been recognized, is to 'treat' his idea, which involves neglecting none of those that directly minister to interest; the degree of that directness remaining meanwhile a matter of highly difficult appreciation, and one on which felicity of form and composition, as a part of the total effect, mercilessly rests. Up to what point is such and such a development *indispensable* to the interest? What is the point beyond which it ceases to be rigorously so? Where, for the complete expression of one's subject, does a particular relation stop – giving way to some other not concerned in that expression?

Really, universally, relations stop nowhere, and the exquisite problem of the artist is eternally but to draw, by a geometry of his own, the circle within which they shall happily *appear* to do so. He is in the perpetual predicament that the continuity of things is the whole matter, for him, of comedy and tragedy; that this continuity is never, by the space of an instant or an inch, broken, and that, to do anything at all, he has at once intensely to consult and intensely to ignore it. All of which will perhaps pass but for a supersubtle way of pointing the plain moral that a young embroiderer of the canvas of life soon began to work in terror, fairly, of the vast expanse of that surface, of the boundless number of its distinct perforations for the needle, and of the tendency inherent in his many-coloured flowers and figures to cover and consume as many as possible of the little holes. The development of the flower, of the figure, involved thus an immense counting of holes and a careful selection among them. That would have been, it seemed to him, a brave enough process, were it not the very nature of the holes so to invite, to solicit, to persuade, to practise positively a thousand lures and deceits. The prime effect of so sustained a system, so prepared a surface, is to lead on and on; while the fascination of following resides, by the same token, in the presumability *somewhere* of a convenient, of a visibly-appointed stopping-place. Art would be easy indeed if, by a fond power disposed to 'patronize' it, such conveniences, such simplifications, had been provided. We have, as the case stands, to invent and establish them, to arrive at them by a difficult, dire process of selection and comparison, of surrender and sacrifice. The very meaning of expertness is acquired courage to brace one's self for the cruel crisis from the moment one sees it grimly loom.

Roderick Hudson was further, was earnestly pursued during a summer partly spent in the Black Forest and (as I had returned to America early in September) during three months passed near Boston. It is one of the silver threads of the recoverable texture of that embarrassed phase, however, that the book was not finished when it had to begin appearing in monthly fragments: a fact in the light of which I find myself live over again, and quite with wonderment and tenderness, so intimate an experience of difficulty and delay. To have 'liked' so much writing it, to have worked out with such conviction the pale embroidery, and yet not, at the end of so many months, to have come through, was clearly still to have fallen short of any facility and any confidence: though the long-drawn process now most appeals to memory, I confess, by this very quality of shy and groping duration. One fact about it indeed outlives all others; the fact that, as the loved Italy was the scene of my fiction – so much more loved than one has ever been able, even after fifty efforts, to say! – and as having had to leave it persisted as an inward ache, so there was soreness in still contriving, after a fashion, to hang about it and in prolonging, from month to month, the illusion of the golden air. Little enough of that medium may the novel, read over to-day, seem to supply; yet half the actual interest lurks for me in the earnest, baffled intention of making it felt. A whole side of the old consciousness, under this mild pressure, flushes up and prevails again; a reminder, ever so penetrating, of the quantity of 'evocation' involved in my plan, and of the quantity I must even have supposed myself to achieve. I take the lingering perception of all this, I may add – that is of the various admonitions of the whole reminiscence – for a signal instance of the way a work of art, however small, if but sufficiently sincere, may vivify and even dignify the accidents and incidents of its growth.

I must that winter (which I again like to put on record that I spent in New York) have brought up my last instalments in due time, for I recall no haunting anxiety: what I do recall perfectly is the felt pleasure, during those months – and in East Twenty-fifth Street! – of trying, on the other side of the world, still to surround with the appropriate local glow the characters that had combined, to my vision, the previous year in Florence. A benediction, a great advantage, as seemed to me, had so from the first rested on them, and to nurse them along was really to sit again in the high, charming, shabby old room which had originally overarched them and which, in the hot May and June, had looked out, through the slits of cooling shutters, at the rather dusty but ever-romantic glare of Piazza Santa Maria Novella. The house formed the corner (I delight to specify) of Via della Scala, and I fear that what the early chapters of the book most 'render' to me to-day is not the umbrageous air of their New England town, but the view of the small cab-stand sleepily disposed – long before the days of strident electric cars – round the rococo obelisk of the Piazza, which is supported on its pedestal, if I remember rightly, by four delightful little elephants. (That, at any rate, is how the object in question, deprecating verification, comes back to me with the clatter of the horse-pails, the discussions, in the intervals of repose under well-drawn hoods, of the unbuttoned *cocchieri*, sons of the most garrulous of races, and the occasional stillness as of the noonday desert.)

Pathetic, as we say, on the other hand, no doubt, to reperusal, the manner in which the evocation, so far as attempted, of the small New England town of my first two chapters, fails of intensity – if intensity, in such a connexion, had been indeed to be looked for. *Could* I verily, by the terms of my little plan, have 'gone in' for it at the best, and even though one of these terms was the projection, for my fable, at the outset, of some more or less vivid antithesis to a state of civilization providing for 'art'? What I wanted, in essence, was the image of some perfectly humane community which was yet all incapable of providing for it, and I had to take what my scant experience furnished me. I remember feeling meanwhile no drawback in this scantness, but a complete, an exquisite little adequacy, so that the presentation arrived at would quite have served its purpose, I think, had I not misled myself into naming my place. To name a place, in fiction, is to pretend in some degree to represent it – and I speak here of course but of the use of existing names, the only ones that carry weight. I wanted one that carried weight – so at least I supposed; but obviously I was wrong, since my effect lay, so superficially, and could only lie, in the local *type*, as to which I had my handful of impressions. The particular local case was another matter, and I was to see again, after long years, the case into which, all recklessly, the opening passages of *Roderick Hudson* put their foot. I was to have nothing then, on the spot, to sustain me but the rather feeble plea that I had not *pretended* so very much to 'do' Northampton Mass. The plea was charmingly allowed, but nothing could have been more to the point than the way in which, in such a situation, the whole question of the novelist's 'doing', with its eternal wealth, or in other words its eternal torment of interest, once more came up. He embarks, rash adventurer, under the star of 'representation', and is pledged thereby to remember that the art of interesting us in things – once these things are the right ones for his case – can *only* be the art of representing them. This relation to them, for invoked interest, involves his accordingly 'doing'; and it is for him to settle with his intelligence what that variable process shall commit him to.

Its fortune rests primarily, beyond doubt, on somebody's having, under suggestion, a *sense* for it – even the reader will do, on occasion, when the writer, as so often happens, completely falls out. The way in which this sense has been, or has not been, applied constitutes, at all events, in respect to any fiction, the very ground of critical appreciation. Such appreciation takes account, primarily, of the thing, in the case, to have *been* done, and I now see what, for the first and second chapters of *Roderick*, that was. It was a peaceful, rural New England community *quelconque* – it was not, it was under no necessity of being, Northampton Mass. But one nestled, technically, in those days, and with yearning, in the great shadow of Balzac; his august example, little as the secret might ever be guessed, towered for me over the scene; so that what was clearer than anything else was how, if it was a question of Saumur, of Limoges, of Guérande, he 'did' Saumur, did Limoges, did Guérande. I remember how, in my feebler fashion, I yearned over the preliminary presentation of my small square patch of the American scene, and yet was not sufficiently on my guard to see how easily his high practice might be delusive for my case. Balzac talked of Nemours and Provins: therefore why shouldn't one, with fond fatuity, talk of almost the only small American *ville de province* of which one had happened to lay up, long before, a pleased vision? The reason was plain: one was not in the least, in one's prudence, emulating his systematic closeness. It didn't confuse the question either that he would verily, after all, addressed as he was to a due density in his material, have found little enough in Northampton Mass to tackle. He tackled no group of appearances, no presented face of the social organism (conspicuity thus attending it), *but* to make something of it. To name it simply and not in some degree tackle it would have seemed to him an act reflecting on his general course the deepest dishonour. Therefore it was that, as the moral of these many remarks, I 'named', under his contagion, when I was really most conscious of not being held to it; and therefore it was, above all, that for all the effect of representation I was to achieve, I might have let the occasion pass. A 'fancy' indication would have served my turn – except that I should so have failed perhaps of a pretext for my present insistence.

Since I do insist, at all events, I find this ghostly interest perhaps even more reasserted for me by the questions begotten within the very covers of the book, those that wander and idle there as in some sweet old overtangled walled garden, a safe paradise of self-criticism. Here it is that if there be air for it to breathe at all, the critical question swarms, and here it is, in particular, that one of the happy hours of the painter's long day may strike. I speak of the painter in general and of his relation to the old picture, the work of his hand, that has been lost to sight and that, when found again, is put back on the easel for measure of what time and the weather may, in the interval, have done to it. Has it too fatally faded, has it blackened or 'sunk', or otherwise abdicated, or has it only, blest thought, strengthened, for its allotted duration, and taken up, in its degree, poor dear brave thing, some shade of the all appreciable, yet all indescribable grace that we know as pictorial 'tone'? The anxious artist has to wipe it over, in the first place, to see; he has to 'clean it up', say, or to varnish it anew, or at the least to place it in a light, for any right judgment of its aspect or its worth. But the very uncertainties themselves yield a thrill, and if subject and treatment, working together, have had their felicity, the artist, the prime creator, may find a strange charm in this stage of the connexion. It helps him to live back into a forgotten state, into convictions, credulities too early spent perhaps, it breathes upon the dead reasons of things, buried as they are in the texture of the work, and makes them revive, so that the actual appearances and the old motives fall together once more, and a lesson and a moral and a consecrating final light are somehow disengaged.

All this, I mean of course, if the case will wonderfully take any such pressure, if the work doesn't break down under even such mild overhauling. The author knows well enough how easily that may happen – which he in fact frequently enough sees it do. The old reasons then are too dead to revive; they were not, it is plain, good enough reasons to live. The only possible relation of the present mind to the thing is to dismiss it altogether. On the other hand, when it is not dismissed – as the only detachment is the detachment of aversion – the creative intimacy is reaffirmed, and appreciation, critical apprehension, insists on becoming as active as it can. Who shall say, granted this, where it shall not begin and where it shall consent to end? The painter who passes over his old sunk canvas the wet sponge that shows him what may still come out again makes his criticism essentially active. When having seen, while his momentary glaze remains, that the canvas *has* kept a few buried secrets, he proceeds to repeat the process with due care and with a bottle of varnish and a brush, he is 'living back', as I say, to the top of his bent, is taking up the old relation, so workable apparently, yet, and there is nothing logically to stay him from following it all the way. I have felt myself then, on looking over past productions, the painter making use again and again of the tentative wet sponge. The sunk surface has here and there, beyond doubt, refused to respond: the buried secrets, the intentions, are buried too deep to rise again, and were indeed, it would appear, not much worth the burying. Not so, however, when the moistened canvas does obscurely flush and when resort to the varnish-bottle is thereby immediately indicated. The simplest figure for my revision of this present array of earlier, later, larger, smaller, canvases, is to say that I have achieved it by the very aid of the varnish-bottle. It is true of them throughout that, in words I have had occasion to use in another connexion (where too I had revised with a view to 'possible amendment of form and enhancement of meaning'), I have 'nowhere scrupled to re-write a sentence or a passage on judging it susceptible of a better turn'.

To re-read *Roderick Hudson* was to find one remark so promptly and so urgently prescribed that I could at once only take it as pointing almost too stern a moral. It stared me in the face that the time-scheme of the story is quite inadequate, and positively to that degree that the fault but just fails to wreck it. The thing escapes, I conceive, with its life: the effect sought is fortunately more achieved than missed, since the interest of the subject bears down, auspiciously dissimulates, this particular flaw in the treatment. Everything occurs, none the less, too punctually and moves too fast: Roderick's disintegration, a gradual process, and of which the exhibitional interest is exactly that it *is* gradual and occasional, and thereby traceable and watchable, swallows two years in a mouthful, proceeds quite *not* by years, but by weeks and months, and thus renders the whole view the disservice of appearing to present him as a morbidly special case. The very claim of the fable is naturally that he *is* special, that his great gift makes and keeps him highly exceptional; but that is not for a moment supposed to preclude his appearing typical (of the general type) as well; for the fictive hero successfully appeals to us only as an eminent instance, as eminent as we like, of our own conscious kind. My mistake on Roderick's behalf – and not in the least of conception, but of composition and expression – is that, at the rate at which he falls to pieces, he seems to place himself beyond our understanding and our sympathy. These are not our rates, we say; we ourselves certainly, under like pressure – for what is it after all? – would make more of a fight. We conceive going to pieces – nothing is easier, since we see people do it, one way or another, all round us; but this young man must either have had less of the principle of development to have had so much of the principle of collapse, or less of the principle of collapse to have had so much of the principle of development. 'On the basis of so great a weakness,' one hears the reader say, 'where was your idea of the interest? On the basis of so great an interest, where is the provision for so much weakness?' One feels indeed, in the light of this challenge, on how much too scantly projected and suggested a field poor Roderick and his large capacity for ruin are made to turn round. It has all begun too soon, as I say, and too simply, and the determinant function attributed to Christina Light, the character of well-nigh sole agent of his catastrophe that this unfortunate young woman has forced upon her, fails to commend itself to our sense of truth and proportion.

It was not, however, that I was at ease on this score even in the first fond good faith of composition; I felt too, all the while, how many more ups and downs, how many more adventures and complications my young man would have had to know, how much more experience it would have taken, in short, either to make him go under or to make him triumph. The greater complexity, the superior truth, was all more or less present to me; only the question was, too dreadfully, how make it present to the reader? How boil down so many facts in the alembic, so that the distilled result, the produced appearance, should have intensity, lucidity, brevity, beauty, all the merits required for my effect? How, when it was already so difficult, as I found, to proceed even as I *was* proceeding? It didn't help, alas, it only maddened, to remember that Balzac would have known how, and would have yet asked no additional credit for it. All the difficulty I could dodge still struck me, at any rate, as leaving more than enough; and yet I was already consciously in presence, here, of the most interesting question the artist has to consider. To give the image and the sense of certain things while still keeping them subordinate to his plan, keeping them in relation to matters more immediate and apparent, to give all the sense, in a word, without all the substance or all the surface, and so to summarize and foreshorten, so to make values both rich and sharp, that the mere procession of items and profiles is not only, for the occasion, superseded, but is, for essential quality, almost 'compromised' – such a case of delicacy proposes itself at every turn to the painter of life who wishes both to treat his chosen subject and to confine his necessary picture. It is only by doing such things that art becomes exquisite, and it is only by positively becoming exquisite that it keeps clear of becoming vulgar, repudiates the coarse industries that masquerade in its name. This eternal time-question is accordingly, for the novelist, always there and always formidable; always insisting on the *effect* of the great lapse and passage, of the 'dark backward and abysm', by the terms of truth, and on the effect of compression, of composition and form, by the terms of literary arrangement. It is really a business to terrify all but stout hearts into abject omission and mutilation, though the terror would indeed be more general were the general consciousness of the difficulty greater. It is not by consciousness of difficulty, in truth, that the story-teller is mostly ridden; so prodigious a number of stories would otherwise scarce get themselves (shall it be called?) 'told'. None was ever very well told, I think, under the law of mere elimination – inordinately as that device appears in many quarters to be depended on. I remember doing my best not to be reduced to it for *Roderick*, at the same time that I did so helplessly and consciously beg a thousand questions. What I clung to as my principle of simplification was the precious truth that I was dealing, after all, essentially with an Action, and that no action, further, was ever made historically vivid without a certain factitious compactness; though this logic indeed opened up horizons and abysses of its own. But into these we must plunge on some other occasion.

It was at any rate under an admonition or two fished out of their depths that I must have tightened my hold of the remedy afforded, such as it was, for the absence of those more adquate illustrations of Roderick's character and history. Since one was dealing with an Action one might borrow a scrap of the Dramatist's all-in-all, his intensity — which the novelist so often ruefully envies him as a fortune in itself. The amount of illustration I could allow to the grounds of my young man's disaster was unquestionably meagre, but I might perhaps make it lively; I might produce illusion if I should be able to achieve intensity. It was for that I must have tried, I now see, with such art as I could command; but I make out in another quarter above all what really saved me. My subject, all blissfully, in face of difficulties, had defined itself — and this in spite of the title of the book — as not directly, in the least, my young sculptor's adventure. This it had been but indirectly, being all the while in essence and in final effect another man's, his friend's and patron's, view and experience of him. One's luck was to have felt one's subject right — whether instinct or calculation, in those dim days, most served; and the circumstance even amounts perhaps to a little lesson that when this has happily occurred faults may show, faults may disfigure, and yet not upset the work. It remains in equilibrium by having found its centre, the point of command of all the rest. From this centre the subject has been treated, from this centre the interest has spread, and so, whatever else it may do or may not do, the thing has acknowledged a principle of composition and contrives at least to hang together. We see in such a case why it should so hang; we escape that dreariest displeasure it is open to experiments in this general order to inflict, the sense of any hanging-together precluded as by the very terms of the case.

The centre of interest throughout *Roderick* is in Rowland Mallet's consciousness, and the drama is the very drama of that consciousness — which I had of course to make sufficiently acute in order to enable it, like a set and lighted scene, to hold the play. By making it acute, meanwhile, one made its own movement – or rather, strictly, its movement in the particular connexion – interesting; this movement really being quite the stuff of one's thesis. It had, naturally, Rowland's consciousness, not to be *too* acute – which would have disconnected it and made it superhuman: the beautiful little problem was to keep it connected, connected intimately, with the general human exposure, and thereby bedimmed and befooled and bewildered, anxious, restless, fallible, and yet to endow it with such intelligence that the appearances reflected in it, and constituting together there the situation and the 'story', should become by that fact intelligible. Discernible from the first the joy of such a 'job' as this making of his relation to everything involved a sufficiently limited, a sufficiently pathetic, tragic, comic, ironic, personal state to be thoroughly natural, and yet at the same time a sufficiently clear medium to represent a whole. This whole was to be the sum of what 'happened' to him, or in other words his total adventure; but as what happened to him was above all to feel certain things happening to others, to Roderick, to Christina, to Mary Garland, to Mrs Hudson, to the Cavaliere, to the Prince, so the beauty of the constructional game was to preserve in everything its especial value for *him*. The ironic effect of his having fallen in love with the girl who is herself in love with Roderick, though he is unwitting, at the time, of that secret – the conception of this last irony, I must add, has remained happier than my execution of it; which should logically have involved the reader's being put into position to take more closely home the impression made by Mary Garland. The ground has not been laid for it, and when that is the case one builds all vainly in the air: one patches up one's superstructure, one paints it in the prettiest colours, one hangs fine old tapestry and rare brocade over its window-sills, one flies emblazoned banners from its roof – the building none the less totters and refuses to stand square.

It is not really *worked-in* that Roderick himself could have pledged his faith in such a quarter, much more at such a crisis, before leaving America: and that weakness, clearly, produces a limp in the whole march of the fable. Just so, though there was no reason on earth (unless I except one, presently to be mentioned) why Rowland should *not*, at Northampton, have conceived a passion, or as near an approach to one as he was capable of, for a remarkable young

woman there suddenly dawning on his sight, a particular fundamental care was required for the vivification of that possibility. The
care, unfortunately, has not been skilfully enough taken, in spite of
the later patching-up of the girl's figure. We fail to accept it, on the
actual showing, as that of a young person irresistible at any moment,
and above all irresistible at a moment of the liveliest *other* preoccupation, as that of the weaver of (even the highly conditioned)
spell that the narrative imputes to her. The spell of attraction is cast
upon young men by young women in all sorts of ways, and the novel
has no more constant office than to remind us of that. But Mary
Garland's way doesn't, indubitably, convince us; any more than we
are truly convinced, I think, that Rowland's destiny, or say his
nature, would have made him accessible at the same hour to two
quite distinct commotions, each a very deep one, of his whole
personal economy. Rigidly viewed, each of these upheavals of his
sensibility must have been exclusive of other upheavals, yet the
reader is asked to accept them as working together. They are
different vibrations, but the whole sense of the situation depicted is
that they should each have been of the strongest, too strong to walk
hand in hand. Therefore it is that when, on the ship, under the stars,
Roderick suddenly takes his friend into the confidence of his engagement, we instinctively disallow the friend's title to discomfiture. The
whole picture presents him as for the time on the mounting wave,
exposed highly enough, no doubt, to a hundred discomfitures, but
least exposed to that one. The damage to verisimilitude is deep.

The difficulty had been from the first that I required my antithesis—
my antithesis to Christina Light, one of the main terms of the subject.
One is ridden by the law that antitheses, to be efficient, shall be both
direct and complete. Directness seemed to fail unless Mary should
be, so to speak, 'plain', Christina being essentially so 'coloured'; and
completeness seemed to fail unless she too should have her potency.
She could moreover, by which I mean the antithetic young woman
could, perfectly have had it; only success would have been then in the
narrator's art to attest it. Christina's own presence and action are, on
the other hand, I think, all firm ground; the truth probably being that
the ideal antithesis rarely does 'come off', and that it has to content
itself for the most part with a strong term and a weak term, and even
then to feel itself lucky. If one of the terms *is* strong, that perhaps may

pass, in the most difficult of the arts, for a triumph. I remember at all
events feeling, toward the end of *Roderick*, that the Princess Casamassima had been launched, that, wound-up with the right silver
key, she would go on a certain time by the motion communicated;
thanks to which I knew the pity, the real pang of losing sight of her. I
desired as in no other such case I can recall to preserve, to recover the
vision; and I have seemed to myself in re-reading the book quite to
understand why. The multiplication of touches had produced even
more life than the subject required, and that life, in other conditions,
in some other prime relation, would still have somehow to be spent.
Thus one would watch for her and waylay her at some turn of the
road to come – all that was to be needed was to give her time. This I
did in fact, meeting her again and taking her up later on.

57

Preface to The American.

THE AMERICAN, which I had begun in Paris early in the winter of 1875–76, made its first appearance in *The Atlantic Monthly* in June of the latter year and continued there, from month to month, till May of the next. It started on its course while much was still unwritten, and there again come back to me, with this remembrance, the frequent hauntings and alarms of that comparatively early time; the habit of wondering what would happen if anything *should* 'happen', if one should break one's arm by an accident or make a long illness or suffer, in body, mind, fortune, any other visitation involving a loss of time. The habit of apprehension became of course in some degree the habit of confidence that one would pull through, that, with opportunity enough, grave interruption never yet *had* descended, and that a special Providence, in short, despite the sad warning of Thackeray's *Denis Duval* and of Mrs Gaskell's *Wives and Daughters* (that of Stevenson's *Weir of Hermiston* was yet to come) watches over anxious novelists condemned to the economy of serialization. I make myself out in memory as having at least for many months and in many places given my Providence much to do: so great a variety of scenes of labour, implying all so much renewal of application, glimmer out of the book as I now read it over. And yet as the faded interest of the whole episode becomes again mildly vivid what I seem most to recover is, in its pale spectrality, a degree of joy, an eagerness on behalf of my recital, that must recklessly enough have overridden anxieties of every sort, including any view of inherent difficulties.

I seem to recall no other like connexion in which the case was met, to my measure, by so fond a complacency, in which my subject can have appeared so apt to take care of itself. I see now that I might all the while have taken much better care of it; yet, as I had at the time no sense of neglecting it, neither acute nor rueful solicitude, I can but speculate all vainly to-day on the oddity of my composure. I ask myself indeed if, possibly, recognizing after I was launched the danger of an inordinate leak — since the ship has truly a hole in its side more than sufficient to have sunk it — I may not have managed, as a counsel of mere despair, to stop my ears against the noise of waters and *pretend* to myself I was afloat; being indubitably, in any case, at sea, with no harbour of refuge till the end of my serial voyage. If I succeeded at all in that emulation (in another sphere) of the pursued ostrich I must have succeeded altogether; must have buried my head in the sand and there found beatitude. The explanation of my enjoyment of it, no doubt, is that I was more than commonly enamoured of my idea, and that I believed it, so trusted, so imaginatively fostered, not less capable of limping to its goal on three feet than on one. The lameness might be what it would: I clearly, for myself, felt the thing *go* — which is the most a dramatist can ever ask of his drama; and I shall here accordingly indulge myself in speaking first of how, superficially, it did so proceed; explaining then what I mean by its practical dependence on a miracle.

It had come to me, this happy, halting view of an interesting case, abruptly enough, some years before: I recall sharply the felicity of the first glimpse, though I forget the accident of thought that produced it. I recall that I was seated in an American 'horse-car' when I found myself, of a sudden, considering with enthusiasm, as the theme of a 'story', the situation, in another country and an aristocratic society, of some robust but insidiously beguiled and betrayed, some cruelly wronged, compatriot: the point being in especial that he should suffer at the hands of persons pretending to represent the highest possible civilization and to be of an order in every way superior to his own. What would he 'do' in that predicament, how would he right himself, or how, failing a remedy, would he conduct himself under his wrong? This would be the question involved, and I remember well how, having entered the horse-car without a dream of it, I was presently to leave that vehicle in full possession of my answer. He would behave in the most interesting manner — it would all depend on that: stricken, smarting, sore, he would arrive at his just vindication and then would fail of all triumphantly and all vulgarly enjoying it. He would hold his revenge and cherish it and feel its sweetness, and then in the very act of forcing it home would sacrifice it in disgust. He would let them go, in short, his haughty contemners, even while feeling them, with joy, in his power, and he would obey, in so doing, one of the large and easy impulses *generally* characteristic of his type. He wouldn't 'forgive' – that would have, in the case, no application; he would simply turn, at the supreme moment, away, the bitterness of his personal loss yielding to the very force of his aversion. All he would have at the end would be therefore just the moral convenience, indeed the moral necessity, of his practical, but quite unappreciated, magnanimity; and one's last view of him would be that of a strong man indifferent to his strength and too wrapped in fine, too wrapped above all in *other* and intenser, reflexions for the assertion of his 'rights'. This last point was of the essence and constituted in fact the subject: there would be no subject at all, obviously – or simply the commonest of the common – if my gentleman should enjoy his advantage. I was charmed with my idea, which would take, however, much working out; and precisely because it had so much to give, I think, must I have dropped it for the time into the deep well of unconscious cerebration: not without the hope, doubtless, that it might eventually emerge from that reservoir, as one had already known the buried treasure to come to light, with a firm iridescent surface and a notable increase of weight.

This resurrection then took place in Paris, where I was at the moment living, and in December 1875; my good fortune being apparently that Paris had ever so promptly offered me, and with an immediate directness at which I now marvel (since I had come back there, after earlier visitations, but a few weeks before), everything that was needed to make my conception concrete. I seem again at this distant day to see it become so quickly and easily, quite as if filling itself with life in that air. The objectivity it had wanted it promptly put on, and if the questions had been, with the usual intensity, for my hero and his crisis – the whole formidable list, the who? the what? the where? the when? the why? the how? – they gathered their answers in the cold shadow of the Arc de Triomphe, for fine reasons, very much as if they had been plucking spring flowers for the weaving of a frolic garland. I saw from one day to another my particular cluster of circumstances, with the life of the splendid city playing up in it like a flashing fountain in a marble basin. The very splendour seemed somehow to witness and intervene; it was important for the effect of my friend's discomfiture that it should take place on a high and lighted stage, and that his original ambition, the project exposing him, should have sprung from beautiful and noble suggestions – those that, at certain hours and under certain impressions, we feel the many-tinted medium by the Seine irresistibly to communicate. It was all charmingly simple, this conception, and the current must have gushed, full and clear, to my imagination, from the moment Christopher Newman rose before me, on a perfect day of the divine Paris spring, in the great gilded Salon Carré of the Louvre. Under this strong contagion of the place he would, by the happiest of hazards, meet his old comrade, now initiated and domiciled; after which the rest would go of itself. If he was to be wronged he would be wronged with just that conspicuity, with his felicity at just that pitch and with the highest aggravation of the general effect of misery mocked at. Great and gilded the whole trap set, in fine, for his wary freshness and into which it would blunder upon its fate. I have, I confess, no memory of a disturbing doubt; once the man himself was imaged to me (and *that* germination is a process almost always untraceable) he must have walked into the situation as by taking a pass-key from his pocket.

But what then meanwhile would be the affront one would see him as most feeling? The affront of course done him as a lover; and yet not that done by his mistress herself, since injuries of this order are the stalest stuff of romance. I was not to have him jilted, any more than I was to have him successfully vindictive: both his wrong and his right would have been in these cases of too vulgar a type. I doubtless even then felt that the conception of Paris as the consecrated scene of rash infatuations and bold bad treacheries belongs, in the Anglo-Saxon imagination, to the infancy of art. The right renovation of any such theme as *that* would place it in Boston or at Cleveland, at Hartford or at Utica – give it some local connexion in which we had not already had so much of it. No, I should make my heroine herself, if heroine there was to be, an equal victim – just as Romeo was not less the sport of fate for not having been interestedly sacrificed by Juliet; and to this end I had but to imagine 'great people' again, imagine my hero confronted and involved with them, and impute to them, with a fine free hand, the arrogance and cruelty, the tortuous behaviour, in given conditions, of which great people have been historically so often capable. But as this was the light in which they were to show, so the essence of the matter would be that he should at the right moment find them in his power, and so the situation would reach its highest interest with the question of his utilization of that knowledge. It would be here, in the possession and application of his power, that he would come out strong and would so deeply appeal to our sympathy. Here above all it really was, however, that my conception unfurled, with the best conscience in the world, the emblazoned flag of romance; which venerable ensign it had, though quite unwittingly, from the first and at every point sported in perfect good faith. I had been plotting arch-romance without knowing it, just as I began to write it that December day without recognizing it and just as I all serenely and blissfully pursued the process from month to month and from place to place; just as I now, in short, reading the book over, find it yields me no interest and no reward comparable to the fond perception of this truth.

The thing is consistently, consummately – and I would fain really make bold to say charmingly – romantic; and all without intention, presumption, hesitation, contrition. The effect is equally undesigned and unabashed, and I lose myself, at this late hour, I am bound to add, in a certain sad envy of the free play of so much unchallenged instinct. One would like to woo back such hours of fine precipitation. They represent to the critical sense which the exercise of one's *whole* faculty has, with time, so inevitably and so thoroughly waked up, the happiest season of surrender to the invoked muse and the projected fable: the season of images so free and confident and ready that they brush questions aside and disport themselves, like the artless school-boys of Gray's beautiful Ode, in all the ecstasy of the ignorance attending them. The time doubtless comes soon enough when questions, as I call them, rule the roost and when the little victim, to adjust Gray's term again to the creature of frolic fancy, doesn't dare propose a gambol till they have all (like a board of trustees discussing a new outlay) sat on the possibly scandalous case. I somehow feel, accordingly, that it was lucky to have sacrificed on this particular altar while one still could; though it is perhaps droll – in a yet higher degree – to have done so not simply because one was guileless, but even quite under the conviction, in a general way, that, since no 'rendering' of any object and no painting of any picture can take effect without some form of reference and control, so these guarantees could but reside in a high probity of observation. I must decidedly have supposed, all the while, that I was acutely observing – and with a blest absence of wonder at its being so easy. Let me certainly at present rejoice in that absence; for I ask myself how without it I could have written *The American*.

Was it indeed meanwhile my excellent conscience that kept the charm as unbroken as it appears to me, in rich retrospect, to have remained? – or is it that I suffer the mere influence of remembered, of associated places and hours, all acute impressions, to palm itself off as the sign of a finer confidence than I could justly claim? It is a pleasure to perceive how again and again the shrunken depths of old work yet permit themselves to be sounded or – even if rather terrible the image – 'dragged': the long pole of memory stirs and rummages the bottom, and we fish up such fragments and relics of the submerged life and the extinct consciousness as tempt us to piece them together. My windows looked into the Rue de Luxembourg – since then meagerly re-named Rue Cambon – and the particular light Parisian click of the small cab-horse on the clear asphalt, with its sharpness of detonation between the high houses, makes for the faded page to-day a sort of interlineation of sound. This sound rises to a martial clatter at the moment a troop of cuirassiers charges down the narrow street, each morning, to file, directly opposite my house, through the plain portal of the barracks occupying part of the vast domain attached in a rearward manner to one of the Ministères that front on the Place Vendôme; an expanse marked, along a considerable stretch of the street, by one of those high painted and administratively-placarded garden walls that form deep, vague, recurrent notes in the organic vastness of the city. I have but to re-read ten lines to recall my daily effort not to waste time in hanging over the window-bar for a sight of the cavalry the hard music of whose hoofs so directly and thrillingly appealed; an effort that inveterately failed – and a trivial circumstance now dignified, to my imagination, I may add, by the fact that the fruits of this weakness, the various items of the vivid picture, so constantly recaptured, must have been in themselves suggestive and inspiring, must have been rich strains, in their way, of the great Paris harmony. I have ever, in general, found it difficult to write of places under too immediate an impression – the impression that prevents standing off and allows neither space nor time for perspective. The image has had for the most part to be dim if the reflexion was to be, as is proper for a reflexion, both sharp and quiet: one has a horror, I think, artistically, of agitated reflexions.

Perhaps that is why the novel, after all, was to achieve, as it went on, no great – certainly no very direct – transfusion of the immense overhanging presence. It had to save as it could its own life, to keep tight hold of the tenuous silver thread, the one hope for which was that it shouldn't be tangled or clipped. This earnest grasp of the silver thread was doubtless an easier business in other places – though as I remount the stream of composition I see it faintly coloured again: with the bright protection of the Normandy coast (I worked away a few weeks at Etretat); with the stronger glow of southernmost France, breaking in during a stay at Bayonne; then with the fine historic and other 'psychic' substance of Saint-Germain-en-Laye, a purple patch of terraced October before returning to Paris. There comes after that the memory of a last brief intense invocation of the enclosing scene, of the pious effort to unwind my tangle, with a firm hand, in the very light (that light of high, narrowish French windows in old rooms, the light somehow, as one always feels, of 'style' itself) that had quickened my original vision. I was to pass over to London that autumn; which was a reason the more for considering the matter – the matter of Newman's final predicament – with due intensity: to let a loose end dangle over into alien air would so fix upon the whole, I strenuously felt, the dishonour of piecemeal composition. Therefore I strove to finish – first in a small dusky hotel of the Rive Gauche, where, though the windows again were high, the days were dim and the crepuscular court, domestic, intimate, 'quaint', testified to ancient manners almost as if it had been that of Balzac's Maison Vauquer in *Le Père Goriot*: and then once more in the Rue de Luxembourg, where a black-framed Empire portrait-medallion, suspended in the centre of each white panel of my almost noble old salon, made the coolest, discreetest, most measured decoration, and where, through casements open to the last mildness of the year, a belated Saint Martin's summer, the tale was taken up afresh by the charming light click and clatter, that sound as of the thin, quick, quite feminine surface-breathing of Paris, the shortest of rhythms for so huge an organism.

I shall not tell whether I did there bring my book to a close – and indeed I shrink, for myself, from putting the question to the test of memory. I follow it so far, the old urgent ingenious business, and then I lose sight of it: from which I infer – all exact recovery of the matter failing – that I did not in the event drag over the Channel a lengthening chain; which would have been detestable. I reduce to the absurd perhaps, however, by that small subjective issue, any undue measure of the interest of this insistent recovery of what I have called attendant facts. There always has been, for the valid work of art, a history – though mainly inviting, doubtless, but to the curious critic, for whom such things grow up and are formed very much in the manner of attaching young lives and characters, those conspicuous cases of happy development as to which evidence and anecdote are always in order. The development indeed must be certain to have been happy, the life sincere, the character fine: the work of art, to create or repay critical curiosity, must in short have been very 'valid' indeed. Yet there is on the other hand no mathematical measure of that importance – it may be a matter of widely-varying appreciation; and I am willing to grant, assuredly, that this interest, in a given relation, will nowhere so effectually kindle as on the artist's own part. And I am afraid that after all even his best excuse for it must remain the highly personal plea – the joy of living over, as a chapter of experience, the particular intellectual adventure. Here lurks an immense homage to the general privilege of the artist, to that constructive, that creative passion – portentous words, but they are convenient – the exercise of which finds so many an occasion for appearing to him the highest of human fortunes, the rarest boon of the gods. He values it, all sublimely and perhaps a little fatuously, for itself – as the great extension, great beyond all others, of experience and of consciousness; with the toil and trouble a mere sun-cast shadow that falls, shifts and vanishes, the result of his living in so large a light. On the constant nameless felicity of this Robert Louis Stevenson has, in an admirable passage and as in so many other connexions, said the right word: that the partaker of the 'life of art' who repines at the absence of the rewards, as they are called, of the pursuit might surely be better occupied. Much rather should he endlessly wonder at his not having to pay half his substance for his luxurious immersion. He enjoys it, so to speak, without a tax; the effort of labour involved, the torment of expression, of which we have heard in our time so much, being after all but the last refinement of his privilege. It may leave him weary and worn; but how, after his fashion, he will have lived! As if one were to expect at once freedom and ease! That silly safety is but the sign of bondage and forfeiture. Who can imagine free selection – which is the beautiful, terrible *whole* of art – without free difficulty? This is the very franchise of the city and high ambition of the citizen. The vision of the difficulty, as one looks back, bathes one's course in a golden glow by which the very objects along the road are transfigured and glorified; so that one exhibits them to other eyes with an elation possibly presumptuous.

Since I accuse myself at all events of these complacencies I take advantage of them to repeat that I value, in my retrospect, nothing so much as the lively light on the romantic property of my subject that I had not expected to encounter. If in *The American* I invoked the romantic association without malice prepense, yet with a production of the romantic effect that is for myself unmistakeable, the occasion is of the best perhaps for penetrating a little the obscurity of that principle. By what art or mystery, what craft of selection, omission or commission, does a given picture of life appear to us to surround its theme, its figures and images, with the air of romance while another picture close beside it may affect us as steeping the whole matter in the element of reality? It is a question, no doubt, on the painter's part, very much more of perceived effect, effect *after* the fact, than of conscious design – though indeed I have ever failed to see how a coherent picture of anything is producible save by a complex of fine measurements. The cause of the deflexion, in one pronounced sense or the other, must lie deep, however; so that for the most part we recognize the character of our interest only after the particular magic, as I say, has thoroughly operated – and then in truth but if we be a bit critically minded, if we find our pleasure, that is, in these intimate appreciations (for which, as I am well aware, ninety-nine readers in a hundred have no use whatever). The determining condition would at any rate seem so latent that one may well doubt if the full artistic consciousness ever reaches it; leaving the matter thus a case, ever, not of an author's plotting and planning and calculating, but just of his feeling and seeing, of his conceiving, in a word, and of his thereby inevitably expressing himself, under the influence of one value or the other. These values represent different sorts and degrees of the communicable thrill, and I doubt if any novelist, for instance, ever proposed to commit himself to one kind or the other with as little mitigation as we are sometimes able to find for him. The interest is greatest – the interest of his genius, I mean, and of his general wealth – when he commits himself in both directions; not quite at the same time or to the same effect, of course, but by some need of performing his whole possible revolution, by the law of some rich passion in him for extremes.

Of the men of largest responding imagination before the human scene, of Scott, of Balzac, even of the coarse, comprehensive, prodigious Zola, we feel, I think, that the deflexion toward either quarter has never taken place; that neither the nature of the man's faculty nor the nature of his experience has ever quite determined it. His current remains therefore extraordinarily rich and mixed, washing us successively with the warm wave of the near and familiar and the tonic shock, as may be, of the far and strange. (In making which opposition I suggest not that the strange and the far are at all necessarily romantic: they happen to be simply the unknown, which is quite a different matter. The real represents to my perception the things we cannot possibly *not* know, sooner or later, in one way or another; it being but one of the accidents of our hampered state, and one of the incidents of their quantity and number, that particular instances have not yet come our way. The romantic stands, on the other hand, for the things that, with all the facilities in the world, all the wealth and all the courage and all the wit and all the adventure, we never *can* directly know; the things that can reach us only through the beautiful circuit and subterfuge of our thought and our desire.) There have been, I gather, many definitions of romance, as a matter indispensably of boats, or of caravans, or of tigers, or of 'historical characters', or of ghosts, or of forgers, or of detectives, or of beautiful wicked women, or of pistols and knives, but they appear for the most part reducible to the idea of the facing of danger, the acceptance of great risks for the fascination, the very love, of their uncertainty, the joy of success if possible and of battle in any case. This would be a fine formula if it bore examination; but it strikes me as weak and inadequate, as by no means covering the true ground and yet as landing us in strange confusions.

The panting pursuit of danger is the pursuit of life itself, in which danger awaits us possibly at every step and faces us at every turn; so that the dream of an intenser experience easily becomes rather some vision of a sublime security like that enjoyed on the flowery plains of heaven, where we may conceive ourselves proceeding in ecstasy from one prodigious phase and form of it to another. And if it be insisted that the measure of the type is then in the *appreciation* of danger – the sign of our projection of the real being the smallness of its dangers, and that of our projection of the romantic the hugeness, the mark of the distinction being in short, as they say of collars and gloves and shoes, the size and 'number' of the danger – this discrimination again surely fails, since it makes our difference not a difference of kind, which is what we want, but a difference only of degree, and subject by that condition to the indignity of a sliding scale and a shifting measure. There are immense and flagrant dangers that are but sordid and squalid ones, as we feel, tainting with their quality the very defiances they provoke; while there are common and covert ones, that 'look like nothing' and that can be but inwardly and occultly dealt with, which involve the sharpest hazards to life and honour and the highest instant decisions and intrepidities of action. It is an arbitrary stamp that keeps these latter prosaic and makes the former heroic; and yet I should still less subscribe to a mere 'subjective' division – I mean one that would place the difference wholly in the temper of the imperilled agent. It would be impossible to have a more romantic temper than Flaubert's Madame Bovary, and yet nothing less resembles a romance than the record of her adventures. To classify it by that aspect – the definition of the spirit that happens to animate her – is like settling the question (as I have seen it witlessly settled) by the presence or absence of 'costume'. Where again then does costume begin or end? – save with the 'run' of one or another sort of play? We must reserve vague labels for artless mixtures.

The only *general* attribute of projected romance that I can see, the only one that fits all its cases, is the fact of the kind of experience with which it deals – experience liberated, so to speak; experience disengaged, disembroiled, disencumbered, exempt from the conditions that we usually know to attach to it and, if we wish so to put the matter, drag upon it, and operating in a medium which relieves it, in a particular interest, of the inconvenience of a *related*, a measurable state, a state subject to all our vulgar communities. The greatest intensity may so be arrived at evidently – when the sacrifice of community, of the 'related' sides of situations, has not been too rash. It must to this end not flagrantly betray itself; we must even be kept if possible, for our illusion, from suspecting any sacrifice at all. The balloon of experience is in fact of course tied to the earth, and under that necessity we swing, thanks to a rope of remarkable length, in the more or less commodious car of the imagination; but it is by the rope we know where we are, and from the moment that cable is cut we are at large and unrelated: we only swing apart from the globe – though remaining as exhilarated, naturally, as we like, especially when all goes well. The art of the romancer is, 'for the fun of it', insidiously to cut the cable, to cut it without our detecting him. What I have recognized then in *The American*, much to my surprise and after long years, is that the experience here represented is the disconnected and uncontrolled experience – uncontrolled by our general sense of 'the way things happen' – which romance alone more or less successfully palms off on us. It is a case of Newman's own intimate experience all, that being my subject, the thread of which, from beginning to end, is not once exchanged, however momentarily, for any other thread; and the experience of others concerning us, and concerning him, only so far as it touches him and as he recognizes, feels or divines it. There is our general sense of the way things happen – it abides with us indefeasibly, as readers of fiction, from the moment we demand that our fiction shall be intelligible; and there is our particular sense of the way they don't happen, which is liable to wake up unless reflexion and criticism, in us, have been skilfully and successfully drugged. There are drugs enough, clearly – it is all a question of applying them with tact; in which case the way things don't happen may be artfully made to pass for the way things do.

Amusing and even touching to me, I profess, at this time of day, the ingenuity (worthy, with whatever lapses, of a better cause) with which, on behalf of Newman's adventure, this hocus-pocus is attempted: the value of the instance not being diminished either, surely, by its having been attempted in such evident good faith. Yes, all is romantic to my actual vision here, and not least so, I hasten to add, the fabulous felicity of my candour. The way things happen is frankly not the way in which they are represented as having happened, in Paris, to my hero: the situation I had conceived only saddled me with that for want of my invention of something better. The great house of Bellegarde, in a word, would, I now feel, given the circumstances, given the *whole* of the ground, have comported itself in a manner as different as possible from the manner to which my narrative commits it; of which truth, moreover, I am by no means sure that, in spite of what I have called my serenity, I had not all the while an uneasy suspicion. I had dug in my path, 'as, a hole into which I was destined to fall. I was so possessed of my idea that Newman should be ill-used – which was the essence of my subject – that I attached too scant an importance to its fashion of coming about. Almost any fashion would serve, I appear to have assumed, that would give me my main chance for him; a matter depending not so much on the particular trick played him as on the interesting face presented by him to *any* damnable trick. So where I part company with *terra-firma* is in making that projected, that performed outrage so much more showy, dramatically speaking, than sound. Had I patched it up to a greater apparent soundness my own trick, artistically speaking, would have been played; I should have cut the cable without my reader's suspecting it. I doubtless at the time, I repeat, believed I had taken my precautions; but truly they should have been greater, to impart the air of truth to the attitude – that is first to the pomp and circumstance, and second to the queer falsity – of the Bellegardes.

They would positively have jumped then, the Bellegardes, at my rich and easy American, and not have 'minded' in the least any drawback – especially as, after all, given the pleasant palette from which I have painted him, there were few drawbacks to mind. My subject imposed on me a group of closely-allied persons animated by immense pretensions – which was all very well, which might be full of the promise of interest: only of interest felt most of all in the light of comedy and of irony. This, better understood, would have dwelt in the idea not in the least of their not finding Newman good enough for their alliance and thence being ready to sacrifice him, but in that of their taking with alacrity everything he could give them, only asking for more and more, and then adjusting their pretensions and their pride to it with all the comfort in life. Such accommodation of the theory of a noble indifference to the practice of a deep avidity is the real note of policy in forlorn aristocracies – and I meant of course that the Bellegardes should be virtually forlorn. The perversion of truth is by no means, I think, in the displayed acuteness of their remembrance of 'who' and 'what' they are, or at any rate take themselves for; since it is the misfortune of all insistence on 'worldly' advantages – and the situation of such people bristles at the best (by which I mean under whatever invocation of a superficial simplicity) with emphasis, accent, assumption – to produce at times an effect of grossness. The picture of their tergiversation, at all events, however it may originally have seemed to me to hang together, has taken on this rococo appearance precisely because their preferred course, a thousand times preferred, would have been to haul him and his fortune into their boat under cover of night perhaps, in any case as quietly and with as little bumping and splashing as possible, and there accommodate him with the very safest and most convenient seat. Given Newman, given the fact that the thing constitutes itself organically as *his* adventure, that too might very well be a situation and a subject: only it wouldn't have been the theme of *The American* as the book stands, the theme to which I was from so early pledged. Since I had wanted a 'wrong' this other turn might even have been arranged to give me *that*, might even have been arranged to meet my requirement that somebody or something should be 'in his power' so delightfully; and with the signal effect, after all, of 'defining' everything. (It is as difficult, I said above, to trace the dividing-line between north and south; but I am not sure an infallible sign of the latter is not this rank vegetation of the 'power' of bad people that good get into, or *vice versa*. It is so rarely, alas, into *our* power that any one gets!)

It is difficult for me to-day to believe that I had not, as my work went on, *some* shade of the rueful sense of my affront to verisimilitude; yet I catch the memory at least of no great sharpness, no true critical anguish, of remorse: an anomaly the reason of which in fact now glimmers interestingly out. My concern, as I saw it, was to make and to keep Newman consistent; the picture of his consistency was all my undertaking, and the memory of *that* infatuation perfectly abides with me. He was to be the lighted figure, the others – even doubtless to an excessive degree the woman who is made the agent of his discomfiture – were to be the obscured; by which I should largely get the very effect most to be invoked, that of a generous nature engaged with forces, with difficulties and dangers, that it but half understands. If Newman was attaching enough, I must have argued, his tangle would be sensible enough; for the interest of everything is all that it is *his* vision, *his* conception, *his* interpretation: at the window of his wide, quite sufficiently wide, consciousness we are seated, from that admirable position we 'assist'. He therefore supremely matters; all the rest matters only as he feels it, treats it, meets it. A beautiful infatuation this, always, I think, the intensity of the creative effort to get into the skin of the creature; the act of personal possession of one being by another at its completest – and with the high enhancement, ever, that it is, by the same stroke, the effort of the artist to preserve for his subject that unity, and for his use of it (in other words for the interest he desires to excite) that effect of a *centre*, which most economize its value. Its value is most discussable when that economy has most operated; the content and the 'importance' of a work of art are in fine wholly dependent on its *being* one: outside of which all prate of its representative character, its meaning and its bearing, its morality and humanity, are an impudent thing. Strong in that character, which is the condition of its really bearing witness at all, it is strong every way. So much remains true then on behalf of my instinct of multiplying the fine touches by which Newman should live and communicate life; and yet I still ask myself, I confess, what I can have made of 'life', in my picture, at such a juncture as the interval offered as elapsing between my hero's first accepted state and the nuptial rites that are to crown it. Nothing here is in truth 'offered' – everything is evaded, and the effect of this, I recognize, is of the oddest. His relation to Madame de Cintré takes a great stride, but the author appears to view that but as a signal for letting it severely alone.

I have been stupefied, in so thoroughly revising the book, to find, on turning a page, that the light in which he is presented immediately after Madame de Bellegarde has conspicuously introduced him to all her circle as her daughter's husband-to-be is that of an evening at the opera quite alone; as if he wouldn't surely spend his leisure, and especially those hours of it, with his intended. Instinctively, from that moment, one would have seen them intimately and, for one's interest, beautifully together; with some illustration of the beauty incumbent on the author. The truth was that at this point the author, all gracelessly, could but hold his breath and pass; lingering was too difficult – he had made for himself a crushing complication. Since Madame de Cintré was after all to 'back out' every touch in the picture of her apparent loyalty would add to her eventual shame. She had acted in clear good faith, but how could I give the *detail* of an attitude, on her part, of which the foundation was yet so weak? I preferred, as the minor evil, to shirk the attempt – at the cost evidently of a signal loss of 'charm'; and with this lady, altogether, I recognize, a light plank, too light a plank, is laid for the reader over a dark 'psychological' abyss. The delicate clue to her conduct is never definitely placed in his hand: I must have liked verily to think it *was* delicate and to flatter myself it was to be felt with finger-tips rather than heavily tugged at. Here then, at any rate, is the romantic *tout craché* – the fine flower of Newman's experience blooming in a medium 'cut off' and shut up to itself. I don't for a moment pronounce any spell proceeding from it necessarily the less workable, to a rejoicing ingenuity, for that; beguile the reader's suspicion of *his* being shut up, transform it for *him* into a positive illusion of the largest liberty, and the success will ever be proportionate to the chance. Only all this gave me, I make out, a great deal to look to, and I was perhaps wrong in thinking that Newman by himself, and for any occasional extra inch or so I might smuggle into his measurements, would see me through my wood. Anything more liberated and disconnected, to repeat my terms, than his prompt general profession, before the Tristrams, of aspiring to a 'great' marriage, for example, could surely not well be imagined. I had to take that over with the rest of him and fit it in – I had indeed to exclude the outer air. Still, I find on re-perusal that I have been able to breathe at least in my aching void; so that, clinging to my hero as to a tall, protective, good-natured elder brother in a rough place, I leave the record to stand or fall by his more or less convincing image.

58

❧

Preface to The Portrait of a Lady.

THE PORTRAIT OF A LADY was, like *Roderick Hudson*, begun in Florence, during three months spent there in the spring of 1879. Like *Roderick* and like *The American*, it had been designed for publication in *The Atlantic Monthly*, where it began to appear in 1880. It differed from its two predecessors, however, in finding a course also open to it, from month to month, in *Macmillan's Magazine*; which was to be for me one of the last occasions of simultaneous 'serialization' in the two countries that the changing conditions of literary intercourse between England and the United States had up to then left unaltered. It is a long novel, and I was long in writing it; I remember being again much occupied with it, the following year, during a stay of several weeks made in Venice. I had rooms on Riva Schiavoni, at the top of a house near the passage leading off to San Zaccaria; the waterside life, the wondrous lagoon spread before me, and the ceaseless human chatter of Venice came in at my windows, to which I seem to myself to have been constantly driven, in the fruitless fidget of composition, as if to see whether, out in the blue channel, the ship of some right suggestion, of some better phrase, of the next happy twist of my subject, the next true touch for my canvas, mightn't come into sight. But I recall vividly enough that the response most elicited, in general, to these restless appeals was the rather grim admonition that romantic and historic sites, such as the land of Italy abounds in, offer the artist a questionable aid to concentration when they themselves are not to be the subject of it. They are too rich in their own life and too charged with their own meanings merely to help him out with a lame phrase; they draw him away from his small question to their own greater ones; so that, after a little, he feels, while thus yearning toward them in his difficulty, as if he were asking an army of glorious veterans to help him to arrest a peddler who has given him the wrong change.

There are pages of the book which, in the reading over, have seemed to make me see again the bristling curve of the wide Riva, the large colour-spots of the balconied houses and the repeated undulation of the little hunchbacked bridges, marked by the rise and drop again, with the wave, of foreshortened clicking pedestrians. The Venetian footfall and the Venetian cry — all talk there, wherever uttered, having the pitch of a call across the water — come in once more at the window, renewing one's old impression of the delighted senses and the divided, frustrated mind. How can places that speak *in general* so to the imagination not give it, at the moment, the particular thing it wants? I recollect again and again, in beautiful places, dropping into that wonderment. The real truth is, I think, that they express, under this appeal, only too much — more than, in the given case, one has use for; so that one finds one's self working less congruously, after all, so far as the surrounding picture is concerned, than in presence of the moderate and the neutral, to which we may lend something of the light of our vision. Such a place as Venice is too proud for such charities; Venice doesn't borrow, she but all magnificently gives. We profit by that enormously, but to do so we must either be quite off duty or be on it in her service alone. Such, and so rueful, are these reminiscences; though on the whole, no doubt, one's book, and one's 'literary effort' at large, were to be the better for them. Strangely fertilizing, in the long run, does a wasted effort of attention often prove. It all depends on *how* the attention has been cheated, has been squandered. There are high-handed insolent frauds, and there are insidious sneaking ones. And there is, I fear, even on the most designing artist's part, always witless enough good faith, always anxious enough desire, to fail to guard him against their deceits.

Trying to recover here, for recognition, the germ of my idea, I see that it must have consisted not at all in any conceit of a 'plot', nefarious name, in any flash, upon the fancy, of a set of relations, or in any one of those situations that, by a logic of their own, immediately fall, for the fabulist, into movement, into a march or a rush, a patter of quick steps; but altogether in the sense of a single character, the character and aspect of a particular engaging young woman, to which all the usual elements of a 'subject', certainly of a setting, were to need to be superadded. Quite as interesting as the young woman herself, at her best, do I find, I must again repeat, this projection of memory upon the whole matter of the growth, in one's imagination, of some such apology for a motive. These are the fascinations of the fabulist's art, these lurking forces of expansion, these necessities of upspringing in the seed, these beautiful determinations, on the part of the idea entertained, to grow as tall as possible, to push into the light and the air and thickly flower there; and, quite as much, these fine possibilities of recovering, from some good standpoint on the ground gained, the intimate history of the business – of retracing and reconstructing its steps and stages. I have always fondly remembered a remark that I heard fall years ago from the lips of Ivan Turgenieff in regard to his own experience of the usual origin of the fictive picture. It began for him almost always with the vision of some person or persons, who hovered before him, soliciting him, as the active or passive figure, interesting him and appealing to him just as they were and by what they were. He saw them, in that fashion, as *disponibles*, saw them subject to the chances, the complications of existence, and saw them vividly, but then had to find for them the right relations, those that would most bring them out; to imagine, to invent and select and piece together the situations most useful and favourable to the sense of the creatures themselves, the complications they would be most likely to produce and to feel.

'To arrive at these things is to arrive at my "story",' he said, 'and that's the way I look for it. The result is that I'm often accused of not having "story" enough. I seem to myself to have as much as I need – to show my people, to exhibit their relations with each other; for that is all my measure. If I watch them long enough I see them come together, I see them *placed*, I see them engaged in this or that act and in this or that difficulty. How they look and move and speak and behave, always in the setting I have found for them, is my account of them – of which I dare say, alas, *que cela manque souvent d'architecture*. But I would rather, I think, have too little architecture than too much – when there's danger of its interfering with my measure of the truth. The French of course like more of it than I give –

having by their own genius such a hand for it; and indeed one must give all one can. As for the origin of one's wind-blown germs themselves, who shall say, as you ask, where *they* come from? We have to go too far back, too far behind, to say. Isn't it all we can say that they come from every quarter of heaven, that they are *there* at almost any turn of the road? They accumulate, and we are always picking them over, selecting among them. They are the breath of life – by which I mean that life, in its own way, breathes them upon us. They are so, in a manner prescribed and imposed – floated into our minds by the current of life. That reduces to imbecility the vain critic's quarrel, so often, with one's subject, when he hasn't the wit to accept it. Will he point out then which other it should properly have been? – his office being, essentially *to* point out. *Il en serait bien embarrassé.* Ah, when he points out what I've done or failed to do with it, that's another matter: there he's on his ground. I give him up my "architecture",' my distinguished friend concluded, 'as much as he will.'

So this beautiful genius, and I recall with comfort the gratitude I drew from his reference to the intensity of suggestion that may reside in the stray figure, the unattached character, the image *en disponibilité*. It gave me higher warrant than I seemed then to have met for just that blest habit of one's own imagination, the trick of investing some conceived or encountered individual, some brace or group of individuals, with the germinal property and authority. I was myself so much more antecedently conscious of my figures than of their setting – a too preliminary, a preferential interest in which struck me as in general such a putting of the cart before the horse. I might envy, though I couldn't emulate, the imaginative writer so constituted as to see his fable first and to make out its agents afterwards: I could think so little of any fable that didn't need its agents positively to launch it; I could think so little of any situation that didn't depend for its interest on the nature of the persons situated, and thereby on their way of taking it. There are methods of so-called presentation, I believe – among novelists who have appeared to flourish – that offer the situation as indifferent to that support; but I have not lost the sense of the value for me, at the time, of the admirable Russian's testimony to my not needing, all superstitiously, to try and perform any such gymnastic. Other echoes from the same source linger with me, I confess, as unfadingly – if it be not all indeed one much-embracing echo. It was impossible after that not to read, for one's uses, high lucidity into the tormented and disfigured and bemuddled question of the objective value, and even quite into that of the critical appreciation, of 'subject' in the novel.

One had had from an early time, for that matter, the instinct of the right estimate of such values and of its reducing to the inane the dull dispute over the 'immoral' subject and the moral. Recognizing so promptly the one measure of the worth of a given subject, the question about it that, rightly answered, disposes of all others – is it valid, in a word, is it genuine, is it sincere, the result of some direct impression or perception of life? – I had found small edification, mostly, in a critical pretension that had neglected from the first all delimitation of ground and all definition of terms. The air of my earlier time shows, to memory, as darkened, all round, with that vanity – unless the difference to-day be just in one's own final impatience, the lapse of one's attention. There is, I think, no more nutritive or suggestive truth in this connexion than that of the perfect dependence of the 'moral' sense of a work of art on the amount of felt life concerned in producing it. The question comes back thus, obviously, to the kind and the degree of the artist's prime sensibility, which is the soil out of which his subject springs. The quality and capacity of that soil, its ability to 'grow' with due freshness and straightness any vision of life, represents, strongly or weakly, the projected morality. That element is but another name for the more or less close connexion of the subject with some mark made on the intelligence, with some sincere experience. By which, at the same time, of course, one is far from contending that this enveloping air of the artist's humanity – which gives the last touch to the worth of the work – is not a widely and wondrously varying element; being on one occasion a rich and magnificent medium and on another a comparatively poor and ungenerous one. Here we get exactly the high price of the novel as a literary form – its power not only, while preserving that form with closeness, to range through all the differences of the individual relation to its general subject-matter, all the varieties of outlook on life, of disposition to reflect and project, created by conditions that are never the same from man to man (or, so far as that goes, from man to woman), but positively to appear more true to its character in proportion as it strains, or tends to burst, with a latent extravagance, its mould.

The house of fiction has in short not one window, but a million – a number of possible windows not to be reckoned, rather; every one of which has been pierced, or is still pierceable, in its vast front, by the need of the individual vision and by the pressure of the individual will. These apertures, of dissimilar shape and size, hang so, all together, over the human scene that we might have expected of them a greater sameness of report than we find. They are but windows at the best, mere holes in a dead wall, disconnected, perched aloft; they are not hinged doors opening straight upon life. But they have this mark of their own that at each of them stands a figure with a pair of eyes, or at least with a field-glass, which forms, again and again, for observation, a unique instrument, insuring to the person making use of it an impression distinct from every other. He and his neighbours are watching the same show, but one seeing more where the other sees less, one seeing black where the other sees white, one seeing big where the other sees small, one seeing coarse where the other sees fine. And so on, and so on; there is fortunately no saying on what, for the particular pair of eyes, the window may *not* open; 'fortunately' by reason, precisely, of this incalculability of range. The spreading field, the human scene, is the 'choice of subject'; the pierced aperture, either broad or balconied or slit-like and low-browed, is the 'literary form'; but they are, singly or together, as nothing without the posted presence of the watcher – without, in other words, the consciousness of the artist. Tell me what the artist is, and I will tell you of what he has *been* conscious. Thereby I shall express to you at once his boundless freedom and his 'moral' reference.

All this is a long way round, however, for my word about my dim first move toward *The Portrait*, which was exactly my grasp of a single character – an acquisition I had made, moreover, after a fashion not here to be retraced. Enough that I was, as seemed to me, in complete possession of it, that I had been so for a long time, that this had made it familiar and yet had not blurred its charm, and that, all urgently, all tormentingly, I saw it in motion and, so to speak, in transit. This amounts to saying that I saw it as bent upon its fate – some fate or other; *which*, among the possibilities, being precisely the question. Thus I had my vivid individual – vivid, so strangely, in spite of being still at large, not confined by the conditions, not engaged in the tangle, to which we look for much of the impress that constitutes an identity. If the apparition was still all to be placed how came it to be vivid? – since we puzzle such quantities out, mostly, just by the business of placing them. One could answer such a question beautifully, doubtless, if one could do so subtle, if not so monstrous, a thing as to write the history of the growth of one's imagination. One would describe then what, at a given time, had extraordinarily happened to it, and one would so, for instance, be in a position to tell, with an approach to clearness, how, under favour of occasion, it had been able to take over (take over straight from life) such and such a constituted, animated figure or form. The figure has to that extent, as you see, *been* placed – placed in the imagination that detains it, preserves, protects, enjoys it, conscious of its presence in the dusky, crowded, heterogeneous back-shop of the mind very much as a wary dealer in precious odds and ends, competent to make an 'advance' on rare objects confided to him, is conscious of the rare little 'piece' left in deposit by the reduced, mysterious lady of title or the speculative amateur, and which is already there to disclose its merit afresh as soon as a key shall have clicked in a cupboard-door.

That may be, I recognize, a somewhat superfine analogy for the particular 'value' I here speak of, the image of the young feminine nature that I had had for so considerable a time all curiously at my disposal; but it appears to fond memory quite to fit the fact – with the recall, in addition, of my pious desire but to place my treasure right. I quite remind myself thus of the dealer resigned not to 'realize', resigned to keeping the precious object locked up indefinitely rather than commit it, at no matter what price, to vulgar hands. For there *are* dealers in these forms and figures and treasures capable of that refinement. The point is, however, that this single small cornerstone, the conception of a certain young woman affronting her destiny, had begun with being all my outfit for the large building of *The Portrait of a Lady*. It came to be a square and spacious house – or has at least seemed so to me in this going over it again; but, such as it is, it had to be put up round my young woman while she stood there in perfect isolation. That is to me, artistically speaking, the circumstance of interest; for I have lost myself once more, I confess, in the curiosity of analysing the structure. By what process of logical accretion was this slight 'personality', the mere slim shade of an intelligent but presumptuous girl, to find itself endowed with the high attributes of a Subject? – and indeed by what thinness, at the best, would such a subject not be vitiated? Millions of presumptuous girls, intelligent or not intelligent, daily affront their destiny, and what is it open to their destiny to *be*, at the most, that we should make an ado about it? The novel is of its very nature an 'ado', an ado about something, and the larger the form it takes the greater of course the ado. Therefore, consciously, that was what one was in for – for positively organizing an ado about Isabel Archer.

One looked it well in the face, I seem to remember, this extravagance; and with the effect precisely of recognizing the charm of the problem. Challenge any such problem with any intelligence, and you immediately see how full it is of substance; the wonder being, all the while, as we look at the world, how absolutely, how inordinately, the Isabel Archers, and even much smaller female fry, insist on mattering. George Eliot has admirably noted it – 'In these frail vessels is borne onward through the ages the treasure of human affection.' In *Romeo and Juliet* Juliet has to be important, just as, in *Adam Bede* and *The Mill on the Floss* and *Middlemarch* and *Daniel Deronda*, Hetty Sorrel and Maggie Tulliver and Rosamond Vincy and Gwendolen Harleth have to be; with that much of firm ground, that much of bracing air, at the disposal all the while of their feet and their lungs. They are typical, none the less, of a class difficult, in the individual case, to make a centre of interest; so difficult in fact that many an expert painter, as for instance Dickens and Walter Scott, as for instance even, in the main, so subtle a hand as that of R. L. Stevenson, has preferred to leave the task unattempted. There are in fact writers as to whom we make out that their refuge from this is to assume it to be not worth their attempting; by which pusillanimity in truth their honour is scantly saved. It is never an attestation of a value, or even of our imperfect sense of one, it is never a tribute to any truth at all, that we shall represent that value badly. It never makes up, artistically, for an artist's dim feeling about a thing that he shall 'do' the thing as ill as possible. There are better ways than that, the best of all of which is to begin with less stupidity.

It may be answered meanwhile, in regard to Shakespeare's and to George Eliot's testimony, that their concession to the 'importance' of their Juliets and Cleopatras and Portias (even with Portia as the very type and model of the young person intelligent and presumptuous) and to that of their Hettys and Maggies and Rosamonds and Gwendolens, suffers the abatement that these slimnesses are, when figuring as the main props of the theme, never suffered to be sole ministers of its appeal, but have their inadequacy eked out with comic relief and underplots, as the playwrights say, when not with murders and battles and the great mutations of the world. If they are shown as 'mattering' as much as they could possibly pretend to, the proof of it is in a hundred other persons, made of much stouter stuff, and each involved moreover in a hundred relations which matter to *them* concomitantly with that one. Cleopatra matters, beyond bounds, to Antony, but his colleagues, his antagonists, the state of Rome and the impending battle also prodigiously matter; Portia matters to Antonio, and to Shylock, and to the Prince of Morocco, to the fifty aspiring princes, but for these gentry there are other lively concerns; for Antonio, notably, there are Shylock and Bassanio and his lost ventures and the extremity of his predicament. This extremity indeed, by the same token, matters to Portia – though its doing so becomes of interest all by the fact that Portia matters to *us*. That she does so, at any rate, and that almost everything comes round to it again, supports my contention as to this fine example of the value recognized in the mere young thing. (I say 'mere' young thing because I guess that even Shakespeare, preoccupied mainly though he may have been with the passions of princes, would scarce have pretended to found the best of his appeal for her on her high social position.) It is an example exactly of the deep difficulty braved – the difficulty of making George Eliot's 'frail vessel', if not the all-in-all for our attention, at least the clearest of the call.

Now to see deep difficulty braved is at any time, for the really addicted artist, to feel almost even as a pang the beautiful incentive, and to feel it verily in such sort as to wish the danger intensified. The difficulty most worth tackling can only be for him, in these conditions, the greatest the case permits of. So I remember feeling here (in presence, always, that is, of the particular uncertainty of my ground), that there would be one way better than another – oh, ever so much better than any other! – of making it fight out its battle. The frail vessel, that charged with George Eliot's 'treasure', and thereby of such importance to those who curiously approach it, has likewise possibilities of importance to itself, possibilities which permit of treatment and in fact peculiarly require it from the moment they are considered at all. There is always the escape from any close account of the weak agent of such spells by using as a bridge for evasion, for retreat and flight, the view of her relation to those surrounding her. Make it predominantly a view of *their* relation and the trick is played: you give the general sense of her effect, and you give it, so far as the raising on it of a superstructure goes, with the maximum of ease. Well, I recall perfectly how little, in my now quite established connexion, the maximum of ease appealed to me, and how I seemed to get rid of it by an honest transposition of the weights in the two scales. 'Place the centre of the subject in the young woman's own consciousness,' I said to myself, 'and you get as interesting and as beautiful a difficulty as you could wish. Stick to *that* – for the centre; put the heaviest weight into *that* scale, which will be so largely the scale of her relation to herself. Make her only interested enough, at the same time, in the things that are not herself, and this relation needn't fear to be too limited. Place meanwhile in the other scale the lighter weight (which is usually the one that tips the balance of interest): press least hard, in short, on the consciousness of your heroine's satellites, especially the male; make it an interest contributive only to the greater one. See, at all events, what can be done in this way. What better field could there be for a due ingenuity? The girl hovers, inextinguishable, as a charming creature, and the job will be to translate her into the highest terms of that formula, and as nearly as possible moreover into *all* of them. To depend upon her and her little concerns wholly to see you through will necessitate, remember, your really "doing" her.'

So far I reasoned, and it took nothing less than that technical rigour, I now easily see, to inspire me with the right confidence for erecting on such a plot of ground the neat and careful and proportioned pile of bricks that arches over it and that was thus to form, constructionally speaking, a literary monument. Such is the aspect that to-day *The Portrait* wears for me: a structure reared with an 'architectural' competence, as Turgenieff would have said, that makes it, to the author's own sense, the most proportioned of his productions after *The Ambassadors* – which was to follow it so many years later and which has, no doubt, a superior roundness. On one thing I was determined; that, though I should clearly have to pile brick upon brick for the creation of an interest, I would leave no pretext for saying that anything is out of line, scale or perspective. I would build large – in fine embossed vaults and painted arches, as who should say, and yet never let it appear that the chequered pavement, the ground under the reader's feet, fails to stretch at every point to the base of the walls. That precautionary spirit, on re-perusal of the book, is the old note that most touches me: it testifies so, for my own ear, to the anxiety of my provision for the reader's amusement. I felt, in view of the possible limitations of my subject, that no such provision could be excessive, and the development of the latter was simply the general form of that earnest quest. And I find indeed that this is the only account I can give myself of the evolution of the fable: it is all under the head thus named that I conceive the needful accretion as having taken place, the right complications as having started. It was naturally of the essence that the young woman should be herself complex; that was rudimentary – or was at any rate the light in which Isabel Archer had originally dawned. It went, however, but a certain way, and other lights, contending, conflicting lights, and of as many different colours, if possible, as the rockets, the Roman candles and Catherine-wheels of a 'pyrotechnic display', would be employable to attest that she was. I had, no doubt, a groping instinct for the right complications, since I am quite unable to track the footsteps of those that constitute, as the case stands, the general situation exhibited. They are there, for what they are worth, and as numerous as might be; but my memory, I confess, is a blank as to how and whence they came.

I seem to myself to have waked up one morning in possession of them – of Ralph Touchett and his parents, of Madame Merle, of Gilbert Osmond and his daughter and his sister, of Lord Warburton, Caspar Goodwood and Miss Stackpole, the definite array of con-tributions to Isabel Archer's history. I recognized them, I knew them, they were the numbered pieces of my puzzle, the concrete terms of my 'plot'. It was as if they had simply, by an impulse of their own, floated into my ken, and all in response to my primary question: 'Well, what will she *do*?' Their answer seemed to be that if I would trust them they would show me; on which, with an urgent appeal to them to make it at least as interesting as they could, I trusted them. They were like the group of attendants and entertainers who come down by train when people in the country give a party; they represented the contract for carrying the party on. That was an excellent relation with them – a possible one even with so broken a reed (from her slightness of cohesion) as Henrietta Stackpole. It is a familiar truth to the novelist, at the strenuous hour, that, as certain elements in any work are of the essence, so others are only of the form; that as this or that character, this or that disposition of the material, belongs to the subject directly, so to speak, so this or that other belongs to it but indirectly – belongs intimately to the treatment. This is a truth, however, of which he rarely gets the benefit – since it could be assured to him, really, but by criticism based upon perception, criticism which is too little of this world. He must not think of benefits, moreover, I freely recognize, for that way dishonour lies: he has, that is, but one to think of – the benefit, whatever it may be, involved in his having cast a spell upon the simpler, the very simplest, forms of attention. This is all he is entitled to; he is entitled to nothing, he is bound to admit, that can come to him, from the reader, as a result on the latter's part of any act of reflexion or discrimination. He may *enjoy* this finer tribute – that is another affair, but on condition only of taking it as a gratuity 'thrown in', a mere miraculous windfall, the fruit of a tree he may not pretend to have shaken. Against reflexion, against discrimination, in his interest, all earth and air conspire; wherefore it is that, as I say, he must in many a case have schooled himself, from the first, to work but for a 'living wage'. The living wage is the reader's grant of the least possible quantity of attention required for consciousness of a 'spell'. The occasional charming 'tip' is an act of his intelligence over and beyond this, a golden apple, for the writer's lap, straight from the wind-stirred tree. The artist may of course, in wanton moods, dream of some Paradise (for art) where the direct appeal to the intelligence might be legalized; for to such extravagances as these his yearning mind can scarce hope ever completely to close itself. The most he can do is to remember they *are* extravagances.

All of which is perhaps but a gracefully devious way of saying that Henrietta Stackpole was a good example, in *The Portrait*, of the truth to which I just adverted – as good an example as I could name were it not that Maria Gostrey, in *The Ambassadors*, then in the bosom of time, may be mentioned as a better. Each of these persons is but wheels to the coach; neither belongs to the body of that vehicle, or is for a moment accommodated with a seat inside. There the subject alone is ensconced, in the form of its 'hero and heroine', and of the privileged high officials, say, who ride with the king and queen. There are reasons why one would have liked this to be felt, as in general one would like almost anything to be felt, in one's work, that one has one's self contributively felt. We have seen, however, how idle is that pretension, which I should be sorry to make too much of. Maria Gostrey and Miss Stackpole then are cases, each, of the light *ficelle*, not of the true agent; they may run beside the coach 'for all they are worth', they may cling to it till they are out of breath (as poor Miss Stackpole all so visibly does), but neither, all the while, so much as gets her foot on the step, neither ceases for a moment to tread the dusty road. Put it even that they are like the fishwives who helped to bring back to Paris from Versailles, on that most ominous day of the first half of the French Revolution, the carriage of the royal family. The only thing is that I may well be asked, I acknowledge, why then, in the present fiction, I have suffered Henrietta (of whom we have indubitably too much) so officiously, so strangely, so almost inexplicably, to pervade. I will presently say what I can for that anomaly – and in the most conciliatory fashion.

A point I wish still more to make is that if my relation of confidence with the actors in my drama who *were*, unlike Miss Stackpole, true agents, was an excellent one to have arrived at, there still remained my relation with the reader, which was another affair altogether and as to which I felt no one to be trusted but myself. That solicitude was to be accordingly expressed in the artful patience with which, as I have said, I piled brick upon brick. The bricks, for the whole counting-over – putting for bricks little touches and inventions and enhancements by the way – affect me in truth as well-nigh innumerable and as ever so scrupulously fitted together and packed-in. It is an effect of detail, of the minutest; though, if one were in this connexion to say all, one would express the hope that the general, the ampler air of the modest monument still survives. I do at least seem to catch the key to a part of this abundance of small anxious, ingenious illustration as I recollect putting my finger, in my young woman's interest, on the most obvious of her predicates. 'What will she "do"? Why, the first thing she'll do will be to come to Europe; which in fact will form, and all inevitably, no small part of her principal adventure. Coming to Europe is even for the "frail vessels", in this wonderful age, a mild adventure; but what is truer than that on one side – the side of their independence of flood and field, of the moving accident, of battle and murder and sudden death – her adventures are to be mild? Without her sense of them, her sense *for* them, as one may say, they are next to nothing at all; but isn't the beauty and the difficulty just in showing their mystic conversion by that sense, conversion into the stuff of drama or, even more delightful word still, of "story"?' It was all as clear, my contention, as a silver bell. Two very good instances, I think, of this effect of conversion, two cases of the rare chemistry, are the pages in which Isabel, coming into the drawing-room at Garden-court, coming in from a wet walk or whatever, that rainy afternoon, finds Madame Merle in possession of the place, Madame Merle seated, all absorbed but all serene, at the piano, and deeply recog-nizes, in the striking of such an hour, in the presence there, among the gathering shades, of this personage, of whom a moment before she had never so much as heard, a turning-point in her life. It is dreadful to have too much, for any artistic demonstration, to dot one's i's and insist on one's intentions, and I am not eager to do it now; but the question here was that of producing the maximum of intensity with the minimum of strain.

The interest was to be raised to its pitch and yet the elements to be kept in their key; so that, should the whole thing duly impress, I might show what an 'exciting' inward life may do for the person leading it even while it remains perfectly normal. And I cannot think of a more consistent application of that ideal unless it be in the long statement, just beyond the middle of the book, of my young woman's extraordinary meditative vigil on the occasion that was to become for her such a landmark. Reduced to its essence, it is but the vigil of searching criticism; but it throws the action further forward than twenty 'incidents' might have done. It was designed to have all the vivacity of incident and all the economy of picture. She sits up, by her dying fire, far into the night, under the spell of recognitions on which she finds the last sharpness suddenly wait. It is a representation simply of her motionlessly *seeing*, and an attempt withal to make the mere still lucidity of her act as 'interesting' as the surprise of a caravan or the identification of a pirate. It represents, for that matter, one of the identifications dear to the novelist, and even indispensable to him; but it all goes on without her being approached by another person and without her leaving her chair. It is obviously the best thing in the book, but it is only a supreme illustration of the general plan. As to Henrietta, my apology for whom I just left incomplete, she exemplifies, I fear, in her superabundance, not an element of my plan, but only an excess of my zeal. So early was to begin my tendency to *overtreat*, rather than undertreat (when there was choice or danger) my subject. (Many members of my craft, I gather, are far from agreeing with me, but I have always held overtreating the minor disservice.) 'Treating' that of *The Portrait* amounted to never forgetting, by any lapse, that the thing was under a special obligation to be amusing. There was the danger of the noted 'thinness' – which was to be averted, tooth and nail, by cultivation of the lively. That is at least how I see it to-day. Henrietta must have been at that time a part of my wonderful notion of the lively. And then there was another matter. I had, within the few preceding years, come to live in London, and the 'international' light lay, in those days, to my sense, thick and rich upon the scene. It was the light in which so much of the picture hung. But that *is* another matter. There is really too much to say.

59

Preface to The Princess Casamassima. *It is curious that James does not mention Turgenev's* Virgin Soil *as a possible inspiration for this novel. He reviewed it in 1877, about seven years before he started writing the* Princess, *and there are many striking similarities of subject. (On the other hand 'the deep well of unconscious cerebration' is indeed disconcertingly deep – recently, for example, I found that a few points I had thought original about* Emma *were similarly made in a book I read over twenty years ago.)*

THE SIMPLEST account of the origin of *The Princess Casamassima* is, I think, that this fiction proceeded quite directly, during the first year of a long residence in London, from the habit and the interest of walking the streets. I walked a great deal – for exercise, for amusement, for acquisition, and above all I always walked home at the evening's end, when the evening had been spent elsewhere, as happened more often than not; and as to do this was to receive many impressions, so the impressions worked and sought an issue, so the book after a time was born. It is a fact that, as I look back, the attentive exploration of London, the assault directly made by the great city upon an imagination quick to react, fully explains a large part of it. There is a minor element that refers itself to another source, of which I shall presently speak; but the prime idea was unmistakeably the ripe round fruit of perambulation. One walked of course with one's eyes greatly open, and I hasten to declare that such a practice, carried on for a long time and over a considerable space, positively provokes, all round, a mystic solicitation, the urgent appeal, on the part of everything, to be interpreted and, so far as may be, reproduced. 'Subjects' and situations, character and history, the tragedy and comedy of life, are things of which the common air, in such conditions, seems pungently to taste; and to a mind curious, before the human scene, of meanings and revelations the great grey Babylon easily becomes, on its face, a garden bristling with an immense illustrative flora. Possible stories, presentable figures, rise from the thick jungle as the observer moves, fluttering up like startled game, and before he knows it indeed he has fairly to guard himself against the brush of importunate wings. He goes on as with his head in a cloud of humming presences – especially during the younger, the initiatory time, the fresh, the sharply-apprehensive months or years, more or less numerous. We use our material up, we use up even the thick tribute of the London streets – if perception and attention but sufficiently light our steps. But I think of them as lasting, for myself, quite sufficiently long; I think of them as even still – dreadfully changed for the worse in respect to any romantic idea as I find them – breaking out on occasion into eloquence, throwing out deep notes from their vast vague murmur.

There was a moment at any rate when they offered me no image more vivid than that of some individual sensitive nature or fine mind, some small obscure intelligent creature whose education should have been almost wholly derived from them, capable of profiting by all the civilization, all the accumulations to which they testify, yet condemned to see these things only from outside – in mere quickened consideration, mere wistfulness and envy and despair. It seemed to me I had only to imagine such a spirit intent enough and troubled enough, and to place it in presence of the comings and goings, the great gregarious company, of the more fortunate than himself – all on the scale on which London could show them – to get possession of an interesting theme. I arrived so at the history of little Hyacinth Robinson – he sprang up for me out of the London pavement. To find his possible adventure interesting I had only to conceive his watching the same public show, the same innumerable appearances, I had watched myself, and of his watching very much as I had watched; save indeed for one little difference. This difference would be that so far as all the swarming facts should speak of freedom and ease, knowledge and power, money, opportunity and satiety, he should be able to revolve round them but at the most respectful of distances and with every door of approach shut in his face. For one's self, all conveniently, there had been doors that opened – opened into light and warmth and cheer, into good and charming relations; and if the place as a whole lay heavy on one's consciousness there was yet always for relief this implication of one's own lucky share of the freedom and ease, lucky acquaintance with the number of lurking springs at light pressure of which particular vistas would begin to recede, great lighted, furnished, peopled galleries, sending forth gusts of agreeable sound.

That main happy sense of the picture was always there and that retreat from the general grimness never forbidden; whereby one's own relation to the mere formidable mass and weight of things was eased off and adjusted. One learned from an early period what it might be to know London in such a way as that – an immense and interesting discipline, an education on terms mostly convenient and delightful. But what would be the effect of the other way, of having so many precious things perpetually in one's eyes, yet of missing them all for any closer knowledge, and of the confinement of closer knowledge entirely to matters with which a connexion, however intimate, couldn't possibly pass for a privilege? Truly, of course, there are London mysteries (dense categories of dark arcana) for every spectator, and it's in a degree an exclusion and a state of weakness to be without experience of the meaner conditions, the lower manners and types, the general sordid struggle, the weight of the burden of labour, the ignorance, the misery and the vice. With such matters as those my tormented young man would have had contact – they would have formed, fundamentally, from the first, his natural and immediate London. But the reward of a romantic curiosity would be the question of what the total assault, that of the world of his work-a-day life and the world of his divination and his envy together, would have made of him, and what in especial he would have made of them. As tormented, I say, I thought of him, and that would be the point – if one could only see him feel enough to be interesting without his feeling so much as not to be natural.

This in fact I have ever found rather terribly the point – that the figures in any picture, the agents in any drama, are interesting only in proportion as they feel their respective situations; since the consciousness, on their part, of the complication exhibited forms for us their link of connexion with it. But there are degrees of feeling – the muffled, the faint, the just sufficient, the barely intelligent, as we may say; and the acute, the intense, the complete, in a word – the power to be finely aware and richly responsible. It is those moved in this latter fashion who 'get most' out of all that happens to them and who in so doing enable us, as readers of their record, as participators by a fond attention, also to get most. Their being finely aware – as Hamlet and Lear, say, are finely aware – *makes* absolutely the intensity of their adventure, gives the maximum of sense to what befalls them. We care, our curiosity and our sympathy care, comparatively little for what happens to the stupid, the coarse and the blind; care for it, and for the effects of it, at the most as helping to precipitate what happens to the more deeply wondering, to the really sentient. Hamlet and Lear are surrounded, amid their complications, by the stupid and the blind, who minister in all sorts of ways to their recorded fate. Persons of markedly limited sense would, on such a principle as that, play a part in the career of my tormented youth; but he wouldn't be of markedly limited sense himself – he would note as many things and vibrate to as many occasions as I might venture to make him.

There wouldn't moreover simply be the question of his suffering – of which we might soon get enough; there would be the question of what, all beset and all perceptive, he should thus adventurously do, thus dream and hazard and attempt. The interest of the attitude and the act would be the actor's imagination and vision of them, together with the nature and degree of their felt return upon him. So the intelligent creature would be required and so some picture of his intelligence involved. The picture of an intelligence appears for the most part, it is true, a dead weight for the reader of the English novel to carry, this reader having so often the wondrous property of caring for the displayed tangle of human relations without caring for its intelligibility. The teller of a story is primarily, none the less, the listener to it, the reader of it, too; and, having needed thus to make it out, distinctly, on the crabbed page of life, to disengage it from the rude human character and the more or less gothic text in which it has been packed away, the very essence of his affair has been the *imputing* of intelligence. The basis of his attention has been that such and such an imbroglio has got started – on the page of life – because of something that some one has felt and more or less understood.

I recognize at the same time, and in planning *The Princess*

Casamassima felt it highly important to recognize, the danger of filling too full any supposed and above all any obviously limited vessel of consciousness. If persons either tragically or comically embroiled with life allow us the comic or tragic value of their embroilment in proportion as their struggle is a measured and directed one, it is strangely true, none the less, that beyond a certain point they are spoiled for us by this carrying of a due light. They may carry too much of it for our credence, for our compassion, for our derision. They may be shown as knowing too much and feeling too much – not certainly for their remaining remarkable, but for their remaining 'natural' and typical, for their having the needful communities with our own precious liability to fall into traps and be bewildered. It seems probable that if we were never bewildered there would never be a story to tell about us; we should partake of the superior nature of the all-knowing immortals whose annals are dreadfully dull so long as flurried humans are not, for the positive relief of bored Olympians, mixed up with them. Therefore it is that the wary reader for the most part warns the novelist against making his characters too *interpretative* of the muddle of fate, or in other words too divinely, too priggishly clever. 'Give us plenty of bewilderment,' this monitor seems to say, 'so long as there is plenty of slashing out in the bewilderment too. But don't, we beseech you, give us too much intelligence; for intelligence – well, *endangers*; endangers not perhaps the slasher himself, but the very slashing, the subject-matter of any self-respecting story. It opens up too many considerations, possibilities, issues; it *may* lead the slasher into dreary realms where slashing somehow fails and falls to the ground.'

That is well reasoned on the part of the reader, who can in spite of it never have an idea – or his earnest discriminations would come to him less easily – of the extreme difficulty, for the painter of the human mixture, of reproducing that mixture aright. 'Give us in the persons represented, the subjects of the bewilderment (that bewilderment without which there would be no question of an issue or of the fact of suspense, prime implications in any story) as much experience as possible, but keep down the terms in which you report that experience, because we only understand the very simplest': such in effect are the words in which the novelist constantly hears himself addressed, such the plea made him by the would-be victims of his spell on behalf of that sovereign principle the economy of interest, a principle as to which their instinct is justly strong. He listens anxiously to the charge – nothing can exceed his own solicitude for an economy of interest; but feels himself all in presence of an abyss of ambiguities, the mutual accommodations in which the reader wholly leaves to him. Experience, as I see it, is our apprehension and our measure of what happens to us as social creatures – any intelligent report of which has to be based on that apprehension. The picture of the exposed and entangled state is what is required, and there are certainly always plenty of grounds for keeping down the complexities of a picture. A picture it still has to be, however, and by that condition has to deal effectually with its subject, so that the simple device of more and more keeping down may well not see us quite to our end or even quite to our middle. One suggested way of keeping down, for instance, is not to attribute feeling, or feelings, to persons who wouldn't in all probability have had any to speak of. The less space, within the frame of the picture, their feelings take up the more space is left for their doings – a fact that may at first seem to make for a refinement of economy.

All of which is charming – yet would be infinitely more so if here at once ambiguity didn't yawn; the unreality of the sharp distinction, where the interest of observation is at stake, between doing and feeling. In the immediate field of life, for action, for application, for getting through a job, nothing may so much matter perhaps as the descent of a suspended weight on this, that or the other spot, with all its subjective concomitants quite secondary and irrelevant. But the affair of the painter is not the immediate, it is the reflected field of life, the realm not of application, but of *appreciation* – a truth that makes our measure of effect altogether different. My report of people's experience – my report as a 'story-teller' – is essentially my appreciation of it, and there is no 'interest' for me in what my hero, my heroine or any one else does save through that admirable process. As soon as I begin to appreciate simplification is imperilled: the sharply distinguished parts of any adventure, any case of endurance and performance, melt together as an appeal. I then see their 'doing', that of the persons just mentioned, as, immensely, their feeling, their feeling as their doing; since I can have none of the conveyed sense and taste of their situation without becoming intimate with them. I can't be intimate without that sense and taste, and I can't appreciate save by intimacy, any more than I can report save by a projected light. Intimacy with a man's specific behaviour, with his given case, is desperately certain to make us see it as a whole – in which event arbitrary limitations of our vision lose whatever beauty they may on occasion have pretended to. What a man thinks and what he feels are the history and the character of what he does; on all of which things the logic of intensity rests. Without intensity where is vividness, and without vividness where is presentability? If I have called the most general state of one's most exposed and assaulted figures the state of bewilderment – the condition for instance on which Thackeray so much insists in the interest of *his* exhibited careers, the condition of a humble heart, a bowed head, a patient wonder, a suspended judgement, before the 'awful will' and the mysterious decrees of Providence – so it is rather witless to talk of merely getting rid of that displayed mode of reaction, one of the oft-encountered, one of the highly recommended, categories of feeling.

The whole thing comes to depend thus on the *quality* of bewilderment characteristic of one's creature, the quality involved in the given case or supplied by one's data. There are doubtless many such qualities, ranging from vague and crepuscular to sharpest and most critical; and we have but to imagine one of these latter to see how easily – from the moment it gets its head at all – it may insist on playing a part. There we have then at once a case of feeling, of ever so many possible feelings, stretched across the scene like an attached thread on which the pearls of interest are strung. There are threads shorter and less tense, and I am far from implying that the minor, the coarser and less fruitful forms and degrees of moral reaction, as we may conveniently call it, may not yield lively results. They have their subordinate, comparative, illustrative human value – that appeal of the witless which is often so penetrating. Verily even, I think, no 'story' is possible without its fools – as most of the fine painters of life, Shakespeare, Cervantes and Balzac, Fielding, Scott, Thackeray, Dickens, George Meredith, George Eliot, Jane Austen, have abundantly felt. At the same time I confess I never see the *leading* interest of any human hazard but in a consciousness (on the part of the moved and moving creature) subject to fine intensification and wide enlargement. It is as mirrored in that consciousness that the gross fools, the headlong fools, the fatal fools play their part for us – they have much less to show us in themselves. The troubled life mostly at the centre of our subject – whatever our subject, for the artistic hour, happens to be – embraces them and deals with them for its amusement and its anguish: they are apt largely indeed, on a near view, to be all the cause of its trouble. This means, exactly, that the person capable of feeling in the given case more than another of what is to be felt for it, and so serving in the highest degree to *record* it dramatically and objectively, is the only sort of person on whom we can count not to betray, to cheapen or, as we say, give away, the value and beauty of the thing. By so much as the affair matters *for* some such individual, by so much do we get the best there is of it, and by so much as it falls within the scope of a denser and duller, a more vulgar and more shallow capacity, do we get a picture dim and meagre.

The great chroniclers have clearly always been aware of this; they have at least always either placed a mind of some sort – in the sense of a reflecting and colouring medium – in possession of the general adventure (when the latter has not been purely epic, as with Scott, say, as with old Dumas and with Zola); or else paid signally, as to the interest created, for their failure to do so. We may note moreover in passing that this failure is in almost no case intentional or part of a plan, but has sprung from their limited curiosity, their short conception of the particular sensibility projected. Edgar of Ravenswood for instance, visited by the tragic tempest of *The Bride of Lammermoor*, has a black cloak and hat and feathers more than he has a mind; just as Hamlet, while equally sabled and draped and plumed, while at least equally romantic, has yet a mind still more than he has a costume. The situation represented is that Ravenswood loves Lucy Ashton through dire difficulty and danger, and that she in the same way loves him; but the relation so created between them is by this neglect of the 'feeling' question never shown us as primarily taking place. It is shown only in its secondary, its confused and disfigured aspects – where, however, luckily, it is presented with great romantic good faith. The thing has nevertheless paid for its deviation, as I say, by a sacrifice of intensity; the centre of the subject is empty and the development pushed off, all around, toward the frame – which is, so to speak, beautifully rich and curious. But I mention that relation to each other of the appearances in a particular work only as a striking negative case; there are in the connexion I have glanced at plenty of striking positive ones. It is very true that Fielding's hero in *Tom Jones* is but as 'finely', that is but as intimately, bewildered as a young man of great health and spirits may be when he hasn't a grain of imagination: the point to be made is, at all events, that his sense of bewilderment obtains altogether on the comic, never on the tragic plane. He has so much 'life' that it amounts, for the effect of comedy and application of satire, almost to his having a mind, that is to his having reactions and a full consciousness; besides which his author — *he* handsomely possessed of a mind — has such an amplitude of reflexion for him and round him that we see him through the mellow air of Fielding's fine old moralism, fine old humour and fine old style, which somehow really enlarge, make every one and every thing important.

All of which furthers my remarking how much I have been interested, on reading *The Princess Casamassima* over, to recognize my sense, sharp from far back, that clearness and concreteness constantly depend, for any pictorial whole, on some *concentrated* individual notation of them. That notation goes forward here in the mind of little Hyacinth, immensely quickened by the fact of its so mattering to his very life what he does make of things: which passion of intelligence is, as I have already hinted, precisely his highest value for our curiosity and our sympathy. Yet if his highest it is not at all his only one, since the truth for 'a young man in a book' by no means entirely resides in his being either exquisitely sensitive or shiningly clever. It resides in some such measure of these things as may consort with the fine measure of other things too — with that of the other faces of his situation and character. If he's too sensitive and too clever for *them*, if he knows more than is likely or natural — for *him* — it's as if he weren't at all, as if he were false and impossible. Extreme and attaching always the difficulty of fixing at a hundred points the place where one's impelled *bonhomme* may feel enough and 'know' enough — or be in the way of learning enough — for his maximum dramatic value without feeling and knowing too much for his minimum verisimilitude, his proper fusion with the fable. This is the charming, the tormenting, the eternal little matter *to be made right*, in all the weaving of silver threads and tapping on golden nails; and I should take perhaps too fantastic a comfort — I mean were not the comforts of the artist just of the raw essence of fantasy – in any glimpse of such achieved rightnesses, whether in my own work or that of others. In no work whatever, doubtless, are they the felicities the most frequent; but they have so inherent a price that even the traceable attempt at them, wherever met, sheds, I think, a fine influence about.

I have for example a weakness of sympathy with that constant effort of George Eliot's which plays through Adam Bede and Felix Holt and Tito Melema, through Daniel Deronda and through Lydgate in *Middlemarch*, through Maggie Tulliver, through Romola, through Dorothea Brooke and Gwendolen Harleth; the effort to show their adventures and their history – the author's subject-matter all – as determined by their feelings and the nature of their minds. Their emotions, their stirred intelligence, their moral consciousness, become thus, by sufficiently charmed perusal, our own very adventure. The creator of Deronda and of Romola is charged, I know, with having on occasion – as in dealing with those very celebrities themselves – left the figure, the concrete man and woman, too abstract by reason of the quantity of soul employed; but such mischances, where imagination and humour still keep them company, often have an interest that is wanting to agitations of the mere surface or to those that may be only taken for granted. I should even like to give myself the pleasure of retracing from one of my own productions to another the play of a like instinctive disposition, of catching in the fact, at one point after another, from *Roderick Hudson* to *The Golden Bowl*, that provision for interest which consists in placing advantageously, placing right in the middle of the light, the most polished of possible mirrors of the subject. Rowland Mallet, in *Roderick Hudson*, is exactly such a mirror, not a bit autobiographic or formally 'first person' though he be, and I might exemplify the case through a long list, through the nature of such a 'mind' even as the all-objective Newman in *The American*, through the thickly-peopled imagination of Isabel Archer in *The Portrait of a Lady* (her imagination positively the deepest depth of her imbroglio) down to such unmistakeable examples as that of Merton Densher in *The Wings of the Dove*, that of Lambert Strether in *The Ambassadors* (*he* a mirror verily of miraculous silver and quite pre-eminent, I think, for the connexion) and that of the Prince in the first half and that of the Princess in the second half of *The Golden Bowl*. I should note the extent to which these persons are, so far as their other passions permit, intense *perceivers*, all, of their respective predicaments, and I should go on from them to fifty other examples; even to the divided Vanderbank of *The Awkward Age*, the extreme pinch of whose romance is the vivacity in him, to his positive sorrow and loss, of the state of being aware; even to scanted Fleda Vetch in *The Spoils of Poynton*, through whose own delicate vision of everything so little of the human value of her situation is wasted for us; even to the small recording governess confronted with the horrors of *The Turn of the Screw* and to the innocent child patching together all ineffectually those of *What Maisie Knew*; even in short, since I may name so few cases, to the disaffected guardian of an overgrown legend in *The Birthplace*, to the luckless fine artist of *The Next Time*, trying to despoil himself, for a 'hit' and bread and butter, of his fatal fineness, to blunt the tips of his intellectual fingers, and to the hapless butler Brooksmith, ruined by good talk, disqualified for common domestic service by the beautiful growth of his habit of quiet attention, his faculty of appreciation. But though this demonstration of a rooted vice – since a vice it would appear mainly accounted – might yield amusement, the examples referred to must await their turn.

I had had for a long time well before me, at any rate, my small obscure but ardent observer of the 'London world', saw him roam and wonder and yearn, saw all the unanswered questions and baffled passions that might ferment in him – once he should be made both sufficiently thoughtful and sufficiently 'disinherited'; but this image, however interesting, was of course not by itself a progression, an action, didn't by itself make a drama. I got my action however – failing which one has nothing – under the prompt sense that the state of feeling I was concerned with might develop and beget another state, might return at a given moment, and with the greatest vivacity, on itself. To see this was really to feel one's subject swim into one's ken, especially after a certain other ingenious connexion had been made for it. I find myself again recalling, and with the possible 'fun' of it reviving too, how I recognized, as revealed and prescribed, the particular complexion, profession and other conditions of my little presumptuous adventurer, with his combination of intrinsic fineness and fortuitous adversity, his small cluster of 'dingy' London associations and the swelling spirit in him which was to be the field of his strange experience. Accessible through his imagination, as I have hinted, to a thousand provocations and intimations, he would become most acquainted with destiny in the form of a lively inward revolution. His being jealous of all the ease of life of which he tastes so little, and, bitten, under this exasperation, with an aggressive, vindictive, destructive social faith, his turning to 'treasons, stratagems and spoils' might be as vivid a picture as one chose, but would move to pity and terror only by the aid of some deeper complication, some imposed and formidable issue.

The complication most interesting then would be that he should fall in love with the beauty of the world, actual order and all, at the moment of his most feeling and most hating the famous 'iniquity of its social arrangements'; so that his position as an irreconcileable pledged enemy to it, thus rendered false by something more personal than his opinions and his vows, becomes the sharpest of his torments. To make it a torment that really matters, however, he must have got practically involved, specifically committed to the stand he has, under the pressure of more knowledge, found impossible; out of which has come for him the deep dilemma of the disillusioned and repentant conspirator. He has thrown himself into the more than 'shady' underworld of militant socialism, he has undertaken to play a part – a part that with the drop of his exasperation and the growth, simply expressed, of his taste, is out of all tune with his passion, at any cost, for life itself, the life, whatever it be, that surrounds him. Dabbling deeply in revolutionary politics of a hole-and-corner sort, he would be 'in' up to his neck, and with that precarious part of him particularly involved, so that his tergiversation is the climax of his adventure. What was essential with this was that he should have a social – not less than a socialist – connexion, find a door somehow open to him into the appeased and civilized state, into that warmer glow of things he is precisely to help to undermine. To look for this necessary connexion was for me to meet it suddenly in the form of that extremely *disponible* figure of Christina Light whom I had ten years before found left on my hands at the conclusion of *Roderick Hudson*. She had for so long, in the vague limbo of those ghosts we have conjured but not exorcized, been looking for a situation, awaiting a niche and a function.

I shall not pretend to trace the steps and stages by which the imputability of a future to that young woman – which was like the act of clothing her chilled and patient nakedness – had for its prime effect to plant her in my little bookbinder's path. Nothing would doubtless beckon us on further, with a large leisure, than such a chance to study the obscure law under which certain of a novelist's characters, more or less honourably buried, revive for him by a force or a whim of their own and 'walk' round his house of art like haunting ghosts, feeling for the old doors they knew, fumbling at stiff latches and pressing their pale faces, in the outer dark, to lighted windows. I mistrust them, I confess, in general; my sense of a really expressed character is that it shall have originally so tasted of the ordeal of service as to feel no disposition to yield again to the strain. Why should the Princess of the climax of *Roderick Hudson* still have made her desire felt, unless in fact to testify that she had not been – for what she was – completely recorded? To continue in evidence, that had struck me from far back as her natural passion; in evidence at any price, not consenting to be laid away with folded hands in the pasteboard tomb, the doll's box, to which we usually relegate the spent puppet after the fashion of a recumbent worthy on the slab of a sepulchral monument. I was to see this, after all, in the event, as the fruit of a restless vanity: Christina had felt herself, known herself, striking, in the earlier connexion, and couldn't resign herself not to strike again. Her pressure then was not to be resisted – sharply as the question might come up of why she should pretend to strike, just *there*. I shall not attempt to answer it with reasons (one can never tell everything); it was enough that I could recognize her claim to have travelled far – far from where I had last left her: that, one felt, was in character – that was what she naturally *would* have done. Her prime note had been an aversion to the *banal*, and nothing could be of an effect less *banal*, I judged, than her intervention in the life of a dingy little London bookbinder whose sensibility, whose flow of opinions on 'public questions' in especial, should have been poisoned at the source.

She would be world-weary – that was another of her notes; and the extravagance of her attitude in these new relations would have its root and its apparent logic in her need to feel freshly about something or other – it might scarce matter what. She can, or she believes she can, feel freshly about the 'people' and their wrongs and their sorrows and their perpetual smothered ferment; for these things are furthest removed from those others among which she has hitherto tried to make her life. That was to a certainty where I was to have looked for her – quite *off* and away (once granted the wisdom of listening to her anew at all): therefore Hyacinth's encounter with her could pass for natural, and it was fortunately to be noted that she was to serve for his experience in quite another and a more 'leading' sense than any in which he was to serve for hers. I confess I was not averse – such are the possible weaknesses of the artist in face of high difficulties – to feeling that if his appearance of consistency were obtained I might at least try to remain comparatively at my ease about hers. I may add moreover that the resuscitation of Christina (and, on the minor scale, of the Prince and of Madame Grandoni) put in a strong light for me the whole question, for the romancer, of 'going on with a character': as Balzac first of all systematically went on, as Thackeray, as Trollope, as Zola all more or less ingeniously went on. I was to find no small savour in the reflexions so precipitated; though I may treat myself here only to this remark about them – that the revivalist impulse on the fond writer's part strikes me as one thing, a charmingly conceivable thing, but the effect of a free indulgence in it (effect, that is, on the nerves of the reader) as, for twenty rather ineffable reasons, quite another.

I remember at any rate feeling myself all in possession of little Hyacinth's consistency, as I have called it, down at Dover during certain weeks that were none too remotely precedent to the autumn of 1885 and the appearance, in the *Atlantic Monthly* again, of the first chapters of the story. There were certain sunny, breezy balconied rooms at the quieter end of the Esplanade of that cheerful castle-crested little town – now infinitely perturbed by gigantic 'harbour works', but then only faded and over-soldiered and all pleasantly and humbly submissive to the law that snubs in due course the presumption of flourishing resorts – to which I had already more than once had recourse in hours of quickened industry and which, though much else has been swept away, still archaically exist. To have lately noted this again from the old benched and asphalted walk by the sea, the twinkling Channel beyond which on occasion the opposite coast of France used to gleam as an incident of the charming tendency of the whole prospect (immediate picture and fond design alike) amusingly to *shine*, was somehow to taste afresh, and with a certain surprise, the odd quality of that original confidence that the parts of my plan *would* somehow hang together. I may wonder at my confidence now – given the extreme, the very particular truth and 'authority' required at so many points; but to wonder is to live back gratefully into the finer reasons of things, with all the detail of harsh application and friction (that there must have been) quite happily blurred and dim. The finest of reasons – I mean for the sublime confidence I speak of – was that I felt in full *personal* possession of my matter; this really seemed the fruit of direct experience. My scheme called for the suggested nearness (to all our apparently ordered life) of some sinister anarchic underworld, heaving in its pain, its power and its hate; a presentation not of sharp particulars, but of loose appearances, vague motions and sounds and symptoms, just perceptible presences and general looming possibilities. To have adopted the scheme was to have had to meet the question of one's 'notes', over the whole ground, the question of what, in such directions, one had 'gone into' and how far one had gone; and to have answered that question – to one's own satisfaction at least – was truly to see one's way.

My notes then, on the much-mixed world of my hero's both overt and covert consciousness, were exactly my gathered impressions and stirred perceptions, the deposit in my working imagination of all my visual and all my constructive sense of London. The very plan of my book had in fact directly confronted me with the rich principle of the Note, and was to do much to clear up, once for all, my practical view of it. If one was to undertake to tell tales and to report with truth on the human scene, it could be but because 'notes' had been from the cradle the ineluctable consequence of one's greatest inward energy: to take them was as natural as to look, to think, to feel, to recognize, to remember, as to perform any act of understanding. The play of the energy had been continuous and couldn't change; what changed was only the objects and situations pressing the spring of it. Notes had been in other words the things one couldn't *not* take, and the prime result of all fresh experience was to remind one of that. I have endeavoured to characterize the peremptory fashion in which my fresh experience of London – the London of the habitual observer, the preoccupied painter, the pedestrian prowler – reminded me; an admonition that represented, I think, the sum of my investigations. I recall pulling no wires, knocking at no closed doors, applying for no 'authentic' information; but I recall also on the other hand the practice of never missing an opportunity to add a drop, however small, to the bucket of my impressions or to renew my sense of being able to dip into it. To haunt the great city and by this habit to penetrate it, imaginatively, in as many places as possible – *that* was to be informed, *that* was to pull wires, *that* was to open doors, *that* positively was to groan at times under the weight of one's accumulations.

Face to face with the idea of Hyacinth's subterraneous politics and occult affiliations, I recollect perfectly feeling, in short, that I might well be ashamed if, with my advantages – and there wasn't a street, a corner, an hour, of London that was not an advantage – I shouldn't be able to piece together a proper semblance of those things, as indeed a proper semblance of all the odd parts of his life. There was always of course the chance that the propriety might be challenged – challenged by readers of a knowledge greater than mine. Yet knowledge, after all, of what? My vision of the aspects I more or less fortunately rendered *was*, exactly, my knowledge. If I made my appearances live, what was this but the utmost one could do with them? Let me at the same time not deny that, in answer to probable ironic reflexions on the full licence for sketchiness and vagueness and dimness taken indeed by my picture, I had to bethink myself in advance of a defence of my 'artistic position'. Shouldn't I find it in the happy contention that the value I wished most to render and the effect I wished most to produce were precisely those of our not knowing, of society's not knowing, but only guessing and suspecting and trying to ignore, what 'goes on' irreconcileably, subversively, beneath the vast smug surface? I couldn't deal with that positive quantity for itself – my subject had another too exacting side; but I might perhaps show the social ear as on occasion applied to the ground, or catch some gust of the hot breath that I had at many an hour seemed to see escape and hover. What it all came back to was, no doubt, something like *this* wisdom – that if you haven't, for fiction, the root of the matter in you, haven't the sense of life and the penetrating imagination, you are a fool in the very presence of the revealed and assured; but that if you *are* so armed you are not really helpless, not without your resource, even before mysteries abysmal.

60

---- ❖ ----

Preface to The Tragic Muse.

I PROFESS a certain vagueness of remembrance in respect to the origin and growth of *The Tragic Muse*, which appeared in the *Atlantic Monthly* again, beginning January 1889 and running on, inordinately, several months beyond its proper twelve. If it be ever of interest and profit to put one's finger on the productive germ of a work of art, and if in fact a lucid account of any such work involves that prime identification, I can but look on the present fiction as a poor fatherless and motherless, a sort of unregistered and unacknowledged birth. I fail to recover my precious first moment of consciousness of the idea to which it was to give form; to recognize in it – as I like to do in general – the effect of some particular sharp impression or concussion. I call such remembered glimmers always precious, because without them comes no clear vision of what one may have intended, and without that vision no straight measure of what one may have succeeded in doing. What I make out from furthest back is that I must have had from still further back, must in fact practically have always had, the happy thought of some dramatic picture of the 'artist-life' and of the difficult terms on which it is at the best secured and enjoyed, the general question of its having to be not altogether easily paid for. To 'do something about art' – art, that is, as a human complication and a social stumbling-block – must have been for me early a good deal of a nursed intention, the conflict between art and 'the world' striking me thus betimes as one of the half-dozen great primary motives. I remember even having taken for granted with this fond inveteracy that no one of these pregnant themes was likely to prove under the test more full of matter. This being the case, meanwhile, what would all experience have done but enrich one's conviction? – since if on the one hand I had gained a more and more intimate view of the nature of art and the conditions therewith imposed, so the world was a conception that clearly required, and that would for ever continue to take, any amount of filling-in. The happy and fruitful truth, at all events, was that there was opposition – why there *should* be was another matter – and that the opposition would beget an infinity of situations. What had doubtless occurred in fact, moreover, was that just this question of the essence and the reasons of the opposition had shown itself to demand the light of experience; so that to the growth of experience, truly, the treatment of the subject had yielded. It had waited for that advantage.

Yet I continue to see experience giving me its jog mainly in the form of an invitation from the gentle editor of the *Atlantic*, the late Thomas Bailey Aldrich, to contribute to his pages a serial that should run through the year. That friendly appeal becomes thus the most definite statement I can make of the 'genesis' of the book; though from the moment of its reaching me everything else in the matter seems to live again. What lives not least, to be quite candid, is the fact that I was to see this production make a virtual end, for the time, as by its sinister effect – though for reasons still obscure to me – of the pleasant old custom of the 'running' of the novel. Not for many years was I to feel the practice, for my benefit, confidingly revive. The influence of *The Tragic Muse* was thus exactly other than what I had all earnestly (if of course privately enough) invoked for it, and I remember well the particular chill, at last, of the sense of my having launched it in a great grey void from which no echo or message whatever would come back. None, in the event, ever came, and as I now read the book over I find the circumstances make, in its name, for a special tenderness of charity; even for that finer consideration hanging in the parental breast about the maimed or slighted, the disfigured or defeated, the unlucky or unlikely child – with this hapless small mortal thought of further as somehow 'compromising'. I am thus able to take the thing as having quite wittingly and undisturbedly existed for itself alone, and to liken it to some aromatic bag of gathered herbs of which the string has never been loosed; or, better still, to some jar of potpourri, shaped and over-figured and polished, but of which the lid, never lifted, has provided for the intense accumulation of the fragrance within. The consistent, the sustained, preserved *tone* of *The Tragic Muse*, its constant and doubtless rather fine-drawn truth to its particular sought pitch and accent, are, critically speaking, its principal merit – the inner harmony that I perhaps presumptuously permit myself to compare to an unevaporated scent.

After which indeed I may well be summoned to say what I mean, in such a business, by an appreciable 'tone' and how I can justify my claim to it – a demonstration that will await us later. Suffice it just here that I find the latent historic clue in my hand again with the easy recall of my prompt grasp of such a chance to make a story about art. *There* was my subject this time – all mature with having long waited, and with the blest dignity that my original perception of its value was quite lost in the mists of youth. I must long have carried in my head the notion of a young man who should amid difficulty – the difficulties being the story – have abandoned 'public life' for the zealous pursuit of some supposedly minor craft; just as, evidently, there had hovered before me some possible picture (but all comic and ironic) of one of the most salient London 'social' passions, the unappeasable curiosity for the things of the theatre; for every one of them, that is, except the drama itself, and for the 'personality' of the performer (almost any performer quite sufficiently serving) in particular. This latter, verily, had struck me as an aspect appealing mainly to satiric treatment; the only adequate or effective treatment, I had again and again felt, for most of the distinctively social aspects of London: the general artlessly histrionized air of things caused so many examples to spring from behind any hedge. What came up, however, at once, for my own stretched canvas, was that it would have to be ample, give me really space to turn round, and that a single illustrative case might easily be meagre fare. The young man who should 'chuck' admired politics, and of course some other admired object with them, would be all very well; but he wouldn't be enough – therefore what should one say to some other young man who would chuck something and somebody else, admired in their way too?

There need never, at the worst, be any difficulty about the things advantageously chuckable for art; the question is all but of choosing them in the heap. Yet were I to represent a struggle – an interesting one, indispensably – with the passions of the theatre (as a profession, or at least as an absorption) I should have to place the theatre in another light than the satiric. This, however, would by good luck be perfectly possible too – without a sacrifice of truth; and I should doubtless even be able to make my theatric case as important as I might desire it. It seemed clear that I needed big cases – small ones would practically give my central idea away; and I make out now my still labouring under the illusion that the case of the sacrifice for art *can* ever be, with truth, with taste, with discretion involved, apparently and showily 'big'. I dare say it glimmered upon me even then that the very sharpest difficulty of the victim of the conflict I should seek to represent, and the very highest interest of his predica-ment, dwell deep in the fact that his repudiation of the great obvious, great moral or functional or useful character, shall just have to consent to resemble a surrender for absolutely nothing. Those characters are all large and expansive, seated and established and endowed; whereas the most charming truth about the preference for art is that to parade abroad so thoroughly inward and so naturally embarrassed a matter is to falsify and vulgarize it; that as a prefer-ence attended with the honours of publicity it is indeed nowhere; that in fact, under the rule of its sincerity, its only honours are those of contraction, concentration and a seemingly deplorable indifference to everything but itself. Nothing can well figure as less 'big', in an honest thesis, than a marked instance of somebody's willingness to pass mainly for an ass. Of these things I must, I say, have been in strictness aware; what I perhaps failed of was to note that if a certain romantic glamour (even that of mere eccentricity or of a fine perversity) may be flung over the act of exchange of a 'career' for the aesthetic life in general, the prose and the modesty of the matter yet come in with any exhibition of the particular branch of aesthetics selected. Then it is that the attitude of hero or heroine may look too much – for the romantic effect – like a low crouching over proved trifles. Art indeed has in our day taken on so many honours and emoluments that the recognition of its importance is more than a custom, has become on occasion almost a fury: the line is drawn – especially in the English world – only at the importance of heeding what it may mean.

The more I turn my pieces over, at any rate, the more I now see I must have found in them, and I remember how, once well in presence of my three typical examples, my fear of too ample a canvas quite dropped. The only question was that if I had marked my political case, from so far back, for 'a story by itself', and then marked my theatrical case for another, the joining together of these interests, originally seen as separate, might, all disgracefully, betray the seam, show for mechanical and superficial. A story was a story, a picture a picture, and I had a mortal horror of two stories, two pictures, in one. The reason of this was the clearest – my subject was immediately, under that disadvantage, so cheated of its indispensable centre as to become of no more use for expressing a main intention than a wheel without a hub is of use for moving a cart. It was a fact, apparently, that one *had* on occasion seen two pictures in one; were there not for instance certain sublime Tintorettos at Venice, a measureless Crucifixion in especial, which showed without loss of authority half a dozen actions separately taking place? Yes, that might be, but there had surely been nevertheless a mighty pictorial fusion, so that the virtue of composition had somehow thereby come all mysteriously to its own. Of course the affair would be simple enough if composition could be kept out of the question; yet by what art or process, what bars and bolts, what unmuzzled dogs and pointed guns, perform that feat? I had to know myself utterly inapt for any such valour and recognize that, to make it possible, sundry things should have begun for me much further back than I had felt them even in their dawn. A picture without composition slights its most precious chance for beauty, and is moreover not composed at all unless the painter knows *how* that principle of health and safety, working as an absolutely premeditated art, has prevailed. There may in its absence be life, incontestably, as *The Newcomes* has life, as *Les Trois Mousquetaires*, as Tolstoi's *Peace and War*, have it; but what do such large loose baggy monsters, with their queer elements of the accidental and the arbitrary, artistically *mean*? We have heard it maintained, we well remember, that such things are 'superior to art'; but we understand least of all what *that* may mean, and we look in vain for the artist, the divine explanatory genius, who will come to our aid and tell us. There is life and life, and as waste is only life sacrificed and thereby prevented from 'counting', I delight in a deep-breathing economy and an organic form. My business was accordingly to 'go in' for complete pictorial fusion, some such common interest between my two first notions as would, in spite of their birth under quite different stars, do them no violence at all.

I recall with this confirmed infatuation of retrospect that through the mild perceptions I here glance at there struck for *The Tragic Muse* the first hour of a season of no small subjective felicity; lighted mainly, I seem to see, by a wide west window that, high aloft, looked over near and far London sunsets, a half-grey, half-flushed expanse of London life. The production of the thing, which yet took a good many months, lives for me again all contemporaneously in that full projection, upon my very table, of the good fog-filtered Kensington mornings; which had a way indeed of seeing the sunset in and which at the very last are merged to memory in a different and a sharper pressure, that of an hotel bedroom in Paris during the autumn of 1889, with the Exposition du Centenaire about to end – and my long story, through the usual difficulties, as well. The usual difficulties – and I fairly cherish the record as some adventurer in another line may hug the sense of his inveterate habit of just saving in time the neck he ever undiscourageably risks – were those bequeathed as a particular vice of the artistic spirit, against which vigilance had been destined from the first to exert itself in vain, and the effect of which was that again and again, perversely, incurably, the centre of my structure would insist on placing itself *not*, so to speak, in the middle. It mattered little that the reader with the idea or the suspicion of a structural centre is the rarest of friends and of critics – a bird, it would seem, as merely fabled as the phoenix: the terminational terror was none the less certain to break in and my work threaten to masquerade for me as an active figure condemned to the disgrace of legs too short, ever so much too short, for its body. I urge myself to the candid confession that in very few of my productions, to my eye, *has* the organic centre succeeded in getting into proper position.

Time after time, then, has the precious waistband or girdle, studded and buckled and placed for brave outward show, practically worked itself, and in spite of desperate remonstrance, or in other words essential counterplotting, to a point perilously near the knees – perilously I mean for the freedom of these parts. In several of my compositions this displacement has so succeeded, at the crisis, in defying and resisting me, has appeared so fraught with probable dishonour, that I still turn upon them, in spite of the greater or less success of final dissimulation, a rueful and wondering eye. These productions have in fact, if I may be so bold about it, specious and spurious centres altogether, to make up for the failure of the true. As to which in my list they are, however, that is another business, not on any terms to be made known. Such at least would seem my resolution so far as I have thus proceeded. Of any attention ever arrested by the pages forming the object of this reference that rigour of discrimination has wholly and consistently failed, I gather, to constitute a part. In which fact there is perhaps after all a rough justice – since the infirmity I speak of, for example, has been always but the direct and immediate fruit of a positive excess of foresight, the overdone desire to provide for future need and lay up heavenly treasure against the demands of my climax. If the art of the drama, as a great French master of it has said, is above all the art of preparations, that is true only to a less extent of the art of the novel, and true exactly in the degree in which the art of the particular novel comes near that of the drama. The first half of a fiction insists ever on figuring to me as the stage or theatre for the second half, and I have in general given so much space to making the theatre propitious that my halves have too often proved strangely unequal. Thereby has arisen with grim regularity the question of artfully, of consummately masking the fault and conferring on the false quantity the brave appearance of the true.

But I am far from pretending that these desperations of ingenuity have not – as through seeming *most* of the very essence of the problem – their exasperated charm; so far from it that my particular supreme predicament in the Paris hotel, after an undue primary leakage of time, no doubt, over at the great river-spanning museum of the Champ de Mars and the Trocadero, fairly takes on to me now the tender grace of a day that is dead. Re-reading the last chapters of *The Tragic Muse* I catch again the very odour of Paris, which comes up in the rich rumble of the Rue de la Paix – with which my room itself, for that matter, seems impregnated – and which hangs for reminiscence about the embarrassed effort to 'finish', not ignobly, within my already exceeded limits; an effort prolonged each day to those late afternoon hours during which the tone of the terrible city seemed to deepen about one to an effect strangely composed at once of the auspicious and the fatal. The 'plot' of Paris thickened at such hours beyond any other plot in the world, I think; but there one sat meanwhile with another, on one's hands, absolutely requiring precedence. Not the least imperative of one's conditions was thus that one should have really, should have finely and (given one's scale) concisely treated one's subject, in spite of there being so much of the confounded irreducible quantity still to treat. If I spoke just now, however, of the 'exasperated' charm of supreme difficulty, that is because the challenge of economic representation so easily becomes, in any of the arts, intensely interesting to meet. To put all that is possible of one's idea into a form and compass that will contain and express it only by delicate adjustments and an exquisite chemistry, so that there will at the end be neither a drop of one's liquor left nor a hair's breadth of the rim of one's glass to spare – every artist will remember how often that sort of necessity has carried with it its particular inspiration. Therein lies the secret of the appeal, to his mind, of the successfully *foreshortened* thing, where representation is arrived at, as I have already elsewhere had occasion to urge, not by the addition of items (a light that has for its attendant shadow a possible dryness) but by the art of figuring synthetically, a compactness into which the imagination may cut thick, as into the rich density of wedding-cake. The moral of all which indeed, I fear, is, perhaps too trivially, but that the 'thick', the false, the dissembling second half of the work before me, associated throughout with the effort to weight my dramatic values as heavily as might be, since they had to be so few, presents that effort as at the very last a quite convulsive, yet in its way highly agreeable, spasm. Of such mild prodigies is the 'history' of any specific creative effort composed!

But I have got too much out of the 'old' Kensington light of twenty years ago – a lingering oblique ray of which, to-day surely quite extinct, played for a benediction over my canvas. From the moment I made out, at my high-perched west window, my lucky title, that is from the moment Miriam Rooth herself had given it me, so this young woman had given me with it her own position in the book, and so that in turn had given me my precious unity, to which no more than Miriam was either Nick Dormer or Peter Sherringham to be sacrificed. Much of the interest of the matter was immediately therefore in working out the detail of that unity and – always entrancing range of questions – the order, the reason, the relation, of presented aspects. With three *general* aspects, that of Miriam's case, that of Nick's and that of Sherringham's, there was work in plenty cut out; since happy as it might be to say 'My several actions beautifully become one', the point of the affair would be in *showing* them beautifully become so – without which showing foul failure hovered and pounced. Well, the pleasure of handling an action (or, otherwise expressed, of a 'story') is at the worst, for a storyteller, immense, and the interest of such a question as for example keeping Nick Dormer's story his and yet making it also and all effectively in a large part Peter Sherringham's, of keeping Sherringham's his and yet making it in its high degree his kinsman's too, and Miriam Rooth's into the bargain; just as Miriam Rooth's is by the same token quite operatively his and Nick's, and just as that of each of the young men, by an equal logic, very contributively hers – the interest of such a question, I say, is ever so considerably the interest of the system on which the whole thing is done. I see to-day that it was but half a system to say: 'Oh Miriam, a case herself, is the *link* between the two other cases'; that device was to ask for as much help as it gave and to require a good deal more application than it announced on the surface. The sense of a system saves the painter from the baseness of the *arbitrary* stroke, the touch without its reason, but as payment for that service the process insists on being kept impeccably the right one.

These are intimate truths indeed, of which the charm mainly comes out but on experiment and in practice; yet I like to have it well before me here that, after all, *The Tragic Muse* makes it not easy to say which of the situations concerned in it predominates and rules. What has become in that imperfect order, accordingly, of the famous centre of one's subject? It is surely not in Nick's consciousness – since why, if it be, are we treated to such an intolerable dose of Sherringham's? It can't be in Sherringham's – we have for that altogether an excess of Nick's. How on the other hand can it be in Miriam's, given that we have no direct exhibition of hers whatever, that we get at it all inferentially and inductively, seeing it only through a more or less bewildered interpretation of it by others. The emphasis is all on an absolutely objective Miriam, and, this affirmed, how – with such an amount of exposed subjectivity all round her – can so dense a medium be a centre? Such questions as those go straight – thanks to which they are, I profess, delightful; going straight they are of the sort that makes answers possible. Miriam *is* central then to analysis, in spite of being objective; central in virtue of the fact that the whole thing has visibly, from the first, to get itself done in dramatic, or at least in scenic conditions – though scenic conditions which are as near an approach to the dramatic as the novel may permit itself and which have this in common with the latter, th...t they move in the light of *alternation*. This imposes a consistency other than that of the novel at its loosest, and, for one's subject, a different view and a different placing of the centre. The charm of the scenic consistency, the consistency of the multiplication of *aspects*, that of making them amusingly various, had haunted the author of *The Tragic Muse* from far back, and he was in due course to yield to it all luxuriously, too luxuriously perhaps, in *The Awkward Age*, as will doubtless with the extension of these remarks be complacently shown.

To put himself at any rate as much as possible under the protection of it had been ever his practice (he had notably done so in *The Princess Casamassima*, so frankly panoramic and processional); and in what case could this protection have had more price than in the one before us? No character in a play (any play not a mere monologue) has, for the right expression of the thing, a *usurping* consciousness; the consciousness of others is exhibited exactly in the same way as that of the 'hero'; the prodigious consciousness of Hamlet, the most capacious and most crowded, the moral presence the most asserted, in the whole range of fiction, only takes its turn with that of the other agents of the story, no matter how occasional these may be. It is left in other words to answer for itself equally with theirs: wherefore (by a parity of reasoning if not of example) Miriam's might without inconsequence be placed on the same footing; and all in spite of the fact that the 'moral presence' of each of the men most importantly concerned with her – or with the second of whom she at least is importantly concerned – *is* independently answered for. The idea of the book being, as I have said, a picture of some of the personal consequences of the art-appetite raised to intensity, swollen to voracity, the heavy emphasis falls where the symbol of some of the complications so begotten might be made (as I judged, heaven forgive me!) most 'amusing': amusing I mean in the blest very modern sense. I never 'go behind' Miriam; only poor

Sherringham goes, a great deal, and Nick Dormer goes a little, and the author, while they so waste wonderment, goes behind *them*: but none the less she is as thoroughly symbolic, as functional, for illustration of the idea, as either of them, while her image had seemed susceptible of a livelier and 'prettier' concretion. I had desired for her, I remember, all manageable vividness – so ineluctable had it long appeared to 'do the actress', to touch the theatre, to meet that connexion somehow or other, in any free plunge of the speculative fork into the contemporary social salad.

The late R. L. Stevenson was to write to me, I recall – and precisely on the occasion of *The Tragic Muse* – that he was at a loss to conceive how one could find an interest in anything so vulgar or pretend to gather fruit in so scrubby an orchard; but the view of a creature of the stage, the view of the 'histrionic temperament', as suggestive much less, verily, in respect to the poor stage *per se* than in respect to 'art' at large, affected me in spite of that as justly tenable. An objection of a more pointed order was forced upon me by an acute friend later on and in another connexion: the challenge of one's right, in any pretended show of social realities, to attach to the image of a 'public character', a supposed particular celebrity, a range of interest, of intrinsic distinction, greater than any such display of importance on the part of eminent members of the class as we see them about us. There *was* a nice point if one would – yet only nice enough, after all, to be easily amusing. We shall deal with it later on, however, in a more urgent connexion. What would have worried me much more had it dawned earlier is the light lately thrown by that admirable writer M. Anatole France on the question of any animated view of the histrionic temperament – a light that may well dazzle to distress any ingenuous worker in the same field. In those parts of his brief but inimitable *Histoire Comique* on which he is most to be congratulated – for there are some that prompt to reserves – he has 'done the actress', as well as the actor, done above all the mountebank, the mummer and the *cabotin*, and mixed them up with the queer theatric air, in a manner that practically warns all other hands off the material for ever. At the same time I think I saw Miriam, and without a sacrifice of truth, that is of the particular glow of verisimilitude I wished her most to benefit by, in a complexity of relations finer than any that appear possible for the gentry of M. Anatole France.

Her relation to Nick Dormer, for instance, was intended as a superior interest – that of being (while perfectly sincere, sincere for *her*, and therefore perfectly consonant with her impulse perpetually to perform and with her success in performing) the result of a touched imagination, a touched pride for 'art', as well as of the charm cast on other sensibilities still. Dormer's relation to herself is a different matter, of which more presently; but the sympathy she, poor young woman, very generously and intelligently offers him where most people have so stinted it, is disclosed largely at the cost of her egotism and her personal pretensions, even though in fact determined by her sense of their together, Nick and she, postponing the 'world' to their conception of other and finer decencies. Nick can't on the whole see – for I have represented him as in his day quite sufficiently troubled and anxious – why he should condemn to ugly feebleness his most prized faculty (most prized, at least, by himself) even in order to keep his seat in Parliament, to inherit Mr Carteret's blessing and money, to gratify his mother and carry out the mission of his father, to marry Julia Dallow in fine, a beautiful imperative woman with a great many thousands a year. It all comes back in the last analysis to the individual vision of decency, the critical as well as the passionate judgement of it under sharp stress; and Nick's vision and judgement, all on the aesthetic ground, have beautifully coincided, to Miriam's imagination, with a now fully marked, an inspired and impenitent, choice of her own: so that, other considerations powerfully aiding indeed, she is ready to see their interest all splendidly as one. She is in the uplifted state to which sacrifices and submissions loom large, but loom so just because they must write sympathy, write passion, large. Her measure of what she would be capable of for him – capable, that is, of *not* asking of him – will depend on what he shall ask of *her*, but she has no fear of not being able to satisfy him, even to the point of 'chucking' for him, if need be, that artistic identity of her own which she has begun to build up. It will all be to the glory therefore of their common infatuation with 'art': she will doubtless be no less willing to serve his than she was eager to serve her own, purged now of the too great shrillness.

This puts her quite on a different level from that of the vivid monsters of M. France, whose artistic identity is the last thing *they* wish to chuck – their only dismissal is of all material and social overdraping. Nick Dormer in point of fact asks of Miriam nothing but that she shall remain 'awfully interesting to paint'; but that is *his* relation, which, as I say, is quite a matter by itself. He at any rate, luckily for both of them it may be, doesn't put her to the test: he is so busy with his own case, busy with testing himself and feeling his reality. He has seen himself as giving up precious things for an object, and that object has somehow not been the young woman in question, nor anything very nearly like her. She on the other hand has asked everything of Peter Sherringham, who has asked everything of *her*; and it is in so doing that she has really most testified for art and invited him to testify. With his professed interest in the theatre – one of those deep subjections that, in men of 'taste', the Comédie Française used in old days to conspire for and some such odd and affecting examples of which were to be noted – he yet offers her his hand and an introduction to the very best society if she will leave the stage. The power – and her having the sense of the power – to 'shine' in the world is his highest measure of her, the test applied by him to her beautiful human value; just as the manner in which she turns on him is the application of her own standard and touchstone. She is perfectly sure of her own; for – if there were nothing else, and there is much – she has tasted blood, so to speak, in the form of her so prompt and auspicious success with the public, leaving all proba- tions behind (the whole of which, as the book gives it, is too rapid and sudden, though inevitably so: processes, periods, intervals, stages, degrees, connexions, may be easily enough and barely enough named, may be unconvincingly stated, in fiction, to the deep discredit of the writer, but it remains the very deuce to *represent* them, especially represent them under strong compression and in brief and subordinate terms; and this even though the novelist who doesn't represent, and represent 'all the time', is lost, exactly as much lost as the painter who, at his work and given his intention, doesn't paint 'all the time').

Turn upon her friend at any rate Miriam does; and one of my main points is missed if it fails to appear that she does so with absolute sincerity and with the cold passion of the high critic who knows, on sight of them together, the more or less dazzling false from the comparatively grey-coloured true. Sherringham's whole profession has been that he rejoices in her as she is, and that the theatre, the organized theatre, will be, as Matthew Arnold was in those very days pronouncing it, irresistible; and it is the promptness with which he sheds his pretended faith as soon as it feels in the air the breath of reality, as soon as it asks of him a proof or a sacrifice, it is this that excites her doubtless sufficiently arrogant scorn. Where is the virtue of his high interest if it has verily never *been* an interest to speak of and if all it has suddenly to suggest is that, in face of a serious call, it shall be unblushingly relinquished? If he and she together, and her great field and future, and the whole cause they had armed and declared for, have not been serious things they have been base make-believes and trivialities – which is what in fact the homage of society to art always turns out so soon as art presumes not to be vulgar and futile. It is immensely the fashion and immensely edifying to listen to, this homage, while it confines its attention to vanities and frauds; but it knows only terror, feels only horror, the moment that, instead of making all the concessions, art proceeds to ask for a few. Miriam is nothing if not strenuous, and evidently nothing if not 'cheeky', where Sherringham is concerned at least: these, in the all-egotistical exhibition to which she is condemned, are the very elements of her figure and the very colours of her portrait. But she is mild and inconsequent for Nick Dormer (who demands of her so little); as if gravely and pityingly embracing the truth that *his* sacrifice, on the right side, is probably to have very little of her sort of recompense. I must have had it well before me that she was all aware of the small strain a great sacrifice to Nick would cost her – by reason of the strong effect on her of his own superior logic, in which the very intensity of concentration was so to find its account.

If the man, however, who holds her personally dear yet holds her extremely personal message to the world cheap, so the man capable of a consistency and, as she regards the matter, of an honesty so much higher than Sherringham's, virtually cares, 'really' cares, no straw for his fellow struggler. If Nick Dormer attracts and all-indifferently holds her it is because, like herself and unlike Peter, he puts 'art' first; but the most he thus does for her in the event is to let her see how she may enjoy, in intimacy, the rigour it has taught him and which he cultivates at her expense. This is the situation in which we leave her, though there would be more still to be said about the difference for her of the two relations – that to each of the men – could I fondly suppose as much of the interest of the book 'left over' for the reader as for myself. Sherringham for instance offers Miriam marriage, ever so 'handsomely'; but if nothing might lead me on further than the question of what it would have been open to us – us novelists, especially in the old days – to show, 'serially', a young man in Nick Dormer's quite different position as offering or a young woman in Miriam's as taking, so for that very reason such an excursion is forbidden me. The trade of the stage-player, and above all of the actress, must have so many detestable sides for the person exercising it that we scarce imagine a full surrender to it without a full surrender, not less, to every immediate compensation, to every freedom and the largest ease within reach: which presentment of the possible case for Miriam would yet have been condemned – and on grounds both various and interesting to trace – to remain very imperfect.

I feel moreover that I might still, with space, abound in remarks about Nick's character and Nick's crisis suggested to my present more reflective vision. It strikes me, alas, that he is not quite so interesting as he was fondly intended to be, and this in spite of the multiplication, within the picture, of his pains and penalties; so that while I turn this slight anomaly over I come upon a reason that affects me as singularly charming and touching and at which indeed I have already glanced. Any presentation of the artist *in triumph* must be flat in proportion as it really sticks to its subject – it can only smuggle in relief and variety. For, to put the matter in an image, all we then – in his triumph – see of the charm-compeller is the back he turns to us as he bends over his work. 'His' triumph, decently, is but the triumph of what he produces, and that is another affair. His romance is the romance he himself projects; he eats the cake of the very rarest privilege, the most luscious baked in the oven of the gods – therefore he mayn't 'have' it, in the form of the privilege of the hero, at the same time. The privilege of the hero – that is of the martyr or of the interesting and appealing and comparatively floundering *person* – places him in quite a different category, belongs to him only as to the artist deluded, diverted, frustrated or vanquished; when the 'amateur' in him gains, for our admiration or compassion or whatever, all that the expert has to do without. Therefore I strove in vain, I feel, to embroil and adorn this young man on whom a hundred ingenious touches are thus lavished: he has insisted in the event on looking as simple and flat as some mere brass check or engraved number, the symbol and guarantee of a stored treasure. The better part of him is locked too much away from us, and the part we see has to pass for – well, what it passes for, so lamentedly, among his friends and relatives. No, accordingly, Nick Dormer isn't 'the best thing in the book', as I judge I imagined he would be, and it contains nothing better, I make out, than that preserved and achieved unity and quality of tone, a value in itself, which I referred to at the beginning of these remarks. What I mean by this is that the interest created, and the expression of that interest, are things kept, as to kind, genuine and true to themselves. The appeal, the fidelity to the prime motive, is, with no little art, strained clear (even as silver is polished) in a degree answering – at least by intention – to the air of beauty. There is an awkwardness again in having thus belatedly to point such features out; but in that wrought appearance of animation and harmony, that effect of free movement and yet of recurrent and insistent reference, *The Tragic Muse* has struck me again as conscious of a bright advantage.

61

❦

From the Preface to The Awkward Age.

... IT COMES back to me, the whole 'job' [of composing the novel], as wonderfully amusing and delightfully difficult from the first; since amusement deeply abides, I think, in any artistic attempt the basis and groundwork of which are conscious of a particular firmness. On that hard fine floor the element of execution feels it may more or less confidently *dance*; in which case puzzling questions, sharp obstacles, dangers of detail, may come up for it by the dozen without breaking its heart or shaking its nerve. It is the difficulty produced by the loose foundation or the vague scheme that breaks the heart — when a luckless fatuity has over-persuaded an author of the 'saving' virtue of treatment. Being 'treated' is never, in a workable idea, a mere passive condition, and I hold no subject ever susceptible of help that isn't, like the embarrassed man of our proverbial wisdom, first of all able to help itself. I was thus to have here an envious glimpse, in carrying my design through, of that artistic rage and that artistic felicity which I have ever supposed to be intensest and highest, the confidence of the dramatist strong in the sense of his postulate. The dramatist has verily to *build*, is committed to architecture, to construction at any cost; to driving in deep his vertical supports and laying across and firmly fixing his horizontal, his resting pieces — at the risk of no matter what vibration from the tap of his master-hammer. This makes the active value of his basis immense, enabling him, with his flanks protected, to advance undistractedly, even if not at all carelessly, into the comparative fairy-land of the mere minor anxiety. In other words his scheme *holds*, and as he feels this in spite of noted strains and under repeated tests, so he keeps his face to the day. I rejoiced, by that same token, to feel *my* scheme hold, and even a little ruefully watched it give me much more than I had ventured to hope. For I promptly found my conceived arrangement of my material open the door wide to ingenuity. I remember that in sketching my project for the conductors of the periodical I have named I drew on a sheet of paper – and possibly with an effect of the cabalistic, it now comes over me, that even anxious amplification may have but vainly attenuated – the neat figure of a circle consisting of a number of small rounds disposed at equal distance about a central object. The central object was my situation, my subject in itself, to which the thing would owe its title, and the small rounds represented so many distinct lamps, as I liked to call them, the function of each of which would be to light with all due intensity one of its aspects. I had divided it, didn't they see? into aspects – uncanny as the little term might sound (though not for a moment did I suggest we should use it for the public), and by that sign we would conquer . . .

The divine distinction of the act of a play – and a greater than any other it easily succeeds in arriving at – was, I reasoned, in its special, its guarded objectivity. This objectivity, in turn, when achieving its ideal, came from the imposed absence of that 'going behind', to compass explanations and amplifications, to drag out odds and ends from the 'mere' storyteller's great property-shop of aids to illusion: a resource under denial of which it was equally perplexing and delightful, for a change, to proceed. Everything, for that matter, becomes interesting from the moment it has closely to consider, for full effect positively to bestride, the law of its kind. 'Kinds' are the very life of literature, and truth and strength come from the complete recognition of them, from abounding to the utmost in their respective senses and sinking deep into their consistency. I myself have scarcely to plead the cause of 'going behind', which is right and beautiful and fruitful in its place and order; but as the confusion of kinds is the inelegance of letters and the stultification of values, so to renounce that line utterly and do something quite different instead may become in another connexion the true course and the vehicle of effect . . .

62

---✦---

From the Preface to The Spoils of Poynton; A London Life;
The Chaperon.

IT WAS YEARS AGO, I remember, one Christmas Eve when I was
dining with friends: a lady beside me made in the course of talk one of
those allusions that I have always found myself recognizing on the
spot as 'germs'. The germ, wherever gathered, has ever been for me
the germ of a 'story', and most of the stories straining to shape under
my hand have sprung from a single small seed, a seed as minute and
wind-blown as that casual hint for *The Spoils of Poynton* dropped
unwitting by my neighbour, a mere floating particle in the stream of
talk. What above all comes back to me with this reminiscence is the
sense of the inveterate minuteness, on such happy occasions, of the
precious particle – reduced, that is, to its mere fruitful essence. Such
is the interesting truth about the stray suggestion, the wandering
word, the vague echo, at touch of which the novelist's imagination
winces as at the prick of some sharp point: its virtue is all in its
needle-like quality, the power to penetrate as finely as possible. This
fineness it is that communicates the virus of suggestion, anything
more than the minimum of which spoils the operation. If one is given
a hint at all designedly one is sure to be given too much; one's subject
is in the merest grain, the speck of truth, of beauty, of reality, scarce
visible to the common eye – since, I firmly hold, a good eye for a
subject is anything but usual. Strange and attaching, certainly, the
consistency with which the first thing to be done for the communicated and seized idea is to reduce almost to nought the form, the air
as of a mere disjoined and lacerated lump of life, in which we may
have happened to meet it. Life being all inclusion and confusion, and
art being all discrimination and selection, the latter, in search of the

hard latent *value* with which alone it is concerned, sniffs round the mass as instinctively and unerringly as a dog suspicious of some buried bone. The difference here, however, is that, while the dog desires his bone but to destroy it, the artist finds in *his* tiny nugget, washed free of awkward accretions and hammered into a sacred hardness, the very stuff for a clear affirmation, the happiest chance for the indestructible. It at the same time amuses him again and again to note how, beyond the first step of the actual case, the case that constitutes for him his germ, his vital particle, his grain of gold, life persistently blunders and deviates, loses herself in the sand. The reason is of course that life has no direct sense whatever for the subject and is capable, luckily for us, of nothing but splendid waste. Hence the opportunity for the sublime economy of art, which rescues, which saves, and hoards and 'banks', investing and reinvesting these fruits of toil in wondrous useful 'works' and thus making up for us, desperate spendthrifts that we all naturally are, the most princely of incomes ...

Extravagant as the mere statement sounds, one seemed accordingly to handle the secret of life in drawing the positive right truth out of the so easy muddle of wrong truths in which the interesting possibilities of that 'row', so to call it, between mother and son over their household gods might have been stifled ...

For something like Fleda Vetch had surely been latent in one's first apprehension of the theme; it wanted, for treatment, a centre, and, the most obvious centre being 'barred', this image, while I still wondered, had, with all the assurance in the world, sprung up in its place. The real centre, as I say, the citadel of the interest, with the fight waged round it, would have been the felt beauty and value of the prize of battle, the Things, always the splendid Things, placed in the middle light, figured and constituted, with each identity made vivid, each character discriminated, and their common consciousness of their great dramatic part established. The rendered tribute of these honours, however, no vigilant editor, as I have intimated, could be conceived as allowing room for; since, by so much as the general glittering presence should spread, by so much as it should suggest the gleam of brazen idols and precious metals and inserted gems in the tempered light of some arching place of worship, by just so much would the muse of 'dialogue', most usurping influence of all the romancingly invoked, be routed without ceremony, to lay her grievance at the feet of her gods. The spoils of Poynton were not directly articulate, and though they might have, and constantly did have, wondrous things to say, their message fostered about them a certain hush of cheaper sound – as a consequence of which, in fine, they would have been costly to keep up. In this manner Fleda Vetch, maintainable at less expense – though even she, I make out, less expert in spreading chatter thin than the readers of romance mainly like their heroines to-day – marked her place in my foreground at one ingratiating stroke. She planted herself centrally, and the stroke, as I call it, the demonstration after which she couldn't be gainsaid, was the simple act of letting it be seen she had character.

For somehow – that was the way interest broke out, once the germ had been transferred to the sunny south windowsill of one's fonder attention – character, the question of what my agitated friends should individually, and all intimately and at the core, show themselves, would unmistakeably be the key to my modest drama, and would indeed alone make a drama of any sort possible. Yes, it is a story of cabinets and chairs and tables; they formed the bone of contention, but what would merely 'become' of them, magnificently passive, seemed to represent a comparatively vulgar issue. The passions, the faculties, the forces their beauty would, like that of antique Helen of Troy, set in motion, was what, as a painter, one had really wanted of them, was the power in them that one had from the first appreciated. Emphatically, by that truth, there would have to be moral developments – dreadful as such a prospect might loom for a poor interpreter committed to brevity. A character is interesting as it comes out, and by the process and duration of that emergence; just as a procession is effective by the way it unrolls, turning to a mere mob if all of it passes at once. My little procession, I foresaw then from an early stage, would refuse to pass at once; though I could keep it more or less down, of course, by reducing it to three or four persons. Practically, in *The Spoils*, the reduction is to four, though indeed – and I clung to that as to my plea for simplicity – the main agents, with the others all dependent, are Mrs Gereth and Fleda. Fleda's ingratiating stroke, for importance, on the threshold, had been that she would understand; and positively, from that moment, the progress and march of my tale became and remained that of her understanding.

Absolutely, with this, I committed myself to making the affirmation and the penetration of it my action and my 'story'; once more, too, with the re-entertained perception that a subject so lighted, a subject residing in somebody's excited and concentrated feeling about something – both the something and the somebody being of course as important as possible – has more beauty to give out than under any other style of pressure. One is confronted obviously thus with the question of the importances; with that in particular, no doubt, of the weight of intelligent consciousness, consciousness of the whole, or of something ominously like it, that one may decently permit a represented figure to appear to throw. Some plea for this cause, that of the intelligence of the moved mannikin, I have already had occasion to make, and can scarce hope too often to evade it. This intelligence, an honourable amount of it, on the part of the person to whom one most invites attention, has but to play with sufficient freedom and ease, or call it with the right grace, to guarantee us that quantum of the impression of beauty which is the most fixed of the possible advantages of our producible effect. It may fail, as a positive presence, on other sides and in other connexions; but more or less of the treasure is stored safe from the moment such a quality of inward life is distilled, or in other words from the moment so fine an interpretation and criticism as that of Fleda Vetch's – to cite the present case – is applied without waste to the surrounding tangle . . .

The 'things' are radiant, shedding afar, with a merciless monotony, all their light, exerting their ravage without remorse; and Fleda almost demonically both sees and feels, while the others but feel without seeing. Thus we get perhaps a vivid enough little example, in the concrete, of the general truth, for the spectator of life, that the fixed constituents of almost any reproducible action are the fools who minister, at a particular crisis, to the intensity of the free spirit engaged with them. The fools are interesting by contrast, by the salience they acquire, and by a hundred other of their advantages; and the free spirit, always much tormented, and by no means always triumphant, is heroic, ironic, pathetic or whatever, and, as exemplified in the record of Fleda Vetch, for instance, 'successful', only through having remained free . . .

63

From the Preface to What Maisie Knew; The Pupil;
In The Cage.

... NO THEMES are so human as those that reflect for us, out of the
confusion of life, the close connexion of bliss and bale, of the things
that help with the things that hurt, so dangling before us for ever that
bright hard medal, of so strange an alloy, one face of which is
somebody's right and ease and the other somebody's pain and
wrong. To live with all intensity and perplexity and felicity in its
terribly mixed little world would thus be the part of my interesting
small mortal; bringing people together who would be at least more
correctly separate; keeping people separate who would be at least
more correctly together; flourishing, to a degree, at the cost of many
conventions and proprieties, even decencies; really keeping the torch
of virtue alive in an air tending infinitely to smother it; really in short
making confusion worse confounded by drawing some stray
fragrance of an ideal across the scent of selfishness, by sowing on
barren strands, through the mere fact of presence, the seed of the
moral life ...

Small children have many more perceptions than they have terms
to translate them; their vision is at any moment much richer, their
apprehension even constantly stronger, than their prompt, their at all
producible, vocabulary. Amusing therefore as it might at the first
blush have seemed to restrict myself in this case to the terms as well as
to the experience, it became at once plain that such an attempt would
fail. Maisie's terms accordingly play their part – since her simpler
conclusions quite depend on them; but our own commentary constantly attends and amplifies. This it is that on occasion, doubtless,
seems to represent us as going so 'behind' the facts of her spectacle as

to exaggerate the activity of her relation to them. The difference here is but of a shade: it is her relation, her activity of spirit, that determines all our own concern – we simply take advantage of these things better than she herself. Only, even though it is her interest that mainly makes matters interesting for us, we inevitably note this in figures that are not yet at her command and that are nevertheless required whenever those aspects about her and those parts of her experience that she understands darken off into others that she rather tormentedly misses. All of which gave me a high firm logic to observe; supplied the force for which the straightener of almost any tangle is grateful while he labours, the sense of pulling at threads intrinsically worth it – strong enough and fine enough and entire enough . . .

She is not only the extraordinary 'ironic centre' I have already noted; she has the wonderful importance of shedding a light far beyond any reach of her comprehension; of lending to poorer persons and things, by the mere fact of their being involved with her and by the special scale she creates for them, a precious element of dignity. I lose myself, truly, in appreciation of my theme on noting what she does by her 'freshness' for appearances in themselves vulgar and empty enough. They become, as she deals with them, the stuff of poetry and tragedy and art; she has simply to wonder, as I say, about them, and they begin to have meanings, aspects, solidities, connexions – connexions with the 'universal!' – that they could scarce have hoped for . . .

The miracle for the author of The Pupil . . . was when, years ago, one summer day, in a very hot Italian railway-carriage, which stopped and dawdled everywhere, favouring conversation, a friend with whom I shared it, a doctor of medicine who had come from a far country to settle in Florence, happened to speak to me of a wonderful American family, an odd adventurous, extravagant band, of high but rather unauthenticated pretensions, the most interesting member of which was a small boy, acute and precocious, afflicted with a heart of weak action, but beautifully intelligent, who saw their prowling precarious life exactly as it was, and measured and judged it, and measured and judged them, all round, ever so quaintly; presenting himself in short as an extraordinary little person. Here was more than enough for a summer's day even in old Italy – here was a thumping windfall. No process and no steps intervened: I *saw*, on the spot, little Morgan Moreen, I saw all the rest of the Moreens; I felt, to the last delicacy, the nature of my young friend's relation with them (he had become at once my young friend) and, by the same stroke, to its uttermost fine throb, the subjection to *him* of the beguiled, bewildered, defrauded, unremunerated, yet after all richly repaid youth who would to a certainty, under stress of compassion, embark with the tribe on tutorship, and whose edifying connexion with it would be my leading document.

This must serve as my account of the origin of *The Pupil*: it will commend itself, I feel, to all imaginative and projective persons who have had – and what imaginative and projective person hasn't? – any like experience of the suddenly-determined *absolute* of perception. The whole cluster of items forming the image is on these occasions born at once; the parts are not pieced together, they conspire and interdepend; but what it really comes to, no doubt, is that at a simple touch an old latent and dormant impression, a buried germ, implanted by experience and then forgotten, flashes to the surface as a fish, with a single 'squirm', rises to the baited hook, and there meets instantly the vivifying ray . . .

If I speak, as just above, of the *action* embodied, each time, in these so 'quiet' recitals, it is under renewed recognition of the inveterate instinct with which they keep conforming to the 'scenic' law. They demean themselves for all the world – they quite insist on it, that is, whenever they have a chance – as little constituted dramas, little exhibitions founded on the logic of the 'scene', the unit of the scene, the general scenic consistency, and knowing little more than that. To read them over has been to find them on this ground never at fault. The process repeats and renews itself, moving in the light it has once for all adopted. These finer idiosyncrasies of a literary form seem to be regarded as outside the scope of criticism – small reference to them do I remember ever to have met; such surprises of re-perusal, such recoveries of old fundamental intention, such moments of almost ruefully independent discrimination, would doubtless in that case not have waylaid my steps. Going over the pages here placed together has been for me, at all events, quite to watch the scenic system at play. The treatment by 'scene', regularly, quite rhythmically recurs; the intervals between, the massing of the elements to a different effect and by a quite other law, remain, in this fashion, all preparative, just as the scenic occasions in themselves become, at a given moment, illustrative, each of the agents, true to its function, taking up the theme from the other very much as the fiddles, in an orchestra, may take it up from the cornets and flutes, or the wind-instruments take it up from the violins. The point, however, is that the scenic passages are *wholly* and logically scenic, having for their rule of beauty the principles of the 'conduct', the organic development, of a scene – the entire succession of values that flower and bear fruit on ground solidly laid for them. The great advantage for the total effect is that we feel, with the definite alternation, how the theme *is* being treated. That is we feel it when, in such tangled connexions, we happen to care. I shouldn't really go on as if this were the case with many readers.

64

From the Preface to The Aspern Papers; The Turn of the Screw;
The Liar; The Two Faces.

. . . I DELIGHT in a palpable imaginable *visitable* past – in the nearer
distances and the clearer mysteries, the marks and signs of a world
we may reach over to as by making a long arm we grasp an object at
the other end of our own table. The table is the one, the common
expanse, and where we lean, so stretching, we find it firm and
continuous. That, to my imagination, is the past fragrant of all, or of
almost all, the poetry of the thing outlived and lost and gone, and yet
in which the precious element of closeness, telling so of connexions
but tasting so of differences, remains appreciable. With more moves
back the element of the appreciable shrinks – just as the charm of
looking over a garden-wall into another garden breaks down when
successions of walls appear. The other gardens, those still beyond,
may be there, but even by use of our longest ladder we are baffled and
bewildered – the view is mainly a view of barriers. The one partition
makes the place we have wondered about *other*, both richly and
recognizeably so; but who shall pretend to impute an effect of
composition to the twenty? We are divided of course between liking
to feel the past strange and liking to feel it familiar; the difficulty is,
for intensity, to catch it at the moment when the scales of the balance
hang with the right evenness . . .

Portentous evil – how was I to save that, as an intention on the part
of my demon-spirits, from the drop, the comparative vulgarity,
inevitably attending, throughout the whole range of possible brief
illustration, the offered example, the imputed vice, the cited act, the
limited deplorable presentable instance? To bring the bad dead back
to life for a second round of badness is to warrant them as indeed

prodigious, and to become hence as shy of specifications as of a waiting anti-climax. One had seen, in fiction, some grand form of wrong-doing, or better still of wrong-being, imputed, seen it promised and announced as by the hot breath of the Pit – and then, all lamentably, shrink to the compass of some particular brutality, some particular immorality, some particular infamy portrayed: with the result, alas, of the demonstration's falling sadly short. If *my* bad things, for *The Turn of the Screw*, I felt, should succumb to this danger, if they shouldn't seem sufficiently bad, there would be nothing for me but to hang my artistic head lower than I had ever known occasion to do.

The view of that discomfort and the fear of that dishonour, it accordingly must have been, that struck the proper light for my right, though by no means easy, short cut. What, in the last analysis, had I to give the sense of? Of their being, the haunting pair, capable, as the phrase is, of everything – that is of exerting, in respect to the children, the very worst action small victims so conditioned might be conceived as subject to. What would *be* then, on reflexion, this utmost conceivability? – a question to which the answer all admirably came. There is for such a case no eligible *absolute* of the wrong; it remains relative to fifty other elements, a matter of appreciation, speculation, imagination – these things moreover quite exactly in the light of the spectator's, the critic's, the reader's experience. Only make the reader's general vision of evil intense enough, I said to myself – and that already is a charming job – and his own experience, his own imagination, his own sympathy (with the children) and horror (of their false friends) will supply him quite sufficiently with all the particulars. Make him *think* the evil, make him think it for himself, and you are released from weak specifications. This ingenuity I took pains – as indeed great pains were required – to apply; and with a success apparently beyond my liveliest hope. Droll enough at the same time, I must add, some of the evidence – even when most convincing – of this success. How can I feel my calculation to have failed, my wrought suggestion not to have worked, that is, on my being assailed, as has befallen me, with the charge of a monstrous emphasis, the charge of all indecently expatiating? There is not only from beginning to end of the matter not an inch of expatiation, but my values are positively all blanks save so far as an excited horror, a promoted pity, a created expertness – on which punctual effects of strong causes no writer can ever fail to plume himself – proceed to read into them more or less fantastic figures. Of high interest to the author meanwhile – and by the same stroke a theme for the moralist – the artless resentful reaction of the entertained person who has abounded in the sense of the situation. He visits his abundance, morally, on the artist – who has but clung to an ideal of faultlessness. Such indeed, for this latter, are some of the observations by which the prolonged strain of that clinging may be enlivened! . . .

65

From the Preface to Lady Barbarina; The Siege of London; An
International Episode; The Pension Beaurepas; A Bundle of
Letters; The Point of View.

... THE THING OF profit is to *have* your experience – to recognize
and understand it, and for this almost any will do; there being surely
no absolute ideal about it beyond getting from it all it has to give. The
artist – for it is of this strange brood we speak – has but to have his
honest sense of life to find it fed at every pore even as the birds of the
air are fed; with more and more to give, in turn, as a consequence,
and, quite by the same law that governs the responsive affection of a
kindly-used animal, in proportion as more and more is confidently
asked ...

66

------------ ✳ ------------

From the Preface to The Lesson of the Master; The Death of the Lion; The Next Time; The Figure in the Carpet; The Coxon Fund.

... WHEREAS ANY anecdote about life pure and simple, as it were, proceeds almost as a matter of course from some good jog of fond fancy's elbow, some pencilled note on somebody else's case, so the material for any picture of personal states so specifically complicated as those of my hapless friends in the present volume will have been drawn preponderantly from the depths of the designer's own mind. This, amusingly enough, is what, on the evidence before us, I seem critically, as I say, to gather – that the states represented, the embarrassments and predicaments studied, the tragedies and comedies recorded, can be intelligibly fathered but on his own intimate experience. I have already mentioned the particular rebuke once addressed me on all this ground, the question of where on earth, where roundabout us at this hour, I had 'found' my Neil Paradays, my Ralph Limberts, my Hugh Verekers and other such supersubtle fry. I was reminded then, as I have said, that these represented eminent cases fell to the ground, as by their foolish weight, unless I could give chapter and verse for the eminence. I was reduced to confessing I couldn't, and yet must repeat again here how little I was so abashed. On going over these things I see, to our critical edification, exactly why – which was because I was able to plead that my postulates, my animating presences, were all, to their great enrichment, their intensification of value, ironic; the strength of applied irony being surely in the sincerities, the lucidities, the utilities that stand behind it. When it's not a campaign, of a sort, on behalf of the something better (better than the obnoxious, the provoking object) that blessedly, as is assumed, *might* be, it's not worth speaking of. But this is exactly what we mean by operative irony. It implies and projects the possible other case, the case rich and edifying where the actuality is pretentious and vain. So it plays its lamp; so, essentially, it carries that smokeless flame, which makes clear, with all the rest, the good cause that guides it . . .

542

67

From the Preface to The Altar of the Dead; The Beast in the Jungle; The Birthplace; The Private Life; Owen Wingrave; The Friend of Friends; Sir Edmund Orme; The Real Right Thing; The Jolly Corner; Julia Bride.

... WE BUT too probably break down, I have ever reasoned, when we attempt the prodigy, the appeal to mystification, in itself; with its 'objective' side too emphasized the report (it is ten to one) will practically run thin. We want it clear, goodness knows, but we also want it thick, and we get the thickness in the human consciousness that entertains and records, that amplifies and interprets it. That indeed, when the question is (to repeat) of the 'supernatural', constitutes the only thickness we do get; here prodigies, when they come straight, come with an effect imperilled; they keep all their character, on the other hand, by looming through some other history – the indispensable history of somebody's *normal* relation to something. It's in such connexions as these that they most interest, for what we are then mainly concerned with is their imputed and borrowed dignity. Intrinsic values they have none – as we feel for instance in such a matter as the would-be portentous climax of Edgar Poe's *Arthur Gordon Pym*, where the indispensable history is absent, where the phenomena evoked, the moving accidents, coming straight, as I say, are immediate and flat, and the attempt is all at the horrific in itself. The result is that, to my sense, the climax fails – fails because it stops short, and stops short for want of connexions. There *are* no connexions; not only, I mean, in the sense of further statement, but of our own further relation to the elements, which hang in the void: whereby we see the effect lost, the imaginative effort wasted.

I dare say, to conclude, that whenever, in quest, as I have noted, of the amusing, I have invoked the horrific, I have invoked it, in such air as that of *The Turn of the Screw*, that of *The Jolly Corner*, that of *The Friends of the Friends*, that of *Sir Edmund Orme*, that of *The Real Right Thing*, in earnest aversion to waste and from the sense that in art economy is always beauty. The apparitions of Peter Quint and Miss Jessel, in the first of the tales just named, the elusive presence nightly 'stalked' through the New York house by the poor gentleman in the second, are matters as to which in themselves, really, the critical challenge (essentially nothing ever but the spirit of fine attention) may take a hundred forms – and a hundred felt or possibly proved infirmities is too great a number. Our friends' respective minds about them, on the other hand, are a different matter – challengeable, and repeatedly, if you like, but never challengeable without some consequent further stiffening of the whole texture. Which proposition involves, I think, a moral. The moving accident, the rare conjunction, whatever it be, doesn't make the story – in the sense that the story is our excitement, our amusement, our thrill and our suspense; the human emotion and the human attestation, the clustering human conditions we expect presented, only make it. The extraordinary is most extraordinary in that it happens to you and me, and it's of value (of value for others) but so far as visibly brought home to us. At any rate, odd though it may sound to pretend that one feels on safer ground in tracing such an adventure as that of the hero of *The Jolly Corner* than in pursuing a bright career among pirates or detectives, I allow that composition to pass as the measure or limit, on my own part, of any achievable comfort in the 'adventure-story'; and this not because I may 'render' – well, what my poor gentleman attempted and suffered in the New York house – better than I may render detectives or pirates or other splendid desperadoes, though even here too there would be something to say; but because the spirit engaged with the forces of violence interests me most when I can think of it as engaged most deeply, most finely and most 'subtly' (precious term!). For then it is that, as with the longest and firmest prongs of consciousness, I grasp and hold the throbbing subject; *there* it is above all that I find the steady light of the picture . . .

68

---------- ✢ ----------

From the Preface to Daisy Miller; Pandora; The Patagonia;
The Marriages; The Real Thing; Brooksmith; The Beldonald
Holbein; The Story In It; Flickerbridge; Mrs Medwin.

... THERE WAS always the difficulty – I have in the course of these
so numerous preliminary observations repeatedly referred to it, but
the point is so interesting that it can scarce be made too often – that
the simplest truth about a human entity, a situation, a relation, an
aspect of life, however small, on behalf of which the claim to
charmed attention is made, strains ever, under one's hand, more
intensely, *most* intensely, to justify that claim; strains ever, as it were,
toward the uttermost end or aim of one's meaning or of its own
numerous connexions; struggles at each step, and in defiance of one's
raised admonitory finger, fully and completely to express itself. Any
real art of representation is, I make out, a controlled and guarded
acceptance, in fact a perfect economic mastery, of that conflict: the
general sense of the expansive, the explosive principle in one's
material thoroughly noted, adroitly allowed to flush and colour and
animate the disputed value, but with its other appetites and treacheries, its characteristic space-hunger and space-cunning, kept down.
The fair flower of this artful compromise is to my sense the secret of
'foreshortening' – the particular economic device for which one must
have a name and which has in its single blessedness and its determined pitch, I think, a higher price than twenty other clustered
loosenesses; and just because full-fed statement, just because the
picture of as many of the conditions as possible made and kept
proportionate, just because the surface iridescent, even in the short
piece, by what is beneath it and what throbs and gleams through, are

things all conducive to the only compactness that has a charm, to the only spareness that has a force, to the only simplicity that has a grace – those, in each order, that produce the *rich* effect . . .

69

Preface to The Wings of the Dove.

THE WINGS OF THE DOVE, published in 1902, represents to my memory a very old – if I shouldn't perhaps rather say a very young – motive; I can scarce remember the time when the situation on which this long-drawn fiction mainly rests was not vividly present to me. The idea, reduced to its essence, is that of a young person conscious of a great capacity for life, but early stricken and doomed, condemned to die under short respite, while also enamoured of the world; aware moreover of the condemnation and passionately desiring to 'put in' before extinction as many of the finer vibrations as possible, and so achieve, however briefly and brokenly, the sense of having lived. Long had I turned it over, standing off from it, yet coming back to it; convinced of what might be done with it, yet seeing the theme as formidable. The image so figured would be, at best, but half the matter; the rest would be all the picture of the struggle involved, the adventure brought about, the gain recorded or the loss incurred, the precious experience somehow compassed. These things, I had from the first felt, would require much working-out; that indeed was the case with most things worth working at all; yet there are subjects and subjects, and this one seemed particularly to bristle. It was formed, I judge, to make the wary adventurer walk round and round it – it had in fact a charm that invited and mystified alike that attention; not being somehow what one thought of as a 'frank' subject, after the fashion of some, with its elements well in view and its whole character in its face. It stood there with secrets and compartments, with possible treacheries and traps; it might have a great deal to give, but would probably ask for equal services in return, and would collect this debt to the last shilling. It involved, to begin with, the placing in the strongest light a person infirm and ill – a case sure to prove difficult and to require much handling; though giving perhaps, with other matters, one of those chances for good taste, possibly even for the play of the very best in the world, that are not only always to be invoked and cultivated, but that are absolutely to be jumped at from the moment they make a sign.

Yes then, the case prescribed for its central figure a sick young woman, at the whole course of whose disintegration and the whole ordeal of whose consciousness one would have quite honestly to assist. The expression of her state and that of one's intimate relation to it might therefore well need to be discreet and ingenious; a reflexion that fortunately grew and grew, however, in proportion as I focussed my image – roundabout which, as it persisted, I repeat, the interesting possibilities and the attaching wonderments, not to say the insoluble mysteries, thickened apace. Why had one to look so straight in the face and so closely to cross-question that idea of making one's protagonist 'sick'? – as if to be menaced with death or danger hadn't been from time immemorial, for heroine or hero, the very shortest of all cuts to the interesting state. Why should a figure be disqualified for a central position by the particular circumstance that might most quicken, that might crown with a fine intensity, its liability to many accidents, its consciousness of all relations? This circumstance, true enough, might disqualify it for many activities – even though we should have imputed to it the unsurpassable activity of passionate, of inspired resistance. This last fact was the real issue, for the way grew straight from the moment one recognized that the poet essentially *can't* be concerned with the act of dying. Let him deal with the sickest of the sick, it is still by the act of living that they appeal to him, and appeal the more as the conditions plot against them and prescribe the battle. The process of life gives way fighting, and often may so shine out on the lost ground as in no other connexion. One had had moreover, as a various chronicler, one's secondary physical weaklings and failures, one's accessory invalids – introduced with a complacency that made light of criticism. To Ralph Touchett in *The Portrait of a Lady*, for instance, his deplorable state of health was not only no drawback; I had clearly been right in counting it, for any happy effect he should produce, a positive good mark, a direct aid to pleasantness and vividness. The reason of this moreover could never in the world have been his fact of sex; since men, among the mortally afflicted, suffer on the whole more overtly and more grossly than women, and resist with a ruder, an inferior strategy. I had thus to take *that* anomaly for what it was worth, and I give it here but as one of the ambiguities amid which my subject ended by making itself at home and seating itself quite in confidence.

With the clearness I have just noted, accordingly, the last thing in the world it proposed to itself was to be the record predominantly of a collapse. I don't mean to say that my offered victim was not present to my imagination, constantly, as dragged by a greater force than any she herself could exert; she had been given me from far back as contesting every inch of the road, as catching at every object the grasp of which might make for delay, as clutching these things to the last moment of her strength. Such an attitude and such movements, the passion they expressed and the success they in fact represented, what were they in truth but the soul of drama? – which is the portrayal, as we know, of a catastrophe determined in spite of oppositions. My young woman would *herself* be the opposition – to the catastrophe announced by the associated Fates, powers conspiring to a sinister end and, with their command of means, finally achieving it, yet in such straits really to *stifle* the sacred spark that, obviously, a creature so animated, an adversary so subtle, couldn't but be felt worthy, under whatever weaknesses, of the foreground and the limelight. She would meanwhile wish, moreover, all along, to live for particular things, she would found her struggle on particular human interests, which would inevitably determine, in respect to her, the attitude of other persons, persons affected in such a manner as to make them part of the action. If her impulse to wrest from her shrinking hour still as much of the fruit of life as possible, if this longing can take effect only by the aid of others, their participation (appealed to, entangled and coerced as they find themselves) becomes their drama too – that of their promoting her illusion, under her importunity, for reasons, for interests and advantages, from motives and points of view, of their own. Some of these promptings, evidently, would be of the highest order – others doubtless mightn't; but they would make up together, for her, contributively, her sum of experience, represent to her somehow, in good faith or in bad, what she should have *known*. Somehow, too, at such a rate, one would see the persons subject to them drawn in as by some pool of a Lorelei – see them terrified and tempted and charmed; bribed away, it may even be, from more prescribed and natural orbits, inheriting from their connexion with her strange difficulties and still stranger opportunities, confronted with rare questions and called upon for new discriminations. Thus the scheme of her situation would, in a comprehensive way, see itself constituted; the rest of the interest would be in the number and nature of the particulars. Strong among these, naturally, the need that life should, apart from her infirmity, present itself to our young woman as quite dazzlingly liveable, and that if the great pang for her is in what she must give up we shall appreciate it the more from the sight of all she has.

One would see her then as possessed of all things, all but the single most precious assurance; freedom and money and a mobile mind and personal charm, the power to interest and attach; attributes, each one, enhancing the value of a future. From the moment his imagination began to deal with her at close quarters, in fact, nothing could more engage her designer than to work out the detail of her perfect rightness for her part; nothing above all more solicit him than to recognize fifty reasons for her national and social status. She should be the last fine flower – blooming alone, for the fullest attestation of her freedom – of an 'old' New York stem; the happy congruities thus preserved for her being matters, however, that I may not now go into, and this even though the fine association that shall yet elsewhere await me is of a sort, at the best, rather to defy than to encourage exact expression. There goes with it, for the heroine of *The Wings of the Dove*, a strong and special implication of liberty, liberty of action, of choice, of appreciation, of contact – proceeding from sources that provide better for large independence, I think, than any other conditions in the world – and this would be in particular what we should feel ourselves deeply concerned with. I had from far back mentally projected a certain sort of young American as more the 'heir of all the ages' than any other young person whatever (and precisely on those grounds I have just glanced at but to pass them by for the moment); so that here was a chance to confer on some such figure a supremely touching value. To be the heir of all the ages only to know yourself, as that consciousness should deepen, balked of your inheritance, would be to play the part, it struck me, or at least to arrive at the type, in the light on the whole the most becoming. Otherwise, truly, what a perilous part to play *out* – what a suspicion of 'swagger' in positively attempting it! So at least I could reason – so I even think I *had* to – to keep my subject to a decent compactness. For already, from an early stage, it had begun richly to people itself: the difficulty was to see whom the situation I had primarily projected might, by this, that or the other turn, *not* draw in. My business was to watch its turns as the fond parent watches a child perched, for its first riding-lesson, in the saddle; yet its interest, I had all the while to recall, was just in its making, on such a scale, for developments.

What one had discerned, at all events, from an early stage, was that a young person so devoted and exposed, a creature with her security hanging so by a hair, couldn't but fall somehow into some abysmal trap – this being, dramatically speaking, what such a situation most naturally implied and imposed. Didn't the truth and a great part of the interest also reside in the appearance that she would constitute for others (given her passionate yearning to live while she might) a complication as great as any they might constitute for herself? – which is what I mean when I speak of such matters as 'natural'. They would be as natural, these tragic, pathetic, ironic, these indeed for the most part sinister, liabilities, to her living associates, as they could be to herself as prime subject. If her story was to consist, as it could so little help doing, of her being let in, as we say, for this, that and the other irreducible anxiety, how could she not have put a premium on the acquisition, by any close sharer of her life, of a consciousness similarly embarrassed? I have named the Rhine-maiden, but our young friend's existence would create rather, all round her, very much that whirlpool movement of the waters produced by the sinking of a big vessel or the failure of a great business; when we figure to ourselves the strong narrowing eddies, the immense force of suction, the general engulfment that, for any neighbouring object, makes immersion inevitable. I need scarce say, however, that in spite of these communities of doom I saw the main dramatic complication much more prepared *for* my vessel of sensibility than by her – the work of other hands (though with her own imbrued too, after all, in the measure of their never not being, in some direction, generous and extravagant, and thereby provoking).

The great point was, at all events, that if in a predicament she was to be, accordingly, it would be of the essence to create the predicament promptly and build it up solidly, so that it should have for us as much as possible its ominous air of awaiting her. That reflexion I found, betimes, not less inspiring than urgent; one begins so, in such a business, by looking about for one's compositional key, unable as one can only be to move till one has found it. To start without it is to pretend to enter the train and, still more, to remain in one's seat, without a ticket. Well – in the steady light and for the continued charm of these verifications – I had secured my ticket over the tolerably long line laid down for *The Wings of the Dove* from the moment I had noted that there could be no full presentation of Milly Theale as *engaged* with elements amid which she was to draw her breath in such pain, should not the elements have been, with all solicitude, duly prefigured. If one had seen that her stricken state was but half her case, the correlative half being the state of others as affected by her (they too should have a 'case', bless them, quite as much as she!) then I was free to choose, as it were, the half with which I should begin. If, as I had fondly noted, the little world determined for her was to 'bristle' – I delighted in the term! – with meanings, so, by the same token, could I but make my medal hang free, its obverse and its reverse, its face and its back, would beautifully become optional for the spectator. I somehow wanted them correspondingly embossed, wanted them inscribed and figured with an equal salience; yet it was none the less visibly my 'key', as I have said, that though my regenerate young New Yorker, and what might depend on her, should form my centre, my circumference was every whit as treatable. Therefore I must trust myself to know when to proceed from the one and when from the other. Preparatively and, as it were, yearningly – given the whole ground – one began, in the event, with the outer ring, approaching the centre thus by narrowing circumvallations. There, full-blown, accordingly, from one hour to the other, rose one's process – for which there remained all the while so many amusing formulae.

The medal *did* hang free – I felt this perfectly, I remember, from the moment I had comfortably laid the ground provided in my first Book, ground from which Milly is superficially so absent. I scarce remember perhaps a case – I like even with this public grossness to insist on it – in which the curiosity of 'beginning far back', as far back as possible, and even of going, to the same tune, far 'behind', that is behind the face of the subject, was to assert itself with less scruple. The free hand, in this connexion, was above all agreeable – the hand the freedom of which I owed to the fact that the work had ignominiously failed, in advance, of all power to see itself 'serialized'. This failure had repeatedly waited, for me, upon shorter fictions; but the considerable production we here discuss was (as *The Golden Bowl* was to be, two or three years later) born, not otherwise than a little bewilderedly, into a world of periodicals and editors, of roaring 'successes' in fine, amid which it was well-nigh unnotedly to lose itself. There is fortunately something bracing, ever, in the alpine chill, that of some high icy *arête*, shed by the cold editorial shoulder; sour grapes may at moments fairly intoxicate and the story-teller worth his salt rejoice to feel again how many accommodations he can practise. Those addressed to 'conditions of publication' have in a degree their interesting, or at least their provoking, side; but their charm is qualified by the fact that the prescriptions here spring from a soil often wholly alien to the ground of the work itself. They are almost always the fruit of another air altogether and conceived in a light liable to represent *within* the circle of the work itself little else than darkness. Still, when not too blighting, they often operate as a tax on ingenuity – that ingenuity of the expert craftsman which likes to be taxed very much to the same tune to which a well-bred horse likes to be saddled. The best and finest ingenuities, nevertheless, with all respect to that truth, are apt to be, not one's compromises, but one's fullest conformities, and I will remember, in the case before us, the pleasure of feeling my divisions, my proportions and general rhythm, rest all on permanent rather than in any degree on momentary proprieties. It was enough for my alternations, thus, that they were good in themselves; it was in fact so much for them that I really think any further account of the constitution of the book reduces itself to a just notation of the law they followed.

There was the 'fun', to begin with, of establishing one's successive centres – of fixing them so exactly that the portions of the subject commanded by them as by happy points of view, and accordingly treated from them, would constitute, so to speak, sufficiently solid *blocks* of wrought material, squared to the sharp edge, as to have weight and mass and carrying power; to make for construction, that is, to conduce to effect and to provide for beauty. Such a block, obviously, is the whole preliminary presentation of Kate Croy, which, from the first, I recall, absolutely declined to enact itself save in terms of amplitude. Terms of amplitude, terms of atmosphere, those terms, and those terms only, in which images assert their fulness and roundness, their power to revolve, so that they have sides and backs, parts in the shade as true as parts in the sun – these were plainly to be my conditions, right and left, and I was so far from overrating the amount of expression the whole thing, as I saw and felt it, would require, that to retrace the way at present is, alas, more than anything else, but to mark the gaps and the lapses, to miss, one by one, the intentions that, with the best will in the world, were not to fructify. I have just said that the process of the general attempt is described from the moment the 'blocks' are numbered, and that would be a true enough picture of my plan. Yet one's plan, alas, is one thing and one's result another; so that I am perhaps nearer the point in saying that this last strikes me at present as most character-ized by the happy features that *were*, under my first and most blest illusion, to have contributed to it. I meet them all, as I renew acquaintance, I mourn for them all as I remount the stream, the absent values, the palpable voids, the missing links, the mocking shadows, that reflect, taken together, the early bloom of one's good faith. Such cases are of course far from abnormal – so far from it that some acute mind ought surely to have worked out by this time the 'law' of the degree in which the artist's energy fairly depends on his fallibility. How much and how often, and in what connexions and with what almost infinite variety, must he be a dupe, that of his prime object, to be at all measurably a master, that of his actual substitute for it – or in other words at all appreciably to exist? He places, after an earnest survey, the piers of his bridge – he has at least sounded deep enough, heaven knows, for their brave position; yet the bridge spans the stream, after the fact, in apparently complete independence of these properties, the principal grace of the original design. *They* were an illusion, for their necessary hour; but the span itself, whether of a single arch or of many, seems by the oddest chance in the world to be a reality; since, actually, the rueful builder, pass-ing under it, sees figures and hears sounds above: he makes out, with his heart in his throat, that it bears and is positively being 'used'.

The building-up of Kate Croy's consciousness to the capacity for the load little by little to be laid on it was, by way of example, to have been a matter of as many hundred close-packed bricks as there are actually poor dozens. The image of her so compromised and compromising father was all effectively to have pervaded her life, was in a certain particular way to have tampered with her spring; by which I mean that the shame and the irritation and the depression, the general poisonous influence of him, were to have been *shown*, with a truth beyond the compass even of one's most emphasized 'word of honour' for it, to do these things. But where do we find him, at this time of day, save in a beggarly scene or two which scarce arrives at the dignity of functional reference? He but 'looks in', poor beautiful dazzling, damning apparition that he was to have been; he sees his place so taken, his company so little missed, that, cocking again that fine form of hat which has yielded him for so long his one effective cover, he turns away with a whistle of indifference that nobly misrepresents the deepest disappointment of his life. One's poor word of honour has *had* to pass muster for the show. Every one, in short, was to have enjoyed so much better a chance that, like stars of the theatre condescending to oblige, they have had to take small parts, to content themselves with minor identities, in order to come on at all. I haven't the heart now, I confess, to adduce the detail of so many lapsed importances; the explanation of most of which, after all, I take to have been in the crudity of a truth beating full upon me through these reconsiderations, the odd inveteracy with which picture, at almost any turn, is jealous of drama, and drama (though on the whole with a greater patience, I think) suspicious of picture. Between them, no doubt, they do much for the theme; yet each baffles insidiously the other's ideal and eats round the edges of its position; each is too ready to say 'I can take the thing for "done" only when done in *my* way.' The residuum of comfort for the witness of these broils is of course meanwhile in the convenient reflexion, invented for him in the twilight of time and the infancy of art by the Angel, not to say by the Demon, of Compromise, that nothing is so easy to 'do' as not to be thankful for almost any stray help in its getting done. It wasn't, after this fashion, by making good one's dream of Lionel Croy that my structure was to stand on its feet – any more than it was by letting him go that I was to be left irretrievably lamenting. The who and the what, the how and the why, the whence and the whither of Merton Densher, these, no less, were quantities and attributes that should have danced about him with the antique grace of nymphs and fauns circling round a bland Hermes and crowning him with flowers. One's main anxiety, for each one's agents, is that the air of each shall be *given*; but what does the whole thing become, after all, as one goes, but a series of sad places at which the hand of generosity has been cautioned and stayed? The young man's situation, personal, professional, social, was to have been so decanted for us that we should get all the taste; we were to have been penetrated with Mrs Lowder, by the same token, saturated with her presence, her 'personality', and felt all her weight in the scale. We were to have revelled in Mrs Stringham, my heroine's attendant friend, her fairly choral Bostonian, a subject for innumerable touches, and in an extended and above all an *animated* reflexion of Milly Theale's experience of English society; just as the strength and sense of the situation in Venice, for our gathered friends, was to have come to us in a deeper draught out of a larger cup, and just as the pattern of Densher's final position and fullest consciousness there was to have been marked in fine stitches, all silk and gold, all pink and silver, that have had to remain, alas, but entwined upon the reel.

It isn't, no doubt, however – to recover, after all, our critical balance – that the pattern didn't, for each compartment, get itself somehow wrought, and that we mightn't thus, piece by piece, opportunity offering, trace it over and study it. The thing has doubtless, as a whole, the advantage that each piece is true to its pattern, and that while it pretends to make no simple statement it yet never lets go its scheme of clearness. Applications of this scheme are continuous and exemplary enough, though I scarce leave myself room to glance at them. The clearness is obtained in Book First – or otherwise, as I have said, in the first 'piece', each Book having its subordinate and contributive pattern – through the associated consciousness of my two prime young persons, for whom I early recognized that I should have to consent, under stress, to a practical *fusion* of consciousness. It is into the young woman's 'ken' that Merton Densher is represented as swimming; but her mind is not here, rigorously, the one reflector. There are occasions when it plays this part, just as there are others when his plays it, and an intelligible plan consists naturally not a little in fixing such occasions and making them, on one side and the other, sufficient to themselves. Do I sometimes in fact forfeit the advantage of that distinctness? Do I ever abandon one centre for another after the former has been postulated? From the moment we proceed by 'centres' – and I have never, I confess, embraced the logic of any superior process – they must *be*, each, as a basis, selected and fixed; after which it is that, in the high interest of economy of treatment, they determine and rule. There is no economy of treatment without an adopted, a related point of view, and though I understand, under certain degrees of pressure, a represented community of vision between several parties to the action when it makes for concentration, I understand no breaking-up of the register, no sacrifice of the recording consistency, that doesn't rather scatter and weaken. In this truth resides the secret of the discriminated occasion – that aspect of the subject which we have our noted choice of treating either as picture or scenically, but which is apt, I think, to show its fullest worth in the Scene. Beautiful exceedingly, for that matter, those occasions or parts of an occasion when the boundary line between picture and scene bears a little the weight of the double pressure.

Such would be the case, I can't but surmise, for the long passage that forms here before us the opening of Book Fourth, where all the offered life centres, to intensity, in the disclosure of Milly's single throbbing consciousness, but where, for a due rendering, everything has to be brought to a head. This passage, the view of her introduction to Mrs Lowder's circle, has its mate, for illustration, later on in the book and at a crisis for which the occasion submits to another rule. My registers of 'reflectors', as I so conveniently name them (burnished indeed as they generally are by the intelligence, the curiosity, the passion, the force of the moment, whatever it be, directing them), work, as we have seen, in arranged alternation; so that in the second connexion I here glance at it is Kate Croy who is, 'for all she is worth', turned on. She is turned on largely at Venice, where the appearances, rich and obscure and portentous (another word I rejoice in) as they have by that time become and altogether exquisite as they remain, are treated almost wholly through her vision of them and Densher's (as to the lucid interplay of which conspiring and conflicting agents there would be a great deal to say). It is in Kate's consciousness that at the stage in question the drama is brought to a head, and the occasion on which, in the splendid saloon of poor Milly's hired palace, she takes the measure of her friend's festal evening, squares itself to the same synthetic firmness as the compact constructional block inserted by the scene at Lancaster Gate. Milly's situation ceases at a given moment to be 'renderable' in terms closer than those supplied by Kate's intelligence, or, in a richer degree, by Densher's, or, for one fond hour, by poor Mrs Stringham's (since to that sole brief futility is this last participant, crowned by my original plan with the quaintest functions, in fact reduced); just as Kate's relation with Densher and Densher's with Kate have ceased previously, and are then to cease again, to be projected for us, so far as Milly is concerned with them, on any more responsible plate than that of the latter's admirable anxiety. It is as if, for these aspects, the impersonal plate – in other words the poor author's comparatively cold affirmation or thin guarantee – had felt itself a figure of attestation at once too gross and too bloodless, likely to affect us as an abuse of privilege when not as an abuse of knowledge.

Heaven forbid, we say to ourselves during almost the whole Venetian climax, heaven forbid we should 'know' anything more of our ravaged sister than what Densher darkly pieces together, or than what Kate Croy pays, heroically, it must be owned, at the hour of her visit alone to Densher's lodging, for her superior handling and her dire profanation of. For we have time, while this passage lasts, to turn round critically; we have time to recognize intentions and proprieties; we have time to catch glimpses of an economy of composition, as I put it, interesting in itself: all in spite of the author's scarce more than half-dissimulated despair at the inveterate displacement of his general centre. *The Wings of the Dove* happens to offer perhaps the most striking example I may cite (though with public penance for it already performed) of my regular failure to keep the appointed halves of my whole equal. Here the makeshift middle – for which the best I can say is that it's always rueful and never impudent – reigns with even more than its customary contrition, though passing itself off perhaps too with more than its usual craft. No-where, I seem to recall, had the need of dissimulation been felt so as anguish; nowhere had I condemned a luckless theme to complete its revolution, burdened with the accumulation of its difficulties, the difficulties that grow with a theme's development, in quarters so cramped. Of course, as every novelist knows, it is difficulty that inspires; only, for that perfection of charm, it must have been difficulty inherent and congenital, and not difficulty 'caught' by the wrong frequentations. The latter half, that is the false and deformed half, of *The Wings* would verily, I think, form a signal object-lesson for a literary critic bent on improving his occasion to the profit of the budding artist. This whole corner of the picture bristles with 'dodges' – such as he should feel himself all committed to recognize and denounce – for disguising the reduced scale of the exhibition, for foreshortening at any cost, for imparting to patches the value of presences, for dressing objects in an *air* as of the dimensions they can't possibly have. Thus he would have his free hand for pointing out what a tangled web we weave when – well, when, through our mislaying or otherwise trifling with our blest pair of compasses, we have to produce the illusion of mass without the illusion of extent. *There* is a job quite to the measure of most of our monitors – and with the interest for them well enhanced by the preliminary cunning quest for the spot where deformity has begun.

I recognize meanwhile, throughout the long earlier reach of the book, not only no deformities but, I think, a positively close and felicitous application of method, the preserved consistencies of which, often illusive, but never really lapsing, it would be of a certain diversion, and might be of some profit, to follow. The author's accepted task at the outset has been to suggest with force the nature of the tie formed between the two young persons first introduced – to give the full impression of its peculiar worried and baffled, yet clinging and confident, ardour. The picture constituted, so far as may be, is that of a pair of natures well-nigh consumed by a sense of their intimate affinity and congruity, the reciprocity of their desire, and thus passionately impatient of barriers and delays, yet with qualities of intelligence and character that they are meanwhile extraordinarily able to draw upon for the enrichment of their relation, the extension of their prospect and the support of their 'game'. They are far from a common couple, Merton Densher and Kate Croy, as befits the remarkable fashion in which fortune was to waylay and opportunity was to distinguish them – the whole strange truth of their response to which opening involves also, in its order, no vulgar art of exhibition; but what they have most to tell us is that, all unconsciously and with the best faith in the world, all by mere force of the terms of their superior passion combined with their superior diplomacy, they are laying a trap for the great innocence to come. If I like, as I have confessed, the 'portentous' look, I was perhaps never to set so high a value on it as for all this prompt provision of forces unwittingly waiting to close round my eager heroine (to the eventual deep chill of her eagerness) as the result of her mere lifting of a latch. Infinitely interesting to have built up the relation of the others to the point at which its aching restlessness, its need to affirm itself otherwise than by an exasperated patience, meets as with instinctive relief and recognition the possibilities shining out of Milly Theale. Infinitely interesting to have prepared and organized, correspondingly, that young woman's precipitations and liabilities, to have constructed, for Drama essentially to take possession, the whole bright house of her exposure.

These references, however, reflect too little of the detail of the treatment imposed; such a detail as I for instance get hold of in the fact of Densher's interview with Mrs Lowder before he goes to America. It forms, in this preliminary picture, the one patch not strictly seen over Kate Croy's shoulder; though it's notable that immediately after, at the first possible moment, we surrender again to our major convenience, as it happens to be at the time, that of our drawing breath through the young woman's lungs. Once more, in other words, before we know it, Densher's direct vision of the scene at Lancaster Gate is replaced by her apprehension, her contributive assimilation, of his experience: it melts back into that accumulation, which we have been, as it were, saving up. Does my apparent deviation here count accordingly as a muddle? – one of the muddles ever blooming so thick in any soil that fails to grow reasons and determinants. No, distinctly not; for I had definitely opened the door, as attention of perusal of the first two books will show, to the subjective community of my young pair. (Attention of perusal, I thus confess by the way, is what I at every point, as well as here, absolutely invoke and take for granted; a truth I avail myself of this occasion to note once for all – in the interest of that variety of ideal reigning, I gather, in the connexion. The enjoyment of a work of art, the acceptance of an irresistible illusion, constituting, to my sense, our highest experience of 'luxury', the luxury is not greatest, by my consequent measure, when the work asks for as little attention as possible. It is greatest, it is delightfully, divinely great, when we feel the surface, like the thick ice of the skater's pond, bear without cracking the strongest pressure we throw on it. The sound of the crack one may recognize, but never surely to call it a luxury.) That I had scarce availed myself of the privilege of seeing with Densher's eyes is another matter; the point is that I had intelligently marked my possible, my occasional need of it. So, at all events, the constructional 'block' of the first two Books compactly forms itself. A new block, all of the squarest and not a little of the smoothest, begins with the Third – by which I mean of course a new mass of interest governed from a new centre. Here again I make prudent *provision* – to be sure to keep my centre strong. It dwells mainly, we at once see, in the depths of Milly Theale's 'case', where, close beside it, however, we meet a supplementary reflector, that of the lucid even though so quivering spirit of her dedicated friend.

The more or less associated consciousness of the two women deals thus, unequally, with the next presented face of the subject – deals with it to the exclusion of the dealing of others; and if, for a highly particular moment, I allot to Mrs Stringham the responsibility of the direct appeal to us, it is again, charming to relate, on behalf of that play of the portentous which I cherish so as a 'value' and am accordingly for ever setting in motion. There is an hour of evening, on the alpine height, at which it becomes of the last importance that our young woman should testify eminently in this direction. But as I was to find it long since of a blest wisdom that no expense should be incurred or met, in any corner of picture of mine, without some concrete image of the account kept of it, that is of its being organically re-economized, so under that dispensation Mrs Stringham has to register the transaction. Book Fifth is a new block mainly in its provision of a new set of occasions, which readopt, for their order, the previous centre, Milly's now almost full-blown consciousness. At my game, with renewed zest, of driving portents home, I have by this time all the choice of those that are to brush that surface with a dark wing. They are used, to our profit, on an elastic but a definite system;

by which I mean that having to sound here and there a little deep, as a test, for my basis of method, I find it everywhere obstinately present. It draws the 'occasion' into tune and keeps it so, to repeat my tiresome term; my nearest approach to muddlement is to have sometimes – but not too often – to break my occasions small. Some of them succeed in remaining ample and in really aspiring then to the higher, the sustained lucidity. The whole actual centre of the work, resting on a misplaced pivot and lodged in Book Fifth, pretends to a long reach, or at any rate to the larger foreshortening – though bringing home to me, on re-perusal, what I find striking, charming and curious, the author's instinct everywhere for the *indirect* presentation of his main image. I note how, again and again, I go but a little way with the direct – that is with the straight exhibition of Milly; it resorts for relief, this process, whenever it can, to some kinder, some merciful indirection: all as if to approach her circuitously, deal with her at second hand, as an unspotted princess is ever dealt with; the pressure all round her kept easy for her, the sounds, the movements regulated, the forms and ambiguities made charming. All of which proceeds, obviously, from her painter's tenderness of imagination about her, which reduces him to watching her, as it were, through the successive windows of other people's interest in her. So, if we talk of princesses, do the balconies opposite the palace gates, do the coigns of vantage and respect enjoyed for a fee, rake from afar the mystic figure in the gilded coach as it comes forth into the great *place*. But my use of windows and balconies is doubtless at best an extravagance by itself, and as to what there may be to note, of this and other supersubtleties, other arch-refinements, of tact and taste, of design and instinct, in *The Wings of the Dove*, I become conscious of overstepping my space without having brought the full quantity to light. The failure leaves me with a burden of residuary comment of which I yet boldly hope elsewhere to discharge myself.

70

From the Preface to The Ambassadors.

... NO PRIVILEGE of the teller of tales and the handler of puppets is more delightful, or has more of the suspense and the thrill of a game of difficulty breathlessly played, than just this business of looking for the unseen and the occult, in a scheme half-grasped, by the light or, so to speak, by the clinging scent, of the gage already in hand. No dreadful old pursuit of the hidden slave with bloodhounds and the rage of association can ever, for 'excitement', I judge, have bettered it at its best. For the dramatist always, by the very law of his genius, believes not only in possible right issue from the rightly-conceived tight place; he does much more than this – he believes, irresistibly, in the necessary, the precious 'tightness' of the place (whatever the issue) on the strength of any respectable hint. It being thus the respectable hint that I had with such avidity picked up, what would be the story to which it would most inevitably form the centre? It is part of the charm attendant on such questions that the 'story', with the omens true, as I say, puts on from this stage the authenticity of concrete existence. It then *is*, essentially – it begins to be, though it may more or less obscurely lurk; so that the point is not in the least what to make of it, but only, very delightfully and very damnably, where to put one's hand on it.

In which truth resides surely much of the interest of that admirable mixture for salutary application which we know as art. Art deals with what we see, it must first contribute full-handed that ingredient; it plucks its material, otherwise expressed, in the garden of life – which material elsewhere grown is stale and uneatable. But it has no sooner done this than it has to take account of a *process* – from which only when it's the basest of the servants of man, incurring ignominious dismissal with no 'character', does it, and whether under some muddled pretext of morality or on any other, pusillanimously edge away. The process, that of the expression, the literal squeezing-out, of value is another affair – with which the happy luck of mere finding has little to do. The joys of finding, at this stage, are pretty well over; that quest of the subject as a whole by 'matching', as the ladies say at the shops, the big piece with the snippet, having ended, we assume, with a capture. The subject is found, and if the problem is then transferred to the ground of what to do with it the field opens out for any amount of doing. This is precisely the infusion that, as I submit, completes the strong mixture. It is on the other hand the part of the business that can least be likened to the chase with horn and hound. It's all a sedentary part – involves as much ciphering, of sorts, as would merit the highest salary paid to a chief accountant. Not, however, that the chief accountant hasn't *his* gleams of bliss; for the felicity, or at least the equilibrium, of the artist's state dwells less, surely, in the further delightful complications he can smuggle in than in those he succeeds in keeping out. He sows his seed at the risk of too thick a crop; wherefore yet again, like the gentlemen who audit ledgers, he must keep his head at any price. In consequence of all which, for the interest of the matter, I might seem here to have my choice of narrating my 'hunt' for Lambert Strether, of describing the capture of the shadow projected by my friend's anecdote, or of reporting on the occurrences subsequent to that triumph. But I had probably best attempt a little to glance in each direction; since it comes to me again and again, over this licentious record, that one's bag of adventures, conceived or conceivable, has been only half-emptied by the mere telling of one's story. It depends so on what one means by that equivocal quantity. There is the story of one's hero, and then, thanks to the intimate connexion of things, the story of one's story itself. I blush to confess it, but if one's a dramatist one's a dramatist, and the latter imbroglio is liable on occasion to strike me as really the more objective of the two . . .

It may be asked why, if one so keeps to one's hero, one shouldn't make a single mouthful of 'method', shouldn't throw the reins on his neck and, letting them flap there as free as in *Gil Blas* or in *David Copperfield*, equip him with the double privilege of subject and object – a course that has at least the merit of brushing away questions at a sweep. The answer to which is, I think, that one makes that surrender only if one is prepared *not* to make certain precious discriminations.

The 'first person' then, so employed, is addressed by the author directly to ourselves, his possible readers, whom he has to reckon with, at the best, by our English tradition, so loosely and vaguely after all, so little respectfully, on so scant a presumption of exposure to criticism. Strether, on the other hand, encaged and provided for as *The Ambassadors* encages and provides, has to keep in view proprieties much stiffer and more salutary than any our straight and credulous gape are likely to bring home to him, has exhibitional conditions to meet, in a word, that forbid the terrible *fluidity* of self-revelation. I may seem not to better the case for my discrimination if I say that, for my first care, I had thus inevitably to set him up a confidant or two, to wave away with energy the custom of the seated mass of explanation after the fact, the inserted block of merely referential narrative which flourishes so, to the shame of the modern impatience, on the serried page of Balzac, but which seems simply to appal our actual, our general weaker, digestion. 'Harking back to make up' took at any rate more doing, as the phrase is, not only than the reader of to-day demands, but than he will tolerate at any price any call upon him either to understand or remotely to measure; and for the beauty of the thing when done the current editorial mind in particular appears wholly without sense. It is not, however, primarily for either of these reasons, whatever their weight, that Strether's friend Waymarsh is so keenly clutched at, on the threshold of the book, or that no less a pounce is made on Maria Gostrey – without even the pretext, either, of *her* being, in essence, Strether's friend. She is the reader's friend much rather – in consequence of dispositions that make him so eminently require one; and she acts in that capacity, and *really* in that capacity alone, with exemplary devotion, from beginning to end of the book. She is an enrolled, a direct, aid to lucidity; she is in fine, to tear off her mask, the most unmitigated and abandoned of *ficelles*. Half the dramatist's art, as we well know – since if we don't it's not the fault of the proofs that lie scattered about us – is in the use of *ficelles*; by which I mean in a deep dissimulation of his dependence on them. Waymarsh only to a slight degree belongs, in the whole business, less to my subject than to my treatment of it;

the interesting proof, in these connexions, being that one has but to take one's subject for the stuff of drama to interweave with enthusiasm as many Gostreys as need be . . .

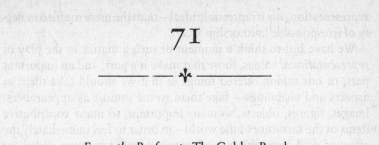

71

From the Preface to The Golden Bowl.

... I HAVE already betrayed, as an accepted habit, and even to extravagance commented on, my preference for dealing with my subject-matter, for 'seeing my story', through the opportunity and the sensibility of some more or less detached, some not strictly involved, though thoroughly interested and intelligent, witness or reporter, some person who contributes to the case mainly a certain amount of criticism and interpretation of it. Again and again, on review, the shorter things in especial that I have gathered into this Series have ranged themselves not as my own impersonal account of the affair in hand, but as my account of somebody's impression of it – the terms of this person's access to it and estimate of it contributing thus by some fine little law to intensification of interest. The somebody is often, among my shorter tales I recognize, but an unnamed, unintroduced and (save by right of intrinsic wit) unwarranted participant, the impersonal author's concrete deputy or delegate, a convenient substitute or apologist for the creative power otherwise so veiled and disembodied. My instinct appears repeatedly to have been that to arrive at the facts retailed and the figures introduced by the given help of some other conscious and confessed agent is essentially to find the whole business – that is, as I say, its effective interest – enriched *by the way*. I have in other words constantly inclined to the idea of the particular attaching case *plus* some near individual view of it; that nearness quite having thus to become an imagined observer's, a projected, charmed painter's or poet's – however avowed the 'minor' quality in the latter – close and sensitive contact with it. Anything, in short, I now reflect, must always have seemed to me better – better for the process and the effect of representation, my irrepressible ideal – than the mere muffled majesty of irresponsible 'authorship' . . .

We have but to think a moment of such a matter as the play of *representational* values, those that make it a part, and an important part, of our taking offered things in that we should take them as aspects and visibilities – take them to the utmost as appearances, images, figures, objects, so many important, so many contributive items of the furniture of the world – in order to feel immediately the effect of such a condition at every turn of our adventure and every point of the representative surface. One has but to open the door to any forces of exhibition at all worthy of the name in order to see the imaging and qualifying agency called at once into play and put on its mettle. We may traverse acres of pretended exhibitory prose from which the touch that directly evokes and finely presents, the touch that operates for closeness and for charm, for conviction and illusion, for communication, in a word, is unsurpassably absent. All of which but means of course that the reader is, in the common phrase, 'sold' – even when, poor passive spirit, systematically bewildered and bamboozled on the article of his dues, he may be but dimly aware of it . . .

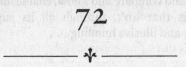

72

On imagination, from a letter to Bernard Shaw, January 1909 (HJL, vol. 4, 512–13). The Saloon is a play, based on 'Owen Wingrave', in which the pacifist hero is killed by a military ghost. Shaw had rejected it on socialist grounds.

... YOU SURELY haven't done all your own so interesting work without learning what it is for the imagination to *play* with an idea – an idea about life – under a happy obsession, for all it is worth. Half the beautiful things that the benefactors of the human species have produced would surely be wiped out if you don't allow this adventurous and speculative imagination its rights. You simplify too much, by the same token, when you limit the field of interest to what you call the scientific – your employment of which term in such a connection even greatly, I confess, confounds and bewilders me. In the one sense in which *The Saloon could* be scientific – that is by being done with all the knowledge and intelligence relevant to its motive, I really think it quite supremely so. That is the only sense in which a work of art can be scientific – though in that sense, I admit, it may be so to the point of becoming an everlasting blessing to man. And if you waylay me here, as I infer you would be disposed to, on the ground that we 'don't want works of art', ah then, my dear Bernard Shaw, I think I take such issue with you that – if we didn't both *like* to talk – there would be scarce use in our talking at all. I think, frankly, even, that we scarce want anything else at all. They are capable of saying more things to man about himself than any other 'works' whatever are capable of doing – and it's only by thus saying as much to him as possible, by saying, as nearly as we can, all there is, and in as many ways and on as many sides, and with a vividness of presentation that 'art', and art alone, is an adequate mistress of, that we enable him to

pick and choose and compare and know, enable him to arrive at any
sort of synthesis that isn't, through all its superficialities and
vacancies, a base and illusive humbug . . .

73

❧

'*The Novel in* The Ring and the Book', Quarterly Review, *July 1912. This was an address given to the Royal Society of Literature on the occasion of Browning's centenary.*

IF ON SUCH an occasion as this – even with our natural impulse to shake ourselves free of reserves – some sharp choice between the dozen different aspects of one of the most copious of our poets becomes a prime necessity, though remaining at the same time a great difficulty, so in respect to the most voluminous of his works the admirer is promptly held up, as we have come to call it; finds himself almost baffled by alternatives. *The Ring and the Book* is so vast and so essentially gothic a structure, spreading and soaring and branching at such a rate, covering such ground, putting forth such pinnacles and towers and brave excrescences, planting its transepts and chapels and porticos, its clustered hugeness or inordinate muchness, that with any first approach we but walk vaguely and slowly, rather bewilderedly, round and round it, wondering at what point we had best attempt such entrance as will save our steps and light our uncertainty, most enable us to reach our personal chair, our indicated chapel or shrine, when once within. For it is to be granted that to this inner view the likeness of the literary monument to one of the great religious gives way a little, sustains itself less than in the first, the affronting mass; unless we simply figure ourselves, under the great roof, looking about us through a splendid thickness and dimness of air, an accumulation of spiritual presences or unprofaned mysteries, that makes our impression heavily general – general only – and leaves us helpless for reporting on particulars. The particulars for our purpose have thus their identity much rather in certain features of the twenty faces – either of one or of another of these – that the structure turns to the outer day and that we can, as it were, sit down before and consider at our comparative ease. I say comparative advisedly, for I cling to the dear old tradition that Browning is 'difficult' – which we were all brought up on and which I think we should, especially on a rich retrospective day like this, with the atmosphere of his great career settling upon us as much as possible, feel it a shock to see break down in too many places at once. Selecting my ground, by your kind invitation, for sticking in and planting before you, to flourish so far as it shall, my little sprig of bay, I have of course tried to measure the quantity of ease with which our material may on that noted spot allow itself to be treated. There are innumerable things in *The Ring and the Book* – as the comprehensive image I began with makes it needless I should say; and I have been above all appealed to by the possibility that one of these, pursued for a while through the labyrinth, but at last overtaken and then more or less confessing its identity, might have yielded up its best essence as a grateful theme under some fine strong economy of *prose* treatment. So here you have me talking at once of prose and seeking that connection to help out my case.

From far back, from my first reading of these volumes, which took place at the time of their disclosure to the world, when I was a fairly young person, the sense, almost the pang, of the novel they might have constituted sprang sharply from them; so that I was to go on through the years almost irreverently, all but quite profanely if you will, thinking of the great loose and uncontrolled composition, the great heavy-hanging cluster of related but unreconciled parts, as a fiction of the so-called historic type, that is as a suggested study of the manners and conditions from which our own have more or less traceably issued, just tragically spoiled – or as a work of art, in other words, smothered in the producing. To which I hasten to add my consciousness of the scant degree in which such a fresh start from our author's documents, such a re-projection of them, wonderful documents as they can only have been, may claim a critical basis. Conceive me as simply astride of my different fancy, my other dream, of the matter – which bolted with me, as I have said, at the first alarm.

Browning worked in this connection literally *upon* documents; no page of his long story is more vivid and splendid than that of his find of the Book in the litter of a market-stall in Florence and the swoop of practised perception with which he caught up in it a treasure. Here was a subject stated to the last ounce of its weight, a living and breathing record of facts pitiful and terrible, a mass of matter bristling with relevations and yet at the same time wrapped over with layer upon layer of contemporary appreciation; which appreciation, in its turn, was a part of the wealth to be appreciated. What our great master saw was his situation founded, seated there in positively packed and congested significance, though by just so much as it was charged with meanings and values were those things undeveloped and unexpressed. They looked up at him, even in that first flush and from their market-stall, and said to him, in their compressed compass, as with the muffled rumble of a slow-coming earthquake, 'Express us, express us, immortalize us as we'll immortalize *you*!' – so that the terms of the understanding were so far cogent and clear. It was an understanding, on their side, with the poet; and since that poet had produced *Men and Women*, *Dramatic Lyrics*, *Dramatis Personae* and sundry plays – we needn't even foist on him *Sordello* – he could but understand in his own way. That way would have had to be quite some other, we fully see, had he been by habit and profession not just the lyric, epic, dramatic commentator, the extractor, to whatever essential potency and redundancy, of the moral of the fable, but the very fabulist himself, the inventor and projector, layer down of the postulate and digger of the foundation. I doubt if we have a precedent for this energy of appropriation of a deposit of *stated* matter, a block of sense already in position and requiring not to be shaped and squared and caused any further to solidify, but rather to suffer disintegration, be pulled apart, melted down, hammered, by the most characteristic of the poet's processes, to powder – dust of gold and silver, let us say. He was to apply to it his favourite system – that of looking at his subject from the point of view of a curiosity almost sublime in its freedom, yet almost homely in its method, and of smuggling as many more points of view together into that one as the fancy might take him to smuggle, on a scale on which even he had never before applied it; this with a courage and a confidence that, in presence of all the conditions, conditions many of them arduous and arid and thankless even to defiance, we can only pronounce splendid, and of which the issue was to be of a proportioned monstrous magnificence.

The one definite forecast for this product would have been that it should figure for its producer as a poem – as if he had simply said, 'I embark at any rate for the Golden Isles'; everything else was of the pure incalculable, the frank voyage of adventure. To what extent the Golden Isles were in fact to be reached is a matter we needn't pretend, I think, absolutely to determine; let us feel for ourselves and as we will about it – either see our adventurer, disembarked bag and baggage and in possession, plant his flag on the highest eminence within his circle of sea, or, on the other hand, but watch him approach and beat back a little, tack and turn and stand off, always fairly in sight of land, catching rare glimpses and meeting strange airs, but not quite achieving the final *coup* that annexes the group. He returns to us under either view all scented and salted with his measure of contact, and that for the moment is enough for us – more than enough for me at any rate, engaged for your beguilement in this practical relation of snuffing up what he brings. He brings, however one puts it, a detailed report, which is but another word for a story; and it is with his story, his offered, not his borrowed one – a very different matter – that I am concerned. We are probably most of us so aware of its general content that if I sum this up I may do so briefly. The Book of the Florentine rubbish-heap is the full account (as full accounts were conceived in those days) of the trial before the Roman courts, with inquiries and judgments by the Tuscan authorities intermixed, of a certain Count Guido Franceschini of Arezzo, decapitated, in company with four confederates – these latter hanged – on February 22, 1698, for the murder of his young wife Pompilia Comparini and her ostensible parents, Pietro and Violante of that ilk.

The circumstances leading to this climax were primarily his marriage to Pompilia, some years before, in Rome – she being then but in her thirteenth year – under the impression, fostered in him by the elder pair, that she was their own child and on this head heiress to moneys settled on them from of old in the event of their having a child. They had in fact had none, and had, in substitution, invented, so to speak, Pompilia, the luckless base-born baby of a woman of lamentable character easily induced to part with her for cash. They bring up the hapless creature as their daughter, and as their daughter they marry her, in Rome, to the middle-aged and impecunious Count Guido, a rapacious and unscrupulous fortune-seeker by whose superior social position, as we say, dreadfully *decaduto* though he be, they are dazzled out of all circumspection. The girl, innocent, ignorant, bewildered, scared and purely passive, is taken home by her husband to Arezzo, where she is at first attended by Pietro and Violante and where the direst disappointments await the three. Count Guido proves the basest of men and his home a place of terror and of torture, from which at the age of seventeen, and shortly prior to her giving birth to an heir to the house, such as it is, she is rescued by a pitying witness of her misery, Canon Caponsacchi, a man of the world and adorning it, yet in holy orders, as men of the world in Italy might then be, who clandestinely helps her, at peril of both their lives, back to Rome, and of whom it is attested that he has had no other relation with her but this of distinguished and all-disinterested friend in need. The pretended parents have at an early stage thrown up their benighted game, fleeing from the rigour of their dupe's domestic rule, disclosing to him vindictively the part they have played and the consequent failure of any profit to him through his wife, and leaving him in turn to wreak his spite, which has become infernal, on the wretched Pompilia. He pursues her to Rome, on her eventual flight, and overtakes her, with her companion, just outside the gates; but having, by the aid of the local powers, re-achieved possession of her, he contents himself for the time with procuring her sequestration in a convent, from which, however, she is presently allowed to emerge in view of the near birth of her child. She rejoins Pietro and Violante, devoted to her, oddly enough, through all their folly and fatuity; and under their roof, in a lonely Roman suburb, her child comes into the world. Her husband meanwhile, hearing of her release, gives way afresh to the fury that had not at the climax of his former pursuit taken full effect; he recruits a band of four of his young tenants or farm-labourers and makes his way, armed, like his companions, with knives, to the door behind which three of the parties to all the wrong done him, as he holds, then lurk. He pronounces, after knocking and waiting, the name of Caponsacchi; upon which, as the door opens, Violante presents herself. He stabs her to death on the spot with repeated blows – like her companions she is off her guard; and he throws himself on each of these with equal murderous effect. Pietro, crying for mercy, falls second beneath him; after which he attacks his wife, whom he literally hacks to death. She survives, by a miracle, long enough, in spite of all her wounds, to testify; which testimony, as may be imagined, is not the least precious part of the case. Justice is on the whole, though deprecated and delayed, what we call satisfactory; the last word is for the Pope in person, Innocent XII. Pignatelli, at whose deliberation, lone and supreme, on Browning's page, we splendidly assist; and Count Guido and his accomplices, bloodless as to the act though these appear to have been, meet their discriminated doom.

That is the bundle of facts, accompanied with the bundle of proceedings, legal, ecclesiastical, diplomatic and other, *on* the facts, that our author, of a summer's day, made prize of; but our general temptation, as I say – out of which springs this question of the other values of character and effect, the other completeness of picture and drama, that the confused whole might have had for us – is a distinctly different thing. The difference consists, you see, to begin with, in the very breath of our poet's genius, already, and so inordinately, at play on them from the first of our knowing them. And it consists in the second place of such an extracted sense of the whole, which becomes, after the most extraordinary fashion, bigger by the extraction, immeasurably bigger than even the most cumulative weight of the mere crude evidence, that our choice of how to take it all is in a manner determined for us: we can only take it as tremendously interesting, interesting not only in itself but with the great added interest, the dignity and authority and beauty, of Browning's general perception of it. We can't not accept this, and little enough on the whole do we want not to: it sees us, with its tremendous push, that of its poetic, esthetic, historic, psychologic shoulder (one scarce knows how to name it), so far on our way. Yet all the while we are in presence not at all of an achieved form, but of a mere preparation for one, though on the hugest scale; so that, you see, we are no more than decently attentive with our question: 'Which of them all, of the various methods of casting the wondrously mixed metal, is he, as he goes, preparing?' Well, as he keeps giving and giving, in immeasurable plenty, it is in our selection from it all and our picking it over that we seek, and to whatever various and unequal effect find, our account. He works over his vast material, and we then work *him* over, though not availing ourselves, to this end, of a grain he himself doesn't somehow give us; and there we are.

I admit that my faith in my particular contention would be a degree firmer and fonder if there didn't glimmer through our poet's splendid hocus-pocus just the hint of one of those flaws that sometimes deform the fair face of a subject otherwise generally appealing or promising – of such a subject in especial as may have been submitted to us, possibly even with the pretension to impose it, in too complete a shape. The idea but half hinted – when it is a very good one – is apt to contain the germ of happier fruit than the freight of the whole branch, waved at us or dropped into our lap, very often proves. This happens when we take over, as the phrase is, established data, take them over from existing records and under some involved obligation to take them as they stand. That drawback rests heavily for instance on the so-called historic fiction – so beautiful a case it is of a muddlement of terms – and is just one of the eminent reasons why the embarrassed Muse of that form, pulled up again and again, and the more often the fine intelligence invokes her, by the need of a superior harmony which shall be after all but a superior truth, catches up her flurried skirts and makes her saving dash for some gap in the hedge of romance. Now the flaw on this so intensely expressive face, that of the general *donnée* of the fate of Pompilia, is that amid the variety of forces at play about her the unity of the situation isn't, by one of those large straight ideal gestures on the part of the Muse, handed to us at a stroke. The question of the whereabouts of the unity of a group of data subject to be wrought together into a thing of art, the question in other words of the point at which the various implications of interest, no matter how many, *most* converge and interfuse, becomes always, by my sense of the affair, quite the first to be answered; for according to the answer shapes and fills itself the very vessel of that beauty – the beauty, exactly, *of* interest, of maximum interest, which is the ultimate extract of any collocation of facts, any picture of life, and the finest aspect of any artistic work. Call a novel a picture of life as much as we will; call it, according to one of our recent fashions, a slice, or even a chunk, even a 'bloody' chunk, of life, a rough excision from that substance as superficially cut and as summarily served as possible, it still fails to escape this exposure to appreciation, or in other words to criticism, that it has had to be selected, selected under some sense for something; and the unity of the exhibition should meet us, does meet us if the work be done, at the point at which that sense is most patent. If the slice or the chunk, or whatever we call it, if *it* isn't 'done', as we say – and as it so often declines to be – the work itself of course isn't likely to be; and there we may dismiss it.

The first thing we do is to cast about for some centre in our field; seeing that, for such a purpose as ours, the subject might very nearly go a-begging with none more definite than the author has provided for it. I find that centre in the embracing consciousness of Capon-sacchi, which, coming to the rescue of our question of treatment, of our search for a point of control, practically saves everything, and shows itself moreover the only thing that *can* save. The more we ask of any other part of our picture that it shall exercise a comprehensive function, the more we see that particular part inadequate; as in-adequate even in the extraordinarily magnified range of spirit and reach of intelligence of the atrocious Franceschini as in the sublime passivity and plasticity of the childish Pompilia, educated to the last point though she be indeed by suffering, but otherwise so untaught that she can neither read nor write. The magnified state is in this work still more than elsewhere the note of the intelligence, of any and every faculty of thought, imputed by our poet to his creatures; and it takes a great mind, one of the greatest, we may at once say, to make these persons express and confess themselves to such an effect of intellectual splendour. He resorts primarily to *their* sense, their sense of themselves and of everything else they know, to exhibit them, and has for this purpose to keep them, and to keep them persistently and inexhaustibly, under the fixed lens of his prodigious vision. He thus makes out in them boundless treasures of truth – truth even when it happens to be, as in the case of Count Guido, but a shining wealth of constitutional falsity. Of the extent to which he may after this fashion unlimitedly draw upon them his exposure of Count Guido, which goes on and on, though partly, I admit, by repeating itself, is a wondrous example. It is not too much to say of Pompilia – Pompilia pierced with twenty wounds, Pompilia on her death-bed, Pompilia but seventeen years old and but a fortnight a mother – that she *acquires* an intellectual splendour just by the fact of the vast covering charity of imagination with which her recording, our commemor-ated, avenger, never so as in this case an avenger of the wronged beautiful things of life, hangs over and breathes upon her. We see her come out to him, and the extremely remarkable thing is that we see it, on the whole, without doubting that it might just have been. Nothing could thus be more interesting, however it may at moments and in places puzzle us, than the impunity, on our poet's part, of most of these over-stretchings of proportion, these violations of the immediate appearance. Browning is deep down below the immediate with the first step of his approach; he has vaulted over the gate, is already far afield and never, so long as we watch him, has occasion to fall back. We wonder, for, after all, the real is his quest, the very ideal of the real, the real most finely mixed with life, which *is* in the last analysis the ideal; and we know, with our dimmer vision, no such reality as a Franceschini fighting for his life, fighting for the vindication of his baseness, embodying his squalor, with an audacity of wit, an intensity of colour, a variety of speculation and illustration, that represent well-nigh the maximum play of the human mind. It is in like sort scarce too much to say of the exquisite Pompilia that on her part intelligence and expression are disengaged to a point at which the angels may well begin to envy her; and all again without our once wincing so far as our consistently liking to see and hear and believe is concerned. Caponsacchi regales us, of course, with the rarest fruit of a great character, a great culture and a great case; but Caponsacchi is acceptedly and naturally, needfully and illustratively, splendid. He *is* the soul of man at its finest – having passed through the smoky fires of life and emerging clear and high. Greatest of all the spirits exhibited, however, is that of the more than octogenarian Pope, at whose brooding, pondering, solitary vigil, by the end of a hard grey winter day in the great bleak waiting Vatican – 'in the plain closet where he does such work' – we assist as intimately as at every other step of the case, and on whose grand meditation we heavily hang. But the Pope strikes us at first – though indeed perhaps only at first – as too high above the whole connection functionally and historically for us to place him within it dramatically. Our novel faces provisionally the question of dispensing with him, as it dispenses with the amazing, bristling, all too indulgently presented Roman advocates on either side of the case, who combine to put together the most formidable monument we possess to Browning's active curiosity and the liveliest proof of his almost unlimited power to give on his readers' nerves without giving on his own.

What remains with us all this time, none the less, is the effect of magnification, the exposure of each of these figures, in its degree, to that iridescent wash of personality, of temper and faculty, that our author ladles out to them, as the copious share of each, from his own great reservoir of spiritual health, and which makes us, as I have noted, seek the reason of a perpetual anomaly. Why, bristling so with references to *him* rather than with references to each other or to any accompanying set of circumstances, do they still establish more truth and beauty than they sacrifice, do they still, according to their chance, help to make *The Ring and the Book* a great living thing, a great objective mass? I brushed by the answer a moment ago, I think, in speaking of the development in Pompilia of the resource of expression, which brings us round, it seems to me, to the justification of Browning's method. To express his inner self – his outward was a different affair! – and to express it utterly, even if no matter how, was clearly, for his own measure and consciousness of that inner self, to *be* poetic; and the solution of all the deviations and disparities or, speaking critically, monstrosities, in the mingled tissue of this work, is the fact that whether or no by such convulsions of soul and sense life got delivered for him, the garment of life (which for him was poetry and poetry alone) got disposed in its due and adequate multitudinous folds. We move with him but in images and references and vast and far correspondences; we eat but of strange compounds and drink but of rare distillations; and very soon, after a course of this, we feel ourselves, however much or however little to our advantage we may on occasion pronounce it, in the world of Expression at any cost. That, essentially, *is* the world of poetry – which in the cases known to our experience where it seems to us to differ from Browning's world does so but through this latter's having been, by the vigour and violence, the bold familiarity, of his grasp and pull at it, moved several degrees nearer us, so to speak, than any other of the same general sort with which we are acquainted; so that, intellectually, we back away from it a little, back down before it, again and again, as we try to get off from a picture or a group or a view which is too much *upon* us and thereby out of focus. Browning is 'upon' us, straighter upon us always, somehow, than anyone else of his race; and we thus recoil, we push our chair back, from the table he so tremendously spreads, just to see a little better what is on it.

This makes a relation with him that it is difficult to express; as if he came up against us, each time, on the same side of the street and not on the other side, across the way, where we mostly see the poets elegantly walk, and where we greet them without danger of concussion. It is on this same side, as I call it, on *our* side, on the other hand, that I rather see our encounter with the novelists taking place; we being, as it were, more mixed with them, or they at least, by their desire and necessity, more mixed with us, and our brush of them, in their minor frenzy, a comparatively muffled encounter.

We have in the whole thing, at any rate, the element of action which is at the same time constant picture, and the element of picture which is at the same time constant action; and with a fusion, as the mass moves, that is none the less effective, none the less thick and complete, from our not owing it in the least to an artful economy. Another force pushes its way through the waste and rules the scene, making wrong things right and right things a hundred times more so – that breath of Browning's own particular matchless Italy which takes us full in the face and remains from the first the felt rich coloured air in which we live. The quantity of that atmosphere that he had to give out is like nothing else in English poetry, any more than in English prose, that I recall; and since I am taking these liberties with him, let me take one too, a little, with the fruit of another genius shining at us here in association – with that great placed and timed prose fiction which we owe to George Eliot and in which *her* projection of the stage and scenery is so different a matter. Curious enough this difference where so many things make for identity – the quantity of talent, the quantity of knowledge, the high equality (or almost) of culture and curiosity, not to say of 'spiritual life'. Each writer drags along a far-sweeping train, though indeed Browning's spreads so considerably furthest; but his stirs up, to my vision, a perfect cloud of gold-dust, while hers, in *Romola*, by contrast, leaves the air about as clear, about as white, and withal about as cold, as before she had benevolently entered it. This straight saturation of our author's, this prime assimilation of the elements for which the name of Italy stands, is a single splendid case, however; I can think of no second one that is not below it – if we take it as supremely expressed in those of his lyrics and shorter dramatic monologues that it has most helped to inspire. The Rome and

Tuscany of the early 'fifties had become for him so at once a medium, a bath of the senses and perceptions, into which he could sink, in which he could unlimitedly soak, that wherever he might be touched afterwards he gave out some effect of that immersion. This places him to my mind quite apart, makes the rest of our poetic record of a similar experience comparatively pale and abstract. Shelley and Swinburne – to name only his compeers – are, I know, a part of the record; but the author of *Men and Women*, of *Pippa Passes*, of certain of the Dramatic Lyrics and other scattered felicities, not only expresses and reflects the matter; he fairly, he heatedly, if I may use such a term, exudes and perspires it. Shelley, let us say in the connection, is a light and Swinburne, let us say, a sound; Browning alone of them all is a temperature. We feel it, we are in it at a plunge, with the very first pages of the thing before us; to which, I confess, we surrender with a momentum drawn from fifty of their predecessors, pages not less sovereign, elsewhere.

The old Florence of the late spring closes round us; the hand of Italy is at once, with the recital of the old-world litter of Piazza San Lorenzo, with that of the great glare and of the great shadow-masses, heavy upon us, heavy with that strange weight, that mixed pressure, which is somehow, to the imagination, at once a caress and a menace. Our poet kicks up on the spot and at short notice what I have called his cloud of gold-dust. I can but speak for myself at least – something that I want to feel both as historic and esthetic truth, both as pictorial and moral interest, something that will repay my fancy tenfold if I can but feel it, hovers before me, and I say to myself that, whether or no a great poem is to come off, I will be hanged if one of the vividest of all stories and one of the sharpest of all impressions doesn't. I beckon these things on, I follow them up, I so desire and need them that I of course, by my imaginative collaboration, contribute to them – from the moment, that is, of my finding myself really in relation to the great points. On the other hand, as certainly, it has taken the author of the first volume, and of the two admirable chapters of the same – since I can't call them cantos – entitled respectively 'Half-Rome' and 'The Other Half-Rome', to put me in relation; where it is that he keeps me more and more, letting the closeness of my state, it must be owned, occasionally drop, letting the finer call on me even, for bad quarters-of-an-hour, considerably languish, but starting up before me again in vivid authority if I really presume to droop or stray. He takes his wilful way with me, but I make it my own, picking over and over as I have said, like some lingering talking pedlar's client, his great unloosed pack; and thus it is that by the time I am settled with Pompilia at Arezzo I have lived into all the conditions. They press upon me close, those wonderful dreadful beautiful particulars of the Italy of the eve of the eighteenth century – Browning himself moving about, darting hither and thither in them, at his mighty ease: beautiful, I say, because of the quantity of romantic and esthetic tradition from a more romantic and esthetic age still visibly, palpably, in solution there; and wonderful and dreadful through something of a similar tissue of matchless and ruthless consistencies and immoralities. I make to my hand, as this infatuated reader, *my* Italy of the eve of the eighteenth century – a vast painted and gilded rococo shell roofing over a scenic, an amazingly figured and furnished earth, but shutting out almost the whole of our own dearly-bought, rudely-recovered spiritual sky. You see I have this right, all the while, if I recognize my suggested material, which keeps coming and coming in the measure of my need, and my duty to which *is* to recognize it, and as handsomely and actively as possible. The great thing is that I have such a group of figures moving across so constituted a scene – figures so typical, so salient, so reeking with the old-world character, so impressed all over with its manners and its morals, and so predestined, we see, to this particular horrid little drama. And let me not be charged with giving it away, the idea of the latent prose fiction, by calling it little and horrid; let me not – for with my contention I can't possibly afford to – appear to agree with those who speak of the Franceschini-Comparini case as a mere vulgar criminal anecdote.

It might have been such but for two reasons – counting only the principal ones; one of these our fact that we see it so, I repeat, in Browning's inordinately-coloured light, and the other – which is indeed perhaps but another face of the same – that, with whatever limitations, it gives us in the rarest manner three characters of the first importance. I hold three a great many; I could have done with it almost, I think, if there had been but one or two; our rich provision shows you at any rate what I mean by speaking of our author's performance as above all a preparation for something. Deeply he felt that with the three — the three built up at us each with an equal genial range of reiterative touches — there couldn't eventually not be something done (artistically done, I mean) if someone would only do it. There they are in their old yellow Arezzo, that miniature milder Florence, as sleepy to my recollection as a little English cathedral city clustered about a Close, but dreaming not so peacefully nor so innocently; there is the great fretted fabric of the Church on which they are all swarming and grovelling, yet after their fashion interesting parasites, from the high and dry old Archbishop, meanly wise or ignobly edifying, to whom Pompilia resorts in her woe and who practically pushes her away with a shuffling velvet foot; down through the couple of Franceschini cadets, Canon Girolamo and Abate Paul, mere minions, fairly in the verminous degree, of the overgrown order or too-rank organism; down to Count Guido himself and to Canon Caponsacchi, who have taken the tonsure at the outset of their careers, but none too strictly the vows, and who lead their lives under some strangest profanest pervertedest clerical category. There have been before this the Roman preliminaries, the career of the queer Comparini, the adoption, the assumption of the parentship, of the ill-starred little girl, with the sordid cynicism of her marriage out of hand, conveying her presumptive little fortune, her poor handful of even less than contingent cash, to hungry middle-aged Count Guido's stale 'rank'; the many-toned note or turbid harmony of all of which recurs to us in the vivid image of the pieties and paganisms of San Lorenzo in Lucina, that banal little church in the old upper Corso — banal, that is, at the worst, with the rare Roman *banalité*; bravely banal, or banal with style — that we have all passed with a sense of its reprieve to our sightseeing, and where the bleeding bodies of the still-breathing Pompilia and her extinct companions are laid out on the greasy marble of the altar-steps. To glance at these things, however, is fairly to be tangled, and at once, in the author's complexity of suggestion, to which our own thick-coming fancies respond in no less a measure; so that I have already missed my time to so much even as name properly the tremendous little chapter we should have devoted to the Franceschini interior as revealed at last to Comparini eyes; the sinister scene or ragged ruin of the Aretine 'palace', where pride and penury and, at once, rabid resentment show their teeth in the dark and the void, and where

Pompilia's inspired little character, clear silver hardened, effectually beaten and battered, to steel, begins to shine at the blackness with a light that fairly outfaces at last the gleam of wolfish fangs – the character that draws from Guido, in his, alas, too boundless harangue of the fourth volume, some of the sharpest specifications into which that extraordinary desert, that indescribable waste of intellectual life, as I have hinted at its being, from time to time flowers.

> 'None of your abnegation of revenge!
> Fly at me frank, tug where I tear again!
> Away with the empty stare! Be holy still,
> And stupid ever! Occupy your patch
> Of private snow that's somewhere in what world
> May now be growing icy round your head,
> And anguish at your foot-print – freeze not me!'

I have spoken of the enveloping consciousness – or call it just the struggling, emerging, comparing, at last intensely living conscience – of Caponsacchi as the indicated centre of our situation or determinant of our form, in the matter of the excellent novel; and know of course what such an indication lets me in for, responsibly speaking, in the way of a rearrangement of relations, in the way of liberties taken. To lift our subject out of the sphere of anecdote and place it in the sphere of drama, liberally considered, to give it dignity by extracting its finest importance, causing its parts to flower together into some splendid special sense, we supply it with a large lucid reflector, which we find only, as I have already noted, in that mind and soul concerned in the business that have at once the highest sensibility and the highest capacity, or that are, as we may call it, most admirably agitated. There is the awkward fact, the objector may say, that by our record the mind and soul in question are not concerned till a given hour, when many things have already happened and the climax is almost in sight; to which we reply, at our ease, that we simply don't suffer that fact to be awkward. From the moment I am taking liberties I suffer *no* awkwardness; I should be very helpless, quite without resource and without vision, if I did. I said it to begin with: Browning works the whole thing over – the whole thing as originally given him – and we work *him*; helpfully, artfully, boldly, which is our whole blest basis. We therefore turn

Caponsacchi on earlier, ever so much earlier; turn him on, with a brave ingenuity, from the very first – that is in Rome if need be; place him there in the field, at once recipient and agent, vaguely conscious and with splendid brooding apprehension, awaiting the adventure of his life, awaiting his call, his real call (the others have been such vain shows and hollow stopgaps), awaiting, in fine, his terrible great fortune. His direct connection with Pompilia begins certainly at Arezzo, only after she has been some time hideously mismated and has suffered all but her direst extremity – that is of the essence; we *take* it; it's all right. But his indirect participation is another affair, and we get it – at a magnificent stroke – by the fact that his view of Franceschini, his fellow-Aretine sordidly 'on the make', his measure of undesired, indeed of quite execrated contact with him, brushed against in the motley hungry Roman traffic, where and while that sinister soul snuffs about on the very vague or the very foul scent of *his* fortune, may begin whenever we like. We have only to have it begin right, only to make it, on the part of two men, a relation of strong irritated perception and restless righteous convinced instinct in the one nature and of equally instinctive hate and envy, jealousy and latent fear, on the other, to see the indirect connection, the one with Pompilia, as I say, throw across our page as portentous a shadow as we need. Then we get Caponsacchi as a recipient up to the brim – as an agent, a predestined one, up to the hilt. I can scarce begin to tell you what I see him give, as we say, or how his sentient and observational life, his fine reactions in presence of such a creature as Guido, such a social type and image and lurid light, as it were, make him comparatively a modern man, breathed upon, to that deep and interesting agitation I have mentioned, by more forces than he yet reckons or knows the names of.

The direct relation – always to Pompilia – is made, at Arezzo, as we know, by Franceschini himself; preparing his own doom, in the false light of his debased wit, by creating an appearance of hidden dealing between his wife and the priest which shall, as promptly as he likes – if he but work it right – compromise and overwhelm them. The particular deepest damnation he conceives for his weaker, his weakest victim is that she shall take the cleric Caponsacchi for her lover, he indubitably willing – to Guido's apprehension; and that her castigation at his hands for this, sufficiently proved upon her, shall be the last luxury of his own baseness. He forges infernally, though grossly enough, an imputed correspondence between them, a series of love-letters, scandalous scrawls, of the last erotic intensity; which we in the event see solemnly weighed by his fatuous judges, all fatuous save the grave old Pope, in the scale of Pompilia's guilt and responsibility. It is this atrocity that at the *dénouement* damns Guido himself most, or well-nigh; but if it fails and recoils, as all his calculations do — it is only his rush of passion that doesn't miss — this is by the fact exactly that, as we have seen, his wife and her friend are, for our perfect persuasion, characters of the deepest dye. There, if you please, is the finest side of our subject; such sides come up, such sides flare out upon us, when we get such characters in such embroilments. Admire with me therefore our felicity in this first-class value of Browning's beautiful critical genial vision of his Caponsacchi — vision of him as the tried and tempered and illuminated *man*, a great round smooth, though as yet but little worn gold-piece, an embossed and figured ducat or sequin of the period, placed by the poet in my hand. He gives me that value to spend for him, spend on all the strange old experience, old sights and sounds and stuffs, of the old stored Italy — so we have at least the wit to spend it to high advantage; which is just what I mean by our taking the liberties we spoke of. I see such bits we can get with it; but the difficulty is that I see so many more things than I can have even dreamed of giving you a hint of. I see the Arezzo life and the Arezzo crisis and every 'i' dotted and every circumstance presented; and when Guido takes his wife, as a possible trap for her, to the theatre — the theatre of old Arezzo: share with me the tattered vision and inhale the musty air! — I am well in range of Pompilia, the tragically exquisite, in her box, with her husband not there for the hour but posted elsewhere; I look at her in fact over Caponsacchi's shoulder and that of his brother-canon Conti, while this light character, a vivid recruit to our company, manages to toss into her lap, and as coming in guise of overture from his smitten friend, 'a papertwist of comfits'. There is a particular famous occasion at the theatre in a work of more or less contemporary fiction — at a petty provincial theatre which isn't even, as you might think, the place where Pendennis had his first glimpse of Miss Fotheringay. The evening at the Rouen playhouse of Flaubert's *Madame Bovary* has a relief not elsewhere equalled — it is the most *done* visit to the play in all literature – but, though 'doing' is now so woefully out of favour, my idea would be to give it here a precious *pendant*; which connection, silly Canon Conti, the old fripperies and levities, the whole queer picture and show of manners, is handed over to us, expressly, as inapt for poetic illustration.

What is equally apt for poetic or for the other, indeed, is the thing for which we feel *The Ring and the Book* preponderantly done – it is at least what comes out clearest, comes out as straightest and strongest and finest, from Browning's genius – the exhibition of the great constringent relation between man and woman at once at its maximum and as the relation most worth while in life for either party; an exhibition forming quite the main substance of our author's message. He has dealt, in his immense variety and vivacity, with other relations, but on this he has thrown his most living weight; it remains the thing of which his own rich experience most convincingly spoke to him. He has testified to it as charged to the brim with the burden of the senses, and has testified to it as almost too clarified, too liberated and sublimated, for traceable application or fair record; he has figured it as never too much either of the flesh or of the spirit for him, so long as the possibility of both of these is in each, but always and ever as the thing absolutely most worth while. It is in the highest and rarest degree clarified and disengaged for Caponsacchi and Pompilia; but what their history most concludes to is how ineffably it was, whatever happened, worth while. Worth while most then for them or for us is the question? Well, let us say worth while assuredly for us, in this noble exercise of our imagination. Which accordingly shows us what we, for all our prose basis, would have found, to repeat my term once more, prepared for us. There isn't a detail of their panting flight to Rome over the autumn Apennines – the long hours when they melt together only *not* to meet – that doesn't positively plead for our perfect prose transcript. And if it be said that the mere massacre at the final end is a lapse to passivity from the high plane, for our pair of protagonists, of constructive, of heroic vision, this is not a blur from the time everything that happens happens most effectively to Caponsacchi's life. Pompilia's is taken, but she is none the less given; and it is in his consciousness and experience that she most intensely flowers – with all her jubilation for doing so. So that *he* contains the whole – unless indeed after all the Pope does, the Pope whom I was leaving out as too transcendent for *our* version. Unless, unless, further and further, I see what I have at this late moment no right to; see, as the very end and splendid climax of all, Caponsacchi sent for to the Vatican and admitted alone to the Papal presence. *There* is a scene if we will; and in the mere mutual confrontation, brief, silent, searching, recognizing, consecrating, almost as august on the one part as on the other. It rounds us off; but you will think I stray too far. I have wanted, alas, to say such still other fond fine things — it being of our poet's great nature to prompt them at every step — that I almost feel I have missed half my points; which will doubtless therefore show you these remarks in their nakedness. Take them and my particular contention as a pretext and a minor affair if you will only feel them at the same time as at the worst a restless refinement of homage. It has been easy in many another case to run to earth the stray prime fancy, the original anecdote or artless tale, from which a great imaginative work, starting off after meeting it, has sprung and rebounded again and soared; and perhaps it is right and happy and final that one should have faltered in attempting by a converse curiosity to clip off or tie back the wings that once have spread. You will agree with me none the less, I feel, that Browning's great generous wings are over us still and even now, more than ever now; and also that they shake down on us his blessing.

—⚹—

On The Reef, *by Edith Wharton, from a letter to Edith Wharton, December 1912 (HJL, vol. 4, 644–5). As I have noted, any praise from James for new literature, at least in private, was rare at this stage in his life; therefore his analytic warmth about this fine novel is remarkable. Compare Mrs Wharton's account of his attitude quoted in my introduction. The Reef, incidentally, contains a fine retrospective re-doing of 'Gilbert Osmond'. See also No. 76.*

... IT ALL SHOWS, partly, what strength of subject is, and how it carries and inspires, inasmuch as I think your subject in its essence, [is] very fine and takes in no end of beautiful things to do. Each of these two figures is admirable for truth and *justesse*: the woman an exquisite thing, and with her characteristic finest, scarce differentiated notes (that is some of them) sounded with a wonder of delicacy. I'm not sure her oscillations are not beyond our notation; yet they are so held in your hand, so felt and known and shown, and everything seems so to come of itself. I suffer or worry a little from the fact that in the Prologue, as it were, we are admitted so much into the consciousness of the man, and that after the introduction of Anna (Anna so perfectly named), we see him almost only as she sees him — which gives our attention a different sort of work to do; yet this is really I think but a triumph of your method, for he remains of an absolute consistent verity, showing himself in that way better perhaps than in any other, and without a false note imputable, not a shadow of one, to his manner of so projecting himself. The beauty of it is that it is, for all it is worth, a Drama and almost, as it seems to me, of the psychologic Racinian unity, intensity and gracility. Anna is really of Racine, and one presently begins to feel her throughout as an Eriphyle or a Bérénice: which, by the way, helps to account a little for something *qui me chiffonne* throughout; which is why the whole thing, unrelated and unreferred save in the most superficial way to its milieu and background, and to any determining or qualifying *entourage* takes place *comme cela*, and in a specified, localized way, in France – these non-French people 'electing', as it were, to have their story out there. This particularly makes all sorts of unanswered questions come up about Owen; and the notorious wickedness of Paris isn't at all required to bring about the conditions of the Prologue. Oh, if you knew how plentifully we could supply them in London and, I should suppose, in New York or in Boston. But the point was, as I see it, that you couldn't really give us the sense of a Boston Eriphyle or Boston Givré, and that an exquisite instinct, 'back of' your Racinian inspiration and settling the whole thing for you, whether consciously or not, absolutely prescribed a vague and elegant French colonnade or gallery, with a French river dimly gleaming through, as the harmonious *fond* you required. In the key of this, with all your reality, you have yet kept the whole thing; and, to deepen the harmony and accentuate the literary pitch, have never surpassed yourself for certain exquisite *moments*, certain images, analogies, metaphors, certain silver correspondences in your *façon de dire*: examples of which I could pluck out and numerically almost confound you with . . . There used to be little notes in you that were like fine benevolent fingermarks of the good George Eliot – the echo of much reading of that excellent woman, here and there, that is, sounding through. But now you are like a lost and recovered 'ancient' whom *she* might have got a reading of (especially were he a Greek) and of whom in *her* texture some weaker reflection were to show.

❧

75

Balzac and George Sand and Dickens, from a review of Balzac
by Émile Faguet, 1913, Times Literary Supplement, *19 June
1913.*

. . . WHATEVER other felicity may have graced the exercise of such a
genius, for instance, as that rare contemporary George Sand, she was
reduced well-nigh altogether to drawing upon resources and enjoying advantages comparatively vague and unassured. She had of
course in a manner her special resource and particular advantage,
which consisted, so to speak, in a finer feeling about what she did
possess and could treat of with authority, and particularly in a finer
command of the terms of expression, than any involved in Balzac's
'happier' example. But her almost fatal weakness as a novelist – an
exponent of the art who has waned exactly as, for our general
long-drawn appreciation, Balzac has waxed – comes from her having
had to throw herself upon ground that no order governed, no frame,
as we have said, enclosed, and no safety attended; safety of the sort,
we mean, the safety of the constitutive, illustrative fact among facts,
which we find in her rival as a warm socialized air, an element
supremely assimilable.

It may freely be pronounced interesting that whereas, in her
instinct for her highest security, she threw herself upon the consideration of love as the *type* attraction or most representable thing
in the human scene, so, assuredly, no student of that field has, in
proportion to the thoroughness of his study, felt he could afford to
subordinate or almost even to neglect it to anything like the tune in
which we see it put and kept in its place through the parts of the
Comédie Humaine that most count. If this passion but too often
exhales a tepid breath in much other fiction – much other of ours at

least – that is apt to come decidedly less from the writer's sense of proportion than from his failure of art, or in other words of intensity. It is rarely absent by intention or by intelligence, it is pretty well always there as the theoretic principal thing – any difference from writer to writer being mostly in the power to put the principal thing effectively forward. It figures as a pressing, an indispensable even if a perfunctory motive, for example, in every situation devised by Walter Scott; the case being simply that if it doesn't in fact attractively occupy the foreground this is because his hand has had so native, so much greater, an ease for other parts of the picture. What makes Balzac so pre-eminent and exemplary that he was to leave the novel a far other and a vastly more capacious and significant affair than he found it, is his having felt his fellow-creatures (almost altogether for him his contemporaries) as quite failing of reality, as swimming in the vague and the void and the abstract, unless their social conditions, to the last particular, their generative and contributive circumstances, of every discernible sort, enter for all these are 'worth' into his representative attempt. This great compound of the total looked into and starting up in its element, as it always does, to meet the eye of genius and patience half way, bristled for him with all its branching connections, those thanks to which any figure could *be* a figure but by showing for endlessly entangled in them.

So it was then that his huge felicity, to re-emphasize our term, was in his state of circulating where recognitions and identifications didn't so much await as rejoicingly assault him, having never yet in all the world, grudged or at the best suspected feeders as they were at the board where sentiment occupied the head, felt themselves so finely important or subject to such a worried intention. They hung over a scene as to which it was one of the forces of his inspiration that history had lately been there at work, with incomparable energy and inimitable art, to pile one upon another, not to say squeeze and dovetail violently into each other, after such a fashion as might defy competition anywhere, her successive deposits and layers of form and order, her restless determinations of appearance – so like those of the different 'states' of an engraver's impression; all to an effect which *should* have constituted, as by a miracle of coincidence it did, the paradise of an extraordinary observer. Balzac lived accordingly, extraordinary since he was, in an earthly heaven so near perfect for his kind of vision that he could have come at no moment more conceivably blest to him. The later part of the eighteenth century, with the Revolution, the Empire and the Restoration, had inimitably conspired together to scatter abroad their separate marks and stigmas, their separate trails of character and physiognomic hits – for which advantage he might have arrived too late, as his hapless successors, even his more or less direct imitators, visibly have done. The fatal fusions and uniformities inflicted on our newer generations, the running together of all the differences of form and tone, the ruinous liquefying wash of the great industrial brush over the old conditions of contrast and colour, doubtless still have left the painter of manners much to do, but have ground him down to the sad fact that his ideals of differentiation, those inherent oppositions from type to type, in which drama most naturally resides, have well-nigh perished. They pant for life in a hostile air; and we may surely say that their last successful struggle, their last bright resistance to eclipse among ourselves, was in their feverish dance to the great fiddling of Dickens. Dickens made them dance, we seem to see, caper and kick their heels, wave their arms, and above all agitate their features, for the simple reason that he couldn't make them stand or sit *at once* quietly and expressively, couldn't make them look straight out as for themselves – quite in fact as though his not daring to, not feeling he could afford to, in a changing hour when ambiguities and the wavering line, droll and 'dodgy' dazzlements and the possibly undetected factitious alone, might be trusted to keep him right with an incredibly uncritical public, a public blind to the difference between a shade and a patch.

Balzac on the other hand, born as we have seen to confidence, the tonic air of his paradise, might make character, in the sense in which we use it, that of the element exposable to the closest verification, sit or stand for its 'likeness' as still as ever it would . . .

76

‑❧‑

*From 'The New Novel', 1914. The first version of this, called
'The Younger Generation', appeared in the* Times Literary
Supplement, *19 March and 2 April 1914. As often in late James
the benign manner conceals (or rather contains surprisingly) an
ability to be quite bluntly dismissive. The essay enraged H. G.
Wells and provoked his insulting satire of James in* Boon. *On
Conrad James seems to have had an intermittent blind spot:
writing to Edith Wharton in February 1914 he refers to* Chance
*as a relief from 'the last three or four impossibilities, wastes of
desolation, that succeeded the two or three final good things of
his earlier time' (HJL, vol. 4, 703). This is vague but it could
refer to* Nostromo, The Secret Agent *and* Under Western Eyes,
*as conjectured by Leon Edel. Perhaps because of his respect for
James, Conrad was hurt by the essay – 'the only time a criticism
affected me painfully', he wrote in 1916.*
The 'truth' at the beginning of the section on Chance *(p. 608)
is that it takes 'blest method' to provide any deep interest in
fiction.*

. . . THE NEW or at least the young novel is up and doing, clearly,
with the best faith and the highest spirits in the world; if we but
extend a little our measure of youth indeed, as we are happily more
and more disposed to, we may speak of it as already chin-deep in
trophies. The men who are not so young as the youngest were but the
other day very little older than these: Mr Joseph Conrad, Mr
Maurice Hewlett and Mr Galsworthy, Mr H. G. Wells and Mr
Arnold Bennett, have not quite perhaps the early bloom of Mr Hugh
Walpole, Mr Gilbert Cannan, Mr Compton Mackenzie and Mr
D. H. Lawrence, but the spring unrelaxed is still, to our perception,

in their step, and we see two or three of them sufficiently related to the still newer generation in a quasi-parental way to make our whole enumeration as illustrational as we need it. Mr Wells and Mr Arnold Bennett have their strongest mark, the aspect by which we may most classify them, in common – even if their three named contemporaries are doubtless most interesting in one of the connections we are not now seeking to make. The author of *Tono-Bungay* and of *The New Machiavelli*, and the author of *The Old Wives' Tale* and of *Clayhanger*, have practically launched the boat in which we admire the fresh play of oar of the author of *The Duchess of Wrexe*, and the documented aspect exhibited successively by *Round the Corner*, by *Carnival* and *Sinister Street*, and even by *Sons and Lovers* (however much we may find Mr Lawrence, we confess, hang in the dusty rear). We shall explain in a moment what we mean by this designation of the element that these best of the younger men strike us as more particularly sharing, our point being provisionally that Mr Wells and Mr Arnold Bennett (speaking now only of them) began some time back to show us, and to show sundry emulous and generous young spirits then in the act of more or less waking up, what the state in question might amount to. We confound the author of *Tono-Bungay* and the author of *Clayhanger* in this imputation for the simple reason that with the sharpest differences of character and range they yet come together under our so convenient measure of value by *saturation*. This is the greatest value, to our sense, in either of them, their other values, even when at the highest, not being quite in proportion to it; and as to be saturated is to be documented, to be able even on occasion to prove quite enviably and potently so, they are alike in the authority that creates emulation. It little signifies that Mr Wells's documented or saturated state in respect to a particular matter in hand is but one of the faces of his *generally* informed condition, of his extraordinary mass of gathered and assimilated knowledge, a miscellaneous collection more remarkable surely than any teller of 'mere' tales, with the possible exception of Balzac, has been able to draw upon, whereas Mr Arnold Bennett's corresponding provision affects us as, though singularly copious, special, exclusive and artfully economic. This distinction avails nothing against that happy fact of the handiest possession by Mr Wells of immeasurably more concrete material, amenable for straight and vivid reference, convertible into apt illustration, than we should know where to look for other examples of. The author of *The New Machiavelli* knows, somehow, to our mystified and dazzled apprehension, because he writes and because that act constitutes for him the need, on occasion a most desperate, of absorbing knowledge at the pores; the chronicler of the Five Towns writing so much more discernibly, on the other hand, because he knows, and conscious of no need more desperate than that particular circle of civilization may satisfy.

Our argument is that each is ideally immersed in his own body of reference, and that immersion in any such degree and to the effect of any such variety, intensity and plausibility is really among us a new feature of the novelist's range of resource. We have seen him, we have even seen *her*, otherwise auspiciously endowed, seen him observant, impassioned, inspired, and in virtue of these things often very charming, very interesting, very triumphant, visibly qualified for the highest distinction before the fact and visibly crowned by the same after it – we have seen him with a great imagination and a great sense of life, we have seen him even with a great sense of expression and a considerable sense of art: so that we have only to reascend the stream of our comparatively recent literature to meet him serene and immortal, brow-bound with the bay and erect on his particular pedestal. We have only to do that, but have only also, while we do it, to recognize that meantime other things still than these various apotheoses have taken place, and that, to the increase of our recreation, and even if our limited space condemns us to put the matter a trifle clumsily, a change has come over our general receptive sensibility not less than over our productive tradition. In these connections, we admit, overstatement is easy and over-emphasis tempting; we confess furthermore to a frank desire to enrich the case, the historic, with all the meaning we can stuff into it. So viewed accordingly it gives us the 'new', to repeat our expression, as an appetite for a closer notation, a sharper specification of the signs of life, of consciousness, of the human scene and the human subject in general, than the three or four generations before us had been at all moved to insist on. They had insisted indeed, these generations, we see as we look back to them, on almost nothing whatever; what was to come to them had come, in enormous affluence and freshness at its best, and to our continued appreciation as well as to the honour of their sweet susceptibility, because again and again the great miracle of genius took place, while they gaped, in their social and sentimental sky. For ourselves that miracle has not been markedly renewed, but it has none the less happened that by hook and by crook the case for appreciation remains interesting. The great thing that saves it, under the drawback we have named, is, no doubt, that we have simply – always for appreciation – learned a little to insist, and that we thus get back on one hand something of what we have lost on the other. We are unable of course, with whatever habit of presumption engendered, to insist upon genius; so that who shall describe the measure of success we still achieve as not virtually the search for freshness, and above all for closeness, in quite a different direction? To this nearer view of commoner things Mr Wells, say, and Mr Arnold Bennett, and in their degree, under the infection communicated, Mr D. H. Lawrence and Mr Gilbert Cannan and Mr Compton Mackenzie and Mr Hugh Walpole, strike us as having all gathered themselves up with a movement never yet undertaken on our literary scene, and, beyond anything else, with an instinctive divination of what had most waved their predecessors off it. What had this lion in the path been, we make them out as after a fashion asking themselves, what had it been from far back and straight down through all the Victorian time, but the fond superstition that the key of the situation, of each and every situation that could turn up for the novelist, was the sentimental key, which might fit into no door or window opening on closeness or on freshness at all? Was it not for all the world as if even the brightest practitioners of the past, those we now distinguish as saved for glory in spite of themselves, had been as sentimental as they could, or, to give the trick another name, as romantic and thereby as shamelessly 'dodgy'? – just in order *not* to be close and fresh, not to be authentic, as that takes trouble, takes talent, and you can be sentimental, you can be romantic, you can be dodgy, alas, not a bit less on the footing of genius than on the footing of mediocrity or even of imbecility? Was it not as if the sentimental had been more and more noted as but another name for the romantic, if not indeed the romantic as but another name for the sentimental, and as if these things, whether separate or united, had been in the same degree recognized as unamenable, or at any rate unfavourable, to any consistent fineness of notation, once the tide of the copious as a condition of the thorough had fairly set in?

So, to express it briefly, the possibility of hugging the shore of the real as it had not, among us, been hugged, and of pushing inland, as far as a keel might float, wherever the least opening seemed to smile, dawned upon a few votaries and gathered further confidence with exercise. Who could say, of course, that Jane Austen had not been close, just as who could ask if Anthony Trollope had not been copious? – just as who could *not* say that it all depended on what was meant by these terms? The demonstration of what was meant, it presently appeared, could come but little by little, quite as if each tentative adventurer had rather anxiously to learn for himself what *might* be meant – this failing at least the leap into the arena of some great demonstrative, some sudden athletic and epoch-making authority. Who could pretend that Dickens was anything but romantic, and even more romantic in his humour, if possible, than in pathos or in queer perfunctory practice of the 'plot'? Who could pretend that Jane Austen didn't leave much more untold than told about the aspects and manners even of the confined circle in which her muse revolved? Why shouldn't it be argued against her that where her testimony complacently ends the pressure of appetite within us presumes exactly to begin? Who could pretend that the reality of Trollope didn't owe much of its abundance to the diluted, the quite extravagantly watered strain, no less than to the heavy hand, in which it continued to be ladled out? Who of the younger persuasion would not have been ready to cite, as one of the liveliest opportunities for the critic eager to see representation searching, such a claim for the close as Thackeray's sighing and protesting 'look-in' at the acquaintance between Arthur Pendennis and Fanny Bolton, the daughter of the Temple laundress, amid the purlieus of that settlement? The sentimental habit and the spirit of romance, it was unmistakably chargeable, stood out to sea as far as possible the moment the shore appeared to offer the least difficulty to hugging, and the Victorian age bristled with perfect occasions for our catching them in the act of this showy retreat. All revolutions have been prepared in spite of their often striking us as sudden, and so it was doubtless that when scarce longer ago than the other day Mr Arnold Bennett had the fortune to lay his hand on a general scene and a cluster of agents deficient to a peculiar degree in properties that might interfere with a desirable density of illustration – deficient, that is, in such connections as might carry the imagination off to some sport on its own account – we recognized at once a set of conditions auspicious to the newer kind of appeal. Let us confess that we were at the same time doubtless to master no better way of describing these conditions than by the remark that they were, for some reason beautifully inherent in them, susceptible at once of being entirely known and of seeming delectably thick. Reduction to exploitable knowledge is apt to mean for many a case of the human complexity reduction to comparative thinness; and nothing was thereby at the first blush to interest us more than the fact that the air and the very smell of packed actuality in the subject-matter of such things as the author's two longest works was clearly but another name for his personal competence in that matter, the fulness and firmness of his embrace of it. This was a fresh and beguiling impression – that the state of inordinate possession on the chronicler's part, the mere state as such and as an energy directly displayed, *was* the interest, neither more nor less, *was* the sense and the meaning and the picture and the drama, all so sufficiently constituting them that it scarce mattered what they were in themselves. Of what they were in themselves their being in Mr Bennett, as Mr Bennett to such a tune harboured them, represented their one conceivable account – not to mention, as reinforcing this, our own great comfort and relief when certain high questions and wonderments about them, or about our mystified relation to them, began one after another to come up.

Because such questions did come, we must at once declare, and we are still in presence of them, for all the world as if that case of the perfect harmony, the harmony between subject and author, were just marked with a flaw and didn't meet the whole assault of restless criticism. What we make out Mr Bennett as doing is simply recording his possession or, to put it more completely, his saturation; and to see him as virtually shut up to that process is a note of all the more moment that we see our selected cluster of his interesting juniors, and whether by his direct action on their collective impulse or not, embroiled, as we venture to call it, in the same predicament. The act of squeezing out to the utmost the plump and more or less juicy orange of a particular acquainted state and letting this affirmation of energy, however directed or undirected, constitute for them the 'treatment' of a theme – *that* is what we remark them as mainly engaged in, after remarking the example so strikingly, so originally set, even if an undue subjection to it be here and there repudiated. Nothing is further from our thought than to undervalue saturation and possession, the fact of the particular experience, the state and degree of acquaintance incurred, however such a consciousness may have been determined; for these things represent on the part of the novelist, as on the part of any painter of things seen, felt or imagined, just one half of his authority – the other half being represented of course by the application he is inspired to make of them. Therefore that fine secured half is so much gained at the start, and the fact of its brightly being there may really by itself project upon the course so much colour and form as to make us on occasion, under the genial force, almost not miss the answer to the question of application. When the author of *Clayhanger* has put down upon the table, in dense unconfused array, every fact required, every fact in any way invocable, to make the life of the Five Towns press upon us, and to make our sense of it, so full-fed, content us, we may very well go on for the time in the captive condition, the beguiled and bemused condition, the acknowledgement of which is in general our highest tribute to the temporary master of our sensibility. Nothing at such moments – or rather at the end of them, when the end begins to threaten – may be of a more curious strain than the dawning unrest that suggests to us fairly our first critical comment: 'Yes, yes – but is this *all*? These are the circumstances of the interest – we see, we see; but where is the interest itself, where and what is its centre, and how are we to measure it in relation to *that*?' Of course we may in the act of exhaling that plaint (which we have just expressed at its mildest) well remember how many people there are to tell us that to 'measure' an interest is none of our affair; that we have but to take it on the cheapest and easiest terms and be thankful; and that if by our very confession we have been led the imaginative dance the music has done for us all it pretends to. Which words, however, have only to happen to be for us the most unintelligent conceivable not in the least to arrest our wonderment as to where our bedrenched consciousness may still not awkwardly leave us for the pleasure of appreciation.

That appreciation is also a mistake and a priggishness, being reflective and thereby corrosive, is another of the fond dicta which we are here concerned but to brush aside – the more closely to embrace the welcome induction that appreciation, attentive and reflective, inquisitive and conclusive, is in this connection absolutely the golden *key* to our pleasure. The more it plays up, the more we recognize and are able to number the sources of our enjoyment, the greater the provision made for security in that attitude, which corresponds, by the same stroke, with the reduced danger of waste in the undertaking to amuse us. It all comes back to our amusement, and to the noblest surely, on the whole, we know; and it is in the very nature of clinging appreciation not to sacrifice consentingly a single shade of the art that makes for that blessing. From this solicitude spring our questions, and not least the one to which we give ourselves for the moment here – this moment of our being regaled as never yet with the fruits of the movement (if the name be not of too pompous an application where the flush and the heat of accident too seem so candidly to look forth), in favour of the 'expression of life' in terms as loose as may pretend to an effect of expression at all. The relegation of terms to the limbo of delusions outlived so far as ever really cultivated becomes of necessity, it will be plain, the great mark of the faith that for the novelist to show he 'knows all about' a certain congeries of aspects, the more numerous within their mixed circle the better, is thereby to set in motion, with due intensity, the pretension to interest. The state of knowing all about whatever it may be has thus only to become consistently and abundantly active to pass for his supreme function; and to its so becoming active few difficulties appear to be descried – so great may on occasion be the mere excitement of activity. To the fact that the exhilaration is, as we have hinted, often infectious, to this and to the charming young good faith and general acclamation under which each case appears to proceed – each case we of course mean really repaying attention – the critical reader owes his opportunity so considerably and so gratefully to generalize.

We should have only to remount the current with a certain energy to come straight up against Tolstoy as the great illustrative master-hand on all this ground of the disconnection of method from matter –

which encounter, however, would take us much too far, so that we must for the present but hang off from it with the remark that of all great painters of the social picture it was given that epic genius most to serve admirably as a rash adventurer and a 'caution', and execrably, pestilentially, as a model. In this strange union of relations he stands alone: from no other great projector of the human image and the human idea is so much truth to be extracted under an equal leakage of its value. All the proportions in him are so much the largest that the drop of attention to our nearer cases might by its violence leave little of that principle alive; which fact need not disguise from us, none the less, that as Mr H. G. Wells and Mr Arnold Bennett, to return to them briefly again, derive, by multiplied if diluted transmissions, from the great Russian (from whose all but equal companion Turgenieff we recognize no derivatives at all), so, observing the distances, we may profitably detect an unexhausted influence in our minor, our still considerably less rounded vessels. Highly attaching as indeed the game might be, of inquiring as to the centre of the interest or the sense of the whole in *The Passionate Friends*, or in *The Old Wives' Tale*, after having sought those luxuries in vain not only through the general length and breadth of *War and Peace*, but within the quite respectable confines of any one of the units of effect there clustered: this as preparing us to address a like friendly challenge to Mr Cannan's *Round the Corner*, say, or to Mr Lawrence's *Sons and Lovers* – should we wish to be *very* friendly to Mr Lawrence – or to Mr Hugh Walpole's *Duchess of Wrexe*, or even to Mr Compton Mackenzie's *Sinister Street* and *Carnival*, discernibly, we hasten to add, though certain betrayals of a controlling idea and a pointed intention do comparatively gleam out of the two fictions last named. *The Old Wives' Tale* is the history of two sisters, daughters of a prosperous draper in a Staffordshire town, who, separating early in life, through the flight of one of them to Paris with an ill-chosen husband and the confirmed and prolonged local pitch of the career of the other, are reunited late in life by the return of the fugitive after much Parisian experience and by her pacified acceptance of the conditions of her birthplace. The divided current flows together again, and the chronicle closes with the simple drying up determined by the death of the sisters. That is all; the canvas is covered, ever so closely and vividly covered, by the exhibition of innumerable small facts and aspects, at which we assist with the most comfortable sense of their substantial truth. The sisters, and more particularly the less adventurous, are at home in their author's mind, they sit and move at their ease in the square chamber of his attention, to a degree beyond which the production of that ideal harmony between creature and creator could scarcely go, and all by an art of demonstration so familiar and so 'quiet' that the truth and the poetry, to use Goethe's distinction, melt utterly together and we see no difference between the subject of the show and the showman's feeling, let alone the showman's manner, about it. This felt identity of the elements – because we at least consciously feel – becomes in the novel we refer to, and not less in *Clayhanger*, which our words equally describe, a source for us of abject confidence, confidence truly *so* abject in the solidity of every appearance that it may be said to represent our whole relation to the work and completely to exhaust our reaction upon it. *Clayhanger*, of the two fictions even the more densely loaded with all the evidence in what we should call the case presented did we but learn meanwhile for what case, or for a case of what, to take it, inscribes the annals, the private more particularly, of a provincial printer in a considerable way of business, beginning with his early boyhood and going on to the complications of his maturity – these not exhausted with our present possession of the record, inasmuch as by the author's announcement there is more of the catalogue to come. This most monumental of Mr Arnold Bennett's recitals, taking it with its supplement of *Hilda Lessways*, already before us, is so describable through its being a monument exactly not to an idea, a pursued and captured meaning, or in short *to* anything whatever, but just simply *of* the quarried and gathered material it happens to contain, the stones and bricks and rubble and cement and promiscuous constituents of every sort that have been heaped in it and thanks to which it quite massively piles itself up. Our perusal and our enjoyment are our watching of the growth of the pile and of the capacity, industry, energy with which the operation is directed. A huge and in its way a varied aggregation, without traceable lines, divinable direction, effect of composition, the mere number of its pieces, the great dump of its material, together with the fact that here and there in the miscellany, as with the value of bits of marble or porphyry, fine elements shine out, it keeps us standing and waiting to the end – and largely just because it keeps us wondering. We surely wonder more what it may all propose to mean than any equal appearance of preparation to relieve us of that strain, any so founded and grounded a postponement of the disclosure of a sense in store, has for a long time called upon us to do in a like connection. A great thing it is assuredly that *while* we wait and wonder we are amused – were it not for that, truly, our situation would be thankless enough; we may ask ourselves, as has already been noted, why on such ambiguous terms we should consent to be, and why the practice doesn't at a given moment break down; and our answer brings us back to that many-fingered grasp of the orange that the author squeezes. This particular orange is of the largest and most rotund, and his trust in the consequent flow is of its nature communicative. Such is the case always, and most naturally, with that air in a person who has something, who at the very least has much to tell us: we *like* so to be affected by it, we meet it half way and lend ourselves, sinking in up to the chin. Up to the chin only indeed, beyond doubt; we even then feel our head emerge, for judgment and articulate question, and it is from that position that we remind ourselves how the real reward of our patience is still to come – the reward attending not at all the immediate sense of immersion, but reserved for the after-sense, which is a very different matter, whether in the form of a glow or of a chill.

If Mr Bennett's tight rotundity then is of the handsomest size and his manipulation of it so firm, what are we to say of Mr Wells's, who, a novelist very much as Lord Bacon was a philosopher, affects us as taking all knowledge for his province and as inspiring in us to the very highest degree the confidence enjoyed by himself – enjoyed, we feel, with a breadth with which it has been given no one of his fellow-craftsmen to enjoy anything. If confidence alone could lead utterly captive we should all be huddled in a bunch at Mr Wells's heels – which is indeed where we *are* abjectly gathered so far as that force does operate. It is literally Mr Wells's own mind, and the experience of his own mind, incessant and extraordinarily various, extraordinarily reflective, even with all sorts of conditions made, of whatever he may expose it to, that forms the reservoir tapped by him, that constitutes his provision of grounds of interest. It is, by our thinking, in his power to name to us, as a preliminary, more of these grounds than all his contemporaries put together, and even to exceed any competitor, without exception, in the way of suggesting that, thick as he may seem to lay them, they remain yet only contributive, are not in themselves full expression but are designed strictly to subserve it, that this extraordinary writer's spell resides. When full expression, the expression of some particular truth, seemed to lapse in this or that of his earlier novels (we speak not here of his shorter things, for the most part delightfully wanton and exempt) it was but by a hand's breadth, so that if we didn't inveterately quite know what he intended we yet always felt sufficiently that *he* knew. The particular intentions of such matters as *Kipps*, as *Tono-Bungay*, as *Ann Veronica*, so swarmed about us, in their blinding, bluffing vivacity, that the mere sum of them might have been taken for a sense over and above which it was graceless to inquire. The more this author learns and learns, or at any rate knows and knows, however, the greater is this impression of his holding it good enough for us, such as we are, that he shall but turn out his mind and its contents upon us by any free familiar gesture and as from a high window forever open – an entertainment as copious surely as any occasion should demand, at least till we have more intelligibly expressed our title to a better. Such things as *The New Machiavelli*, *Marriage*, *The Passionate Friends*, are so very much more attestations of the presence of material than attestations of an interest in the use of it that we ask ourselves again and again why so fondly neglected a state of leakage comes not to be fatal to *any* provision of quantity, or even to stores more specially selected for the ordeal than Mr Wells's always strike us as being. Is not the pang of witnessed waste in fact great just in proportion as we are touched by our author's fine off-handedness as to the value of the stores, about which he can for the time make us believe what he will? so that, to take an example susceptible of brief statement, we wince at a certain quite peculiarly gratuitous sacrifice to the casual in *Marriage* very much as at seeing some fine and indispensable little part of a mechanism slip through profane fingers and lose itself. Who does not remember what ensues after a little upon the aviational descent of the hero of the fiction just named into the garden occupied, in company with her parents, by the young lady with whom he is to fall in love? – and this even though the whole opening scene so constituted, with all the comedy hares its function appears to be to start, remains with its back squarely turned, esthetically speaking, to the quarter in which the picture develops. The point for our mortification is that by one of the first steps in this development, the first impression on him having been made, the hero accidentally meets the heroine, of a summer eventide, in a leafy lane which supplies them with the happiest occasion to pursue their acquaintance – or in other words supplies the author with the liveliest consciousness (as we at least feel it should have been) that just so the relation between the pair, its seed already sown and the fact of that bringing about all that is still to come, pushes aside whatever veil and steps forth into life. To show it step forth and affirm itself as a relation, what is this but the interesting function of the whole passage, on the performance of which what follows is to hang? – and yet who can say that when the ostensible sequence *is* presented, and our young lady, encountered again by her stirred swain, under cover of night, in a favouring wood, is at once encompassed by his arms and pressed to his lips and heart (for celebration thus of their third meeting) we do not assist at a well-nigh heartbreaking miscarriage of 'effect'? We see effect, invoked in vain, simply stand off unconcerned; effect not having been at all consulted in advance she is not to be secured on such terms. And her presence would so have redounded – perfectly punctual creature as she is on a made appointment and a clear understanding – to the advantage of all concerned. The bearing of the young man's act is all in our having begun to conceive it as possible, begun even to desire it, in the light of what has preceded; therefore if the participants have *not* been shown us as on the way to it, nor the question of it made beautifully to tremble for us in the air, its happiest connections fail and we but stare at it mystified. The instance is undoubtedly trifling, but in the infinite complex of such things resides for a work of art the shy virtue, shy at least till wooed forth, of the whole susceptibility. The case of Mr Wells might take us much further – such remarks as there would be to make, say, on such a question as the due understanding, on the part of *The Passionate Friends* (not as associated persons but as a composed picture), of what that composition is specifically *about* and where, for treatment of this interest, it undertakes to find its centre: all of which, we are willing however to grant, falls away before the large assurance and incorrigible levity with which this adventurer carries his lapses – far more of an adventurer as he is than any other of the company. The composition, as we have called it, heaven saving the mark, is simply at any and every moment 'about' Mr Wells's general adventure; which is quite enough while it preserves, as we trust it will long continue to do, its present robust pitch . . .

It is odd and delightful perhaps that at the very moment of our urging this truth we should happen to be regaled with a really supreme specimen of the part playable in a novel by the source of interest, the principle of provision attended to, for which we claim importance. Mr Joseph Conrad's *Chance* is none the less a signal instance of provision the most earnest and the most copious for its leaving ever so much to be said about the particular provision effected. It is none the less an extraordinary exhibition of method by the fact that the method is, we venture to say, without a precedent in any like work. It places Mr Conrad absolutely alone as a votary of the way to do a thing that shall make it undergo most doing. The way to do it that shall make it undergo least is the line on which we are mostly now used to see prizes carried off; so that the author of *Chance* gathers up on this showing all sorts of comparative distinction. He gathers up at least two sorts – that of bravery in absolutely reversing the process most accredited, and that, quite separate, we make out, of performing the manoeuvre under salvos of recognition. It is not in these days often given to a refinement of design to be recognized, but Mr Conrad has made his achieve that miracle – save in so far indeed as the miracle has been one thing and the success another. The miracle is of the rarest, confounding all calculation and suggesting more reflections than we can begin to make place for here; but the sources of surprise surrounding it might be, were this possible, even greater and yet leave the fact itself in all independence, the fact that the whole undertaking was committed by its very first step either to be 'art' exclusively or to be nothing. This is the prodigious rarity, since surely we have known for many a day no other such case of the whole clutch of eggs, and these withal of the freshest, in that one basket; to which it may be added that if we say for many a day this is not through our readiness positively to associate the sight with any very definite moment of the past. What concerns us is that the general effect of *Chance* is arrived at by a pursuance of means to the end in view contrasted with which every other current form of the chase can only affect us as cheap and futile; the carriage of the burden or amount of service required on these lines exceeding surely all other such displayed degrees of energy put together. Nothing could well interest us more than to see the exemplary value of attention, attention given by the author and asked of the reader, attested in a case in which it has had almost unspeakable difficulties to struggle with – since so we are moved to qualify the particular difficulty Mr Conrad has 'elected' to face: the claim for method in itself, method in this very sense of attention applied, would be somehow less lighted if the difficulties struck us as less consciously, or call it even less wantonly, invoked. What they consist of we should have to diverge here a little to say, and should even then probably but lose ourselves in the dim question of why so special, eccentric and desperate a course, so deliberate a plunge into threatened frustration, should alone have seemed open. It has been the course, so far as three words may here serve, of his so multiplying his creators or, as we are now fond of saying, producers, as to make them almost more numerous and quite emphatically more material than the creatures and the production itself in whom and which we by the general law of fiction expect such agents to lose themselves. We take for granted by the general law of fiction a primary author, take him so much for granted that we forget him in proportion as he works upon us, and that he works upon us most in fact by making us forget him.

Mr Conrad's first care on the other hand is expressly to posit or set up a reciter, a definite responsible intervening first person singular, possessed of infinite sources of reference, who immediately proceeds to set up another, to the end that this other may conform again to the practice, and that even at that point the bridge over to the creature, or in other words to the situation or the subject, the thing 'produced', shall, if the fancy takes it, once more and yet once more glory in a gap. It is easy to see how heroic the undertaking of an effective fusion becomes on these terms, fusion between what we are to know and that prodigy of our knowing which is ever half the very beauty of the atmosphere of authenticity; from the moment the reporters are thus multiplied from pitch to pitch the tone of each, especially as 'rendered' by his precursor in the series, becomes for the prime poet of all an immense question – these circumferential tones having not only to be such individually separate notes, but to keep so clear of the others, the central, the numerous and various voices of the agents proper, those expressive of the action itself and in whom the objectivity resides. We usually escape the worst of this difficulty of a tone *about* the tone of our characters, our projected performers, by keeping it single, keeping it 'down' and thereby comparatively impersonal or, as we may say, inscrutable; which is what a creative force, in its blest fatuity, likes to be. But the omniscience, remaining indeed nameless, though constantly active, which sets Marlow's omniscience in motion from the very first page, insisting on a reciprocity with it throughout, this original omniscience invites consideration of itself only in a degree less than that in which Marlow's own invites it; and Marlow's own is a prolonged hovering flight of the subjective over the outstretched ground of the case exposed. We make out this ground but through the shadow cast by the flight, clarify it though the real author visibly reminds himself again and again that he must – all the more that, as if by some tremendous forecast of future applied science, the upper aeroplane causes another, as we have said, to depend from it and that one still another; these dropping shadow after shadow, to the no small menace of intrinsic colour and form and whatever, upon the passive expanse. What shall we most call Mr Conrad's method accordingly but his attempt to clarify *quand même* – ridden as he has been, we perceive at the end of fifty pages of *Chance*, by such a danger of steeping his matter in perfect eventual obscuration as we recall no other artist's consenting to with an equal grace. This grace, which presently comes over us as the sign of the whole business, is Mr Conrad's gallantry itself, and the shortest account of the rest of the connection for our present purpose is that his gallantry is thus his success. It literally strikes us that his volume sets in motion more than anything else a drama in which his own system and his combined eccentricities of recital represent the protagonist in face of powers leagued against it, and of which the *dénouement* gives us the system fighting in triumph, though with its back desperately to the wall, and laying the powers piled up at its feet. This frankly has been *our* spectacle, our suspense and our thrill; with the one flaw on the roundness of it all the fact that the predicament was not imposed rather than invoked, was not the effect of a challenge from without, but that of a mystic impulse from within.

Of an exquisite refinement at all events are the critical questions opened up in the attempt, the question in particular of by what it exactly is that the experiment is crowned. Pronouncing it crowned and the case saved by sheer gallantry, as we did above, is perhaps to fall just short of the conclusion we might reach were we to push further. *Chance is* an example of objectivity, most precious of aims, not only menaced but definitely compromised; whereby we are in presence of something really of the strangest, a general and diffused lapse of authenticity which an inordinate number of common readers – since it always takes this and these to account encouragingly for 'editions' – have not only condoned but have emphatically commended. They can have done this but through the bribe of some authenticity other in kind, no doubt, and seeming to them equally great if not greater, which gives back by the left hand what the right has, with however dissimulated a grace, taken away. What Mr Conrad's left hand gives back then is simply Mr Conrad himself. We asked above what would become, by such a form of practice, of indispensable 'fusion' or, to call it by another name, of the fine process by which our impatient material, at a given moment, shakes off the humiliation of the handled, the fumbled state, puts its head in the air and, to its own beautiful illusory consciousness at least, simply runs its race. Such an amount of handling and fumbling and repointing has it, on the system of the multiplied 'putter into marble', to shake off! And yet behold, the sense of discomfort, as the show here works out, *has* been conjured away. The fusion has taken place, or at any rate *a* fusion; only it has been transferred in wondrous fashion to an unexpected, and on the whole more limited plane of operation; it has succeeded in getting effected, so to speak, not on the ground but in the air, not between our writer's idea and his machinery, but between the different parts of his genius itself. His genius is what is left over from the other, the compromised and compromising quantities – the Marlows and their determinant inventors and interlocutors, the Powells, the Franklins, the Fynes, the tell-tale little dogs, the successive members of a cue from one to the other of which the sense and the interest of the subject have to be passed on together, in the manner of the buckets of water for the improvised extinction of a fire, before reaching our apprehension: all with whatever result, to this apprehension, of a quantity to be allowed for as spilt by the way. The residuum has accordingly the form not of such and such a number of images discharged and ordered, but that rather of a wandering, circling, yearning imaginative *faculty*, encountered in its habit as it lives and diffusing itself as a presence or a tide, a noble sociability of vision. So we have as the force that fills the cup just the high-water mark of a beautiful and generous mind at play in conditions comparatively thankless – thoroughly, unweariedly, yet at the same time ever so elegantly at play, and doing more for itself than it succeeds in getting done for it. Than which nothing could be of a greater reward to critical curiosity were it not still for the wonder of wonders, a new page in the record altogether – the fact that these things are apparently what the common reader has seen and understood. Great then would seem to be after all the common reader! ...

Were it not for a second exception, one at this season rather pertinent, *Chance* then, to return to it a moment, would be as happy an example as we might just now put our hand on of the automatic working of a scheme unfavourable to that treatment of the colloquy by endless dangling strings which makes the current 'story' in general so figure to us a porcupine of extravagant yet abnormally relaxed bristles.

The exception we speak of would be Mrs Wharton's *Custom of the Country*, in which, as in this lady's other fictions, we recognize the happy fact of an abuse of no one of the resources it enjoys at the expense of the others; the whole series offering as general an example of dialogue flowering and not weeding, illustrational and not itself starved of illustration, or starved of referability and association, which is the same thing, as meets the eye in any glance that leaves Mr Wells at Mr Wells's best-inspired hour out of our own account. The truth is, however, that Mrs Wharton is herself here out of our account, even as we have easily recognized Mr Galsworthy and Mr Maurice Hewlett to be; these three authors, with whatever differences between them, remaining essentially votaries of selection and intention and being embodiments thereby, in each case, of some state over and above that simple state of possession of much evidence, that confused conception of what the 'slice' of life must consist of, which forms the text of our remarks. Mrs Wharton, *her* conception of the 'slice' so clarified and cultivated, would herself of course form a text in quite another connection, as Mr Hewlett and Mr Galsworthy would do each in his own, which we abstain from specifying; but there are two or three grounds on which the author of *Ethan Frome*, *The Valley of Decision* and *The House of Mirth*, whom we brush by with reluctance, would point the moral of the treasure of amusement sitting in the lap of method with a felicity peculiarly her own. If one of these is that she too has clearly a saturation – which it would be ever so interesting to determine and appreciate – we have it from her not in the crude state but in the extract, the extract that makes all the difference for our sense of an artistic economy. If the extract, as would appear, is the result of an artistic economy, as the latter is its logical motive, so we find it associated in Mrs Wharton with such appeals to our interest, for instance, as the fact that, absolutely sole among our students of this form, she suffers, she even encourages, her expression to flower into some sharp image or figure of her thought when that will make the thought more finely touch us. Her step, without straying, encounters the living analogy, which she gathers, in passing, without awkwardness of pause, and which the page then carries on its breast as a trophy plucked by a happy adventurous dash, a token of spirit and temper as well as a proof of vision. We note it as one of the *kinds* of proof of vision that most fail us in that comparative desert of the inselective where our imagination has itself to hunt out or call down (often among strange witnessed flounderings or sand-storms) such analogies as may mercifully 'put' the thing. Mrs Wharton not only owes to her cultivated art of putting it the distinction enjoyed when some ideal of expression has the *whole* of the case, the case once made its concern, in charge, but might further act for us, were we to follow up her exhibition, as lighting not a little that question of 'tone', the author's own intrinsic, as to which we have just seen Mr Conrad's late production rather tend to darken counsel. *The Custom of the Country* is an eminent instance of the sort of tonic value most opposed to that baffled relation between the subject-matter and its emergence which we find constituted by the circumvalations of *Chance*. Mrs Wharton's reaction in presence of the aspects of life hitherto, it would seem, mainly exposed to her is for the most part the ironic – to which we gather that these particular aspects have so much ministered that, were we to pursue the quest, we might recognize in them precisely the saturation as to which we a moment ago reserved our judgment. *The Custom of the Country* is at any rate consistently, almost scientifically satiric, as indeed the satiric light was doubtless the only one in which the elements engaged could at all be focussed together. But this happens directly to the profit of something that, as we read, becomes more and more one with the principle of authority at work; the light that gathers is a dry light, of great intensity, and the effect, if not rather the very essence, of its dryness is a particular fine asperity. The usual 'creative' conditions and associations, as we have elsewhere languished among them, are thanks to this ever so sensibly altered; the general authoritative relation attested becomes clear – we move in an air purged at a stroke of the old sentimental and romantic values, the perversions with the maximum of waste of perversions, and we shall not here attempt to state what this makes for in the way of esthetic refreshment and relief; the waste having kept us so dangling on the dark esthetic abyss. A shade of asperity may be in such fashion a security against waste, and in the dearth of displayed securities we should welcome it on that ground alone. It helps at any rate to constitute for the talent manifest in *The Custom* a rare identity, so far should we have to go to seek another instance of the dry, or call it perhaps even the hard, intellectual touch in the soft, or call it perhaps even the humid, temperamental air; in other words of the masculine conclusion tending so to crown the feminine observation . . .

INDEX

———————— ❖ ————————

FOR THE BEST IN PAPERBACKS, LOOK FOR THE (penguin)

FOR THE BEST IN PAPERBACKS, LOOK FOR THE 🐧

PENGUIN CLASSICS

Netochka Nezvanova Fyodor Dostoyevsky

Dostoyevsky's first book tells the story of 'Nameless Nobody' and introduces many of the themes and issues which will dominate his great masterpieces.

Selections from the Carmina Burana A verse translation by David Parlett

The famous songs from the *Carmina Burana* (made into an oratorio by Carl Orff) tell of lecherous monks and corrupt clerics, drinkers and gamblers, and the fleeting pleasures of youth.

Fear and Trembling Søren Kierkegaard

A profound meditation on the nature of faith and submission to God's will which examines with startling originality the story of Abraham and Isaac.

Selected Prose Charles Lamb

Lamb's famous essays (under the strange pseudonym of Elia) on anything and everything have long been celebrated for their apparently innocent charm; this major new edition allows readers to discover the darker and more interesting aspects of Lamb.

The Picture of Dorian Gray Oscar Wilde

Wilde's superb and macabre novella, one of his supreme works, is reprinted here with a masterly Introduction and valuable Notes by Peter Ackroyd.

A Treatise of Human Nature David Hume

A universally acknowledged masterpiece by 'the greatest of all British Philosophers' – A. J. Ayer

FOR THE BEST IN PAPERBACKS, LOOK FOR THE 🐧

PENGUIN CLASSICS

A Passage to India E. M. Forster

Centred on the unresolved mystery in the Marabar Caves, Forster's great work provides the definitive evocation of the British Raj.

The Republic Plato

The best-known of Plato's dialogues, *The Republic* is also one of the supreme masterpieces of Western philosophy whose influence cannot be overestimated.

The Life of Johnson James Boswell

Perhaps the finest 'life' ever written, Boswell's *Johnson* captures for all time one of the most colourful and talented figures in English literary history.

Remembrance of Things Past (3 volumes) Marcel Proust

This revised version by Terence Kilmartin of C. K. Scott Moncrieff's original translation has been universally acclaimed – available for the first time in paperback.

Metamorphoses Ovid

A golden treasury of myths and legends which has proved a major influence on Western literature.

A Nietzsche Reader Friedrich Nietzsche

A superb selection from all the major works of one of the greatest thinkers and writers in world literature, translated into clear, modern English.

FOR THE BEST IN PAPERBACKS, LOOK FOR THE 🐧

PENGUIN CLASSICS

FOR THE BEST IN PAPERBACKS, LOOK FOR THE 🐧

PENGUIN CLASSICS

Benjamin Disraeli	**Sybil**
George Eliot	**Adam Bede**
	Daniel Deronda
	Felix Holt
	Middlemarch
	The Mill on the Floss
	Romola
	Scenes of Clerical Life
	Silas Marner
Elizabeth Gaskell	**Cranford** and **Cousin Phillis**
	The Life of Charlotte Brontë
	Mary Barton
	North and South
	Wives and Daughters
Edward Gibbon	**The Decline and Fall of the Roman Empire**
George Gissing	**New Grub Street**
Edmund Gosse	**Father and Son**
Richard Jefferies	**Landscape with Figures**
Thomas Macaulay	**The History of England**
Henry Mayhew	**Selections from London Labour** and **The London Poor**
John Stuart Mill	**On Liberty**
William Morris	**News from Nowhere** and **Selected Writings and Designs**
Walter Pater	**Marius the Epicurean**
John Ruskin	**'Unto This Last' and Other Writings**
Sir Walter Scott	**Ivanhoe**
Robert Louis Stevenson	**Dr Jekyll and Mr Hyde**
William Makepeace Thackeray	**The History of Henry Esmond**
	Vanity Fair
Anthony Trollope	**Barchester Towers**
	Framley Parsonage
	Phineas Finn
	The Warden
Mrs Humphrey Ward	**Helbeck of Bannisdale**
Mary Wollstonecraft	**Vindication of the Rights of Woman**

FOR THE BEST IN PAPERBACKS, LOOK FOR THE 🐧

PENGUIN CLASSICS

Horatio Alger, Jr.	**Ragged Dick** and **Struggling Upward**
Phineas T. Barnum	**Struggles and Triumphs**
Ambrose Bierce	**The Enlarged Devil's Dictionary**
Kate Chopin	**The Awakening and Selected Stories**
Stephen Crane	**The Red Badge of Courage**
Richard Henry Dana, Jr.	**Two Years Before the Mast**
Frederick Douglass	**Narrative of the Life of Frederick Douglass, An American Slave**
Theodore Dreiser	**Sister Carrie**
Ralph Waldo Emerson	**Selected Essays**
Joel Chandler Harris	**Uncle Remus**
Nathaniel Hawthorne	**Blithedale Romance**
	The House of the Seven Gables
	The Scarlet Letter and Selected Tales
William Dean Howells	**The Rise of Silas Lapham**
Alice James	**The Diary of Alice James**
William James	**Varieties of Religious Experience**
Jack London	**The Call of the Wild and Other Stories**
	Martin Eden
Herman Melville	**Billy Budd, Sailor and Other Stories**
	Moby-Dick
	Redburn
	Typee
Frank Norris	**McTeague**
Thomas Paine	**Common Sense**
Edgar Allan Poe	**The Narrative of Arthur Gordon Pym of Nantucket**
	The Other Poe
	The Science Fiction of Edgar Allan Poe
	Selected Writings
Harriet Beecher Stowe	**Uncle Tom's Cabin**
Henry David Thoreau	**Walden** and **Civil Disobedience**
Mark Twain	**The Adventures of Huckleberry Finn**
	A Connecticut Yankee at King Arthur's Court
	Life on the Mississippi
	Pudd'nhead Wilson
	Roughing It
Edith Wharton	**The House of Mirth**